About Pearson

Pearson is the world's learning company, with presence across 70 countries worldwide. Our unique insights and world-class expertise comes from a long history of working closely with renowned teachers, authors and thought leaders, as a result of which, we have emerged as the preferred choice for millions of teachers and learners across the world.

We believe learning opens up opportunities, creates fulfilling careers and hence better lives. We hence collaborate with the best of minds to deliver you class-leading products, spread across the Higher Education and K12 spectrum.

Superior learning experience and improved outcomes are at the heart of everything we do. This product is the result of one such effort.

Your feedback plays a critical role in the evolution of our products and you can contact us – reachus@pearson.com. *We look forward to it.*

Ninth Edition

LEADERSHIP IN ORGANIZATIONS

Gary Yukl
State University of New York at Albany

William L. Gardner, III
Rawls College of Business
Texas Tech University

Nishant Uppal
Indian Institute of Management Lucknow

Acknowledgments of third-party content appear on the appropriate page within the text.

PEARSON, ALWAYS LEARNING, and MYLAB are exclusive trademarks owned by Pearson Education, Inc. or its affiliates in the U.S. and/or other countries.

Unless otherwise indicated herein, any third-party trademarks, logos, or icons that may appear in this work are the property of their respective owners, and any references to third-party trademarks, logos, icons, or other trade dress are for demonstrative or descriptive purposes only. Such references are not intended to imply any sponsorship, endorsement, authorization, or promotion of Pearson's products by the owners of such marks, or any relationship between the owner and Pearson Education, Inc., or its affiliates, authors, licensees, or distributors.

Authorized adaptation from the United States edition, entitled *Leadership in Organizations*, 9th Edition, ISBN 9780134895130 by Yukl, Gary A. and Gardner, William L., published by Pearson Education, Inc, Copyright © 2020.

Indian Subcontinent Adaptation
Copyright © 2020 Pearson India Education Services Pvt. Ltd

All rights reserved. This book is sold subject to the condition that it shall not, by way of trade or otherwise, be lent, resold, hired out, or otherwise circulated without the publisher's prior written consent in any form of binding or cover other than that in which it is published and without a similar condition including this condition being imposed on the subsequent purchaser and without limiting the rights under copyright reserved above, no part of this publication may be reproduced, stored in or introduced into a retrieval system, or transmitted in any form or by any means (electronic, mechanical, photocopying, recording or otherwise), without the prior written permission of both the copyright owner and the publisher of this book.

ISBN 978-93-895-5245-4

First Impression, 2020
Third Impression, 2022
Fourth Impression

This edition is manufactured in India and is authorized for sale only in India, Bangladesh, Bhutan, Pakistan, Nepal, Sri Lanka and the Maldives. Circulation of this edition outside of these territories is UNAUTHORIZED.

Published by Pearson India Education Services Pvt. Ltd, CIN: U72200TN2005PTC057128.

Head Office:15th Floor, Tower-B, World Trade Tower, Plot No. 1, Block-C, Sector 16, Noida 201 301, Uttar Pradesh, India.
Registered Office: 7th Floor, SDB2, ODC 7, 8 & 9, Survey No.01 ELCOT IT/ ITES SEZ, Sholinganallur, Chennai – 600119, Tamil Nadu, India.
Website: in.pearson.com, Email: companysecretary.india@pearson.com

Printed in India at Saurabh Printers Pvt. Ltd.

For their support, devotion, and love, this book is dedicated to Maureen and Claudia.

BRIEF CONTENTS

TABLE OF CONTENTS

CHAPTER 6 POWER AND INFLUENCE TACTICS

CHAPTER 7 LEADER TRAITS AND SKILLS

CHAPTER 8 CHARISMATIC AND TRANSFORMATIONAL LEADERSHIP

CHAPTER 15 OVERVIEW AND INTEGRATION

ABOUT THE AUTHORS

Gary Yukl

After more than 45 years of studying leadership, Dr. Gary Yukl is highly qualified to write about the subject. His highest academic degree is a Ph.D. in Industrial-Organizational Psychology from the University of California, Berkeley. He is an emeritus professor at UAlbany, State University of New York, where before retiring he taught courses in leadership at the undergraduate, MBA, and doctoral level. He is a member of the editorial boards for several important journals that publish articles on leadership theory and research. His own publications include many articles on leadership, and he has received a number of awards for best research article, most-cited article, and best convention paper. He has also received two lifetime achievement awards for his research and publications: the 2007 Walter Ulmer Applied Research Award from the Center for Creative Leadership, and the 2011 Eminent Leadership Scholar Award from the Academy of Management Network of Leadership Scholars. He has consulted with several business and public-sector organizations to help improve the effectiveness of their managers, and the leadership development programs he designed for a consulting company were used by managers and administrators in many organizations. Some of the practical guidelines presented in this book are from management development programs found to improve the effectiveness of the participants. For his exceptional research and scholarship he was elected a Fellow of the American Psychological Association, the American Psychological Society, the Society for Industrial-Organizational Psychology, and the Academy of Management.

William L. Gardner, III

Drawing on his 40-plus years of teaching and researching leadership, Dr. William (Bill) Gardner is well positioned to share his insights on leaders and effective leadership. His highest academic degree is a Doctor of Business Administration (DBA) from Florida State University. He holds the Jerry S. Rawls Chair in Leadership and serves as the Director of the Institute for Leadership Research in the Rawls College of Business at Texas Tech University. He previously held faculty positions at Southern Illinois University, the University of Mississippi, and the University of Nebraska–Lincoln. During his career, he has taught leadership and management courses at the undergraduate, masters, professional MBA, and doctoral levels. Currently, he serves as the Editor-in-Chief for *Group & Organization Management* and as an Associate Editor for *The Leadership Quarterly.* He has published numerous high-impact articles focused on leadership in top-tier journals and received several best-paper and most-cited-article awards. In 2011, he received the Distinguished Doctoral Alumni Award from the College of Business at Florida State University. In 2015, Texas Tech recognized him as an "Integrated Scholar," an honor bestowed to "a faculty member who not only demonstrates outstanding teaching, research, and service, but is able to generate synergy among the three functions." In recognition of his extensive contributors to the Southern Management Association (SMA), including his service as President and an SMA Fellow, he received the "James G. (Jerry) Hunt Sustained Outstanding Service Award" in 2017.

Nishant Uppal

Nishant Uppal is faculty of Organization Behavior in the Human Resources Management Group, Indian Institute of Management Lucknow. He earned his PhD in Organizational Behavior and Human Resource Management from the Indian Institute of Management Indore.

His books Duryodhanization, Are the Villains Born, Made, or Made Up is a landmark in understanding unique nuances associated with historical and modern corporate villains. His book – Understanding the Theory and Design of Organizations runs successfully as text and reference book in many national and international educational and training institutions.

Additionally, he has published a number of papers in world-renowned journals such as Personality and Individual Differences, Studies in Higher Education, International Journal for Selection and Assessment, Personnel Review, Journal for International Business and Entrepreneurship Development, and Journal for Global Business Advancement, etc. He specializes in the fields of leadership, change management, knowledge management, organizational adaptation, job design, organizational structure, and personality.

PREFACE

This book is about leadership in organizations. Its primary focus is on managerial leadership as opposed to parliamentary leadership, leadership in social movements, or emergent leadership in informal groups. The book presents a broad survey of theory and research on leadership in formal organizations. Topics of special interest are the determinants of leadership effectiveness and how leadership can be improved. William Gardner was added as a second author for this edition to incorporate his knowledge and perspective on effective leadership.

The book is appropriate for use as the primary text in an undergraduate or graduate course in leadership. Such courses are found in many different schools or departments, including business, psychology, sociology, educational administration, public administration, and health-care administration. The book is on the list of required or recommended readings for students in many doctoral programs in leadership, management, and industrial-organizational psychology. With its focus on effective leadership in organizations, the book is especially relevant for students who expect to become a manager or administrator in the near future, for people who will be responsible for training or coaching leaders, and for people who will be teaching courses or workshops that include leadership as one of the key topics. The book is also useful for practicing managers and consultants who are looking for something more than vague theories and superficial answers to difficult questions about leadership. The book is widely used in many different countries, and some editions were translated into other languages, including Chinese, Korean, Indonesian, Spanish, Greek, Croatian, and Swedish.

The content of the book still reflects a dual concern for theory and practice. We have attempted to satisfy two different audiences with somewhat different perspectives. Most academics prefer a book that explains and evaluates major theories and relevant empirical research. They are most interested in how well the research was done, what was found, how well the research supports the theoretical basis for it, and what additional research is needed. Academics tend to be skeptical about the value of prescriptions and guidelines for practitioners and may consider them premature in the absence of further research. In contrast, most practitioners want some immediate answers about what to do and how to do it in order to be more effective as leaders. They need to deal with the current challenges of their job and cannot wait for decades until the academics resolve their theoretical disputes and obtain definitive answers. Practitioners are more interested in finding helpful remedies and prescriptions than in finding out how this knowledge was discovered. Readers who desire to improve their leadership effectiveness will find this edition of the book is even more useful than previous editions.

The different preferences are one of the reasons for the much-lamented gulf between scientists and practitioners in management and industrial-organizational psychology. We believe it is important for managers and administrators to understand the complexity of effective leadership, the source of our knowledge about leadership in organizations, and the limitations of this knowledge. Likewise, we believe it is important for academics to think more about how their theories and research can be used to improve the practice of management. Too much of our leadership research is designed to examine narrow, esoteric questions that only interest a few other scholars who publish in the same journals.

Academics will be pleased to find that major theories are explained and evaluated, findings in empirical research on leadership are summarized, and many references are provided to help readers find sources of additional information about topics of special interest. The field of leadership is still in a state of ferment, with many continuing controversies about conceptual and methodological issues. The book addresses these issues, but the literature review was not intended to be comprehensive. Rather than detailing an endless series of weak theories and inconclusive studies like most handbooks of leadership, this book describes major findings about effective leadership and how they can be applied by readers.

For practitioners and students who desire to become effective managers, we attempted to convey a better appreciation of the complexity of managerial leadership, the importance of having theoretical knowledge about leadership, and the need to be flexible and pragmatic in applying this knowledge. The current edition provides many guidelines and recommendations for improving managerial effectiveness, but it is not a "practitioner's manual" of simple techniques and secret recipes that guarantee instant success. The purpose of the guidelines is to help the reader understand the practical implications of the leadership theory and research, not to prescribe exactly how things must be done by a leader. Most of the guidelines are based on a limited amount of research and they are not infallible or relevant for all situations. Being a flexible, adaptive leader includes determining which guidelines are relevant for each unique situation.

Most chapters end with two short cases designed to help the reader gain a better understanding of the theories, concepts, and guidelines presented in the chapter. Most of the cases describe events that occurred in real organizations, but some cases were modified to make them more useful for learning basic concepts and effective practices. For many of the cases, the names of organizations and individuals were changed to keep the analysis focused on the events that occurred in a defined time period, rather than on recent events that may involve different leaders and a different situation. The cases ask a reader to analyze behavioral processes, identify examples of effective and ineffective behavior, and suggest effective ways to handle the situation that is depicted.

In this ninth edition, the basic structure of most chapters remains the same, but the order of some chapters was changed, a few topics were moved to a different chapter, some new topics were added, and the discussion of some other topics was expanded. Since the book is not intended to be a history of leadership, it seemed appropriate to reduce the amount of detail about early research programs and old theories that are no longer popular, and focus more closely on what we now know about effective leadership.

Preface to the Indian Edition

The Indian edition of *Leadership in Organizations, 9e* aspires to deepen the understanding of leadership in global business, both in knowledge and practice, by drawing perspectives from the latest advancements in international business. The chapters and cases included in this edition focus upon the theoretical, empirical, and policy and practitioner aspects of a wide range of topics including subordinate management, motivation, and job satisfaction among others. The geographical spread of topics and cases presented in the present edition provide a truly global flavor.

The leaders in an organization can be an asset that could be leveraged upon to improve business performance. Leadership has always remained a topic of academic exploration and discussion as an important aspect of organizational behavior, one that greatly influences organizations, workers, and workplace in the extremely volatile and uncertain business environment. This book attempts to interpret and discuss the complex person-job-organization-environment relationship.

The ninth edition is organized in the following way:

- The first three chapters focus on individual as leader and attempts to simplify otherwise complex nature of leadership.

- Chapter 4 then presents the role of feedback in terms of usefulness of views from varied sources in decision making.
- Managing and leadership change have become the primary function of leaders in volatile, uncertain, complex and ambiguous business situations. Chapter 5 explains the role and responsibility of leaders in such situations.
- Chapters 6 to 10 explain and critically analyze another critical role of the leader, more specifically in perpetually transforming and evolving business environment, and dealing with people.
- Chapter 10 also links behaviors and dispositions of a leader with the vision and mission of organizations. Leaders are not only responsible for crafting socially relevant business goals, but also for embarking upon them while taking the organization with them.
- While leaders are responsible for designing socially relevant organizations, they must be attentive to the definition of society for their organizations. Organizations engage into boundary spanning and finding places in each corner of society. This makes leaders responsible for ensuring high ethical and moral standards so that their organizations can make decisions that are least ambiguous and most benefitting for the larger segment of the society. This is the main theme of chapters 13 and 14.

Finally, in order to meet the objectives and functions of leaders in organization, the book also outlines various methods through which leaders can develop themselves. Leadership skills are dynamic and contextual and hence deserve continuous attention. The last chapter deals with this leadership issue and presents some scientific ways in which leaders are currently being trained and nurtured.

It is hoped that this edition shall provide stimulus for research and propel further development in international business entwined with the global business diaspora including academics, policy makers, and organizations.

Lastly, I would like to acknowledge the peers and the editors who have reviewed and worked tirelessly towards evaluating the current edition. I am also grateful to Dr Archana Shukla, Director, Indian Institute of Management Lucknow, who consistently encourage to link theory with practice motivated me to take up the current project. I would also like to acknowledge the immense support offered by my mother, Shivani and wife, Deepti. Without their contribution, this project would not have been possible.

New to This Edition

Following is a list of changes we made to make the book easier to understand and more useful to most readers:

- The number of chapters was reduced from 16 to 15 to improve the organization of content.
- The order of chapters was modified to improve the explanation of related topics.
- Every chapter has been updated and revised for clarity and understanding.
- New examples of effective and ineffective leadership were added to most chapters.
- Personal Reflection exercises were added to most chapters to help students think critically and apply the leadership concepts.
- Several new cases were added, and there are now two cases for all but the introduction and overview chapters.
- Over 500 citations to recent research were added throughout.
- The design of the book was updated, and two colors are used for this edition.

Chapter by Chapter Changes

- In Chapter 1 (*The Nature of Leadership)* we added a discussion of the research methods used to study leadership, including new methods such as social networks, biosensor methods, and behavioral genetics. The description of different theoretical approaches for studying leadership was expanded.
- In Chapter 2 (*Leadership Behavior*) the description of distinct types of leadership behavior was revised to include new knowledge and theories about these subjects. A new case on leadership behavior was added to the chapter.
- In Chapter 3 (*The Leadership Situation and Adaptive Leadership*) the ways in which leaders are influenced by the leadership situation was expanded to include the discussion of leadership in extreme situations such as hospital emergency rooms, SWAT teams, and police work. This chapter also includes some theories of situational determinants and adaptive leadership that were included in a separate chapter on managerial work in the previous edition.
- In Chapter 4 (*Decision Making and Empowerment by Leaders*) we added a discussion of the threshold effect of participative leadership, which explains how there is a minimum level of participative leadership that must be reached before the positive effects on employee performance are realized. In addition, we expanded the discussion of psychological empowerment and empowering leadership.
- In Chapter 5 *(Leading Change and Innovation)* we added a discussion of the differences among developmental, transitional, and transformational change, and organizational cynicism about change was added as another reason for rejecting change. A discussion of the strategic fitness process is included, and it involves a nine-step process of organizational change that combats the "silent killers" of organizational effectiveness. This chapter also includes a new case about leading change.
- In Chapter 6 (*Power and Influence Tactics*) the description of how leaders can effectively use their power and several different influence tactics was expanded. A new case about power and influence was added to the chapter.
- In Chapter 7 *(Leader Traits and Skills)* we added a discussion of core self-evaluations about a leader's worthiness, effectiveness, and capacity as a person. In addition, the concept of political skill is discussed in more detail, along with the associated research and practical implications of this skill.
- In Chapter 8 *(Charismatic and Transformational Leadership*) we added a discussion of specific charismatic leadership tactics that leaders use to manage impressions. We also describe how leaders can learn to effectively use these tactics. The discussion of contextual factors that contribute to the emergence and impact of charismatic leadership was expanded to include attributional ambiguity.
- In Chapter 9 (*Value-Based and Ethical Leadership)* we added an explanation of the factors that increase the moral intensity of an ethical issue and the effects of moral intensity on ethical leadership. The constructs of ethical culture and ethical climate, and the differences between them, are discussed, along with their effects on leader and follower behaviors in organizations. We also refined the discussion of authentic leadership by describing the four components: self-awareness, balanced processing, relational transparency, and an internalized moral perspective.

- In Chapter 10 *(Dyadic Relations and Followership)* we added a discussion of how a leader's affective expressions serve as cues about the leader's enthusiasm for the relationship, which in turn evoke emotional reactions from followers. We also describe how leaders and followers sometimes attribute performance problems to their relationship rather than to internal or external causes, and how leaders and followers may engage in relational work for the purpose of improving the relationship and future performance.
- In Chapter 11 (*Leadership in Teams and Decision Groups*) we added a discussion of how a team's composition affects the emergence of identity-based, resource-based, and knowledge-based subgroups, and the implications of these subgroups are explained. A new case was also added to this chapter.
- In Chapter 12 (*Strategic Leadership in Organizations*) we added a detailed discussion of strategic human resource management, which calls for an alignment and coordination of the firm's human resource practices across organizational levels to ensure that human capital is deployed strategically to foster enhanced competitiveness.
- In Chapter 13 (*Cross-Cultural Leadership and Diversity*) we introduced the concept of global leadership and added a set of guidelines for effective global leadership and the practical challenges that confront leaders of multinational organizations. We also added a discussion of the "glass cliff" phenomenon, which refers to the tendency of women to be more likely to be appointed to leadership positions that are risky and precarious. We included a discussion of findings from research that investigates the relationships between gender composition on corporate boards and key organizational outcomes. A new case was also added to this chapter.
- In Chapter 14 (*Developing Leadership Skills*) we added a discussion of how return on development investment (RODI) can be used as a metric for assessing the impact of leadership development programs and activities. In addition, we expanded the description of factors that facilitate leader development to include the concept of developmental readiness, which is a function of the leader's ability and motivation to develop. We also added a new case to this chapter.
- In Chapter 15 (*Overview and Integration*) we updated the summary of major findings about effective leadership to include new findings since the eighth edition was written. Ways to improve leadership research in the future are suggested, and we briefly summarize some general guidelines for effective leadership.

Gary Yukl
The Villages, Florida

William L. Gardner
Lubbock, Texas
August, 2018

Nishant Uppal
IIM Lucknow

Instructor Resource Center

The following supplements are available with this text:

- Instructor's Resource Manual
- Test Bank
- TestGen®
- PowerPoint Presentation

Chapter 1

The Nature of Leadership

Learning Objectives

After studying this chapter, you should be able to:

- Understand the different ways leadership has been defined.
- Understand the major types of leadership theories that have been studied.
- Understand the different ways leadership effectiveness is determined.
- Understand what aspects of leadership have been studied the most.
- Understand the organization of this book.

Introduction

Leadership is a subject that has long excited interest among people. The term connotes images of powerful, dynamic individuals who command victorious armies, direct corporate empires from atop gleaming skyscrapers, or shape the course of nations. The exploits of brave and clever leaders are the essence of many legends and myths. Much of our description of history is the story of military, political, religious, social, and business leaders who are credited or blamed for important historical events, even though we do not understand very well how the events were caused or how much influence the leader really had. The widespread fascination with leadership may be because it is such a mysterious process, as well as one that touches everyone's life. Why did certain leaders (e.g., Gandhi, Mohammed, Martin Luther King, Jr., Mao Tse-tung) inspire such intense fervor and dedication? How did certain leaders (e.g., Julius Caesar, Alexander the Great) build great empires? Why did some rather undistinguished people (e.g., Adolf Hitler, Claudius Caesar) rise to positions of great power? Why were certain leaders (e.g., Winston Churchill, Indira Gandhi) suddenly deposed, despite their apparent power and record of successful accomplishments? Why do some leaders have loyal followers who are willing to sacrifice their lives, whereas other leaders are so despised that subordinates conspire to murder them?

Questions about leadership have long been a subject of speculation, but scientific research on leadership did not begin until the twentieth century. The focus of much of the research has been on the determinants of leadership effectiveness. Social scientists have attempted to discover what traits, abilities, behaviors, sources of power, or aspects of the situation determine how well a leader is able to influence followers and accomplish task objectives. There is also a growing interest in understanding leadership as a shared process in a team or organization and the reasons why this process is effective or ineffective. Other important questions include the reasons why some people emerge as leaders, and the determinants of a leader's actions, but the predominant concern has been leadership effectiveness.

Some progress has been made in probing the mysteries surrounding leadership, but many questions remain unanswered. In this book, major theories and research findings on leadership effectiveness will be reviewed, with particular emphasis on managerial leadership in formal organizations such as business corporations, government agencies, hospitals, and universities. This chapter introduces the subject by considering different conceptions of leadership, different ways of evaluating its effectiveness, and different approaches for studying leadership. Finally, the chapter explains the basis for placement of key topics in different parts of the book.

Definitions of Leadership

The term leadership is a word taken from the common vocabulary and incorporated into the technical vocabulary of a scientific discipline without being precisely redefined. As a consequence, it carries extraneous connotations that create ambiguity of meaning (Calder, 1977; Janda, 1960). Additional confusion is caused by the use of other imprecise terms such as power, authority, management, administration, control, and supervision to describe similar phenomena. An observation by Bennis (1959, p. 259) is as true today as when he made it many years ago:

> Always, it seems, the concept of leadership eludes us or turns up in another form to taunt us again with its slipperiness and complexity. So we have invented an endless proliferation of terms to deal with it... and still the concept is not sufficiently defined.

Researchers usually define leadership according to their individual perspectives and the aspects of the phenomenon of most interest to them. After a comprehensive review of the leadership literature, Stogdill (1974, p. 259) concluded that "there are almost as many definitions of leadership as there are persons who have attempted to define the concept." The stream of new definitions has continued unabated since Stogdill made his observation. Leadership has been defined in terms of traits, behaviors, influence, interaction patterns, role relationships, and occupation of an administrative position. Table 1-1 shows some representative definitions presented over the past 50 years.

Most definitions of leadership reflect the assumption that it involves a process whereby intentional influence is exerted over other people to guide, structure, and facilitate activities and relationships in a group or organization. The numerous definitions of leadership appear to have little else in common. They differ in many respects, including who exerts influence, the intended purpose of the influence, the manner in which influence is exerted, and the outcome of the influence attempt. The differences are not just a case of scholarly nit-picking; they reflect deep disagreement about the identification of leaders and leadership processes. Researchers who differ in their conception of leadership select different phenomena to investigate and interpret the

TABLE 1-1 Definitions of Leadership

- Leadership is "the behavior of an individual ... directing the activities of a group toward a shared goal" (Hemphill & Coons, 1957, p. 7).
- Leadership is "the influential increment over and above mechanical compliance with the routine directives of the organization" (Katz & Kahn, 1978, p. 528).
- Leadership is "the process of influencing the activities of an organized group toward goal achievement" (Rauch & Behling, 1984, p. 46).
- "Leadership is about articulating visions, embodying values, and creating the environment within which things can be accomplished" (Richards & Engle, 1986, p. 206).
- "Leadership is a process of giving purpose (meaningful direction) to collective effort, and causing willing effort to be expended to achieve purpose" (Jacobs & Jaques, 1990, p. 281).
- Leadership "is the ability to step outside the culture ... to start evolutionary change processes that are more adaptive" (Schein, 1992, p. 2).
- "Leadership is the process of making sense of what people are doing together so that people will understand and be committed" (Drath & Palus, 1994, p. 4).
- Leadership is "the ability of an individual to influence, motivate, and enable others to contribute toward the effectiveness and success of the organization ..." (House et al., 1999, p. 184).
- "Leadership is a formal or informal contextually rooted and goal-influencing process that occurs between a leader and a follower, groups, of followers, or institutions" (Antonakis & Day, 2018, p. 5).

results in different ways. Researchers who have a very narrow definition of leadership are less likely to discover things that are unrelated to or inconsistent with their initial assumptions about effective leadership.

Because leadership has so many different meanings to people, some theorists question whether it is even useful as a scientific construct (e.g., Alvesson & Sveningsson, 2003; Calder, 1977; Miner, 1975). Nevertheless, most behavioral scientists and practitioners seem to believe leadership is a real phenomenon that is important for the effectiveness of organizations. Interest in the subject remains high, and the number of articles and books about leadership continues to increase.

Specialized Role or Shared Influence Process?

A major controversy involves the issue of whether leadership should be viewed as a specialized role or as a shared influence process. One view is that all groups have role specialization, and the leadership role has responsibilities and functions that cannot be shared too widely without jeopardizing the effectiveness of the group. The person with primary responsibility to perform the specialized leadership role is designated as the "leader." Other members are called "followers," even though some of them may assist the primary leader in carrying out leadership functions. The distinction between leader and follower roles does not mean that a person cannot perform both roles at the same time. For example, a department manager who is the leader of department employees is also a follower of higher-level managers in the organization. Researchers who view leadership as a specialized role are likely to pay more attention to the attributes that determine selection of designated leaders, the typical behavior of designated leaders, and the effects of this behavior on other members of the group or organization.

Another way to view leadership is in terms of an influence process that occurs naturally within a social system and is diffused among the members. Writers with this perspective believe it is more useful to study leadership as a social process or pattern of relationships rather than as a specialized role. According to this view, various leadership functions may be carried out by different people who influence what the group does, how it is done, and the way people in the group relate to each other. Leadership may be exhibited both by formally selected leaders and by informal leaders. Important decisions about what to do and how to do it are made through the use of an interactive process involving many different people who influence each other. Researchers who view leadership as a shared, diffuse process are likely to pay more attention to the complex influence processes that occur among members, the context and conditions that determine when and how they occur, the processes involved in the emergence of informal leaders, and the consequences for the group or organization.

Type of Influence Process

Controversy about the definition of leadership involves not only who exercises influence, but also what type of influence is exercised and the outcome. Some theorists would limit the definition of leadership to the exercise of influence resulting in enthusiastic commitment by followers, as opposed to indifferent compliance or reluctant obedience. These theorists argue that the use of control over rewards and punishments to manipulate or coerce followers is not really "leading" and may involve the unethical use of power.

An opposing view is that this definition is too restrictive because it excludes some influence processes that are important for understanding why a leader is effective or ineffective in a given situation. How leadership is defined should not predetermine the answer to the research question of what makes a leader effective. The same outcome can be accomplished with different influence methods, and the same type of influence attempt can result in different outcomes, depending on the nature of the situation. Even people who are forced or manipulated into doing something may become committed to it if they subsequently discover that it really is the best option for them and the organization. The ethical use of power is a legitimate concern for leadership scholars, but it should not limit the definition of leadership or the type of influence processes that are studied.

Purpose of Influence Attempts

Another controversy about which influence attempts are part of leadership involves their purpose and outcome. One viewpoint is that leadership occurs only when people are influenced to do what is ethical and beneficial for the organization and themselves. This definition of leadership does not include influence attempts that are irrelevant or detrimental to followers, such as a leader's attempts to gain personal benefits at the follower's expense.

An opposing view would include all attempts to influence the attitudes and behavior of followers in an organizational context, regardless of the intended purpose or actual beneficiary. Acts of leadership often have multiple motives, and it is seldom possible to determine the extent to which they are selfless rather than selfish. The outcomes of leader actions usually include a mix of costs and benefits, some of which are unintended, making it difficult to infer purpose. Despite good intentions, the actions of a leader are sometimes more detrimental than beneficial for followers. Conversely, actions motivated solely by a leader's personal needs sometimes result in unintended benefits for followers and the organization. Thus, the domain of leadership processes to study should not be limited by the leader's intended purpose.

Influence Based on Reason or Emotions

Most of the leadership definitions listed earlier emphasize rational, cognitive processes. For many years, it was common to view leadership as a process wherein leaders influence followers to believe it is in their best interest to cooperate in achieving a shared task objective. Until the 1980s, few conceptions of leadership recognized the importance of emotions as a basis for influence.

In contrast, some recent conceptions of leadership emphasize the emotional aspects of influence much more than reason. According to this view, only the emotional, value-based aspects of leadership influence can account for the exceptional achievements of groups and organizations. Leaders inspire followers to willingly sacrifice their selfish interests for a higher cause. For example, leaders can motivate soldiers to risk their lives for an important mission or to protect their comrades. The relative importance of rational and emotional processes and how they interact are issues to be resolved by empirical research, and the conceptualization of leadership should not exclude either type of process.

Direct and Indirect Leadership

Most theories about effective leadership focus on behaviors used to directly influence immediate subordinates, but a leader can also influence other people inside the organization, including peers, bosses, and people at lower levels who do not report to the leader. Some theorists make a distinction between direct and indirect forms of leadership to help explain how a leader can influence people when there is no direct interaction with them (Hunt, 1991; Lord & Maher, 1991; Yammarino, 1994).

A chief executive officer (CEO) has many ways to influence people at lower levels in the organization. Direct forms of leadership involve attempts to influence followers when interacting with them or using communication media to send messages to them. Examples include sending memos or reports to employees, sending e-mail and text messages, presenting speeches on television, holding face-to-face or virtual meetings with small groups of employees, and participating in activities involving employees (e.g., attending orientation or training sessions, company picnics). Most of these forms of influence can be classified as direct leadership.

Indirect leadership has been used to describe how a chief executive can influence people at lower levels in the organization who do not interact directly with the leader (Bass, Waldman, Avolio, & Bebb, 1987; Hunter et al., 2013; Mayer, Kuenzi, Greenbaum, Bardes, & Salvador, 2009; Park & Hassan, 2018; Waldman & Yammarino, 1999; Yammarino, 1994). One form of indirect leadership by a CEO is called "cascading." It occurs when the direct influence of the CEO is transmitted down the authority hierarchy of an organization from the CEO to middle managers, to lower-level managers, to regular employees. The influence can involve changes in employee attitudes, beliefs, values, or behaviors. For example, a CEO who sets a good example of ethical and supportive behavior may influence similar behavior by employees at lower levels in the organization.

Another form of indirect leadership involves influence over formal programs, management systems, and structural forms (Hunt, 1991; Lord & Maher, 1991; Yukl & Lepsinger, 2004). Many large organizations have programs or management systems intended to influence the attitudes, skills, behavior, and performance of employees. Examples include programs for recruitment, selection, and promotion of employees. Structural forms and various types of programs can be used to increase control, coordination, efficiency, and innovation. Examples include formal rules and procedures, specialized subunits, decentralized product divisions, standardized facilities, and self-managed teams. In most organizations only top executives have sufficient authority to implement new programs or change the structural forms (see Chapter 12).

A third form of indirect leadership involves leader influence over the organization culture, which is defined as the shared beliefs and values of members (Day, Griffin, & Louw, 2014; Schein, 1992; Trice & Beyer, 1991). Leaders may attempt either to strengthen existing cultural beliefs and values or to change them. There are many ways for leaders to influence an organization's culture. Some ways involve direct influence (e.g., communicating a compelling vision or leading by example), and some involve forms of indirect influence, such as changing the organizational structure, reward systems, and management programs (see Chapter 12). For example, a CEO can implement programs to recruit, select, and promote people who share the same values (Giberson, Resick, & Dickson, 2005).

The interest in indirect leadership is useful to remind scholars that leadership influence is not limited to the types of observable behavior emphasized in many leadership theories. However, it is important to remember that a simple dichotomy does not capture the complexity involved in these influence processes. Some forms of influence are not easily classified as either direct or indirect leadership. Moreover, direct and indirect forms of influence are not mutually exclusive, and when used together in a consistent way, it is possible to magnify their effects (see Chapter 12).

Leadership or Management

There is a continuing controversy about the difference between leadership and management (Gardner & Schermerhorn, 1992; Kotter, 1990; Zaleznik, 1977). It is obvious that a person can be a leader without being a manager (e.g., an informal leader), and a person can have the job title "manager" with no subordinates to lead. Nobody has proposed that managing and leading are equivalent, but the degree of overlap is a point of sharp disagreement. The most useful perspective is probably to view leadership as one of several managerial roles (Mintzberg, 1973).

Defining managing and leading as distinct roles, processes, or relationships may obscure more than it reveals if it encourages simplistic theories about effective leadership. Most scholars seem to agree that success as a manager or administrator in modern organizations also involves leading. How to integrate the two processes has emerged as a complex and important issue in organizational literature (Yukl & Lepsinger, 2005). The answer will not come from debates about ideal definitions. Questions about what to include in the domain of essential leadership processes should be explored with empirical research, not predetermined by subjective judgments. Whenever feasible, leadership research should be designed to provide information relevant to a wide range of definitions, so that over time it will be possible to compare the utility of different conceptions and arrive at some consensus on the matter.

Our Definition of Leadership

In this book, leadership is defined broadly in a way that takes into account several things that determine the success of a collective effort by members of a group or organization to accomplish meaningful tasks. The following definition is used:

> Leadership is the process of influencing others to understand and agree about what needs to be done and how to do it, and the process of facilitating individual and collective efforts to accomplish shared objectives.

TABLE 1-2 What Leaders Can Influence

- The choice of objectives and strategies to pursue
- The motivation of members to achieve the objectives
- The mutual trust and cooperation of members
- The organization and coordination of work activities
- The allocation of resources to activities and objectives
- The development of member skills and confidence
- The learning and sharing of new knowledge by members
- The enlistment of support and cooperation from outsiders
- The design of formal structure, programs, and systems
- The shared beliefs and values of members

The definition includes efforts not only to influence and facilitate the current work of the group or organization, but also to ensure that it is prepared to meet future challenges. Both direct and indirect forms of influence are included. The influence process may involve only a single leader or it may involve many leaders. Table 1-2 shows the wide variety of ways leaders can influence the effectiveness of a group or organization.

In this book, leadership is treated as both a specialized role and a social influence process. Both rational and emotional processes are viewed as essential aspects of leadership. No assumptions are made about the actual outcome of the influence processes, because the evaluation of outcomes is difficult and subjective. Thus, the definition of leadership is not limited to processes that necessarily result in "successful" outcomes. The focus is clearly on the process, not the person, and the two are not assumed to be equivalent.

The terms leader, manager, and boss are used interchangeably in this book to indicate people who occupy positions in which they are expected to perform the leadership role, but without any assumptions about their actual behavior or success. The terms subordinate and direct report are used interchangeably to denote someone whose primary work activities are directed and evaluated by the focal leader.

Some writers use the term staff as a substitute for subordinate, but this practice creates unnecessary confusion. The term connotes a special type of advisory position, and most subordinates are not staff advisors. Moreover, the term staff is used both as a singular and plural noun, which creates a lot of unnecessary confusion. The term associate has become popular in business organizations as another substitute for subordinate, because it conveys a relationship in which employees are valued and supposedly empowered. However, this vague term fails to differentiate between a direct authority relationship and other types of formal relationships (e.g., peers, partners). To clarify communication, this book continues to use the term subordinate to denote the existence of a formal authority relationship.

The term follower is used to describe a person who acknowledges the focal leader as the primary source of guidance about the work, regardless of how much formal authority the leader actually has over the person. Although the term is often used to describe subordinates, followers may also include people who are not direct reports (e.g., coworkers, team members, partners, outsiders). However, the term is not used to describe members of an organization who completely reject the formal leader and seek to remove the person from office; such people are more appropriately called "rebels" or "insurgents."

Indicators of Leadership Effectiveness

Like definitions of leadership, conceptions of leader effectiveness differ from one writer to another. The criteria selected to evaluate leadership effectiveness reflect a researcher's explicit or implicit conception of good leadership. Most researchers evaluate leadership effectiveness in terms of the consequences of influence on a single individual, a team or group, or an organization.

One very relevant indicator of leadership effectiveness is the extent to which the performance of the team or organization is enhanced and the attainment of goals is facilitated (Bass, 2008; Kaiser, Hogan, & Craig, 2008). Examples of objective measures of performance include sales, net profits, profit margin, market share, return on investment, return on assets, productivity, cost per unit of output, costs in relation to budgeted expenditures, and change in the value of corporate stock. Subjective measures of effectiveness include ratings obtained from the leader's superiors, peers, or subordinates.

Follower attitudes and perceptions of the leader are another common indicator of leader effectiveness, and they are usually measured with questionnaires or interviews. How well does the leader satisfy the needs and expectations of followers? Do they like, respect, and admire the leader? Do they trust the leader and perceive him or her to have high integrity? Are they strongly committed to carrying out the leader's requests, or will they resist, ignore, or subvert them? Does the leader improve the quality of work life, build the self-confidence of followers, increase their skills, and contribute to their psychological growth and development? Follower attitudes, perceptions, and beliefs also provide an indirect indicator of dissatisfaction and hostility toward the leader. Examples of such indicators include absenteeism, voluntary turnover, grievances, complaints to higher management, requests for transfer, work slowdowns, and deliberate sabotage of equipment and facilities.

Leader effectiveness is occasionally measured in terms of the leader's contribution to the quality of group processes, as perceived by followers or by outside observers. Does the leader enhance group cohesiveness, member cooperation, member task commitment, and member confidence that the group can achieve its objectives? Does the leader enhance problem solving and decision making by the group, and help to resolve disagreements and conflicts in a constructive way? Does the leader contribute to the efficiency of role specialization, the organization of activities, the accumulation of resources, and the readiness of the group to deal with change and crises?

A final type of criterion for leadership effectiveness is the extent to which a person has a successful career as a leader. Is the person promoted rapidly to positions of higher authority? Does the person serve a full term in a leadership position, or is he or she removed or forced to resign? For elected positions in organizations, is a leader who seeks reelection successful? It is difficult to evaluate the effectiveness of a leader when there are so many alternative measures of effectiveness, and it is not clear which measure is most relevant. Some researchers attempt to combine several measures into a single, composite criterion, but this approach requires subjective judgments about how to assign a weight to each measure. Multiple criteria are especially troublesome when trade-offs occur among criteria, such that as one increases, others decrease. For example, increasing sales and market share (e.g., by reducing price and increasing advertising) may result in lower profits. Likewise, an increase in production output (e.g., by inducing people to work faster) may reduce product quality or employee satisfaction.

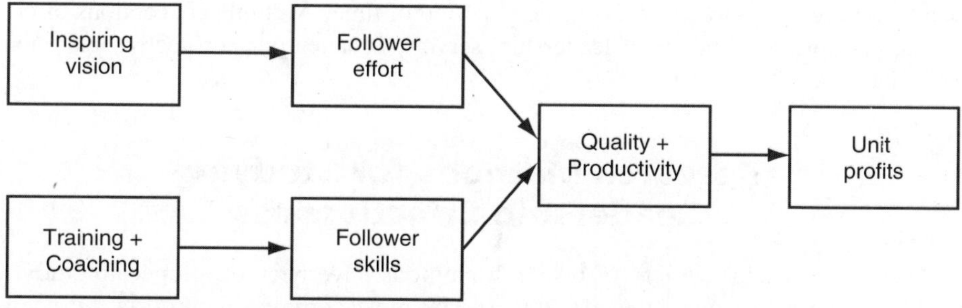

FIGURE 1-1 Causal Chain of Effects from Two Types of Leader Behavior

Immediate and Delayed Outcomes

Some outcomes are more immediate than others. For example, the immediate result of an influence attempt is whether followers are willing to do what the leader asks, but a delayed effect is how well followers actually perform the assignment. The effects of a leader can be viewed as a causal chain of variables, with each mediating variable explaining the effects of the preceding one on the next one. An example is shown in Figure 1-1. Leader training and coaching of a subordinate will improve the person's task skills, and an inspiring vision is likely to increase subordinate task motivation. These changes will jointly improve subordinate performance. The farther along in the causal chain, the longer it takes for the effect to occur. For outcomes at the end of a long causal chain, there may be a considerable delay before the effects of the leader's actions on an individual subordinate, the leader's work unit, or the organizational subunit are evident. The end-result outcomes are more likely to be influenced by other variables that are not measured. When the delay is long and there is considerable "contamination" of end-result criteria by extraneous events, then these criteria may be less useful for assessing leadership effectiveness than more immediate outcomes.

In many cases, a leader has both immediate and delayed effects on the same criterion. The two types of effects may be consistent or inconsistent. When they are inconsistent, the immediate outcome may be very different from the delayed outcomes. For example, profits may be increased in the short run by eliminating costly activities that have a delayed effect on profits, such as equipment maintenance, research and development, investments in new technology, and employee skill training. In the long run, the net effect of cutting these essential activities is likely to be lower profits because the negative consequences slowly increase and eventually outweigh any benefits. The opposite effect can also occur: increased investment in these activities is likely to reduce immediate profits but increase long-term profits.

What Criteria to Use

There is no simple answer to the question of how to evaluate leadership effectiveness. The selection of appropriate criteria depends on the objectives and values of the person making the evaluation, and people have different values. For example, top management may prefer different criteria than other employees, customers, or shareholders. To cope with the problems of incompatible criteria, delayed effects, and the preferences of different stakeholders, it is usually best to include a variety of criteria in research on leadership effectiveness and to examine the impact of the leader on each criterion over an extended period of time. Multiple conceptions of effectiveness, like multiple conceptions of leadership, serve to broaden our perspective and enlarge the scope of inquiry.

Research Methods for Studying Leadership Effectiveness

Over time, a wide variety of research methods have been developed to study leadership effectiveness (Antonakis et al., 2004). The most common method is the use of survey research with questionnaires filled out by the leaders themselves or by subordinates and other people who interact with the leader, such as a leader's boss or other managers in the organization. The questionnaires usually measure how much a leader uses different types of behavior, and researchers examine how a leader's pattern of behavior is related to measures of outcomes influenced by the leader, such as subordinate satisfaction, task commitment, and performance.

Another type of study uses descriptions of leader actions and decisions obtained from observation, diaries, critical incidents, or interviews with leaders and their subordinates or followers. The behavior descriptions are coded into categories and related to measures of leadership effectiveness. Case studies and biographies of famous leaders can also be content analyzed to identify behaviors used by effective and ineffective leaders.

A third type of study involves the use of experiments in which the researchers assess the effects of different patterns of leader behavior on group processes and outcomes. Sometimes the studies (called "lab experiments") involve temporary task groups of students with a leader instructed to use the type of behavior being studied. Sometimes the researchers use a scenario method that has participants read incidents or view videos that each show a different pattern of leader behavior, and then participants indicate how they would likely respond to each type of leader. Field experiments involve actual leaders who are randomly assigned to different treatment conditions. Leaders in the "experimental group" are trained or otherwise influenced to use specific types of behavior, and these leaders are compared to the untrained leaders in a "control group" on measures of leadership effectiveness. Leader behavior and effectiveness are usually measured before the intervention (the "premeasures") and at an appropriate time after the intervention (the "postmeasures") to verify that the desired changes were achieved and undesired changes did not occur. Since being selected to participate in the intervention can influence a person's attitudes and behavior, the control group sometimes includes a placebo treatment such as training that is not directly related to the outcomes. When it is not feasible to have a control group or placebo condition, some quasi-experimental field studies use only one group of leaders and compare their effectiveness before and after the manipulation or intervention.

In recent years, leadership researchers have begun to make more use of new methods that can provide novel insights into how and why leaders emerge and exert influence (Jacquart, Cole, Gabriel, Koopman, & Rosen, 2018; Schyns, Hall, & Neves, 2017). One type of study examines social networks within organizations to determine which individuals exert influence and leadership within the network. Other studies use implicit measures to tap into automatic cognitive processes that people use without conscious awareness to describe leaders by using broad classifications such as charismatic, authentic, ethical, and empowering. Another stream of research uses biosensor methods that combine biology (e.g., genetic assessments of DNA), chemistry (e.g., drawing blood to examine chemical markers), and technology (e.g., neuroimaging using MRI) to identify the physical and psychological mechanisms that underlie leader traits and behaviors, follower reactions to leaders, and the development of leader–follower relationships. Yet another cutting-edge line of research employs behavioral genetics approaches such as studies that compare the attributes of identical twins who were raised apart, or fraternal twins who were raised together, to determine the relative influence of genetic ("nature") versus environmental ("nurture") forces on leadership emergence and effectiveness. Still another emerging field of inquiry focuses on what we can learn about leadership from people's reactions to leaders' facial expressions.

Each type of method for studying leadership has advantages and limitations, and the most appropriate method depends in part on the research question. The use of multiple methods is highly recommended to minimize the limitations of a single method. Unfortunately, multimethod studies are very rare. It is more common for researchers to select a method that is familiar, well accepted, and easy to use rather than determining the most appropriate method for the research question.

Major Perspectives in Leadership Theory and Research

The attraction of leadership as a subject of research and the many different conceptions of leadership have created a vast and bewildering literature. Attempts to organize the literature according to major approaches or perspectives show only partial success. One of the more useful ways to classify leadership theory and research is according to the type of variable that is emphasized the most. Three types of variables that are relevant for understanding leadership effectiveness include (1) characteristics of leaders, (2) characteristics of followers, and (3) characteristics of the situation. Examples of key variables within each category are shown in Table 1-3. Figure 1-2 depicts likely causal relationships among the variables.

Most leadership theories emphasize one category more than the others as the primary basis for explaining effective leadership, and leader characteristics have been emphasized most often over the past half-century. Another common practice is to limit the focus to one type of leader characteristic, namely traits, behavior, or power. To be consistent with most of the leadership literature, the theories and empirical research reviewed in this book are classified into the following five approaches: (1) the trait approach, (2) the behavior approach, (3) the power-influence approach, (4) the situational approach, and (5) the values-based approach, although some theories and research involve more than one approach.

Trait Approach

One of the earliest approaches for studying leadership was the trait approach. This approach emphasizes attributes of leaders such as personality, motives, values, and skills. Underlying this approach was the assumption that some people are natural leaders, endowed with certain traits not possessed by other people. Early leadership theories attributed managerial success to extraordinary abilities such as tireless energy, penetrating intuition, uncanny foresight, and irresistible persuasive powers. Hundreds of trait studies conducted during the 1930s and 1940s sought to discover these elusive qualities. The predominant research method was to look for a significant correlation between individual leader attributes and a criterion of leader success without examining any explanatory processes. This research failed to find any traits that would

TABLE 1-3 Key Variables in Leadership Theories

Characteristics of the Leader

- Traits (motives, personality)
- Values, integrity, and moral development
- Confidence and optimism
- Skills and expertise
- Leadership behavior
- Influence tactics
- Attributions about followers
- Affect (e.g., emotions and moods) and affective displays
- Mental models (beliefs and assumptions)

Characteristics of the Followers

- Traits (needs, values, self-concepts)
- Confidence and optimism
- Skills and expertise
- Attributions about the leader
- Identification with the leader
- Affect (e.g., emotions and moods) and affective displays
- Task commitment and effort
- Satisfaction with job and leader
- Cooperation and mutual trust

Characteristics of the Situation

- Type of organizational unit
- Size of organizational unit
- Position power and authority of leader
- Task structure and complexity
- Organizational culture
- Environmental uncertainty and change
- External dependencies and constraints
- National cultural values
- Temporal factors

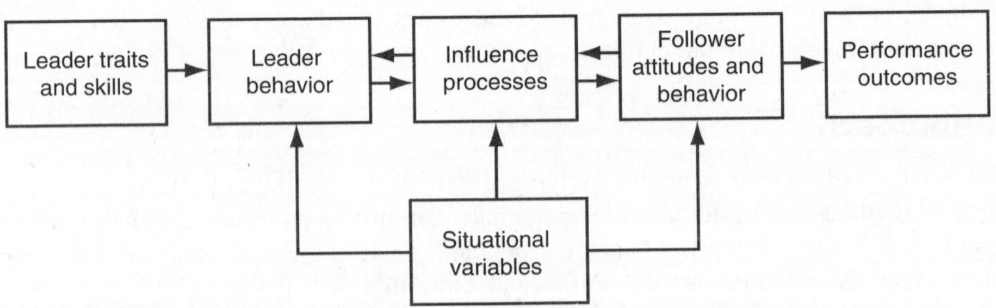

FIGURE 1-2 Causal Relationships Among the Primary Types of Leadership Variables

guarantee leadership success. However, as evidence from better designed research slowly accumulated over the years, researchers made progress in discovering how leader attributes are related to leadership behavior and effectiveness.

Behavior Approach

The behavior approach began in the early 1950s after many researchers became discouraged with the trait approach and began to pay closer attention to what managers actually do on the job. After identifying observable types of leader behavior, these behaviors were related to measures of outcomes such as the performance of the leader's group or work unit. Most behavior studies examined only one or two broadly defined categories of leader behavior, but the failure to find strong, consistent results encouraged more research on specific types of leader behavior. For example, instead of focusing on task-oriented behavior, the researcher could examine specific types of task-oriented behavior (e.g., clarifying, planning, monitoring, problem solving).

The most common research method in the behavior approach has been a survey field study with a behavior description questionnaire filled out by each leader or by subordinates of each leader. Hundreds of survey studies examined how the leadership behaviors are related to indicators of leadership effectiveness, such as subordinate satisfaction, task commitment, and performance. A much smaller number of studies used laboratory experiments, field experiments, or critical incidents to determine how effective leaders differ in behavior from ineffective leaders.

Power-Influence Approach

This line of research seeks to explain leadership effectiveness in terms of the amount and type of power possessed by a leader and how power is exercised. Power is viewed as important not only for influencing subordinates, but also for influencing peers, superiors, and people outside the organization, such as clients and suppliers. The favorite research method has been the use of survey questionnaires to relate leader power to various measures of leadership effectiveness.

Research on influence behavior has been used to determine how leaders influence followers and other people whose cooperation and support are needed by a leader. The study of influence tactics can be viewed as a bridge linking the power-influence approach and the behavior approach. The use of different influence tactics is compared in terms of their relative effectiveness for getting people to do what the leader wants. The research has used several different methods, including survey studies, influence incidents, lab experiments, and field experiments.

Situational Approach

The situational approach emphasizes the importance of contextual factors that influence leader behavior and how it influences outcomes such as subordinate satisfaction and performance. Major situational variables include the characteristics of followers, the nature of the work performed by the leader's unit, the type of organization, and the nature of the external environment. One line of research is an attempt to discover the extent to which aspects of the leadership situation influence leader behavior. The primary research method is a comparative study of leaders in different situations, and several methods have been used to measure leader behavior. The other type of situational research attempts to identify aspects of the situation that determine which leader traits, skills, or behaviors are most likely to enhance leadership effectiveness. The assumption is that the optimal pattern of leader behavior will depend on aspects of the situation. Theories describing this relationship are sometimes called "contingency theories" of leadership. Most of the contingency theories involve leader behavior, but a few involve leader traits and skills.

Values-Based Approach

Values-based approaches to leadership differ from the previously discussed approaches in that they highlight the importance of deeply held leader values that appeal to and influence followers. While there are differences in the points that they emphasize, theories of ethical leadership, authentic leadership, servant leadership, and spiritual leadership, all view leader values as the foundation for the leader's goals and behaviors and their impact on followers. That is, followers are often drawn to and identify with a leader because they share the leader's expressed values, or they see the leader as a person of character who they admire and they emulate the leader's values and behavior.

Some leadership approaches emphasize leader and follower values as well as leader behavior. Examples include charismatic and transformational leadership. Central to these theories is the notion that the leaders inspire and motivate followers to pursue an idealized vision involving their shared values.

Level of Conceptualization for Leadership Theories

Another way to classify leadership theories is in terms of the "level of conceptualization" used to describe a leader's influence on others. Leadership can be described as (1) an intra-individual process for leaders, (2) a dyadic process involving leader interaction with one subordinate, (3) a group process, or (4) an organizational process. The levels can be viewed as a hierarchy, as depicted in Figure 1-3. What level is emphasized will depend on the primary research question, the type of criterion variables used to evaluate leadership effectiveness, and the type of mediating processes used to explain leadership influence. Typical research questions for each level are listed in Table 1-4. The four levels of conceptualization, and their relative advantages and disadvantages, are described next.

Intra-Individual Processes

A number of scholars have used psychological theories of personality traits, values, skills, motives, cognitions, and emotions to explain the decisions and behavior of an individual leader. Examples can be found in theories about the leader attributes essential for different types

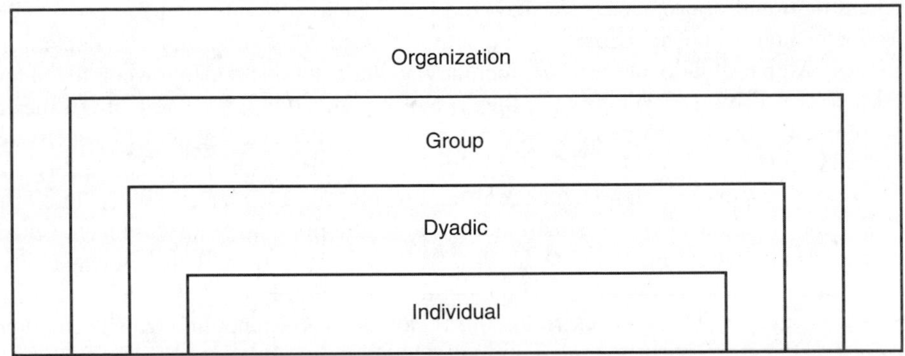

FIGURE 1-3 Levels of Conceptualization for Leadership Processes

TABLE 1-4 Research Questions at Different Levels of Conceptualization

Intra-Individual Theories

- How leader traits and values influence leadership behavior
- How leader skills are related to leader behavior
- How leaders make decisions
- How leaders manage their time
- How leaders are influenced by role expectations and constraints
- How leaders react to feedback and learn from experience
- How leaders experience and display affect (e.g., emotions and moods)
- How leaders form leadership identities
- How leaders can use self-development techniques

Dyadic Theories

- How a leader influences subordinate motivation and task commitment
- How a leader facilitates the work of a subordinate
- How a leader interprets information about a subordinate
- How a leader develops a subordinate's skills and confidence
- How a leader influences subordinate loyalty and trust
- How a leader uses influence tactics with a subordinate, peer, or boss
- How a leader and a subordinate influence each other
- How a leader develops a cooperative exchange relationship with a subordinate
- How a leader influences a follower to identify with the leader
- How a leader elicits and impacts follower emotions and vice versa

Group-Level Theories

- How different leader–member relations affect each other and team performance
- How leadership is shared in the group or team
- How leaders organize and coordinate the activities of team members
- How leaders influence cooperation and resolve disagreements in the team or unit
- How leaders influence collective efficacy and optimism for the team or unit
- How leaders influence collective learning and innovation in the team or unit
- How leaders influence collective identification of members with the team or unit
- How leaders influence the shared mental models of team members
- How unit leaders obtain resources and support from the organization and other units

Organizational-Level Theories

- How top executives influence members at other levels
- How leaders are selected at each level (and implications of process for the firm)
- How leaders influence organizational culture
- How leaders influence the efficiency and the cost of internal operations
- How leaders influence human relations and human capital in the organization
- How leaders make decisions about competitive strategy and external initiatives
- How conflicts among leaders are resolved in an organization
- How leaders influence innovation and major change in an organization

of leadership positions (see Chapter 7). Individual traits and skills are also used to explain a person's motivation to seek power and positions of authority (see Chapter 7), and individual values are used to explain ethical leadership and the altruistic use of power (see Chapter 9). Knowledge of leader attributes provides helpful insights for developing better theories of effective leadership.

However, the potential contribution of the intra-individual approach to leadership is limited, because it does not explicitly describe and explain how leaders influence subordinates, peers, bosses, and outsiders.

Dyadic Processes

The dyadic approach focuses on the relationship between a leader and another individual who is usually a subordinate. The need to influence direct reports is shared by leaders at all levels of authority from chief executives to department managers and work crew supervisors. The explanation of leader influence is usually in terms of how the leader causes the subordinate to be more motivated and more capable of accomplishing task assignments. These theories usually focus on leadership behavior as the source of influence over the attitudes, beliefs, feelings, motivation, and behavior of an individual subordinate. Reciprocal influence may be included in the theory, but subordinate influence over the leader is usually much less important than leader influence over the subordinate.

An example of a dyadic leadership theory is the leader–member exchange (LMX) theory described in Chapter 10, which describes how dyadic relationships evolve over time and take different forms, ranging from a casual exchange to a cooperative alliance with shared objectives and mutual trust. Although the LMX theory recognizes that the leader has multiple dyadic relationships, the focus is clearly on what happens within a single relationship. Much of the research on power and influence tactics (see Chapter 6) is also conceptualized in terms of dyadic processes.

Since real leaders seldom have only a single subordinate, some assumptions are necessary to make dyadic explanations relevant for explaining a leader's influence on the performance of a group or work unit. One assumption is that subordinates have work roles that are similar and independent. Subordinates may not be homogeneous with regard to skills and motives, but they have similar jobs. There is little potential for subordinates to affect each other's job performance, and group performance is the sum of the performances by individuals. An example of minimum interdependence is a district sales unit in which sales representatives work separately and independently of each other and sell the same product in different locations or to different customers. However, when there is high interdependence among group members, a group-level theory can better explain how leadership can influence overall group performance.

The dyadic theories do not include some of the leadership behaviors that are necessary to facilitate collective performance by a team or organization. Moreover, some of the dyadic behaviors that are effective in terms of dyadic influence will not be effective with regard to team performance or organizational performance. For example, attempts to develop a closer relationship with one subordinate (e.g., by providing more benefits) may create perceptions of inequity by other subordinates. Efforts to empower individual subordinates may create problems in achieving coordination among subordinates with interdependent jobs. The extra time needed by a leader to maximize performance by an individual subordinate (e.g., providing intensive coaching) may be more effectively used to deal with problems that involve the team or work group (e.g., obtaining necessary resources, facilitating cooperation and coordination).

Group Processes

When effective leadership is viewed from a group-level perspective, the focus is on the influence of leaders on collective processes that determine team performance. The explanatory influence processes include determinants of group effectiveness that can be influenced by leaders, and they usually involve all members of a group or team, not only a single subordinate. Examples of these collective explanatory processes include how well the work is organized to utilize personnel and resources, how committed members are to perform their work roles effectively, how confident members are that the task can be accomplished successfully, and the extent to which members trust each other and cooperate in accomplishing task objectives. Behavioral theories describing leadership processes in various types of groups and teams are discussed in Chapter 11, and leadership in executive teams is discussed in Chapter 12.

The leadership behaviors identified in dyadic theories are still relevant for leadership in teams, but other behaviors are also important. The focus is on behaviors used by a leader to influence group processes. Behaviors used to influence people outside the leader's work unit are also examined, but the focus is on the implications for the work unit, not for effects on other groups or the parent organization, which may not be positive ones. For example, getting more resources may enhance performance by the leader's department but harm the performance by another department for which the resources were critical. A group usually exists in a larger social system, and its effectiveness cannot be understood if the focus of the research is limited to the group's internal processes.

Organizational Processes

The organizational level of analysis describes leadership as a process that occurs in a larger "open system" in which groups are subsystems (Davison, Hollenbeck, Barnes, Sleesman, & Ilgen, 2012; Fleishman et al., 1991; Katz & Kahn, 1978; Mumford, 1986; Murase, Carter, DeChurch, & Marks, 2014). The survival and prosperity of an organization depend on adaptation to the environment and the acquisition of necessary resources. Some examples of leadership behaviors relevant for successful adaptation include gathering and interpreting information about the environment, identifying threats and opportunities, developing an effective strategy, negotiating favorable agreements for the organization, influencing outsiders to have a favorable impression of the organization and its products, and gaining cooperation and support from outsiders upon whom the organization is dependent. Survival and prosperity also depend on the efficiency of the transformation process used by the organization to produce its products and services. Efficiency is increased by finding more rational ways to organize and perform the work, and by deciding how to make the best use of available technology, resources, and personnel. Some examples of leadership responsibilities include designing an appropriate organizational structure, determining authority relationships, and coordinating operations across specialized subunits of the organization. All of these aspects of "strategic leadership" are discussed in Chapter 12.

As compared to dyadic or group-level theories of leadership, organization-level theories usually provide a better explanation of financial performance by an organization. Distributed leadership is less likely to be ignored in an organization-level theory, because it is obvious that an organization has many designated leaders whose actions must be coordinated. Management practices and systems (e.g., human resource management, operations management, strategic management) are also ignored or downplayed in dyadic and team leadership theories, but in theories of organizational leadership the need to integrate leading and managing is more obvious (Yukl & Lepsinger, 2004). More attention is given to subjects such as organizational structure and culture, organizational change, executive succession, and influence processes between the CEO and the top management team or board of directors.

Multi-level Theories

Multi-level theories include constructs from more than one level of explanation (Klein, Dansereau, & Hall, 1994; Rousseau, 1985). For example, the independent and dependent variables are at the same level of conceptualization, but moderator variables are at a different level. An even more complex type of multi-level theory may include leader influence on explanatory processes at more than one level and reciprocal causality among some of the variables. Multi-level theories of effective leadership provide a way to overcome the limitations of single-level theories, but it is very difficult to develop a multi-level theory that is parsimonious and easy to apply. The level of conceptualization has implications for the measures and methods of analysis used to test a theory, and multi-level theories are usually more difficult to test than single-level theories (Yammarino, Dionne, Chun, & Dansereau, 2005; Yammarino & Gooty, 2017). Despite the difficulties, there is growing interest in developing and testing multi-level theories of leadership. Efforts to develop multi-level theories, similarities in explanatory processes at different levels, and approaches for multi-level analysis are described in Chapter 15.

Other Bases for Comparing Leadership Theories

Key variables and level of conceptualization are not the only ways to compare leadership theories. This section briefly describes three other types of distinctions commonly used in the leadership literature: (1) leader-centered versus follower-centered theory, (2) universal versus contingency theory, and (3) descriptive versus prescriptive theory. Each type of distinction is better viewed as a continuum along which a theory can be located, rather than as a sharp dichotomy. For example, it is possible for a theory to have some descriptive elements as well as some prescriptive elements, some universal elements as well as some contingency elements, and an equal focus on leaders and followers.

Leader-Centered or Follower-Centered Theory

The extent to which a theory is focused on either the leader or followers is another useful way to classify leadership theories. Most leadership theories emphasize the characteristics and actions of the leader without much concern for follower characteristics. The leader focus is strongest in theory and research that identifies traits, skills, or behaviors that contribute to leader effectiveness. Most of the contingency theories (in Chapter 3) also emphasize leader characteristics more than follower characteristics.

Only a small amount of research and theory has emphasized follower characteristics. Empowerment theory describes how followers view their ability to influence important events (see Chapter 4). Attribution theory describes how followers view a leader's influence on events and outcomes (see Chapter 10), and other theories in the same chapter explain how followers can actively influence their work role and relationship with the leader, rather than being passive recipients of leader influence. The leader substitutes theory (see Chapter 3) describes aspects of the situation and follower attributes that make a hierarchical leader less important. The emotional contagion theory of charisma (see Chapter 8) describes how followers influence each other. Finally, theories of self-managed groups emphasize sharing of leadership functions among the members of a group; in this approach, the followers are also the leaders (see Chapter 11).

Theories that focus almost exclusively on either the leader or the follower are less useful than theories that offer a more balanced explanation. For example, most theories of leader power (Chapter 6) emphasize that influence over followers depends on follower perceptions of the leader as well as on objective conditions and the leader's influence behavior.

Descriptive or Prescriptive Theory

Another important distinction among leadership theories is the extent to which they are descriptive or prescriptive. Descriptive theories explain leadership processes, describe the typical activities of leaders, and explain why certain behaviors occur in particular situations. Prescriptive theories specify what leaders must do to become effective, and they identify any necessary conditions for using a particular type of behavior effectively.

The two perspectives are not mutually exclusive, and a theory can have both types of elements. For example, a theory that explains why a particular pattern of behavior is typical for leaders (descriptive) may also explain which aspects of behavior are most effective (prescriptive). However, the two perspectives are not always consistent. For example, the typical pattern of behavior for leaders is not always the optimal one. A prescriptive theory is especially useful when a wide discrepancy exists between what leaders typically do and what they should do to be most effective.

Universal or Contingency Theory

A universal theory describes some aspect of leadership that applies to all types of situations, and the theory can be either descriptive or prescriptive. A descriptive universal theory may describe typical functions performed to some extent by all types of leaders, whereas a prescriptive universal theory may specify functions all leaders must perform to be effective.

A contingency theory describes some aspects of leadership that apply to some situations but not to others, and these theories can also be either descriptive or prescriptive. A descriptive contingency theory may explain how leader behavior varies from one situation to another, whereas a prescriptive contingency theory describes effective behavior in a specific situation.

The distinction between universal and contingency theories is a matter of degree, not a sharp dichotomy. Some theories include both universal and situational aspects. For example, a prescriptive theory may specify that a particular type of leadership is always relevant but is more effective in some situations than in others. Even when a leadership theory is initially proposed as a universal theory, limiting and facilitating conditions are usually found in later research on the theory.

Organization of the Book

The diversity and complexity of the relevant literature make it difficult to organize a survey book on leadership. No single way of classifying the literature captures all of the important distinctions. The basis for organizing chapters in this edition of the book involves the type of leadership variable, the leadership context, and the amount and scope of the available theory and research on each subject. Some chapters focus on a type of leadership variable that has been studied extensively, such as task-oriented and relations-oriented behavior (Chapter 2), leader decision behavior (Chapter 4), change-oriented leader behavior (Chapter 5), charismatic and transformational leadership (Chapter 8), leader use of power and influence tactics

(Chapter 6), and leader traits, skills, and values (Chapters 7 and 9). Some chapters deal with special contexts for leadership, such as dyadic relations with individual followers (Chapter 10), leadership of teams and task groups (Chapter 11), strategic leadership of organizations (Chapter 12), and leadership in different cultures (Chapter 13). Ways for developing leaders are described in Chapter 14, and the final chapter (Chapter 15) provides an overview and summary of major findings about effective leadership and some concluding ideas about the essence of leadership.

Summary

Leadership has been defined in many different ways, but most definitions share the assumption that it involves an influence process for facilitating the performance of a collective task. Otherwise, the definitions differ in many respects, such as who exerts the influence, the intended beneficiary of the influence, the manner in which the influence is exerted, and the outcome of the influence attempt. Some theorists advocate treating leading and managing as separate roles or processes, but the proposed definitions do not resolve important questions about the scope of each process and how they are interrelated. No single, "correct" definition of leadership covers all situations. What matters most is how useful the definition is for increasing our understanding of effective leadership.

Most researchers evaluate leadership effectiveness in terms of the consequences for followers and other organization stakeholders, but the choice of outcome variables has differed considerably from researcher to researcher. Criteria differ in many important respects, including how immediate they are, and whether they have subjective or objective measures. When evaluating leadership effectiveness, multiple criteria should be considered to deal with these complexities and the different preferences of various stakeholders.

Leadership has been studied in different ways, depending on the researcher's methodological preferences and definition of leadership. The various methods all have limitations, and a multi-method approach is more likely to yield accurate results. Most researchers deal only with a narrow aspect of leadership, and most empirical studies fall into distinct lines of research such as the trait, behavior, power, value-based, and situational approaches. In recent years, there has been an increased effort to cut across and integrate these diverse approaches.

Level of analysis is another basis for classifying leadership theory and research. The levels include intra-individual, dyadic, group, and organizational. Each level provides some unique insights, but more research is needed on group and organizational processes, and more integration across levels is needed.

Another basis for differentiating theories is the relative focus on leader or follower. For many years, the research focused on leader characteristics and followers were studied only as the object of leader influence. A more balanced approach is needed, and some progress is being made in that direction.

Leadership theories can be classified as prescriptive versus descriptive, according to the emphasis on "what should be" rather than on "what occurs now." A final basis for differentiation (universal versus contingency) is the extent to which a theory describes leadership processes and relationships that are similar in all situations or that vary in specified ways across situations. Because the requirements for effective leadership are highly dependent on the leadership situation, and flexible leadership is needed to adapt to changing situations, more development and testing of contingency theories are desirable.

Review and Discussion Questions

1. What are some similarities and differences in the way leadership has been defined?
2. Why is it so difficult to measure leadership effectiveness?
3. What different criteria have been used to evaluate leadership effectiveness?
4. What different research methods have been used to study effective leadership?
5. Compare descriptive and prescriptive theories of leadership, and explain why both types of theory are useful.
6. Compare universal and contingency theories. Is it possible to have a theory with both universal and contingent aspects?

Key Terms

behavior approach
contingency theory
criteria of leadership effectiveness
descriptive theory
dyadic processes
follower-centered theory
leader-centered theory
level of conceptualization
mediating variable
power-influence approach
prescriptive theory
situational approach
trait approach
universal theory
values-based approach

Chapter 2 Leadership Behavior

Learning Objectives

After studying this chapter, you should be able to:

- Understand the different ways leader behavior has been described and examined.
- Understand the major types of leader behavior in leadership theory and research.
- Understand why task and relations behaviors are both important for leadership.
- Understand how specific types of task and relations behavior can be used effectively.

Introduction

The most frequently examined aspect of leadership is the type of behavior used by a leader in interactions with subordinates and other people. A major problem in research on the content of leadership behavior has been the identification of behavior categories that are relevant and meaningful for all leaders. The past half century of research has produced a bewildering variety of behavior concepts pertaining to managers and leaders. Sometimes different terms are used to refer to the same type of behavior. At other times, the same term is defined differently by various theorists. What is treated as a general behavior category by one theorist is viewed as two or three distinct categories by another theorist. What is a key behavior in one taxonomy may be missing in some other taxonomies. With so many divergent taxonomies, it is difficult to translate from one set of behaviors to another.

The chapter begins by explaining why there is so much diversity is leader behavior taxonomies. Next is a brief description of several broadly defined behaviors that have been used in much of the leadership research over the past half century. The final part of the chapter describes some specific types of task and relations behaviors that are important for effective leadership, with guidelines for using the behaviors. Other types of leadership behavior are described in later chapters of the book.

Reasons for Diverse Taxonomies of Leadership Behavior

There are several reasons why taxonomies developed to describe leadership behavior are so diverse. Behavior categories are abstractions rather than tangible attributes of the real world. The categories are derived from observed behavior in order to organize perceptions of the world and make them meaningful, but they do not exist in any objective sense. No absolute set of "correct" behavior categories can be established. Thus, taxonomies that differ in purpose can be expected to have somewhat different constructs. For example, taxonomies designed to facilitate research and theory on effective leadership behaviors differ from taxonomies designed to describe managerial roles, activities, or position responsibilities. Taxonomies of behaviors for leaders of small teams are not identical to taxonomies for top executives of large organizations.

Another source of diversity among taxonomies, even for those with the same purpose, is the possibility that behavior constructs can be formulated at different levels of abstraction or generality. For example, task-oriented behavior is a broad construct, whereas planning and clarifying are specific types of task-oriented behaviors. The scope of behavior taxonomies also differs. Some taxonomies attempt to include all relevant aspects of leader behavior, whereas other taxonomies focus on one aspect of behavior, such as specific procedures for making decisions.

A third source of diversity among behavior taxonomies is the method used to develop them. Some taxonomies are developed by examining the pattern of relationships among items on a behavior description questionnaire describing actual managers (e.g., with factor analysis). Some taxonomies are developed by having judges group behavior examples according to perceived similarity in content or purpose (judgmental classification). Some taxonomies are developed by deduction from a leadership theory (theoretical-deductive approach). Each method has its own biases and limitations, and the use of different methods results in somewhat different taxonomies, even when the purpose is the same. When different taxonomies are compared, it is obvious that there are substantial differences in the number of behaviors, the range of behaviors, and the level of abstraction of the behavior concepts. Some taxonomies have only a few broad behaviors, some have only specific behaviors, and some (called a "hierarchical taxonomy") have two or more broad behaviors with specific component behaviors for each broad behavior. Some taxonomies are intended to cover the full range of leader behaviors, whereas others only include the behaviors identified in a leadership theory.

Some Important Types of Leadership Behavior

Most of the theories and research on effective leadership behavior have involved one or two broadly defined behaviors. This section of the chapter briefly describes several of the broad behaviors that have been examined extensively in leadership research during the past half century, including task-oriented and relations-oriented behavior, change-oriented behavior, transformational leadership, empowering leadership, external behavior, and proactive influence tactics. A more detailed explanation of each behavior and guidelines for using it are provided later in this chapter or in other chapters.

Task-Oriented and Relations-Oriented Behaviors

Much of the early theory and research on effective leadership behavior involved broadly defined task-oriented and relations-oriented behaviors. Task-oriented behavior is primarily concerned with accomplishing the task in an efficient and reliable way. Relations-oriented behavior is primarily concerned with increasing mutual trust, cooperation, job satisfaction, and identification with the team or organization. Different labels that have been used to describe task-oriented and relations-oriented behavior are shown in Table 2-1.

TABLE 2-1 Similar Broadly Defined Behaviors in Early Leadership Research

Task-Oriented	Relations-Oriented	Source
Initiating Structure	Consideration	Fleishman (1953); Halpin & Winer (1957)
Concern for Production	Concern for People	Blake & Mouton (1964)
Instrumental Leadership	Supportive Leadership	House (1971)
Goal Emphasis; Work	Supportive Leadership	Bowers & Seashore (1966)
Facilitation	Interaction Facilitation	Taylor & Bowers (1972)
Performance Behavior	Maintenance Behavior	Misumi & Peterson (1985)

The task-oriented categories usually include specific behaviors such as clarifying work roles and task objectives, assigning specific tasks to subordinates, planning activities and tasks for the work group, and monitoring performance by subordinates. However, the definition for the two broad behaviors varies somewhat for different scholars, and the definitions sometimes include other types of specific behaviors. For example, a task-oriented behavior may include solving operational problems, and a relations-oriented behavior may include involving subordinates in making decisions affecting them. Moreover, some specific behaviors can be useful for improving more than one type of objective (e.g., task performance and relationships).

Scholars have reviewed and analyzed the results from the large number of studies on task-oriented and relations-oriented behaviors (e.g., Behrendt, Matz, & Göritz, 2017; Gottfredson & Aguinis, 2017; Judge, Piccolo, & Illies, 2004), but interpretation of overall results for the two broad types of behavior was made difficult by differences among studies in the behavior measures, types of criteria, and research methods that were used. Most studies found that subordinates were more satisfied with a leader who was considerate and supportive, although the relationship was weaker when the measures of behavior and satisfaction were not from the same source. Leader task-oriented behavior was not consistently related to subordinate satisfaction. In some studies, subordinates were more satisfied with a structuring leader, but in other studies they were less satisfied or there was no significant effect on satisfaction. Results are also inconsistent for studies on how the two broad behaviors are related to indicators of effective leadership. The findings suggest that all leaders need to use some task-oriented and relations-oriented behaviors, but the effects depend on the leader's ability to identify and use specific component behaviors that are relevant for the leadership situation. A detailed description of specific task-oriented and relations-oriented behaviors and guidelines for their use is presented later in the chapter.

Change-Oriented Behaviors

The early leadership theory and research paid little attention to behaviors directly concerned with encouraging and facilitating change. In the 1980s, some change-oriented behaviors were included in theories of charismatic and transformational leadership (see Chapter 8), but leading change was still not explicitly recognized as a type of behavior that is distinct from task-oriented and relations-oriented behaviors. Evidence for a distinct change-oriented category was found in later research (Anzengruber, Goetz, Nold, & Woelfle, 2017; Ekvall & Arvonen, 1991; Yukl, 1997, 1999a; Yukl, Gordon, & Taber, 2002). Four specific types of change-oriented behaviors include communicating an appealing vision of what could be changed, proposing specific changes, implementing a change, and encouraging innovation. Change leadership is discussed in Chapter 5.

Empowering and Participative Leadership

Another behavior category identified in the early leadership research involves decision-making procedures that a leader can use to involve others such as subordinates or team members in decisions about the work. Terms used to describe the frequent use of such procedures with subordinates include participative leadership, empowering leadership, and democratic leadership. Specific types of empowering decision procedures include consultation, joint decisions, and delegation. The frequent use of these decision procedures may reflect a strong concern for relations objectives such as subordinate commitment and development, as well as for task objectives such as decision quality. A participative leader may, in fact, be perceived as weak in the Indian context (Sinha 1980). Some of the research on empowering leadership includes other types of leader behaviors in addition to decision procedures (e.g., sharing information, providing resources). Participative and empowering leadership is discussed in Chapter 4.

Transformational Leadership

Another broadly defined leader behavior that was identified in the 1980s is usually called transformational leadership (Bass, 1985), although other terms for it include visionary leadership and inspirational leadership. The component behaviors vary for different theories, but they usually include a few relations-oriented behaviors such as supporting and developing, a few change-oriented behaviors such as articulating an appealing vision and encouraging innovative thinking, and a few other behaviors (e.g., leading by example, talking about personal values, making self-sacrifices for the team or organization). A participative leader may, in fact, be perceived as weak in the Indian context (Sinha 1980). Some of these behaviors are also described in theories of charismatic leadership. Theories and research involving transformational and charismatic leadership are described in Chapter 8.

External Leadership Behaviors

Most of the theories and research on leader behavior only involve behavior used in interactions with subordinates, but many leaders must also interact with other people in the same organization, such as bosses and people in other subunits, and with people outside their organization, such as customers, clients, suppliers, subcontractors, government officials, important people in the community, and managers from other organizations (Kotter, 1982). These interactions reflect the need for information about complex and uncertain events that influence subunit operations and depend on the cooperation and assistance of numerous people outside the immediate chain of command. Three distinct and broadly defined categories of external behavior are networking, external monitoring, and representing (Hassan, Prussia, Mahsud, & Yukl, 2018; Luthans & Lockwood, 1984; Stogdill, Goode, & Day, 1962; Yukl et al., 2002; Yukl & Van Fleet, 1982; Yukl, Wall, & Lepsinger, 1990).

Networking involves building and maintaining favorable relationships with peers, superiors, and outsiders who can provide desired information, resources, and political support. The behavior category includes attending professional conferences and ceremonies, joining social networks, socializing informally with people outside the leader's work unit, doing favors for peers or outsiders, and using impression management tactics such as ingratiation.

External monitoring includes collecting information about relevant events and changes in the external environment, identifying threats and opportunities for the leader's group or organization, and identifying best practices that can be imitated or adapted. The external monitoring may involve using a leader's network of contacts, studying relevant publications and industry reports, conducting market research, and studying the decisions and actions of competitors and opponents.

Representing includes lobbying for resources and assistance from superiors, promoting and defending the reputation of the leader's group or organization, negotiating agreements with peers and outsiders such as clients and suppliers, and using political tactics to influence decisions made by superiors or governmental agencies. The types and amount of external behaviors that are needed for a leader depend to a great extent on the leadership situation, and these behaviors are discussed in Chapters 11 and 12.

Proactive Influence Tactics

Several types of influence tactics are used in influence attempts made by leaders with subordinates, peers, bosses, and people outside their organization, such as clients and suppliers. This type of behavior is important to gain compliance or commitment to requests and proposals, especially ones that are not routine and unlikely to be successful if the leader makes only a simple request. Influence tactics can also be used by a leader to resist or modify influence attempts made by others. Types of tactics and guidelines for using them effectively are discussed in Chapter 6.

Specific Task-Oriented Leader Behaviors

This section of the chapter describes some specific types of task-oriented behaviors found to be related to effective leadership (Yukl, 2012; Yukl et al., 2002). The behaviors include planning, clarifying, monitoring, and problem solving. After each type of behavior is described, guidelines for using the behavior are provided. The guidelines are based on applied research in leadership, on suggestions by practitioners, and on relevant theory and research in the management literature (e.g., project management, operations management, performance management, and human resources management).

Planning Work Activities

Short-term planning of work activities means deciding what to do, how to do it, who will do it, and when it will be done. The purpose of planning is to ensure efficient organization of the work unit, coordination of activities, and effective utilization of resources. Planning is a broadly defined behavior that includes making decisions about objectives, priorities, strategies, organization of the work, assignment of responsibilities, scheduling of activities, and allocation of resources among different activities according to their relative importance. Special names are sometimes used for subvarieties of planning. For example, operational planning is the scheduling of routine work and determination of task assignments for the next day or week. Action planning is the development of detailed action steps and schedules for implementing a new policy or carrying out a project. Contingency planning is the development of procedures for avoiding or coping with potential problems or disasters. Finally, planning also includes determining how to allocate time to different responsibilities and activities ("time management").

TABLE 2-2 Guidelines for Action Planning

- Identify necessary action steps.
- Identify the optimal sequence of action steps.
- Estimate the time needed to carry out each action step.
- Determine starting times and deadlines for each action step.
- Estimate the cost of each action step.
- Determine who will be accountable for each action step.
- Develop procedures for monitoring progress.

Planning is mostly a cognitive activity that involves analyzing information and making decisions about how task objectives will be accomplished. Planning seldom occurs in a single behavior episode; instead it tends to be a prolonged process that occurs over a period of weeks or months. Because planning is a cognitive activity that seldom occurs as a single discrete episode, it is difficult to observe (Snyder & Glueck, 1980). Nevertheless, some observable aspects include writing plans, preparing written budgets, developing written schedules, and meeting with others to formulate objectives and strategies. Planning is most observable when a manager takes action to implement plans by communicating them to others and making specific task assignments.

The importance of planning and organizing has long been recognized in the management literature (Carroll & Gillen, 1987; Drucker, 1974; Fayol, 1949; Quinn, 1980; Urwick, 1952). Evidence of a relationship between planning and managerial effectiveness is provided by a variety of different types of studies (e.g., Boyatzis, 1982; Carroll & Gillen, 1987; Kim & Yukl, 1995; Kotter, 1982; Morse & Wagner, 1978; Shipper & Wilson, 1992; Yukl, 2012; Yukl et al., 1990). Recommended steps for action planning are shown in Table 2-2.

Clarifying Roles and Objectives

Clarifying is the communication of plans, policies, and role expectations. Major subcategories of clarifying include (1) defining job responsibilities and requirements, (2) setting performance goals, and (3) assigning specific tasks. The purpose of clarifying behavior is to guide and coordinate work activity and make sure people know what to do and how to do it. It is essential for each subordinate to understand what duties, functions, and activities are required in the job and what results are expected. Even a subordinate who is highly competent and motivated may fail to achieve a high level of performance if confused about responsibilities and priorities. Such confusion results in misdirected effort and neglect of important responsibilities in favor of less important ones. The more complex and multifaceted the job, the more difficult it is to determine what needs to be done.

Clarifying behavior is likely to be more important when there is substantial role ambiguity or role conflict for members of the work unit. Less clarifying is necessary if the organization has elaborate rules and regulations dictating how the work should be done and subordinates understand them, or if subordinates are highly trained professionals who have the expertise to do their jobs without much direction from superiors. Contingency theories about the amount of clarifying behavior needed in different situations are described in Chapter 3.

Several studies have found a positive relationship between clarifying and managerial effectiveness (Alexander, 1985; Bauer & Green, 1998; Kim & Yukl, 1995; Van Fleet & Yukl, 1986b; Yukl et al., 1990). Evidence from many studies (including some field experiments)

TABLE 2-3 Guidelines for Clarifying Roles and Objectives

- Clearly explain an assignment.
- Explain the reason for the assignment.
- Check for understanding of the assignment.
- Provide any necessary instruction in how to do the task.
- Explain priorities for different objectives or responsibilities.
- Set specific goals and deadlines for important tasks.

indicates that setting specific, challenging goals usually improves performance (see Locke & Latham, 1990).

The following guidelines indicate how leaders can effectively assign tasks to subordinates and clarify subordinate roles and responsibilities (see Table 2-3 for summary).

- **Clearly explain an assignment.**

When assigning tasks, use clear language that is easy to understand. If more than one task is involved, explain one task at a time to avoid confusion. Describe what needs to be done, say when it should be done, and describe the expected results. Explain any organization rules or standard procedures that must be followed by anyone who does that type of task.

- **Explain the reason for the assignment.**

Unless it is obvious already or there is no time for it, explain why the task is necessary and important and why you have selected the person to be responsible for it. Understanding the purpose of an assignment can increase task commitment and facilitate subordinate initiative in overcoming obstacles.

- **Check for understanding of the assignment.**

Be alert for indications that the person does not understand your instructions or is reluctant to do what is asked (e.g., a puzzled expression or hesitant response). For a complex task that the person has not done previously, it is useful to probe for understanding. For example, ask how the person expects to carry out the task.

- **Provide any necessary instruction in how to do the task.**

If the person needs instruction in how to do a task, demonstrate and explain the procedures one step at a time using simple, clear language. Point out both correct and incorrect procedures, and explain the cues that indicate whether a procedure has been done correctly. If the task involves an observable procedure that only takes a short time to complete, and the person lacks experience doing it, demonstrate the procedure, and then have the person practice it while you observe and provide feedback and coaching.

- **Explain priorities for different objectives or responsibilities.**

Tasks often involve more than one type of objective, and there may be trade-offs among the objectives. For example, the objectives may involve both quantity and quality of the work, and when too much time is devoted to one objective the other may suffer. There is no simple way to determine priorities, but they should reflect the importance of the task for the manager's unit and the organization. It is essential to explain the relative priorities of different objectives and provide guidance on how to achieve an effective balance among them.

- **Set specific goals and deadlines for important tasks.**

Clear, specific performance goals are often useful to guide efforts and increase task motivation. The goals may involve the performance of individual subordinates or the overall performance of a team or work unit. The goals should be challenging but realistic given the difficulty of the task, subordinate skills, and available resources needed for the work. For a task that needs to be completed by a definite time and date, it is useful to set a specific deadline for the overall task and sometimes for each important step.

Monitoring Operations and Performance

Monitoring involves gathering information about the operations of the manager's organizational unit, including the progress of the work, the performance of individual subordinates, the quality of products or services, and the success of projects or programs. Monitoring can take many forms, including observation of work operations, reading written reports, watching computer screen displays of performance data, inspecting the quality of samples of the work, and holding progress review meetings with an individual or group. Many organizations use video cameras to observe operations and increase security, and monitoring of telephone calls and Internet correspondence is sometimes used to check on quality for customer service representatives. To assess performance for retail facilities and service centers, it is sometimes useful to have someone acting as a customer visit the facility to observe how well the employees provide customer service. The appropriate type of monitoring depends on the nature of the task and other aspects of the situation.

Monitoring provides much of the information needed for planning and problem solving, which is why it is so important for managerial effectiveness (Meredith & Mantel, 1985). Information gathered from monitoring is used to identify problems and opportunities, as well as to formulate and modify objectives, strategies, plans, policies, and procedures. Monitoring provides the information needed to evaluate subordinate performance, recognize achievements, identify performance deficiencies, assess training needs, provide coaching and assistance, and allocate rewards such as a pay increase or promotion. When monitoring is insufficient, a manager will be unable to detect problems before they become serious (problems such as declining quality, low productivity, cost overruns, behind-schedule projects, employee dissatisfaction, and conflicts among employees).

The appropriate degree of monitoring will depend on the competence of the subordinate and the nature of the work. More frequent monitoring is desirable when subordinates are inexperienced and insecure, when mistakes have serious consequences, when the tasks of subordinates are highly interdependent and require close coordination, and when disruptions in the workflow are likely from equipment breakdowns, accidents, materials shortages, personnel shortages, and so forth. Monitoring of performance is most difficult when the work involves unstructured, unique tasks for which results can be determined only after a long time interval. For example, it is more difficult to evaluate the performance of a research scientist or human resource manager than the performance of a sales representative or production manager. Monitoring too closely or in ways that communicate distrust can undermine subordinate self-confidence and reduce intrinsic motivation.

TABLE 2-4 Guidelines for Monitoring Operations

- Identify and measure key performance indicators.
- Monitor key process variables as well as outcomes.
- Measure progress against plans and budgets.
- Develop independent sources of information about performance
- Conduct progress review meetings at appropriate times.
- Observe operations directly when it is feasible.
- Ask specific questions about the work.
- Encourage reporting of problems and mistakes.
- Use information from monitoring to guide other behaviors.

As noted previously, monitoring indirectly affects a manager's performance by facilitating the effective use of other behaviors. The amount of research on the effects of monitoring by leaders is still limited, but evidence that monitoring is related to managerial effectiveness is provided by several studies using a variety of research methods (e.g., Amabile, Schatzel, Moneta, & Kramer, 2004; Jenster, 1987; Kim & Yukl, 1995; Komaki, 1986; Komaki, Desselles, & Bowman, 1989; Komaki & Minnich, 2002; Yukl et al., 1990).

The following guidelines describe effective ways to monitor operations and the performance of subordinates (see summary in Table 2-4).

- **Identify and measure key indicators of performance.**

Accurate, timely information about the operations and performance of the work unit is essential for effective leadership by the work unit manager. When performance involves multiple criteria, they should all be measured and used for evaluation performance. It is a common mistake to focus on one or two indicators that are easy to measure, even though they do not provide a complete and accurate picture of unit performance.

- **Monitor key processes as well as outcomes.**

Processes that determine outcomes should be measured in addition to the outcomes themselves to gain a better understanding of causal relationships and to detect problems earlier. For example, quality problems can be resolved more effectively by identifying the critical steps in the production process or service activity where they occur and measuring them continuously to detect and resolve them quickly.

- **Measure progress against plans and budgets.**

Interpretation of information about operations is aided by relating it to plans, forecasts, and budgets. For example, at appropriate times (e.g., monthly or quarterly) compare actual expenditures to budgeted amounts to identify any discrepancies. If expenditures exceed budgeted amounts, investigate to determine the reason for the discrepancy and determine if there is a problem that requires corrective action.

- **Develop independent sources of information.**

Instead of relying on a single source for information, it is better to compare information from multiple sources. Using multiple sources makes it less likely that important information will be lost or discounted. Multiple sources can be found by enlisting the aid of other people who have relevant information, such as peers, customers and clients, or members of the organization below the level of immediate subordinates. For example, a top executive in one company made it known that he would have breakfast in the company cafeteria at a particular time on certain days, and he invited any employees who were interested to join him for an informal discussion of company operations.

- **Conduct progress review meetings at appropriate times.**

Progress review meetings provide an opportunity to review and discuss a subordinate's progress in a project or assignment. The optimal frequency and timing for progress review meetings depend on the nature of the task and the competence of the subordinate. More frequent meetings are appropriate for a subordinate who is learning a new job or who is unreliable. The timing of meetings depends partly on when performance data will be available and when key action steps are scheduled for completion.

- **Observe operations directly.**

Information about operations can be obtained from reports and progress review meetings, but there is no substitute for direct observation. Walking around to observe operations and talk to employees is especially useful for middle managers and top executives who tend to become isolated from day-to-day operations. Visiting worksites and different facilities of the company is also a way to see for yourself how things are going and check on the accuracy of reports about operations. The success of a visit to a worksite depends partly on how the visit is arranged and conducted. Most visits should be unannounced and made by the manager alone. If advance notice is provided, people will probably try to make a favorable impression, making it difficult to assess how things are normally done. If the manager brings along several staff assistants, employees are likely to be more inhibited about what they say.

- **Ask specific questions.**

When conducting progress review meetings or observing operations, managers should use their knowledge about the work processes and their subordinates to ask specific questions and obtain vital information about the work. A probing but nonjudgmental style of questioning is better than a critical tone. Questions usually elicit better information if worded in an open-ended way rather than asking for a simple yes or no answer. Since questions reflect a manager's concerns, it is an effective way to communicate those concerns to people even while getting information from them.

- **Encourage reporting of problems and mistakes.**

The success of monitoring depends on getting accurate information from people who may be reluctant to provide it. Subordinates are often afraid to inform their boss about problems, mistakes, and delays. Even a subordinate who is not responsible for a problem may be reluctant to report it if the leader's reaction is likely to be an angry outburst (the "kill the messenger" syndrome). Thus, it is essential to react to information about problems in a constructive, non-punitive way. Show appreciation for accurate information, even if it is not favorable, and help subordinates learn from mistakes rather than punishing them.

- **Use information from monitoring to guide other behaviors.**

When monitoring reveals that a subordinate has been highly effective, it is an opportunity to provide praise. If performance is below targeted levels or a project is behind schedule, the leader should acknowledge the problem rather than ignoring it and initiate actions to deal with it. It may be necessary to revise the action plan and schedule if it is unrealistic, to provide more resources for the task, or to provide coaching if the subordinate lacks adequate skills.

Solving Operational Problems

Problem solving is a type of behavior used by leaders to deal with disruptions of normal operations and member behavior that is illegal, destructive, or unsafe. Leaders face an endless stream of operational problems and disturbances in their work, and examples include serious accidents, power failures, equipment breakdowns, natural disasters, terrorist attacks, quality problems, supply shortages, and strikes by labor unions. Several survey studies found that problem solving was related to effective leadership (e.g., Kim & Yukl, 1995; Morgeson, 2005; Yukl & Van Fleet, 1982; Yukl et al., 1990). The descriptive research using critical incidents, diaries, and comparative case studies also provides evidence that effective leaders deal with operational problems in a timely and appropriate way (e.g., Amabile et al., 2004; Boyatzis, 1982; Van Fleet & Yukl, 1986; Yukl & Van Fleet, 1982). The descriptive research also found that ineffective leaders ignore signs of a serious problem, avoid responding until it becomes much worse (e.g., by forming a committee to study it and write a detailed report), make a hasty response before identifying the cause of the problem, discourage useful input from subordinates, or react in ways that create more serious problems at a later time.

It is desirable to evaluate whether a problem can be solved within a reasonable time period with available resources and (2) whether it is worthwhile to invest the time, effort, and resources on this problem rather than on others (Isenberg, 1984; McCall & Kaplan, 1985). Descriptive research on effective managers suggests that they give priority to important problems that can be solved, rather than ignoring these problems or trying to avoid responsibility for them by passing the problem to someone else or involving more people than necessary to diffuse responsibility for decisions (Peters & Austin, 1985; Peters & Waterman, 1982). For problems that are either trivial or intractable, it is often best to postpone attempts to resolve them and use the time more effectively. Of course, some problems are so important that they should not be postponed even when the initial probability of a successful solution is low.

When serious disruptions in the work occur, people look to their leader to explain the problem and what is being done to deal with it. In the absence of timely, appropriate information, harmful rumors may occur and people may become discouraged and afraid. A leader can help to avoid unnecessary stress or panic by explaining how the problem is being resolved and showing confidence that the actions will be successful. Effective leaders provide firm, confident direction to their team or work unit as they cope with the problem.

Problem solving can be proactive as well as reactive, and effective leaders take the initiative to identify likely problems and determine how to avoid them or minimize their adverse effects. Many things can be done to prepare the work unit or organization to respond effectively to predictable types of disruptions such as accidents, equipment failures, natural disasters, health emergencies, supply shortages, computer hacking, and terrorist attacks.

Researchers and some practitioners have identified types of leader actions that are effective for dealing with operational problems and disruptions of the work (e.g., DeChurch et al., 2011; Heifetz, Grashow, & Linsky, 2009; Mitroff, 2004; Muffet-Willett & Kruse, 2008). The amount of

TABLE 2-5 Guidelines for Solving Operational Problems

- Anticipate operational problems and prepare for them.
- Learn to recognize early warning signs for an impending problem.
- Quickly identify the cause and scope of the problem.
- Look for connections among problems.
- Direct the response to the problem in a confident and decisive way.
- Keep people informed about the problem and what is being done to resolve it.
- Be willing to explore innovative solutions

research is limited, but the findings suggest some practical guidelines for leaders to use problem-solving behaviors (see summary in Table 2-5).

- **Anticipate operational problems and prepare for them.**

Many types of problems that occur only infrequently can be very disruptive and costly. Examples include accidents, medical emergencies, terrorist attacks, supply shortages, strikes, sabotage, and natural disasters. If possible, it is worthwhile to plan in advance how to avoid them. For problems that are unavoidable, contingency plans should be made to cope with them effectively when they eventually occur. Look for best practices found in analyses of past experience with similar problems. Implement training on how to respond to different types of disruptions and emergencies. If appropriate, have the team or work unit practice procedures for handling an emergency, and conduct after-activity reviews to assess preparedness and facilitate learning.

- **Learn to recognize early warning signs for an impending problem.**

Some types of problems have early warning signs, and a leader should learn to recognize them. A common response to signs that unpleasant events will soon occur is to deny the signs and do nothing in the hope that the problem will go away. However, for some types of disruptions an early response can reduce the impact and costs. The responsibility for detecting emerging problems should be shared with all employees who have opportunities to observe these signs.

- **Quickly identify the cause and scope of the problem.**

A common reason for ineffective problem solving is the failure to correctly identify the reasons for the problem. An incorrect diagnosis can result in actions that not only fail to solve the problem, but also waste resources, create new problems, and result in delays that allow the problem to get worse. It is essential for the leader to make a quick but systematic analysis of the situation. However, despite the pressure to act quickly, the analysis should not be hasty and superficial. Unless the cause of the problem is identified correctly, time and resources will be wasted in trying to solve the wrong problem. Even when the cause of the problem is obvious, the scope of the problem may not be known initially, and it can be a factor in selecting an appropriate response. Either underestimating or overestimating the scope of a problem can result in an inappropriate response.

- **Look for connections among problems.**

In the process of trying to make sense out of the streams of problems, issues, and opportunities encountered by a manager, it is important to look for relationships among them rather than assuming that they are distinct and independent (Isenberg, 1984). A broader view of problems provides better insights for understanding them. By relating problems to each other and to informal strategic objectives, a manager is more likely to recognize opportunities to take actions that contribute to the solution of several related problems at the same time. Finding these connections is more likely if the manager is able to remain flexible and open-minded about the definition of a problem and actively considers multiple definitions for each problem.

- **Direct the response to the problem in a confident and decisive way.**

The need for more direction is especially great for a team that must react quickly in a coordinated way to cope with a serious crisis or emergency for which it is unprepared. Knowing how to remain calm and deal with a crisis in a systematic but decisive manner requires a leader with considerable skill and confidence. The leader should provide clear, confident direction to guide the response of the team or unit. However, the leader should also remain receptive to relevant information and suggestions from followers. Followers often have important information and useful suggestions on how to deal with a crisis, especially when it is a novel one.

- **Keep people informed about the problem and what is being done to resolve it.**

In the absence of timely and accurate information about a crisis, harmful rumors are likely to occur, and people may become discouraged and afraid. A manager can help prevent unnecessary stress for subordinates by interpreting threatening events and emphasizing positive elements rather than leaving people to focus on negatives. When feasible, it is helpful to provide short, periodic briefings about progress in efforts to deal with the crisis.

- **Be willing to explore innovative solutions.**

When no effective remedy is obvious for a problem and a rapid resolution is not needed, it may be useful to initially conduct one or more small-scale experiments to gain more information about the causes and good solutions. Sometimes taking limited action is the only way to develop an adequate understanding of the problem (Isenberg, 1984; Quinn, 1980). Peters and Waterman (1982, p. 13) found that managers in effective companies had a bias for action characterized as "do it, fix it, try it."

Specific Relations-Oriented Leader Behaviors

This section of the chapter describes some specific types of relations-oriented behaviors found to be related to effective leadership (Yukl, 2012; Yukl et al., 2002). The behaviors include Supporting, Developing, and Recognizing. After each behavior is described, guidelines for using the behavior are provided.

Supportive Leadership

Supportive leadership (or "supporting") includes a wide variety of behaviors that show consideration, acceptance, and concern for the needs and feelings of other people. Supportive leadership helps to build and maintain effective interpersonal relationships. A manager who is considerate and friendly toward people is more likely to win their friendship and loyalty. The emotional ties that are formed make it easier to gain cooperation and support from people on whom the manager must rely to get the work done. It is more satisfying to work with someone who is friendly, cooperative, and supportive than with someone who is cold and impersonal, or worse, hostile and uncooperative. Improvements in job satisfaction are likely to result in less absenteeism, less turnover, less alcoholism, and less drug abuse (Brief, Schuler, & Van Sell, 1981; Ganster, Fusilier, & Mayes, 1986; Kessler, Price, & Wortman, 1985). Supportive leadership may increase a subordinate's acceptance of the leader, trust of the leader, and willingness to do extra things for the leader.

Some forms of supporting behavior increase subordinate self-confidence and reduce the amount of stress in the job. Stress is reduced by showing appreciation, listening to problems and complaints, providing assistance when necessary, expressing confidence in the person, doing things to make the work environment more enjoyable, and buffering the person from unnecessary demands by outsiders. Stress is increased by making unreasonable demands, pressuring the person to work faster, being overly critical, and insisting on compliance with unnecessary bureaucratic requirements. Although results in research on the effects of considerate, supportive leadership are not consistent, it is likely this type of behavior will improve subordinate satisfaction and performance in many situations.

The following guidelines indicate ways that managers can use supporting behavior effectively with subordinates and others (see Table 2-6 for summary).

- **Show acceptance and positive regard.**

Due to the considerable position power of most managers, subordinates are especially sensitive to indications of acceptance and approval (or rejection and criticism). Outbursts of anger, harsh criticism, and personal insults are stressful regardless of the source, but especially when the source is someone who has considerable position power. There are many ways to show acceptance and concern for people in your day-to-day behavior. Supportive leadership means being polite and considerate. Maintain a pleasant, cheerful disposition. Spend some time with subordinates to get to know them better and find out about their interests, recreational activities, family, and hobbies. Remember prior conversations with the person, including details about the person's family and activities. If necessary, keep a notebook with this type of information about each subordinate. Be discreet about things that are told to you in confidence (don't spread gossip about the personal lives of subordinates or team members).

- **Show interest in the person as an individual.**

Most people want to be appreciated as individuals as well as valued for their contributions to the tasks performed by the leader's group or organizational subunit. One way to show interest in a person is to gather and remember important details about work and non-work subjects that are important for the person (e.g., career aspirations, interests and hobbies, family members,

TABLE 2-6 Guidelines for Supporting

- Show acceptance and positive regard.
- Show interest in the person as an individual
- Provide sympathy and support when the person is anxious or upset.
- Bolster the person's self-esteem and confidence.
- Be willing to help with personal problems.

leisure activities). In *The 21 Irrefutable Laws of Leadership*, John C. Maxwell (2007, p. 118), describes a key guideline for achieving his "Law of Connection" as follows:

> If you got on an elevator with me and asked me to tell you the secret to good communication before I got off at the next floor, I'd tell you to focus on others, not yourself. That is the number one problem of inexperienced speakers, and it is also the number one problem of ineffective leaders. You will always connect faster when your focus is not on yourself.

- **Provide sympathy and support when the person is anxious or upset.**

Show understanding and sympathy for someone who is upset by stress and difficulties in the work. Take time to listen to the person's concerns. Try to understand why the person is anxious or frustrated, and when appropriate, offer coaching, advice, and personal assistance. For example, pitching in to help subordinates do their work when the workload is unusually high is an effective way to demonstrate support. Job stress for subordinates can be reduced by buffering them from frivolous complaints and unrealistic demands made by outsiders or by higher management.

- **Bolster the person's self-esteem and confidence.**

Indicate that the person is a valued member of the organization. Express confidence in the person when assigning a difficult task. When someone is discouraged due to job problems and setbacks in a difficult task, supportive managers will say things to help boost a person's self-confidence. When mistakes or performance problems occur, supportive managers deal with them in a constructive manner instead of "blowing up" and criticizing the person harshly. It is important to indicate a sincere desire to help someone learn from mistakes and overcome performance problems.

- **Be willing to help with personal problems.**

Effective managers are willing to help an employee deal with personal problems (e.g., family problems, financial problems, substance abuse) when assistance is requested or it is clearly needed because the person's performance is being adversely affected. Examples of things that a manager can do include helping the person identify and express concerns and feelings, helping the person understand the reasons for a personal problem, providing factual information that will help the person, referring the person to professionals who can provide assistance, helping the person identify alternatives, and offering advice (Burke, Wier, & Duncan, 1976; Kaplan & Cowen, 1981).

Developing Subordinate Skills

Developing includes several managerial practices that are used to increase a subordinate's skills and facilitate job adjustment and career advancement. Key component behaviors include mentoring, coaching, and providing developmental opportunities. Developing is usually done with a subordinate, but it may also be done with a peer, a colleague, or even with a new, inexperienced boss. Responsibility for developing subordinates can be shared with other members of the work unit who are competent and experienced. For example, some leaders assign an experienced subordinate to serve as a mentor and coach for a new employee.

The descriptive research suggests that most effective managers take an active role in developing the skills and confidence of subordinates (Bradford & Cohen, 1984; McCauley, 1986). Developing is usually regarded as primarily a relations-oriented behavior, but it can also contribute to the attainment of task-related objectives, such as improved quantity and quality

TABLE 2-7 Guidelines for Developing Subordinates

- Show concern for each person's development.
- Help the person identify ways to improve performance.
- Be patient and helpful when providing coaching.
- Provide helpful career advice.
- Help the person prepare for a job change.
- Encourage attendance at relevant training activities.
- Provide opportunities to learn from experience.
- Encourage coaching by peers when appropriate.
- Promote the person's reputation.

of employee performance. Developing offers a variety of potential benefits for the manager, the subordinate, and the organization. One benefit is to foster mutually cooperative relationships. Potential benefits for subordinates include better job adjustment, more skill learning, greater self-confidence, and faster career advancement. The leader can gain a sense of satisfaction from helping others grow and develop. Potential benefits for the organization include higher employee commitment, higher performance, and better preparation of people to fill positions of greater responsibility in the organization as openings occur.

Guidelines for developing subordinate skills and confidence are described in this section and summarized in Table 2-7.

- **Show concern for each person's development.**

The most basic principle of mentoring is to have a genuine concern about the personal development and career progress of subordinates. A manager should encourage each subordinate to set ambitious career goals that are realistic in terms of the person's ability and consistent with the person's interests. Encourage the person to set specific goals for self-development. Respond enthusiastically to requests for advice or assistance. Provide social–emotional support as well as career-related support. Doc Rivers, head coach of the Los Angeles Clippers, describes how he learns what his players need to foster their development as follows:

> I communicate to my team. Not just collectively as a team but individually. I have to know where each person is in order to lead them where they need to be. Since I communicate often with them, I know who is struggling with a personal issue. I know who needs encouragement. I know who needs to be challenged (Gordon, 2017, 105).

- **Help the person identify ways to improve performance.**

Before trying to improve task performance, it is essential to discover what is being done correctly and incorrectly. One diagnostic approach is to jointly review step-by-step how the person carries out the task to determine whether any essential steps are omitted, unnecessary steps are included, or key steps are performed incorrectly. When discussing ways to improve performance, it is usually better to begin by inviting the person to do a self-assessment rather than by making your own diagnosis of the person's performance. The person may already be aware of weaknesses and will be less defensive if asked to identify them rather than being told by you. However, in some cases, the person does not understand why his or her performance is not better. Even a highly motivated person may be unable to improve beyond the current level of performance without assistance. When appropriate, suggest additional things the person should consider to improve performance.

- **Be patient and helpful when providing coaching.**

An essential quality for effective coaching is patience. Don't expect people to learn everything immediately or do everything right the first time. It takes time to learn complex skills, and learning is inhibited when someone is anxious and frustrated. A person who is experiencing difficulty in doing a task will become even more anxious and upset if you are critical and impatient. Be helpful and supportive when a person is frustrated and discouraged by slow progress or repeated mistakes. For example, tell the person how you experienced the same frustrations in mastering a particularly difficult aspect of the task. If the person lacks self-confidence, say you are confident that he or she will be able to learn a new procedure or skill.

- **Provide helpful career advice.**

Provide career guidance and advice about how to deal with career problems, such as lack of advancement, interpersonal conflicts, burnout, and mid-career crisis. Many subordinates need help in developing specific strategies for achieving their career objectives. It may be useful to identify career paths and promotion opportunities in the organization and explain the advantages and pitfalls of various assignments or potential job changes. Share insights learned from experience with problems or choices similar to those now faced by a subordinate. If appropriate, introduce the person to other people in the organization who can be trusted to provide good career advice. To avoid being overbearing about career advice, ask a subordinate to indicate ways you can be helpful in the career-planning process.

- **Encourage attendance at relevant training activities.**

Another way to facilitate skill development by subordinates is to encourage them to attend relevant workshops and courses. Inform subordinates about developmental opportunities and explain why they are relevant to a subordinate's needs, interests, and career ambitions. Encourage subordinates to take advantage of opportunities to attend assessment centers or multisource feedback workshops that provide useful feedback about strengths and weaknesses. Make it easier for subordinates to attend developmental activities by planning work schedules to allow time for them. If feasible, provide financial compensation to pay for outside courses. Bring in outside experts to conduct special training sessions for subordinates.

- **Provide opportunities to learn from experience.**

Provide special projects and assignments that require the subordinate to assume new responsibilities and apply new skills. Some of these assignments may involve delegation of responsibilities previously carried out by the manager (e.g., prepare a budget, conduct a meeting, present a proposal to top management). Sometimes the best approach for developing skills is to assign a challenging task without giving detailed instructions, and allow the person to discover how to carry out the task and to deal with problems encountered along the way. In a developmental assignment, provide coaching when needed to help the person learn from successes and failures.

- **Encourage coaching by peers when appropriate.**

The responsibility to develop subordinates may be shared with other members of the work unit who are competent and experienced. Peers are a valuable source of advice and support in organizations. Although coaching and mentoring by peers occur informally, both can be encouraged and facilitated by the manager. One example is the practice of assigning a competent subordinate to serve as a mentor and coach for a new employee. It is also useful to have a subordinate with special knowledge coach other employees who are less experienced.

- **Promote the person's reputation.**

A manager can promote the reputation of a subordinate by telling superiors and peers about the person's achievements and expertise. It is also helpful to introduce the person to important people in the organization. A subordinate's visibility and contacts can be enhanced by selecting the person to serve on committees or projects that provide an opportunity to interact with important people in the organization. High-visibility assignments provide an opportunity for a subordinate to demonstrate competence in carrying out important responsibilities.

Providing Praise and Recognition

Recognizing involves giving praise and showing appreciation to others for effective performance, significant achievements, and important contributions to the organization. Although it is most common to think of recognition as being given by a manager to subordinates, this managerial practice can also be used with peers, superiors, and people outside the work unit. The primary purpose of recognizing, especially when used with subordinates, is to strengthen desirable behavior and task commitment. Recognizing is primarily a relations behavior, but like developing, it can contribute to the attainment of task objectives as well.

Three major forms of recognizing are praise, awards, and recognition ceremonies. Praise consists of oral comments, expressions, or gestures that acknowledge a person's accomplishments and contributions. It is the easiest form of recognition, but it is underutilized by many managers. Most praise is given privately, but it can be used in a public ritual or ceremony as well. Leaders usually have less discretion in the use of awards or recognition ceremonies, because organizations often have programs and policies specifying the criteria and procedures for this type of recognition. Nevertheless, even low-level leaders have options to be very creative about informal awards.

Awards include things such as a certificate of achievement, a letter of commendation, a plaque, a trophy, a medal, or a ribbon. Awards can be announced in many different ways, including an article in the company newsletter, a notice posted on a bulletin board or website, a picture of the person (e.g., "employee of the month") hung in a prominent place, over a public address system, in regular meetings, and at special ceremonies or rituals. Giving formal awards is a symbolic act that communicates a manager's values and priorities to people in the organization. Thus, it is important for awards to be based on meaningful criteria rather than favoritism or arbitrary judgments. An award that is highly visible allows others to share in the process of commending the recipient and showing appreciation for his or her contributions to the success of the organization. The basis for making the award is more important than the form of the award. A recognition ceremony ensures that an individual's achievements are acknowledged not only by the manager but also by other members of the organization.

Recognition ceremonies can be used to celebrate the achievements of a team or work unit as well as those of an individual. Special rituals or ceremonies to honor particular employees or teams can have strong symbolic value when attended by top management, because they demonstrate concern for the aspects of behavior or performance being recognized. Milliken & Company (Peters & Austin, 1985) use a unique version of a recognition ceremony:

> Once each quarter a "Corporate Sharing Rally" is held to allow work teams to brag about their achievements and contributions. Each of the "fabulous bragging sessions" has a particular theme such as improved productivity, better product quality, or reduced

costs. Attendance is voluntary, but hundreds of employees show up to hear teams make short five-minute presentations describing how they have made improvements relevant to the theme. Every participant receives a framed certificate, and the best presentations (determined by peer evaluation) get special awards. In addition to celebrating accomplishments and emphasizing key values (represented by the themes), these ceremonies increase the diffusion of innovative ideas within the company.

Survey research on the effects of praise and recognition suggest that this type of behavior can be beneficial when used in a skillful way (e.g., Kim & Yukl, 1995; Yukl et al., 1990). Descriptive studies in organizations suggest that effective leaders provide more recognition to subordinates for their achievements and contributions (Kouzes & Posner, 1987; Peters & Austin, 1985). In a rare field experiment on the effects of praise, Wikoff, Anderson, and Crowell (1983) found that increasing the use of praise by supervisors resulted in improved performance by employees.

The following guidelines for recognizing are based on the research literature on positive reinforcement and the descriptive literature on practices of managers in effective organizations. The guidelines are concerned with the following questions: what to recognize, when to give recognition, who to recognize, and what form of recognition to use (see summary in Table 2-8).

- **Recognize a variety of contributions and achievements.**

Managers tend to think of recognition as appropriate only for major achievements, thereby limiting their opportunity to gain the benefits from this potent managerial practice. Recognition should be provided for a variety of other things, including demonstration of initiative and extra effort in carrying out an assignment or task; achievement of challenging performance goals and standards; personal sacrifices made to accomplish a task or objective; helpful suggestions and innovative ideas for improving efficiency, productivity, or the quality of the work unit's products or services; special efforts to help someone else (e.g., coworker, customer) deal with a problem; and significant contributions made to the success of other individuals or teams.

- **Actively search for contributions to recognize.**

Before recognition can be given for contributions and accomplishments, it is necessary to determine what things are important for the success of the work unit and consistent with the values and ideals of the organization. It is helpful to spend some time each day looking for examples of effective behavior to recognize. Many managers tend to notice and criticize ineffective behavior by subordinates or peers but fail to notice and praise effective behavior. It is also

TABLE 2-8 Guidelines for Recognizing

- Recognize a variety of contributions and achievements.
- Actively search for contributions to recognize.
- Recognize improvements in performance.
- Recognize commendable efforts that failed.
- Do not limit recognition to high-visibility jobs.
- Do not limit recognition to a few best performers.
- Provide specific recognition.
- Provide timely recognition.
- Use an appropriate form of recognition.

helpful to establish periodic awards, such as the "employee of the week," that require a manager to spend some time on a regular basis looking for examples of effective performance among subordinates. Kouzes and Posner (1987) recommend setting a personal goal to find and praise at least one subordinate each day for some exemplary behavior or significant contribution.

- **Recognize improvements in performance.**

Some managers believe that it is inappropriate to recognize performance improvements if an individual's level of performance is still only average or substandard. However, some form of recognition for improvements is important to encourage and strengthen efforts toward additional improvement. Improvements can be recognized in a way that also communicates an expectation of continuing progress toward excellence. Recognition of improvement is especially relevant for new employees who are just learning a new task and for employees who do not have much self-confidence.

- **Recognize commendable efforts that failed.**

Another fallacy is that recognition must be limited to successful efforts. Sometimes recognition is necessary for unsuccessful efforts to perform an important activity with a low probability of success. For example, Ore-Ida fires off a cannon to celebrate the "perfect failure" when research scientists terminate a project that is failing rather than prolong it at great cost to the company (Peters & Waterman, 1982). In another example, when someone suggests an improvement but it does not appear to be feasible, the manager should thank the person and explain why the idea could not be implemented in order to encourage further suggestions in the future.

- **Do not limit recognition to high-visibility jobs.**

Everyone has a desire for recognition and appreciation, and even people who are a little embarrassed by recognition still desire and value it. It is a common tendency to provide recognition to individuals whose performance and achievements are highly visible, while largely ignoring people whose contributions are less visible and whose performance is harder to measure. It is better to recognize contributions and achievements by employees in all jobs, regardless of their status or visibility. Recognition should be given to people in support functions as well as to people in line functions with easily quantifiable performance, such as production and sales. With a little effort, it is possible to find examples of effective behavior and indicators of successful performance for any type of job.

- **Do not limit recognition to a few best performers.**

The question of who to recognize also relates closely to the basis for giving recognition and the amount of recognition. Some managers believe that recognition should be limited to a few best performers in each type of job, thereby creating strong competition among people. However, Peters and Austin (1985) found that effective organizations recognize many winners rather than only a few. For example, it is better to provide awards for the top 75 percent of sales representatives than only for the top 10 percent. It is better to give an award to everyone who exceeds a challenging performance standard rather than to recognize only the person with the best performance. Extreme forms of competition create undesirable side effects, such as unwillingness to help competitors and resentment by people who perform exceptionally well but receive little or no recognition merely because someone else does a little better, often due to a lucky break. It is feasible to recognize many "heroes" or "winners" and still have different amounts of recognition for different levels of performance. Unless the people with the best performance receive a greater amount of recognition, their accomplishments will be unnecessarily diminished and the desired benefits from recognition may not be realized.

- **Provide specific recognition.**

Praise is more likely to be successful if it is specific. Instead of a general comment commending someone for doing an assignment well, it is better to explain why you think the person did the assignment well. Indicate the basis for your judgment, point out examples of special effort or effective behavior, and explain why the person's accomplishments are important to you and to the organization. In the case of praise for good suggestions, explain how the person's ideas were used and how they benefited the organization or contributed to the success of a project. Specific praise is more believable than general praise, because it shows that you actually know what the person has done and have a sound basis for a positive evaluation. In addition, citing specific examples of effective behavior communicates what behaviors you value and guides the person toward repeating these behaviors in the future.

- **Provide timely recognition.**

Research on positive reinforcement suggests that it is more effective when given reasonably soon after the behavior to be reinforced. Thus, managers should try to identify effective behavior and provide recognition for it promptly. As Peters and Waterman (1982) point out, one of the benefits of "management by walking around" is to help find examples of good behavior and provide immediate praise for it. However, recognition for any particular type of achievement or contribution by a person can be overdone. It is not necessary or effective to praise someone every day for the same thing.

- **Use an appropriate form of recognition.**

There is no simple, mechanical formula for determining what type of recognition to use. The appropriate form of recognition will depend on the type and importance of the achievement to be recognized, the norms and culture of the organization, and the characteristics of the manager and recipient. Whatever form of recognition is used, it must be sincere. Most people are able to detect efforts to manipulate them with praise or awards. Managers should avoid overusing a particular form of recognition, because its effect can be diminished if it becomes too commonplace.

Summary

Many types of leadership behavior have been identified, and much of the research on it has been focused on broadly defined behaviors such as task-oriented behavior and relations-oriented behavior. Hundreds of studies were conducted to see how the two types of behavior were related to measures of leadership effectiveness, such as subordinate satisfaction and performance. The results were weak and inconsistent for studies that examined only broad measures of task-oriented and relations-oriented behavior.

There has been less research on specific types of leader behavior. The specific task-oriented behaviors that have been examined include planning, clarifying, monitoring, and solving operational problems. The specific relations-oriented behaviors that have been examined include supporting, developing, and recognizing. The overall pattern of results suggests that effective leaders have a high concern for task objectives and interpersonal relationships, but they use specific types of behavior that are relevant for their leadership situation. In addition to the specific task-oriented and relations-oriented behaviors described in this chapter, effective leaders use other types of specific behaviors that are described in later chapters of the book.

Review and Discussion Questions

1. How do task-related behaviors affect subordinate satisfaction and performance?
2. How do relations-oriented behaviors affect subordinate satisfaction and performance?
3. What are some guidelines for clarifying and monitoring?
4. What are some guidelines for planning and problem solving?
5. What are some guidelines for supporting, developing, and recognizing?

Key Terms

clarifying
monitoring
planning
problem solving
recognizing
supporting
developing
relations-oriented behavior
task-oriented behavior

PERSONAL REFLECTION

Think about a leader who you have had an opportunity to observe over a period of several months. This leader could be a work supervisor, sports coach, elected leader of a student organization, or a member of a temporary project team. What types of task- and relations-oriented behaviors did this leader use and how effective did the leader appear to be?

CASE

HomeStay

HomeStay was an initiative of Anil Anand, with the aim of providing home-like comfort to its customers. Anil's son, Akash, was appointed the hotel manager. Akash felt that that the hotel should not only offer a comfortable stay to its customers, but also an amicable and positive working condition for its employees. Therefore, he decided to design a recreational room meant exclusively for the employees, where they could engage in fun-filled activities and as well relax in-between the work schedule. Akash opines that only when the hotel employees felt happy and content with their work, would they serve others with dedication. He believed that when employees are treated properly, they develop a sense of belonging and loyalty towards the organization—which ensures higher rate of employee retention and a lot more employee commitment. Akash also, made it a point to interact on a one-on-one basis with the employees regularly, talking about not just work, but life otherwise—encompassing the problems they might be facing in their everyday life. Akash would organize monthly picnics where all the employees and their families would get the chance to socialise and interact with one another, so that the feeling of being one family would be reinforced.

Akash's managerial style had positive impact on the organization's turnover rate making it lower than usual. Employees were seldom laid off, and in the event of accident or injury, the department or allotted tasks of the employee(s) would be changed to a more suitable job within the organization. The all-round training provided to the hotel's employees would come in handy in such cases. Akash believed in providing his employees autonomy at work. This meant that the employees had the freedom to make their decisions within the framework of their job. He did not enforce his ideas or command the ways of working. Akash felt that all the employees are adults and their judgment about their roles and responsibilities deserved to be trusted. He acted more like a guide than a supervisor. But the result of this was low productivity on the part of the employees. It turned out, they got a little too comfortable at their workplace, and since Akash did not do much to discipline them or set any target for them to fulfil, they got a little too carried away by the freedom they were given.

Slowly with time, the hotel started losing out its customers, owing to its sloppy services. It was then that Anil decided to get in a professional to handle the task of managing the hotel. The newly appointed manager, Rohit Kalra had pursued his degree in management. His way of working was drastically different from that of Akash's. Unlike his predecessor, Rohit believed that employees perceive the passive attitude of a lenient manager as a weakness, and hence, tend to overlook and not show respect towards the manager. Therefore, when Rohit took over, he revolutionized the way things at HomeStay functioned. Each employee specialized at a task, and so he/she, clearly, belonged to a set department. Each department had its own set of targets or tasks to complete. All employees were governed by a universal set of policies. The recreational room that was built for employees, was converted into fitness and entertainment rooms for the guests.

In case employees failed to fulfil their set target or satisfactorily complete the task given to them, they would be given a warning. If there was no improvement in performance post warning, they would be fired. Rohit believed that training everyone in all aspects was a waste of time and only resulted in sub-standard quality of work, as not everyone is meant for or good at all kinds of work. Therefore, he focused on specializing i.e. the employee would be trained to become better at his area of expertise or interest. A register was maintained to record the work done by each employee. Based on this, performance was reviewed at the end of each month and bonuses or penalties were awarded accordingly. Meetings were held at the end of each week to review progress and discuss any issues that needed attention.

Rohit also preferred all decision to be run through him. He had established a clear set of policies that the organization and its employees were expected to follow. Although he was open to ideas and suggestions, the end verdict was always his, in order to ensure that all decisions that were taken were in harmony with the organization's philosophy and policies. While the hotel witnessed a great upsurge in its clientele, with more and more customers going back satisfied and recommending the hotel's services to more people, the employee turnover also increased. With time, finding replacement of these employees became more and more difficult.

—*Written by* Nishant Uppal

Questions

1. Describe and compare the managerial behavior of Akash and Rohit. To what extent does each manager display specific relations behaviors (supporting, developing, recognizing) and specific task behaviors (clarifying, planning, monitoring)?
2. Compare Akash and Rohit in terms of their influence on employee attitudes, short-term performance, and long-term plant performance, and explain the reasons for the differences.
3. If you were selected to be the manager of this hotel, what would you do to achieve both high employee satisfaction and performance?

CASE

Superior Staffing

Shakti is a Delhi-based NGO, that works towards the skill and career development of the economically weaker sections of the society. The organization has regional supervisors who are responsible for recruiting and providing necessary training to its trainers, who would eventually train the trainees. Additionally, the regional supervisors are also responsible for bringing in companies that recruit their trainees.

Akansha Jain, the founder and head of the organization manages all the supervisors' working at the various centres of the organization in Delhi. Akansha was liked by all her employees, i.e. her immediate subordinates (supervisors), as well as the trainers. She made it a point to interact with them as much as possible, especially the supervisors. She tried to establish and maintain a relationship that was beyond the professional space as well. She tried to build a camaraderie with them by taking steps such as organizing picnics for them, hosting parties at her home, and meeting them for coffee occasionally. The aim of these informal meets was to create a rapport on personal level, and to assist the team during problems that were not just of a professional nature. Whenever any of her employees faced any difficulty, she tried to provide them help to the best of her ability. Her genuine interest in the well-being of her employees reflected in her attitude towards them. As a result, the employees also respected and loved her, and this led to the creation of a highly supportive work environment.

The supervisors as well as the trainers are appreciative of the time and attention she gives to each of them. She closely observes their work, and wherever deems fit, appreciates and rewards their performance. Where needed, she gives her suggestions about ways to improve and become more efficient. Being an NGO, the organization is not able to pay its employees very highly, yet no employee has resigned as a result of feeling dissatisfied with their job or their work environment. When asked about what made them stick around for so long, employees commented that it was the personal touch with which Akansha managed them.

Akansha would lay down monthly goals that each supervisor and trainer was expected to fulfil. A review process at the end of each month would be held wherein individual progress would be discussed and monitored. In cases that the employees would successfully achieve their given target, they would be appreciated for their efforts and encouraged to work harder, however, in cases that an employee would fail to achieve the set target, Akansha would suggest improvements that were needed from her end, and help the employee work towards achieving them. In case an employee ever faced any problems, Akansha would always encourage them to share so that they could work together towards its quick resolution. Shakti's success so far can thus be attributed to Akansha's managerial skills.

—*Written by* Nishant Uppal

Questions

1. What specific task-oriented behaviors are used by Akansha?
2. What specific relations-oriented behaviors are used by Akansha?
3. What are some other specific task and relations behaviors that were not described in the case but may also be relevant for Akansha to use?

The Leadership Situation and Adaptive Leadership

Learning Objectives

After studying this chapter, you should be able to:

- Understand how aspects of the situation can influence leader behavior.
- Understand how aspects of the situation can enhance or diminish effects of leader behavior.
- Understand how to adapt leader behavior to the situation.
- Understand how to deal with demands, constraints, and role conflicts.

Introduction

Much of the early research on effective leadership reflects an implicit assumption that some leader traits (e.g., intelligence, self-confidence) or broadly defined behaviors (e.g., task-oriented, relations-oriented, participative) are positively related to subordinate performance or satisfaction the same way in all situations. However, the research failed to provide strong support for universal conceptions of effective leadership. The lack of consistent results stimulated interest in studying how aspects of the leadership situation help to determine what actions a leader takes and the effects of the behavior on outcomes such as subordinate satisfaction and performance.

The purpose of this chapter is to describe what has been learned about the effects of the leadership situation on the behavior and effectiveness of leaders. The chapter begins by briefly explaining three ways that aspects of the situation can influence the effectiveness of leaders. Next, the chapter describes findings in descriptive research on aspects of the job situation that influence the actions and decisions of leaders in that situation. Then the chapter examines three contingency theories that explain how aspects of the situation can enhance or diminish the effects of leader behavior. Practical guidelines for adapting to different or changing situations are provided at various points in the chapter.

Different Ways Situations Affect Leaders

Aspects of the leadership situation can have different types of causal effects, and more than one type of effect can occur for the same situational variable (Howell, Dorfman, & Kerr, 1986; James & Brett, 1984; Oc, 2018; Osborn, Uhl-Bien, & Milosevic, 2014; Yukl, 2009).

Situation Directly Influences Leader Behavior

A situational variable may directly influence a leader's behavior but only indirectly influence the dependent variables. Aspects of the situation such as formal rules, policies, role expectations, and organizational values can encourage or constrain a leader's behavior. In addition to the direct effect of the situation on leader behavior, there may be an indirect effect on dependent variables. For example, a company establishes a new policy requiring sales managers to provide bonuses to any sales representative with sales exceeding a minimum standard; sales managers begin awarding bonuses, and the performance and satisfaction of the sales representatives increase.

Situation Moderates Effects of Leader Behavior

A situational variable is called an enhancer if it increases the effects of leader behavior on the dependent variable but does not directly influence the dependent variable. For example, leader task expertise enables the leader to provide better coaching, and subordinates are more likely to follow advice from a leader who is perceived to be an expert. A situational moderator variable is called a neutralizer when it decreases the effect of leader behavior on the dependent variable or prevents any effect from occurring. For example, leader instruction in how to do a task has little effect on the performance of employees who already know how to do it.

Situation Directly Affects Outcomes or Mediators

A situational variable can directly influence an outcome such as subordinate satisfaction or performance, or a mediating variable that is a determinant of the outcomes. When a situational variable can make a mediating variable or an outcome more favorable, it is sometimes called a substitute for leadership. An example is when subordinates have extensive prior training and experience, the need for clarifying and coaching by the leader is reduced, because subordinates already know what to do and how to do it. A substitute can indirectly influence leader behavior if it becomes obvious to the leader that some types of behavior are redundant and unnecessary. A situational variable can also affect the relative importance of a mediating variable as a determinant of performance outcomes. For example, employee skill is a more important determinant of performance when the task is very complex and variable than when the task is simple and repetitive. Here again, the situational variable can indirectly influence leader behavior if it is obvious that some types of behavior are more relevant than others to improve performance for the leader's team or work unit.

Stewart Model of Situational Determinants

Much of the knowledge about how the situation influences leader behavior comes from descriptive research using observation, interviews, and diaries. This research indicates that there are unique role requirements for many types of leadership positions. Based on extensive research with different methods for collecting data, Stewart (1967, 1976, 1982, 2002) formulated a model for describing different types of managerial jobs and understanding how managers do them.

Demands

Demands are the required duties, activities, and responsibilities for someone in a managerial position. Demands include standards, objectives, and deadlines for work that must be met, and bureaucratic procedures that cannot be ignored or delegated, such as preparing budgets and reports, attending certain meetings, authorizing expenditures, signing documents, and conducting performance appraisals.

Constraints

Constraints are characteristics of the organization and external environment limiting what a manager can do. They include bureaucratic rules, policies, and regulations that must be observed, and legal constraints such as labor laws, environmental regulations, securities regulations, and safety regulations. Another type of constraint involves the availability of resources, such as facilities, equipment, budgetary funding, supplies, personnel, and support services. The technology used to do the work constrains the options for how the work will be done. The physical location of facilities and distribution of personnel among work sites limit the opportunities for face-to-face interaction.

Choices

Choices include the opportunities available to someone in a particular type of managerial position to determine what to do and how to do it. Demands and constraints limit choices in the short run, but over a longer time period, a manager has some opportunities to modify demands and remove or circumvent constraints, thereby expanding choices. Examples of major choices include the objectives for the manager's unit, the priorities attached to different objectives, the strategies selected to pursue objectives, the aspects of the work in which the manager gets personally involved, how the manager spends time, what responsibility is delegated, and how the manager attempts to influence different people. By their choices, managers can also influence demands. For example, agreeing to serve on a committee adds to a manager's demands. Moreover, people differ in the way they interpret role expectations, and one person will perceive a demand where another may not. For example, one operations manager believes that a bureaucratic regulation must be observed exactly, whereas another operations manager in the same company perceives more flexibility in what can be done.

Pattern of Relationships

The demands made on a manager by superiors, subordinates, peers, and persons outside the organization influence how the manager's time is spent and how much skill is needed to fulfill role requirements. More time is needed to deal with subordinates when new assignments must be made frequently, subordinates must be closely coordinated, and it is important but difficult to monitor their performance. More time is needed to deal with superiors when the manager is highly dependent on them for resources or assignments, and superiors make unpredictable demands. More time is needed to deal with peers when the manager is dependent on them for services, supplies, cooperation, or approval of work outputs. More time is needed for outsiders (e.g., clients, customers, suppliers, subcontractors) when the manager is highly dependent on them and must negotiate agreements, carry out public relations activities, and create a good impression. Having to establish relationships with many people for short periods of time, as opposed to dealing with the same people repeatedly, further complicates the manager's job, especially when it is necessary to impress and influence people quickly. The extent to which subordinates, peers, and superiors make incompatible demands on a manager determines how much role conflict the manager will experience.

Work Patterns

Stewart found that the pattern of role requirements and demands affected managerial behavior, and somewhat different patterns of behavior were associated with different types of managerial jobs. The following factors were useful for classifying managerial jobs: (1) the extent to which managerial activities are either self-generating or a response to the requests, instructions, and problems of other people; (2) the extent to which the work is recurrent and repetitive rather than variable and unique; (3) the amount of uncertainty in the work; (4) the extent of managerial activities requiring sustained attention for long periods of time; and (5) the amount of pressure to meet deadlines. For example, more initiative and planning of activities are required in a predominantly self-generating job (e.g., product manager, research manager, training director) than for a predominantly responding job with unpredictable problems and workload variations that are beyond the manager's control (e.g., production manager, service manager). Stewart suggested that the work pattern associated with some kinds of managerial jobs tends to be habit forming. A person who spends a long time in one position may grow accustomed to acting in a particular way and will find it difficult to adjust to another managerial position with different behavioral requirements.

Exposure

Another aspect of a managerial job that determines what behavior and skills are required is the amount of responsibility for making decisions with potentially serious consequences, and the amount of time before a mistake or poor decision can be discovered. There is more "exposure" when decisions and actions have important, highly visible consequences for the organization, and mistakes or poor judgment can result in loss of resources, disruption of operations, and risk to human health and life. There is less exposure when decisions do not have immediate consequences, or when decisions are made by a group that has shared accountability for them. Examples of high-exposure jobs include product managers who must recommend expensive marketing programs and product changes that may quickly prove to be a disaster, project managers who may fail to complete projects on schedule and within budget, and managers of profit centers (e.g., managers of each company store or service facility) who are held accountable for their unit's costs and profits.

Leader Discretion

A managerial or administrative position makes various demands on the person who occupies it, and the actions of the occupant are constrained by laws, policies, regulations, traditions, and scope of formal authority. Demands and constraints are not determined entirely by objective job conditions, they also depend on the leader's objectives and skills. There are choices for what aspects of the job are emphasized, how much time is devoted to various activities, and how much time is spent with different people. The descriptive research showed that even for managers with similar jobs, there was considerable variability of behavior (Fondas & Stewart, 1994; James & White, 1983; Kotter, 1982; Stewart, 1976, 1982, 1991). For example,

Stewart (1976, 1982) found that some bank managers emphasized staff supervision, whereas others delegated much of the internal management to the assistant manager and concentrated on actively seeking out new business. Stewart's (1991) study showed the relationships between the CEO of a company and the chairperson of the company board of directors varied widely depending on their personalities and contextual factors such as the organizational structure. More recently, an interview study by Morais, Kakabadse, and Kakabadse (2018) revealed that higher levels of communication and trust enabled a CEO and chairperson to more effectively address and resolve problems and conflicts.

In part, variability of behavior within the same job occurs because of its multiple performance dimensions. Within the boundaries imposed by the priorities of higher management, a person may choose to devote more effort to some objectives than to others. For example, activities involving development of new products may get more attention than cost reduction, quality improvements, development of new export markets, or improvement of safety practices. Development of subordinates to groom them for promotion may get more attention than team building or training in skills necessary to improve performance in the current job.

The trade-offs inherent among different aspects of the job and the lack of time to do everything well make it inevitable that different people will define the same job in different ways. How this job definition is done will reflect a leader's interests, skills, and values, as well as the role expectations other people have for the leader. Leaders differ with regard to their skill in dealing with role conflicts and inconsistent demands, and a highly skilled leader may be able to reconcile role requirements that were initially incompatible. Moreover, leaders with a record of successful decisions and demonstrated loyalty to the organization are given more freedom to redefine their role and initiate innovations.

Other Situational Determinants of Leader Behavior

Unlike Stewart's broad perspective, most of the studies on situational determinants have included only one or two aspects of the situation. This narrow approach makes it difficult to detect the influence of unmeasured situational variables or to compare results across studies. However, despite these limitations the research found some other situational variables that can influence leader behavior, including level of management, subunit size, external dependencies, and extreme contexts.

Level of Management

Job responsibilities and the skills necessary to carry them out vary somewhat for managers at different authority levels in the organization (Anzengruber et al., 2017; Chun, Yammarino, Dionne, Sosik, & Moon, 2009; DeChurch, Hiller, Murase, Doty, & Salas, 2010; Jacobs & Jaques, 1987; Jacobs & McGee, 2001; Katz & Kahn, 1978; Lucas & Markessini, 1993; Mumford, Campion, & Morgeson, 2007). Higher-level managers are usually more concerned with the exercise of broad authority in making long-range plans, formulating policy, modifying the organization structure, and initiating new ways of doing things. Decisions at this level usually have a long-time perspective, because it is appropriate for top executives to be thinking about what will happen 10 to 20 years in the future. Middle managers are primarily concerned with interpreting and implementing policies and programs, and they usually have a moderately long-time perspective (two to five years). Low-level managers are primarily concerned with structuring, coordinating, and facilitating work activities. Objectives are more specific, issues are less complex and more focused, and managers typically have a shorter time perspective (a few weeks to two years).

A manager at a high level in the authority hierarchy of an organization typically has more responsibility for making important decisions, including determination of organizational objectives, planning of strategies to obtain objectives, determination of general policies, design of the organizational structure, and allocation of resources. Managers at lower levels in the authority hierarchy have less discretion and freedom of action, because they must operate within the constraints imposed by formalized rules and policy decisions made at higher levels. Blankenship and Miles (1968) found that lower-level managers had less discretion, were required more often to consult with superiors before taking action on decisions, and made the final choice in a decision less often.

Consistent with this difference in job requirements and discretion across levels is the relative importance and amount of time devoted to different managerial activities and roles (Allan, 1981; Anzengruber et al., 2017; Korica, Nicolini, & Johnson, 2017; Luthans, Rosenkrantz, & Hennessey, 1985; McCall & Segrist, 1980; Martinko & Gardner, 1985; Mintzberg, 1973; Mumford et al., 2007). The job description research found that planning, strategic decision making, and public relations are more important activities for top managers than for lower-level managers (Hemphill, 1959; Katzell, Barrett, Vann, & Hogan, 1968; Mahoney, Jerdee, & Carroll, 1965; Tornow & Pinto, 1976). The research on managerial roles found that allocating resources in the organization and serving as the external representative of the organization are more important roles for top-level managers than for lower-level managers. High-level managers are usually more dependent on people outside the organization, and research on managerial activities and networking shows that they spend more time interacting with outsiders than do most managers at lower levels (Korica et al., 2017; Luthans et al., 1985; Martinko & Gardner, 1985; McCall, Morrison, & Hannan, 1978; Michael & Yukl, 1993). Research on social networks finds that external ties with important people are a valuable resource to top executives, but spending too much time in external relations can distract from their internal management responsibilities and undermine their effectiveness (Balkundi & Kilduff, 2005). Lower-level managers tend to be more concerned with technical matters, staffing (personnel selection and training), scheduling work, and monitoring subordinate performance (Anzengruber et al., 2017; Korica et al., 2017; Mumford et al., 2007). The number of activities carried out each day is greater for lower-level managers, and the time spent on each activity tends to be less (Korica et al., 2017; Kurke & Aldrich, 1983; Martinko & Gardner, 1985; Mintzberg, 1973; Thomason, 1967).

Size of Organizational Unit

The implications of work unit size or "span of control" for leader behavior have been investigated in several types of research, ranging from studies with small groups to studies on chief executives. Kotter (1982) studied general managers and concluded that managers of the larger organizational subunits had more demanding jobs in comparison to managers of smaller units. Decisions are more difficult due to the sheer volume of issues and activities and the lack of detailed knowledge a manager is likely to have. Because larger units are likely to have a more bureaucratic structure, managers must cope with more constraints (e.g., rules, standard procedures, and required authorizations). Consistent with this analysis, general managers in larger organizational units had larger networks and attended more scheduled meetings.

When a manager has a large number of subordinates, it is more difficult to get all of them together for meetings, or to consult individually with each subordinate. Such leaders tend to use less participative leadership or to limit it to an "executive committee" or to a few trusted "lieutenants." Heller and Yukl (1969) found that as span of control increased, upper-level managers made more autocratic decisions, but they also used more delegation. Both decision styles allow a manager who is overloaded with responsibilities to reduce the amount of time needed to make decisions. Lower-level managers in this study also made more autocratic decisions as span of control increased, but they did not use more delegation, perhaps because delegation was less feasible for them. Blankenship and Miles (1968) found that as span of control increased, managers relied more on subordinates to initiate action on decisions, and this trend was much more pronounced for upper-level managers than for lower-level managers.

As the size of a work unit increases, so does the administrative workload. Managers spend more time on planning, coordinating, staffing, and budgeting activities (Cohen & March, 1974; Hemphill, 1950; Katzell et al., 1968). In an observational study of school principals, Martinko and Gardner (1990) found that principals with larger staffs spent more time giving information, scheduling, conducting reviews, and developing strategy than principals from smaller schools, who devoted more time to nonmanagerial work. These findings are consistent with Stewart's (1967) observation that managers in larger organizations devoted more time to formal communication, as well as Mintzberg's (1973) conclusion that managers in large organizations had more extensive and well-developed communication networks and spent more time on formal communications (e.g., memos and scheduled meetings). The increase in coordination requirements is magnified when the subordinates have highly uncertain and interdependent tasks. Sometimes part of the increased administrative burden can be delegated to a second in command, to a coordinating committee composed of subordinates, or to new coordinating specialists who serve as staff assistants. In many cases, however, the leader is expected to assume the responsibility for providing direction and integration of group activities.

While studies of managerial work in small firms indicate that their CEOs spend most of their time with subordinates (Floren, 2006), managers of large work units have less opportunity for interacting with individual subordinates and maintaining effective interpersonal relationships with them (Ford, 1981). Less time is available to provide support, encouragement, and recognition to individual subordinates (Goodstadt & Kipnis, 1970). Problems with subordinates are likely to be handled in a more formalized, impersonal manner, and managers are more likely to use warnings and punishment (Kipnis & Cosentino, 1969; Kipnis & Lane, 1962). When a subordinate has a performance problem, the manager is less likely to provide individualized instruction and coaching.

As a group or work unit grows larger, separate subgroups, cliques, or factions are likely to emerge. The subgroups often compete for power and resources, creating conflicts and posing a threat to group cohesiveness and teamwork. Thus, the leader of a large group or work unit needs to devote more time to building group identification, promoting cooperation, and managing conflict. The pressure to carry out more administrative activities may cause the leader to neglect group maintenance activities until serious problems arise.

External Dependencies

The extent to which a leader's subunit is dependent on other subunits in the same organization ("lateral interdependence") or on external groups will affect leader behavior to a considerable extent. As interdependence increases with other subunits, coordination with them becomes more important and there is more need for mutual adjustments in plans, schedules, and activities (Galbraith, 1973; Mintzberg, 1979). Lateral interdependence represents a threat to the subunit because routine activities must be modified more frequently to accommodate the needs of other subunits, with a resulting loss in autonomy and stability (Hunt & Osborn, 1982; Sayles, 1979). Research on activity patterns of managers finds results consistent with this picture. As lateral interdependence increases, the external activities of a leader become more important, managers spend more time in lateral interactions, and they build larger networks with contacts in other parts of the organization (Hammer & Turk, 1987; Kaplan, 1984; Kotter, 1982; Michael & Yukl, 1993; Stewart, 1976).

The leader's role in lateral relations includes functions such as gathering information from other subunits, obtaining assistance and cooperation from them, negotiating agreements, reaching joint decisions to coordinate unit activities, defending the unit's interests, promoting a favorable image for the unit, and serving as a spokesperson for subordinates. The extent to which a leader emphasizes each of these activities depends on the nature of the lateral relationship. For example, when a unit provides services on demand to other units, acting as a buffer for subordinates against these external demands is a primary concern of the leader (Sayles, 1979).

Just as the leader tries to reconcile demands from above and below, so also is it necessary to make compromises in seeking to reach agreements with other units. Subordinates expect the leader to represent their interests, but it will not be possible to maintain an effective working relationship with other units unless the leader is also responsive to their needs. Salancik, Calder, Rowland, Leblebici, and Conway (1975) conducted a study of managers in an insurance company to investigate this kind of role conflict. The study found that to maintain a cooperative effort, managers with interdependent work activities tended to become more responsive to each other's needs. The greater the number of peers a manager had to interact with on a regular basis, the less responsive the manager was to the desires of subordinates.

External dependencies are also increased by reliance on outside suppliers, consultants, and contractors that provide supplies, materials, or services when needed on a just-in-time basis. Many companies now use a "virtual" or "networked" form of organization and outsource most activities to other organizations. Some of the leaders in these organizations are expected to function more like entrepreneurs than traditional managers, which requires more knowledge about information technology and more skills in project management (Horner-Long & Schoenberg, 2002). The managers must identify strategic opportunities, negotiate joint ventures with people in other organizations, build strategic alliances, and coordinate interdependent activities in dozens of locations spread around the globe.

More external behavior is needed when the leader is highly dependent on information, resources, and cooperation from other parts of the organization, from higher management, and from outsiders such as clients, customers, suppliers of materials, and government agencies that regulate some aspects of the work. External dependencies increase the need to develop and maintain a large network of contacts and sources of timely, relevant information. A coalition of internal and external supporters is especially important when it is necessary to make changes that require their approval and cooperation.

Extreme Contexts

Some of the greatest leadership challenges arise when there is an immediate crisis or disruption of normal operations, such as a terrorist attack, a serious accident or shooting incident with many fatalities, a natural disaster (flood, tornados, earthquake), a cyberattack, a financial crisis or hostile takeover attempt, or a health emergency with widespread illness or deaths (Hannah & Parry, 2014; Hannah, Uhl-Bien, Avolio, & Cavarretta, 2009). Such extreme events are more likely in extreme contexts, and because many people work in settings that are inherently extreme, the practical significance of leadership in such contexts should not be underestimated. For instance, it is estimated that more than 89 million people worldwide are engaged in military service (International Institute for Strategic Studies, 2010). The International Firefighters Association identifies nearly 300,000 full-time firefighters serving in the United States and Canada, and the United Nations crime database indicates that there are nearly 4 million police officers serving in just the 10 largest countries (Hannah & Parry, 2014).

When operating within extreme contexts, and particularly when extreme events arise, the role expectations for the leader are likely to change. Leaders of organizations affected by such crises will be expected to be more assertive, directive, and decisive (Mulder & Stemerding, 1963). Peterson and Van Fleet (2008) found that respondents from nonprofit organizations preferred leaders to use more problem-solving and directive behavior and less supportive behavior in crisis situations than in noncrisis situations. A study conducted aboard warships found that in crisis situations navy officers were more directive, autocratic, and goal-oriented (Mulder, Ritsema van Eck, & de Jong, 1970). Officers who showed initiative and exercised power in a confident and decisive manner were usually more effective. A study of bank managers found that effective managers were more flexible in their behavior when a crisis disrupted normal operations (Mulder, de Jong, Koppelaar, & Verhage, 1986).

Clair and Dufresne (2007) described leadership strategies that enable organizations to go beyond resilience in the face of a crisis to achieve "hyper-resilience" that serves as a catalyst for positive transformation. As an example, they offered the story of how Reuters America responded to the tragic events of September 11, 2001:

> On that day over 1,200 employees of the renowned news agency were placed in harms' way and eight died as a result of the attacks. Through constant communication with employees, their families, clients, and affiliated firms, a newfound sense of humanity emerged. "What was previously considered a sterile and values-free workplace became a hub of compassion" (p. 70).

Hannah and colleagues (2009) distinguish between four general types of organizations that operate within extreme contexts that pose unique challenges to leadership: (1) naïve organizations, (2) trauma organizations, (3) high-reliability organizations, and (4) critical action organizations. Naïve organizations are those that face extreme events or are thrust into extreme contexts by chance. Examples include organizations that are confronted with unexpected events such as natural disasters (e.g., earthquakes, tornadoes, hurricanes), robberies, and catastrophic fires that destroy facilities. Because such events are unusual and unexpected, naïve organizations have typically taken only minimal steps to prepare and have limited systems in place to respond. Indeed, leaders of naïve organizations too often assume "It won't happen here" and consequently find it difficult to overcome complacency, resulting in a lack of preparation for extreme events (Pauchant & Mitroff, 1992).

Trauma organizations include disaster response units, hospital emergency rooms, and emergency medical technicians and ambulance teams. Such organizations are typically highly specialized and highly reactive, since they are primarily "on call" and have little control over when and where they face extreme conditions (Hannah & Parry, 2014). This is an extreme work setting where highly skilled professionals cooperate in teams to perform urgent, interdependent, unpredictable, and highly consequential tasks while dealing with common changes in team composition and the on-the-job training of novice members. For such teams to function effectively, a dynamic system of delegation is required. When appropriate, senior leaders rapidly delegate key leadership roles to junior leaders of the team, but these leadership roles are retained or taken back when necessary to meet the demands of the situation. Benefits of such dynamic delegation include enhancement of the ability of such "improvisational" teams to adroitly adapt to rapidly changing emergencies while simultaneously developing the skills of novice team members. Because trauma organizations are confronted with extreme events on a routine basis, their members come to perceive such events as "normal" and progressively less risky and threatening. Furthermore, repeated exposure to such events provides an opportunity for high levels of organizational learning and the refinement of team processes and systems for addressing extreme events. A qualitative study by Klein, Ziegert, Knight, and Xiao (2006, pg. 590) sheds light on how dynamic delegation can occur in this unique context:

> The patient arrives by helicopter or ambulance at the City Trauma Center (a pseudonym), one of the best and busiest trauma care centers in the world. The victim of a shooting, stabbing, car crash, or some other traumatic blow to the body, the patient is transported to the center's Trauma Resuscitation Unit (TRU) and is immediately surrounded by a team of doctors, nurses, and technicians. The team's task is to stabilize, diagnose, and treat the patient as quickly as possible. Errors or delays in this process may result in the death of the patient; quick and appropriate treatment is likely to save the patient's life. Several members of the team have never before worked together. Further, some of the doctors are relative novices. They are residents who joined the TRU days ago, seeking additional experience and training; they will leave the organization at the end of the month. Throughout the coming day and night, more patients will arrive, at unpredictable times, bearing unpredictable and uncertain injuries. And throughout the day and night, the team will change repeatedly in composition, as team members end their shifts of varying lengths and are replaced by other members of the TRU. In the months ahead, hundreds of trauma victims will enter the TRU. Scores of residents will cycle through. Evolving interdisciplinary teams of doctors, nurses, and technicians, often unfamiliar to one another, will provide treatment, repeatedly facing tasks necessitating swift coordination, reliable performance, adaptation, and learning.

The primary focus of high-reliability organizations (Weick & Sutcliffe, 2001) is on preventing or containing extreme events (Hannah & Parry, 2014). Examples include airlines, nuclear power plants, and "normal" police operations that focus on crime prevention. While high-reliability organizations and their members can certainly encounter extreme events, as the Fukushima nuclear reactor incident in Japan demonstrates, their goal is to avoid such events. The leaders must focus on the creation and maintenance of well-developed administrative and control processes that employ risk detection systems designed to avert potential failures.

Critical action organizations can be distinguished from high-reliability organizations in that they purposely and proactively engage in extreme events, rather than trying to avoid them (Hannah et al., 2009). Examples include a SWAT team raiding a meth lab and a special operations military unit launching a surprise attack on an enemy. While critical-action organizations typically face extreme events with less frequency than trauma units, the intensity and potential consequences (e.g. death, destruction) of the events tend to be more extensive. Members encounter higher levels of personal risk and are especially sensitive to leadership decisions that have a direct bearing on their safety (Hannah & Parry, 2014).

As yet, there is a limited but growing amount of research on leadership in extreme contexts, including those involving a serious crisis or disruption (Baur et al., 2018; DeChurch et al., 2011; Geier, 2016; Hannah & Parry, 2014; Hannah et al., 2009; Stewart, 1967, 1976). Given the number of people working in extreme contexts and the increasing frequency of extreme events for many types of organizations, much more research is needed.

Guidelines for Coping with Demands and Constraints

The chaotic and demanding nature of managerial work makes time management one of the most important administrative skills for leaders. This section of the chapter presents guidelines for managing time wisely, coping with demands, reducing constraints, and handling role conflicts (see summary in Table 3-1). The guidelines are based on research, practical experience, and recommendations by consultants.

- **Learn the reasons for demands and constraints.**

It is essential to learn how others perceive the manager's role and what they expect. Perception of demands and constraints inevitably involves subjective judgments, but many managers fail to take the time necessary to gather sufficient information on which to base these judgments. Do not assume that everyone agrees with your vision, priorities, or ideas about effective management. Before one can satisfy people or modify their expectations, it is necessary to understand what they really desire. Understanding role expectations requires frequent face-to-face interaction, asking questions, listening to others rather than constantly preaching, being sensitive to negative reactions (including nonverbal cues), and trying to discover the values and needs underlying a person's opinions and preferences.

- **Expand the range of available choices.**

Too many managers focus on the demands and constraints and fail to give adequate consideration to opportunities to define the job in different ways. It is essential to step back from the job and see it in a broader strategic perspective. It is usually possible to be proactive with superiors about defining the job in a way that allows more discretion, especially when role ambiguity is already present due to poorly defined responsibilities. Choices

TABLE 3-1 General Guidelines for Coping with Demands and Constraints

- Learn the reasons for demands and constraints.
- Expand the range of available choices.
- Determine what you want to accomplish.
- Analyze how you use your time.
- Plan daily and weekly activities.
- Avoid unnecessary activities.
- Conquer procrastination.
- Take advantage of reactive activities.
- Make time for reflective analysis and planning.
- Plan and prepare for extreme events.

may be expanded by finding ways to avoid demands and reduce constraints. A manager's planning and agenda development should include a conscious analysis of the demands and constraints limiting current effectiveness and how they can be reduced, eliminated, or circumvented. For instance, Jocko Willink and Leif Babin (2017, p. 237), two former U.S. Navy SEALs who have applied the lessons they learned from their military careers to create high-performance teams within the corporate world, offer the following advice to lower-level managers for "leading up":

> Leading up the chain of command requires tactful engagement with the immediate boss (or in military terms, higher headquarters) to obtain the decisions and support necessary to enable your team to accomplish its mission and ultimately win. To do this, a leader must push situational awareness up the chain of command. Leading up, the subordinate leader must use . . . influence, experience, knowledge, communication, and maintain the highest professionalism.

- **Determine what you want to accomplish.**

Time is a scarce resource that must be used well if the manager is to be effective. The key to effective time management is knowing what you want to accomplish. A person with a clear set of objectives and priorities can identify important activities and plan the best way to use time. Without clear objectives, no amount of planning will improve time management. The objectives and priorities may be informal, as with Kotter's (1982) mental agendas, but they need to be identified by a deliberate, conscious process.

- **Analyze how you use your time.**

It is difficult to improve time management without knowing how time is actually spent. Most managers are unable to estimate very accurately how much time they spend on different activities. Most time management systems recommend keeping a daily log of activities for one or two weeks. The log should list each activity in 15-minute blocks of time. It is helpful to indicate the source of control over each activity (e.g., self, boss, subordinates, others, organizational requirements) and whether the activity was planned in advance or is an immediate reaction to requests and problems. Typical time wasters should be noted on the log (e.g., unnecessary interruptions, meetings that run too long, searching for misplaced items, excessive use of online social networks). The time log should be analyzed to identify how important and necessary each activity is. Consider whether the activity can be eliminated, combined with others, or given less time. Identify whether too many activities are initiated by others, and whether adequate time is allowed for activities that are important but not urgent.

- **Plan daily and weekly activities.**

The extensive practitioner-oriented literature on time management shows considerable agreement about the importance of planning daily and weekly activities in advance (e.g., Webber, 1980). When planning daily activities, the first step is to make a to-do list for the day and assign priorities to each activity. This type of prioritized activity list may be used with a calendar showing required meetings and scheduled appointments to plan the next day's activities. Most of the discretionary time should be allocated to high-priority activities. If insufficient time is available to do important activities with immediate deadlines, reschedule or delegate some activities that are less important. The task of juggling the various activities and deciding which to do is a difficult but essential component of managerial work. Remember that it is more efficient to do a series of similar tasks than to keep switching from one type of task to another. Sometimes it is possible to schedule similar activities (e.g., several telephone calls, several letters) at the same time during the day. In addition, it is wise to take into account natural energy cycles and biorhythms. Peak alertness and efficiency occur at different times of the day for different people, and peak periods should be used for difficult tasks that require creativity.

- **Avoid unnecessary activities.**

Managers who become overloaded with unnecessary tasks are likely to neglect activities that are important for attaining key objectives. Managers may accept unnecessary tasks because they are afraid of offending subordinates, peers, or the boss, and they lack the self-confidence and assertiveness to turn down requests. One way to avoid unnecessary tasks is to prepare and use tactful ways to say no (e.g., say that you could only do the task if the person does some of your work for you; suggest other people who could do the task faster or better; point out that an important task will be delayed or jeopardized if you do what the person requests). Some unnecessary but required tasks can be eliminated by showing how resources will be saved or other benefits attained. Unessential tasks that cannot be eliminated or delegated can be put off until slack times. Sometimes when a task is put off long enough, the person who requested it will discover that it is not needed after all.

- **Conquer procrastination.**

Even when it is obvious that an activity is important, some people delay doing it in favor of a less important activity. One reason for procrastination is the fear of failure. People find excuses for delaying a task because they lack self-confidence. One remedy for a long, complex task is to divide it into smaller parts, each of which is easier and less intimidating. Deadlines are also helpful for overcoming procrastination. When setting deadlines for completion of difficult tasks, it is better to allow some slack and set a deadline that is earlier than the date when the task absolutely must be completed. However, having some slack should not become an excuse for not starting the task. Schedule a definite time early in the day to begin working on unpleasant tasks that tend to be procrastinated. Such tasks are more likely to get done if tackled first before the daily stream of demands provides excuses to avoid them.

- **Take advantage of reactive activities.**

Although some degree of control over the use of one's time is desirable, it is not feasible for a manager to plan in advance exactly how each minute of the day will be spent. The unpredictable nature of the environment makes it essential to view chance encounters, interruptions, and unscheduled meetings initiated by others not just as intrusions on scheduled activities, but rather as opportunities to gain important information, discover problems, influence others, and move forward on implementation of plans and informal agendas. Obligations that might otherwise be time wasters, such as required attendance at some meetings and ceremonial occasions, can be turned to one's advantage (Kotter, 1982; Mintzberg, 1973).

- **Make time for reflective analysis and planning.**

Managers face relentless pressures for dealing with immediate problems and responding to requests for assistance, direction, or authorization. Some of these problems require immediate attention, but if managers become too preoccupied with reacting to day-to-day problems, they have no time left for the reflective planning that would help them to avoid many of the problems, or for the contingency planning that would help them cope better with unavoidable problems. Therefore, it is desirable to set aside some time on a regular basis for reflective analysis and planning. One approach is to set aside a block of private time (at least one to two hours) each week for individual planning. Another approach is to schedule periodic strategy sessions with subordinates to encourage discussion of strategic issues. Still another approach is to initiate a major improvement project, delegate primary responsibility to a subordinate or task force, and schedule regular meetings with the individual or group to review plans and progress.

- **Plan and prepare for extreme events.**

Planning and preparing for a crisis are especially important for leaders in organizations that have extreme contexts. However, even for leaders in organizations unlikely to encounter extreme events such as natural disasters, terrorist attacks, and accidents involving explosions and fires, it is important to anticipate and plan for such crisis situations. Developing a plan for responding to such events and training members how to respond can help to avoid or reduce terrible consequences for the organization and its members.

Early Contingency Theories of Effective Leader Behavior

Contingency theories describe aspects of the situation that determine what type of leader behavior is most likely to be effective in each type of situation. Two early contingency theories that involve observable leader behaviors are the path-goal theory and the leadership substitutes theory. These theories are briefly reviewed, followed by a review of a more recent and broader contingency theory called the multiple-linkage model. A few contingency theories such as the Vroom and Yetton normative decision theory are described in other chapters. The least useful of the early contingency theories, such as situational leadership theory (Hersey & Blanchard, 1977) and the LPC contingency model (Fiedler, 1967) are described and evaluated in other publications (e.g., Ayman & Lauritsen, 2018; Yukl, 1993).

Path-Goal Theory

The initial versions of path-goal theory described how a leader's task-oriented behavior ("instrumental leadership") and relations-oriented behavior ("supportive leadership") influence subordinate satisfaction and performance in different situations (Evans, 1970; House, 1971). The theory was later extended to include participative leadership and achievement-oriented leadership (e.g., Evans, 1974; House, 1996; House & Mitchell, 1974).

As in the expectancy theory of motivation, leaders can motivate subordinates by influencing their perceptions about the likely consequences of different levels of effort. Subordinates will perform better when they have clear and accurate role expectations, they perceive that a high level of effort is necessary to attain task objectives, they are optimistic that it is possible to achieve the task objectives, and they perceive that high performance will result in beneficial outcomes. The effect of a leader's behavior is primarily to modify these perceptions and beliefs. Leader behavior can also affect subordinate satisfaction with the leader.

The effect of leader behavior on subordinate satisfaction and effort depends on aspects of the situation, including task characteristics and subordinate characteristics. These situational moderator variables determine both the potential for increased subordinate motivation and the manner in which the leader must act to improve motivation. Situational variables also influence subordinate preferences for a particular pattern of leadership behavior, thereby influencing the impact of the leader on subordinate satisfaction.

One key proposition of the theory involves the moderating influence of situational variables on instrumental leadership. Task-oriented behavior has a stronger effect on role clarity, self-efficacy, effort, and performance when subordinates are unsure about how to do their work, which occurs when they have a complex and difficult task and little prior experience with it. Another key proposition is that supportive leadership has a stronger effect when the task is very tedious, dangerous, and stressful. In this situation supportive leadership increases subordinate confidence, effort, and satisfaction.

Leadership Substitutes Theory

Kerr and Jermier (1978) identified aspects of the situation that make task-oriented behavior ("instrumental leadership") or relations-oriented behavior ("supportive leadership") by the designated leader redundant or ineffective. Later versions included additional behaviors such as contingent reward behavior (Howell, Bowen, Dorfman, Kerr, & Podsakoff, 1990; Podsakoff, Niehoff, MacKenzie, & Williams, 1993).

The situational variables include characteristics of the subordinates, task, and the organization that serve as substitutes by directly affecting the dependent variable and making the leader behavior redundant. The substitutes for instrumental leadership include a highly structured and repetitive task, extensive rules and standard procedures, and extensive prior training and experience for subordinates. The substitutes for supportive leadership include a cohesive work group in which the members support each other, and an intrinsically satisfying task that is not stressful.

In a situation with many substitutes, the potential impact of leader behavior on subordinate motivation and satisfaction may be greatly reduced. For example, little direction is necessary when subordinates have extensive prior experience or training, and they already possess the skills and knowledge to know what to do and how to do it. Likewise, professionals who are internally motivated by their values, needs, and ethics do not need to be encouraged by the leader to do high-quality work.

Some situational variables (called neutralizers) prevent a leader from using forms of behavior that would improve subordinate satisfaction or unit performance. For example, a leader with no authority to change ineffective work procedures cannot make changes that would improve efficiency. Howell et al. (1990) contend that some situations have so many neutralizers that it is difficult or impossible for a leader to succeed. In this event, the remedy is to change the situation and make it more favorable for the leader by removing neutralizers, and in some cases by increasing substitutes.

Multiple-Linkage Model

The multiple-linkage model (Yukl, 1981, 1989) describes how specific types of leader behavior and situational variables jointly influence performance by individual subordinates and by the leader's work unit. The broadly defined behaviors used in most earlier contingency theories were replaced with specific types of leader behaviors. The model includes a larger number of mediating variables that explain the effects of leader behaviors and situational variables, and there is more explicit description of group-level processes. However, the model does not deal directly with organizational processes involving adaptive leadership by top management to threats and opportunities in the external environment of the organization, and that subject is discussed in Chapter 12. The four types of variables in the multiple-linkage model include leader behaviors, explanatory mediating variables, outcome variables, and situational variables.

Mediating Variables

The mediating variables in the model are based on earlier research and theory on determinants of individual and group performance (e.g., Hackman, Brousseau, & Weiss, 1976; Likert, 1967; McGrath, 1984; Porter & Lawler, 1968), but they are defined primarily at the group level, as with theories of team leadership (see Chapter 11).

Task commitment: members strive to attain a high level of performance and show a high degree of personal commitment to unit task objectives.

Ability and role clarity: members understand their individual job responsibilities, know what to do, and have the skills to do it.

Organization of the work: effective performance strategies are used and the work is organized to ensure efficient utilization of personnel, equipment, and facilities.

Cooperation and mutual trust: members trust each other, share information and ideas, help each other, and identify with the work unit.

Resources and support: the group has budgetary funds, tools, equipment, supplies, personnel, facilities, information, and assistance needed to do the work.

External coordination: the activities of the group are synchronized with the interdependent activities in other subunits and organizations (e.g., suppliers, clients).

The mediating variables interact with each other to determine the effectiveness of a group or organizational subunit. A serious deficiency in one mediating variable may lower group effectiveness, even though the other mediating variables are not deficient. The greater the relative importance of a particular mediating variable, the more group performance will be reduced by a deficiency in this variable. The relative importance of the mediating variables depends on the type of work unit and other aspects of the situation.

Situational Variables

Situational variables directly influence mediating variables and can make them either more or less favorable. Situational variables also determine the relative importance of the mediating variables as a determinant of group performance. Mediating variables that are both important and deficient should get top priority for corrective action by a leader. Conditions that make a mediating variable more favorable are similar to "substitutes" for leadership. In a very favorable situation, some of the mediating variables may already be at their maximum short-term level, making the job of the leader much easier.

Situational variables that can influence task commitment include the formal reward system and the intrinsically motivating properties of the work itself. Subordinate task commitment is more important for complex tasks that require high effort and initiative and have a high cost for any errors. Member commitment to perform the task effectively will be greater if the organization has a reward system that provides attractive rewards contingent on performance, as in the case of many sales jobs. Intrinsic motivation is likely to be higher for subordinates if the work requires varied skills, is interesting and challenging, and provides automatic feedback about performance.

Situational variables that affect subordinate ability and role clarity include the nature of the work, the prior training and experience of the leader's subordinates, and the effectiveness of the organization's recruitment and selection processes. Subordinate skills are more important when tasks are complex and difficult to perform, they require strong technical skills, the cost of errors is high, and disruptions in the work are likely. An organization with effective recruiting and high salaries is more likely to attract qualified people with relevant job skills and prior experience. Role requirements are easier to understand and the work is easier to perform when the task is simple and repetitive, subordinates have extensive prior experience, and the organization has clear rules and standard procedures for the work. Role ambiguity is more likely to be a problem when the task has multiple performance criteria and unclear priorities, when the nature of the work or technology is changing, or when the work is affected by frequent changes in plans or priorities determined by clients or higher management.

Situational variables that affect the organization of the work and assignment of tasks to individuals include the type of technology, the variety of tasks performed by the leader's work unit, the variation in subordinate skills, and the amount of work rules and standard procedures that are determined by staff experts or union contracts. When the work unit performs one basic type of task and subordinates are all highly skilled, it is easy to organize unit activities and make task assignments that will achieve a high level of efficiency. An effective performance strategy for organizing activities and assigning tasks is more important when the work unit has complex, unique, and important projects and members who differ with regard to their skills. For some types of projects, an efficient organization of activities can be achieved by qualified staff experts who use operations management and project management software.

Situational variables that affect cooperation and teamwork include the nature of the work, the size of the group, the stability of membership, the similarity among members in values and background, and the reward system. Cooperation and teamwork are more important when the group has specialized, interdependent tasks or when members work alone but must share equipment and scarce resources. More cohesiveness and cooperation are likely in small groups with a stable, homogeneous membership. Cooperation is increased by rewards that are based primarily on contributions to group performance rather than on individual performance.

The adequacy of resources that are necessary to do the work is influenced by the nature of the work, the organization's formal budgetary systems, procurement systems, and inventory control systems, as well as by economic conditions at the time. Ensuring an adequate level of resources is more important when work unit performance is highly dependent on getting scarce resources from the organization or outside sources, and when the providers of resources are unreliable. An adequate level of resources is more likely to be provided to a work unit when the organization is prosperous and growing than when the organization is in decline and faces severe resource shortages.

The need for external coordination is affected by the formal structure of the organization. High lateral interdependence increases the amount of necessary coordination with other subunits, but this coordination may be facilitated by special integrating mechanisms such as integrator positions and cross-functional committees (Galbraith, 1973; Lawrence & Lorsch, 1969. A high level of dependency on outsiders such as clients or subcontractors for resources or approvals increases the need for external coordination with them, but it may be achieved by designated project managers or liaison specialists rather than by work unit managers.

Short-Term Actions to Correct Deficiencies

A basic proposition of the model is that leader actions correct any deficiencies in the mediating variables that determine group performance. A leader who fails to recognize opportunities to correct deficiencies in key mediating variables, who recognizes the opportunities but fails to act, or who acts but is not skilled will be less than optimally effective. An ineffective leader may make things worse by acting in ways that increase rather than decrease the deficiency in one or more mediating variables. For example, a leader who is very manipulative and coercive may reduce subordinate effort rather than increase it.

Table 3-2 summarizes ways to deal with deficiencies in the mediating variables. Leaders may influence group members to work faster or do better-quality work by offering special

TABLE 3-2 Types of Specific Actions for Improving Weak Performance Determinants

Low subordinate task commitment or confidence

- Set challenging goals and express confidence they can be achieved.
- Articulate an appealing vision of what the group can accomplish.
- Use influence tactics to influence task commitment.
- Offer more incentives for goal attainment.

Low subordinate task knowledge and skills

- Make clear assignments.
- Provide more direction and clarification of procedures.
- Provide instruction and coaching when needed.
- Find skilled people to do difficult tasks.

Low coordination and inefficient procedures for the work

- Find ways to make better use of members, resources, and equipment.
- Identify and eliminate inefficient or unnecessary activities.
- Provide clear, decisive direction of activities.
- Develop better plans for achieving task objectives.

Inadequate resources to do the work

- Find more reliable or alternative sources of resources.
- Request more resources from the organization.
- Identify ways to avoid wasted sources.
- Find more efficient ways to use resources.

Weak external coordination

- Develop better plans to avoid external coordination problems.
- Improve external relations with interdependent units.
- Consult more often with interdependent units to coordinate actions.
- Monitor closely to detect external coordination problems quickly.

incentives, by giving an inspiring talk about the importance of the work, or by setting challenging goals. Leaders may increase member ability to do the work by clarifying objectives and providing relevant training and coaching. Leaders may organize and coordinate activities in a more efficient way by finding ways to reduce delays, duplication of effort, and wasted effort; by more effective matching of people to tasks; or by finding better ways to use people and resources. Leaders may obtain resources needed immediately to do the work, such as information, personnel, equipment, materials, or supplies. Leaders may act to improve external coordination by meeting with outsiders to plan activities and resolve conflicting demands on the work unit.

Some aspects of the situation limit a leader's discretion in making changes and reacting to problems, and they are similar to Stewart's (1976, 1982) "constraints" and Kerr and Jermier's (1978) "neutralizers." The extent to which a leader is capable of doing something in the short run to improve any of the mediating variables is limited by the position power, organizational policies, technology used to do the work, and legal-contractual restrictions (e.g., labor–management agreements, contracts with suppliers, requirements mandated by government agencies). Constraints may prevent a leader from rewarding or punishing members, changing work assignments or procedures, and procuring supplies and equipment.

The model does not imply that there is only one optimal pattern of managerial behavior in any given situation. Leaders usually have some choice among mediating variables in need of improvement, and different patterns of behavior are usually possible to correct a particular deficiency. The overall pattern of leadership behavior by the designated leader and other group members is more important than any single action. In this respect, the model is similar to Stewart's (1976, 1982) "choices" (see Chapter 2). However, a leader whose attention is focused on mediating variables that are not deficient or not important will fail to improve unit performance.

Long-Term Actions to Improve the Situation

Over a longer period of time, leaders can make larger improvements in group performance by modifying the situation to make it more favorable. Effective leaders act to reduce constraints, increase substitutes, and reduce the importance of mediating variables that are not amenable to improvement. These effects usually involve sequences of related behaviors carried out over a long time period. Useful insights are provided by literature on leading change, making strategic decisions, and representing the team or work unit (see Chapters 5, 11, and 12). Some examples of possible actions a leader may take to improve the situation are as follows:

1. Gain more access to resources needed for the work by cultivating better relationships with suppliers, finding alternative sources, and reducing dependence on unreliable sources.
2. Gain more control over the demand for the unit's products and services by finding new customers, opening new markets, advertising more, and modifying the products or services to be more acceptable to clients and customers.
3. Initiate new, more profitable activities for the work unit that will make better use of personnel, equipment, and facilities.
4. Initiate long-term improvement programs to upgrade equipment and facilities in the work unit (e.g., replace old equipment, implement new technology).
5. Improve selection procedures to increase the level of employee skills and commitment.
6. Modify the formal structure of the work unit to solve chronic problems and reduce demands on the leader for short-term problem solving.

Evaluation of Research on the Contingency Theories

Review articles and meta-analyses describe relevant research on path-goal theory (Ayman & Lauritsen, 2018; Osborn et al., 2014; Podsakoff, MacKenzie, Ahearne, & Bommer, 1995; Wofford & Liska, 1993), and leadership substitutes theory (Ayman & Lauritsen, 2018; Dionne, Yammarino, Atwater, & James, 2002; Osborn et al., 2014; Podsakoff, MacKenzie, & Bommer, 1996a; Podsakoff et al., 1993; Podsakoff et al., 1995; Wu, 2010; Xu, Zhong, & Wang, 2013). Several research methods have been used to test the multiple-linkage model, but no studies have directly tested all aspects of the model (e.g., Peterson & Van Fleet, 2008; Yukl & Van Fleet, 1982; Yukl, 2012).

The evidence supporting contingency theories of effective leadership is limited, and the findings are difficult to interpret. The complexity, ambiguity, and conceptual problems in the theories make them more difficult to test. The lack of strong and consistent results is probably due in part to overreliance on weak research methods, such as survey studies with convenience samples and data for all variables obtained from the same respondents (Dionne et al., 2002; Podsakoff et al., 1996a; Schriesheim & Kerr, 1974; Wu, 2010; Xu et al., 2013; Yukl, 1989; Yukl, 2012). It is desirable to make more use of other relevant research methods, including comparative field studies of effective and ineffective leaders in different situations, longitudinal studies of how well leaders adapt to changes in the situation over time, field experiments with leaders trained to diagnose the situation accurately and select appropriate behaviors, and laboratory experiments with observation of leaders in team simulations conducted over a period of several weeks. Other methods for measuring leadership behavior (e.g., observation, diaries, interviews, and critical incidents) should be used more often, and ineffective forms of leadership behavior should be examined in addition to effective forms of behavior (e.g., Amabile et al., 2004; Yukl & Van Fleet, 1982).

Other improvements in the research are also desirable, and some deal with limitations already described for the behavior research in Chapter 2. Most studies only examined how much leaders used one or two broad behaviors such as task-oriented and relations-oriented behaviors, and the studies only examined simple linear relationships between the broad behaviors and outcomes. To understand adaptive leadership, it is also necessary to examine how specific types of leader behavior affect outcomes in different situations (Uhl-Bien & Arena, 2018; Yukl & Mahsud, 2010). It is essential to consider the optimal amount of behavior in each situation and the optimal timing of the behavior.

Researchers should also pay more attention to the overall pattern of leadership behavior rather than examining each type of behavior separately. Effective leaders use behaviors that are complementary and mutually enhancing (Kaplan, 1988). More than one pattern of specific behaviors may be equally effective in the same situation. It is essential for leaders to find a good balance between competing objectives, such as controlling versus empowering, strategic versus operational objectives, and concern for people versus concern for task performance (Hooijberg, 1996; Kaiser & Overfield, 2010; Kaplan & Kaiser, 2006; Quinn, Spreitzer, & Hart, 1992; Yukl & Mahsud, 2010). The importance of competing objectives and flexibility for strategic leadership, and ways to make the situation more favorable by implementing management programs and systems that enhance leader behaviors or reduce the need for some of them, are discussed in Chapter 12.

Guidelines for Flexible, Adaptive Leadership

Despite the many limitations for many studies on contingency theories, the combined results found in many different types of research suggest the following general guidelines for flexible, adaptive leadership:

- **Understand your leadership situation and try to make it more favorable.**

Identify demands, constraints, and choices, and look for ways to increase substitutes and reduce constraints. Find new sources of resources, advice, and assistance. Use a pattern of behavior that is relevant for the situation and likely to help achieve desired objectives.

- **Learn how to use a wide range of relevant behaviors.**

Learn how to use a wide range of behaviors that may be relevant for any situation or challenge you are likely to face in the job. The first step is to identify the types of behaviors and skills that are likely to be useful and assess your current strengths and weaknesses for them. Ways to assess and develop leadership skills are described in Chapter 14.

- **Identify effective behaviors for your objectives and situation.**

Avoid the common assumption that the same form of behavior that was effective in the past will always be effective in the future. Identify the optimal type and amount of a behavior for the situation and when the behavior should be used. A moderate amount is usually better than very little or a maximum amount of the behavior, and the behavior may be less effective if used too early or too late.

- **Use more planning for a long, complex task.**

For a long, complex task with many interrelated activities performed by a large group of people over a considerable period of time (e.g., weeks or months), careful planning is necessary to complete the task on time and within budget. Planning is easier when the steps necessary to carry out the task are known in advance, and the environment is relatively predictable. Some examples of such activities include a construction project, installation of new equipment, introduction of new information systems, and the design and execution of a training program. Guidelines for project planning include the following steps: (1) identify the list of necessary activities, (2) determine the optimal sequence for them, (3) estimate when each activity should begin and end, (4) determine who should be responsible for performing each activity, and (5) identify the resources needed for it.

- **Provide more direction to people with interdependent roles.**

Role interdependence among group members increases role ambiguity, because it requires frequent mutual adjustments in behavior. A team will not achieve high performance unless the actions of its members are closely coordinated. Even when the individual tasks seem relatively structured, members may be confused about how to make mutual adjustments to coordinate their actions. Confusion is greater when team members lack prior experience in performing a particular task together, which is likely in a newly formed team, a team with new members, or a team with a new type of task. Intensive direction by the leader is sometimes needed to coordinate the interdependent actions of different team members, but the amount of required direction may be reduced if the team practices complex activities and members become accustomed to working together closely. Examples include sports teams (e.g., basketball, ice hockey), rescue teams, combat teams, and teams that operate complex equipment (e.g., airplanes, submarines). Team leadership behaviors are described in more detail in Chapter 11.

- **Monitor a critical task or unreliable person more closely.**

Monitoring provides information needed to detect and correct performance problems. More frequent and intensive monitoring is appropriate for a critical task that involves high exposure, so that problems can be detected before they get so bad that they will be costly and difficult to correct. However, the appropriate amount of monitoring depends also on the reliability of the subordinates who are doing the task. The less dependable and competent a subordinate is, the more monitoring is needed.

- **Provide more instruction and coaching to an inexperienced subordinate.**

When the work is complex and a subordinate is inexperienced at doing it, more instruction and coaching by the leader are needed. Lack of experience is likely for subordinates who are new to the job, but it also occurs when there is a major change in how the work is done (e.g., new technology, reconfigured jobs). A leader with strong expertise can help a person discover the reasons for weak performance and provide any necessary coaching or instruction.

- **Be more supportive to someone with a highly stressful task.**

A person who becomes emotionally upset will have more difficulty performing a task successfully, especially if it requires reasoning and problem solving. Sources of stress include unreasonable demands, uncontrollable problems, difficult interpersonal relations (e.g., critical, abusive customers), dangerous conditions (e.g., firefighting, combat, police work), and the risk of costly errors (surgery, financial advisor, aircraft maintenance). People in such situations have more need for emotional support from leaders and coworkers.

Summary

The job situation for most leaders is too complex and unpredictable to rely on the same set of standardized responses for all situations. Effective leaders are continuously reading the situation and determining how to adapt their behavior to it. They seek to understand the task requirements, situational constraints, and interpersonal processes that determine which course of action is most likely to be successful.

This chapter examined some contingency theories that prescribe different patterns of leader behavior (or traits) for different situations. The path-goal theory of leadership examines how aspects of the situation determine the optimal level of each type of leadership behavior for improving subordinate satisfaction and effort. Leadership substitutes theory identifies aspects of the situation that make leadership behavior redundant or irrelevant. The multiple-linkage model describes how leader behavior and aspects of the situation jointly influence individual or group performance. A leader can improve group performance by taking direct action to correct any deficiencies in the mediating variables, and over time the leader can improve group performance by taking action to make the situation more favorable.

The early contingency theories have conceptual weaknesses such as overemphasis on broadly defined behaviors, exclusion of relevant situational variables, and unclear explanation of causal relationships and mediating processes. Most studies conducted to test the early contingency theories used weak research methods, and the results are difficult to interpret. Additional knowledge about situational variables has been gained in research on specific types of leader behavior, such as those in the multiple linkage model and in some contingency theories described in other chapters of the book.

In an increasingly turbulent and uncertain world, flexible adaptive leadership seems even more relevant today than it was decades ago when the contingency theories were first proposed, and especially for extreme contexts (e.g., trauma organizations, high-reliability and critical-action organizations) and extreme events (e.g., natural disasters, terrorist attacks). Better contingency theories are needed to help managers understand and overcome the challenges confronting them. In future theories it is desirable to include both universal elements (e.g., general principles) and situational elements (e.g., guidelines to help identify desirable behaviors for a particular type of situation).

Review and Discussion Questions

1. What situational variables influence leader behavior?
2. What are some guidelines for coping with demands and constraints?
3. Briefly explain the path-goal and leader-substitutes theories.
4. Briefly explain the multiple-linkage model.
5. Briefly describe four types of extreme contexts for leadership.
6. In what situations are planning, clarifying, and monitoring most likely to be effective?
7. In what situations are supporting, developing, and recognizing most likely to be effective?
8. What are specific ways to deal with short-term deficiencies in performance determinants?
9. What are specific ways to improve the leadership situation?
10. What are some ways to become a more flexible, adaptive leader?

Key Terms

demands, constraints, and choices
extreme contexts
extreme events
contingency theories
situational variable
mediating variable
moderator variable
substitutes
neutralizers

PERSONAL REFLECTION

Think about a current leadership role or one you had in the past. It could be a formal role such as supervisor, coach, team captain, or an informal one such as in a student project team. In this role, what demands were made of you? What constraints did you face? Finally, describe any choices you made that defined the role to suit your strengths.

CASE

KKN Advertising

Chandan, the head of print media advertising department at the KKN Advertising Agency, Indore, reached an hour late to office for work. He had an important meeting to attend for which he had been feeling extremely anxious, and spent the previous night almost sleepless. By the time he managed to catch some sleep, it was quite late, and as a result he overslept and woke up very late the next morning. He rushed for the meeting as soon as he reached his office. In the meeting, when the Chairman asked him about his suggestions on the new layout they were thinking of adopting, Chandan was completely blank. He vaguely remembered having received a mail about it and had thought of getting back to it later, but then completely forgot about it. The Chairman was visibly annoyed as he asked another employee to briefly orient Chandan about the strategy they were planning to adopt so that the meeting could be conducted.

Post meeting, Chandan received a call from a client asking if he had completed their project or not. Chandan was a little taken aback, since the deadline was still a week away according to him. However, the client reminded him of an email that was sent a week back, informing about the sudden urgency of the project. So, Chandan searched for the email in his inbox, he found it in the large collection of unread mails. He apologized to his client and requested for an extension of two days. Just as he got done with this call, his secretary Jyoti arrived. She was sent by the digital media advertising head, Amit, to call Chandan to his office to discuss an upcoming project. The three of them discussed the plan to for the project, after which they went out for lunch.

As soon as he got back to his office, he was called by the head of the Human Resources Department with the monthly employee feedback and production report. Chandan who had not finished the report, informed the HR head that due to other more important projects that needed his urgent attention, the monthly report would be slightly delayed. The HR head was quite annoyed at this as he needed Chandan's report in order to complete his monthly report to the Chairman. Now, there would be a delay in his work because of Chandan.

On the way back to his office, Chandan was stopped by his assistant who needed his help with a project he was working on. The two of them spent almost an hour discussing about it. By the time Chandan reached back to his office, it was time for him to leave for home. As Chandan took a moment to sit down and reflect on his day, he realized that he was falling behind in his work a lot. There were still so many things to do and he felt exhausted just thinking about them. On his way out from office, he wondered what steps he could take to manage his job more efficiently.

—*Written by* Nishant Uppal

Questions

1. What are the things that Chandan did wrong, and what should he have done in each case?
2. What steps should Chandan take in order to become more efficient at his job?

CASE

The Auto Shop

Part 1

Kabir owned and managed a car servicing workshop. His shop was known for its quick, reliable and quality service and attracted a very loyal client base because of it. The mechanics at the shop are well equipped and trained to manage both repair and maintenance related tasks. There is a standard procedure for every task that each mechanic follows. Customers are requested to provide their valuable feedback when they come to pick-up their car as well as after a few days of use. Kabir was known for his friendly and warm attitude with not only his customers but also his employees. He rarely passed directives to his employees. He would suggest ways of handling a problem and give technical advice to them, but would ultimately give them the freedom to handle a given task in a manner they deemed to be suitable. He would demonstrate how to do a lot of tasks. When not occupied with administrative work, Kabir would work alongside his employees. He followed a very collaborative form of leadership wherein his employees were a part of the workshop's decision-making process as well. He always encouraged his employees to share their knowledge and ideas with others for the personal as well as the workshop's betterment. Just like his nature, Kabir's style of supervision and management was also easy-going like him. It was because of this reason that his employees also liked and respected him a lot. They never felt that they were being bossed around or were being treated as inferior in any way. They understood that Kabir genuinely sought their advice, opinion and participation for the advancement of the workshop, and not just to manipulate them so they don't oppose his decisions.

—*Written by* Nishant Uppal

Questions

1. What is the usual leadership situation in the car service workshop (consider the nature of the task, subordinates, and environment)?
2. Describe Kabir's typical leadership style and evaluate whether it is appropriate for the leadership situation.

Part 2

On a monsoon Monday, it had been raining heavily for two hours continuously, and according to the weather forecasts, it did not seem like the rain would have slowed down anytime soon. There was water dripping from parts of the roof, and eventually, it was beginning to seep into the workshop through the gate as well. Kabir was worried that if it continued to rain like this, his workshop, especially the workstation would soon get flooded. He felt that quick action was needed, and immediately he instructed his employees to relocate the cars and the workshop equipment to a higher platform or the storage room, to prevent them from getting wet. Although everyone heard Kabir's instruction, they seemed unmoved by it. They felt that Kabir was panicking for no reason. It was only when Kabir said, "You'll do as I say", assertively, that they made a move.

The employees realizing the seriousness in Kabir's tone, immediately stopped whatever they were doing and began to relocate the cars and the workshop equipment and supplies. Just before the water began to enter the shop, everything had been relocated in time. After about four hours of incessant pour, it finally stopped raining. It took another 2–3 hours for the water to recede, after which the workers helped clean up the workshop and put everything back to its original place. As a gesture of gratitude, Kabir thanked each of his employees for their individual efforts, and gave them an off the next day.

The following day, when all the employees returned to work, Kabir made an informal speech wherein he credited the mechanics for helping him avoid a lot of damage to the workshop. He pointed out the contribution made by each employee separately, which made them feel even more valued and respected. It was after his speech that one of his employees told him that they were taken aback by his behavior the previous day, as they could not believe that the mild mannered Kabir could suddenly transform into this assertive boss. His employees told him that because of his attitude in general, they had forgotten that he was their boss.

Questions

1. Describe Kabir's leadership style during the flood, and evaluate how appropriate it was for the leadership situation.
2. Identify effective behaviors by Kabir after the flood subsided.
3. How should Kabir behave toward his employees in the future?

Decision Making and Empowerment by Leaders

Learning Objectives

After studying this chapter, you should be able to:

- Understand different forms of participative and empowering leadership.
- Understand the major findings in research on consequences of participative and empowering leadership.
- Understand the situations in which participative and empowering leadership are most likely to be effective.
- Understand empowerment programs and psychological empowerment.
- Understand when and how to use consultation and delegation.

Introduction

Making decisions is one of the most important functions performed by leaders. Many of the activities of managers and administrators involve making and implementing decisions. Involving others in making decisions is often a necessary part of the political process for getting decisions approved and implemented in organizations. Participative leadership involves efforts by a leader to enlist the aid of others in making important decisions. Delegation and consultation are distinct types of power-sharing processes that leaders can use to empower subordinates. Psychological empowerment involves the perception by members of an organization that they have the opportunity to determine their work roles, accomplish meaningful work, and influence important events. Empowering leadership promotes a sense of psychological empowerment for followers by sharing power with them and by providing emotional and developmental support.

Empowering and participative leadership are subjects that bridge the power and behavior approaches to leadership. The research on participative and empowering leadership emphasizes the leader's perspective on power sharing. The research on psychological empowerment emphasizes the follower's perspective. Taken together, the two different perspectives provide a better understanding of effective leadership in organizations. This chapter describes the theory and research findings on these subjects. The chapter begins with a brief review of findings about the way important decisions are usually made in organizations.

Decision Making by Managers

An important responsibility of formal leaders is to make decisions about objectives, strategies, operational procedures, and the allocation of resources. The literature on decision making is extensive, and much progress has been made studying how important decisions are made in organizations. Descriptive studies and analyses of cognitive processes have both been useful for understanding how decisions are made in groups and organizations (Bromiley & Rau, 2015; Butler, O'Broin, Lee, & Senior, 2016; Combe & Carrington, 2015; Mazutis & Eckardt, 2017; Mumford, Watts, & Partlow, 2015; Narayanan, Zane, & Kemmerer, 2011). Some of the findings are reviewed in this section of the chapter.

Emotions and Intuition Are Often Involved

Decision processes are often characterized more by confusion and emotionality than by rationality. Instead of careful analysis of likely outcomes in relation to predetermined objectives, information is often distorted or suppressed to serve preconceptions and biases about the best course of action. The emotional shock of discovering a serious problem and anxiety about choosing among unattractive alternatives may result in denial of negative evidence, wishful thinking, procrastination, vacillation between choices, and panic reactions by individual managers or by decision groups (Janis & Mann, 1977). The greater the job demands and stress for a manager, the less likely it is that a prolonged search or careful analysis of potential costs and benefits will be made (Hambrick, Finkelstein, & Mooney, 2005). Instead, a highly stressed executive is more likely to respond to serious threats and problems by relying on solutions used in the past or by imitating the practices of similar companies. Individuals with strong negative affect (fear, anger, depression) are more likely to use dysfunctional methods for decision making than individuals with positive affect (Ganster, 2005; Scheibehenne & von Helversen, 2015).

Decisions often reflect the influence of intuition rather than conscious rational analysis of available alternatives and their likely outcomes (Akinci & Sadler-Smith, 2012; Dane & Pratt, 2007; Salas, Rosen, & DiazGranados, 2010; Simon, 1987). Experienced managers try to determine if a problem is familiar or novel, and for familiar ones they can apply past experience and learned procedures to determine the best course of action. However, failure to classify a problem accurately is likely to result in a poor decision on how to resolve it. When managers have mental models that are no longer adequate, it is more difficult to recognize novel problems or innovative solutions (Combe & Carrington, 2015; Narayanan et al., 2011). Involving other people can improve the quality of problem diagnosis and decision choice, but only if appropriate processes are used. Decision making by a group is described in Chapter 11.

Important Decisions Are Disorderly and Political

Much of the management literature describes decisions as discrete events made by a single manager or group in an orderly, rational manner. This picture is sharply contradicted by the descriptive research on managerial activities and decision making (Akinci & Sadler-Smith, 2012; Cohen & March, 1974; Korica et al., 2017; McCall & Kaplan, 1985; Schweiger, Anderson, & Locke, 1985; Simon, 1987). Managers are seldom observed to make major decisions at a single point in time, and some major decisions are the result of many small actions or incremental choices taken without regard to larger strategic issues.

Important decisions in organizations typically require the support and authorization of many different people at different levels of management and in different subunits of the organization. It is common practice for a manager to consult with subordinates, peers, or superiors about important decisions when an immediate decision is not required. The person who initiates the decision process may not be the person who makes the final choice among action alternatives. For example, a section supervisor with a problem may point out the need for a decision to the department manager, who may consult with the plant manager or with managers in other departments affected by the decision. Even when not consulted in advance, the plant manager may review the department manager's decision and approve, reject, or modify it.

The different people involved in making a decision often disagree about the true nature of a problem and the likely outcomes of the proposed solutions, due to the different perspectives, assumptions, and values typical of managers from different functional specialties and backgrounds. When managers have different mental models for explaining the cause of a problem, it is more difficult to reach agreement about a good solution (Gary & Wood, 2016; Mumford, Friedrich, Caughron, & Byrne, 2007).

A prolonged, highly political decision process is likely when decisions involve important and complex problems for which no ready-made, good solutions are available, when many affected parties have conflicting interests, and when a diffusion of power exists among the parties. The decision process may drag on for weeks or months due to delays and interruptions as a proposal is sidetracked by opponents, preempted by immediate crises, or recycled back to its initiators for revisions necessary to make it suitable to managers whose support is needed (Mintzberg, Raisinghani, & Theoret, 1976). For decisions involving major changes in organizational strategies or policies, the outcome will depend to a great extent on the influence, skills, and persistence of the individual managers who desire to initiate change and on the relative power of the various coalitions involved in making or authorizing these decisions (Battilana, Gilmartin, Sengul, Pache, & Alexander, 2010; Kanter, 1983; Kotter, 1982, 1985).

Many Decisions Are Informal and Adaptive

An important type of decision for managers involves determining how to achieve key task objectives, implement changes, and conduct required activities. This type of decision making is often described in the managerial literature as primarily a formal planning process that involves written objectives, strategies, policies, and budgets. However, the descriptive studies found that important decisions are often made in a way that is informal and implicit. Kotter (1982) found that general managers developed agendas consisting of goals and plans related to their job responsibilities and involving a variety of short-term and long-term issues. The short-term (1–30 days) objectives and plans were usually quite specific and detailed, but the longer-term agenda items were usually vague, incomplete, and only loosely connected. For a new manager the process of developing this agenda is likely to be rough and incomplete. Over time, as managers gather more information about their organization or subunit, the agendas are refined and expanded (Gabarro, 1985; Kotter, 1982). Kotter also found that the implementation of agenda items is a gradual, continuous process. Managers use a variety of influence techniques during their daily interactions with other people to mobilize support and shape events. The agenda guides the manager in making efficient use of random encounters and brief interactions with people in the network of contacts.

In his study of top executives, Quinn (1980) found that most of the important strategic decisions were made outside the formal planning process, and strategies were formulated in an incremental, flexible, and intuitive manner. In response to major unforeseen events, the executives developed tentative, broad strategies that allowed them to keep their options open until they had more opportunity to learn from experience about the nature of the environment and the feasibility of their initial actions. Strategies were refined and implemented simultaneously in a cautious, incremental manner that reflected the need to develop a political coalition in support of a strategy as well as to avoid the risks of an initial, irreversible commitment to a particular course of action. Instead of a top-down, formal process, overall objectives and strategies for the firms were more likely to be the result of a bottom-up political process in which the objectives and strategies of powerful individuals and organizational subunits are reconciled and integrated. The formal, annual plans were merely a confirmation of strategic decisions already reached through the informal political process.

Routine Decisions Are Different

Not all decisions involve major changes or prolonged political processes. Managers make many less momentous decisions in the process of solving operational problems, setting short-term goals, assigning work to subordinates, setting up work schedules, authorizing the expenditure of funds for supplies or equipment, and approving pay increases. These decisions often involve the use of established procedures or solutions, the manager has the authority to make a decision, few important people will be affected by the decision, little conflict exists about objectives or solutions, and pressure is felt for a quick decision due to a deadline or a crisis. Managers usually make this type of decision either alone or after briefly consulting with a few people, and only a short period of problem analysis and search for solutions is likely to occur (McCall & Kaplan, 1985). Although these decisions are less important, they require appropriate technical knowledge by the manager and the capacity to find a good balance between lengthy, systematic analysis and quick, decisive action. A hasty decision based on limited information may fail to solve the problem, but the problem may get worse and be more difficult to resolve if the manager delays a decision to get more information.

Participative Leadership

Participative leadership involves the use of decision procedures that allow other people some influence over the leader's decisions. Other terms commonly used to refer to aspects of participative leadership include consultation, joint decision making, power sharing, decentralization, empowerment, and democratic management. Participative leadership can take many forms and includes several specific decision procedures. Although usually classified as primarily a relations-oriented behavior, participative leadership also has implications for achieving task objectives and leading change.

Types of Decision Procedures

The type of decision procedure used by a manager determines how much influence subordinates or group members have over the decision. Scholars have proposed several different taxonomies of decision procedures, and there is no agreement about the optimal number of decision procedures or the best way to define them. However, most leadership scholars would recognize the following four decision procedures as distinct and meaningful:

Autocratic Decision. The manager makes a decision alone without asking for the opinions or suggestions of other people, and these people have no direct influence on the decision; there is no participation.

Consultation. The manager asks other people for their opinions and ideas and then makes the decision alone after seriously considering their suggestions and concerns.

Joint Decision. The manager meets with others to discuss the decision problem and make a decision together; the manager has no more influence over the final decision than any other participant.

Delegation. The manager gives an individual or group the authority and responsibility for making a decision; the manager usually specifies limits within which the final choice must fall, and prior approval may or may not be required before the decision can be implemented.

The four decision procedures can be ordered along a continuum ranging from no influence by other people to high influence (see Figure 4-1). Some researchers also identify subtypes for these four basic procedures. For example, Tannenbaum and Schmidt (1958) distinguished two forms of autocratic decisions: one in which the leader merely announces an autocratic decision ("tell" decision) and the other in which the leader makes the decision alone but uses influence tactics such as rational persuasion to gain support for it ("sell" decision). Vroom and Yetton (1973) distinguished between consulting with individuals and consulting with a group. A joint decision may involve only a single subordinate or several people, and a number of different decision procedures can be used for group decisions (see Chapter 11). Varieties of delegation are described later in this chapter.

Decision procedures are abstract descriptions of pure or ideal types, and the actual behavior of managers seldom occurs in ways that neatly fit these descriptions. Consultation often occurs informally during the course of repeated interactions with other people rather than at a single point in time in a formal meeting. Consultation may occur during brief contacts in the hall, after a meeting or social event, at lunch, or on the golf course. Actual behavior may involve a mix of elements from different decision procedures, such as consulting about problem diagnosis but not about final choice among solutions, or consulting about final choice among a limited set of predetermined solutions. Participative leadership has a dynamic quality and may change over time. For example, what was initially consultation may become a joint decision as it becomes evident that there is consensus about the best alternative. What was initially a group decision may become consultation after it becomes obvious that the group is deadlocked and the leader must make the final decision.

It is also important to distinguish between overt procedures and actual influence. Sometimes what appears to be participation is only pretense. For example, a manager may solicit ideas and suggestions from others but ignore them when making the decision. Likewise, the manager may ask subordinates to make a decision, but make the request in such a way that the subordinates are afraid to show initiative or deviate from the choice they know their boss prefers.

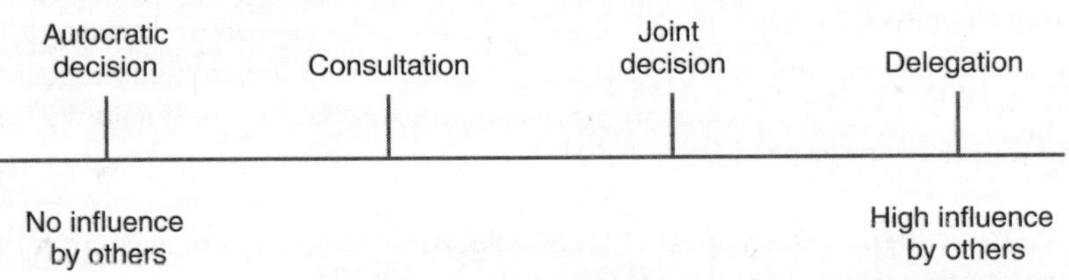

FIGURE 4-1 Continuum of Decision Procedures

Potential Benefits of Participative Leadership

Participative leadership offers a variety of potential benefits, but whether the benefits are achieved depends on who the participants are, how much influence they have, and other aspects of the decision situation (see Figure 4-2). Four potential benefits include higher decision quality, higher decision acceptance by participants, more satisfaction with the decision process, and more development of their decision-making skills. Several explanations have been proposed for the positive effects, and the explanations also identify conditions that make a positive effect more likely to occur (Anthony, 1978; Cooper & Wood, 1974; Huang, Iun, Liu, & Gong, 2010; Lam, Huang, & Chan, 2015; Likert, 1967; Maier, 1963; Mitchell, 1973; Strauss, 1963; Vroom & Yetton, 1973). The conditions that enhance or limit the effects of each decision procedure are also identified in the situational theories of participative and empowering leadership that are described later in the chapter.

Decision Quality. Involving other people in making a decision is likely to increase the quality of a decision when participants have information and knowledge lacked by the leader and are willing to cooperate in finding a good solution to a decision problem. Cooperation and sharing of knowledge will depend on the extent to which participants trust the leader and view the process as legitimate and beneficial. If participants and the leader have incompatible goals, cooperation is unlikely to occur. In the absence of cooperation, participation may reduce rather than increase decision quality. Even high cooperation does not guarantee that participation will result in a better decision. The decision process used by the group will determine whether members are able to reach agreement, and it will determine the extent to which any decision incorporates the members' expertise and knowledge (see Chapter 11). When members have different perceptions of the problem or different priorities for the various outcomes, it is difficult to discover a high-quality decision. The group may fail to reach agreement or settle for a poor compromise. Finally, other aspects of the decision situation such as time pressures, the number of participants, and formal policies may make some forms of participation impractical.

Decision Acceptance. People who have considerable influence in making a decision tend to identify with it and perceive it to be their decision. This feeling of ownership increases their

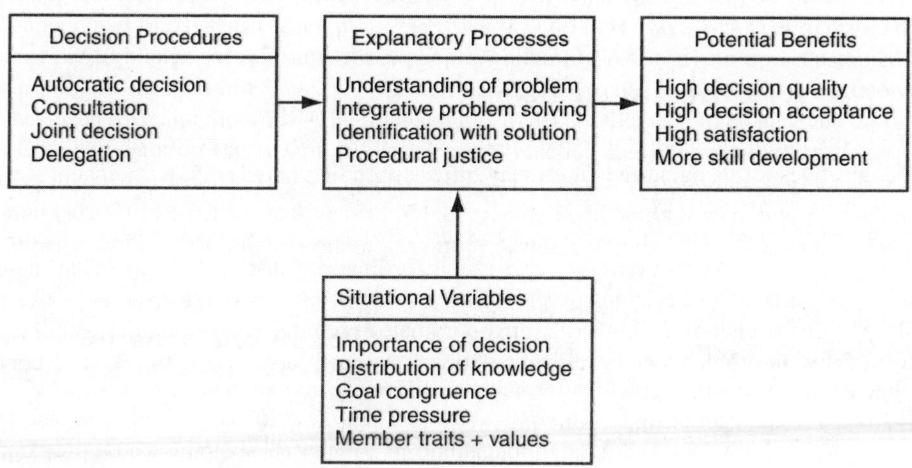

FIGURE 4-2 Causal Model of Participative Leadership

motivation to implement it successfully. Participation also provides a better understanding of the nature of the decision problem and the reasons why a particular alternative was accepted and others rejected. Participants gain a better understanding of how they will be affected by a decision, which is likely to reduce any unwarranted fears and anxieties about it. When adverse consequences are likely, participation allows people an opportunity to express their concerns and help to find a solution that deals with these concerns. Finally, when a decision is made by a participative process that most members consider legitimate, then the group is likely to apply social pressure on any reluctant members to do their part in implementing the decision.

Satisfaction with the Decision Process. Research on procedural justice found that the opportunity to express opinions and preferences before a decision is made (called "voice") can have beneficial effects on work attitudes and job performance regardless of the amount of actual influence participants have over the final decision (called "choice") (Chamberlin, Newton, & Lepine, 2017; Colquitt, Conlon, Wesson, Porter, & Ng, 2001; Colquitt et al., 2013; Earley & Lind, 1987; Lind & Tyler, 1988). People are more likely to perceive that they are being treated with dignity and respect when they have an opportunity to express opinions and preferences about a decision that will affect them. The likely result is more perception of procedural justice and stronger satisfaction with the decision process (Roberson, Moye, & Locke, 1999). However, in the absence of real influence over a decision, members may not have a strong commitment to implement the decision. Furthermore, the process may reduce rather than increase satisfaction if participants perceive that the leader is attempting to manipulate them into supporting an undesirable decision.

Development of Participant Skills. The experience of helping to make a complex decision can result in the development of more skill and confidence by participants. Whether the potential benefits are realized depends on how much involvement participants actually have in the process of diagnosing the cause of the problem, generating feasible solutions, evaluating solutions to identify the best one, and planning how to implement it. Participants who are involved in all the aspects of the decision process learn more than participants who merely contribute to one aspect. For participants with little experience in making complex decisions, learning also depends on the extent to which participants receive coaching and encouragement from the leader during difficult stages of the decision process.

Objectives for Different Participants

The potential benefits of participation are not identical for all types of participants. The leader's objectives for using participation may differ depending on whether participants are subordinates, peers, superiors, or outsiders.

Downward consultation may be used to increase the quality of decisions by drawing on the knowledge and problem-solving expertise of subordinates. Another objective is to increase subordinate acceptance of decisions by providing a sense of ownership. A third objective may be to develop the decision-making skills of subordinates by giving them experience in helping to analyze decision problems and evaluate solutions. A fourth objective is to facilitate conflict resolution and team building.

Lateral consultation with people in different subunits may be used to increase decision quality when peers have relevant knowledge about the cause of a problem and likely solutions. When cooperation from other managers is necessary to implement a decision, consultation is a way to increase their understanding and commitment. Lateral consultation facilitates coordination and cooperation among managers of different organizational subunits with interdependent tasks. However, consultation should be limited to decisions for which it is appropriate, so that time is not wasted in unnecessary meetings.

Upward consultation by a manager makes it possible to draw on the expertise of the boss, which may be greater than the manager's expertise. In addition, upward consultation allows a manager to find out how the boss feels about a problem and is likely to react to various proposals. On the other hand, excessive consultation with a boss suggests a lack of self-confidence and initiative for the subordinate. A manager with authority to make decisions is wise to avoid becoming too dependent on the boss when making these decisions.

Consulting with outsiders such as clients and suppliers helps ensure that decisions affecting them are understood and accepted. It is also a way to learn more about their needs and preferences, strengthen external networks, improve coordination, and solve mutual problems.

Research on Effects of Participative Leadership

Since the pioneering studies by Lewin, Lippitt, and White (1939) and Coch and French (1948), social scientists have been interested in assessing the consequences of participative leadership. The research has continued for more than a half century using a variety of methods. Survey field studies assessed how a leader's use of participative decision making was related to subordinate satisfaction with the leader, task commitment, task performance, organizational citizenship behavior, turnover, and ratings of leader effectiveness by higher management (e.g., Buengeler, Homan, & Voelpel, 2016; Huang et al., 2010; Kim & Yukl, 1995; Lam et al., 2015; Miao, Newman, & Huang, 2014; Likert, 1967; Yukl & Van Fleet, 1982). Field experiments compared leaders who used participative procedures to leaders who made autocratic decisions (e.g., Coch & French, 1948; Fleishman, 1965; French, Israel, & As, 1960; Latham & Yukl, 1975, 1976; Lawrence & Smith, 1955; Morse & Reimer, 1956). Following is an example of a quasi-experimental study by Bragg and Andrews (1973) in a hospital laundry department:

> The foreman of the laundry department typically made decisions in an autocratic manner, and he was persuaded by the chief administrator to try a participative approach. The 32 workers in the laundry department were told that the purpose of the group meetings was to make their jobs more interesting, not to increase productivity, which was already high. The workers and union were told that the participation program would be discontinued if they found it unsatisfactory. Over the next 18 months, meetings were held whenever the workers wanted to discuss specific proposals about hours of work, working procedures, working conditions, minor equipment modifications, and safety matters. In addition to these group meetings, the foreman consulted regularly with individuals and smaller groups of workers to discuss problems and new ideas.
>
> Worker attitudes were measured at two-month intervals for 14 months with a questionnaire. The attitude data showed some initial doubts about the participation program, after which workers became increasingly more favorable toward it. Productivity during the first 18 months of the program increased 42 percent over that for the department during the prior year, whereas for similar departments in two other hospitals (the comparison groups), productivity declined slightly during the same period of time. Attendance in the department, which was high initially, became even better after the participation program was introduced, whereas for other nonmedical departments in the same hospital (the comparison groups), it became worse. The results showed that the participation program was highly successful.

After the program had been in effect for three years, neither the workers nor the supervisor had any desire to return to the old autocratic style of management. The success of the program encouraged the introduction of participation in the medical records section, where it resulted in the elimination of grievances and a sharp reduction in turnover. However, an attempt to introduce a participation program in the nursing group was much less successful, due primarily to lack of support by the head nurse and resistance by administrative medical personnel.

The Threshold Effect of Participative Leadership

Recent research by Lam et al. (2015) revealed that there is a minimum threshold for the level of participative leadership that must be reached before positive effects on employee performance are realized. Further, the extent to which this threshold effect was realized depended upon how much information the leader shared with followers.

Two studies were conducted to explore when and how this threshold effect occurs. Study 1 collected survey data from office and call-center employees and their supervisors who worked in a textile manufacturing firm headquartered in Hong Kong and a state-owned telecommunication services company located in China. Employees completed measures of participative leadership and leader information sharing, while their supervisors rated employee task performance. Study 2 collected data from a random sample of workers and their direct supervisors within a large garment-manufacturing firm located in Southern China. Employees again completed survey measures of participative leadership and leader information sharing, as well as perceived leadership effectiveness. In addition, objective measures of subordinate productivity were obtained.

In both studies, participative leadership was unrelated to employee performance below a moderate, threshold level, but once that threshold was surpassed, gains in employee performance were achieved. This curvilinear relationship was stronger when information sharing by the leader with subordinates was high, and weaker when information sharing was low. Finally, Study 2 found that employee perceptions of leadership effectiveness mediated the combined effects of participative leadership and information sharing on objective work performance.

Lam and colleagues (2015) explained their findings by suggesting that some leaders are reluctant to embrace participative leadership because they fear doing so will lessen their power or cause them to be blamed if employees fail to meet expectations. In such cases, leaders may elect to exhibit a moderate degree of participative leadership, assuming that doing so will be enough to pacify subordinates' desires for input. However, if subordinates perceive that the leader's commitment to participative leadership is half-hearted, they may decline to invest the extra effort and resources that their participation would require. In contrast, when followers perceive that the leader is fully committed to securing their input, they are more likely to provide it, which will subsequently improve their work performance.

The extent to which the leader shares information with subordinates was shown to further complicate this threshold effect. When employees perceived that their leader readily shared information relevant to decision making with them, the threshold effect was strengthened. In contrast, if they saw the leader as being reluctant to share information, it was weakened. When leaders express a desire to involve followers in decision making but do not give them the knowledge required to make informed decisions, it sends followers a mixed message that undermines the effects of participative leadership. Similarly, a leader who shares information with followers but does allow them to participate in decisions discourages them from providing input to improve the decisions. Followers perceive their leaders to be most effective when they combine participative leadership with high levels of information sharing, and this combination of empowering behaviors was necessary to secure the level of follower commitment required to achieve gains in work performance.

Findings in Participation Research

Findings in the quantitative research on the effects of participative leadership are summarized in several literature reviews and meta-analyses (Cotton, Volrath, Froggatt, Lengnick-Hall, & Jennings, 1988; Leana, Locke, & Schweiger, 1990; Miller & Monge, 1986; Sagie & Koslowsky, 2000; Spector, 1986; Wagner & Gooding, 1987; Wagner, Leana, Locke, & Schweiger, 1997). All the reviewers noted the lack of consistent strong results in the research.

Survey studies with all data from the same respondents (the subordinates) usually found positive effects of participation, whereas survey studies with independent measures of outcomes had weaker and less consistent results. No effort was made in most survey studies to identify the particular mix of decision procedures that were used or to determine whether these procedures were appropriate for the types of decisions being made. In effect, the studies tested only the general hypothesis that more is better when it comes to participation.

Results from the laboratory experiments were weak and inconsistent. Most field experiments and quasi-experimental studies showed positive results. However, these studies usually involved a participation program introduced by the organization rather than participative behavior by an individual manager, and participation was usually combined with other types of interventions, such as more supportive behavior by the leader, better training of subordinates, use of goal setting, or better procedures for planning and problem solving, making it difficult to determine which consequences were due to participation.

Most descriptive case studies support the benefits of participative leadership (Benn, Teo, & Martin, 2015; Bradford & Cohen, 1984; Kanter, 1983; Kouzes & Posner, 1987; Peters & Austin, 1985; Peters & Waterman, 1982; Skordoulis & Dawson, 2007). This type of research found that effective managers used a substantial amount of consultation and delegation to empower subordinates and give them a sense of ownership for activities and decisions.

Overall, the results from research on the effects of participative leadership are not sufficiently strong and consistent to draw any firm conclusions. Participative leadership sometimes results in higher satisfaction, effort, and performance, and at other times it does not. The lack of consistent results about the effectiveness of participative leadership probably reflects the fact that each type of participative decision procedure is more effective in some situations than in others, and the effects depend on other behaviors not usually measured such as information sharing. Few studies incorporated situational variables in a systematic manner or investigated whether different procedures are more effective for different types of decisions. This question is the subject of a contingency theory called the normative decision model that was developed by Vroom and Yetton (1973).

Normative Decision Model

The importance of using decision procedures that are appropriate for the situation has been recognized for some time. Building on earlier approaches, the normative decision model proposed by Vroom and Yetton (1973) describes aspects of the decision situation that determine whether a specific type of decision procedure will be effective.

TABLE 4-1 Decision Procedures in Normative Decision Model

A-I	You solve the problem or make the decision yourself, using information available to you at the time.
A-II	You obtain the necessary information from your subordinates, then decide the solution to the problem yourself. You may or may not tell your subordinates what the problem is in getting the information from them. The role played by your subordinates in making the decision is clearly one of providing necessary information to you, rather than generating or evaluating alternative solutions.
C-I	You share the problem with the relevant subordinates individually, getting their ideas and suggestions, without bringing them together as a group. Then you make the decision, which may or may not reflect your subordinates' influence.
C-II	You share the problem with your subordinates as a group, obtaining their collective ideas and suggestions. Then you make the decision, which may or may not reflect your subordinates' influence.
G-II	You share the problem with your subordinates as a group. Together you generate and evaluate alternatives and attempt to reach agreement (consensus) on a solution. Your role is much like that of chairman. You do not try to influence the group to adopt your preferred solution, and you are willing to accept and implement any solution that has the support of the entire group.

Based on Vroom & Yetton, 1973, p. 13.

Vroom and Yetton identified five decision procedures for decisions involving multiple subordinates, including two types of autocratic decision (A-I and A-II), two types of consultation (C-I and C-II), and one type of joint decision making by the leader and subordinates as a group (G-II). The procedures are defined in Table 4-1. The decision procedure used by a leader affects the quality of a decision and decision acceptance by the people who are responsible for implementing the decision. These two mediating variables jointly determine how the decision will affect the performance of the leader's team or work unit. Aspects of the situation determine the importance of the mediating variables.

Decision Acceptance and Quality

Decision acceptance is the degree of commitment to implement a decision effectively. Acceptance is important whenever a decision must be implemented by subordinates or has implications for their work motivation. In some cases, subordinates are highly motivated to implement a decision made by the leader because it is clearly beneficial to them or because the leader uses influence tactics to gain their commitment to the decision. However, subordinates may not accept an autocratic decision if they resent not being consulted, they do not understand the reasons for the decision, or they see it as detrimental to their interests. A basic assumption of the model is that participation increases decision acceptance if it is not already high, and the more influence subordinates have in making a decision, the more they will be motivated to implement it successfully. Thus, decision acceptance is likely to be greater for joint decision making than for consultation, and for consultation than for an autocratic decision.

Decision quality refers to the objective aspects of the decision that affect group performance aside from any effects mediated by decision acceptance. The quality of a decision is high when the best alternative is selected. For example, an efficient work procedure is selected instead of less efficient alternatives, or a challenging performance goal is set instead of an easy goal. Decision quality is important when there is a great deal of variability among alternatives and the decision has important consequences for group performance. If the available alternatives are approximately equal in consequences, or if the decision has no important consequences for group performance, then decision quality is not important. Examples of task decisions that are usually important include determination of goals and priorities, assignment of tasks to subordinates who differ in skills, determination of work procedures for complex tasks, and determination of ways to solve technical problems.

Situational Variables

The effect of the decision procedures on decision quality and acceptance depends on various aspects of the situation, and a procedure that is effective in some situations may be ineffective in other situations. The effectiveness of a decision procedure depends on several aspects of the decision situation, including the importance and complexity of the decision, the distribution of relevant information, subordinate attitudes regarding the decision, and leader dependence on subordinates to implement the decision. The causal relationships among the variables are shown in Figure 4-3.

The effect of participation on decision quality depends on how much relevant information and problem-solving expertise is possessed by the leader and the subordinates (or group members). The model assumes that participation will result in better decisions if subordinates possess relevant information lacked by the leader and are willing to cooperate with the leader in making a good decision. Cooperation depends on the extent to which subordinates share the leader's task objectives and have a relationship of mutual trust with the leader. The model assumes that consultation and joint decision making are equally likely to facilitate decision quality when subordinates share the leader's objectives. However, when subordinates have incompatible objectives, consultation usually results in higher-quality decisions than joint decision making, because the leader retains control over the final choice.

Decision Rules

The model provides a set of rules for identifying any decision procedure that is not appropriate in a given situation because using that procedure would jeopardize decision quality and acceptance (see Table 4-2). The rules are based on the assumptions discussed earlier about the consequences of different decision procedures under different conditions. For some decision situations, the model prescribes more than one feasible decision procedure. Any decision procedure not excluded in a decision rule can be used for that situation. Vroom and Yetton (1973) developed decision process flowcharts to simplify the application of the rules and assist managers in identifying the feasible set of decision procedures for each situation. When more than one decision procedure remains in the "feasible set," then other criteria can be used to determine which decision procedure to use. Both time pressure and subordinate development are included in the extended model by Vroom and Jago (1978, 1988).

One limitation of the normative decision model is its complexity, and the extended model is even more complex than the original one. A simplified model that is easier for managers to use was proposed by Yukl (1990), and it is shown in Table 4-3. This simplified model indicates which of three decision procedures (autocratic, consultation, or joint decision) is optimal when the priorities are (1) protect decision quality, (2) gain decision acceptance, and (3) save time.

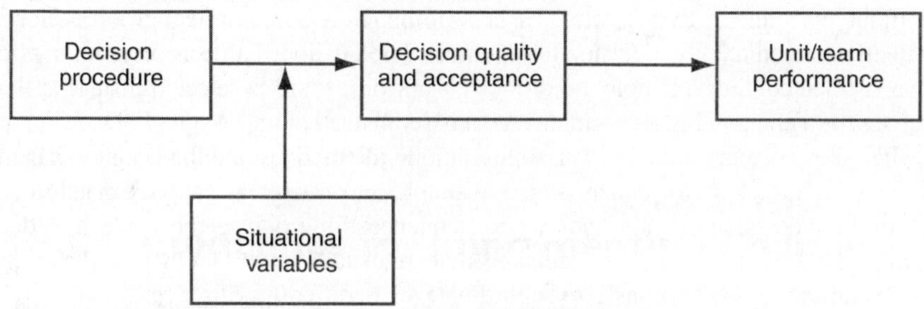

FIGURE 4-3 Causal Relationships in the Normative Decision Model

TABLE 4-2 Decision Rules in the Normative Decision Model

1. When the decision is important and subordinates possess relevant information lacked by the leader, an autocratic decision (A-I, A-II) is not appropriate, because an important decision would be made without all of the relevant, available information.
2. When decision quality is important and subordinates do not share the leader's concern for task goals, a group decision (G-II) is not appropriate, because these procedures would give too much influence over an important decision to uncooperative or even hostile people.
3. When decision quality is important, the decision problem is unstructured, and the leader does not possess the necessary information and expertise to make a good decision, then the decision should be made by interaction among the people who have the relevant information (C-II, G-II).
4. When decision acceptance is important and subordinates are unlikely to accept an autocratic decision, then an autocratic decision (A-I, A-II) is not appropriate, because the decision may not be implemented effectively.
5. When decision acceptance is important and subordinates are likely to disagree among themselves about the best solution to an important problem, autocratic procedures (A-I, A-II) and individual consultation (C-I) are not appropriate, because these procedures do not provide the opportunity to resolve differences through discussion and negotiation among subordinates and between the subordinates and the leader.
6. When decision quality is not important but acceptance is important and unlikely to result from an autocratic decision, then the only appropriate procedure is a group decision (G-II), because acceptance is maximized without risking quality.
7. When decision acceptance is important and not likely to result from an autocratic decision, and subordinates share the leader's task objectives, subordinates should be given equal partnership in the decision process (G-II), because acceptance is maximized without risking quality.

Based on Vroom & Yetton, 1973.

Evaluation of the Theory

The normative decision model is probably the best supported contingency theory of effective leadership. It focuses on specific aspects of behavior, it includes meaningful intervening variables, and it identifies important aspects of the situation moderating the relationship between behavior and outcomes. However, the model deals with only a small part of leadership, and the complexity of the model makes it difficult for leaders to apply.

TABLE 4-3 Simplified Version of the Normative Decision Model

	Subordinate Acceptance of Decision	
Decision Quality	**Not Important or Assured with Autocratic Decision**	**Important and Not Assured with Autocratic Decision**
Not Important	AUTOCRATIC	GROUP
Important, the leader has sufficient information, and members share leader's goals	AUTOCRATIC	GROUP
Important, the leader has sufficient information, but members do not share the leader's goals	AUTOCRATIC	CONSULTATION
Important, the leader lacks essential information, and members share leader goals	CONSULTATION	GROUP
Important and the leader lacks essential information, but members don't share leader goals	CONSULTATION	CONSULTATION

Based on Yukl (1990).

Guidelines for Participative Leadership

Building on the participation research and the normative decision model, some tentative guidelines are proposed for using participative leadership. Guidelines for diagnosing the situation are presented first, followed by some guidelines for encouraging participation (see Table 4-4).

TABLE 4-4 Guidelines for Participative Leadership

How to Diagnose Decision Situations:

- Evaluate how important the decision is.
- Identify people with relevant knowledge or expertise.
- Evaluate likely cooperation by participants.
- Evaluate likely acceptance without participation.
- Evaluate whether it is feasible to hold a meeting.

How to Encourage Participation:

- Keep people informed.
- Encourage people to express their concerns.
- Describe a proposal as tentative.
- Record ideas and suggestions.
- Look for ways to build on ideas and suggestions.
- Be tactful in expressing concerns about a suggestion.
- Listen to dissenting views without getting defensive.
- Try to utilize suggestions and deal with concerns.
- Show appreciation for suggestions.

Determining the Feasibility of Participation

The following sequence is a relatively easy way to determine whether a participative procedure is feasible and appropriate for a particular decision situation.

- **Evaluate how important the decision is.**

Decision quality is likely to be important if the decision has important consequences for the manager's work unit or the overall organization and if some of the alternatives are much better than others. Decision quality is also more important when the manager's position has high exposure (i.e., mistakes are very visible and will reflect poorly on the manager).

- **Identify people with relevant knowledge or expertise.**

Participative decision procedures are appropriate when a manager lacks relevant information possessed by others such as subordinates, peers, or outsiders. This situation is likely when the decision problem is complex and the best way to resolve the problem is not evident from the data or from the manager's prior experience with similar problems. A decision is more complex when it involves many possible alternatives, the outcomes of each alternative are difficult to predict, and the alternatives involve trade-offs among several important criteria. For complex decisions, it is essential to identify people who have relevant knowledge and expertise, and a good network of contacts is invaluable for identifying such people.

- **Evaluate likely cooperation by participants.**

Participation is unlikely to be successful unless the prospective participants are willing to cooperate in finding a good solution to the decision problem. Cooperation is more likely when the decision is important to followers and they perceive that they will actually have some influence over the final decision. If people perceive that a leader is trying to manipulate them, then consultation is unlikely to increase either decision quality or decision acceptance.

Cooperation is also unlikely if potential participants have task objectives that are incompatible with those of the manager. When there is doubt about the motives of potential participants, it is advisable to consult with a few of them individually to determine whether a group meeting would be productive. It is unwise to hold a meeting with a hostile group of people who want to make decisions that are contrary to the interests of the manager. When people with relevant information have different objectives, then some consultation may be useful to diagnose the cause of a problem and identify promising alternatives, but the final choice of an alternative must remain with the manager.

Another reason for lack of cooperation is that the potential participants simply do not want to become involved in making decisions they view as the manager's responsibility. The opportunity to participate may be rejected by people who are already overloaded with work, especially when the decisions do not affect them in any important way. Just as some people decline to vote in local elections, not everyone will be enthusiastic about the opportunity to participate in making organizational decisions.

- **Evaluate likely acceptance without participation.**

A time-consuming participative procedure is not necessary if the manager has the knowledge to make a good decision and it is likely to be accepted by people who must implement it or who will be affected by it. An autocratic decision is more likely to be accepted if made by someone with considerable power and the persuasive skills needed to "sell" the decision successfully. Acceptance of an autocratic decision is also likely if the decision involves something people already want to do, or the decision appears to be a reasonable response to a crisis situation. Finally, acceptance of autocratic decisions is more likely when people have cultural values that emphasize obedience to authority figures (see Chapter 13).

- **Evaluate whether it is feasible to hold a meeting.**

Consulting with people separately or holding a group meeting usually requires more time than making an autocratic decision and telling people to implement it. It is especially difficult to hold a meeting if the number of people who need to be involved is large and they are widely dispersed, although this issue has become less of a concern with the dissemination of virtual meeting software. In many crisis situations, time is not available either for extensive consultation with individuals or for a lengthy group meeting to decide how to react to the crisis. In this situation, a leader who knows what to do and takes charge in a decisive way is likely to be more effective than one who uses a form of participation that does not yield a quick decision (e.g., Yun, Samer, & Sims, 2005). Nevertheless, even in a crisis situation, a leader should remain responsive to suggestions made by knowledgeable subordinates. Under the stress of a crisis, a leader is unlikely to notice all of the problems that require attention or to think of all the actions that need to be taken.

Using Participative Decision Making

Consultation and joint decision-making procedures will not be effective unless people are actively involved in generating ideas, making suggestions, stating their preferences, and expressing their concerns. Some guidelines for encouraging and using participative decision making include the following:

- **Share relevant information.**

It is important to share relevant information with subordinates to convince them that you are serious about seeking their input, and to ensure they can help to make a high-quality decision. A failure to share relevant information may also yield cynicism about your real interest in meaningful employee participation.

- **Encourage people to express their concerns.**

Consult with people before making a change that will affect them in important ways, and encourage them to express any concerns about it. This guideline applies to peers and outsiders as well as subordinates. One form of consultation that is often appropriate is to hold special meetings with people who will be affected by a change to identify and deal with their concerns.

- **Describe a proposal as tentative.**

More participation is likely if you present a proposal as tentative and encourage people to improve it, rather than announcing a plan that appears to be complete, which will inhibit people from expressing concerns that appear to be criticism of the plan.

- **Record ideas and suggestions.**

When someone makes a suggestion, it is helpful to acknowledge the idea and show that it is not being ignored. One approach is to list ideas on a flipchart or computer display as they are expressed. In an informal meeting, if there is no easy way to display ideas, make notes to avoid forgetting a person's ideas and suggestions.

- **Look for ways to build on ideas and suggestions.**

Most people quickly focus on the weaknesses of an idea or suggestion made by someone else without giving enough consideration to its strengths. It is helpful to make a conscious effort to find positive aspects of a suggestion and mention them before mentioning negative aspects. Many times an initial idea is incomplete, but it can be turned into a much better idea with a little conscious effort. Thus, rather than automatically rejecting a suggestion with obvious weaknesses, it is useful to discuss how the weaknesses could be overcome and to consider other ideas that build on the initial one.

- **Be tactful in expressing concerns about a suggestion.**

If you have concerns about a suggestion, express them tactfully to avoid threatening the self-esteem of the person who made the suggestion and discouraging future suggestions. Avoid negative responses such as the following:

> You can't be serious about that suggestion?
> That idea has been tried before and it doesn't work.

Concerns should be expressed in a way that indicates qualified interest rather than outright rejection. It is usually possible to express concerns in the form of a question using the terms *we* and *us* to emphasize a shared effort, as shown in the following example:

> Your suggestion is a promising one, but I am concerned about the cost. Is there any way we could do it without exceeding our budget?

- **Listen to dissenting views without getting defensive.**

In order to encourage people to express concerns and criticisms of your plans and proposals, it is essential to listen carefully without getting defensive or angry. Use restatement of a person's concerns in your own words to verify that you understand them and to show you are paying attention. Avoid making weak excuses, and instead try to consider objectively whether revisions are needed.

- **Try to utilize suggestions and deal with concerns.**

People will stop making suggestions if you dismiss them without serious consideration or simply ignore them in making a final decision. It is important to make a serious effort to utilize suggestions and deal with concerns expressed by people who are being consulted. The potential benefits from participation will not occur if people perceive that a request for suggestions was made just to manipulate them.

- **Show appreciation for suggestions.**

People will be more likely to cooperate in making decisions and solving problems if they receive appropriate credit for their helpful suggestions and ideas. Compliment someone for good ideas and insights. It is important to thank people and show appreciation for their helpful suggestions. Explain how an idea or suggestion was used in the final decision or plan.

Explain how the proposal or plan was modified to incorporate participant suggestions and concerns. If a suggestion is not used, thank the contributor and explain why it was not feasible to use the suggestion.

Delegation

As noted earlier, delegation involves the assignment of new responsibilities to subordinates and additional authority to carry them out. Although delegation is usually regarded as a variety of participative leadership, it is different in some important ways from the other forms of participative leadership such as consulting and joint decision making. A manager may consult with subordinates, peers, or superiors, but in most cases delegation is appropriate only with subordinates. Delegation has somewhat different situational determinants than consultation (Leana, 1987). For example, a manager who is overloaded with work is likely to use more delegating but less consulting. Delegation often involves the shifting of primary responsibility for a particular type of decision to an individual or group, whereas the other participative procedures do not involve a similar redefinition of roles. With all these differences, it is not surprising that a factor analysis of leader behavior questionnaires usually yields a distinct factor for delegating (Yukl & Fu, 1999).

Varieties of Delegation

The term delegation is commonly used to describe a variety of different forms and degrees of power sharing with individual subordinates. Major aspects of delegation include the variety and magnitude of responsibilities, the amount of discretion or range of choice allowed in deciding how to carry out responsibilities, the authority to take action and implement decisions without prior approval, the frequency and nature of reporting requirements, and the flow of performance information (Sherman, 1966; Webber, 1981).

In its most common form, delegation involves assignment of new and different tasks or responsibilities to a subordinate. For example, a person who is responsible for manufacturing something is also given responsibility for inspecting the product and correcting any defects that are found. When new tasks are assigned, the additional authority necessary to accomplish the tasks is usually delegated also. For example, a production worker who is given new responsibility for ordering materials is given the authority (within specified constraints) to sign contracts with suppliers.

Sometimes delegation involves only the specification of additional authority and discretion for the same tasks and assignments already performed by the subordinate. For example, a sales representative is allowed to negotiate sales within a specified range of prices, quantities, and delivery dates, but cannot exceed these limits without prior approval from the sales manager. Delegation is increased by giving the sales representative more latitude in setting prices and delivery dates.

The extent to which a subordinate must check with the manager before taking action is another aspect of delegation. There is little or no delegation for someone who must ask for guidance whenever there is a problem or something unusual occurs. There is moderate delegation when the subordinate is allowed to determine what to do but must get approval before implementing decisions. There is substantial delegation when the subordinate is allowed to make important decisions and implement them without getting prior approval. For example, a sales representative who was not allowed to make adjustments for damaged goods and late deliveries without checking first is given permission to resolve these matters in the future without getting prior approval.

Reporting requirements are another aspect of delegation that is subject to considerable variation. The amount of subordinate autonomy is greater when reports are required only infrequently. For example, a department manager must report department performance on a weekly basis rather than on a daily basis. Autonomy is also greater when reports describe only results rather than also describing the procedures used to accomplish them. For example, a training director must report to the vice president for human resources the number of employees who were trained in each subject area and the overall training expenses for the month, but not the types of training methods used, the number of trainers, or the training expenses in different categories.

The flow of performance information involved in monitoring a subordinate's activities is also subject to variation. Subordinate autonomy is greater when detailed information goes directly to the subordinate, who is then allowed to correct any problems. A subordinate is likely to have less autonomy when detailed performance information goes first to the boss, and there is an intermediate amount of subordinate autonomy when detailed performance information goes to both parties simultaneously.

Potential Benefits from Delegation

There are many different reasons for delegating (Leana, 1986; Newman & Warren, 1977; Preston & Zimmerer, 1978; Yukl & Fu, 1999). Table 4-5 shows the results found in a study that asked managers in several organizations about the importance of various reasons for delegation to a subordinate. Delegation offers a number of potential advantages if carried out in an appropriate manner by a manager. One potential advantage is the improvement of decision quality. Delegation is likely to improve decision quality if a subordinate has more expertise in how to do the task than the manager. Delegation is also likely to improve decision quality when the subordinate's job requires quick responses to a changing situation and the lines of communication do not permit the manager to monitor the situation closely and make rapid adjustments. A subordinate who is closer to the problem than the manager and has more relevant information can make quicker and better decisions about how to resolve the problem. The result may be better customer service and reduced administrative costs. However, delegation is not

TABLE 4-5 Percent of Managers Who Rated a Reason for Delegating As Moderately or Very Important

Reason	Percent
Develop subordinate skills and confidence.	97%
Enable subordinates to deal with problems quickly.	91%
Improve decisions by moving them close to the action.	89%
Increase subordinate commitment to a task.	89%
Make the job more interesting for subordinates.	78%
Reduce your workload to manage time better.	68%
Satisfy superiors who want you to delegate more.	24%
Get rid of tedious tasks you don't want to do.	23%

Adapted from Yukl & Fu (1999).

likely to improve decision quality if the subordinate lacks the skills to make good decisions, fails to understand what is expected, or has goals incompatible with those of the manager.

Another potential advantage of delegation is greater subordinate commitment to implement decisions effectively. The commitment results from identification with the decision and a desire to make it successful. However, commitment is unlikely to improve if a subordinate views delegation as a manipulative tactic by the manager, considers the task impossible to do, or believes the newly delegated responsibilities are an unfair increase in workload.

Delegation of additional responsibilities and authority can make a subordinate's job more interesting, challenging, and meaningful. Enriched jobs are sometimes necessary to attract and retain competent employees, especially when the organization has limited opportunities for advancement to higher-level positions. Giving junior managers more responsibility and authority, with a commensurate increase in salary, reduces the likelihood that they will be lured away to other companies in times of stiff competition for managerial talent. However, delegation will only increase job satisfaction for a subordinate who desires more responsibility, has the skills necessary to handle new responsibilities, and is able to experience some success in accomplishing a challenging task. Delegation will decrease job satisfaction if the subordinate is constantly frustrated due to a lack of sufficient authority and resources to carry out new responsibilities, or to a lack of ability to do the work.

Delegation is an important form of time management for a manager who is overloaded with responsibilities. By delegating less important duties and functions to subordinates, a manager frees additional time for more important responsibilities. Even when a manager could do the delegated tasks better than subordinates, it is a more efficient use of the manager's time to concentrate on those functions that will have the greatest influence on the performance of the manager's organizational unit. Without delegation, a manager is not likely to have sufficient discretionary time to do some complex tasks that are important but not urgent.

Delegation can be an effective method of management development. Organizations need to develop managerial talent to fill vacant positions at higher levels of authority. Delegation is a way to facilitate development of the skills necessary to perform key responsibilities in a higher position. When delegation is used for developmental purposes, however, it is usually necessary for the manager to do more monitoring and coaching. Thus, when used for this purpose, delegation may not reduce a manager's workload.

Reasons for Lack of Delegation

With all of these potential advantages from delegation, it would seem as if it should occur whenever appropriate. However, there are several reasons some managers fail to delegate as much as they should (Leana, 1986; Newman & Warren, 1977; Preston & Zimmerer, 1978; Yukl & Fu, 1999). Results from a study that asked managers in several companies about the importance of different reasons for not delegating are shown in Table 4-6.

Some aspects of a manager's personality are associated with failure to delegate, including a strong need for power, insecurity, a high need for achievement, and difficulty in forming relationships. Some managers enjoy the exercise of power over subordinates and the feeling of being in charge. Delegation would require sharing power with subordinates and reducing their dependence.

Delegation is never absolute, because a manager continues to be responsible for the work activities of subordinates. To avoid the risk of mistakes, a manager who is insecure may delegate sensitive tasks only to a few trusted subordinates, or not at all. Furthermore, allowing a

TABLE 4-6 Percentage of Managers Who Rated a Reason for Not Delegating As Moderately or Very Important

Reason	%
Keep decisions involving confidential information.	87%
Keep tasks and decisions that are very important.	76%
Keep tasks and decisions central to your role.	73%
Keep tasks for which mistakes are highly visible.	58%
Keep tasks you can do better than subordinates.	51%
Keep tasks that are difficult to explain to subordinates.	43%
Keep tasks that are difficult to monitor.	39%
Keep tasks that are interesting and enjoyable.	24%

Adapted from Yukl & Fu (1999).

subordinate to demonstrate competence in performing managerial responsibilities may create a competitor for the manager's job.

Managers with a high need for achievement often prefer to retain important, challenging tasks rather than delegating them to subordinates (Miller & Toulouse, 1986). Managers who take pride in solving important problems may be reluctant to relinquish that activity or admit that others could do it as effectively. Reluctance to delegate may be supported by biases in perception of one's own performance. One experiment found that managers rated quality of performance higher when they were directly involved in supervising a task, even though actual quality was the same as for a delegated task (Pfeffer, Cialdini, Hanna, & Knopoff, 1998).

Failure to delegate is also related to characteristics of the subordinates, such as task expertise and shared objectives. Managers are reluctant to delegate significant responsibilities to subordinates who lack the necessary expertise (Ashour & England, 1972; Leana, 1986; Yukl & Fu, 1999). Even if a subordinate has the expertise, delegation of significant responsibility is unlikely if the person seems indifferent about task objectives (McGregor, 1960). This perception may be inaccurate initially, but distrust by the manager may eventually make it a self-fulfilling prophecy (Argyris, 1964). Sometimes distrust of subordinates is determined more by personality problems in the manager than by the actual characteristics of the subordinates (Johnston, 2000). However, it is not only insecure, power-hungry managers who are reluctant to delegate. Even managers who become successful at empowering people often say it was personally difficult, as the following example shows (O'Toole, 1995):

> Ben Cohen, the cofounder of Ben and Jerry's (Ice Cream), believes strongly in empowerment. When describing how difficult it was, he explained how it was not natural to ask questions of employees when he already knew the answer, to listen patiently when they said something that wasn't right, or to ask them for ideas when he was eager to express ideas of his own.

The potential for delegation also depends on the nature of the work and the amount of authority possessed by the leader. A lack of leader authority to make decisions or change how the work is done limits the potential for delegation. Another constraint is when subordinates have highly interdependent jobs. Even if people have shared objectives, they may disagree about priorities and the best way to accomplish the objectives. In this situation, empowering individuals to act on their own increases the danger they will be working at cross-purposes. To achieve coordination and avoid destructive conflicts, it will be necessary to devote more time to meetings to plan joint activities and solve operational problems. In this type of situation, it is more feasible to use consultation or to delegate authority for a task to a team rather than to individual subordinates. Self-managed teams are discussed in Chapter 11.

Research on Consequences of Delegation

Much less empirical research is available on leader delegation than on leader consultation with individuals or a group. Studies on the amount of delegation used by supervisors find that it is correlated with subordinate performance (e.g., Bauer & Green, 1996; Leana, 1986; Schriesheim, Neider, & Scandura, 1998). However, the direction of causality is difficult to determine in survey research. It is not clear whether delegation improves performance, if improved performance results in more delegation, or if both effects are occurring simultaneously. Moreover, descriptive studies of leaders make it evident that delegation can harm performance if used when it is not appropriate for the situation. More longitudinal, experimental research is needed to investigate direction of causality and the facilitating conditions (e.g., mutual trust, shared objectives, leader's self-confidence, and the subordinate's desire for more responsibility).

Guidelines for Delegating

This section of the chapter provides some tentative guidelines for effective use of delegation by managers. Although research on delegation is still very limited, there is considerable agreement in the practitioner literature about when and how to use delegation effectively. Guidelines for what to delegate are presented here first, followed by guidelines on how to delegate.

What to Delegate

The selection of tasks to delegate depends in part on the purpose of the delegation. Some guidelines on what to delegate are the following (see Table 4-7):

- **Delegate tasks that can be done better by a subordinate.**

Some responsibilities can be done better by a subordinate than by a manager. Better performance by a subordinate is likely when the person has more expertise, when the person is closer to the problem and can obtain more timely information about it, or because the manager

TABLE 4-7 Guidelines for What to Delegate

- Tasks that can be done better by a subordinate
- Tasks that are urgent but not high priority
- Tasks relevant to a subordinate's career
- Tasks of appropriate difficulty
- Both pleasant and unpleasant tasks
- Tasks not central to the manager's role

simply does not have the time necessary to do the task properly. Such responsibilities are usually good candidates for delegation, regardless of the purpose.

- **Delegate tasks that are urgent but not high priority.**

When the purpose is to reduce excessive workload, the best tasks for delegation are ones that are urgent but not high priority. These tasks must get done quickly, but the manager does not have time to do all of them. Some of the tasks may be things that a subordinate cannot do as well as the manager, but it is better for them to be done by a subordinate than not at all. Delegation of these tasks frees more time for a manager to do higher-priority tasks.

- **Delegate tasks relevant to a subordinate's career.**

If the purpose of delegation is to develop subordinate skills, the responsibilities must be ones relevant to the subordinate's career objectives. Developmental delegation is likely to include special projects that allow a subordinate the opportunity to struggle with a challenging task and exercise initiative and problem solving. Preparation of a subordinate to take over the manager's job or to advance to a management position in another work unit may require delegating some important leadership responsibilities, including some that the subordinate may not do as well as the manager. Some of these delegated tasks may be irrelevant to the subordinate's current job and, in fact, may take time away from the subordinate's regular work.

- **Delegate tasks of appropriate difficulty.**

Delegated tasks should be challenging for a subordinate, but not so difficult as to offer little hope of doing them successfully. The tasks should be difficult enough so that some mistakes are likely to occur, because mistakes are an integral part of the learning experience. However, the task should not be so difficult and important that mistakes will undermine the subordinate's self-confidence and ruin his or her reputation. Delegation for developmental purposes should be carried out gradually. As the subordinate learns how to handle the initial responsibilities, additional responsibilities can be delegated.

- **Delegate both pleasant and unpleasant tasks.**

Some managers keep all the pleasant tasks for themselves and delegate only tedious, boring tasks to subordinates. Such tasks will not enrich subordinate jobs and are likely to reduce rather than increase subordinate job satisfaction. On the other hand, some managers with a martyr complex delegate only pleasant tasks and retain for themselves all the disagreeable ones. This approach leaves a gap in the development of subordinates and is likely to make the manager's job more stressful than it should be. Delegation should include both pleasant and unpleasant tasks. The unpleasant tasks should be shared by subordinates or rotated among them to avoid perceptions of favoritism and inequity in work assignments.

- **Delegate tasks not central to the manager's role.**

Tasks that are symbolically important and central to a manager's role should not be delegated to subordinates. These responsibilities include such things as setting objectives and priorities for the work unit, allocating resources among subordinates, evaluating the performance of subordinates, making personnel decisions about pay increases and promotions for subordinates, directing the group's response to a crisis, and various figurehead activities for which an appearance by the manager is expected (Korica et al., 2017; Mintzberg, 1973). When it is necessary to develop subordinate skills related to these responsibilities, another form of participation such as consultation and group decisions can be used rather than delegation. For example, strategic planning may be carried out in planning meetings in which subordinates provide ideas and suggestions, but the responsibility for strategic decisions is not delegated to individual subordinates.

How to Delegate

The success of delegation depends as much on how it is carried out as on what is delegated. The following guidelines are designed to minimize problems and avoid common pitfalls related to assignment of tasks and delegation of authority (see Table 4-8). The first four guidelines are for the initial meeting held to delegate responsibilities to a subordinate. The last four guidelines describe other steps the manager should take at appropriate times to ensure that delegation will be successful.

- **Specify responsibilities clearly.**

When delegating, it is essential to make sure the subordinate understands the new responsibilities. Explain the results expected for a delegated task or assignment, clarify objectives and priorities, and inform the person about any deadlines that must be met. Check for comprehension by asking the subordinate to restate your expectations, or by questioning the subordinate about important aspects of the task. In the case of an inexperienced subordinate, you may want to ask the person to prepare action plans for you to review before the plans are implemented.

- **Provide adequate authority and specify limits of discretion.**

When assigning new responsibilities, determine the appropriate amount of authority needed by the subordinate to carry them out. Specify clearly the subordinate's scope of authority and limits of discretion. Authority includes funds that can be committed, resources that can be used, decisions that can be made without prior approval, and agreements that can be negotiated directly with outsiders or other units in the organization.

- **Specify reporting requirements.**

It is important for a subordinate to understand the types of information that must be reported, how often reports are expected, and the manner in which progress will be monitored

TABLE 4-8 Guidelines for How to Delegate

- Specify responsibilities clearly.
- Provide adequate authority and specify limits of discretion.
- Specify reporting requirements.
- Ensure subordinate acceptance of responsibilities.
- Arrange for the subordinate to get necessary information.
- Provide support and assistance, but avoid reverse delegation.
- Monitor progress in appropriate ways.
- Make mistakes a learning experience.

(e.g., written reports, progress review meetings, presentations in department meetings, and formal performance evaluations). The frequency and timing of progress reviews will depend on the nature of the task and the competence of the subordinate. More frequent checking is appropriate for critical tasks with high exposure and high cost of mistakes and for subordinates who lack experience and confidence. As a subordinate demonstrates the ability to perform delegated tasks, the frequency of reporting can be reduced. Progress reports should emphasize results, but the means for accomplishing delegated tasks should not be ignored entirely. It is important to ensure use of procedures that are legal, ethical, and consistent with organizational policy.

- **Ensure subordinate acceptance of responsibilities.**

If delegation is to be successful, the subordinate must accept the new assignments and be committed to carrying them out. In some cases, acceptance is not a problem, because the assignments are interesting and important for the subordinate's career advancement. However, a subordinate may be reluctant to admit doubts and concerns about new assignments. It is useful to allow the subordinate to participate in determining what tasks will be assigned and how much authority will be delegated. With developmental delegation, it is useful to discuss how the delegated tasks are relevant to the person's career advancement. If the subordinate lacks self-confidence, it is helpful to express confidence in the person's ability to do a good job.

- **Inform others who need to know.**

People who are affected by the delegation and people whose cooperation and assistance are necessary for the subordinate to do the delegated tasks should be informed about the subordinate's new responsibilities and authority. Unless informed about the delegation by you, these people may doubt the subordinate's authority to make a decision. The people who need to be informed may include other subordinates, subordinates of your subordinate, peers in other units, your boss, and outsiders such as clients and suppliers.

- **Monitor progress in appropriate ways.**

With delegated tasks, as with all tasks, it is important to monitor progress and provide feedback to the subordinate. It is difficult to achieve an optimal balance between control and delegation, and progress review meetings enable a manager to monitor subordinate progress without having to supervise too closely on a day-to-day basis. The subordinate is given considerable latitude to deal with problems without interference, yet is free to ask for advice and assistance whenever it is needed. When authority is delegated, a manager and subordinate should decide on the type of performance measures and progress indicators to collect.

- **Arrange for the subordinate to receive necessary information.**

It is usually best to have all detailed information about the subordinate's performance flow directly to the subordinate, with less detailed summary information coming to the manager at less frequent intervals. However, in the case of developmental delegation with an inexperienced subordinate, detailed information may be collected more frequently to check closely on the progress of the subordinate. In addition to performance information, the subordinate will need various types of technical and general information to carry out the delegated tasks effectively. Keep the subordinate informed about changes that affect his or her plans and schedules. If possible, arrange for relevant technical information to flow directly to the subordinate and help the subordinate establish his or her own sources of essential information.

- **Provide support and assistance, but avoid reverse delegation.**

A manager should provide psychological support to a subordinate who is discouraged or frustrated, and encourage the person to keep going. For newly delegated tasks, it may be necessary to provide more advice and coaching about procedures for doing some aspect of the work. However, it is important to avoid reverse delegation, in which control is reasserted over a task that was previously delegated. When a subordinate requests help with problems, he or she should be asked to recommend a solution, and the manager can help the person evaluate whether the solution is feasible and appropriate.

- **Make mistakes a learning experience.**

It is important to recognize that mistakes are inevitable for delegated tasks. Mistakes and failures should be treated seriously, but the response should not be one of criticism and blame. Instead, the episode should become a learning experience for both parties as they discuss the reason for the mistake and identify ways to avoid similar mistakes in the future. If it becomes obvious that the subordinate does not know how to do some essential aspect of the work, the manager should provide additional instruction and coaching.

Psychological Empowerment

The theory and research described earlier in this chapter examine power sharing and participation from the perspective of leader behavior and decision procedures. The emphasis has been on what is done to allow more influence over work-related decisions and to create conditions that foster initiative and self-determination, but additional insights can be gained by examining follower perceptions, needs, and values.

Theories of psychological empowerment help to explain when and why efforts to empower people are likely to be successful (Conger & Kanungo, 1988). For example, allowing people to determine how to do a trivial and demeaning task is unlikely to increase their feelings of self-worth and self-fulfillment. Delegating responsibility for a more significant task will not be empowering if people lack the skills and knowledge required to perform the task successfully and are worried about failure. The opportunity to elect a leader may do little to reduce feelings of powerlessness if the choice is between candidates who are equally unsatisfactory.

The defining elements of psychological empowerment have been suggested by various scholars (e.g., Bowen & Lawler, 1995; Conger & Kanungo, 1988; Kanter, 1983; Maynard, Gilson, & Mathieu, 2012; Spreitzer, 2008; Thomas & Velthouse, 1990). A study by Spreitzer (1995) found support for the proposition that psychological empowerment includes four defining elements: (1) meaning, (2) self-determination, (3) self-efficacy, and (4) impact. More empowerment will be felt when the content and consequences of the work are consistent with a person's values, the person has the capability to determine how and when the work is done, the person has high confidence about being able to do it effectively, and the person believes it is possible to influence important events and outcomes. The emphasis on these four elements links psychological empowerment to earlier theory and research on work motivation (e.g., Bandura, 1986; Shamir, 1991), job design (e.g., Fried & Ferris, 1987; Hackman & Oldham,

1976), participative leadership (e.g., Sagie & Koslowsky, 2000; Vroom & Jago, 1978), and organizational programs for employee involvement (e.g., Cotton, 1993; Lawler, 1986). Spreitzer's (1995) conceptualization of psychological empowerment has proven to be highly influential, stimulating a considerable amount of research over the past two decades (for a review and a meta-analysis, see Maynard et al., 2012, and Seibert, Wang, & Courtright, 2011).

The theory and research on psychological empowerment make it evident that participative leadership and delegation are not the only types of leadership behavior that can help make people feel empowered. Some scholars have introduced a broader conception of empowering leadership that encompasses participative leadership, delegation, and other types of leadership behavior that can increase feelings of psychological empowerment (Ahearne, Mathieu, & Rapp, 2005; Forrester, 2000; Sharma & Kirkman, 2015; Vecchio, Justin, & Pearce, 2010; Zhang & Bartol, 2010). For example, the leader can encourage a subordinate to view problems as opportunities, encourage innovative thinking, provide necessary information and resources, remove unnecessary bureaucratic restraints, recognize important achievements and contributions, and avoid being defensive when subordinates question the leader's decisions.

Some studies on effects of a broader conception of empowering leadership have found that it is related to the psychological empowerment of direct reports and to their performance (Fong & Snape, 2015; Lee, Willis, & Tian, 2018). However, as with other broadly defined leader behaviors, it fails to provide clear knowledge about the independent effects of the specific component behaviors or the situations in which each specific behavior is most relevant.

Empowerment Programs

Efforts to increase employee empowerment often involve organizational programs rather than empowering behaviors by leaders with their direct subordinates. A variety of different empowerment programs have been used, including self-managed teams (see Chapter 11), democratic structures and processes, and employee ownership of the company (Heller, 2000; Lawler, Mohrman, & Benson, 2001; Yukl & Becker, 2007; Yukl & Lepsinger, 2004). Some of these empowerment programs for organizations are described briefly.

Leader Selection and Assessment

More empowerment is likely when members elect their leaders for limited terms, which is a common practice in voluntary organizations, professional associations, and democratic political units (e.g., city councils, school boards, state legislatures). Most private business organizations have leaders who are appointed rather than elected, but some companies use a hybrid form of selection. The leaders are selected by a council of representatives who were elected by the members (c.f., de Jong & van Witteloostuijn, 2004). For example, in some employee-owned companies, the employees select top management and can vote to replace them if their performance is not satisfactory (Heller, 2000). Regardless of how a leader is selected, the influence of members is greater when they participate actively in assessing leader performance, especially if they are able to remove a leader with unsatisfactory performance.

Formal Decision Procedures

Empowerment is also increased when the formal procedures for making important decisions give members significant influence over these decisions. In some organizations, the charter specifies that a meeting or referendum must be held to allow members to decide important matters by a majority vote. In large organizations where direct participation is not feasible, an alternate form of empowerment that is sometimes used is to have elected representatives from each major subunit on the governing council, or to allow lower-level members to elect one or more representatives to serve on the board of directors. In many public sector organizations, members also have the right to attend open meetings of the board or council to express opinions about important issues before a decision is made. The election of leaders and the use of policy-making councils or boards with elected members are common in public sector organizations and professional associations, but they are rare in private sector business organizations in the United States.

In some European countries, the board of directors for a company is required by law to include members representing employees, and some organizations have an employee council with elected representatives from different subunits (Heller, 2000). In Germany, for example, the labor union members of the board can vote on important decisions and have a voice in the selection of the CEO. The European Union has adopted guidelines for increasing empowerment with works councils and other structural arrangements and processes.

Shared Leadership Responsibilities

Empowerment is also increased when leadership responsibilities are shared by members of a small organization or team rather than invested in a single leader. One example is the growing use of self-managed teams in business organizations (see Chapter 11). The most extreme form of shared leadership occurs when all important decisions are made collectively, and leadership responsibilities for daily operations are distributed among the members and rotated frequently. This form of empowerment is most likely to be found in small employee-owned businesses, cooperatives, and voluntary organizations. An example of a "bossless organization" is provided by Vanderslice (1988) in her case study of the Moosewood Restaurant:

> Moosewood is a small, collectively owned organization that has been financially sound for the 15 years it has existed. The restaurant has 18 members, and all of them are involved in making important decisions such as policy changes, selection and dismissal of members, financial issues, wages and benefits, and selection of suppliers. In addition, there are usually 4 to 6 temporary workers who are not involved in decision making but who may be accepted as regular members after a year of apprenticeship. Areas of responsibility are rotated among the members. The time an individual remains responsible for a particular job depends on the logical cycle of the task and the individual's interest in doing it. All jobs are open to any member who wants to learn to do them, and members are encouraged to take a turn at every job. Job rotation spreads expertise and responsibility among collective members rather than lodging it in one or two managers. All jobs pay the same hourly rate, and income from the 15% service charge is shared by all members. Some power differences exist, but they are based on demonstrated expertise and commitment to the organization. Accountability is regulated through internalized values and group pressure. However, confronting a member about inappropriate behavior is still an unresolved problem.

Information Sharing

As was found in the study by Lam and colleagues (2015) on participative leadership, it is difficult for employees to influence decisions or assess the effectiveness of top executives unless they have access to accurate information about business performance, plans, goals, and strategies. Unfortunately, many companies are reluctant to share such information with their employees (Lawler, Mohrman, & Ledford, 1998). Open-book programs are one way to empower employees through communication and learning. As the name suggests, top management "opens the books" to employees to give them a clear understanding of financial information, such as revenues, profits, and costs. To be successful, this type of program should also provide training that will enable employees to understand the information and use it to improve company performance.

Example of a Creative Empowerment Program

In his *New York Times* best-selling book, Daniel Pink (2009, p. 91) describes a creative empowerment program developed by Mike Cannon-Brookes, the co-founder of Atlassian, a software development firm:

> At two P.M. on a Thursday, the day begins. Engineers, including Cannon-Brookes himself, crash out new code or an elegant hack – any way they want, with anyone they want. Many work through the night. Then, at four P.M. on Friday, they show the results to the rest of the company in a wild-and-woolly all-hands meeting stocked with ample quantities of cold beer and chocolate cake. Atlassian calls these twenty-four-hour bursts of freedom and creativity "FedEx Days" – because people have to deliver something overnight. Over the years, this odd little exercise has produced an array of software fixes that might otherwise never have emerged. Says one engineer, "Some of the coolest stuff we have in our product today has come from FedEx Days."

Benefits of Empowering Leadership and Programs

Scholars have identified several potential benefits of empowering leadership and empowerment programs (e.g., Fong & Snape, 2015; Lee et al., 2018; Maynard et al., 2012; Seibert et al., 2011; Sharma & Kirkman, 2015; Spreitzer, 2008; Thomas & Velthouse, 1990; Vecchio et al., 2010). They include (1) stronger task commitment, (2) greater initiative in carrying out role responsibilities, (3) greater persistence in the face of obstacles and temporary setbacks, (4) more creativity, innovation, and learning, and stronger optimism about the eventual success of the work, (5) higher job satisfaction, (6) stronger organizational commitment, (8) greater trust in the leader, (9) higher levels of organizational citizenship behaviors, (10) elevated levels of employee performance, and (11) less turnover.

Some potential costs and risks have also been identified (e.g., Baloff & Doherty, 1989; Bowen & Lawler, 1995; Eccles, 1993; Sharma & Kirkman, 2015). Examples include (1) higher costs for selection and training, (2) higher labor costs for skilled employees, (3) inconsistent service quality, (4) inappropriate decisions by some employees, (5) customer feelings of inequity about unequal treatment, (6) opposition by middle managers who feel threatened, and (7) conflicts from raising employee expectations beyond what top management is willing to concede.

The combined evidence from research on participative leadership, psychological empowerment, and empowerment programs demonstrates the potential benefits and costs of employee empowerment, while indicating that the benefits are unlikely to occur unless conditions are favorable (Lee et al., 2018; Maynard et al., 2012; Seibert et al., 2011; Sharma & Kirkman, 2015; Spreitzer, 2008). Positive correlation has been found between most of the subvariables of psychological empowerment and organizational commitment. Overall organizational learning capability and psychological empowerment correlations are positive (Bhatnagar, 2007). The conditions that can strengthen or weaken feelings of empowerment have been suggested by a number of writers (e.g., Argyris, 1998; Forrester, 2000; Gratton, 2004; Randolph, 1995; Maynard et al., 2012; Sharma & Kirkman, 2015; Spreitzer, 2008; Yukl & Becker, 2007), and they include characteristics of the organization, the members, and the national culture (see Table 4-9).

TABLE 4-9 Conditions Facilitating Psychological Empowerment

Condition	Unfavorable	Favorable
Organization structure	High centralization and formalization	Very decentralized, low formalization
Competitive strategy	Low-cost, standard product or service	Customized, highly differentiated product/service
Task design and technology	Simple, repetitive task and reliable technology	Complex, nonroutine task, unreliable technology
Duration of relation with customers/clients	Brief transactions during a short time interval	Repeated interaction in a continuing relationship
Dominant cultural values in the organization	Reliable, efficient operations without any mistakes	Flexibility, learning, and participation
Employee traits	Low achievement motivation, external locus of control, and emotional stability	High need for achievement, internal locus of control, and emotional stability
Employee ability	Unskilled, inexperienced	Highly skilled professional
Employee tenure	Temporary employee	Regular, continuing employee
Employee ownership and rewards for success	None or very little	Employees are shareholders or co-owners
Employee involvement programs	None	Extensive programs strongly supported by top management
Mutual trust	Low	High

Summary

The descriptive research on decisions by managers found that decision processes are highly political, and most planning is informal and adaptive. This pattern of decision making occurs in part because managers need to obtain recent, relevant information that exists only in the heads of people who are widely scattered within and outside the organization; they need to make decisions based on information that is both overwhelming and incomplete; and they need to get cooperation from people over whom they have no formal authority.

Participative leadership involves efforts to encourage and facilitate participation by others in making decisions for which a leader has primary responsibility. Participation can take many forms, ranging from revising a tentative decision after receiving protests, to asking for suggestions before making a decision, to asking an individual or group to jointly make a decision, to allowing others to make a decision subject to the leader's final authorization. Involving others in making decisions is often necessary for getting decisions approved and implemented in organizations. Even when it is not necessary to involve others in making a decision, it can yield potential benefits, including better decision quality and greater acceptance of decisions.

Many studies have been conducted on the outcomes of using decision participation, but the research evidence is not sufficiently strong and consistent to draw any firm conclusions. Lack of consistent results occurs in part because the effects from using each type of participation depend on the leader's skill in using it and on several aspects of the situation. Participation is unlikely to be effective if potential participants do not share the leader's objectives, if they do not want to take responsibility for helping to make decisions, if they distrust the leader, or if time pressures and the dispersion of participants make it difficult to hold group meetings. Group forms of participation are unlikely to be effective unless the manager has sufficient skills in managing conflict, facilitating constructive problem solving, and dealing with common process problems that occur in groups (see Chapter 11).

The normative decision model identifies some widely used decision procedures and situational variables that determine how each decision procedure will likely affect decision quality and decision acceptance. Research on the model is limited, but the findings suggest that managers are likely to be more effective if they use decision procedures that are appropriate for the situation.

Delegation involves the assignment of new responsibilities and additional authority to individual subordinates or to a team. The potential benefits of delegation include better decisions, increased subordinate motivation, more satisfying jobs for subordinates, development of subordinate skills, and reduction of work overload for a manager. Lack of confidence in subordinates and desire to consolidate power prevent some managers from delegating as much as they should. Research on the consequences of using delegation is still limited, but the findings suggest it can be effective when used for appropriate decisions and carried out in a competent manner.

Leaders can affect the psychological empowerment of followers in many ways, and participative leadership and delegation are only two of the relevant forms of empowering leadership. The effects of empowering leadership are better understood by examining the reasons for feelings of psychological empowerment. Whether a person feels powerful or powerless depends not only on leader behavior but also on aspects of the job, the work group, and the organization. Organizations can implement empowerment programs to make the work more satisfying, increase the influence of employees on important decisions, and give members more influence over the selection and assessment of leaders.

Review and Discussion Questions

1. What does the descriptive research reveal about decision making by managers and administrators in most organizations?
2. How does the Vroom–Yetton normative model explain the effects of a decision procedure?
3. What are some ways to encourage participation in making a decision?
4. What are the potential benefits of delegation, and when is it most likely to be successful?
5. What are some guidelines for effective use of delegation?
6. Why do some managers find it so difficult to delegate or share power?
7. What are the essential elements of psychological empowerment?
8. How is empowering leadership related to participative leadership and delegation.

Key Terms

autocratic decision
consultation
decision acceptance
decision quality
delegation
employee involvement programs
empowering leadership
normative decision model
psychological empowerment
self-efficacy
self-determination

PERSONAL REFLECTION

Think about a previous or current job, or your experience as a member of a sports team, social group, or project team. In that type of situation, how much influence do you prefer to have over leadership decisions that affect you? Does it depend on the type of work or activity? What are the reasons for your preference?

CASE

Groove Electronics

Abhinav Chandra was the production manager of Groove Electronics, a local company in Agra, that manufactured low-end mobile handsets and accessories. His immediate subordinates were supervisors of different production departments in the company's manufacturing plant. A year back, the engineering manager at the company, came up with a proposal of upgrading the equipment at their workstations by computerizing as much as possible, in order to increase productivity. Abhinav approved the idea and gave instructions for this change to be carried out as soon as possible. Within a span of six months, all the equipment at the manufacturing plant had been upgraded.

After a year, when Abhinav looked at the production reports, he was disappointed to see that the expected increase in productivity had not occurred. Conversely, both productivity as well as the quality of their products had gone down, resulting an increase in consumer complaints. Abhinav was sure that the problem lay not in the workstations but somewhere else, since the recent round of workstations review by technicians had revealed that all the machinery were operating properly. Conversation with the company's other production managers who used similar kind of machinery further strengthened this belief as they had achieved success with it.

Abhinav then decided to discuss the issue with the production supervisors. Although they shared the concern, their views about where the problem lay differed vastly. While some were of the view that the decline in company's productivity could be attributed to the poor workstation design, some felt that inadequate training of the production workers responsible for operating the machinery was behind the problem. There were others who felt that lack of financial incentives could also be responsible for the declining productivity. Employees who were not comfortable with the changes introduced and could not adjust to the new style of work, eventually quit.

Today, Abhinav received a call from the company's CEO who, after reading the annual production report, was worried about the situation in which the company's productivity had reached post the changes introduced. The CEO informed Abhinav that the latter needs to come up with quick strategies to resolve the issue, and that the plan of action for the corrective measures for the future should be worked out by the following next week.

—*Written by* Nishant Uppal

Questions

1. What actions could Abhinav have taken to prevent the problem?
2. What steps should Abhinav take now to deal with the problem?

CASE

Grasim Textiles

Shivam Bhatnagar was the production manager at Grasim, a textile company that manufactured material for men's suits, shirts and pants. Workers at Grasim were not unionized. However, when Shivam read an article that stressed the benefits of participative management, he felt that these benefits could be realised at Grasim as well, if workers are allowed to participate in the decision-making process of the company on issues concerning them.

The first decision was regarding the vacation schedule of the employees. The company had a policy that each worker could seek a two-week paid leave during summers, but on the condition, that not more than two workers can be on leave at the same time. Initially, Shivam decided whom to give permission for leave based on—

- the preferred dates mentioned by the workers, and
- how their absence would affect the work.

The priority for which employee's leave, to permit or to reject, depended on the employee's productivity—if two employees with similar skill-set were contesting for a leave during the same period, the employee with the higher productivity would be granted leave first. Hence, when planning a vacation schedule, it was important that adequate staffing for all essential operations was maintained at all times.

The second decision was regarding the production standards. Owing to the increasing sales over the past few years, the company had decided to install new equipment that would help them increase their productivity. According to the company's pay incentive system, a worker would receive a piece-rate for each unit above the designated amount that they produced. Every product had a separate standard. Now, with the advent of the new equipment, the top management at the company wanted to readjust these standards, so that they reflected the change brought about by the new equipment; the new equipment enabled workers to earn more without having to put in more effort. The management felt that this way, the savings made from higher productivity could be used to pay for the new equipment.

As part of his participative management plan, Shivam invited his workers to discuss about these two issues and make recommendations. However, he felt that the workers may be hesitant in openly expressing themselves in his presence, so he allowed them to have discussion on their own. Meanwhile he met with the quality control manager to discuss the quality issues they were facing ever since the new equipment had been installed. In addition, industrial engineers had been asked to study why instead of an improvement, there had been a decline in the company's product quality.

When Shivam returned from his meeting to see what conclusion the workers at his company had arrived at, it surprised him to learn that the workers were of the opinion that the standards should be kept the same. He was expecting that since the workers were aware of the pay incentives no longer being fair, they would ask for a higher standard to be set. However, the workers explained how their base pay had not kept up with inflation, and so the higher incentive pay compensated for their real income lost.

On the issue of the vacation schedule, the workers had reached an impasse, with most of them wanting to take their two-week leave. While some workers argued that leave should be permitted based on one's seniority level, others were of the opinion that priority should be given based on the productivity level of a worker, as in the past. In the end, the workers felt that since they could not arrive at a consensus, Shivam should resolve the dispute himself, also as it was a part of his job, and he was being paid for it.

—*Written by* Nishant Uppal

Questions

1. Were the two decisions appropriate for a group decision procedure according to the Vroom–Yetton model?
2. What mistakes were made in using participation, and what could have been done to avoid the difficulties the manager encountered?
3. Were these two situations appropriate ones for introducing participation into the department?

Leading Change and Innovation

Learning Objectives

After studying this chapter, you should be able to:

- Understand reasons for resisting change.
- Understand the psychological processes involved in making major changes.
- Understand how to develop an appealing vision for the organization.
- Understand how to implement a major change in an organization.
- Understand how leaders can increase learning and innovation.

Introduction

Leading change is one of the most important and difficult responsibilities for managers and administrators. It involves guiding, encouraging, and facilitating the collective efforts of members to adapt and survive in an uncertain and sometimes hostile environment. For some theorists, this is the essence of leadership. The subject became especially relevant when many private and public sector organizations were confronted with the need for major changes to cope with globalization, deregulation, sweeping social and political changes, and the technological revolution in products and services.

Major change in an organization is usually guided by the top management team, but other members of the organization can initiate change or contribute to its success. This chapter begins with a description of different types of change, common change processes, and reasons for member resistance to change. Conditions affecting the success of change are described, and the importance of a change vision is discussed. Guidelines for advocating and implementing change are presented. The chapter also explains the importance of collective learning in teams and organizations, and guidelines are presented for encouraging and facilitating collective learning and innovation.

Types of Change in Teams and Organizations

Many types of changes can be made by leaders, and some types are more difficult than others. The focus of a change effort may involve roles, attitudes, technology, strategy, economics, or people.

Roles or Attitudes

One useful distinction is between efforts to change attitudes versus efforts to change roles, structures, and procedures (Beer, Eisenstat, & Spector, 1990). The attitude-centered approach involves changing attitudes and values with persuasive appeals, training programs, team-building activities, or a culture change program. In addition, technical or interpersonal skills may be increased with a training program. The underlying assumption is that new attitudes and skills will cause behavior to change in a beneficial way. The leader seeks to convert resisters into change agents who will transmit the vision to other people in the organization.

The role-centered approach involves changing work roles by reorganizing the workflow, redesigning jobs to include different activities and responsibilities, modifying authority relationships, changing the criteria and procedures for evaluation of work, and changing the reward system. The assumption is that when work roles require people to act in a different way, they will change their attitudes to be consistent with the new behavior. Effective behavior is induced by the new role requirements and reinforced by the evaluation and reward system. An example will clarify the difference between the two approaches to organizational change:

> A company is having difficulty getting people in different functionally specialized departments to cooperate in developing new products rapidly and getting them into the marketplace. One approach is to talk about the importance of cooperation and use a process analysis intervention or team-building activity to increase understanding and mutual respect among people from different functions. This approach assumes that increased trust and understanding will increase cooperation back in the workplace. Another approach is to create cross-functional teams that are responsible for the development of a new product, and then reward people for contributions to the success of the team. This approach assumes that people who cooperate to achieve a common goal will come to understand and trust each other.

Over the years, there has been controversy about which approach is the most effective. Either approach can succeed or fail depending on how well it is implemented. Beer and colleagues (1990) argue that a role-centered program is more likely to be successful than an attitude-centered program. However, the two approaches are not incompatible, and the best strategy is to use them together in a mutually supportive way. Efforts to change attitudes and skills to support new roles reduce the chance that the role change will be subverted by opponents before it has a chance to succeed.

Technology

Another type of change is in the technology used to do the work. Many organizations have attempted to improve performance by implementing new information and decision support systems. Examples include networked workstations, human resource information systems, inventory and order processing systems, sales tracking systems, or an intranet with groupware for communication and idea sharing among employees. Such changes often fail to yield the desired benefits, because without consistent changes in work roles, attitudes, and skills, the new technology will not be accepted and used in an effective way.

Strategy

Still another major type of change is in the competitive strategy for achieving the major objectives of the team or organization (see Chapter 12). Examples of strategy changes for a company include introduction of new products or services, entering new markets, use of new forms of marketing, initiation of Internet sales in addition to direct selling, forming alliances or joint ventures with other organizations, and modifying relationships with suppliers (e.g., partnering with a few reliable suppliers). To be successful, changes in the competitive strategy may require consistent changes in people, work roles, organization structure, and technology. For example, the decision to begin providing a more intensive type of customer service may require service personnel with additional skills and better technology for communicating with customers.

Economics or People

Internal changes in an organization may emphasize economics or people (Beer & Nohria, 2000). The first approach seeks to improve financial performance with changes such as downsizing, restructuring, and adjustments in compensation and incentives. The second approach seeks to improve human capability, commitment, and creativity by increasing individual and organizational learning, strengthening cultural values that support flexibility and innovation, and empowering people to initiate improvements. Attempts to make large-scale change in an organization often involve some aspects of both approaches, but incompatible elements can undermine the change effort if not carefully managed. For example, making drastic layoffs of employees to reduce costs can undermine the trust and loyalty needed to improve collective learning and innovation. It is difficult to improve organizational performance unless a leader can find ways to deal with the trade-offs and competing values involved in making major change, and this aspect of strategic leadership is discussed in Chapter 12.

Developmental, Transitional, or Transformational Change

A useful distinction can also be made between three types of planned change: developmental, transitional, and transformational (Anderson & Ackerman-Anderson, 2010; Packard & Shih, 2014). Developmental change involves improving a skill, process, or method or making refinements in existing operations to bridge a gap between the organization's current and desired standards. Examples include routine training, improving communications, and basic problem solving. Transitional change involves abandoning old ways of operating or implementing a new way of functioning. Examples include implementing a new program, a basic reorganization, or the introduction of new technology systems. The most extreme type of change is transformational change, which requires dramatic shifts in vision, systems, strategy, or structure. The necessity for such change might arise from major technological innovations, or the entry of an aggressive competitor. Transformational change in organizational goals, functions, and processes is often accompanied by large-scale transitional change, and each type of change will benefit from evidence-based knowledge of how to effectively lead planned change.

Change Processes

Change process theories describe a typical pattern of events that occur from the beginning of a change to the end, and in some cases they describe how earlier changes affect subsequent changes. The theories may identify distinct phases in the process, stages in the reaction of individuals, or effects of repeated changes on people.

Stages in the Change Process

One of the earliest process theories was Lewin's (1951) force-field model. He proposed that the change process can be divided into three phases: unfreezing, changing, and refreezing. In the unfreezing phase, people come to realize that the old ways of doing things are no longer adequate. This recognition may occur as a result of an obvious crisis, or it may result from an effort to describe threats or opportunities that were not evident to most people in the organization. In the changing phase, people look for new ways of doing things and select a promising approach. In the refreezing phase, the new approach is implemented and it becomes established. All three phases are important for successful change. An attempt to move directly to the changing phase without first unfreezing attitudes is likely to meet with apathy or strong resistance. Lack of systematic diagnosis and problem solving in the changing phase will result in a weak change plan. Lack of attention to consensus building and maintenance of enthusiasm in the third stage may result in the change being reversed soon after it is implemented.

According to Lewin, change may be achieved by two types of actions. One approach is to increase the driving forces toward change (e.g., increase incentives and use position power to force change). The other approach is to reduce restraining forces that create resistance to change (e.g., reduce fear of failure or economic loss, co-opt, or remove opponents). If the restraining forces are weak, it may be sufficient merely to increase driving forces. However, when restraining forces are strong, a dual approach is advisable. Unless restraining forces can be reduced, an increase in driving forces will create an intense conflict over the change, and continuing resistance will make it more difficult to complete the refreezing phase.

Stages in Reaction to a Change

Another process theory describes a typical pattern of reactions to changes imposed upon people (Gebert, Boerner, & Lanwehr, 2003; Jick, 1993; Krause, 2004; Woodward & Bucholz, 1987). The theory builds on observations about the typical sequence of reactions to sudden, traumatic events such as the death of a loved one, the breakup of a marriage, or a natural disaster that destroys one's home (Lazarus, 1991). The reaction pattern has four stages: denial, anger, mourning, and adaptation. The initial reaction is to deny that change will be necessary ("This isn't happening" or "It's just a temporary setback"). The next stage is to get angry and look for someone to blame. At the same time, people stubbornly resist giving up accustomed ways of doing things. In the third stage, people stop denying that change is inevitable, acknowledge what has been lost, and mourn it. The final stage is to accept the need to change and go on with one's life. The duration and severity of each type of reaction can vary greatly, and some people get stuck in an intermediate stage. Understanding these stages is important for change leaders, who must learn to be patient and helpful. Many people need help to overcome denial, channel their anger constructively, mourn without becoming severely depressed, and have optimism about adjusting successfully.

Prior Experience and Reactions to Change

Despite the extensive literature providing guidance on how to initiate and manage change, it is argued that as much as 70% of change efforts fail to meet expectations (Burke, 2002; Higgs & Rowland, 2005). Large-scale change in organizations is difficult to study, and much of the research involves anecdotal accounts or case studies in a single organization (Barends, Janssen, ten Have, W. & ten Have, S., 2013; Packard & Shih, 2014). However, recent years have seen an increase in research on conditions affecting the success of change efforts in organizations (Beer, 2014). The research has examined how contextual factors and individual factors jointly determine the amount of resistance or commitment to change (Beer, 2011).

How a person reacts to change depends in part on the person's general confidence about coping with change successfully. This confidence is affected by prior experience with change as well as by traits, such as self-confidence, risk tolerance, openness to new experiences, and internal locus of control orientation (Erwin & Garman, 2010). The effects of experiencing repeated, difficult change are not clear (Jick, 1993). One possibility is that experiencing traumatic change will "inoculate" people and leave them better prepared to change again without such an intense or prolonged period of adjustment. For example, having experienced and survived the loss of two jobs in five years, Sally is confident about taking more risky, less secure jobs in the future. However, it is also possible that repeated change leaves a person less resilient and more vulnerable to adverse effects from subsequent change. The explanation involves prolonged stress and the inability to completely resolve the emotional trauma of an earlier change. For example, after losing two jobs in five years as a result of downsizing, Linda cannot deal with the threat of losing another job and seeks early retirement.

Research on the cumulative effects of experiencing repeated, intense changes is still limited, but it suggests that the more common effect is to increase stress and frustration (Rafferty & Griffin, 2006). The stress caused by earlier changes and a person's self-efficacy for change jointly determine how the person will react to more changes (Herold, Fedor, & Caldwell, 2007). Even for people with strong confidence in their ability to handle change, multiple changes in a short period of time can undermine commitment. People are likely to feel frustration and a sense of injustice if the burden of implementing change is placed on them without adequate support from the organization. Feelings of being unjustly treated are intensified when most of the benefits of the changes will accrue to others, such as owners and top management.

Reasons for Accepting or Rejecting Change

Many efforts to implement major change in an organization are unsuccessful, and resistance to change is a major reason for failure. One explanation for the outcome of a proposed change is in terms of leader power and the types of influence processes that leaders use (see Chapter 6). Compliance with the change is likely if people believe that it is a legitimate exercise of leader authority (legitimate power), or if they fear punishment for resisting the change (coercive power). Commitment to support a change initiative is likely when people trust their leaders and believe that the change is necessary and effective (strong referent and expert power). However, resistance to change is common in organizations, and it can occur for several reasons that are not mutually exclusive (Connor, 1995; Fedor, Caldwell, & Herold, 2006; Szabla, 2007).

The Proposed Change Is Not Necessary

A change is likely to be resisted if there is no clear evidence of a serious problem or opportunity that would justify major change. The signs of a developing problem are usually ambiguous at the early stage, and it is easy for people to ignore or discount them. Even when a problem is finally recognized, the usual response is to make incremental adjustments in the present strategy, or to do more of the same, rather than to do something different.

The Proposed Change Is Not Feasible

Another reason for resistance is the belief that a proposed change cannot be implemented successfully. Making a change that is radically different from anything done previously will appear difficult if not impossible to most people. If earlier change programs initiated by the same leaders were unsuccessful, it creates cynicism and makes people doubtful the next one will be any better. The self-confidence of people who must implement change also influences how they view it. Change makes some expertise obsolete and requires learning new ways of doing the work. Individuals who lack self-confidence will be reluctant to give up established procedures for new ones that may be too difficult to master.

The Proposed Change Is Not Cost Effective

A change may be resisted because the benefits would not justify the costs necessary to implement the change. Major change always entails some costs, and they may be higher than any likely benefits. Resources are necessary to implement change, and resources already invested in doing things the traditional way will be lost. Performance invariably suffers during the transition period as the new ways are learned and new procedures are debugged. More resistance is likely when it is not possible to accurately estimate costs in relation to benefits and people are pessimistic about the benefits.

The Change Would Cause Personal Losses

Even if a change would benefit the organization, it may be resisted by people who would suffer personal loss of income, benefits, or job security. Major changes in organizations invariably result in some shift in power and status for individuals and subunits. Some jobs may be eliminated or modified, resulting in layoffs or transfers to new locations. People responsible for activities that will be cut back or eliminated may lose the basis for their current status and power. A change will be perceived as unfair by people if it has adverse consequences for them and they have little or no influence over decisions about the change.

The Proposed Change Is Inconsistent with Values

Another reason for resistance is that the proposed change appears inconsistent with an individual's values and ideals. If a proposed change is viewed as unethical, illegal, or inconsistent with strong beliefs about proper behavior, it is more likely to be resisted, even if it would provide tangible benefits to the person. When the values violated by a proposed change are embedded in a strong organization culture, resistance will be widespread.

The Leaders Are Not Trusted

In some organizations, change is resisted because the leaders who propose it are distrusted, and this distrust can magnify the effect of other sources of resistance. Even without an obvious threat, a change may be resisted if people imagine hidden, ominous implications that will not be discovered until it is too late to do anything about them. Mutual mistrust may encourage a leader to be secretive about the real reasons for change or some of the risks, thereby further increasing suspicion and resistance. Resistance may also reflect resentment that changes were proposed by leaders who are not viewed as having legitimate authority to make them, or who are seen as using the changes to further personal ambitions and desire for more power.

Organizational Cynicism About Change

Some organizations have a history of failed change efforts based on popular management programs that are ineffective. The employees may become cynical that the latest organizational change effort simply reflects another "fad" that will either fail or soon be abandoned (Bommer, Rich, & Rubin, 2005; Rubin, Dierdorff, Bommer, & Baldwin, 2009). Such cynicism may be the product of a lack of top management commitment to prior change efforts that fell by the wayside, or a deep-rooted distrust of the underlying motives for change. Other factors that may contribute to organizational cynicism and hence resistance to change include an organizational history of layoffs, excessive executive compensation, and self-serving decisions that foster feelings of contempt, frustration, and distrust of organizational leaders. Under these circumstances, leaders may find it difficult to secure the requisite buy-in for the change, and active or passive resistance is likely.

Alternative Reasons for Resistance

Resistance to change is not merely the result of ignorance or inflexibility. It can occur for several reasons and is a natural reaction by people who want to protect their self-interests and sense of self-determination. Rather than viewing resistance only as an obstacle to batter down or circumvent, it can be viewed as energy that can be redirected to improve change (Ford, J. D., Ford, L. W., & D'Amelio, 2008; Jick, 1993; Maurer, 1996). Active resistance indicates the presence of strong values and emotions that could serve as a source of commitment if opponents are converted to supporters. It is essential to discuss a proposed change with the people who will be affected to learn about their concerns and their ideas about the best course of action.

Implementing Change

Organization scholars have been interested in determining how the approach used to implement change affects the success of the effort. It is likely that the outcome will depend in part on what is changed, how and when the change is implemented, who participates in the process, and how much influence each participant has. The outcomes for a change can be judged in different ways, including commitment of people to the change, successful implementation of the change, and the extent to which the change results in the desired benefits and avoids negative consequences.

Determining What to Change

Before initiating major changes, leaders need to be clear about the nature of the problem and the objectives to be achieved. Just as in the treatment of a physical illness, the first step is a careful diagnosis to determine what is wrong with the patient. The organizational diagnosis can be conducted by the top management team, by outside consultants, or by a task force composed of representatives of the various key stakeholders in the organization.

An incorrect diagnosis or an inappropriate change program will not provide the desired benefits. A common mistake is to implement a generic change program that is currently popular without a careful diagnosis of the problems confronting the organization. Some examples of popular change programs in past years include downsizing, delayering, total quality management, quality circles, lean management, re-engineering, self-managed teams, outsourcing, and partnering with suppliers (Barends et al., 2013). Change programs often fail to solve organizational problems and sometimes make them worse (Beer, 2011; Beer et al., 1990). The benefits obtained from changes made in one part of the organization often fail to improve the overall performance of the organization and may cause new problems for other subunits (Goodman & Rousseau, 2004).

Understanding Systems Dynamics

To understand the reasons for a problem and how to deal with it requires a good understanding of the complex relationships and systems dynamics that occur in organizations (Beer, 2011; Gharajedaghi, 1999; Goodman & Rousseau, 2004; Senge, 1990). Knowledge of systems dynamics is helpful both for identifying the nature of a problem and for anticipating the likely effects of changes made to resolve it.

Systems dynamics involve complex relationships, multiple causes and outcomes, delayed effects, and cyclical causality. Problems have multiple causes, which may include actions taken earlier to solve other problems. If the diagnosis only identifies one of several problems, the changes may fail to achieve the desired outcome. In large systems such as organizations, actions have multiple outcomes, including unintended side effects. A change in one part of a system will eventually affect other parts, and reactions to the change may cancel out the effects. Changes that have delayed effects tend to obscure the real nature of the relationship. Sometimes actions that appear to offer quick relief may actually make things worse in the long run, whereas the best solution may offer no immediate benefits, but the delayed benefits are substantial. A leader who is impatient for quick results may keep repeating inappropriate remedies, rather than pursuing better remedies that require patience and short-term sacrifice.

Understanding the complex interdependencies among organizational processes and the implications of efforts to make changes requires cognitive skills and "systems thinking" (Senge, 1990). When making decisions or diagnosing the cause of problems, it is essential to understand how the different parts of the organization are interrelated. Even when the immediate objective is to deal with one type of challenge, such as improving efficiency, leaders need to consider the likely consequences for other performance determinants and the possibility that any immediate benefits will be nullified by delayed effects. An example is when a manager downsizes the workforce to reduce costs, but pressure to maintain the same output requires expensive overtime and use of consultants (including some of the same people who were downsized), thereby negating most of the cost savings.

Another common phenomenon is a reinforcing cycle wherein small changes grow into much bigger changes that may or may not be desirable. A positive example is when a change made to improve processes in one subunit is successful, and other subunits are encouraged to imitate it, resulting in more benefits for the organization than initially expected. A negative example is when rationing is introduced to conserve a scarce resource and people stockpile more of it than they currently need, thereby causing more shortages and problems.

Responsibility for Implementing Major Change

Large-scale change in an organization is unlikely to be successful without the support of top management. However, contrary to common assumptions, major changes are not always initiated by top management, and they may not become involved until the process is well under way (Beer, 1988, 2011; Belgard, Fisher, & Rayner, 1988). Major changes suggested by lower levels may be resisted by top managers who are strongly committed to traditional approaches and do not understand that the old ways of doing things are no longer appropriate. As noted in Chapter 12, the major transformation of an organization often requires the replacement of top management by new leaders with a mandate for radical change.

The essential role of top management in implementing change is to formulate an integrating vision and general strategy, build a coalition of supporters who endorse the strategy, then guide and coordinate the process by which the strategy will be implemented. Complex changes usually involve a process of experimentation and learning, because it is impossible to anticipate all the problems or to prepare detailed plans for how to carry out all aspects of the change. Instead of specifying detailed guidelines for change at all levels of the organization, it is much better to encourage middle- and lower-level managers to transform their own units in a way that is consistent with the vision and strategy. Top management should provide encouragement, support, and necessary resources to facilitate change, but should not try to dictate the details of how to do it.

Based on a 20-year action research program, Michael Beer of the Harvard Business School and his colleagues developed a "Strategic Fitness Process" (SFP) that reflects these recommendations for the leadership of planned change. Beer (2011, p. 1) describes SFP as "a platform by which senior leaders, working with the help of consultants, can have an honest, collective, and public conversation about their organization's alignment with espoused strategy and values." While senior leaders assume responsibility for initiating these conversations and the resultant change process, a key to their success is to engage as many employees as possible in discussions of problems, solutions, and commitments. The goal of these conversations is to combat six barriers to organizational effectiveness: "(1) unclear strategy, values, and conflicting priorities; (2) an ineffective senior team; (3) a top-down or laissez faire leader; (4) poor coordination and communication across functions, business, or geographic entities; (5) inadequate leadership development and leadership resources below the top; and (6) poor vertical communication – down and up" (Beer, 2011, pgs. 12–13). Beer calls these barriers "silent killers" because like hypertension and cholesterol in humans, they can cause severe damage to an organization and are often unrecognized by top management. An example of the negative consequences is provided by one observation of conditions at the Hewlett-Packard's Santa Rosa Systems Division (SRSD):

> The division is not sure about what kind of business it wants to be. Two competing strategies are battling for the same resources, and the factions supporting these strategies are tearing the division apart. The top managers of the functional departments refuse to cooperate effectively for fear that they will lose power.

SFP is designed to combat the "silent killers" of organizational effectiveness through the following nine steps: (1) a one-day meeting of the senior team is held to develop a statement of organizational direction; (2) a fitness task force is appointed and trained to conduct interviews throughout the organization to obtain candid feedback about barriers to execution; (3) the fitness task force conducts interviews with 100 employees, typically over a three-week period, and identifies themes regarding organizational strengths and barriers; (4) the fitness task force prepares a report that summarizes the unvarnished truth to the senior team; (5) task force feedback, senior team diagnosis, and plans for changing the system occur within a three-day Fitness Meeting, which is the key catalytic SFP event; (6) the senior team meets with the fitness task force to present an action plan for organizational redesign and realignment; (7) the task force meets alone to discuss the quality of the action plan and prospects for implementation; (8) the senior team and task force meet to revise the organization design and change plan; and (9) the senior team, ideally with task force participation, meets with the interviewees and other key employees to communicate what they heard from the task force, their diagnosis of the issues, their action plan for change, and to mobilize support. The application of SFP at Hewlett-Packard resulted in dramatic changes in the Santa Rosa Systems Division's performance that are described in the following example (Beer, 2011, pg. 13):

> The division has done a terrific job after a year of struggling to figure out what their business is and how to get it going. They have turned weakness into strengths and are now one of the top divisions in terms of growth in profitability, return on assets, and customer satisfaction.

As this example illustrates, SFP facilitates honest, safe, collective, and public conversations about organizational problems throughout an organization, and it can help to ensure that responsibility for the planned change and commitment to its implementation are shared across organizational levels and subunits.

The Pace and Sequencing of Changes

A debate continues among change scholars about the optimal pace and sequencing of desired changes. Some scholars have advocated rapid introduction of changes throughout the organization to prevent the buildup of resistance, whereas other scholars favor a more gradual introduction of change to different parts of the organization at different times. The limited amount of longitudinal research does not yet provide clear answers to these questions, but some evidence favors the gradual approach (e.g., Beer, 1988, 2011; Hinings & Greenwood, 1988; Pettigrew, Ferlie, & McKee, 1992). In a 12-year study of 36 national sports organizations, Amis, Slack, and Hinings (2004) found evidence that major change was more successful when it was implemented slowly and in highly visible ways that made it clear the change was a serious, long-lasting effort. Controversial aspects were modified to deal with opponent concerns or postponed until a time when opponents would be more receptive to them. This process provided opportunities for the change agents to establish trust and use collaborative problem solving for contentious issues.

Whenever feasible, it seems beneficial to change interdependent subunits of the organization simultaneously so that the effects will be mutually supporting. However, in a large organization with semiautonomous subunits (e.g., separate product divisions) simultaneous change is not essential, and it may not be feasible to implement change in all subunits at the same time. One way to demonstrate the success of a new strategy is to implement it on a small scale in one subunit or facility on an experimental basis. A successful change that is carried out in one part of an organization can help to stimulate similar changes throughout the organization. However, it is unwise merely to assume that the same changes will be appropriate in all subunits, especially when they are very diverse. This type of mistake is more likely to be avoided when middle managers are allowed to have a major voice in determining how to implement a strategy in their own organizational subunits (Beer, 2011; Beer et al., 1990).

Successful implementation of a major new strategy usually requires changes in the organizational structure to make it consistent with the strategy. However, when structural change is likely to be resisted, it may be easier to create an informal structure to support the new strategy and postpone changes in the formal structure until people realize that they are needed.

Informal teams can be created to facilitate the transition, without any expectation that these temporary structures will become permanent. For example, after temporary task forces were created to plan and coordinate changes in one company, they eventually evolved into permanent cross-functional committees with formal authority to plan and monitor continuing improvements in product quality and operational procedures.

Guidelines for Implementing Change

Successful implementation of change in organizations requires a wide range of leadership behaviors. Some of the behaviors involve political and administrative aspects, and others involve motivating, supporting, and guiding people. Even the people who initially endorse a change will need support and assistance to sustain their enthusiasm and optimism as the inevitable difficulties and setbacks occur. Major change is always stressful and painful for people, especially when it involves a prolonged transition period of adjustment, disruption, and dislocation. The following guidelines describe current thinking about good ways to gain support for a major change and to implement it in an organization (see summary in Table 5-1). The guidelines are based on theory, research findings, and practitioner insights (Battilana et al., 2010; Beer, 1988, 2011, 2014; Connor, 1995; Higgs & Rowland, 2005; Jick, 1993; Kotter, 1996; Nadler, Shaw, Walton, & Associates, 1995; Pettigrew & Whipp, 1991; Rubin et al., 2009; Self & Schraeder, 2009; Tichy & Devanna, 1986). Although the guidelines describe actions a chief executive can take, many of them also apply to other leaders who want to make major changes in their team or department.

- **Create a sense of urgency about the need for change.**

When changes in the environment are gradual and no obvious crisis has occurred, many people fail to recognize emerging threats (or opportunities). An important role of the leader is to persuade other key people in the organization of the need for major changes rather than incremental adjustments. To mobilize support for proposed changes, it is essential to explain why they are necessary and to create a sense of urgency about them. Explain why not changing will eventually be more costly than making the proposed changes now. If people have little

TABLE 5-1 Guidelines for Implementing a Major Change

- Create a sense of urgency about the need for change.
- Communicate a clear vision of the benefits to be gained.
- Identify likely supporters, opponents, and reasons for resistance.
- Build a broad coalition to support the change.
- Fill key positions with competent change agents.
- Use task forces to guide the implementation of changes.
- Empower competent people to help plan and implement change.
- Make dramatic, symbolic changes that affect the work.
- Prepare people for change by explaining how it will affect them.
- Help people deal with the stress and difficulties of major change.
- Provide opportunities for early successes to build confidence.
- Monitor the progress of change and make any necessary adjustments.
- Keep people informed about the progress of change.
- Demonstrate continued optimism and commitment to the change.

knowledge of the problems, it is important for the leader to provide relevant information and help people understand them. For example, distribute a summary of customer complaints each week with selective quotes from irate customers. Arrange for people to meet with dissatisfied customers. Prepare analyses of costs involved in correcting quality problems. Compare the performance of the organizational unit to the performance of key competitors as well as to unit performance in prior years.

- **Communicate a clear vision of the benefits to be gained from change.**

When it is necessary to make major changes in an organization, a vision of what the changes will do to achieve shared objectives and values is very helpful in gaining commitment for the change. The desirable characteristics of a vision and guidelines for developing an appealing vision are described later in this chapter, and guidelines for communicating an inspiring vision are explained in Chapter 8.

- **Identify likely supporters, opponents, and reasons for resistance.**

To evaluate the feasibility of various strategies for accomplishing major change in the organization, a leader must understand the political processes, the distribution of power, and the identity of people whose support is necessary to make the change happen. Before beginning a major change effort, it is useful to identify likely supporters and opponents. Time should be set aside to explore each of the following questions: Which key people will determine whether a proposal will be successfully implemented? Who is likely to support the proposal? How much resistance is likely and from whom? What would be necessary to overcome the resistance? How could skeptics be converted into supporters? How long will it take to get approval from all of the key parties?

- **Build a broad coalition to support the change.**

The task of persuading people to support major change is not easy, and it is too big of a job for a single leader to do alone. Successful change in an organization requires cooperative effort by people who have the power to facilitate or block change. It is essential to build a coalition of supporters, both inside and outside the organization. A supportive coalition may be even more important in pluralistic organizations that have collective leadership (e.g., hospitals, universities, professional associations) than in hierarchical business organizations where the top management team may have sufficient power to authorize major change (Denis, Lamothe, & Langley, 2001). The first step is to ensure that the executive team is prepared to undertake the difficult task of implementing major change in the organization, and some changes in the team may be necessary. Supporters are needed not only within the top executive team, but also among middle and lower levels of management. In a study by Beer (1988) of six companies undergoing a major change effort, the companies with a successful transformation had more middle managers who supported the changes and possessed relevant skills to facilitate it. The external members of the coalition may be consultants, labor union leaders, important clients, executives in financial institutions, or officials in government agencies.

- **Use task forces to guide implementation of changes.**

Temporary task forces are often useful to guide the implementation of major change in an organization, especially when it involves modification of the formal structure and the relationships among subunits. Examples of typical responsibilities for a task force include exploring how key values in the vision can be expressed more fully; developing action plans for implementing a new strategy that cuts across subunits; designing procedures for performing new types of activities; and studying how the appraisal and reward structure can be modified to make it more consistent with the new vision and strategy. The composition of each task force should be appropriate for its responsibilities. For example, a task force to improve customer service should include people from all the functions that affect the quality of this service, and the task force should actually meet with some important customers. The leader of each task force should be someone who understands and supports the new vision and has skills in how to conduct meetings, manage conflict, and involve people in constructive problem solving.

- **Fill key positions with competent change agents.**

It is especially important to get the commitment of people directly responsible for implementing the change—the people in key positions who will make it happen. These "change agents" must support the change with their actions as well as their words. They should be people who are committed to the vision and have the ability to communicate it clearly. Whenever possible, people in key positions who cannot be won over to the new vision and strategy should be replaced. If left in place, opponents may go beyond passive resistance and use political tactics in an effort to block additional change. Pockets of resistance can develop and grow strong enough to prevent the new strategy from being implemented successfully. Acting quickly to remove opponents who symbolize the old order not only removes people who will resist change, but also signals that you are serious about the change.

- **Empower competent people to help plan and implement the change.**

A major change is less likely to be successful if top management tries to dictate in detail how it will be implemented in each part of the organization. Whenever feasible, the authority to make decisions and deal with problems should be delegated to the individuals or teams responsible for implementing change. Competent supporters in key positions should be empowered to determine the best way to implement a new strategy or support a new program, rather than telling them in detail what to do. Empowering people also means reducing bureaucratic constraints that will impede their efforts and providing the resources they need to implement change successfully.

- **Make dramatic, symbolic changes that affect the work.**

If feasible, make dramatic, symbolic changes that affect the everyday lives of organization members in significant ways. When members are immediately affected, it becomes more obvious that the change is really going to happen and they need to adjust to it. One type of symbolic change involves how the work is done and the authority of various parties over the work. For example, in a manufacturing company that adopted a new strategy of total product quality, the position of quality inspector was eliminated, production employees were given the responsibility for checking quality and correcting any quality problems, quality circles were established to identify ways to improve quality, and employees were empowered to stop the production line to correct quality problems. Another type of symbolic change involves where the work is done. In a large insurance company that reorganized from a functionally specialized hierarchy into 14 small, semiautonomous divisions, the chief executive officer (CEO) sold the old high-rise office building and relocated each division into its own, separate, low-rise facility. The move emphasized to employees the new strategy of empowering each division to find its own ways to improve customer service. Symbolic changes may also involve cultural forms such as symbols, ceremonies, and rituals.

- **Prepare people for change by explaining how it will affect them.**

Even when a change is necessary and beneficial, it will require difficult adjustments by the people who are most affected. If people are unable to handle the stress and trauma of change, they will become depressed or rebellious. Even enthusiastic change agents are not immune from the difficulties experienced in a long-term change effort. Alternating successes and setbacks may leave change agents feeling as if they are on an emotional roller coaster ride. Ambiguity about progress and the recurring discovery of new obstacles will increase fatigue and frustration. These negative aspects of change are easier to deal with if people expect them and know how to cope with them. Rather than presenting change as a panacea without any costs or problems, it is better to help people understand what adjustments will be necessary. However, it is essential to be enthusiastic and optimistic about the likely success of the change, despite serious obstacles. Change agents should be careful to avoid any cynicism, because it will undermine confidence and commitment. One approach to prepare people for change is to provide a realistic preview of some typical types of problems and difficulties, and then discuss what can be done to avoid or resolve these problems. It may be useful to ask people who have experienced a similar change to speak about their experiences and what they did to get through the change successfully. Social networks can be used to enable people to get advice and support from each other more easily.

- **Help people deal with the stress and difficulties of major change.**

When radical changes are made, many people experience personal pain at the loss of familiar things to which they had become attached. The trauma of change may be experienced regardless of whether the change involves new strategies and programs, new equipment and procedures for doing the work, new facilities, new management practices, or new leaders. It is difficult for people to accept the failure of past decisions and policies, and it may be necessary to help them accept the need for change without feeling personally responsible for the failure. Leaders can encourage people to take advantage of available training on how to manage stress, anxiety, and depression. It may be useful to form support groups to help people cope with the disruptions caused by a major change. Sometimes ceremonies or rituals are useful to help people express their grief and anger over the loss of sentimental elements of the old organization. An example is provided by the following description of a special management conference held in a large electronics company that had recently undergone many changes (Deal, 1985, p. 321):

> The conference opened with a general discussion of culture and then continued with three successive small-group sessions of thirty participants each. When asked for metaphors to capture the essence of the company, the group overwhelmingly came up with transitive images: afloat in a stormy sea without an anchor, a two-headed animal, and so on. Each group specifically addressed the issue of loss. In the last session, the CEO was present; the word had spread that the discussions were yielding some significant perceptions. The tension in the room was obvious. At one point, the participants were asked to name what they had lost, and these were written on a flip chart. The list included values, symbols, rituals, ceremonies, priests, and heroes. As people contributed specific losses, someone got up and dimmed the lights. The emotion was obviously high. The group then launched into a discussion of the positive features of the company in its new incarnation. The CEO incorporated much of the preceding discussion into an excellent closing speech, and the company moved ahead.

- **Provide opportunities for early successes to build confidence.**

The confidence of an individual or team can be increased by making sure people experience successful progress in the early phases of a new project or major change. Some skeptics will only become supporters after they see evidence of progress in initial efforts to do things a new way. Kouzes and Posner (1987) recommend breaking up a challenging task into initial small steps or short-term goals that do not appear too difficult. People are more willing to undertake an activity if they perceive that their efforts are likely to be successful and that the costs of failure would not be great. As the initial steps or goals are accomplished, people experience success and gain more self-confidence. Then, they are willing to try for larger wins and to invest more resources in the effort.

- **Monitor the progress of change and make any necessary adjustments.**

Innovative changes are by nature ventures into uncharted waters, and it is impossible to predict all of the obstacles and difficulties that will be encountered. Many things must be learned by doing, and monitoring is essential for this learning. Feedback about the effects of change should be collected and analyzed to evaluate progress and refine mental models about the relationship among key variables that affect the organization's performance. Monitoring is also important to help coordinate different aspects of the change. Accurate, timely information is needed about the effect of the changes on people, processes, and performance. This information can be gathered in a variety of ways, one of which is to hold frequent progress review meetings with people in key positions.

- **Keep people informed about the progress of change.**

A major change, like any other crisis, creates anxiety and stress in people who are affected by it. When a new strategy does not require many visible changes in the early stages of implementation, people will begin to wonder whether the effort has died and things are going back to the way they were. People will be more enthusiastic and optimistic if they know that the change program is progressing successfully. One way to convey a sense of progress is to communicate what steps have been initiated, what changes have been completed, and what improvements have occurred in performance indicators. Hold ceremonies to announce the inauguration of major activities, to celebrate significant progress or success, and to give people recognition for their contributions and achievements. These celebrations provide an opportunity to increase optimism, build commitment, and strengthen identification with the organizational unit. Recognizing the contributions and accomplishments of individuals makes the importance of each person's role in the collective effort more evident. When obstacles are encountered, explain what they are and what is being done about them. If the implementation plan must be revised, explain why it was necessary. Otherwise, people may interpret any revisions in the plan or schedule as a sign of faltering commitment.

- **Demonstrate optimism and continued commitment to the change.**

Responsibility for guiding various aspects of the change can be delegated to other change agents, but the leader who is identified as the primary proponent and sponsor of the change must continue to provide the attention and endorsement that signal commitment to see it through to the end. Initial enthusiasm and support for a major change may decline as problems are encountered, setbacks occur, and people come to understand the necessary costs and sacrifices. People look to their leaders for signs of continued commitment to the change objectives and vision. Any indication that the change is no longer viewed as important or feasible may have ripple effects that undermine the change effort. Supporters will be lost and opponents encouraged to increase overt resistance. Continued attention and endorsement signal a leader's commitment to see the change program through to a successful conclusion. The leader should persistently promote the vision guiding the change process and display optimism that the inevitable setbacks and difficulties will be overcome. The leader should reject easy solutions for dealing with immediate problems when these solutions are inconsistent with the underlying objectives of the change effort. Demonstrating commitment is more than just talking about the importance of the change; the leader must invest time, effort, and resources in resolving problems and overcoming obstacles. When appropriate, the leader should participate in activities related to the change. For example, attendance at a special meeting or ceremony relevant to the change effort has a clear symbolic meaning for other people in the organization that the change must be important.

How Visions Influence Change

The success of a major change will depend to a great extent on how well leaders communicate the reasons why proposed change is necessary and beneficial. Success is more likely if leaders articulate a vision of a better future that is attractive enough to justify the sacrifices and hardships the change will require. The vision can provide a sense of continuity for followers by linking past events and present strategies to a vivid image of a better future for the organization. The vision provides hope for a better future and the faith that it will be attained someday. In the hectic and confusing process of implementing change, a clear vision helps to guide and coordinate the decisions and actions of many people in widely dispersed locations.

The reason behind the success of Patanjali products was the fact that they were marketed as historically and culturally indigenous. The vision of bringing in products that competed with those of the MNC's, but without the use of any chemicals or any compromise in the quality, and using only natural ingredients encouraged the consumers to shift to Patanjali products as it was a reminder of the famous Swadeshi campaign. Consumers were motivated to buy Patanjali's products as they were free from any synthetic and artificial ingredients and were ayurvedic. The country's penchant for culturally rooted products was well tapped by the Patanjali products. The advent of Patanjali increased the sales of not only other ayurvedic and herbal brands but also forced MNC's to come up with more naturally made alternatives to their existing products. For example, Coalgate came up with a new tootpaste which consisted *neem* in it.

Desirable Characteristics for a Vision

A number of writers have attempted to describe the essential qualities of a successful vision (Bennis & Nanus, 1985; Kantabutra, 2009; Kotter, 1996; Kouzes & Posner, 1995; Nanus, 1992; Tichy & Devanna, 1986; Zaccaro & Banks, 2004). A vision should be simple and idealistic, a picture of a desirable future, not a complex plan with quantitative objectives and detailed action steps. The vision should appeal to the values, hopes, and ideals of organization members and other stakeholders whose support is needed. The vision should emphasize distant ideological objectives rather than immediate tangible benefits. The vision should be challenging but realistic. To be meaningful and credible, it should not be a wishful fantasy, but rather an attainable future grounded in the present reality. The vision should address basic assumptions about what is important for the organization, how it should relate to the environment, and how people should be treated. The vision should be focused enough to guide decisions and actions, but general enough to allow initiative and creativity in the strategies for attaining it. Finally, a successful vision should be simple enough to be communicated clearly in five minutes or less.

Elements of a Vision

The term vision has many different meanings, which creates widespread confusion. It is unclear whether a mission statement, strategic objective, value statement, or slogan constitutes an effective vision. In the absence of direct research on this question, one way to answer it is to examine each construct in relation to the desirable characteristics for a vision.

The mission statement usually describes the purpose of the organization in terms of the type of activities to be performed for constituents or customers. In contrast, an effective vision tells us what these activities mean to people. The core of the vision is the organization's mission, but different aspects of it may be emphasized. A successful vision tells you not only what the organization does, but also why it is worthwhile and exciting to do it. A successful vision makes the typical dull mission statement come alive, infusing it with excitement, arousing emotions, and stimulating creativity to achieve it. Consider this vision for a car company:

> We will create an empowered organization to unleash our creativity and focus our energies in cooperative effort that will enable us to develop and build the best personal vehicles in the world, vehicles that people will treasure owning because they are fun to use, they are reliable, they keep people comfortable and safe, and they enable people to have freedom of movement in their environment without harming it.

This vision conveys an image of what can be achieved, why it is worthwhile, and how it can be done. Note that the vision is flexible enough to encourage the possibility of finding alternative power sources in the future and developing other types of vehicles besides conventional ground cars (e.g., fusion-powered air cars, as in the movie *Back to the Future*).

Values statements are a list of the key values or ideological themes considered important for an organization. The values usually pertain to treatment of customers, treatment of organization members, core competencies, and standards of excellence. Common themes include satisfying customers, achieving excellence in products or services, providing an innovative product or service, developing and empowering employees, and making important contributions to society. A values statement provides a good beginning for developing a more complete vision. However, just listing values does not clearly explain their relative priority, how they are interrelated, or how they will be expressed and achieved. An effective vision statement provides a glimpse of a possible future in which all the key values are realized at the same time.

Slogans are statements used to summarize and communicate values in simple terms. However, a slogan is limited in how many values can be expressed. Consider the following examples: Technology is our business, quality is job one, we feel good when you feel good, all the news people want to read, and partners in making dreams come true. Only the last slogan has more than one value; it describes the ideal service provided to customers and the ideal relationship among the providers. Slogans can be useful as part of a larger vision, but overemphasis on a simplistic slogan can trivialize the vision and diminish important values not included in the slogan (Richards & Engle, 1986).

Strategic objectives are tangible outcomes or results to be achieved, sometimes by a specific deadline. A performance objective may be stated in terms of the absolute level of performance (e.g., profits, sales, return on investment), or the relative level of performance (e.g., becoming number one in the industry or region, outperforming a traditional rival). Neither type of objective is likely to involve enduring, ideological themes. Performance objectives are useful to guide planning and facilitate evaluation of progress, but the focus of a vision should be on values and ideological themes, not on improvement of economic outcomes or outperforming rivals. If performance objectives are included in a vision, they should be regarded as milestones along the way toward achieving ideological objectives.

Project objectives are defined in terms of the successful completion of a complex activity (e.g., developing a new type of product, implementing a new MBA program, establishing a subsidiary in China). These objectives can emphasize economic outcomes, ideological outcomes, or both. For example, a pharmaceutical company has a project to develop a new vaccine that will prevent a disease; successful completion of the project will improve profits, provide health benefits to society, and enhance scientific knowledge. A limitation of most project objectives is their relatively short time perspective. When the project is completed, the vision is ended. Project objectives can be included in the long-term vision for an organization, or a supplementary vision can be built around an especially important project. However, no single project should be allowed to eclipse the fuller, more enduring vision for the organization.

To understand what an effective project vision looks like, it is helpful to examine a specific example. When Walt Disney conceived the idea of Disneyland, it was an entirely new type of activity for his company, and it was unlike any earlier amusement park. It would be expensive to build, and it was uncertain whether enough visitors would be attracted to yield a profit. At the time it was not obvious that Disneyland would become such a phenomenal success, and people were skeptical about the risky project. An inspiring vision was needed to gain support from other key members of top management and outside investors. Disney's vision for the park was described in the following way (Thomas, 1976, p. 246):

> The idea of Disneyland is a simple one. It will be a place for people to find happiness and knowledge. It will be a place for parents and children to spend pleasant times in one another's company: a place for teachers and pupils to discover greater ways of understanding and education. Here the older generation can recapture the nostalgia of days gone by, and the younger generation can savor the challenge of the future. Here will be the wonders of Nature and Man for all to see and understand. Disneyland will be based upon and dedicated to the ideals, the dreams and hard facts that have created America. And it will be uniquely equipped to dramatize these dreams and facts and send them forth as a source of courage and inspiration to all the world. Disneyland will be something of a fair, an exhibition, a playground, a community center, a museum of living facts, and a showplace of beauty and magic. It will be filled with the accomplishments, the joys and hopes of the world we live in. And it will remind us and show us how to make those wonders part of our own lives.

Research on Effects of Visions

Most of the evidence about the importance of a vision for successful change in organizations comes from leadership research that is focused more on the process of envisioning than on the content of the vision. The visions articulated by effective leaders are sometimes elaborate and sometimes simple. Descriptive studies on the content of organizational visions found that most of them were expressed in the form of a performance objective or values statement that was very brief, strategic, and future oriented (Larwood, Falbe, Kriger, & Miesing, 1995; Ruvio, Rosenblatt, & Hertz-Lazarowitz, 2010). A study by Berson, Shamir, Avolio, and Popper (2001) found that leaders who were rated as highly transformational were more likely to develop visions that were future oriented and reflected a high level of optimism and confidence. A study of small entrepreneurial firms by Baum, Locke, and Kirkpatrick (1998) found that CEOs for the fastest-growing firms were more likely to communicate a vision that emphasized future growth. A qualitative, interview-based study by Perkins, Lean, and Newbery (2017, p. 83) of small and medium enterprises (SMEs) revealed that an organizational vision plays a key role in the guidance of idea generation, with more relevant ideas being offered when a vision is in place. The results from these studies seem to suggest that few organizations actually have a well-developed vision with significant ideological content. However, in recent years, some scholars have begun to question whether the importance of an explicit vision for organization change has been overstated. More research is needed to determine what type of vision is sufficient to guide and inspire change in organizations and the conditions where an ideological vision is most important.

Guidelines for Developing a Vision

It is extremely difficult to develop a vision that will elicit commitment from the many diverse stakeholders whose support is needed for major change. Such a vision cannot be generated by a mechanical formula. Judgment and analytical ability are needed to synthesize the vision, but intuition and creativity are important as well. To develop an appealing vision, it is essential to have a good understanding of the organization (its operations, products, services, markets, competitors, and social-political environment), its culture (shared beliefs and assumptions about the world and the organization's place in it), and the underlying needs and values of employees and other stakeholders. In most cases, a successful vision is not the creation of a single, heroic leader working alone, but instead it reflects the contributions of many diverse people in the organization (Tichy & Devanna, 1986). The vision is seldom created in a single moment of revelation, but instead it takes shape during a lengthy process of exploration, discussion, and refinement of ideas. The following guidelines for developing visions (see summary in Table 5-2) are based on leadership theories, empirical research, and practitioner insights (e.g., Conger, 1989; Kotter, 1996; Kouzes & Posner, 1987; Nadler et al., 1995; Nanus, 1992; Peters, 1987; Peters & Austin, 1985; Strange & Mumford, 2005; Tichy & Devanna, 1986; Trice & Beyer, 1993; Zaccaro & Banks, 2004).

- **Involve key stakeholders.**

A single leader is unlikely to have the knowledge needed to develop a vision that will appeal to all the stakeholders whose support is necessary to accomplish major organizational change. Even when the initial ideas for a vision originate with the leader, it is desirable to involve key stakeholders in refining these ideas into a vision with widespread appeal. Key stakeholders may include owners, executives, other members of the organization, customers, investors, joint venture partners, and labor unions.

Often, the best place to begin is with senior executives, the group most likely to have the broad perspective and knowledge necessary to understand the need for change. An important source of

TABLE 5-2 Guidelines for Formulating a Vision

- Involve key stakeholders.
- Identify shared values and ideals.
- Identify strategic objectives with wide appeal.
- Identify relevant elements in the old ideology.
- Link the vision to core competencies and prior achievements.
- Continually assess and refine the vision.

ideas for a vision is to discuss beliefs and assumptions about the determinants of performance for the organization and changes that will affect future performance. It is easier to develop an ambitious but realistic vision for the organization if the key executives have accurate shared beliefs about the determinants of company performance and opportunities for the future. A shared "mental model" is useful both for developing a credible vision and for strategic planning (see Chapter 12).

Executives are not the only stakeholders to consult when formulating a vision. It is also essential to understand the values, hopes, and aspirations of other people in the organization. Gaining this insight can be difficult if people are unable or reluctant to explain what is really important to them. Kouzes and Posner (1987, p. 115) described how leaders may learn about the needs and values of followers:

> Leaders find the common thread that weaves together the fabric of human needs into a colorful tapestry. They seek out the brewing consensus among those they would lead. In order to do this, they develop a deep understanding of the collective yearnings. They listen carefully for quiet whisperings in dark corners. They attend to the subtle cues. They sniff the air to get the scent. They watch the faces. They get a sense of what people want, what they value, what they dream about.

- **Identify shared values and ideals.**

The appeal of a vision depends on its ideological content as well as on its relevance for the challenges facing the organization. If the vision embodies shared values and ideals for most members of the organization, it is more likely to elicit their commitment. Thus, another useful procedure is to identify and understand what values and ideals can be incorporated in the vision. Discovery of shared values often requires considerable time and effort, and there is no guarantee of success. If serious disagreement exists about the essential qualities for an ideal organization, then it will be difficult to find a vision that transcends these differences.

One approach for identifying shared values and ideals is to ask people to describe what the best possible future would look like for the organization. One technique suggested by Tichy and Devanna (1986) is to ask executives to write a magazine article in journalistic style describing the organization as they would like it to be at a specified time in the future. A variation of this technique is a role-play in which half of the executives (the "reporters") interview the remaining executives and ask them to describe how they would like the organization to be in 10 years. Still another technique is to have people describe a fictitious organization that would be able to compete effectively with the leading companies in a specified market. The group then determines how the current organization differs from the fictitious one and looks for ways to close the gaps.

- **Identify strategic objectives with wide appeal.**

It is sometimes easier to get agreement on strategic objectives than on a more elaborate vision, and a group discussion of objectives can provide insight about values and ideals to include in a vision. The first step is to ask people to identify specific performance objectives that are challenging and relevant to the mission of the organization. Then ask people to discuss the relative importance of the various objectives and the reasons why an objective is important. Look for shared values and ideals that can become the basis for a vision with wide appeal.

- **Identify relevant elements in the old ideology.**

Even when radical change is necessary in an organization, some elements in the current ideology may be worthy of preservation. Look for values and ideals that will continue to be relevant for the organization in the foreseeable future. Sometimes traditional values that were subverted or ignored can serve as the basis for a new vision, as in the following example:

> A manufacturing company that once had a reputation for making the best products in the industry decided to pursue a strategy of cost reduction to compete with the inexpensive products of foreign competitors. The strategy was not successful. After several years of declining sales the company lost its dominant position in the market and its products were perceived to be of inferior quality. Major changes were made to implement a new strategy that emphasized quality and innovation rather than low price. The strategy was justified as a return to key values from the glorious early years of the firm.

- **Link the vision to core competencies and prior achievements.**

A successful vision must be credible. People will be skeptical about a vision that promises too much and seems impossible to attain. Leaders face a difficult task in crafting a vision that is both challenging and believable. Lofty visions often require innovative strategies, and untested strategies are risky and difficult to assess. In the absence of a tested strategy, people need a basis for believing the vision is attainable. One way to build follower optimism about the vision is to link it to their ability to collectively solve problems and overcome difficult obstacles. If people have been successful in past efforts to accomplish difficult objectives, the leader can use these successes to build confidence in their ability to do it again.

> When President Kennedy first articulated his visionary objective to land a man on the moon by the end of the decade, only about 15 percent of the necessary technology and procedures had been developed, and it was not evident that so many difficult things could be done successfully in such a short time. However, the availability of scientists and engineers with the necessary expertise and confidence to tackle these formidable problems made the vision more credible. The objective was successfully achieved in less time than initially expected.

- **Continually assess and refine the vision.**

A successful vision is likely to evolve over time. As strategies to achieve the vision are implemented, people can learn more about what is feasible and what is not. As progress is made toward achieving the vision, new possibilities may be discovered, and objectives that seemed unrealistic may suddenly become attainable. Although some continuity in the vision is desirable, it is helpful to keep looking for ways to make the vision more appealing and credible (e.g., new metaphors, slogans, and symbols that capture the essence of the vision). The development of a vision is an interactive, circular process, not a simple, linear progression from vision to strategy to action. A review of strategy may provide the ideas for a new vision, and information about changing conditions may require major revisions rather than just minor adjustments.

Collective Learning and Innovation

The environment of most organizations is becoming increasingly dynamic and competitive. Competition is becoming more intense, customer expectations are rising, less time is available to develop and market new products and services, and they become obsolete sooner. To succeed in this turbulent environment, organizations need to have people at every level who are oriented toward learning and continuous improvement.

Organizational learning involves acquiring and using new knowledge. The new knowledge can be created internally or acquired from outside the organization (Berson, Nemanich, Waldman, Galvin, & Keller, 2006; Nevis, Dibella, & Gould, 1995). After new knowledge is acquired, it must be conveyed to the people who need it and applied to improve the organization's products, services, and work processes (Crossan, Lane, & White, 1999; Hannah & Lester, 2009). How knowledge is acquired, disseminated, and applied will be described in more detail in this part of the chapter.

Internal Creation of New Knowledge

Many organizations have formal subunits with primary responsibility for research and development of new products and services, and some organizations also have subunits with responsibility for continually assessing and improving work processes. These dedicated subunits can be an important source of innovation in organizations, but they are not the only internal source; many important innovations are developed informally by employees apart from their regular job activities. Efforts to help employees find better ways to do the work or to make improvements in products usually require only a small investment of resources in the developmental stage.

Many good ideas die before having a chance to be tested, because it is not possible to gain approval for them in an organization where traditional ways of doing things are favored, or where there is no good process to determine the value of new ideas. Sometimes important discoveries are made in an organization, but their potential value is not recognized, as shown in the following example about Xerox (Finkelstein, 2003; Smith & Alexander, 1988):

> Several major discoveries were made at the Palo Alto Research Center, including the graphic user interface, the mouse, the Ethernet, and the laser printer. Except for the laser printer, executives at Xerox failed to recognize the potential value of these discoveries. Microsoft and Apple would eventually earn billions of dollars from the sale of products that incorporated the unused discoveries. According to Steve Jobs, the CEO of Apple, Xerox missed the opportunity to become the dominant company in the computer industry.

To facilitate the development and approval of innovations, it is helpful to have sponsors or champions who will shepherd new ideas through the long and tedious review and approval process in organizations. Also important is an impartial but systematic process for reviewing and assessing new ideas suggested by individual employees or teams. Examples include "venture boards" or "innovation teams" to identify high-potential ideas and determine which ideas will receive additional funding and development (Pryor & Shays, 1993).

External Acquisition of New Knowledge

An important leadership function is to encourage and facilitate external acquisition of relevant knowledge. New ideas and knowledge may also be acquired from a variety of outside sources, including: publications on results of applied research, books or articles describing practitioner experiences, and observation of best practices used elsewhere. Other sources include purchasing the right to use specific knowledge from another organization, getting advice from consultants who have relevant expertise, hiring outsiders with special expertise, entering joint ventures with another organization to increase learning opportunities, and acquiring another organization that has relevant expertise and patents.

The process of examining best practices used in successful organizations is sometimes called "benchmarking" (Camp, 1989), and an example is provided by Main (1992):

> The benchmarking manager for Xerox read an article about the success of L.L.Bean, the catalog retailer, in filling customer orders quickly and accurately. He organized a fact-finding visit to the headquarters office of L.L.Bean in Freeport, Maine. The team found that good planning and software support helped to make Bean three times faster than Xerox in filling small orders. The team used this knowledge to help redesign the procedures used at Xerox warehouses, resulting in significant improvements.

Another example is provided by Larsen and Turbo:

> Larsen and Turbo, an Indian multinational conglomerate company has benchmarked against global players like: M/s Bechtel Coporation, which is one the world's largest engineering-construction firms and M/s Fluor Daniel, one of the world's largest, publicly owned engineering, procurement, construction, and maintenance services organizations. The benchmarking activity was carried out with the help of M/s Mckinsey to boost the skill levels of its human resources.

Imitating the best practices of others can be beneficial, but it is essential to evaluate their relevance before adopting them. It is also important to remember that imitation alone seldom provides much of a competitive advantage. Rather than simply copying what others are doing, it is usually better to improve their best practices, and to invent new approaches not yet discovered by competitors.

Integrating Exploration and Exploitation Learning Processes

When describing the objectives of collective learning in organizations, a distinction is often made between exploration and exploitation (Berson et al., 2006; Benner & Tushman, 2003; March, 1991; Sariol & Abebe, 2017). Exploration involves finding innovative new products, services, processes, or technology, whereas exploitation involves learning how to make incremental improvements in existing products, services, or processes. Both learning processes are necessary in organizations, and their relative importance will depend on the competitive strategy and the pace of change in the external environment (e.g., He & Wong, 2003; O'Reilly & Tushman, 2004; O'Reilly & Tushman, 2013; Tushman & O'Reilly, 1996). There is growing evidence that successful firms are able to develop new products and services (involving exploration) simultaneously with delivery of existing ones in an efficient way (which involves exploitation).

A difficult challenge for leaders is how to gain the benefits of both learning processes and avoid adverse side effects (Miller, 1990; Sariol & Abebe, 2017; Yukl & Lepsinger, 2004). Too much emphasis on exploration may result in excessive costs for acquiring new knowledge (e.g., for R&D), but too much emphasis on exploitation can reduce flexibility and discourage development of new products and services. Introducing new products too quickly can reduce the profitability of established products that are still selling well and paying off their developmental costs, but waiting too long can result in the loss of competitive advantage. Effective leaders balance the trade-offs and integrate the processes in a way that is appropriate for the situation.

Effective leaders also recognize opportunities for integrating the two types of learning across multiple organizational levels (Berson et al., 2006). For example, methods usually associated with exploitation by senior management at the strategic level can be used to reduce costs for expensive forms of exploration, such as research by teams of scientists in the pharmaceutical industry. Methods usually associated with exploration such as technological breakthroughs can be used to redesign employee jobs and gain efficiencies in established processes to reduce the cost of traditional products and services.

Knowledge Diffusion and Application

New knowledge is of little value unless it is made available to people who need it and is used by them. Some organizations are successful at discovering knowledge, but fail to apply it effectively (Ferlie, Fitzgerald, Wood, & Hawkins, 2005; Hansen, Mors, & Løvås, 2005). One example is provided by a multinational company that established a "center of marketing excellence" in its Australian operations (Ulrich, Jick, & Von Glinow, 1993). Successful pilot programs increased market share by 25 percent, but the lessons learned never reached the European and U.S. divisions, where the benefits would have been even greater. Similar examples can be found in many organizations.

Secrecy is the enemy of learning, and easy access to information about the organization's operations, including problems and failures, facilitates learning. There are several different approaches to encourage and facilitate knowledge sharing in organizations (Earl, 2001). An increasing number of companies have sophisticated information systems to facilitate easy access by employees to relevant information. An employee with a difficult task can discover how other people in the organization handled a similar task in the past, and employees can interact with each other to get advice and support about common problems.

A more formalized mechanism for translating learning into practice is to describe best practices and effective procedures in written manuals or computer files. For example, when the U.S. Army discovers an effective way to conduct some type of operation, it is translated into doctrine to guide others who will be performing the same operation. Formal doctrine can be useful, but it is not as flexible or easily updated as posting best practices and lessons learned on an interactive network. Moreover, formal doctrine often ends up being used in a way that discourages subsequent learning and innovation.

Another approach for diffusing new knowledge in an organization is a special-purpose conference to facilitate sharing of new knowledge and ideas among the subunits of an organization. General Electric conducts "best practice" workshops to encourage sharing of ideas among managers. A large government agency holds a conference each year to enable participants from different facilities to present new ideas and informally discuss how to improve service quality.

Seminars and workshops can be used to teach people how to perform new activities or use new technology. When it is not feasible for people to attend a conference or workshop, a team of experts can be dispatched to different worksites to show people how to use new procedures. An alternative approach is to transfer individuals with new knowledge to other units, or assign them on a temporary basis to teach others. A person who has participated in a successful change can serve as a catalyst and consultant for change in another unit.

Learning Organizations

All organizations learn things, but some do it much better than others. The term learning organization has been used to describe organizations that learn rapidly and use the knowledge to become more effective (e.g., Crossan et al., 1999; Fiol & Lyles, 1985; Hannah & Lester, 2009; Huber, 1991; Levitt & March, 1988). In these organizations, the values of learning, innovation, experimentation, flexibility, and initiative are firmly embedded in the culture of the organization (Baer & Frese, 2003; Berson et al., 2006; Hogan & Coote, 2014; James, 2002; Kotter & Heskett, 1992; Miron, Erez, & Naveh, 2004; Popper & Lipshitz, 1998). Resources are invested in promoting learning, knowledge is made easily available to anyone who needs it, and people are encouraged to apply it to their work. The advantage of a learning culture is shown by the way a hospital responded to a physicians' strike (Meyer, 1982):

> The hospital that adapted most successfully had a culture in which innovation, professional autonomy, and entrepreneurial activity were strong values. The administrator anticipated the strike and asked a task force to develop scenarios describing how it would affect the hospital. Supervisors were asked to read the scenarios and develop contingency plans. When the strike actually occurred, the hospital was able to adapt quickly and continue making profits, despite a drastic drop in the number of patients. When the strike ended, the hospital was able to re-adapt quickly. In the process the hospital even discovered some new ways to cut operating costs.

Most organizations fall short of this ideal. A major obstacle is the common belief that top management should have most of the responsibility for leading change and innovation. This belief encourages a top-down approach to innovation, rather than a collaborative approach that includes emergent processes. Many CEOs are too insulated to recognize opportunities and threats immediately, and bottom-up initiatives help an organization to be more flexible and adaptive. Top management can help to avoid or overcome this obstacle by implementing systems and programs that support local initiatives and emergent processes of learning and innovation. People at all levels should be empowered to deal with problems and find better ways of doing the work. Innovation programs should nurture ideas and support changes initiated by people at lower levels in the organization. The process of discovery and diffusion of knowledge can be accelerated by encouraging accurate communication, implementing appropriate information systems, allowing greater access to information, and encouraging people to use social networks to increase their access to relevant information and ideas. All leaders in the organization need to communicate and model values relevant for a learning culture. Finally, the appraisal and compensation system should provide equitable rewards for knowledge creation, sharing, and application (Bartol & Srivastava, 2002; Yukl, 2009).

Guidelines for Enhancing Learning and Innovation

Leaders at all levels can help to create conditions favorable to learning and innovation. The following guidelines (see Table 5-3) are based on theory, research findings, and practitioner insights (e.g., Berson et al., 2006; Cavaleri & Fearon, 1996; Chaston, Badger, Mangles, & Sadler-Smith, 2001; Garvin, 1993; Hannah & Lester, 2009; Hogan & Coote, 2014; James, 2002; Madsen & Desai, 2010; McGill, Slocum, & Lei, 1993; Nadler et al., 1995; Sabherwal & Becerra-Fernandez, 2003; Schein, 1993; Senge, 1990; Ulrich et al., 1993; Vera & Crossan, 2004; Yeung, Ulrich, Nason, & Von Glinow, 1999; Yukl, 2009; Zhang & Bartol, 2010).

TABLE 5-3 Guidelines for Increasing Learning and Innovation

- Recruit talented, creative people and empower them to be innovative.
- Encourage appreciation for flexibility and innovation.
- Encourage and facilitate learning by individuals and teams.
- Help people improve their mental models.
- Evaluate new ideas with small-scale experiments.
- Leverage learning from surprises and failures.
- Encourage and facilitate sharing of knowledge and ideas.
- Preserve past learning and ensure continued use of relevant knowledge.
- Set innovation goals.
- Reward entrepreneurial behavior.

- **Recruit talented, creative people and empower them to be innovative.**

New and better ways to accomplish work unit objectives are more likely to be found by people who are talented and creative. One way for a leader to facilitate innovation is to recruit people who have the skills and enthusiasm to develop new ideas, and then empower them to pursue these ideas by providing necessary time and resources. An example of this type of leadership is provided by Anne Sweeney (Bisoux, 2006):

> Sweeney is the president of Disney-ABC Television Group and one of the most powerful and successful women in business. Her achievements include the successful creation of new ventures such as Nickelodeon. Sweeney has a passion for innovation and uses her leadership skills to encourage and facilitate change. She hires people who are talented, enthusiastic about their work, and unafraid of change. She expects them to serve as internal entrepreneurs to keep the company relevant, and she gives them the autonomy they need to be creative.

- **Encourage appreciation for flexibility and innovation.**

Major change will be more acceptable and less disruptive if people develop pride and confidence in their capacity to adapt and learn. Confident people are more likely to view change as an exciting challenge rather than an unpleasant burden. To develop an appreciation for flexibility and adaptation, encourage people to view all practices as temporary. Each activity should be examined periodically to determine whether it is still needed and how it can be improved or eliminated. Encourage subordinates and peers to question traditional assumptions about the work and to "think outside the box" when solving problems. Encourage people to apply creative ideas for improving work processes. Encourage and support relevant learning practices and quality improvement programs (e.g., benchmarking, Six Sigma, TQM, quality circles).

- **Encourage and facilitate learning by individuals and teams.**

Organizations can learn only when individual members of the organization are learning (Senge, 1990). More individual learning will occur if the organization has strong cultural values for personal development and lifelong education, and it provides training and development programs to help individuals learn new skills (see Chapter 15). Opportunities for learning are also increased by empowering individuals or teams to try new and innovative approaches for doing the work. Leaders should keep subordinates informed about relevant learning opportunities (e.g., workshops, training programs, college courses) and make it easier for them to pursue these opportunities (e.g., allowing time and providing education subsidies). Leaders can also encourage and facilitate collective learning in teams by using procedures such as after-activity reviews (see Chapter 11). Finally, leaders can provide tangible rewards to encourage individuals to acquire new knowledge and apply it to improve their job performance.

- **Help people improve their mental models.**

People have conscious beliefs and implicit assumptions about the causes of performance and the source of problems. These "mental models" influence how they interpret events and information about the effects of decisions and actions (Cannon-Bowers, Salas, & Converse, 1993; Senge, 1990; Gary & Wood, 2016; Mumford & Strange, 2002). Leaders can help people improve their mental models about the way things work in organizations and the reasons for success or failure. One form of collective learning is to analyze feedback about prior performance. How such feedback is interpreted depends on what assumptions are made about the causal relationships among variables and how much time is necessary for decisions and actions to have visible effects. A poor mental model about causal relationships is likely to result in inaccurate interpretation of performance feedback. For collective learning to be successful, team members must be able to develop a shared mental model that is accurate and use it to interpret performance feedback. As noted earlier in this chapter, to develop a better understanding of complex problems often requires systems thinking. By helping people to understand complex systems, a leader can increase their ability to learn and solve problems. In this way, the leader also helps people understand that they are not powerless and can collectively influence events in the organization.

- **Evaluate new ideas with small-scale experiments.**

One way to assess the feasibility of new ideas is to test them on a small scale. In recent years, the trend has been for more organizations to use small experiments and controlled tests to facilitate learning. A well-known example of an organization with an experimental orientation is Walmart, which regularly conducts hundreds of tests in its stores on sales promotions, displays, and improving customer service. Small-scale experiments provide an opportunity to try out new ideas without the risks entailed by major change programs. People who are skeptical about a controversial new approach may be willing to experiment on a small scale to evaluate it. The amount of learning that results from an experiment depends on how well it is designed and executed. Even a simple experiment can provide useful information. However, experiments do not always produce useful knowledge, and the results may even be misleading. Careful planning is needed to ensure that a controlled test yields clear, meaningful results.

- **Leverage learning from surprises and failures.**

Surprises usually provide a good opportunity for learning. Things that turn out just as expected confirm existing theories or assumptions but do not provide new insights. Many people tend to discount or ignore unexpected information that does not fit their theories or assumptions about how things work. Some of the most important scientific discoveries resulted from investigating unexpected "accidents" or "anomalies" that would be overlooked by people only interested in confirming prior beliefs or favorite theories. It is helpful to specify in advance what results are expected from an activity or change and the underlying assumptions on which the prediction is based. Otherwise, instead of using unexpected results to reevaluate the model, people are more likely to overlook them. Make specific predictions and the reasons for them a regular part of the planning process, and make evaluation of outcomes in relation to predictions a regular part of the review process for activities. Use unexpected failures as an opportunity to learn more about a strategy or process, rather than looking for someone to blame for them.

- **Encourage and facilitate sharing of knowledge and ideas.**

Leaders at all levels should facilitate the timely dissemination of new ideas and knowledge in the organization. Attend meetings with people from different subunits of the organization (or send a representative) to discuss ideas for solving common problems. Encourage subordinates to share relevant ideas and knowledge with other people in the organization who can use it to improve their own performance. Encourage subordinates to support and make use of knowledge management programs (e.g., a resource directory, databases, and groupware). Invite experts or outside consultants to inform members of the unit or team about relevant discoveries, new technology, and improved practices.

- **Preserve past learning and ensure continued use of relevant knowledge.**

A common mistake is to assume that once something has been learned in an organization it remains in the "organizational memory." However, knowledge that is not being used may not be retained in an accessible form, and knowledge that resides only in the heads of individuals may be lost when they leave the organization. Sometimes an organization implements best practices for avoiding serious problems, but the practices are later abandoned and the organization eventually has a disaster that could have been prevented (Kletz, 1993). It is important for leaders to ensure that useful knowledge is preserved and relevant practices continue to be used. Advances in the technology for information processing have made it easier to find relevant knowledge quickly, while still preserving the security of proprietary knowledge.

- **Set innovation goals.**

The pressure of meeting normal task deadlines tends to leave little time for reflective thinking about ways to make things better. A leader should encourage entrepreneurial activity and help employees find the time to pursue their ideas for new or improved products and processes. One way to increase the number of creative ideas is to set innovation goals for individuals or teams. A special meeting is scheduled on a monthly or quarterly basis to discuss these ideas and review progress. Goals can also be set for the application of ideas to improve products and work processes. For example, some companies set a goal to have new products or services (e.g., those introduced within the last three years) account for a substantial percentage of sales each year.

- **Reward entrepreneurial behavior.**

Employees who invent new products or suggest ways to improve existing products and processes should receive appropriate recognition and equitable rewards. The support and cooperation of many people are needed to get new ideas accepted and implemented effectively in an organization. It is essential to provide recognition and equitable rewards not only to the individuals or teams who contribute creative ideas, but also to individuals who serve as sponsors, advocates, and champions for innovations.

Summary

One of the most important and difficult leadership responsibilities is to guide and facilitate the process of making a major change in an organization. A major change may involve a variety of different objectives, including attitudes, roles, technology, competitive strategy, economics, and people. The change process can be described as having different stages, such as unfreezing, changing, and refreezing. Moving too quickly through the stages can endanger the success of a change effort. People typically transit through a series of emotional stages as they adjust to the need for a drastic change in their lives. Understanding each of these change processes helps leaders guide and facilitate change.

A major change is unlikely to be successful unless it is based on an adequate diagnosis of the problem or opportunity that was the reason for making it. This diagnosis should include systems thinking about complex relationships, multiple causes and outcomes, delayed effects, cyclical causality, and the potential for unintended consequences. When planning a major change, it is also desirable to anticipate likely resistance and plan how to avoid or resolve it. There are many reasons for resisting, and resistance should be viewed as a normal defensive response, not as a character weakness or a sign of ignorance.

People are more likely to support radical change if they have a vision of a better future that is attractive enough to justify the sacrifices and hardships the change will require. To be inspiring, the vision must include strong ideological content that appeals to shared values and ideals concerning customers, employees, and the mission of the organization. The vision can be created in an interactive process involving key stakeholders.

A leader can do many things to facilitate the successful implementation of change. Political actions include identifying likely supporters and opponents, creating a coalition to approve changes, forming teams to guide the implementation of changes, filling key positions with competent change agents, making symbolic changes that affect the work, and monitoring the progress of change to detect problems that require attention. People-oriented actions include creating a sense of urgency, articulating a clear vision of the likely benefits, preparing people for change, helping them cope with change, providing opportunities for early successes, keeping people informed, demonstrating continued commitment to the change program, and empowering people to help plan and implement change.

It is important for leaders to influence the acquisition, retention, and application of relevant knowledge that can provide a competitive advantage. Leaders can help to create the conditions favorable to organizational learning and an appropriate balance of exploration and exploitation. New knowledge and innovative ideas can be discovered through reflection, research, and systematic learning activities, or acquired externally by imitation, purchase of expertise, or participation in joint ventures. The discovery of new knowledge is of little use unless it is disseminated to people who need it and used to improve products, services, and processes. Individual leaders can do many things to encourage and facilitate learning and innovation in their work unit or organization.

Review and Discussion Questions

1. What are the major reasons for resistance to change?
2. What are the process theories of change and how are they useful?
3. What are the desirable characteristics for a vision?
4. What are some guidelines for developing a compelling vision?
5. What are some reasons why efforts to change organizations often fail?
6. What are some guidelines to help leaders implement change?
7. What is a learning organization and what kind of learning occurs in it?
8. How can leaders increase collective learning and innovation?

Key Terms

benchmarking
change agents
core competencies
developmental change
diffusion of knowledge
exploitation
exploration
innovation
learning organization
mental models
mission statement
organizational cynicism about change
organizational diagnosis
resistance to change
stakeholders
symbolic changes
systems dynamics
transformational change
transitional change
value statement
vision

PERSONAL REFLECTION

Think about a time when an organization that you currently or previously belonged to embarked on a planned change effort. How successful was the change effort? Why did you support or resist the change effort?

CASE

Universals Stationery and Office Products

Universals Stationery and Office Products (USOP) is an established stationery and office supplies manufacturing company that is facing distribution challenges from the new superstores and discount merchandisers that were spreading rapidly. These growing superstores were changing the traditional distribution channels that used to be dominated by wholesalers and small retail stores. They were forcing the traditional manufacturers to improve their customer service. New companies in office supplies business were willing to cut prices and make use of new technology-enabled processes that the superstores favoured, such as electronic ordering and billing. Due to such growing trends, traditionally operated companies like USOP were losing their market share and their profits were on a decline.

Realizing the need of the hour, Gautam Prasad, the CEO of USOP created a new position of director of information systems Gautam Prasad. Dheeraj Pandey was appointed to the position. During the discussion of Dheeraj's job objectives and responsibilities, Gautam clearly informed his expectation on speeding up the order processing and improving customer service. Knowing that the company's current order processing system was obsolete, Dheeraj decided to embrace technology and prepared a plan to automate the system. He took Gautam's approval for this purpose and purchased new computer workstations and a software package to support it. The software was meant to allow the customers to order electronically. This, Dheeraj believed, would improve order processing, billing and inventory control. However, the equipment and software kept waiting to be used, even months after their arrival. This was because of the non-consensus of the managers from sales, production, accounting, shipping, and customer service, regarding the requirements of the new system, that was subject to a go-ahead from all the managers.

Since these managers happens to be Gautam's peers, he had no direct authority over them. So, even though he encouraged them to cooperate, their meetings would invariably end up in heated arguments and accusations regarding who was responsible for the company's problems. Some even questioned the need for such an expensive new system. Meanwhile, Gautam was growing impatient due to the lack of progress. He told Dheeraj about his intention to see positive results after having spent a fortune on purchasing the new technology and expected the latter to figure out a way to resolve the issue, irrespective of the present hurdles.

Thus, Dheeraj decided that it was time to take a different approach. He investigated the probable issues that caused delays in processing and filling of orders. He asked his staff to map the workflow from the time orders were received to the time the filled orders were shipped. As suspected, a lot of unrequired activities were responsible for the bottlenecks that had been created. Removal of these would help speed up the process. This problem did not pertain to any one function but extended across functional boundaries and so changes needed to be made in all departments.

These preliminary results were shown to Gautam, who seemed to be on board with the need for drastic improvements, and so, authorized Dheeraj to start reengineering the process. Despite Gautam's support, Dheeraj knew that in order for these changes to be successful, widespread commitment would be required. To ensure this Dheeraj met with the managers of all the departments and sought their assistance in forming cross-functional task forces. Although he knew that one task force would be sufficient for the change process, he decided to involve as many people as possible, so that they would understand and support the process.

A consultant was hired to advise and assist the task force in their work. Each task force was responsible for examining a different aspect of the problem—starting from analyzing the process, then meeting key customers to understand their requirement and expectations and finally visiting other companies to study how they processed orders more efficiently. The seriousness of the problems faced by USOP was realized only when all the departments started working together to understand the system. This exercise helped them keep their biases aside, to come together and work towards finding ways to improve efficiency and serve the customers better. Each task force came up with their own set of recommendations to the steering committee that was made up of Dheeraj and the various department managers.

Gautam would also attend all these meetings in order to stress their importance. Whenever the managers were at loggerheads and opposed a change, everyone turned to Gautam to take the final call, who would invariably support the unanimous suggestions made by the task forces. As a result of these efforts, the company was able to get rid of the bottlenecks that hampered and slowed down the order processing previously. Now, the average number of days required to complete an order was reduced to almost half. Orders were now processed electronically, as a result of which, errors in the billing process were eliminated as well. USOP employees discovered how their efforts could actually bring about positive changes for the company—in fact, many of them volunteered to serve as teams that would continue to look for ways to improve quality and customer service.

—*Written by* Nishant Uppal

Questions

1. Why did Dheeraj fail in his first attempt to implement change?
2. Identify subsequent actions by Dheeraj that were more effective for implementing change in the organization.
3. Evaluate the change leadership provided by the CEO.

CASE

Ready Foods Company

Ready Foods is a regional packaged food company that makes and sells food products in supermarkets. The company's most popular brands have traditionally been nonperishable foods that are easy to prepare, often with little regard for nutritional value. For the last 20 years, these brands have made the company highly profitable and its employees have become accustomed to big paychecks and generous benefits, including a three-week annual paid holiday, a well-funded retirement program, and college tuition reimbursement for children of employees. However, in recent years, company sales and profits have declined because consumer preferences have shifted to favor fresher, healthier foods not currently provided by the company.

Bruce Berry has been the CEO of the company for five years, and the shift in customer preferences to healthier options has been his major management problem. Over the past few years Bruce has made incremental changes to the company's products, but none of these changes have reduced the decline in sales and profits. He knew that for the company to survive, it would be necessary in the coming year to make more significant changes in the company's products and marketing strategy.

After considerable marketing research, Bruce determined that the company needed to expand its offerings and invest in a program to develop and offer fresh, organic foods to support the healthier lifestyle of many potential customers. However, this program would require funds that would not be available as the company's profits continued to decline. Bruce did not like the idea of employee layoffs as a means of securing the necessary funds, and he decided instead to cut some employee benefits that seemed excessive and unnecessary for his type of company. He assumed that most employees would be willing to lose these benefits to enable the company to pay for the new fresh foods program without having to lay off any employees. However, he did not try to explain the need for his decision or seek the suggestions and support of employees. Bruce believed that he had the responsibility and authority to make this type of decision, and that it was why he was paid more than most CEOs of similar companies.

When the changes were announced, many employees were very upset that their benefits were being cut. Most employees believed the fresh foods program was unnecessary. They saw it as an overreaction to a temporary change in customer preferences, and they believed company sales and profits would recover to the levels achieved for many years without such a program. Many employees believed the cut in benefits was excessive and felt like the company did not value their years of service. This resentment caused some employees to seek employment elsewhere, and others found ways to delay the development and implementation of the fresh foods program. It took months to find qualified replacements for the employees who left and to regain employee trust. Meanwhile, the lack of healthier options continued to hurt company performance.

—*Written by* Daniel P. Gullifor and William L. Gardner

Questions

1. Why did Bruce fail to successfully implement the changes?
2. What could Bruce have done differently to plan and implement the new program more successfully?

Power and Influence Tactics

Learning Objectives

After studying this chapter, you should be able to:

- Understand how power is acquired or lost in organizations.
- Understand how power is related to leadership effectiveness.
- Understand how to use power effectively.
- Understand the different types of influence tactics.
- Understand effective ways to use the influence tactics.

Introduction

Influence is the essence of leadership. To be effective as a leader, it is necessary to influence people to carry out requests, support proposals, and implement decisions. In large organizations, the effectiveness of managers depends on influence over superiors and peers as well as influence over subordinates.

The concept of power is useful for understanding how people are able to influence each other in organizations (Mintzberg, 1983; Pfeffer, 1981, 1992). However, the term has been used in different ways by different writers, and the differences can create confusion. In the first part of this chapter, power is defined, different sources and types of power are described, and the way power is gained or lost is described. The implications of power for leadership effectiveness are explained, and guidelines for using power effectively are provided.

The second part of the chapter explains how power is related to a leader's influence behavior. Different types of influence behavior are described, and research on effects of this behavior is reviewed. The chapter ends with guidelines for using eleven proactive influence tactics.

Sources of Power

Power involves the capacity of one party (the "agent") to influence another party (the "target"), but this influence has been described and measured in several different ways. The term may refer to the agent's influence over a single target person, or over multiple target persons.

Sometimes the term refers to potential influence over things or events as well as attitudes and behavior. Sometimes the agent is a group or organization rather than an individual. Sometimes power is defined in relative rather than absolute terms, in which case it means the extent to which the agent has more influence over the target than the target has over the agent.

It is difficult to describe the power of an agent without specifying the target person(s) and influence objectives. An agent will have more power over some people than over others and more influence for some types of objectives than for others. Furthermore, power is a dynamic variable that changes as conditions change. How power is used and the outcomes of influence attempts can increase or reduce an agent's subsequent power. In this book, the term power is defined as the potential of an individual agent to influence the behavior or attitudes of one or more designated target persons at a given point in time.

Position and Personal Power

Efforts to classify types of power usually involve differences in the source or basis for potential influence over another person or event. The most general way to classify power sources is the distinction between position power and personal power (Bass, 1960; Etzioni, 1961; Rahim, 1988; Yukl & Falbe, 1991). These broadly defined categories involve power sources that are either inherent in an agent's position in the organization, or that involve attributes of the agent and the agent–target relationship. Position power includes potential influence derived from legitimate authority to make important decisions, control over the use of resources and access to information, and control over the use of rewards and punishments. Personal power includes potential influence derived from agent expertise and friendship with the target person. The two broad power constructs are less useful than specific types of power, such as the ones identified in the early power research by French and Raven (1959). Six specific types of power are described in this section of the chapter.

Legitimate Power

Legitimate power is based on formal authority, and it involves the rights, prerogatives, obligations, and duties associated with a particular position in an organization. A leader's authority usually includes the right to make decisions and requests consistent with this authority. For example, a manager usually has the legitimate right to establish work rules and give work assignments to subordinates. Authority also involves the right to exercise control over things, such as money, resources, equipment, and materials, and this control is another source of power. The scope of authority for the leader is the range of requests that can properly be made and the range of actions that can properly be taken. The scope of authority is much greater for some managers than for others, and it depends in large part on the influence needed to accomplish role requirements and organizational objectives (Barnard, 1952).

The influence processes associated with legitimate power are complex. Some theorists emphasize the downward flow of authority from owners and top management, but the potential influence derived from authority depends as much on the consent of the governed as on the ownership and control of property (Jacobs, 1970). Members of an organization usually agree to comply with rules and directions from leaders in return for the benefits of membership. However, this agreement is usually an implicit mutual understanding rather than an explicit formal contract.

Compliance with legitimate rules and requests is more likely for members who identify with the organization and are loyal to it. Compliance is also more likely for members who have an internalized value that it is proper to obey authority figures, show respect for the law, and follow tradition. Acceptance of authority also depends on whether the agent is perceived to be a legitimate occupant of his or her leadership position. The specific procedures for selecting a leader are usually based on tradition and the provisions of a legal charter or constitution. Any deviation from the selection process considered legitimate by members will weaken a new leader's authority.

The amount of legitimate power is also related to a person's scope of authority. Higher-level managers usually have more authority than lower-level managers, and a manager's authority is usually much stronger in relation to subordinates than in relation to peers, superiors, or outsiders. However, even for a target person who is not a subordinate, the agent may have the legitimate right to make requests necessary to carry out job responsibilities, such as requests for information, supplies, support services, technical advice, and assistance in carrying out interrelated tasks.

A manager's scope of authority is usually delineated by documents such as an organization charter, a written job description, or an employment contract, but considerable ambiguity about it often remains (Davis, 1968; Reitz, 1977). People evaluate not only whether a request or order falls within a leader's scope of authority, but also whether it is consistent with the basic values, principles, and traditions of the organization or social system. The legitimacy of a request may be questioned if it contradicts basic values of the organization or the larger society to which members of the organization belong. For example, soldiers may disobey an order to shoot everyone in a village that has aided insurgents, because the soldiers perceive this use of excessive force to be contrary to basic human rights.

Reward Power

Reward power is the perception by the target person that an agent can provide important resources and rewards desired by the target person. Reward power stems in part from formal authority to allocate resources and rewards, and it varies greatly across organizations and from one type of management position to another within the same organization. More control over scarce resources is usually authorized for high-level executives than for lower-level managers. Executives have authority to make decisions about the allocation of resources to various subunits and activities, and they have the right to review and modify resource allocation decisions made at lower levels.

Reward power depends not only on a manager's actual control over resources and rewards, but also on the target person's perception that the agent has the capacity and willingness to provide promised rewards. The target person's perception of agent reward power is more important than the agent's actual control over rewards. Sometimes reward power can influence people even when the agent makes no overt influence attempt. People are likely to act more deferential and helpful toward someone with high reward power in the hopes of getting rewards in the future.

The authority relationship is an important determinant of reward power. Managers usually have much more reward power over subordinates than over peers or superiors. One form of reward power over subordinates is the authority to give pay increases, bonuses, or other economic incentives to deserving subordinates. Reward power is derived also from control over tangible benefits such as a promotion, a better job, a better work schedule, a larger operating budget, a larger expense account, and status symbols such as a larger office or a reserved parking space. Possible constraints on a manager's reward power include any formal policies or agreements that specify how rewards must be allocated.

A source of reward power in lateral relations is dependence of a peer on the agent for some types of resources, information, and assistance. Trading of favors needed to accomplish task objectives is a common form of influence among peers in organizations, and research indicates that it is important for the success of middle-level managers (Cohen & Bradford, 1989; Kaplan, 1984; Kotter, 1982; Strauss, 1962).

Upward reward power of subordinates over their boss is limited in most organizations. Few organizations provide a formal mechanism for subordinates to evaluate leaders. Nevertheless, subordinates usually have some indirect influence over the leader's reputation and prospects for a pay increase or promotion. If subordinates perform well, the reputation of their manager will usually be enhanced. Some subordinates may also have upward reward power based on their ability to acquire resources outside of the formal authority system of the organization, as in the following example:

> A department chairperson was able to obtain discretionary funds from grants and contracts. Sharing these funds with the college dean who lacked discretionary funds provided more influence over decisions affecting the department.

Coercive Power

A leader's coercive power over subordinates is based on authority over punishments, which varies greatly across different types of organizations. The coercive power of military and political leaders is usually greater than that of corporate managers. Over the last two centuries, there has been a general decline in use of coercive power by most types of leaders. For example, most managers once had the right to dismiss employees for any reason they thought was justified. The captain of a ship could flog sailors who were disobedient or who failed to perform their duties diligently. Military officers could execute a soldier for desertion or failure to obey an order during combat. Nowadays, these forms of coercive power are prohibited or sharply restricted in many nations.

Lateral relations provide few opportunities for using coercion in a way that is considered legitimate. If the peer is dependent on the manager for assistance in performing important tasks, the manager may threaten to withhold cooperation if the peer fails to carry out a request. However, because mutual dependencies usually exist between managers of different subunits, coercion may elicit retaliation and escalate into a conflict that benefits neither party.

The coercive power that subordinates have over superiors varies greatly from one kind of organization to another. In many organizations, subordinates have the capacity to indirectly influence the performance evaluation of their boss. Subordinates can damage the reputation of the boss if they restrict production, sabotage operations, initiate grievances, hold demonstrations, or make complaints to higher management. In many organizations subordinates have sufficient counterpower to remove a leader or prevent the leader from being reelected. For an unpopular political leader, the ultimate form of coercive power for opponents of the leader is a violent revolution that results in the leader's imprisonment, death, or exile.

Referent Power

Referent power is derived from a target person's strong feelings of affection, admiration, and loyalty toward the agent. People are usually willing to do special favors for a friend, and they are more likely to carry out requests made by someone who is greatly admired. The strongest form of referent power involves the influence process called personal identification (Kelman, 1958).

Strong referent power will tend to increase the agent's influence over the target person even without any explicit effort by the agent to invoke this power. People are more likely to carry out requests made by an agent with strong referent power. When the relationship is characterized by a strong bond of love or friendship, the target person may do things the agent is perceived to want, even without being asked.

Referent power is an important source of influence over subordinates, peers, and superiors, but it has limitations. A request based solely on referent power should be commensurate with the extent of the target person's loyalty and friendship toward the leader. Some things are simply too much to ask, given the nature of the relationship. When requests are extreme or made too frequently, the target person may feel exploited. The result of such behavior may be to undermine the relationship and reduce the agent's referent power.

Expert Power

Task-relevant knowledge and skill are major sources of personal power in organizations. Unique knowledge about the best way to perform a task or solve an important problem provides potential influence over subordinates, peers, and superiors. However, expertise is a source of power only if others are dependent on the agent for advice. The more important a problem is to the target person, the greater the power derived by the agent from possessing the necessary expertise to solve it. Dependency is increased when the target person cannot easily find another source of advice besides the agent (Hickson, Hinings, Lee, Schneck, & Pennings, 1971; Patchen, 1974).

It is not enough for the agent to possess expertise; the target person must recognize this expertise and perceive the leader to be a reliable source of information and advice. In the short run, perceived expertise is more important than real expertise, and an agent may be able to fake it for a time by acting confident and pretending to be an expert. However, over time, as the agent's knowledge is put to the test, target perceptions of the agent's expertise are likely to become more accurate. Thus, it is essential for leaders to develop and maintain a reputation for strong expertise and credibility.

Actual expertise is gained through a continual process of education and practical experience. For example, in many professions it is important to keep informed about new developments by reading technical publications and attending workshops and seminars. Evidence of expertise can be displayed in the forms of diplomas, licenses, and awards. However, the most convincing way to demonstrate expertise is by solving important problems, making good decisions, providing sound advice, and successfully completing challenging but highly visible projects. An extreme tactic is to intentionally but covertly precipitate crises just to demonstrate the ability to deal with them (Goldner, 1970; Pfeffer, 1977a).

Specialized knowledge and technical skill will remain a source of power only as long as dependence on the person who possesses them continues. If a problem is permanently solved or others learn how to solve it by themselves, the agent's expertise is reduced. Thus, people sometimes try to protect their expert power by keeping procedures and techniques shrouded in secrecy, by using technical jargon to make the task seem more complex and mysterious, and by destroying alternate sources of information about task procedures such as written manuals, diagrams, blueprints, and computer programs (Hickson et al., 1971).

When the agent has a lot of expert power and is trusted as a reliable source of information and advice, the target person may carry out a request without receiving any explanation for it. One example is a patient who takes medicine prescribed by a doctor without knowing much about the medicine.

Another example is an investor who purchases stocks recommended by a financial consultant without knowing much about the companies that issued the stocks. However, it is rare for leaders to possess this much expert power. A leader's expertise can be used to present logical arguments and evidence that appears credible. Successful influence depends on the leader's credibility and persuasive communication skills in addition to technical knowledge and analytical ability.

Information Power

Another important source of power is control over information (Raven, 1965). This type of power involves both the access to vital information and control over its distribution to others. Managerial positions often provide opportunities to obtain information that is not directly available to subordinates or peers. Boundary role positions (e.g., marketing, purchasing, public relations) provide easier access to important information about events in the external environment of an organization. However, regardless of the type of position, useful information does not appear as if by magic, and one must actively cultivate a network of sources to provide it (Kotter, 1982).

A leader who controls the flow of vital information about outside events has an opportunity to interpret these events for subordinates and influence their perception and attitudes. Some managers distort information to persuade people that a particular course of action is desirable. Examples of information distortion include selective editing of reports and documents, biased interpretation of data, and presentation of false information. Some managers use their control over the distribution of information as a way to enhance their expert power and increase subordinate dependence. If the leader is the only one who "knows what is going on," subordinates will lack evidence to dispute the leader's claim that an unpopular decision is justified by circumstances. Control of information also makes it easier for a leader to cover up failures and mistakes that would otherwise undermine a carefully cultivated image of expertise (Pfeffer, 1977a). It has been common practice for political dictators to limit follower access to sources of information, and in recent times this practice has included limiting access to the Internet and preventing opponents from communicating any criticism of the leader's decisions.

Control over information can be a source of upward influence as well as downward and lateral influence. When subordinates have exclusive access to information needed by superiors to make decisions, this advantage can be used to influence the superior's decisions. Some subordinates actively seek this type of influence by gradually assuming more responsibility for collecting, storing, analyzing, and reporting operating information. If a leader is completely dependent on a subordinate to interpret complex analyses of operating information, the subordinate may be invited to participate directly in making decisions based on these analyses (Korda, 1975). Even when not actively participating in the decision process, a subordinate who provides most of the information for a decision has substantial influence over it (Pettigrew, 1972). Control over operating information also enables subordinates to magnify accomplishments, cover up mistakes, and exaggerate the amount of expertise and resources needed to do their work.

How Power Is Gained or Lost

Power is not a static condition; it changes over time due to changing conditions and the actions of individuals and coalitions. How power is gained or lost in organizations is described in social exchange theory, strategic contingencies theory, and theories about institutionalization of power.

Social Exchange Theory

In a group, the amount of status and power accorded to an elected or emergent leader by other members depends on the person's loyalty, demonstrated competence, and contribution to the attainment of shared objectives (Hollander, 1958, 1980; Jacobs, 1970). The contribution may involve control over scarce resources, access to vital information, or skill in dealing with critical task problems. In addition to increased status and influence, a person who has demonstrated good judgment accumulates "idiosyncrasy credits" and is allowed more latitude to deviate from nonessential group norms. The authority and position power for appointed leaders make them less dependent on subordinate evaluation of their competence, but they will also gain influence from repeated demonstration of expertise and loyalty to subordinates.

Innovation by a leader can be a double-edged sword. Success resulting from innovation leads to greater credit, but failure leads to greater blame. When a member makes an innovative proposal that proves to be successful, the group's trust in the person's expertise is confirmed, and even more status and influence may be accorded to the person. When an innovative proposal results in failure, the person is likely to lose status and influence. More power is lost if failure appears to be due to poor judgment or incompetence rather than to circumstances beyond the leader's control, or if the leader is perceived to have pursued selfish motives rather than loyally serving the group. Selfish motives and irresponsibility are more likely to be attributed to a leader who willingly deviates from group norms and traditions. The extent of a leader's loss of status and influence following failure depends in part on how serious the failure is to the group. A major disaster results in greater loss of esteem than a minor setback. Loss of status also depends on the amount of status the leader had prior to the failure. More is expected of a leader with high status, and such a leader will lose more status if perceived to be responsible for failure. Innovation is not only accepted but also expected of leaders when necessary to deal with serious problems and obstacles. A leader who fails to show initiative and deal decisively with serious problems will lose esteem and influence, just as a leader who proposes actions that are unsuccessful.

Social exchange theory emphasizes expert power and authority, and other forms of power do not receive much attention. For example, the theory does not explain how reciprocal influence processes affect a leader's reward and referent power. Most of the evidence for the theory is from research with small groups in a laboratory setting, and the results are not consistent across studies (Hollander, 1960, 1961, 1980; Stone & Cooper, 2009). Longitudinal field research in organizations would be useful to test the theory and determine if it applies to other types of power.

Strategic Contingencies Theory

Strategic contingencies theory explains how some organizational subunits gain or lose power to influence important decisions such as determination of the organization's competitive strategy and the allocation of resources to subunits and activities (Hickson et al., 1971). The theory postulates that the power of a subunit depends on three factors: (1) expertise in coping with important problems, (2) centrality of the subunit within the workflow, and (3) the extent to which the subunit's expertise is unique rather than substitutable.

All organizations must cope with critical contingencies, especially problems in the technological processes used to carry out operations and problems in adapting to unpredictable events in the environment. Success in solving important problems is a source of expert power for subunits, just as it is for individuals. The opportunity to demonstrate expertise and gain power from it is much greater for a subunit that has responsibility for dealing with critical problems. A problem is critical if it is clearly essential for the survival and prosperity of the organization.

The importance of a particular type of problem is greater as the degree of interdependence among subunits increases; other subunits cannot perform their own functions unless this type of problem is handled effectively. An individual or subunit will gain more power over important decisions if the critical functions cannot be performed by someone else or made easier by development of standard procedures. In other words, the more unique and irreplaceable the expertise required to solve critical problems, the more power is gained from possessing this expertise.

Increased expert power can result in increased legitimate power. People with valuable expertise are more likely to be appointed or elected to positions of authority in the organization. Subunits with critical expertise are likely to have more representation on boards or committees that make important decisions for the organization.

Some support for the theory was found in several studies (Brass, 1984, 1985; Hambrick, 1981; Hills & Mahoney, 1978; Hinings, Hickson, Pennings, & Schneck, 1974; Pfeffer & Moore, 1980; Pfeffer & Salancik, 1974). However, the theory fails to take into account the possibility that a powerful subunit or coalition can use its power to protect its dominant position in the organization by enhancing its perceived expertise and by denying potential rivals an opportunity to demonstrate their greater expertise.

Institutionalization of Power

The process for using political tactics to increase influence or protect existing power sources is called "institutionalization." Having power makes it easier to use political tactics for influencing important decisions in the organization. A powerful subunit can get its members appointed to key leadership positions where they will promote the subunit's objectives. When it is not possible to control key decisions directly, it may be possible to influence them indirectly by determining the procedures and criteria that will be used in making the decisions.

A powerful subunit or coalition is often able to use its power to maintain a dominant position even after their expertise is no longer critical to the organization (Pfeffer, 1981; Salancik & Pfeffer, 1977). Ambiguity about the nature of the environment and how it is changing provides an opportunity for top executives to interpret events in a biased manner, to magnify the importance of their expertise, and to justify their policies. Control over distribution of information about how well the organization is performing allows top executives to exaggerate the success of past decisions and cover up mistakes. The power of top management can also be used to deny others the resources and opportunity needed to demonstrate their superior expertise. Critics and potential rivals can be silenced, co-opted, or expelled from the organization (Pfeffer, 1981).

The evolutionary shift in power described by strategic contingencies theory can be delayed by the use of these political tactics, but if top management lacks the expertise to develop an appropriate strategy for responding to changes in the environment, the performance of the organization will decline. This process will occur much faster when the organization has strong competition for its products and services, and competitors are able to adapt more rapidly to changes in the environment. Unless the organization replaces top management, it will eventually go bankrupt or be taken over by outsiders who desire its assets.

Consequences of Power

The amount of overall power that is necessary for effective leadership and the mix of different types of power are questions that research has only begun to answer. Studies on the consequences of leader power are inconclusive, but findings indicate that effective leaders have more expert and referent power than less effective leaders, and they rely on their personal power more than on their position power (Hinkin & Schriesheim, 1989; Podsakoff & Schriesheim, 1985; Rahim, 1989; Yukl & Falbe, 1991). However, several of the power studies also indicate that it is beneficial for leaders to have at least a moderate amount of position power (e.g., Dunne, Stahl, & Melhart, 1978; Rahim & Afza, 1993; Thambain & Gemmill, 1974; Warren, 1968; Yukl & Falbe, 1991).

The amount of necessary power for a leader will depend on what needs to be accomplished and on the leader's skill in using the available power. Some leadership situations require more power than others for the leader to be effective. More influence is necessary in an organization where major changes are required, but there is strong initial opposition to the leader's proposals for change. It is especially difficult for a leader who recognizes that the organization will face a major crisis in coming years, a crisis that can be overcome only if preparations are begun immediately and short-term sacrifices are made, but the evidence of the coming crisis is not yet sufficiently strong to convince key members to support the necessary changes. In such situations, a leader will need sufficient expert and referent power to persuade people that change is necessary and desirable, or sufficient position and political power to overcome the opposition and buy time to show that the proposed changes are necessary and effective. A combination of personal and position power increases the likelihood of success, but forcing change is always risky. Maurer (1996, p. 177) describes one successful example:

> When Leonard Bernstein became conductor of the Vienna Philharmonic, he reintroduced the symphonies of Gustav Mahler. The orchestra hated Mahler; they felt his music was overblown and pompous... Although Bernstein certainly had the power to program whatever he wished, it was a risky move. Orchestras notoriously show their disdain for conductors they disrespect by engaging in malicious compliance. All the notes are correct—so no one can be reprimanded—but they play without spirit... Although [they did not agree with Bernstein's] decision... he was highly respected by the members of the orchestra... He was a world class musician. So, for Leonard Bernstein they played Mahler beautifully. Eventually, it seems, most of the orchestra grew to enjoy playing the music of their hometown boy.

Questions about the optimal mix of power for leaders are complicated by the interdependence among different sources of power. The distinction between position and personal power is sometimes convenient, but it should not be overdrawn. Position power is important, not only as a source of influence but also because it can be used to enhance a leader's personal power. Control over information complements expert power based on technical skill by giving the leader an advantage in solving important problems and by enabling a leader to cover up mistakes and exaggerate accomplishments. Reward power facilitates development of a deeper exchange relationship with subordinates, and when used skillfully in a way that is generous and fair, it can enhance a leader's referent power. The authority to make decisions and the upward influence to get them approved enable a leader to demonstrate expertise in problem solving, and it also facilitates development of stronger exchange relationships with subordinates. Some coercive power is necessary to buttress legitimate and expert power when a leader needs to influence compliance with rules and procedures that are unpopular but necessary to do the work and avoid serious accidents. Likewise, coercive power is needed by a leader to restrain or banish rebels and criminals who would otherwise disrupt operations, steal resources, harm other members, and cause the leader to appear weak and incompetent.

However, too much position power may be as detrimental as too little if the leader is tempted to rely on it instead of developing personal power or using other approaches (e.g., consultation, persuasion) for influencing people to comply with a request or support a change. The negative effects of high position power on a leader have been found in laboratory and field experiments as well as survey studies (Bendahan, Zehnder, Pralong, & Antonakis, 2015; Foulk, Lanaj, Tu, Erez, & Archambreau, 2015; Glad, 2002; Kipnis, 1972; Tost, Gino, & Larrick, 2013). Leaders with strong position power perceived subordinates as objects of manipulation, used rewards more often to influence subordinates, maintained more social distance from subordinates, and were less likely to involve subordinates in making decisions. When the power of such leaders is threatened, even more disruptive forms of behavior may be used by leaders (Williams, 2014). In general, a leader should have only a moderate amount of position power, although the optimal amount will vary somewhat depending on the situation. Personal power is less susceptible to misuse, because it erodes quickly when a leader acts contrary to the interests of followers. Nevertheless, the potential for corruption remains. A leader with extensive expert power or charismatic appeal will be tempted to act in ways that will eventually lead to failure (McClelland, 1975).

The corrupting influence of high power can be reduced by holding leaders accountable for the way they use their power (Rus, Van Knippenberg, & Wisse, 2012). Rules and policies can be enacted to regulate the exercise of position power, especially reward and coercive power. Grievance and appeals procedures can be enacted, and independent review boards established to protect subordinates against misuse of power by leaders. Bylaws, charter provisions, and official policies can be drafted to require leaders to consult with subordinates and obtain their approval on specified types of decisions. Regular attitude surveys can be conducted to measure subordinate satisfaction with their leaders. When appropriate, periodic elections or votes of confidence can be held to determine whether the leader should continue in office. Recall procedures can be established to remove incompetent leaders in an orderly manner.

Studies of the amount of influence exercised by people at different levels in the authority hierarchy of an organization reveal that effective leaders create relationships in which they have strong influence over subordinates but are also receptive to influence from them. Leaders can facilitate reciprocal influence by encouraging subordinates to participate in making important decisions, and by fostering and rewarding innovation. Instead of using their power to dictate how things will be done, effective executives empower members of the organization to discover and implement new and better ways of doing things.

Guidelines for Using Power

The research on power is still too limited to provide clear guidelines on the best ways to exercise it. Nevertheless, by drawing on the findings from research in many different social science disciplines, it is possible to develop some tentative guidelines for leaders (Yukl & Taber, 1983). The guidelines are usually worded in terms of influencing subordinates, but many apply as well to influencing other people. Some guidelines involve using influence tactics described later in the chapter.

Legitimate Power

Authority is usually exercised with a request, order, or instruction that is communicated orally or in writing. The way in which legitimate power is exercised affects the outcome (see Table 6-1). A polite request is more effective than an arrogant demand, because it does not emphasize a status gap or imply target dependence on the agent. Use of a polite request is

TABLE 6-1 Guidelines for Using Legitimate Authority

- Make polite, clear requests.
- Explain the reasons for a request.
- Don't exceed your scope of authority.
- Verify authority if necessary.
- Follow proper channels.
- Follow up to verify compliance.
- Insist on compliance if appropriate.

especially important for people who are likely to be sensitive about status differentials and authority relationships, such as someone who is older than the agent or who is a peer rather than a subordinate.

Making a polite request does not imply you should plead or appear apologetic about a request. To do so risks the impression that the request is not worthy or legitimate, and it may give the impression that compliance is not really expected. A legitimate request should be made in a firm, confident manner. In an emergency situation, it is more important to be assertive than polite. A direct order by a leader in a commanding tone of voice is sometimes necessary to shock subordinates into immediate action in an emergency. In this type of situation, subordinates associate confident, firm direction with expertise as well as authority. To express doubts or appear confused risks the loss of influence over subordinates.

The order or request should be stated very clearly using language that the target person can understand. If the request is complex, it is advisable to communicate it in writing (e.g., work order, memo, email) as well as orally. Oral requests should be made directly to the target person rather than relying on someone else to relay it to the target person. An intermediary may misinterpret the message, and you also lose the opportunity to assess the target person's reaction. If there is any question about your right to make a request or assignment, then it is important to verify this authority, which is a type of "legitimating tactic" described later.

Instances of outright refusal by subordinates to carry out a legitimate order or request undermine the leader's authority and increase the likelihood of future disobedience. Orders that are unlikely to be carried out should not be given. Sometimes a subordinate will delay in complying with an unusual or unpleasant request to test whether the leader is really serious about it. If the leader does not follow up the initial request to check on compliance, the subordinate is likely to conclude that the request may be ignored.

Reward Power

Reward power can be used in several ways (see Table 6-2). When the agent offers to give the target person a reward for carrying out a request or performing a task, it is called an exchange tactic, and the use of such tactics is described in more detail later in this chapter. Another way to use reward power is to create a formal incentive system that provides tangible rewards for good behavior or a monetary bonus for performance that exceeds standards.

Studies have revealed that verbal approval, encouragement and praise can very often be very positive substitutes in place of tangible rewards. Experiments involving positive reinforcement and behavior modification in the classroom or work setting revealed that verbal rewards could consist of: 'extreme politeness', 'compliments', and 'praise' for past behavior.

TABLE 6-2 Guidelines for Using Reward Power

- Offer the type of rewards that people desire.
- Offer rewards that are fair and ethical.
- Don't promise more than you can deliver.
- Explain the criteria for giving rewards and keep it simple.
- Provide rewards as promised if requirements are met.
- Use rewards symbolically (not in a manipulative way).

Non-verbal rewards might comprise: "Giving individuals in the other party more space at the table" Nodding of the head to signal your acceptance and that you approve; "Eye contact to indicate attention"; and "By using open and non-aggressive gestures to designate acceptance and respect."

How reward power is used affects the outcome. Since compliance is most likely if the reward is something valued by the target person, it is essential to determine what rewards are valued, which will not be the same for everyone. Another essential condition is that the agent must be perceived as a credible source of the reward, and credibility is undermined by making unrealistic promises or failing to provide a promised reward.

Even when the conditions are favorable for using rewards, they seldom motivate someone to put forth extra effort beyond what is required to complete the task and get the reward. The target person may be tempted to neglect aspects of the task not included in the specification of performance criteria or aspects not easily monitored by the agent. If rewards are used in a manipulative manner, they may result in resistance rather than compliance. The power to give or withhold rewards may cause resentment among people who dislike being dependent on the whims of a powerful authority figure, or who believe that the agent is manipulating them to his or her own advantage. Even an attractive reward may be ineffective if it is seen as a bribe to get the target person to do something improper or unethical.

When rewards are used frequently as a source of influence, people may come to perceive their relationship to the leader in purely economic terms. They will expect a reward every time they are asked to do something new or unusual. It is more satisfying for both parties to view their relationship in terms of mutual loyalty and friendship. Rather than using rewards as incentives in an impersonal, mechanical way, they should be used in a more symbolic manner to recognize accomplishments and express personal appreciation for special contributions or exceptional effort. Used in this way, reward power can be a source of increased referent power.

Coercive Power

Coercive power is invoked by a threat or warning that the target person will suffer undesirable consequences for noncompliance with a request, rule, or policy. The threat may be explicit, or it may be only a vague comment that the person will be sorry for failing to do what the agent wants. The likelihood of compliance is greatest when the threat is perceived to be credible, and the target person strongly desires to avoid the threatened punishment. Credibility will be undermined by rash threats that are not carried out despite noncompliance by the target person. Sometimes it is necessary to establish credibility by demonstrating the will and ability to cause unpleasant consequences for the target person. However, even a credible threat may be unsuccessful if the target person refuses to be intimidated or believes that a way can be found to avoid compliance without being detected by the agent.

Coercive power could take the form of a threatened strike action by a labour union; the threat of preventing promotion or transfer of a subordinate for poor performance; it could be a threat of litigation; it could be at threat of non-payment; it could be the threat to go public; and it could even be a threat of physical injury.

It is best to avoid using coercion except when absolutely necessary, because it is difficult to use and likely to result in undesirable side effects. Coercion often arouses anger or resentment, and it may result in retaliation. In work organizations, the most appropriate use of coercion is to deter behavior detrimental to the organization, such as illegal activities, theft, violation of safety rules, reckless acts that endanger others, and direct disobedience of legitimate requests. Coercion is not likely to result in commitment, but when used skillfully in an appropriate situation, there is a reasonably good chance that it will result in compliance. Table 6-3 has guidelines for using coercion primarily to maintain discipline with subordinates (Arvey & Ivancevich, 1980; Preston & Zimmerer, 1978; Schoen & Durand, 1979).

Expert Power

Some guidelines for using expert power are shown in Table 6-4. When an agent clearly has much more relevant expertise than target persons, the effects of the expert power will be automatic. For example, a renowned expert physician recommends a form of treatment, and the patient accepts the recommendation without any doubts. However, in many cases an agent will

TABLE 6-3 Guidelines for Using Coercive Power to Maintain Discipline

1. Explain rules and requirements, and ensure that people understand the serious consequences of violations.
2. Respond to infractions promptly and consistently without showing any favoritism to particular individuals.
3. Investigate to get the facts before using reprimands or punishment, and avoid jumping to conclusions or making hasty accusations.
4. Except for the most serious infractions, provide sufficient oral and written warnings before resorting to punishment.
5. Administer warnings and reprimands in private, and avoid making rash threats.
6. Stay calm and avoid the appearance of hostility or personal rejection.
7. Express a sincere desire to help the person comply with role expectations and thereby avoid punishment.
8. Invite the person to suggest ways to correct the problem, and seek agreement on a concrete plan.
9. If noncompliance continues after warnings have been made, use punishments that are legitimate, fair, and commensurate with the seriousness of the infraction.

TABLE 6-4 Ways to Use and Maintain Expert Power

- Explain the reasons for a request or proposal and why it is important.
- Provide evidence that a proposal will be successful.
- Don't make rash, careless, or inconsistent statements.
- Don't lie, exaggerate, or misrepresent the facts.
- Listen seriously to the person's concerns and suggestions.
- Act confident and decisive in a crisis.

not have such an obvious advantage in expertise, and it will be necessary to use the expertise to provide information, explanations, and evidence that support a request or proposal. If there is any question about the agent's expertise, it is helpful to verify it by providing appropriate documents and evidence, or by describing prior success in dealing with similar problems.

Proposals or requests should be made in a clear, confident manner, and the agent should avoid making contradictory statements or vacillating between inconsistent positions. However, it is important to remember that superior expertise can also cause resentment if used in a way that implies the target person is ignorant or helpless. The agent may lecture target persons in an arrogant, condescending manner, rudely interrupt any attempted replies, and dismiss any objections or concerns without serious consideration. Even when the agent is acknowledged to have more expertise, the target person usually has some relevant information, ideas, and concerns that should be considered.

Referent Power

Some specific ways to gain and use referent power are summarized in Table 6-5. Referent power is increased by showing concern for the needs and feelings of others, demonstrating trust and respect, and treating people fairly. However, to achieve and maintain strong referent power usually requires more than just flattery, favors, and charm. Referent power ultimately depends on the agent's character and integrity. Over time, actions speak louder than words, and someone who tries to appear friendly but manipulates and exploits people will lose referent power. Integrity is demonstrated by being truthful, expressing a consistent set of values, acting in a way that is consistent with one's espoused values, and carrying out promises and agreements (French & Raven, 1959). Governments that negotiate internationally understand how vital it is to send professional negotiators or individuals who possess special qualities of referent power when negotiating on their behalf.

One way to exercise referent power is through "role modeling." A person who is well liked and admired can have considerable influence over others by setting an example of proper and desirable behavior for them to imitate. When there is strong personal identification, imitation of agent behavior is likely to occur even without any conscious intention by the agent. However, because people also imitate undesirable behavior in someone they admire, it is important to be aware of the examples that one sets.

An agent with limited referent power may find it useful to remind the target person of favors done in the past or events when their friendship was very important. Finally, when relying on referent power as a source of influence, it is important to ensure that the target person understands how important a request is for you. An example is to say: "I would really appreciate it if you can do this, because it is really important to me."

TABLE 6-5 Ways to Gain and Use Referent Power

- Show acceptance and positive regard.
- Be supportive and helpful.
- Use sincere forms of ingratiation.
- Keep promises and commitments.
- Make self-sacrifices to benefit others.
- Lead by example (use role modeling).
- Explain the personal importance of a request.

Influence Tactics and Outcomes

Knowledge about effective leadership is also provided by studying influence processes involving managers and their subordinates, bosses, other members of the organization, and outsiders (e.g., clients, customers, suppliers, government officials). This introduction describes three general types of influence tactics and three distinct task-related outcomes for an influence attempt involving proactive tactics. The final part of the chapter describes eleven specific types of proactive influence tactics, their likely outcomes, and guidelines for using the tactics.

General Types of Influence Tactics

The type of behavior used intentionally to influence the attitudes and behavior of another person is usually called an influence tactic. Three general types of influence tactics can be differentiated according to their primary purpose. Some specific influence tactics can be used for more than one purpose but may not be equally effective for the different purposes.

Impression Management Tactics. These tactics are intended to influence people to like the agent (e.g., provide praise, act friendly, offer assistance) or to have a favorable evaluation of the agent (e.g., describe past achievements). Impression management tactics can be used by leaders to influence followers, or by followers to influence a leader (see Chapter 10).

Political Tactics. These tactics are used to influence organizational decisions or otherwise gain benefits for an individual or group. One type of political tactic involves an attempt to influence how important decisions are made and who makes them. Examples include influencing the agenda for meetings to include your issues, influencing decision makers to use criteria that will bias decisions in your favor, and selecting decision makers who will promote and defend your interests. Political tactics are also used to defend against opponents and silence critics. Some political tactics involve deception, manipulation, and abuse of power, and ethical aspects of power and influence are discussed in Chapter 9.

Proactive Tactics. These tactics have an immediate task objective, such as getting the target person to carry out a new task, change the procedures used for a current task, provide assistance on a project, or support a proposed change. The proactive influence tactics are useful when a simple request or command is unlikely to have the desired outcome. Eleven types of proactive tactics are described later in this chapter. Some of the eleven tactics can also be used to resist or modify a request from someone who is attempting to influence you.

Influence Outcomes for Proactive Tactics

One useful basis for evaluating the success of an influence attempt involving proactive tactics is to examine the outcome. The agent may achieve the intended effects on the target, or the outcome may be less than was intended. For an influence attempt that involves a single target person, it is useful to differentiate among three distinct outcomes that involve the target person's willingness to carry out the agent's request or proposal.

Commitment. The target person makes a great effort to carry out the request or implement the decision effectively. This outcome is usually the most successful one for a complex, difficult task that requires enthusiasm, initiative, and persistence by the target person in overcoming obstacles.

Compliance. The target person is willing to carry out a request but is not enthusiastic about it and will make only a minimal effort. With compliance, the target person is not convinced that the decision or action is the best thing to do or even that it will be effective for accomplishing its purpose. However, for a simple, routine request, compliance may be all that is necessary to accomplish the agent's task objectives.

Resistance. The target person is opposed to the proposal or request, rather than merely indifferent about it. Resistance can take several different forms: (1) refuse to carry out the request, (2) explain why it is impossible to carry out the request, (3) try to persuade the agent to withdraw or change the request, (4) ask higher authorities to overrule the agent's request, (5) delay acting in the hope that the agent will forget about the request, and (6) make a pretense of complying but try to sabotage the task. Resistance is usually regarded as an unsuccessful outcome, but it can be beneficial if it helps the agent avoid a serious mistake. For example, you develop a detailed plan for a new project, but people find some serious flaws that need to be fixed before they will implement the plan.

The target person's reaction to the agent's request is not the only basis for evaluating success. The proactive tactics can also affect interpersonal relationships and the way other people perceive the agent (e.g., ethical, supportive, likable, competent, trustworthy, strong). A few of the proactive tactics (i.e., ingratiation, collaboration, consultation, apprising) may improve the agent–target relationship, and the use of hard-pressure tactics can weaken the relationship.

Types of Proactive Influence Tactics

As explained earlier, behavior used intentionally to gain acceptance of a request or support for a proposal is called a proactive influence tactic. Two research programs used inductive and deductive approaches to identify distinct types of proactive tactics.

In an early research program (Kipnis, Schmidt, & Wilkinson, 1980), a preliminary taxonomy was developed by analyzing critical incidents that described successful and unsuccessful influence attempts. Then, the tactics identified with this inductive approach were used to develop an agent self-report questionnaire called the Profiles of Organizational Influence Strategies (POIS). The POIS was used in a follow-up study by Schriesheim and Hinkin (1990) with samples of agents who rated their own use of the tactics in upward influence attempts with their boss. The study found support for six of the proposed tactics (i.e., rationality, exchange, ingratiation, assertiveness, coalition, and upward appeal). Limited support for a revised version of the questionnaire was also found in a subsequent study of upward influence (Hochwarter, Pearson, Ferris, Perrewe, & Ralston, 2000). The original and revised versions of the POIS have been used in many studies on proactive tactics (see Ammeter, Douglas, Gardner, Hochwarter, & Ferris, 2002).

A more recent program of research was carried out to identify proactive tactics used to influence subordinates and peers as well as bosses (Yukl, Chavez, & Seifert, 2005; Yukl, Lepsinger, & Lucia, 1992; Yukl, Seifert, & Chavez, 2008). The research program involved a series of studies conducted over a period of more than a decade using several different research methods (i.e., critical incidents, diaries, questionnaires, experiments, and scenarios). The eleven proactive influence tactics identified in this research program are defined in Table 6-6. Five of the tactics are similar to ones in the POIS (rational persuasion, ingratiation, exchange, pressure, and coalition), and upward appeals are treated as a type of coalition tactic. Seven other tactics were also identified in the critical incidents or suggested by theories about leadership and power. The Influence Behavior Questionnaire (IBQ) was developed in the survey research to measure target ratings of agent influence behavior. Target

TABLE 6-6 Definition of the 11 Proactive Influence Tactics

Rational Persuasion: The agent uses logical arguments and factual evidence to show a proposal or request is feasible and relevant for attaining important task objectives.

Apprising: The agent explains how carrying out a request or supporting a proposal will benefit the target personally or help advance the target person's career.

Inspirational Appeals: The agent makes an appeal to values and ideals or seeks to arouse the target person's emotions to gain commitment for a request or proposal.

Consultation: The agent encourages the target to suggest improvements in a proposal or to help plan an activity or change for which the target person's support and assistance are desired.

Collaboration: The agent offers to provide relevant resources and assistance if the target will carry out a request or approve a proposed change.

Ingratiation: The agent uses praise and flattery before or during an influence attempt, or expresses confidence in the target's ability to carry out a difficult request.

Personal Appeals: The agent asks the target to carry out a request or support a proposal out of friendship, or asks for a personal favor before saying what it is.

Exchange: The agent offers an incentive, suggests an exchange of favors, or indicates willingness to reciprocate at a later time if the target will do what the agent requests.

Coalition Tactics: The agent seeks the aid of others to persuade the target to do something, or uses the support of others as a reason for the target to agree.

Legitimating Tactics: The agent seeks to establish the legitimacy of a request or to verify authority to make it by referring to rules, policies, contracts, or precedent.

Pressure: The agent uses demands, threats, frequent checking, or persistent reminders to influence the target to carry out a request.

Source: Yukl et al. (2008).

ratings are usually more accurate than the type of agent's self-ratings used in the POIS. The remainder of this section describes each type of tactic and how it is commonly used in organizations to influence a subordinate, peer, or boss. Ansari and Kapoor (1987) found that the subjects used rational persuasion, upward appeal, and blocking when pursuing organizational goals and ingratiation tactics to meet personal ends.

Rational Persuasion

Rational persuasion involves the use of explanations, logical arguments, and factual evidence to explain why a request or proposal will benefit the organization or help to achieve an important task objective. This tactic may also involve presentation of factual evidence that a project or change is likely to be successful. A strong form of rational persuasion (e.g., a detailed proposal, elaborate documentation) is much more effective than a weak form of rational persuasion (e.g., a brief explanation, an assertion without supporting evidence). Rational persuasion is a flexible tactic that can be used for most influence attempts and target persons. This tactic is very useful when the target person shares the agent's objectives but does not initially recognize that the agent's request or proposal is the best way to attain their shared objectives. The use of a rational appeal that involves evidence and predicted outcomes is more effective if the agent is perceived to have high expertise and credibility. Rational persuasion is unlikely to be effective if the agent and target have incompatible objectives, or the agent lacks expertise and credibility. Rational Persuasion (the use of facts and logic to support a proposal) is the most frequently used tactic in all 12 countries and the one considered most effective by managers regardless of country (Kennedy, J. C., Fu, P. P., & Yukl, G., 2003).

Apprising

Apprising involves an explanation of how a request or proposal is likely to benefit the target person as an individual. The benefits may involve the person's career advancement, job satisfaction, or compensation. Apprising may involve the use of facts and logic, but unlike rational persuasion, the benefits described are for the target person, not for the organization or the mission. Unlike exchange tactics, the benefits to be obtained by the target person are not something the agent will provide to the target, but rather something that is likely to happen when the agent's request is carried out or the proposal is implemented.

This tactic is more likely to be used with subordinates or peers than with bosses. Successful use of apprising requires unique knowledge about the likely personal benefits associated with an activity or change, and a subordinate is much less likely than a superior to be a credible source of such knowledge. An exception is the situation where the subordinate is experienced but the boss is new to the organization.

Inspirational Appeals

This tactic involves an emotional or value-based appeal, in contrast to the logical arguments used in rational persuasion and apprising. An inspirational appeal is an attempt to develop enthusiasm and commitment by arousing strong emotions and linking a request or proposal to a person's needs, values, hopes, and ideals. Some bases for appealing to most people include their desire to be important, to feel useful, to support their values, to accomplish something worthwhile, to perform an exceptional feat, to be a member of the best team, or to participate in an exciting effort to make things better.

This tactic can be used in any direction, but it is especially appropriate for gaining commitment to work on a new project, and this type of request is most likely to be made with subordinates or peers. An inspirational appeal is also an appropriate tactic to gain support for a proposed change that involves values and ideals.

Consultation

This tactic involves inviting the target person to participate in planning how to carry out a request, revise a strategy, or implement a proposed change. Consultation can take a variety of forms, but unlike the leadership behavior with the same name, the target person is only invited to help determine how the objective should be attained, not to help decide what the objective should be. As with rational persuasion, consultation is more likely to be effective if the agent and target have shared objectives. Consultation is useful for discovering if the target person has concerns about the feasibility of a proposal or likely adverse consequences. The agent can explore ways to avoid or resolve any issues that are revealed (which involves the tactic called collaboration).

Consultation can be used in any direction, but it is likely to be used more often with subordinates and peers than with bosses. This tactic is especially appropriate when the agent has the authority to plan a task or make a change, and such authority is greatest in a downward direction. Consultation can be used in an attempt to gain support or approval from superiors for a proposed change or new project, but superiors already have authority to review such decisions and do not need an invitation from the subordinate to modify the proposal. In a lateral direction, consultation is very useful to elicit concerns and suggestions from peers who may not be committed to support an activity or change unless their needs and opinions are taken into account.

Exchange

This influence tactic involves the explicit or implicit offer to reward a person for doing what is requested. The tactic is especially appropriate for a request that offers no important benefits for the target person and would involve considerable effort and inconvenience. The benefit should be something valued enough by the target person to motivate compliance with a request. The promised benefit may involve tangible rewards, scarce resources, information, advice or assistance on another task, career support, or political support. An exchange tactic is unlikely to be effective unless the target person believes the agent is able to provide the promised benefit and can be trusted to actually deliver it.

Exchange tactics are more likely to be used in influence attempts with subordinates and peers than with bosses. Control over rewards is greatest in a downward direction and least in an upward direction. One type of reward that can be offered only to subordinates is a pay increase, bonus, promotion, better assignments, or a better work schedule. It is also more socially acceptable to offer incentives to subordinates than to bosses. Managers have little to offer bosses that is not already expected as part of their job responsibilities, and any incentive offered to a boss may be viewed as a bribe. Managers usually have some control over rewards desired by peers, but the rewards are more likely to be task related (e.g., provide resources, assistance, information, political support) rather than personal benefits.

Collaboration

This influence tactic involves an offer to provide necessary resources and/or assistance if the target person agrees to carry out a request or approve a proposal. Collaboration may seem similar to exchange in that both tactics involve an offer to do something for the target person. However, there are important differences in the underlying motivational processes and facilitating conditions. Exchange involves increasing the benefits to be obtained by carrying out a request, and it is especially appropriate when the benefits of compliance would otherwise be low for the target person. Collaboration involves reducing the difficulty or costs of carrying out a request, and it is especially appropriate when compliance would be difficult for the target person. Exchange usually involves an impersonal trade of unrelated benefits, whereas collaboration usually involves a joint effort to accomplish the same task.

Collaboration is used least often in an upward direction. A boss usually has more control over discretionary resources than subordinates and can usually require subordinate assistance on an essential activity. With subordinates and peers, there is more opportunity to propose ways to facilitate the target person's ability to carry out a request.

Ingratiation

Forms of ingratiation include giving compliments, doing unsolicited favors, acting deferential and respectful, and acting especially friendly and helpful before making a request. When ingratiation is perceived to be sincere, it tends to strengthen positive regard and make a target person more willing to consider a request.

This tactic is more likely to be used in influence attempts with subordinates or peers than with bosses. Praise and compliments can be used with anyone, but they are more credible and meaningful when the agent has higher status and expertise than the target person. Thus, ingratiation is likely to be viewed as less sincere when used in an influence attempt with a boss. Ingratiation may be viewed as manipulative if it is used just before asking for something; so in general, it is more useful as part of a long-term strategy for building cooperative relations than as a proactive influence tactic.

Personal Appeals

A personal appeal involves asking someone to do a favor based on friendship or loyalty to the agent, or it may also involve an appeal to the person's kindness and generosity. This influence tactic is not feasible when the target person dislikes the agent or is indifferent about what happens to the agent. A personal appeal is most useful for getting assistance or information or for requesting a personal favor unrelated to the work. The tactic is more socially acceptable with a peer or outsider than with a subordinate or boss. It is awkward to request a personal favor from a subordinate or boss and should not be necessary except in very unusual circumstances.

Legitimating Tactics

Legitimating tactics involve attempts to establish one's legitimate authority or right to make a particular type of request. Legitimacy is unlikely to be questioned for a routine request that has been made and complied with many times before. However, legitimacy is more likely to be questioned when the request is unusual or the agent's authority is unclear. There are several different types of legitimating tactics, most of which are mutually compatible.

Legitimating tactics are most often relevant for influence attempts with peers or outsiders, where role relationships are often ambiguous and agent authority less well defined. For downward influence attempts with subordinates, legitimating may be used when implementing major changes or for dealing with an unusual crisis. For upward influence attempts, legitimating may be used for requests involving personnel matters, especially if the superior is new and unfamiliar with relevant policies, contract agreements, and standard practices.

Pressure

Pressure tactics include threats, warnings, and assertive behavior such as repeated demands or frequent checking to see if the person has complied with a request. Pressure tactics are sometimes successful in eliciting compliance with a request, particularly if the target person is just lazy or apathetic rather than strongly opposed to it. However, pressure is not likely to result in commitment and may have serious side effects. The harder forms (e.g., threats, warnings, demands) are likely to cause resentment and undermine working relationships. The softer forms (e.g., persistent requests, reminders that the person promised to do something) are more likely to gain compliance without undermining the agent's relationship with the target person.

Pressure tactics are most likely to be used with subordinates and least likely to be used with bosses. The authority and power needed to make threats or warnings credible is much greater in a downward direction than in a lateral or upward direction, and pressure is often considered more appropriate for influence attempts with subordinates than with peers or bosses. Pressure Tactics and Appeals to a Higher Authority were consistently rated as least frequently used and least effective across countries (Kennedy, J. C., Fu, P. P., & Yukl, G. (2003).

Coalition Tactics

Coalition tactics involve getting help from other people to influence the target person to comply with a request or support a proposal. The coalition partners may be peers, subordinates, superiors, or outsiders. Coalition partners may actively participate in influence attempts with the target person, or the agent may only use their endorsement of a request or proposal. When a coalition partner actively participates in the effort to influence the target person, the influence attempt usually involves other influence tactics as well. For example, the coalition partner may use rational persuasion, exchange, or pressure to help influence the target person. When the other party who is helping the agent is the immediate superior of the target person, the process is sometimes called an upward appeal, but it is still an example of a coalition tactic rather than an entirely different type of proactive tactic.

Coalition tactics are more likely to be used to influence peers or bosses than subordinates, and it is especially appropriate to gain their support for a proposed change or new initiative. It is seldom necessary to use coalition tactics to influence subordinates. Managers have many ways to influence subordinates, and in Western countries they are expected to do so without getting help from other people.

Power and Influence Behavior

Power and influence behavior are distinct constructs, but the relationship among specific forms of power, specific influence tactics, and influence outcomes is complex. Different types of effects are possible, and they are not mutually exclusive (see Figure 6-1).

Agent power may directly affect the agent's choice of influence tactics (as depicted by arrow #1). Some tactics require a particular type of power to be effective, and a leader with relevant power is more likely to use these tactics. For example, exchange tactics require reward power, which provides an agent with something of value to exchange with the target person. Strong forms of pressure such as warnings and threats are more likely to be used by an agent who has some coercive power over the target person. Rational persuasion is more likely to be used when the agent has expert power that includes the knowledge to explain why a request is important and feasible.

Some influence tactics may have a direct effect on target attitudes and/or behavior, regardless of the agent's power. However, in the majority of influence attempts, it is likely that power acts as a moderator variable to enhance or diminish the effectiveness of the tactics used by the

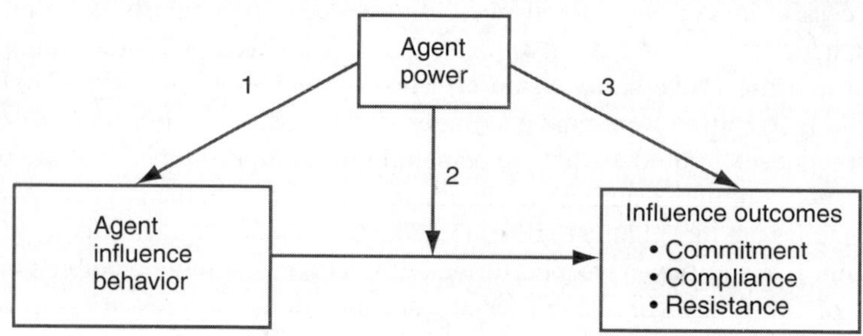

FIGURE 6-1 Relationships Among Agent Power, Influence Behavior, and Influence Outcomes

agent. This moderator effect of power (depicted by arrow #2) is most likely to occur for the types of power directly relevant to the tactics used in an influence attempt. For example, expert power increases the effectiveness of rational persuasion. An agent with high reward power is likely to have more success offering an exchange than an agent with little reward power.

It is also possible that agent power can enhance the success of an influence tactic for which the power is not directly relevant (also depicted by arrow #2). An agent with strong referent power may be more successful when using rational persuasion to gain support for a proposal, because the target person will see the agent as more trustworthy. An agent with strong coercive power may be more successful in gaining compliance with a simple request, even though no pressure or exchange tactics are used. Strong expert power may increase the credibility of a request unrelated to the agent's expertise. For example, a famous scientist influences people to participate in a risky financial venture that does not involve the scientist's field of expertise.

Another possibility (depicted by arrow #3) is that agent power can influence the target person regardless of whether the agent makes any overt influence attempt. In organizations, people act more deferential toward somebody who has high position power, because they are aware of the possibility that the person can affect their job performance and career advancement. People are less likely to criticize or contradict a powerful agent, because they do not want to risk the agent's displeasure. People are more likely to cooperate with an agent who has strong referent power, even if the agent does nothing to encourage such cooperation.

Effectiveness of Proactive Tactics

Proactive influence tactics are not always needed in an influence attempt. When a request is clearly legitimate, relevant for the work, and something the target person knows how to do, then it is often possible to get target compliance by using a "simple request" based on legitimate power. However, when a person is likely to resist a simple request, the use of proactive influence tactics can help to make the influence attempt more successful. The influence tactics are especially useful for a request or proposal that is unusual, controversial, or difficult to do, or when the agent has little authority over the target person (e.g., a peer, boss, or client).

The effectiveness of each type of proactive tactic depends on several aspects of the situation in which it is used (e.g., Kipnis et al., 1980; Yukl & Falbe, 1990; Yukl, Falbe, & Youn, 1993; Yukl, Guinan, & Sottolano, 1995; Yukl, Kim, & Chavez, 1999; Yukl, Kim, & Falbe, 1996; Yukl & Tracey, 1992). Relevant aspects of the situation include the type of agent–target relationship, the agent's power and authority, the agent's interpersonal skills, the type of influence objective, and the extent to which the request is seen as appropriate and acceptable by the target person. A tactic is more likely to be successful if the target person perceives it to be a socially acceptable form of influence behavior, the agent has sufficient position and personal power, the agent has strong interpersonal skills, and if the tactic is used for a request that is legitimate and consistent with target values and needs.

The outcome of an influence attempt also depends on the extent to which the agent is trusted by the target and perceived to have integrity. Any tactic can be used in a way that is unethical. To preserve a reputation for integrity it is essential to avoid using tactics in a way that is deceptive or manipulative. The proactive tactics should be used in ethical ways to accomplish worthwhile objectives, not to exploit others for personal gain.

Even though the outcome of an influence attempt depends on the situation, research on consequences of influence attempts finds that some tactics tend to be generally more effective than others (e.g., Falbe & Yukl, 1992; Fu & Yukl, 2000; Lee, Han, Cheong, Kim, & Yun, 2017; Yukl, Fu, & McDonald, 2003; Yukl & Tracey, 1992). Findings in the research on tactic effectiveness and how the tactics are commonly used in different situations are summarized in Table 6-7. Research on how the tactics are used with different targets and how tactics are combined and sequenced is still limited, but those findings are also summarized in the table. This section of the chapter describes the findings about the relative effectiveness of the tactics when used individually and when combined and sequenced in different ways.

Effects of Individual Tactics

The five tactics that are generally most effective include rational persuasion, consultation, collaboration, inspirational appeals, and apprising. These "core tactics" are often successful for influencing target commitment to carry out a request or support a proposal. However, even these tactics have limitations and their effects depend greatly on how appropriate they are for the situation.

TABLE 6-7 Summary of Findings for Proactive Influence Tactics

Influence Tactic	Directional Use of Tactic	Sequencing Results	Used Alone or in Combination	General Effectiveness
Rational Persuasion	Widely used in all directions	Used more for initial request	Used frequently both ways	High
Inspirational Appeal	More down than up or lateral	No difference	Used most with other tactics	High
Consultation	More down and lateral than up	No difference	Used most with other tactics	High
Collaboration	More down and lateral than up	Not studied	Used most with other tactics	High
Apprising	More down than lateral or up	Not studied	Used most with other tactics	High
Ingratiation	More down and lateral than up	Used more for initial request	Used most with other tactics	Moderate
Exchange	More down and lateral than up	Used most for quick follow-up	Used both ways equally often	Moderate
Personal Appeal	More lateral than down or up	Used more for initial request	Used both ways equally often	Low/Moderate
Coalition Tactic	More lateral and up than down	Used most for delayed follow-up	Used both ways equally often	Low/Moderate
Legitimating Tactic	More down and lateral than up	Used most for quick follow-up	Used most with other tactics	Low/Moderate
Pressure	More down than lateral or up	Used most for delayed follow-up	Used both ways equally often	Low

For example, apprising can be effective when the target person would benefit greatly by carrying out a request or supporting a proposal, but it is not useful if the person already recognizes the potential benefits or does not believe the agent's claims.

Exchange tactics are moderately effective for influencing subordinates and peers, but these tactics are difficult to use for proactive influence attempts with superiors, because subordinates usually lack control over resources and rewards desired by superiors. Personal appeals can be useful for influencing a target person with whom the agent has a friendly relationship, but this tactic is only relevant for certain types of requests (e.g., getting assistance, getting a personal favor, changing a scheduled meeting), and it is likely to result in target compliance rather than commitment.

Pressure and legitimating tactics are not likely to result in target commitment, but these tactics can be useful for eliciting compliance. As noted earlier, compliance is sometimes all that is needed to accomplish the objective of an influence attempt.

A coalition can be effective for influencing a peer or superior to support a change or innovation, especially if the coalition partners use direct tactics such as rational persuasion and inspirational appeals. However, use of a coalition is less likely to be effective if it involves the use of pressure tactics by coalition partners and is viewed as an attempt to "gang up" on the target person. An upward appeal to an authority person should only be used as a last resort for resolving a conflict with a peer who can cause the failure of an important project.

Combining Tactics

It is often feasible for a manager to use more than one direct influence tactic at the same time or in a sequence. An influence attempt is more likely to be successful if two or more different tactics are combined. However, the outcome will depend on the potency of the component tactics and the extent to which they are compatible with each other. Compatible tactics are easy to use together and they enhance each other's effectiveness. The research on tactic combinations is very limited, but it suggests that some tactics are more easily combined than others.

Rational persuasion is a very flexible tactic, and it is usually compatible with any of the other tactics. For example, rational persuasion can be used to clarify why a proposed change is important, and consultation can be used to involve the target person in finding an acceptable way to implement the change. When consultation reveals target person concerns about a proposed change, collaboration can be used to help alleviate them. An inspirational appeal that involves values and ideals can also involve reasons why the request or proposal is important to the organization or mission. The explanation of why a request is beneficial for the organization can also include reasons why it is beneficial to the person. For example, a proposed change to increase profits may also help the target person get a promotion.

Some tactics are clearly incompatible. For example, a hard form of pressure is incompatible with personal appeals or ingratiation because it undermines the feelings of friendship and loyalty that are the basis for these soft tactics. A hard form of pressure also tends to undermine the trust necessary for tactics such as consultation and collaboration. The use of pressure tactics to gain compliance requires considerable skill, and it should be used only when other tactics are not feasible or have already failed.

Sequencing Tactics

Influence attempts often involve a series of separate influence episodes that occur over a period of days or weeks. Some tactics are used more in initial influence attempts and other tactics are used more in follow-up influence attempts. The reasons for tactic selection described earlier can be used to explain sequencing differences in the use of different influence tactics. In general, it is reasonable to assume that a manager will initially select tactics that are likely to accomplish an objective with the least effort and cost. Most initial influence attempts involve either a simple request or a relatively weak form of rational persuasion. These tactics are easy to use and entail little in the way of agent costs.

Ingratiation is likely to be used early in an influence attempt, because common forms of this tactic (e.g., say that the person is highly qualified to do a task) are more credible at that point in the influence process. If some target resistance is anticipated, then the agent is likely to use a stronger form of rational persuasion, and "soft" tactics, such as personal appeals, consultation, collaboration, apprising, and inspirational appeals. In the face of continued resistance by a target, the agent will either escalate to "harder" tactics or abandon the effort if the request does not justify the risks of escalation. Pressure, exchange, and coalitions are likely to be saved for follow-up influence attempts, because they involve the greatest costs and risks. Legitimating may be used either early or late, depending on how the target is likely to perceive the legitimacy of a request. This tactic should be used early if the agent believes that the target person is likely to have any doubts about legitimacy.

Using the Tactics to Resist Influence Attempts

Most of the tactics used for proactive influence attempts can also be used to resist or modify a request made by someone else such as a boss, peer, subordinate, or client, although a different form of the tactic is usually appropriate. For example, when used as a resistance tactic, rational persuasion may involve explaining why the agent's request or proposal is unlikely to be successful. Collaboration may involve an offer to help accomplish an objective in a different way than the one proposed by the agent. Apprising may involve explaining why a proposed activity or change is likely to result in unfavorable personal outcomes for the agent. Legitimating may involve explaining how the agent's request is inconsistent with company rules or a formal contract.

Pressure is another tactic that can be used in upward influence if the agent is willing to take the necessary risks. The agent can make a threat to resign or to pursue legal action against the agent if an unethical request or an unacceptable demand is not withdrawn. An example is provided by the following incident:

> A man and his wife rented a cabin on a lake for their vacation. The first morning the husband spent several hours fishing in the lake from his boat, then returned to the cabin to take a nap. The wife does not fish and is not familiar with the lake, but she decides to take the boat out to look at the view and read her book. She motors out a short distance, anchors in a shady cove, and begins reading her book. Shortly afterward a Game Warden stops his boat next to the woman and says: "You are in a Restricted Fishing Area." She replies: "I did not know that, but I am only reading a book, not fishing." The Game Warden, who likes to exercise his authority, says: "Yes, but you have all the equipment and could start at any moment. Unless you leave now I will have to give you a citation." She thinks for a moment and says: "If you do that, I will charge you with sexual assault. My husband is a criminal attorney and a friend of the Sheriff for this county." The Game Warden is stunned by this response and says: "But I haven't even touched you." She replies: "Yes, but you have all the equipment and could start at any moment." The Game Warden mutters: "Have a nice day ma'am" and quickly leaves.

Guidelines for Using Proactive Influence Tactics

Specific guidelines for using each core tactic in a proactive influence attempt are presented next, and guidelines for using the other proactive tactics can be found in Table 6-8 at the end of this section. The guidelines are suggestions rather than prescriptions, because it is always necessary to evaluate the situation and determine whether a tactic is feasible and relevant. Some

TABLE 6-8 Ways to Use the Other Tactics

Apprising

- Explain how the person could benefit from carrying out a requested task.
- Explain how the task you want the person to do would help his/her career.
- Explain why a proposed activity or change would be good for the person.
- Explain how a proposed change would solve some of the person's problems.

Exchange

- Offer something the person wants in exchange for providing help on a task or project.
- Offer to do a specific task or favor in return for compliance with a request.
- Promise to do something for the person in the future in return for his/her help now.
- Offer to provide an appropriate reward if the person carries out a difficult request.

Ingratiation

- Say that the person has the special skills or knowledge needed to carry out a request.
- Praise the person's past achievements when asking him/her to do another task.
- Show respect and appreciation when asking the person to do something for you.
- Say that there is nobody more qualified to do a task.

Legitimating

- Explain that your request or proposal is consistent with official rules and policies.
- Point out that your request or proposal is consistent with a prior agreement or contract.
- Use a document to verify that a request is legitimate (e.g., a policy manual, contract, charter).
- Explain that a request or proposal is consistent with prior precedent and established practice.

Personal Appeal

- Ask the person to do a favor for you as a friend.
- Ask for his/her help as a personal favor.
- Say that you are in a difficult situation and would really appreciate the person's help.
- Say you need to ask for a favor before telling the person what it is.

Pressure

- Keep asking the person in a persistent way to say yes to a request.
- Insist in an assertive way that the person must do what you ask.
- Repeatedly check to see if the person has carried out a request.
- Warn the person about the penalties for not complying with a request.

Coalition

- Mention the names of others who endorse a proposal when asking the person to support it.
- Get others to explain to the person why they support a proposed activity or change.
- Bring someone along for support when meeting with the person to make a request or proposal.
- Ask someone with higher authority to help influence the target person.

of the tactics can take many different forms, and it is important to determine the best way to use a tactic to achieve the desired outcome.

Rational Persuasion

This tactic involves the use of logical arguments and factual evidence that a proposal or request is desirable because it is important for the organization or team and is feasible to do.

- **Explain the reason for a request or proposal.**

People are more likely to comply with a request if they understand the reason why it is necessary and important. When asked to do something unusual, people may wonder whether it is really necessary or just an impulsive whim. Explain how a proposed activity would solve a problem in your work or help you carry out your job responsibilities more effectively. Explain how a proposal would help to achieve an important objective you share in common with the person, such as improved quality, service, or productivity.

- **Provide evidence that your proposal is feasible.**

It is not enough for a request or proposal to be relevant; it must also be seen as practical and realistic to gain the person's enthusiastic support and cooperation. The target person may exaggerate the difficulties or anticipate obstacles that are unlikely to occur. If the person has doubts about the feasibility of a request or proposal, provide supporting evidence for it. Explain the underlying theoretical rationale for assuming that a proposed plan of action will lead to the desired objective. Describe a specific sequence of action steps that could be used to accomplish the objective. Cite supporting evidence from empirical research (e.g., a pilot study, a survey showing a favorable response to a proposed new product, service, or change). Describe how a similar approach was successful when used in the past by yourself or someone else. If appropriate, provide an actual demonstration for the person to observe (seeing is believing).

- **Explain why your proposal is better than competing ones.**

Sometimes your proposal is competing with other proposals for the person's support. In this case, it is not only necessary to show that your proposal is feasible, but also to show that it is better than any of the alternatives. Point out the advantages of your proposal in comparison to the alternatives (e.g., more likely to accomplish the objective, less costly, more likely to be approved, easier to implement, less risk of undesirable side effects). Point out the weaknesses and problems with each competing proposal. Your comparison will be more credible if you also acknowledge some advantages of competing proposals rather than ignoring them altogether, especially if the person is already aware of these advantages. If feasible, cite evidence from a test of the competing proposals to show that yours is better.

- **Explain how likely problems or concerns would be handled.**

All proposals and plans have weaknesses and limitations. A proposal is more likely to be accepted if you anticipate any obvious limitations and find ways to deal with them. Explain how you propose to avoid potential problems, overcome likely obstacles, and minimize risks. If the person expresses any unanticipated concerns about your proposal, describe ways to deal with these concerns rather than ignoring them or dismissing them as unworthy of consideration.

Inspirational Appeals

This tactic is an attempt to develop enthusiasm and commitment by appealing to the target person's emotions and values.

- **Appeal to the person's ideals and values.**

Most people aspire to be important, to feel useful, to accomplish something worthwhile, to make an important contribution, to perform an exceptional feat, to be a member of the best team, or to participate in an exciting effort to make things better. These aspirations are a good basis for emotional appeals. Some values and ideals that may be the basis for an inspirational appeal include patriotism, loyalty, liberty, freedom, justice, fairness, equality, excellence, altruism, and saving the environment.

- **Link the request to the person's self-image.**

A proposed activity or assignment may be linked to values that are central to the person's self-image as a professional, a member of an organization, an adherent of a particular religion, or a member of a political party. For example, most scientists have strong values about the discovery of new knowledge and its application to improve humanity; most physicians and nurses have strong values about healing people and keeping them healthy. A proposed change or activity may be described as something that will advance new knowledge, improve health care, enrich the lives of all members of the organization, serve one's god, or demonstrate loyalty to one's country.

- **Link the request to a clear and appealing vision.**

Efforts to introduce major changes or innovations are more likely to be successful when they involve an appealing vision of what could be accomplished or how the future could look if the proposed activity or change is implemented successfully. The vision may be an existing one the target person is known to embrace, or one you created to help gain commitment to a new project or activity. The vision should emphasize ideological values rather than tangible economic benefits (used in rational appeals to self-interest). However, it is not necessary to ignore economic benefits; they may be integrated into the overall vision of what can be accomplished as long as it is clear that they are not the primary objective.

- **Use a dramatic, expressive style of speaking.**

A dramatic, expressive style of speaking often increases the effectiveness of an emotional appeal. Conviction and intensity of feeling are communicated by one's voice (e.g., tone, inflection, pause), facial expressions, gestures, and body movement. Use a strong, clear tone of voice, but vary the pace and intensity. Use pauses at appropriate times to emphasize key words, maintain interest, and arouse excitement. Maintain strong eye contact, use strong gestures, and move around to display energy and intensity of feeling.

- **Use positive, optimistic language.**

Confidence and optimism about a project or change can be contagious. It is especially important to show optimism when the task is very difficult and people lack self-confidence. State your personal belief in the project and your strong commitment to see it through to a successful conclusion. Use positive language to communicate your confidence that a proposed project or change will be successful. For example, talk about the wonderful things that "will" happen when a change is made, rather than what "may" happen.

Consultation

This tactic involves inviting the target person to help plan a task or improve a proposed change in order to gain more commitment for it.

- **State your objective and ask what the person can do to help.**

When you do not expect the target person to be enthusiastic about helping you accomplish an objective, it is useful to explain why it is important (rational persuasion) before asking the person what he or she can do to help you attain it. If you have a good relationship, the target person is likely to suggest some ways to be of assistance. Show appreciation for any suggestions and discuss how they could be used. Once the person has agreed to provide some assistance, it is easier to ask for additional things that build on the initial offer.

- **Ask for suggestions on how to improve a tentative proposal.**

More participation is likely if you present a proposal as tentative and encourage people to improve it, rather than asking people to react to an elaborate plan that appears complete. People will be less inhibited about expressing concerns for a proposal that appears to be in the development stage rather than complete. The agent and target person should jointly explore ways to deal with any serious concerns or incorporate promising suggestions. A stronger version of this tactic is to ask the target person to write the initial draft of a proposal that you want him or her to support. Of course, this procedure is only feasible if the person shares your objectives and has the expertise to develop a credible proposal.

- **Involve the person in planning how to attain an objective.**

Present a general strategy, policy, or objective and ask the target person to suggest specific action steps for implementing it. If the action plan will be detailed, it is best to schedule a meeting at a later time to review the plan and reach a mutual agreement about it. This tactic is especially useful for assigning responsibilities to a subordinate or asking a peer to carry out supporting activities on a project. To be feasible, the target person should have at least moderate agreement with the strategy or objective.

- **Respond to the person's concerns and suggestions.**

Consultation is used mostly as a proactive influence tactic, but opportunities arise to use it also as a reactive tactic. Sometimes when asking the target person to carry out an assignment or provide assistance on a task, the person expresses concerns about it or suggestions for improving it. Whenever feasible, try to deal with the target person's concerns, even if it requires some modification of your initial plans. Ask the person for suggestions about how to deal with concerns. Good suggestions for improving an activity should be utilized whenever feasible.

Collaboration

This tactic involves an offer to help the target person carry out a request or to help reduce the difficulty or cost of carrying out a request.

- **Offer to show the person how to perform a requested task.**

If a request involves a new task or the person is worried about performing the task successfully, offer to show the person how to do the task or to arrange for someone else who is qualified to provide instruction.

- **Offer to provide necessary resources.**

Sometimes the target person is reluctant to do a requested task because it requires supplies, equipment, information, or other resources that are not readily available. If the task requires additional resources that are essential for task performance but difficult to obtain, offer to provide them or help the person get them.

- **Offer to help the person solve problems caused by a request.**

A request is more likely to be resisted if it will cause new problems that will increase the cost of compliance beyond an acceptable level. Try to anticipate such problems and be prepared to offer ways to avoid them or help the person deal with them. In many cases, the agent will not be aware of the problems caused by a request, but target concerns can be elicited with the skillful use of consultation and active listening by the agent.

- **Offer to help the person implement a proposed change.**

A major source of resistance to change is the extra work that would be involved in implementing it in the target person's unit or job. To gain the person's support and approval for a proposed change, offer to help the person implement it. A requirement for the use of this tactic is the capability to actually provide assistance in implementing the proposed change, which is most likely when the target person is a subordinate.

Summary

Power is the capacity to influence the attitudes and behavior of people in the desired direction. Potential influence derived from a manager's position in the organization is called position power, and it includes legitimate power, reward power, coercive power, and information power. Potential influence derived from the characteristics of the person who occupies a leadership position is called personal power, and it includes expert and referent power.

Power for an individual or group can increase or decrease as conditions change. Social exchange theory explains how power is gained and lost as reciprocal influence processes occur over time between leaders and followers in small groups. Strategic contingencies theory explains the acquisition and loss of power by different subunits of an organization (e.g., functional departments or product divisions) and the implications of this power distribution for the effectiveness of the organization in a changing environment. Theories of power institutionalization explain how political tactics are used to increase power and protect existing power.

The amount of power necessary for leader effectiveness depends on the nature of the organization, task, and subordinates. A leader with extensive position power is tempted to rely on it too much, which can cause resentment and rebellion. Throughout history many political leaders with strong position power have used it to dominate and exploit subordinates. The ethical and unethical use of power is discussed in Chapter 9. On the other hand, a leader lacking sufficient position power to reward competent subordinates, make necessary changes, and punish chronic troublemakers will find it difficult to develop a high-performing group or organization. A moderate amount of position power is usually optimal.

The success of a manager depends greatly on the manner in which power is exercised. Effective leaders rely more on personal power than on position power and they use power in a subtle, careful fashion that minimizes status differentials and avoids threats to the target person's self-esteem. In contrast, leaders who exercise power in an arrogant, manipulative, domineering manner are likely to engender resentment and resistance.

The relationship between power and influence behavior is complex. Power can influence the leader's choice of tactics and it can enhance their effectiveness. Leader power may also influence others even without a direct influence attempt by the leader. More research is needed to clarify these relationships.

Three broad types of influence tactics are impression management tactics, political tactics, and proactive tactics. Eleven proactive tactics have been identified, and they are useful when a simple request is not sufficient for eliciting the desired level of compliance or commitment for a request or proposal. What tactics are used depends on the situation, and the choice of tactics will vary somewhat depending on whether the target person is a subordinate, peer, or superior.

The outcome of an influence attempt may be target commitment, compliance, or resistance. Some tactics tend to be more effective than others, and the ones most likely to elicit target commitment are rational persuasion, consultation, collaboration, inspirational appeals, and apprising. However, these core tactics do not always result in task commitment, because the outcome of any particular influence attempt is affected strongly by other factors in addition to the type of influence tactics used by the agent. Any tactic may fail if not used in a way that is ethical and appropriate for the influence objective and situation. Combining different influence tactics can be beneficial, but it requires considerable insight and skill on the part of the agent.

Review and Discussion Questions

1. What types of power are related most strongly to leadership effectiveness?
2. How much power do leaders need to be effective?
3. What are some guidelines for using position power effectively?
4. What are some guidelines for using personal power effectively?
5. Which proactive tactics are most likely to result in target commitment?
6. What are some guidelines for combining and sequencing the use of proactive tactics?
7. How can the proactive tactics be used to resist or modify influence attempts by others?
8. How are leader power, influence behavior, and influence outcomes related to each other?

Key Terms

apprising
coercive power
collaboration
commitment
compliance
consultation
exchange tactics
expert power
information power
ingratiation
inspirational appeals
institutionalization of power
legitimate power
legitimating tactic
personal appeal
personal power
position power
pressure tactics
rational persuasion
referent power
resistance
reward power
scope of authority

PERSONAL REFLECTION

Think about a time when someone influenced you to become a strong supporter for a proposed change that you initially opposed. Describe the influence tactics used by the person to gain your support for the proposed change.

CASE

Aoun Naqvi and his Store

Aoun Naqvi became the new manager of a books and stationery shop in Lucknow, which is a part of a nationwide chain of bookstores. Aoun, who is 26 years old has been working for the company for three years. Aoun is faced with the challenge of improving the store's profits which have been below average so far. As an assistant manager, he was mostly allotted paperwork and minor administrative duties, which made this assignment his first opportunity to show his effectiveness as a manager.

According to the company's policy, the base salaries of the employees would be set by the company. However, the size of annual merit raise for each employee would be subject to the store manager's appraisal rating. Whatever recommendations the store manager makes, needs to be justified to the regional manager, especially in cases of recommendations that are inconsistent with individual and department sales. Although in theory, Aoun has the authority to suspend or fire an employee with his boss's approval, in practice any such recommendation needs to be backed by a strong case, in order to be implemented.

The store manager can influence store's performance only to a certain degree. One way to do this is to keep the cost of employees low—by ensuring that they work efficiently, and well as take as few leaves as possible. Another way is to ensure that employees provide a high level of customer service to ensure customer satisfaction and loyalty. How good is one's customer service depends on certain factors—thorough knowledge of the product, polite attitude, prompt service, and ensuring that inventories of popular goods are maintained, so that customers can find what they want.

However, in a set-up of a retail outlet, pay to the employees is usually low, and turnover consequently high. Since gaining thorough product knowledge takes some time, it becomes important to satisfy established and competent employees well enough, in order to retain them. Although it has been only ten days since Aoun joined the store, he has already discovered some of its problems. Among the various products that the store sells, school books and bags have the highest potential for earning profit during spring, which is when the new session of various schools begins. Currently, the store's sales are around average it has the potential for great improvement in the future.

Aoun would often notice a long queue of customers waiting at the school books and bag section, owing to delayed service. He would occasionally hear customers complaining about waiting time at this store and often contemplated going to another store that offered them prompt service. Aoun observed Anurag, the department manager (of school book and bags), often spend a lot of time socializing with his colleagues as well his customers, including random visits from his own friends.

—*Written by* Nishant Uppal

Questions

1. How much of each type of power does Aoun have at this time?
2. What influence tactics could be used in this situation to influence Anurag? Explain what you would actually say to Anurag in the process of using each tactic.
3. What should Aoun do to improve store performance?

CASE

The New Dean

When the Dean of the Business School was recruited by another university, the Associate Dean was asked to serve as the Acting Dean until a new dean was selected. The Associate Dean had been doing staff work that included planning how to make good use of the new building already approved for the Business School. He told the Provost and University President that in order to be effective in obtaining additional funds for the new building, he needed more status and authority. They decided to appoint him as the new Dean of the Business School without consulting the faculty or conducting a regular dean search. The new Dean planned to use his power to support budget requests, faculty appointments, and decisions about tenure, promotion, and sabbaticals to change some things that he did not like.

The Business School had very successful master's degree programs with excellent placement of graduates in good jobs. One unique feature of the MBA program was the option for MBA students in three of the five departments in the Business School to do a field project instead of writing a master's thesis. The field projects involved a team of two or three students in the final year of the program who conducted a mini-consulting project in a local organization under faculty supervision. The field projects provided the students an opportunity to learn more skills relevant for their career, and many of the MBA graduates were hired for good jobs in the companies where they had conducted a field project. Except for nonprofit organizations, project clients were charged a fee that was used to cover project expenses and to support faculty research. The new Dean resented his lack of control over the use of funds generated by the field projects. In conversations with the Provost, who had responsibility for administration of academic programs, he falsely claimed that the field projects were improper, ineffective, and should be eliminated.

The new Dean also failed to appreciate the importance and benefits of the small doctoral program that was housed in the Business School. It was a low-cost program because much of the required coursework involved using some of the MBA courses and some doctoral courses in other parts of the university such as the School of Public Administration. The Business School only needed to provide a few doctoral courses, and members of the program faculty did not get workload credit for supervising doctoral research projects and dissertations. Because he lacked the publications and research skills needed to supervise doctoral research, the new Dean had never been invited to join the doctoral program faculty, and it was a source of resentment for him. In conversations with the Academic Vice President, the new Dean claimed that doctoral students funded by graduate assistantships made no worthwhile contribution to faculty research and were less effective than adjuncts for teaching undergraduate courses. Both claims were false. The research supported by doctoral students was being published and had even won best paper awards. The careful selection and training of doctoral students for teaching undergraduate courses yielded high student ratings for these courses. It was difficult to find qualified adjuncts, and adding more of them would reduce the chance that the upcoming accreditation review for the undergraduate programs would be successful. Without consulting the doctoral program director and faculty, the Dean made a decision to eliminate the funding of most assistantships for doctoral students. He figured that the members of the Business School faculty who did not participate in the doctoral program would not care if it was ended.

The new Dean made little effort to socialize with members of the Business School faculty or to keep informed about their activities and challenges. Unlike previous deans, he did not host an annual party for faculty at his house or a country club. When the Dean's efforts to eliminate the doctoral program and MBA field projects were discovered, a secret meeting was held for full-time faculty and most of them voted to remove the Dean. The Provost was informed about the Dean's lies, arbitrary bad decisions, and lack of faculty approval. Her initial resistance was overcome when she was reminded that his qualifications for the position were weak and there was no affirmative action search, which is a university requirement for selection of deans. A decision was soon made to dismiss the Dean and initiate a proper search for a replacement.

—*Written by* Gary Yukl

Questions

1. What influence tactics were used by the Acting Dean to get promoted?
2. How much of each type of power did the new Dean possess over the Business School faculty?
3. What power bases and influence tactics were used to get the new Dean dismissed?

Chapter 7

Leader Traits and Skills

Learning Objectives

After studying this chapter, you should be able to:

- Understand how leader traits and skills are related to effective leadership.
- Understand what traits and skills are most relevant for effective leadership.
- Understand what traits and skills best predict success in a managerial career.
- Understand how the relevance of a trait or skill depends on the situation.
- Understand the limitations of the trait approach.

Introduction

One of the earliest approaches to studying leadership was the search for personality traits and skills that predict whether a person will attain positions of leadership and be effective in those positions. This approach is commonly called the "trait approach" to differentiate it from other approaches used to explain effective leadership. This chapter reviews research on the personality traits and skills that contribute to leadership effectiveness and advancement to higher levels of management in organizations. The chapter begins with an explanation of basic concepts and research methods, then major findings about personality traits and skills related to effective leadership are reviewed, and some situations that affect their relevance are described. The chapter ends with guidelines for managers based on the findings.

Different Types of Leader Attributes

A variety of individual attributes have been examined in the leadership research, including aspects of personality, temperament, needs, motives, and values. Personality traits are relatively stable dispositions to behave in a particular way, and some examples are self-confidence, extroversion, emotional maturity, and energy level. Social needs and motives are also important traits, because they influence a person's attention to information and events, and they guide, energize, and sustain behavior. Examples include the need for achievement, esteem, affiliation, power, and independence. Considerable evidence shows that most traits are jointly determined by learning and by an inherited capacity to gain satisfaction from particular types of stimuli or experiences (Arvey, Li, & Wang, 2016; Bouchard, Lykken, McGue, Segal, & Tellegen, 1990; Zhang, Ilies, & Arvey, 2009). Some traits (e.g., social needs) are probably more influenced by learning than others (temperament, physiological needs).

Values are internalized attitudes about what is right and wrong, ethical and unethical, moral and immoral. Examples include fairness and justice, honesty, freedom, equality, altruism, loyalty, civility (courtesy and politeness), pragmatism, and performance orientation (excellence). Values are important because they influence a person's preferences, perception of problems, and choice of behavior. Values relevant for ethical leadership are discussed in Chapter 9, and values studied in cross-cultural research are discussed in Chapter 13.

Self-concepts, self-identities, and social identities involve values and beliefs about a person's occupation, relationships to others, and worthwhile roles and activities. It is usually assumed that people are intrinsically motivated to defend their self-esteem and to maintain consistency among their core values, social identities, and behavior.

Skills are the ability to do something in an effective manner, and as with traits they are determined jointly by learning and heredity (Arvey, Zhang, Avolio, & Krueger, 2007). Skills may be defined at different levels of abstraction, ranging from general, broadly defined abilities (e.g., intelligence, interpersonal skills, conceptual skills, technical skills) to narrower, more specific abilities (verbal reasoning, problem-solving skill).

A competency may involve traits, skills, or a combination of related skills and traits. Competencies are often used to describe qualities considered relevant for managers in a particular organization, profession, or situation.

Types of Research on Leader Traits and Skills

Several types of research have been used to learn how leader traits and skills are related to measures of leadership effectiveness, such as subordinate satisfaction and performance, unit performance, or ratings of leader effectiveness by bosses (Bass, 1990, 2008; Boyatzis, 1982; Stogdill, 1974). In studies to discover traits and skills that predict whether a person will pursue a leadership career (Lord, DeVader, & Alliger, 1986; Stogdill, 1974), leaders are compared to non-leaders in the same profession. Other studies have identified the traits and skills of individuals who emerge as informal leaders in a group problem-solving exercise.

Many studies examine how the traits and skills for leaders in similar managerial or administrative positions are related to measures of their leadership effectiveness. The leader traits and skills are usually measured by tests, coded critical incidents, leader self-ratings, or ratings by other people such as subordinates or bosses. Some studies measure the traits and skills after leaders have been in their current position long enough to assess their performance. Other studies are conducted over a period of several years to discover the traits and skills that predict effectiveness in the leader's current position or later advancement to higher levels of management and career success. Relevant traits and skills are measured with tests, interviews, and biographical information collected during the selection process for a managerial job or in assessment centers used to identify promising candidates for promotion (e.g., Bray, Campbell, & Grant, 1974; Howard & Bray, 1988; McClelland & Boyatzis, 1982; Miner, 1978).

Some longitudinal studies compare managers who advanced successfully to top management position to managers who initially advanced but then "derailed" in their careers because they were dismissed, took early retirement, or simply reached a "plateau" without any chance of further advancement (Braddy, Gooty, Fleenor, & Yammarino, 2014;

McCall & Lombardo, 1983a; McCartney & Campbell, 2006). Information about the traits, skills, and career experiences of each manager is collected and analyzed to identify similarities and differences for derailed and successful managers. In a cross-cultural version of this research, executives and middle managers rated the extent to which various flaws are likely to derail a management career in the United States and Europe (Lombardo & McCauley, 1988; Van Velsor & Leslie, 1995). Subsequent cross-cultural research suggests that individuals who lack awareness and engage in self-enhancement are seen by their bosses as being highly likely to derail in collectivistic, but not individualistic cultures, because they violate cultural norms for modesty (Cullen, Gentry, & Yammarino, 2015).

Some other studies have attempted to determine the extent to which leader traits and skills are the result of heredity or learning. By comparing identical twins (who share 100% of their genetic background) to fraternal twins (who share roughly 50% of their genetic background), insights into the influence of genetic versus environmental factors can be gained. The evidence suggests that genetic factors account for 30% of the variance in the attainment of leadership roles, as well as the possession of personality traits associated with leadership, such as self confidence and need for achievement (Arvey, Rotundo, Johnson, Zhang, & McGue, 2006). Cutting-edge genetic research also reveals that people who possess "r64950, a single nucleotide polymorphism (SNP) residing on a neuronal acetylcholine receptor gene (*CHRNB3*)" are more likely to occupy leadership positions (De Neve, Mikhaylov, Dawes, Christakis, & Fowler, 2013, p. 45), while those who have the dopamine transporter gene DAT1 are less likely to have a proactive personality, and hence less likely to hold leadership roles (Li et al., 2015). The research indicates that leadership success involves a combination of inherited and learned attributes.

Overview of Findings in the Research

How the emergence, effectiveness, and career advancement of leaders is related to their traits and skills has been investigated in hundreds of studies, and the results have been reported in several reviews and meta-analyses (Bass, 1990, 2008; Judge, Piccolo, & Kosalka, 2009; Stogdill, 1974; Zaccaro, 2007, 2012; Zaccaro, Dubrow, & Kolze, 2018). Some traits and skills increase the likelihood that a person will be selected or elected to fill a leadership position. Some traits and skills increase the effectiveness of a leader, but they do not guarantee it. A leader with certain traits can be effective in one situation but ineffective in a different situation. The pattern of traits and skills that best predicts leader effectiveness also varies somewhat for different outcomes, such as leader selection, advancement, performance by the leader's work unit, and subordinate satisfaction.

Personality Traits and Effective Leadership

Over a period of several decades, researchers examined a variety of different personality traits related to managerial effectiveness and advancement. The choice of traits and the labels used for them have varied from study to study, but the results have been fairly consistent across different research methods. This section summarizes and integrates the findings regarding the most relevant aspects of personality for effective leadership by managers and administrators in large organizations (see also Table 7-1). For some of the traits and skills, it is possible to explain why they affect outcomes by examining how they affect the leader behaviors described in other chapters.

TABLE 7-1 Specific Traits Related to Leadership Effectiveness

- High energy level and stress tolerance
- Internal locus of control orientation
- Emotional stability and maturity
- High core self-evaluations
- Personal integrity
- Socialized power motivation
- Moderately high achievement orientation
- Moderately high self-confidence
- Moderately low need for affiliation

Energy Level and Stress Tolerance

The trait research finds that energy level, physical stamina, and stress tolerance are associated with managerial effectiveness (Bass, 1990, 2008; Howard & Bray, 1988). High energy level and stress tolerance help managers cope with the hectic pace, long hours, and unrelenting demands of most managerial jobs. Physical vitality and emotional resilience make it easier to cope with stressful interpersonal situations, such as a punitive boss, a troubled subordinate, an uncooperative peer, or a hostile client. Effective problem solving requires an ability to remain calm and stay focused on a problem rather than panicking, denying the problem exists, or attempting to shift responsibility to someone else. In addition to making better decisions, a leader with high stress tolerance and composure is more likely to stay calm and provide confident, decisive direction to subordinates in a crisis.

Managerial jobs often have a high level of stress, especially when there is pressure to make important decisions without adequate information and the need to resolve role conflicts and satisfy incompatible demands made by different parties. Tolerance of stress is especially important for executives who must deal with adverse situations where the leader's reputation and career, or the lives and jobs of subordinates, may hang in the balance. Narasimha Murthy, Founder and CEO of Connectivity Solutions opines that:

> "Stress is a combination of multiple factors in everyday work. One has to be on the toes to acquire a new customer or cater to the existing customer demand, handle internal stakeholders. It is not just one thing."

Self-Confidence

The term self-confidence is defined in a general way to include several related concepts such as self-esteem and self-efficacy. Most studies on leader self-confidence or self-efficacy found that it is related positively to effectiveness and advancement (see Bass, 1990, 2008; Hannah, Avolio, Luthans, & Harms, 2008). Self-confidence differentiated between effective and ineffective managers in a study of critical incidents by Boyatzis (1982), and self-confidence predicted subsequent advancement to higher levels of management in the assessment center research at AT&T (Howard & Bray, 1988). Other research finds that self-confidence is essential for charismatic leadership (see Chapter 8).

The relationship of self-confidence to leadership effectiveness can be understood by examining how this trait affects a leader's behavior. Leaders with high self-confidence are more likely to attempt difficult tasks and to set challenging objectives for themselves. Confident leaders take more initiative to solve problems and introduce desirable changes (Paglis & Green, 2002). Leaders who have high expectations for themselves are likely to have high expectations for subordinates as well (Kouzes & Posner, 1987). These leaders are more persistent in pursuit of difficult objectives, despite initial problems and setbacks. Their optimism and persistence in efforts to accomplish a task or mission are likely to increase commitment by subordinates, peers, and superiors to support the effort. Leaders with self-confidence are likely to be more decisive in a crisis, where success often depends on the perception by subordinates that the leader has the knowledge and courage necessary to deal with the crisis effectively. Finally, self-confidence is related to an action-oriented approach for dealing with problems. Leaders with low self-confidence are more likely to put off dealing with difficult problems or to shift responsibility to someone else (Kipnis & Lane, 1962).

There are some clear advantages of having self-confidence, but if it becomes excessive some dysfunctional behaviors may occur. Excessive self-confidence may make a leader overly optimistic about the likely success of a risky venture, and it may result in rash decisions and denial of evidence that a plan is flawed. A manager with extremely high self-confidence is inclined to be arrogant, autocratic, and intolerant of dissenting viewpoints, especially if the manager is not emotionally mature. Because the manager is unresponsive to ideas and concerns expressed by others, the benefits of participative leadership are unlikely to be realized. Thus, in situations where the leader does not have vastly superior expertise than subordinates, a moderately high amount of self-confidence may be better than either extremely high self-confidence or low self-confidence.

The arrogance and know-it-all attitude associated with excessive self-confidence have another negative side effect. An arrogant manager will have difficulty in developing cooperative relationships with people who are not dependent on the manager's specialized expertise. Acting arrogant toward people who have more expertise than the manager may create enemies who are able to derail the manager's career.

Internal Locus of Control

Another trait that appears to be relevant to managerial effectiveness is called the locus of control orientation, which is measured with a personality scale developed by Rotter (1966). People with a strong internal locus of control orientation (called "internals") believe that events in their lives are determined more by their own actions than by chance or uncontrollable forces. In contrast, people with a strong external control orientation (called "externals") believe that events are determined mostly by chance or fate and they can do little to improve their lives.

Because internals believe that they can influence their own destiny, they take more responsibility for their own actions and for the performance of their organization. Internals have a more future-oriented perspective, and they are more likely to proactively plan how to accomplish objectives. They take more initiative than externals in discovering and solving problems. They are confident in their ability to influence people and are more likely to use persuasion rather than coercive or manipulative influence tactics (Goodstadt & Hjelle, 1973). They are more flexible, adaptive, and innovative in their response to a problem and in their management strategies (Miller, Kets de Vries, & Toulouse, 1982). When setbacks or failures occur, they are more likely to learn from them rather than just dismissing them as bad luck.

Research on the relationship of this trait to managerial effectiveness is still limited, but the results suggest that a strong internal locus of control orientation is positively associated with managerial effectiveness. For example, Miller and Toulouse (1986) conducted a study of chief executive officers in 97 firms and found that internals were more effective than externals in terms of objective criteria such as profitability and sales growth. The relationship was stronger for firms in dynamic environments where it is more important to have major product innovations. Howell and Avolio (1993) conducted a study of 76 executives in a large financial institution and found that internals had better business-unit performance than externals for the year following the measurement of personality. However, there is also evidence that an internal locus of control is not always linked to socially responsible behavior. Keller and Foster (2012), for example, found that U.S. presidents with an internal versus external locus of control were more likely to engage in risky diversionary strategies for domestic political purposes. Internality of locus of control was positively and significantly related with overall managerial effectiveness; (ii) internally controlled managers were significantly higher on overall managerial effectiveness as compared to externally controlled managers (Nair & Yuvaraj, 2000).

Emotional Stability and Maturity

The term emotional maturity may be defined broadly to encompass several interrelated motives, traits, and values. A person who is emotionally mature is well adjusted and does not suffer from severe psychological disorders. Emotionally mature people have more self-awareness of strengths and weaknesses, and they are oriented toward self-improvement instead of denying weaknesses and fantasizing success. People with high emotional maturity are less self-centered (they care more about other people), they have more self-control (are less impulsive and more able to resist hedonistic temptations), they have more stable emotions (are not prone to extreme mood swings or outbursts of anger), and they are less defensive (are more receptive to criticism and more willing to learn from mistakes). They are also more likely to be at a high level of cognitive moral development (see Chapter 9). As a result, leaders with high emotional maturity maintain more cooperative relationships with subordinates, peers, and superiors. The following description (George, 2003, p. 15) includes many of these attributes:

> I too have struggled in getting comfortable with my weaknesses—my tendency to intimidate others with an overly challenging style, my impatience, and my occasional lack of tact. Only recently have I realized that my strengths and weaknesses are two sides of the same coin. By challenging others in business meetings, I am able to get quickly to the heart of the issues, but my approach unnerves and intimidates less confident people. My desire to get things done fast leads to superior results, but it exposes my impatience with people who move more slowly. Being direct with others gets the message across clearly but often lacks tact. Over time I have moderated my style and adapted my approach to make sure that people are engaged and empowered and that their voices are fully heard.

Most of the empirical research on traits shows that key components of emotional maturity are associated with managerial effectiveness and advancement (Bass, 1990, 2008). A study by McCauley and Lombardo (1990) with a measure called benchmarks found that managers with good self-awareness and a desire to improve had higher advancement. Self-objectivity and general adjustment predicted advancement in the AT&T research by Howard and Bray (1988). Other research has found that effective executives have a good understanding of their own strengths and weaknesses, and they are oriented toward self-improvement rather than being defensive (e.g., Bennis & Nanus, 1985; Tichy & Devanna, 1986). More recently, evidence that women leaders tend to believe that they are seen by bosses as less capable than male leaders reflects a lack of self-awareness and self-confidence that has negative consequences for their advancement and causes organizations to underutilize their talents (Sturm, Taylor, Atwater, & Braddy, 2014). The research on socialized and personalized power orientation also provides evidence about the importance of emotional maturity for effective leadership.

Core Self-Evaluation

While there is ample evidence that the traits of self-confidence (also known as generalized self-efficacy), internal locus of control, and emotional stability are linked to leadership emergence and effectiveness, some of the research also indicates that the combination of these traits, coupled with high self-esteem, is especially important. Such core self-evaluations reflect a broad personality trait that involves "a basic, fundamental appraisal of one's worthiness, effectiveness, and capability as a person" (Judge, Erez, Bono, & Thoresen, 2003, p. 304). A study of 75 CEOs of Major League Baseball teams over a 100-year time period revealed that CEOs with high core self-evaluations had teams that won more games and had better attendance by fans (Resick, Whitman, Wengarden, & Hiller, 2009). Another study of 150 leaders and 464 employees of three Chinese organizations (Hu, Wang, Liden, & Sun, 2012) found that leaders with high core self-evaluations were more likely to instill confidence in followers and inspire them to achieve better outcomes.

Power Motivation

Someone with a high need for power enjoys influencing people and events and is more likely to seek positions of authority. Most studies find a strong relationship between need for power and advancement to higher levels of management in large organizations (e.g., Howard & Bray, 1988; McClelland & Boyatzis, 1982; Stahl, 1983). People with a strong need for power seek positions of authority and power, and they are likely to be more attuned to the power politics of organizations.

A strong need for power is relevant to managerial role requirements involving the use of power and influence. Managers in large organizations must exercise power to influence subordinates, peers, and superiors. People who are low in need for power usually lack the desire and assertiveness necessary to organize and direct group activities, to negotiate favorable agreements, to lobby for necessary resources, to advocate and promote desirable changes, and to impose necessary discipline. A person who finds such behavior difficult and emotionally disturbing or who believes it is wrong to exercise power over others is unlikely to satisfy the role requirements of a managerial job (Miner, 1985).

A strong need for power is desirable, but a manager's effectiveness also depends on how this need finds expression. The empirical research indicates that a socialized power orientation is more likely to result in effective leadership than a personalized power orientation (Boyatzis, 1982; House, Spangler, & Woycke, 1991; McClelland & Boyatzis, 1982; McClelland & Burnham, 1976; Steinmann, Dörr, Schultheiss, & Maier, 2015). Only a few studies have examined the behaviors associated with each power orientation, but the results indicate significant differences (McClelland, 1975, 1985; Steinmann et al., 2015).

Managers with a personalized power orientation use power to aggrandize themselves and satisfy their strong need for esteem and status. They have little inhibition or self-control, and they exercise power impulsively. According to McClelland and Burnham (1976, p. 103), "They are more rude to other people, they drink too much, they try to exploit others sexually, and they collect symbols of personal prestige such as fancy cars or big offices." Personalized power leaders seek to dominate subordinates by keeping them weak and dependent. Authority for making important decisions is centralized in the leader, information is restricted, and rewards and punishments are used to manipulate and control subordinates. The leader tries to play off different individuals or factions against each other to keep them weak. Assistance and advice to a subordinate are provided in a way that demonstrates personal superiority and the inferiority and dependence of the subordinate. Sometimes personalized power leaders are able to inspire subordinate loyalty and team spirit, but adverse consequences are more likely to occur. When problems are encountered in the work, subordinates are reluctant to take any initiative in solving them. Instead of acting quickly to deal with a problem, they ignore it or wait for explicit directions from the leader.

Managers with a socialized power orientation are more emotionally mature. They exercise power more for the benefit of others, are hesitant about using power in a manipulative manner, are less egoistic and defensive, accumulate fewer material possessions, have a longer-range view, and are more willing to take advice from people with relevant expertise. Their strong need for power is expressed by using influence to build up the organization and make it successful. Because of their orientation toward building organizational commitment, this kind of leader is more likely to use a participative, coaching style of managerial behavior and is less likely to be coercive and autocratic. Such leaders "help make their subordinates feel strong and responsible, bind them less with petty rules, help produce a clear organizational structure, and create pride in belonging to the unit" (McClelland, 1975, p. 302).

Personal Integrity

Integrity means that a person's behavior is consistent with espoused values, and the person is honest, ethical, and trustworthy (Bauman, 2013; Palanski & Yammarino, 2009). Integrity is a primary determinant of interpersonal trust. Unless one is perceived to be trustworthy, it is difficult to retain the loyalty of followers or to obtain cooperation and support from peers and superiors. Moreover, a major determinant of expert and referent power is the perception by others that a person is trustworthy. Values related to integrity include honesty, loyalty, fairness, justice, and altruism.

Several types of behaviors are related to integrity. One important indicator of integrity is the extent to which one is honest and truthful rather than deceptive. Leaders lose credibility when people discover that they have lied or made claims that are grossly distorted. Another indicator of integrity is keeping promises. People are reluctant to negotiate agreements with a leader who cannot be trusted to keep promises. A third indicator of integrity is the extent to which a leader fulfils the responsibility of service and loyalty to followers. The trust of followers will be lost if they discover the leader exploited or manipulated them in pursuit of self-interest. A fourth indicator of integrity is the extent to which a leader can be trusted not to indiscriminately repeat something said in the utmost confidence. People will not pass on important but sensitive information to a leader who cannot be trusted to keep a secret. A key determinant of perceived integrity is the extent to which a leader's behavior is consistent with values articulated repeatedly to followers. A leader who hopes to inspire others to support an ideology or vision must set an example in his or her own behavior. Finally, integrity also means taking responsibility for one's actions and decisions. Leaders appear weak and undependable when they make a decision or take a position on an issue, then try to deny responsibility later if the decision is unsuccessful or the position becomes controversial.

Integrity was mentioned as an important value by most of the 45 British chief executives in a study by Cox and Cooper (1989). The CCL research described earlier found that lack of integrity was common among the managers whose careers derailed, whereas managers who succeeded were regarded as having strong integrity. The successful managers were honest and dependable; they would carry out promised actions and inform people in advance about any necessary changes. The Project GLOBE (Global Leadership Organizational Behavior Effectiveness) study of 62 cultures identified integrity as a universally endorsed attribute of outstanding leadership (Den Hartog et al., 1999). Integrity is an important aspect of ethical, authentic, and spiritual leadership, which is discussed in Chapter 9.

Narcissism

Narcissism is a personality syndrome that includes several traits relevant to effective leadership, such as a strong need for esteem (e.g., prestige, status, attention, admiration, adulation), a strong personalized need for power, low emotional maturity, and low integrity. This personality syndrome can be measured with a self-report scale called the Narcissistic Personality Inventory (Raskin & Hall, 1981).

Researchers with a background in clinical psychology and psychoanalysis have described the origins of narcissism and the behaviors associated with it (Kets de Vries & Miller, 1984, 1985; Raskin, Novacek, & Hogan, 1991). People whose parents have been emotionally unresponsive and rejecting may come to believe that they cannot depend on anyone's love or loyalty. In an effort to cope with their inner loneliness and fear, they become preoccupied with establishing their power, status, and control. They have fantasies of success and power, and a grandiose, exaggerated sense of their own self-importance and unique talents. To support this self-deception, they seek continuous attention and admiration from others.

Because they are so preoccupied with their own ego needs, narcissists have little empathy or concern for the feelings and needs of others. They exploit and manipulate others to indulge their desire for self-aggrandizement without feeling any remorse. They expect special favors from others without feeling any need for reciprocity. Narcissists tend to oversimplify human relationships and motives and see everything in extreme good and bad terms. People are viewed either as loyal supporters or as enemies. Narcissists are very defensive and view criticism by others as a sign of rejection and disloyalty. Narcissists can be charming and helpful when they want to impress someone who is important, but they are likely to be aggressive and cruel with people who have little power, especially someone who opposes them or stands in their way. The following example describes a narcissistic manager:

> He was very talented in handling technical problems, but his remarkable results were achieved at a horrible cost to others. He was moody, volatile, and completely devoid of sensitivity, kindness, or patience. Any subordinate who made a serious mistake was loudly criticized in front of others with scathing remarks or questions such as "How could you be so stupid?" He did not tolerate any disagreement, and subordinates were afraid to suggest changes that would make the unit more effective. Ironically, he could be charming and pleasant when it suited his purpose, which was usually when interacting with top management.

The research on narcissism provides additional insights into the difficulties encountered by leaders with low emotional maturity and a personalized power orientation (House & Howell, 1992; Rosenthal & Pittinsky, 2006). Narcissists in leadership positions have a number of characteristic flaws (Glad, 2002; Kets de Vries & Miller, 1984, 1985). They surround themselves with subordinates who are loyal and uncritical. They make decisions without gathering adequate information about the environment. In the belief that they alone are sufficiently informed and talented to decide what is best, objective advice is not sought or accepted from subordinates and peers. They tend to undertake ambitious, grandiose projects to glorify themselves, but in the absence of an adequate analysis of the situation, the projects are likely to be risky and unrealistic. When a project is not going well, they tend to ignore or reject negative information, thereby missing the opportunity to correct problems in time to avert a disaster. When failure is finally evident, the narcissistic leader refuses to admit any responsibility, but instead finds scapegoats to blame. Even initiatives that involve improving corporate social responsibility are likely to be short-lived and unsustainable (Petrenko, Aime, Ridge, & Hill, 2016). Given the dysfunctional nature of such behaviors, it is not surprising that research has shown that firms led by narcissistic CEOs are more likely to manipulate accounting data (Ham, Lang, Seybert, & Sean, 2017), they tend to overpay for acquisitions (Chatterjee & Hambrick, 2007, 2011), and they are more vulnerable to litigation (O'Reilly III, Doerr, & Chatman, 2018). Finally, because they exploit the organization to compensate for their own sense of inadequacy, extreme narcissists are unable to plan for an orderly succession of leadership. They see themselves as indispensable and cling to power, in contrast to emotionally mature executives who are able to retire gracefully when their job is done and it is time for new leadership.

Despite the many negative aspects of narcissism, this personality syndrome may also have some positive aspects, at least in limited situations (Rosenthal & Pittinsky, 2006). Research on U.S. presidents (Deluga, 1998) and CEOs of computer and software companies (Chatterjee & Hambrick, 2007) found that some of the most and least successful leaders were narcissistic. The strong self-confidence and optimism of narcissistic leaders facilitates their efforts to influence others to pursue bold, innovative objectives, which may or may not prove to be feasible and worthwhile. Despite questionable motives for proposing risky new initiatives, a narcissistic person is sometimes successful in leading an organization's response to serious threats or unusual opportunities. However, a narcissistic leader is less likely to be effective than a leader who has strong self-confidence and optimism combined with a socialized power orientation and high emotional maturity.

Achievement Orientation

Achievement orientation includes a set of related needs and values, including need for achievement, willingness to assume responsibility, performance orientation, and concern for task objectives. Many studies have been conducted on the relationship of achievement orientation to managerial advancement and effectiveness (see Bass, 1990, 2008). However, the results have not been consistent for different criteria (e.g., advancement, effectiveness) and for different types of managerial positions (e.g., entrepreneurial managers, corporate general managers, technical managers).

The relationship of achievement motivation to managerial effectiveness is complex. Some studies find a positive relationship between achievement motivation and effectiveness (e.g., Stahl, 1983; Wainer & Rubin, 1969), but other studies find a negative relationship (House, Spangler, & Woycke, 1991) or no evidence of a strong, significant relationship (Miller & Toulouse, 1986). One possible explanation for these inconsistent findings is that the relationship of achievement motivation to managerial effectiveness is curvilinear rather than linear. In other words, managers with a moderately high amount of achievement motivation are more effective than managers with low achievement motivation, or managers with very high achievement motivation.

Research on the behavioral correlates of achievement orientation is still limited, but some relationships appear likely. Compared to managers with a weak achievement orientation, managers with a strong achievement orientation are likely to have a strong concern for task objectives; they are more willing to assume responsibility for solving task-related problems; they are more likely to take the initiative in discovering these problems and acting decisively to solve them; and they prefer solutions that involve moderate levels of risk rather than solutions that are either very risky or very conservative. These managers are likely to engage in task behaviors such as setting challenging but realistic goals and deadlines, developing specific action plans, determining ways to overcome obstacles, organizing the work efficiently, and emphasizing performance when talking to others (Boyatzis, 1982). In contrast, a manager with a weak achievement orientation is not motivated to seek opportunities involving challenging objectives and moderate risks and is less willing to take the initiative to identify problems and to assume responsibility for solving them.

A strong achievement orientation may also result in behavior that undermines managerial effectiveness. If need for achievement is the dominant motive, it is likely that a manager will seek personal achievement and advancement rather than achievements by the team or work unit. The manager will try to accomplish everything alone, be reluctant to delegate, and fail to develop a strong sense of responsibility and task commitment among subordinates (McClelland & Burnham, 1976; Miller & Toulouse, 1986). It is especially difficult for this type of person to function effectively in a management team in which leadership responsibility is shared.

The way in which achievement orientation finds expression in behavior depends on the manager's overall motive pattern. Achievement motivation enhances leadership effectiveness only if it is subordinated to a stronger need for socialized power, so that the manager's efforts are directed toward building a successful team. When combined with a personalized need for power, strong achievement motivation may be focused on career advancement at any cost. This type of manager will neglect task objectives and the development of subordinates in an effort to build a personal reputation as a fast-rising star. Task decisions will be guided by a desire for short-term achievements, even though unit performance may suffer in the longer run. The manager is likely to take personal control over promising, highly visible projects and will take most of the credit for success. A manager who is very competitive may refuse to cooperate with peers who are viewed as potential rivals. As found in the CCL study, the result is likely to be initial advancement but eventual derailment when a manager with overriding personal ambition and excessive competitiveness makes too many powerful enemies.

Additional insights are provided by research on the Type A personality, which appears to combine a strong achievement orientation with a strong need for control over events (Baron, 1989; Nahavandi, Mizzi, & Malekzadeh, 1992; Strube, Turner, Cerro, Stevens, & Hinchey, 1984). Managers with this personality syndrome have high expectations for themselves and are very competitive. They set high performance objectives, compare themselves with others, and want to win any contest. Type A managers are also highly concerned about time; they feel rushed much of the time, try to do more than one thing at a time, and are impatient with delays. They prefer to maintain control over all aspects of their work, which makes them poor delegators and reluctant to work in a team (Miller, Lack, & Asroff, 1985). Finally, Type A managers tend to be more angry and inclined to express their hostility when unable to control events. They are demanding, intolerant of mistakes, and critical of people who are not as intensely dedicated. This behavior pattern makes it more difficult for them to maintain cooperative relationships.

Need for Affiliation

As noted earlier in this chapter, people with a strong need for affiliation receive great satisfaction from being liked and accepted by others, and they enjoy working with people who are friendly and cooperative. Most studies find a negative correlation between the need for affiliation and managerial effectiveness. The ineffectiveness of managers with a high need for affiliation can be understood by examining the typical pattern of behavior for such managers. These managers are concerned primarily about interpersonal relationships rather than the task, and they are unwilling to allow the work to interfere with harmonious relationships (Litwin & Stringer, 1966; McClelland, 1975). They seek to avoid conflicts or smooth them over rather than confront genuine differences. They avoid making necessary but unpopular decisions. They dispense rewards in a way designed to gain approval, rather than rewarding effective performance. They show favoritism to personal friends in making assignments and allowing exceptions to rules. This pattern of behavior often leaves subordinates feeling "weak, irresponsible, and without a sense of what might happen next, of where they stand in relation to their manager, or even of what they ought to be doing" (McClelland & Burnham, 1976, p. 104).

It is clearly undesirable for a manager to have a strong need for affiliation, but a very low need for affiliation can also have undesirable consequences. A person with low need for affiliation tends to be a "loner" who does not like to socialize with others, except perhaps the immediate family or a few close friends. This type of person may lack the motivation to engage in the many social and public relations activities that are essential for a manager, including those involved in establishing effective interpersonal relationships with subordinates, superiors, and peers. As a result, this type of person may fail to develop effective interpersonal skills and may lack confidence in being able to influence others. Thus, it is likely that a moderate level of affiliation motivation is best rather than either a high or very low level.

The Big Five Personality Traits

Describing leaders in terms of their individual profiles would be easier if there was an integrative conceptual framework with a small number of meta-categories that encompass all of the relevant traits. The proliferation of personality traits identified over the past century has resulted in efforts to find a small number of broadly defined categories that would simplify the development of trait theories. One such effort that appears promising is referred to as the five-factor model of personality or the "Big Five" model (e.g., Digman, 1990; Hough, 1992; McCrae & Costa, 1999, 2008). The five broadly defined personality traits in the taxonomy have somewhat different labels from one version to another. The traits include surgency (or extroversion), dependability (or conscientiousness), adjustment (or neuroticism), intellectance (or openness to experience), and agreeableness.

In the ensuing years, leadership scholars have shown increasing interest in using this taxonomy to facilitate interpretation of results in the massive and confusing literature on leadership traits (e.g., Abatecola, Mandarelli, & Poggesi, 2013; De Hoogh, Den Hartog, & Koopman, 2005; Hofmann & Jones, 2005; Oh & Berry, 2009). Table 7-2 shows how the five broad trait categories correspond to many of the specific traits found relevant for leadership emergence, advancement, or effectiveness in the trait studies reviewed earlier in this chapter.

Reviews and meta-analyses of studies on the five factors find that most of them are related to leader emergence and effectiveness (e.g., Bono & Judge, 2004; Judge, Bono, Ilies, & Gerhardt, 2002). Effective leaders had higher scores on extroversion, conscientiousness, and openness to learning from experience, and lower scores on neuroticism. However, the results were not consistent across studies or for different types of organizations. One likely reason for inconsistent results is the use of different measures to represent the five factors, including surrogate measures that do not adequately represent a factor. Another reason for inconsistent results may be the use of different criterion variables (e.g., leadership emergence, advancement, or effectiveness; subjective or objective measures).

TABLE 7-2 Correspondence of the Big Five Traits with Specific Traits

Big Five Personality Traits	Specific Traits
Surgency	Extroversion (outgoing)
	Energy/Activity Level
	Need for Power (assertive)
Conscientiousness	Dependability
	Personal Integrity
	Need for Achievement
Agreeableness	Cheerful and Optimistic
	Nurturance (sympathetic, helpful)
	Need for Affiliation
Adjustment	Emotional Stability
	Self-Esteem
	Self-Control
Intellectance	Curious and Inquisitive
	Open Minded
	Learning Oriented

Based on Hogan, Curphy, & Hogan (1994).

While research on the five-factor model suggests that extraversion is positively related to leadership emergence, care should be taken not to assume the leadership is the sole province of extraverts. Susan Cain (2012, p. 2) offers the following powerful example of a quiet and reserved leader who permanently changed our world for the better:

> I had always imagined Rosa Parks as a stately woman with a bold temperament, someone who could easily stand up to a busload of glowering passengers. But when she died in 2005 at the age of ninety-two, the flood of obituaries recalled her as soft-spoken, sweet, and small in stature. They said she was "timid and shy" but had the "courage of a lion."

Thus, while extraverts who speak forcefully and demand attention fit the stereotype of the confident and effective leader, a more reserved individual who reflects on a problem before rushing to action may ultimately produce more creative solutions to perplexing problems. As Susan Cain (2012, p. 6) observes, this may explain "how figures like Eleanor Roosevelt, Al Gore, Warren Buffet, Gandhi—and Rosa Parks—achieved what they did, not in spite of but because of their introversion."

Not all scholars agree that the Big Five model of personality is better than taxonomies with more specific traits (cf., Block, 1995; Hough, 1992). If both relevant and irrelevant traits are included in a broadly defined factor, the accuracy of prediction will be lower. Even when the component traits are all relevant, they may not have the same relationship with different criteria of leadership effectiveness. More research is needed to determine whether the Big Five traits predict and explain leadership effectiveness better than the specific component traits. Such research should be based on a theory that clearly describes how the leader traits are related to specific types of behavior that can explain why the traits are related to leadership effectiveness.

Skills and Effective Leadership

The early research on leader characteristics identified several skills that are related to the advancement and effectiveness of leaders. Many different taxonomies have been proposed for classifying managerial skills, but the most useful and parsimonious taxonomy uses the three broadly defined skill categories called technical skills, interpersonal skills, and conceptual skills (see Table 7-3). Similar versions of this taxonomy were proposed by Katz (1955) and Mann (1965). The technical skills are primarily concerned with things, the interpersonal skills (or "social skills") are primarily concerned with people, and the conceptual skills (or "cognitive skills") are primarily concerned with ideas and concepts.

Some writers also differentiate a fourth category of skills (called administrative skills or strategic management skills) that includes selected aspects of the other three categories and are defined in terms of the ability to perform a particular type of managerial function or behavior such as planning, negotiating, and coaching (e.g., Hooijberg, Hunt, & Dodge, 1997; Hunt, 1991; Mumford et al., 2007). These administrative skills are discussed along with related behaviors relevant for strategic leadership in Chapter 12.

Technical Skills

Technical skills include knowledge about methods, processes, and equipment for conducting the specialized activities of the manager's organizational unit. Technical skills also include factual knowledge about the organization (rules, structure, management systems, employee characteristics), and knowledge about the organization's products and services (technical specifications, strengths, and limitations). This type of knowledge is acquired by a combination of formal education, training, and job experience. Acquisition of technical knowledge is facilitated by a good memory for details and the ability to learn technical material quickly. Effective managers are able to obtain information and ideas from many sources and store it away in their memory for use when they need it.

TABLE 7-3 Three-Factor Taxonomy of Broadly Defined Skills

Technical Skills: Knowledge about methods, processes, procedures, and techniques for conducting a specialized activity, and the ability to use tools and equipment relevant to that activity

Interpersonal Skills: Knowledge about human behavior and interpersonal processes, ability to understand the feelings, attitudes, and motives of others from what they say and do (empathy, social sensitivity), ability to communicate clearly and effectively (speech fluency, persuasiveness), and ability to establish effective and cooperative relationships (tact, diplomacy, listening skill, knowledge about acceptable social behavior)

Conceptual Skills: General analytical ability, logical thinking, proficiency in concept formation and conceptualization of complex and ambiguous relationships, creativity in idea generation and problem solving, ability to analyze events and perceive trends, anticipate changes, and recognize opportunities and potential problems (inductive and deductive reasoning)

Managers who supervise the work of others need extensive knowledge of the techniques and equipment used by subordinates to perform the work. Technical knowledge of products and processes is necessary to plan and organize work operations, to direct and train subordinates with specialized activities, and to monitor and evaluate their performance. Technical expertise is needed to deal with disruptions in the work due to equipment breakdowns, quality defects, accidents, insufficient materials, and coordination problems. Ample evidence indicates that technical skills are related to the effectiveness of civilian and military leaders, especially at lower levels of management (see Bass, 1990, 2008). The CCL study (McCall & Lombardo, 1983a) on derailed managers found that technical knowledge about products and work processes is related to effectiveness and advancement at lower levels of management, but it becomes relatively less important at higher levels of management.

Technical knowledge is also relevant for entrepreneurial managers. The inspirational vision of a new product or service may seem to spring from out of nowhere, but it is actually the result of many years of learning and experience. Research on entrepreneurs who started successful companies or introduced important new products in established companies suggests that their technical knowledge is the fertile ground in which the seeds of inspiration take root to yield innovative products (Westley & Mintzberg, 1989). Some examples include Edwin Land, the inventor of the instant camera and founder of Polaroid Corporation; Steve Jobs, the cofounder of Apple Computer; Mark Zukerberg, the cofounder of Facebook; Azim Premji, the founder of Wipro. It is not enough to have an intimate knowledge of the products and processes for which a manager is responsible. Managers also need to have extensive knowledge of the products and services provided by competitors. Strategic planning is unlikely to be effective unless a manager can make an accurate evaluation of the organization's products (or services) in comparison to those of competitors (Peters & Austin, 1985).

Conceptual Skills

In general terms, conceptual (or cognitive) skills involve good judgment, foresight, intuition, creativity, and the ability to find meaning and order in ambiguous, uncertain events. Specific conceptual skills that can be measured with aptitude tests include analytical ability, logical thinking, concept formation, inductive reasoning, and deductive reasoning. Cognitive complexity involves a combination of these specific skills and is defined as the ability to develop concepts and categories for describing things, the ability to identify patterns and understand complex relationships, and the ability to develop creative solutions to problems. A person with low cognitive complexity sees things in simplistic black and white terms and has difficulty in seeing how many diverse elements fit together to make a meaningful whole. A person with high cognitive complexity is able to see many shades of gray and is able to identify complex patterns of relationships and predict future events from current trends.

Conceptual skills are essential for effective planning, organizing, and problem solving. A major administrative responsibility is coordination of the separate, specialized parts of the organization. To accomplish effective coordination, a manager needs to understand how the various parts of the organization relate to each other and how changes in one part of the system affect the other parts. Managers must also be able to comprehend how changes in the external environment will affect the organization. Strategic planning requires considerable ability to analyze events and perceive trends, anticipate changes, and recognize opportunities and potential problems. A manager with high cognitive complexity is able to develop a better mental model of the organization to help understand the most critical factors and the relationships among them. A model is like a road map that depicts the terrain for a region, shows where things are located in relation to each other, and helps you decide how to get from one place to another. Managers with weak conceptual skills tend to develop a simplistic mental model that is not especially useful because it is unable to describe the complex processes, causal relationships, and flow of events in the organization and external environment. In the CCL study described earlier, weak conceptual skills were one reason for managers who derailed (McCall & Lombardo).

Conceptual skills have been measured with a variety of different methods, including traditional aptitude tests, situational tests, interviews, critical incidents, and constructed response tasks. Research with traditional pencil-and-paper measures of conceptual skills finds strong evidence that they are related to managerial effectiveness, especially in high-level managerial positions (Bass, 1990, 2008). Cognitive skills measured with incident interviews differentiated between effective and ineffective managers in a study by Boyatzis (1982). Cognitive skills measured in an assessment center predicted advancement to higher levels of management in a study at AT&T (Howard & Bray, 1988). In a longitudinal study of managers in four companies, cognitive complexity measured with an individual assessment interview predicted managerial advancement remarkably well four to eight years later (Stamp, 1988). With constructed response tasks, leaders say how they would solve representative types of problems described in a set of scenarios, and raters determine the level of skill demonstrated by the answers. In a large sample of army officers at different ranks, complex problem-solving skills that were measured in this way were related to career achievement (Connelly, Gilbert, Zaccaro, Marks, & Mumford, 2000). Based on a review of the accumulated research on cognitive skills and leadership performance, Mumford, Todd, Higgs, and McIntosh (2017) identified nine important cognitive skills: (1) problem definition, (2) cause/goal analysis, (3) constraint analysis, (4) planning, (5) forecasting, (6) creative thinking, (7) idea evaluation, (8) wisdom, and (9) sensemaking/visioning.

Interpersonal Skills

Interpersonal (or social) skills include knowledge about human behavior and group processes, ability to understand the feelings, attitudes, and motives of others, and ability to communicate clearly and persuasively. Specific types of interpersonal skills such as empathy, social insight, charm, tact and diplomacy, persuasiveness, and oral communication ability are essential to develop and maintain cooperative relationships with subordinates, superiors, peers, and outsiders. Someone who is charming, tactful, and diplomatic will have more cooperative relationships than a person who is insensitive and offensive.

Interpersonal skills are essential for influencing people. Empathy is the ability to understand another person's motives, values, and emotions, and social insight is the ability to understand what types of behavior are socially acceptable in a particular situation. Understanding what people want and how they perceive things makes it easier to select an appropriate influence strategy, and persuasiveness and oral communication make influence attempts more successful. Another interpersonal skill is the ability to use cues from others to understand one's own behavior and how it affects other people. This skill is sometimes called "self-monitoring," and it helps a person adjust behavior to fit the requirements of the situation (Bedeian & Day, 2004; Day & Schleicher, 2006; Snyder, 1974; Zaccaro, Foti, & Kenny, 1991). Influence tactics and impression management tactics (see Chapter 6) are used more effectively by people who have strong interpersonal skills.

Interpersonal skills also enhance the effectiveness of relationship-oriented behaviors. Strong interpersonal skills help a manager listen in an attentive, sympathetic, and nonjudgmental way to somebody with a personal problem, complaint, or criticism. Empathy is important for understanding the needs and feelings of others and determining how to provide support and sympathy. Empathy is also useful for determining effective ways to resolve conflicts. Even managerial behaviors that are primarily task-oriented (e.g., making assignments and giving instructions) require considerable interpersonal skill to be enacted in a way that reflects a concern for people as well as task objectives. Some people have a misconception that interpersonal skill is nothing more than considerate behavior to be "turned on" in special situations. However, as noted by Katz (1955, p. 34): "Real skill in working with others must become a natural, continuous activity, since it involves sensitivity not only at times of decision making but also in the day-by-day behavior of the individual."

The trait research described earlier in this chapter shows consistently that interpersonal skills are important for managerial effectiveness and advancement (Bass, 1990, 2008). In the AT&T study, interpersonal skills predicted managerial advancement. In research on leadership competencies by Boyatzis (1982), interpersonal skills differentiated between effective and ineffective managers, regardless of the situation. In the CCL research (McCall & Lombardo, 1983b), deficiencies in interpersonal skills (including abusive treatment of subordinates) were a major reason for managers who eventually derailed in their management careers.

Political Skill

While the thought of politics in organizations often conjures up negative images of manipulative individuals taking advantage of others for personal gain, the reality is that organizational politics often enable leaders to accomplish goals that benefit others and would not be attainable without them. Some individuals are particularly skilled at navigating organizational politics and using political tactics to achieve their goals. Political skill involves "the ability to effectively understand others at work, and to use such knowledge to influence others to act in ways that enhance one's personal and/or organizational objectives" (Ferris et al., 2005, p. 127). The dimensions of political skill include social astuteness, interpersonal influence, networking ability, and apparent sincerity. Social astuteness involves the ability to understand social interactions and interpret one's own and others' behavior in social settings. Interpersonal influence stems from the ability of politically skilled persons to adapt and calibrate their behavior to fit the situation and elicit desired responses from others. Networking ability involves the ability to form and use diverse social networks with others; politically skilled persons develop friendships easily and build strong and beneficial coalitions and alliances that enable them to create and take advantage of opportunities. People with strong political skills are seen by others as possessing high levels of authenticity, genuineness, and integrity; they are viewed as open, honest, and trustworthy. Because such individuals are not deemed to be coercive or manipulative, they inspire confidence and trust in their colleagues (Ferris, Perrewe, Anthony, & Gilmore, 2000; Ferris et al., 2007).

Political skill is most commonly measured using a survey instrument, the Political Skill Inventory (Ferris et al., 2005). A recent meta-analysis concluded that political skill is positively related to work productivity, job satisfaction, organizational commitment, self-efficacy, organizational citizenship behavior, personal reputation, and career success, and negatively related to physiological strain (Munyon, Summers, Thompson, & Ferris, 2015). Political skill also predicted task performance above and beyond general mental ability and the Big Five personality traits. Politically skilled leaders have been shown to achieve higher levels of team performance (Ahearn, Ferris, & Hochwarter, 2004), and are seen by subordinates as being more effective (Blickle, Meurs, Wihler, Ewen, & Peiseler, 2014). The reasons for the success of politically skilled leaders stem from their heightened abilities to read others and the situation, build and deploy extensive social networks to gain influence, and foster the impression that they are authentic, sincere, and non-manipulative colleagues who have the interests of others at heart.

Managerial Competencies

Although competencies are commonly regarded as skills, they usually involve a combination of specific skills and complementary traits. Competencies are frequently used to describe desirable attributes for managers in a particular company or profession, but some scholars have proposed generally relevant competencies for managers. Examples include emotional intelligence, social intelligence, and learning ability. These competencies include some of the same skills and traits described earlier in the chapter, but they are defined and measured in unique ways.

Emotional Intelligence

Emotions are strong feelings that demand attention and are likely to affect cognitive processes and behavior. Some examples of emotions include anger, fear, sadness, joy, shame, and surprise. Even after the intensity of an emotion fades, it is likely to linger as a positive or negative mood, which can also affect leadership behavior (George, 1995). Emotional intelligence includes several interrelated component skills. Empathy is the ability to recognize moods and emotions in others, to differentiate between genuine and false expression of emotions, and to understand how someone is reacting to your emotions and behavior. Self-regulation is the ability to channel emotions into behavior that is appropriate for the situation, rather than responding with impulsive behavior (e.g., lashing out at someone who made you angry, or withdrawing into a state of depression after experiencing disappointment). Emotional self-awareness is an understanding of one's own moods and emotions, how they evolve and change over time, and the implications for task performance and interpersonal relationships. Another aspect of emotional intelligence that requires both self-awareness and communication skills is the ability to accurately express one's feelings to others with language and nonverbal communication (e.g., facial expressions, gestures). Emotional intelligence can be learned, but a significant improvement probably requires intensive individual coaching, relevant feedback, and a strong desire for significant personal development (Goleman, 1995).

Emotional intelligence is relevant for leadership effectiveness in several ways (Goleman, 1995; Goleman, Boyatzis, & McKee, 2002; Mayer & Salovey, 1995). Leaders with a high level of emotional intelligence are more capable of solving complex problems, planning how to use their time effectively, adapting their behavior to the situation, and managing crises. Self-awareness makes it easier to understand one's own needs and likely reactions if certain events occurred, thereby facilitating evaluation of alternative solutions. Self-regulation facilitates emotional stability and information processing in stressful situations, and it helps leaders maintain their own optimism and enthusiasm about a project or mission in the face of obstacles and setbacks. Empathy is associated with strong social skills that are needed to develop cooperative interpersonal relationships. Examples include the ability to listen attentively, communicate effectively, and express appreciation and positive regard. The ability to understand and influence emotions in others will help a leader who is attempting to arouse enthusiasm and optimism for a proposed activity or change. A leader with high emotional intelligence will have more insight about the type of rational or emotional appeal that is most likely to be effective in a particular situation.

In research on the consequences of emotional intelligence, some studies use a self-report measure (e.g., Wong & Law, 2002), but other studies use a performance-based measure (e.g., Mayer, Salovey, Caruso, & Sitarenios, 2003). Although emotional intelligence has received a great deal of attention within the popular press (Goleman, 1995, 1998; Goleman et al., 2002), considerable controversy exists regarding how important it is for effective leadership (Antonakis, Ashkanasy, & Dasborough, 2009). Despite skepticism about exaggerated claims for its importance (e.g., Landy, 2005; Locke, 2005), there is sufficient evidence at this time to conclude that a high level of emotional intelligence enhances leadership success (Walter, Cole, & Humphrey, 2011).

Social Intelligence

Social intelligence is defined as the ability to determine the requirements for leadership in a particular situation and select an appropriate response (Cantor & Kihlstrom, 1987; Ford, 1986; Zaccaro, Gilbert, Thor, & Mumford, 1991). The two primary components of social intelligence are social perceptiveness and behavioral flexibility.

Social perceptiveness is the ability to understand the functional needs, problems, and opportunities that are relevant for a group or organization, and the member characteristics, social relationships, and collective processes that will enhance or limit attempts to influence the group or organization. A leader with high social perceptiveness understands what needs to be done to make a group or organization more effective and how to do it. Social perceptiveness involves the conceptual skills and specific knowledge needed for strategic leadership, including the ability to identify threats and opportunities that are jointly determined by environmental events and the core competencies of the organization, and the ability to formulate an appropriate response. Social perceptiveness also involves interpersonal skills (e.g., empathy, social sensitivity, understanding of group processes) and knowledge of the organization (structure, culture, power relationships), which jointly determine whether it is feasible to initiate change and the best way to do it.

Behavioral flexibility is the ability and willingness to vary one's behavior to accommodate situational requirements. A leader with high behavioral flexibility knows how to use a variety of different behaviors and is able to evaluate and modify the behavior when needed. High behavioral flexibility implies a mental model with fine distinctions among different types of leadership behavior rather than a simplistic taxonomy. The person must have a large repertoire of skilled behaviors from which to select, as well as knowledge about the effects and limiting conditions for each type of behavior. Behavioral flexibility is facilitated by self-monitoring, because leaders who rate high on self-monitoring are more aware of their own behavior and how it affects others. Whether social intelligence is used primarily to achieve collective rather than personal objectives probably depends on the leader's emotional maturity and socialized power motivation.

Considerable overlap is apparent between social intelligence and emotional intelligence, although the latter construct seems to be more narrowly defined (Kobe, Reiter-Palmon, & Rickers, 2001; Salovey & Mayer, 1990). Social intelligence also appears to overlap with political skill, in that socially intelligent leaders will understand how decisions are made in organizations and how to use political tactics to influence decisions and events. However, Ferris and colleagues (2000) argue that political skill differs from social and emotional intelligence because it focuses specifically on interactions that seek to achieve success in organizations. More research is needed to clarify how social intelligence is related to emotional intelligence and political skill, and to assess how each component skill in social intelligence is related to leadership effectiveness.

Learning Ability

In a turbulent environment in which organizations must continually adapt, innovate, and reinvent themselves, leaders must be flexible enough to learn from mistakes, change their assumptions and beliefs, and refine their mental models. One of the most important competencies for successful leadership in changing situations is the ability to learn from experience and adapt to change (Argyris, 1991; Dechant, 1990; Heslin & Keating, 2017; Hirst, Mann, Bain, Pirola-Merlo, & Richver, 2004; Marshall-Mies et al., 2000; Mumford & Connelly, 1991; Yukl, 2009). It involves "learning how to learn," which is the ability to introspectively analyze your own cognitive processes (e.g., the way you define and solve problems) and to find ways to improve them. It also involves self-awareness, which is an understanding of your own strengths and limitations (including both skills and emotions).

In a study of 1,800 high-level military officers, this competency predicted self-reported career achievements (Zaccaro et al., 1997). A study of military officers by Marshall-Mies and colleagues (2000) provides additional evidence that the ability to learn and adapt is important for leadership effectiveness. In research on derailment by civilian managers, this ability was considered an important success factor by American and European executives (Van Velsor & Leslie, 1995). More recently, global leaders who possess a divergent style of experiential learning that emphasizes concrete experience and reflective observation were shown to be most inclined to develop heightened cultural intelligence from an overseas assignment (Li, Mobley, & Kelly, 2013). Personal adaptability and cultivating learning agility were identified as two of the critical leadership capabilities for success in today's complex and global business landscape (Axon, Friedman, & Jordan, 2015).

The ability to learn from experience and adapt to change probably involves traits as well as skills (Spreitzer, McCall, & Mahoney, 1997). Traits that appear relevant include achievement orientation, emotional stability, and an internal locus of control orientation. Managers with these traits are motivated to achieve excellence; they are inquisitive and open-minded; they have the confidence and curiosity to experiment with new approaches; and they actively seek feedback about their strengths and weaknesses.

Situational Relevance of Traits and Skills

Managers need many types of skills to fulfill their role requirements, but the relative importance of the skills depends on the leadership situation. Relevant situational moderator variables include managerial level, type of organization, leader stress, and the nature of the external environment.

Level of Management

One aspect of the situation influencing skill importance is a manager's position in the authority hierarchy of the organization (Boyatzis, 1982; De Meuse, Dai, & Wu, 2011; Gentry, Harris, Baker, & Leslie, 2008; Jacobs & Jaques, 1987; Katz, 1955; Mann, 1965; Mumford & Connelly, 1991; Mumford, Marks, Connelly, Zaccaro, & Reiter-Palmon, 2000; Mumford et al., 2007). Skill priorities at different levels of management are related to the differing role requirements at each level. Managerial level affects not only the relevance of the three broad categories of skills described earlier (i.e., conceptual, interpersonal, technical), but also the relative importance of specific types of skills within each category.

In general, higher levels of management have a greater number and variety of activities to be coordinated; the complexity of relationships that need to be understood and managed is greater; and the problems that need to be solved are more unique and ill-defined (Axon et al., 2015; Jacobs & Jaques, 1987, 1990; Jaques, 1989; Mumford & Connelly, 1991; Mumford et al., 2007). Whereas a department supervisor may have to coordinate the work of employees with mostly similar jobs, a CEO must coordinate the diverse activities of several organizational units, each with large numbers of people. Increasing complexity as one ascends to higher levels in an organization is reflected in increased requirements for conceptual skills. Top executives need to analyze vast amounts of ambiguous and contradictory information about the environment in order to make strategic decisions and to interpret events for other members of the organization. Executives need to have a long-term perspective and the ability to comprehend complex relationships among variables relevant to the performance of the organization. A top executive must be able to anticipate future events and know how to plan for them. The quality of strategic decisions ultimately depends on conceptual skills, even though some technical knowledge is necessary to make these decisions, and interpersonal skills are necessary for developing relationships, obtaining information, and influencing subordinates to implement decisions (De Meuse et al., 2011; Katz & Kahn, 1978; Mumford et al., 2000).

The role of middle-level managers is primarily one of supplementing existing structure and developing ways to implement policies and goals established at higher levels (Katz & Kahn, 1978). This role requires a roughly equal mix of technical, interpersonal, and conceptual skills. Low-level managers are mainly responsible for implementing policy and maintaining the workflow within the existing organizational structure. For these managers, technical skills are relatively more important than conceptual skills or interpersonal skills (De Meuse et al., 2011).

The skill requirements for managers at each level vary somewhat depending on the type of organization, its size, the organization structure, and the degree of centralization of authority (McLennan, 1967). For example, technical skills are more important for top executives in organizations where operating decisions are highly centralized. Likewise, more technical skill is needed by top executives who have functionally specialized roles (e.g., selling to key customers, product design) in addition to general administrative responsibilities. More conceptual skills are needed by middle- and lower-level managers who are expected to participate in strategic planning, product innovation, and leading change.

Research at the Center for Creative Leadership (CCL) on managers who succeed or derail in their careers provides some interesting insights about traits and skills that determine advancement to an executive position and success in the position (McCall & Lombardo, 1983b). Most of the managers had strong technical skills; they had a string of prior successes; and they were initially viewed by others as "fast risers" in their company. Every manager had both strengths and weaknesses, but none of the successful executives had all of the strengths, and none of the derailed managers had all of the weaknesses. Sometimes the reason for derailing was obvious, but other times it appeared to be just a matter of bad luck involving events beyond a manager's control (e.g., unfavorable economic conditions or losing political battles). Sometimes the importance of a success factor seemed to depend in part on the organization culture. For example, derailment often involved weak interpersonal skills, but this type of skill was more important in some organizations than in others.

The researchers used a mix of traits, skills, and other competencies (e.g., ability to build and lead a team, ability to adapt to change) to describe their interpretation of the descriptive data they collected. Managers who derailed were less able to handle pressure. They were more prone to moodiness, angry outbursts, and inconsistent behavior, which undermined their interpersonal relationships with subordinates, peers, and superiors. In contrast, the successful managers were calm, confident, and predictable during crises. The ability to learn and adapt to change was an especially important success factor.

Managers who derailed were more likely to be defensive about weaknesses and failures. They reacted by attempting to cover up mistakes or blame other people. The successful managers admitted mistakes, accepted responsibility, and then took action to fix the problem. Moreover, having dealt with the problem, they did not continue to dwell on it, but turned their attention to other things. The successful managers were more focused on the immediate task and the needs of subordinates than on competing with rivals or impressing superiors. In contrast, many of the derailed managers were too ambitious about advancing their career at the expense of others, and they were more likely to betray a trust or break a promise.

Managers who derailed usually had fewer interpersonal skills. The most common reason for derailment was insensitivity, which was reflected in abrasive or intimidating behavior toward others. This flaw had been tolerated when the person was a lower-level manager, especially when the person had outstanding technical skills, but at higher levels the technical skills could not compensate for being insensitive. Some of the derailed managers could be charming when they wanted to, but over time it became evident that beneath the facade of charm and concern for others was a selfish, inconsiderate, and manipulative person. In contrast, the successful managers were more sensitive, tactful, and considerate. They were able to understand and get along with all types of people, and they developed a larger network of cooperative relationships. When they disagreed with someone, they were direct but diplomatic, whereas the derailed managers were more likely to be outspoken and offensive. These interpersonal skills are especially relevant for building and leading a cooperative team, which was a key success factor in the recent studies.

For most managers who derailed, their technical brilliance was a source of successful problem solving and technical achievement at lower levels of management where their expertise was usually greater than that of subordinates. However, at higher levels this strength could become a weakness if it led to overconfidence and arrogance, causing the manager to reject sound advice, to offend others by acting superior, and to micro-manage subordinates who had more expertise. Some managers were unable to shift from a focus on technical problems to the more strategic perspective needed at a higher level of management. Some derailed managers had technical expertise only in a narrow functional area, and they advanced too quickly to learn skills needed to perform higher-level jobs effectively. Successful managers usually had experience in a variety of different types of situations where they acquired a broader perspective and expertise in dealing with different types of problems.

Some rare leaders, such as Steve Jobs, Apple's legendary co-founder and CEO, possess the ability to both "know the big picture and the details," as described by Jobs's biographer, Walter Isaacson (2012, p. 100), in his *Harvard Business Review* article titled, "The Real Leadership Lessons of Steve Jobs."

> Jobs's passion was applied to issues both large and miniscule. Some CEOs are great at vision; some are managers who know that God is in the details. Jobs was both. Time Warner CEO Jeff Bewkes says that one of Jobs's salient traits was his ability and desire to envision overarching strategy while also focusing on the tiniest aspects of design. For example, in 2000 he came up with the grand vision that the personal computer should become a "digital hub" for managing all of a user's music, videos, photos, and content, and thus got Apple into the personal-device business with the iPod and then the iPad. In 2010 he came up with the successor strategy — the "hub" would move to the cloud — and Apple began building a huge server farm so that all a user's content could be uploaded and then seamlessly synced to other personal devices. But even as he was laying out these grand visions, he was fretting over the shape and color of the screws inside the iMac.

Type of Organization

An interesting question about managerial skills is the extent to which they are transferable from one type of organization to another. Writers generally agree that lower-level managers cannot easily transfer to a different functional specialty (e.g., from sales manager to engineering manager), because the technical skills needed at this level of management are so different across functions. However, less agreement is evident about the transferability of skills across organizations at the executive level.

Katz (1955) proposed that top-level managers with ample human relations and conceptual skills can be shifted from one industry to another with great ease and no loss of effectiveness. However, some other writers contend that the transferability of skills for top executives is limited due to variations in ownership, traditions, organizational climate, and culture (Dale, 1960; Groysberg, McLean, & Nohria, 2006; Kotter, 1982; McLennan, 1967; Shetty & Peery, 1976). Different industries have unique economic, market, and technological characteristics. Familiarity with technical matters, products, personalities, and tradition is a type of knowledge that is acquired only through long experience in the organization. Only the general components of conceptual and technical skills can be used in a different situation; the unique knowledge component of these skills must be relearned. Moreover, an executive who moves to a different industry must develop a new network of external contacts, whereas the old network would still be relevant for a move to another organization in the same industry. In general, it seems to be more difficult for an executive to make a successful transition to a different industry or type of organization, especially if the new position requires extensive technical expertise and an extensive network of external contacts (Groysberg et al., 2006; Kotter, 1982; Shetty & Peery, 1976).

Stress on the Leader

Cognitive resources theory (Fiedler, 1986; Fiedler & Garcia, 1987) describes the conditions under which leader intelligence and experience are related to group performance. According to the theory, stress for the leader moderates the relation between leader intelligence and subordinate performance. Stress may be due to an overly demanding boss, frequent work crises, and serious conflicts with subordinates. Under low stress, leader intelligence facilitates information processing and problem solving, and it is likely to improve the quality of leader decisions. However, when there is high interpersonal stress, strong emotions are likely to disrupt cognitive information processing and make intelligence difficult to apply. The leader may become distracted and unable to focus on the task. In this stressful situation, a leader who has already learned a high-quality solution in previous experience with similar problems is usually more effective than an intelligent but inexperienced leader who tries to find new solutions. Based on a meta-analysis of the relationship between intelligence and leadership, Judge, Colbert, and Ilies (2004) obtained evidence for the predictions of cognitive resources theory. The relationship between intelligence and leadership was stronger when leaders exhibited directive behaviors and leader stress was low.

External Environment

Recent research and theory on how organizations evolve and adapt to a changing environment suggests that the mix of skills needed for effective leadership may change as the situation changes. The skills needed by an entrepreneurial manager to build a new organization are not identical to the skills needed by the chief executive of a large, established organization. The skills needed to lead an organization with a stable, supportive environment are not identical to the skills needed to lead an organization facing a turbulent, competitive environment (Hunt, 1991; Osborn, Hunt, & Jauch, 2002; Porter & McLaughlin, 2006; Quinn, Faerman, Thompson, McGrath, & St. Clair, 2006). Hannah and colleagues (2009) describe the unique skills required for leaders in extreme contexts that involve great challenges or peril such as those encountered in medical, military, fire, law enforcement, and crisis response organizations. It is essential for leaders in such situations to have the skills needed to respond quickly to extreme events.

As noted in earlier chapters, unprecedented changes affecting organizations are changing the nature of managerial work. To cope with these changes, most managers may need more of the new competencies as well as the skills identified in earlier research. As the pace of globalization, technological development, and social change continues to increase, so will the premium on competencies such as cognitive complexity, empathy, self-awareness, cultural sensitivity, behavioral flexibility, systems thinking, and the ability to learn from experience and adapt to change (Conger, 1993; Gentry et al., 2008; Hunt, 1991; Nadkarni & Herrmann, 2010; Quinn et al., 2006; Van Velsor & Leslie, 1995).

Evaluation of the Trait Approach

Considerable progress has been made in identifying traits and skills relevant for managerial effectiveness and advancement. Nevertheless, this line of research has been hindered by some methodological and conceptual limitations. Most trait studies are not guided by a theory that explains how traits are related to managerial effectiveness and advancement. It is difficult to interpret the relevance of abstract traits except by examining how they are expressed in the actual behavior of leaders and the effects of leader decisions and actions. Few trait studies include mediating processes to explain why leadership traits and skills are relevant for predicting effectiveness in the current position or career success.

Another limitation of the trait approach is the lack of attention in many studies to the leadership situation. As in the behavior research, the relevance of different traits and skills will depend in part on the nature of the leadership position, the types of challenges facing the leader, and the criteria used to assess effectiveness.

Most trait studies on the relationship of traits and skills to effective leadership only test for simple, linear relationships. However, the relationship is often curvilinear, and a moderate amount of the trait is usually optimal rather than the maximum amount. Examples of traits for which either a very low or very high level is undesirable are shown in Table 7-4. When the

TABLE 7-4 Negative Aspects of Very Low or Very High Trait Scores

Self-confidence

- Too little: indecisive, avoids risks, and does not seek to influence others
- Too much: arrogant, acts too quickly, and takes too many risks

Need for Esteem

- Too little: does not seek recognition or build a reputation for high expertise and reliability
- Too much: preoccupied with reputation and status, exaggerates achievements, covers up mistakes and failures or blames others

Need for Affiliation

- Too little: does not try to form strong relationships or build a social support network
- Too much: overly concerned about being liked and accepted by others, overuses ingratiation, and will not risk popularity by asking for sacrifices or insisting on better performance

Need for Independence

- Too little: dependent on others for direction, rule oriented, avoids taking initiative
- Too much: resents authority, too quick to ignore rules and standard procedures

Altruism (value)

- Too little: selfish, indifferent about the needs of others, may exploit them for personal gain
- Too much: overly generous and forgiving, unable to ask for sacrifices or maintain discipline

Performance Orientation (value)

- Too little: accepts weak performance and does not push for improvement
- Too much: is a perfectionist and is overly demanding and never satisfied

relationship is curvilinear, a study that only tests for a linear relationship will yield incorrect results, and the practical implications for leaders may be incorrect.

Most trait studies examined how single traits or skills are related to leadership effectiveness or advancement. This approach fails to consider how the traits are interrelated and how they interact to influence leader behavior and effectiveness. A broader perspective is needed to examine patterns of leader traits and skills in relation to leader effectiveness (Kaplan & Kaiser, 2006; McCall, Lombardo, & Morrison, 1988; Quinn, 1988; Quinn et al., 2006). Sometimes the optimal pattern requires a balance among related traits. For example, effective leaders balance a high need for power with the emotional maturity required to ensure that subordinates are empowered rather than dominated.

The concept of balance has been described for individuals, but it applies to shared leadership as well (Pearce & Conger, 2003). For example, balance may involve several different leaders in a management team who have complementary attributes that compensate for each other's weaknesses and enhance each other's strengths (Bradford & Cohen, 1984). A better understanding of leadership in an organization may be gained by examining the pattern of traits for the executive team rather than focusing on the traits of a single leader such as the chief executive officer (see Chapter 12).

Guidelines for Leaders

The finding that particular skills and traits are positively related to managerial effectiveness and advancement has some practical implications for people in planning their own managerial careers. The following guidelines (summarized in Table 7-5) are based on research, theory, and practitioner findings about traits and skills.

TABLE 7-5 Guidelines for Understanding and Improving Relevant Competencies

- Learn about your strengths and weaknesses.
- Maintain self-awareness.
- Identify and develop skills relevant for a future leadership position.
- Remember that a strength can become a weakness.
- Compensate for weaknesses.

- **Learn about your strengths and weaknesses.**

It is essential for leaders to understand what is required for success in their current position and how well their traits and skills will enable them to do what is required. Understanding of strengths makes it easier to build on them and become more effective. Understanding of weaknesses makes it easier to correct them or compensate for them. Take advantage of opportunities to gain systematic feedback about strengths and weaknesses from multisource feedback programs and assessment centers (see Chapter 14).

- **Maintain a high level of self-awareness.**

Self-awareness includes a good understanding of one's own needs, emotions, abilities, and behavior. Awareness of your emotional reactions to events facilitates information processing and decision making in stressful situations, and it helps you maintain optimism and enthusiasm about a project or mission in the face of obstacles and setbacks. Awareness of your behavior and its influence on others makes it easier to learn from experience and to assess your strengths and weaknesses. Insights can be gained by monitoring your own behavior and its consequences. It is also important to be receptive to feedback from others about positive and negative aspects of behavior as they perceive it.

- **Identify and develop skills relevant for a future leadership position.**

Effective managers are more oriented toward continuous learning and self-development. Learn what traits and skills are useful for the type of leadership role or position you want to have in the future. Determine which skills need to be strengthened and seek opportunities to develop them. Some training may be obtained in specialized management development workshops run by one's employer or by consulting companies. Other approaches for developing new skills include challenging assignments, personal coaching by a mentor, and self-development activities (see Chapter 14).

- **Remember that a strength can become a weakness.**

A trait or skill that is a strength in one situation can later become a weakness when the situation changes. For example, a study conducted by CCL researchers found that staff managers who performed brilliant analytical work could not develop the action orientation necessary to implement ideas when they moved into a line position. Successful line managers had the opposite problem; they seemed incapable of the reflective analysis and cooperative teamwork that was necessary in a staff position. Any trait taken to an extreme can also become a weakness, even when the situation has not changed. Confidence can become arrogance, innovation can become recklessness, decisiveness can become rashness, integrity can become fanaticism, and global vision can become lack of focus.

- **Compensate for weaknesses.**

One way to compensate for weaknesses is to select subordinates who have complementary strengths and allow them to assume responsibility for aspects of the work they are more qualified to perform. Sometimes it is appropriate to delegate responsibilities to qualified individuals, and other times it is better to have a management team (in which you are a member) share the responsibility for a particular problem or challenge.

Summary

Some personality traits found to be relevant for leadership advancement or effectiveness include energy level and stress tolerance, self-confidence, internal control orientation, emotional stability, extroversion, conscientiousness, integrity, and core self-evaluations. The motive pattern characteristic of many effective managers includes a socialized power orientation and a moderately strong need for achievement, with an emphasis on collective performance rather than individual performance.

To be successful, a leader also needs interpersonal, cognitive, and technical skills. The relative priority of the three types of skills and the optimal mix of specific skills probably depends on the type of organization, the level of management, and the nature of the challenges confronting a leader. Some skills such as political skill, persuasiveness, analytical ability, speaking ability, and memory for details are relevant for most types of leaders, whereas some other skills are not easily transferred to a different type of position. Competencies involve a combination of traits and skills, and some competencies examined in recent leadership research include emotional intelligence, social intelligence, and the ability to learn and adapt to change.

The research on personality traits and skills of leaders has provided some useful knowledge about individual attributes that can affect the success of a leader. Nevertheless, much of the trait research continues to have weaknesses. As in the case of leadership behavior, some scholars have emphasized broadly defined categories of traits and skills that can make it more difficult to identify and understand important relationships. Much of the research has failed to pay adequate attention to situational variables, curvilinear relationships, the joint effects of different traits and skills, and how traits and skills influence leader behavior.

The trait approach has important implications for improving managerial effectiveness. Information about traits and skills relevant for different types of managerial positions is useful for people who are planning a managerial career. The information is also useful for selecting people to fill managerial positions, for identifying training needs for managers in their current position, and for planning management development activities to prepare people for promotion to higher-level jobs (see Chapter 14).

Review and Discussion Questions

1. What traits are the best predictors of managerial performance and advancement?
2. What are the major reasons for managers to derail in their careers?
3. Why is it important to consider the joint effects of different traits and skills?
4. Which skills are more important at higher levels of management than at lower levels?
5. How are technical, conceptual, and interpersonal skills related to managerial effectiveness?
6. How are the effects of traits and skills dependent on the situation?

Key Terms

Big Five personality traits
cognitive skills
conceptual skills
core self-evaluation
emotional intelligence
emotional maturity
emotional stability
interpersonal skills
locus of control orientation
need for achievement
need for affiliation
need for power
personalized power orientation
political skill
self-awareness
self-confidence
social intelligence
socialized power orientation
technical skills

PERSONAL REFLECTION

Think about a leader who has had a positive influence on your life. This leader could be a teacher, coach, manager, or someone else who has served as a role model for you. Which leadership traits, skills, and competencies described in this chapter are embodied by the leader you selected? How did these qualities shape the leader's behavior and ability to influence others and achieve desired goals?

CASE

Community Empowerment Lab

Sarah Nathan is the head of Human Resources at Community Empowerment Lab, Lucknow. It is a NGO working for the well-being of newborn babies and mothers. The organization is involved in a variety of works such as research, creation and conduction of assessment and testing of various kinds, creation of equipment to conduct various mental and physical tests, fieldwork at the ground level, call centres etc. The organization in all, had a team of around 200 members. There was an opening for the position of general manager for one of their new fieldwork projects. Sarah was asked to review the backgrounds of the three employees who were eligible for a promotion and had applied for the post. She had the option of either recommending any one of the internal applicants, or recruit a external candidate. The candidates from within the organization were Mohit Singh, Shreya Mishra and Avantika Sharma. Information about all three candidates obtained from their performance records, their interviews and the feedback of their superiors is given below.

Mohit Singh

Mohit has been the manager with the design department for the past five years. An outgoing person who loves to crack jokes, tell stories, and keep the environment light, does not like conflicts of any kind. Thus, he tries to smoothen them as soon as possible by finding an acceptable compromise. He emphasizes on the significance of teamwork and collaboration for the success of an organization.

Mohit believes in helping whoever and wherever possible. Thus, he would not only help the less experienced co-workers by giving them advice, but would also lend his support to them as well as his superiors on their assignments. This attitude gave him the tag of a "loyal company man" and a "good team player". Coming from a background where importance of close family ties is stressed upon, Mohit had a high desire of being accepted, liked and appreciated by everybody. Therefore, he would hold get-togethers for his entire family almost every Sunday. On Saturdays, he would play some sport with his friends from work as well as outside.

Mohit wants the organization to perform well, however, he is afraid that his relationship with his subordinates might suffer if he pushed them too much in order to improve their performances. He also felt that their current level of functioning was optimal. Thus, when he gives out performance bonuses to his subordinates, he tries to see that everyone receives something worth the efforts.

Shreya Mishra

Shreya has been the manager of the research and development department for the past three years. She was promoted to this position because she proved to be the best in this field within the organization, and has contributed immensely towards the construction of a comprehensive assessment tool. When Shreya joined the team, she had little idea of the kind of work that lay ahead of her because her previous work experience was in a corporate setting. But, rather than being pulled back by this hurdle, she decided to grab this challenge as a great learning opportunity.

Shreya is an introvert individual. She is not comfortable in the company of too many people around her, and is averse to the idea of socializing in office or business parties and get-togethers where she does not know everyone that well.

Shreya also prefers work assignments that requires her to work alone rather than in a team. Although she has a good rapport with her current superior, mainly because there is much autonomy at work and she can do things her way, she finds it difficult to deal with bureaucratic authority figures in general.

Since Shreya likes challenging projects and sees them as opportunities, she puts her heart and soul into them, and often ends up performing well. However, the downside of her preoccupation with the assignments is that she is not left with much time for her managerial activities such as mentoring her subordinates.

Avantika Sharma

Avantika has been a fieldwork manager for the past four years. Coming from a very humble background, she is able to understand and connect better with the people, who too do not have a very sound financial background and live a hard life to make ends meet. Avantika has worked hard to get where she is today, but she has done so not because she enjoys her work but in order to rise in life and do good financially. She wishes to leave behind her life of struggle, and embrace a lavish and comfortable lifestyle in the near future. As soon as she got her last promotion, she bought herself new expensive clothes and gadgets.

Avantika looks at the organization as a political jungle and is quick to defend herself against any threat that is made to her position or reputation. She tries to discredit anyone who criticizes her and undermines anyone who opposes her. She keeps a tight control over her departments and insists that any decision that does not fall under the routine work, should have her approval first.

—*Written by* Nishant Uppal

Questions

1. What are the dominant motives of each candidate?
2. What are the implications of personality characteristics (traits) mentioned above for the success of each candidate, if selected for the general manager position?
3. Should Sarah recommend one of these candidates for the position or look for external candidates?

CASE

Prestige Marketing

Prestige Marketing Inc. is a full-service marketing firm located in the Midwest with a focus on digital marketing. Prestige's typical customers include local entertainment organizations such as restaurants, concert venues, and even the town's minor league baseball team. Initially founded to create websites when they became important to the entertainment industry, Prestige has since become a full-service agency that offers the market analysis, strategic planning, and creative services necessary to develop and implement a comprehensive marketing campaign. Despite Prestige's full-service capabilities, a majority of the company's business continues to be generated by its specialty in digital marketing. When top management became aware that the full-service capabilities of the company are currently underutilized, they decided to increase efforts to sign customers up for a comprehensive marketing service package.

A potential new customer is a popular micro-brewery/restaurant (Andrea's Ale House) in another state that has decided to expand and open a new restaurant within the local area. They have signaled that they are looking for a local full-service marketing firm to generate proposals for a comprehensive marketing campaign that will promote a successful opening and ongoing operations. Top management has created three different teams to develop competing marketing proposals, and the best one will be presented to Andrea's Ale House. Each team is composed of six members and has a team leader who is also the manager of a functional department. The team leader is responsible for organizing, directing, and coordinating the activities required to develop a competitive team proposal.

The leader of Team 1 is Jerry Davis. He has been a member of Prestige's client services department for over eight years, and during four of those years he served as the client services director. Jerry relates well to others, finds it easy to identify common interests, and is viewed by many as a valuable member of Prestige. However, several sales associates from his work unit described him as being "obsessed with success" and "willing to do anything to make a sale." One former team member who was recently promoted said that although Jerry is able to increase team performance, his hard-driving style can become excessive and overly stressful to some team members.

The leader of Team 2 is Sandy Newton. She has been a part of the Market Research Department at Prestige for seven years, and during the last four years she served as the market research director. She joined Prestige right out of college and immediately conducted some highly sophisticated market analyses that were seen as exceptional. There has never been a problem too complex for Sandy to solve, and this ability has led to her rapid rise within the company. However, some team members have complained about a lack of challenge in the work because Sandy is unwilling to delegate any tasks of real significance. One current member noted that although Sandy is the best analyst in the building, she needs to understand that solving problems for members can inhibit their development of problem-solving skills, reduce their satisfaction with the work, and detract from other supervisory responsibilities. Trying to do too much of the work herself has also created high levels of stress for Sandy.

The leader of Team 3 is Austin James. Austin has been part of the Creative Services Department at Prestige for nearly 15 years, and during the past seven years he has served as the department manager. Austin's department performs at a high level. He has good relations with other departments and spends considerable time ensuring that they receive any assistance they need from his department. Since he became the manager of his department, Austin has frequently conducted team-building exercises. He also invites members to his home for cookouts and the chance to get to know one another outside the office. However, some members of his department have expressed a concern that too much team bonding can be a distraction from the work, and it also makes members reluctant to openly express disagreements about the ways to resolve problems regarding work.

—*Written by* Daniel P. Gullifor and William L. Gardner

Questions

1. What are the key leadership traits, skills, and competencies of each team leader?
2. Identify any attributes that have contributed to each team leader's career success.
3. What attributes of each team leader are seen by others as a weakness, and how would these attributes make it more difficult for the team to develop a high-quality proposal?

Chapter 8

Charismatic and Transformational Leadership

Learning Objectives

After studying this chapter, you should be able to:

- Understand similarities and differences for charismatic and transformational leadership
- Understand how leaders, followers, and the situation affect attributions of charisma.
- Understand the traits, behaviors, and influence processes included in theories of charismatic and transformational leadership.
- Understand the benefits and costs of charismatic leadership for followers and the organization.
- Understand how to inspire more follower commitment and optimism.

Introduction

In the 1980s, management researchers became very interested in the emotional and symbolic aspects of leadership. These processes help us to understand how leaders influence followers to make self-sacrifices and put the needs of the mission or organization above their materialistic self-interests. Theories of charismatic and transformational leadership describe this important aspect of leadership. This chapter describes the key aspects of the two types of theories, compares and evaluates them, and provides some practical guidelines for how leaders can use what has been learned about them.

The first part of the chapter describes charismatic leadership theories, including insights regarding leader behaviors, influence processes and mediating variables, leader traits and skills, positive and negative charismatics, and aspects of the leadership situation that facilitate the emergence of charismatic leaders. Positive and negative implications of charismatic leadership for organizations are described.

The second part of the chapter describes theories of transformational leadership, the essential behaviors and influence processes, and the implications of such leadership for organizations. Transformational leadership is compared to charismatic leadership, the research evidence for the two types of theories is evaluated, and the chapter ends with guidelines for inspirational leadership.

Charismatic Leadership

Charisma is a Greek word that means "divinely inspired gift," such as the ability to perform miracles or predict future events. Weber (1947) used the term to describe a form of influence based not on tradition or formal authority but rather on follower perceptions that the leader is endowed with exceptional qualities. According to Weber, charisma occurs during a social crisis when a leader emerges with a radical vision that offers a solution to the crisis and attracts followers who believe in the vision. The followers experience some successes that make the vision appear attainable, and they come to perceive the leader as extraordinary. The early conceptions of charisma defined it primarily in terms of the effect of the leader on followers and the type of situation where it was most likely to occur, rather than identifying the leader traits and behaviors that explain these effects.

In the 1980s and 1990s, several social scientists formulated newer theories to describe charismatic leadership in organizations (e.g., Choi & Mai-Dalton, 1998; Conger & Kanungo, 1987, 1998; Gardner & Avolio, 1998; House, 1977; Shamir, House, & Arthur, 1993). These "neo-charismatic" theories incorporate some of Weber's ideas, but they also extend his initial conception of charismatic leadership (Beyer, 1999; Conger, 1989). Some of these theories describe the motives and behaviors of charismatic leaders and the processes that explain how these leaders influence followers (Antonakis, 2018; Jacobsen & House, 2001; Mhatre & Riggio, 2014). However, these neo-charismatic theories differ with regard to the essential attributes for charismatic leaders and the explanation of leader influence on followers.

In more recent years leadership scholars have attempted to find better ways to describe charismatic leadership. After examining many different conceptions of charismatic leadership, Antonakis and colleagues (Antonakis, Bastardoz, Jacquart, & Shamir, 2016) identified three important ways charismatics communicate their leadership qualifications and expectations to potential followers: (1) appealing to follower values, (2) communicating in symbolic ways that are clear and vivid, and (3) displaying emotional conviction and passion for the mission. These communication processes may be common for charismatic leaders, but their use does not automatically guarantee a leader will be regarded as charismatic. Additional insights about charismatic leadership are provided by examining more specific types of leader behavior, influence processes, and the leadership situation. Other scholars have recently proposed complex theories to explain the influence and effects of charismatic leaders (Castelnovo, Popper, & Koren, 2017; Grabo, Spisak, & van Vugt, 2017; Reh, Van Quaquebeke, & Giessner, 2017; Sy, Horton & Riggio, 2018), but more research is needed to evaluate these theories.

Behavior of Charismatic Leaders

Follower attributions of charisma depend on several specific types of leader behavior, but not all are included in every theory of charismatic leadership, and how they are used depends to some extent on the leadership situation.

A Novel and Appealing Vision. Charisma is more likely to be attributed to leaders who advocate a vision that is highly discrepant from the status quo, but not so radical that followers will view the leader as incompetent or insane. A leader who supports the status quo or advocates only small, incremental changes will not be viewed as charismatic. The ability to see opportunities that others fail to recognize is another reason for a leader to be viewed as extraordinary. Attributions of charisma are likely for leaders who have influenced people to collectively achieve objectives that initially seemed impossible.

Emotional Appeals to Values. Leaders are more likely to appear charismatic if the emotional appeals to follower values and ideals. Sometimes charismatic leaders influence followers to embrace new values, but it is more common to articulate a vision describing task objectives in ideological terms that reflect existing follower values. Charismatic leaders use language that includes symbols, slogans, imagery, and metaphors that are relevant to the experience and values of followers.

Expression of Confidence and Optimism. Leaders who express enthusiasm and optimism about a proposed new initiative, project, or strategy are more likely to be viewed as charismatic than leaders who appear doubtful and confused. If the leader does not express strong confidence in an innovative strategy, success may be attributed more to luck than to leader expertise. Followers who believe the leader knows how to attain the vision will have more confidence and enthusiasm, and they will work harder, thereby increasing the actual probability of success.

Self Sacrifices. Leaders are more likely to be viewed as charismatic if they make self-sacrifices and take personal risks to achieve the vision they espouse. Trust appears to be an important component of charisma, and followers have more trust in a leader who seems less motivated by self-interest than by concern for followers. Most impressive is a leader who actually risks substantial personal loss in terms of status, money, leadership position, or membership in the organization.

Unconventional Behavior and Methods. Charisma is more likely to be attributed to leaders who use unconventional and innovative strategies that appear to be succeeding. The use of unconventional behavior can sometimes increase the attribution of charisma to a leader by followers, even when it is not directly related to the vision.

Demonstrate Exceptional Abilities. Attributions of charisma to a leader are increased when the leader demonstrates the ability to do things that appear exceptional to followers. An example is when a religious leader appears to perform miracles, or when a business leader shows that a very innovative idea can quickly yield unusual financial success. As with magic tricks, the demonstration of exceptional ability may involve the use of deception and illusions. An example is when a con artist reports greatly exaggerated returns from past investments to lure new investors.

Influence Processes and Mediating Variables

The theories of charismatic leadership describe several types of influence processes and other mediating variables to explain how the leader can increase follower commitment to achieve the vision, although not every theory includes all of the influence processes.

Personal Identification. Followers may identify a charismatic leader as an idealized self who exemplifies their wishes and fantasies, and who serves as an ideal role model to emulate. Followers who identify with the leader are more likely to imitate the leader's behavior, carry out the leader's requests, and make an extra effort to please the leader. Leader approval becomes a measure of the follower's own self-worth and it is an important source of motivation. Followers are also motivated by fear of disappointing the leader and being rejected.

Social Identification. Strong social identification with the group or organization occurs when people regard membership in it as one of their most important social identities. They see how their efforts and work roles are related to a larger entity, making their work more meaningful and important. They are more willing to place the needs of the group above individual needs and make self-sacrifices for the sake of the group. Moreover, social identification results in strengthening of shared values, beliefs, and behavior norms among members of the group. By emphasizing the ideological importance of the mission and the group's unique qualifications to perform it, the leader can imbue the group with a unique collective identity. Social identification can also be increased by the skillful use of slogans, symbols (e.g., flags, emblems, uniforms), rituals (singing the organization's song or anthem, saluting the flag, reciting the creed), and ceremonies (e.g., initiation of new members). Other relevant ways to increase social identification include telling stories about past successes, heroic deeds by members, and symbolic actions by the founder or former leaders.

Internalization. With this influence process, followers embrace the leader's mission or objectives as being worthy of their commitment. An inspirational vision can influence followers to internalize attitudes and beliefs that will subsequently serve as a source of intrinsic motivation to carry out the mission of the organization. By emphasizing the symbolic and ideological aspects of the work, the leader makes it seem more meaningful, noble, heroic, and morally correct. Even a routine task can be made more meaningful. For example, a bricklayer who had viewed the work as making a wall was influenced to view it as building a wonderful cathedral. The ultimate form of internalization occurs when followers come to view their work role as inseparably linked to their self-concepts and self-worth. They carry out the role because it is a part of their essential nature and destiny.

Self-Efficacy and Collective Efficacy. Task motivation also depends on individual self-efficacy and collective efficacy. Individual self-efficacy is the belief that one is competent and capable of attaining difficult task objectives. People with high self-efficacy are willing to expend more effort and persist longer in overcoming obstacles to the attainment of task objectives. Collective efficacy refers to the perception of group members that they can accomplish exceptional feats by working together. When collective efficacy is high, people are more willing to cooperate with members of their group in a joint effort to carry out their mission. A leader can enhance follower self-efficacy and collective efficacy by articulating an inspiring vision, expressing confidence that it can be accomplished, and providing necessary coaching and assistance.

Impression Management. Charismatic leaders are skilled at managing the impressions of followers and other key stakeholders to promote a positive image of themselves, as well as the groups and organizations they represent (Gardner & Avolio, 1998). The positive attributes that are sometimes associated with charismatic leaders (such as confident, creative, trustworthy, and visionary) are often the result of the leader's conscious efforts to portray these qualities. Charismatic leaders are usually able to understand the needs and values of followers and appear uniquely qualified to satisfy these needs and promote these values. Charismatic leaders are also skilled at fostering desired impressions through the use of symbols (e.g., flags, logos), their own appearance (e.g., personal grooming and clothing), and the physical setting for speeches or meetings.

Emotional Contagion. A leader who is very positive and enthusiastic can influence the enthusiasm of followers for the work and their perception that they can accomplish difficult objectives (e.g., collective efficacy). Moreover, emotional contagion can occur among the followers themselves. Feelings of excitement and optimism can spread quickly in a group or organization and increase follower enthusiasm and devotion to the leader. The qualities attributed to a leader may become highly exaggerated as rumors and stories circulate among people who have no direct contact with the leader. For example, stories about a leader's heroic deeds and exceptional feats may spread among members of a political movement; stories about miracles performed by the leader may spread among members of a religious cult.

Traits and Values of Charismatic Leaders

Some personality traits and values have been identified for charismatic leaders, and they predict leader behavior and effects on followers (House & Howell, 1992; Howell, 1988). Banks et al. (2017) conducted a meta-analysis to examine the relationships of the Big Five personality traits and cognitive ability with charismatic leadership. The results revealed that persons who are above average in intelligence, open to new experiences, extraverted, conscientious, agreeable, and emotionally stable were more likely to be perceived as charismatic leaders. Interpreting these findings, the authors suggest that: (1) intelligence increases the ability to identify an appealing vision; (2) openness to experience facilitates innovative and unconventional behavior; (3) extraversion increases a leader's efforts to influence others; (4) conscientiousness contributes to the leader's commitment to the vision and mission; (5) agreeableness encourages articulation of values with wide appeal that will promote harmony among followers; and (6) emotional stability fosters the emotional expressiveness and ability to connect with followers.

Positive and Negative Charismatics

Other research reveals that charismatic leaders with mostly positive effects on followers have somewhat different traits and behaviors from leaders with mostly negative effects (House & Howell, 1992; Howell, 1988). Negative charismatics are usually narcissists with a personalized power orientation, they intentionally seek follower devotion to themselves more than to ideals, and their influence results more from personal identification than from internalization. They may use ideological appeals, but merely as a means to gain power, after which the ideology is ignored or arbitrarily changed to serve the leader's personal objectives. They seek to dominate and subjugate followers by keeping them weak and dependent on the leader. Authority for making important decisions is centralized in the leader, rewards and punishments are used to manipulate and control followers, and information is restricted and used to maintain an image of leader infallibility or to exaggerate external threats to the organization. Decisions of these leaders reflect a greater concern for self-glorification and maintaining power than for the welfare of followers. Typical dysfunctional attributes of negative charismatics are shown in Table 8-1.

TABLE 8-1 Dysfunctional Attributes of a Narcissistic Charismatic Leader

- Fails to manage important details for the success of a project
- Pays too much attention to superficial aspects of the job
- Informal, impulsive leader actions create chaos and confusion
- Autocratic decisions fail to use available expertise from others
- Controlling style of managing creates excessive dependence by others
- Creates disruptive rivalries among favored and unfavored groups of employees
- Makes exaggerated claims of unique personal expertise and commitment
- Makes exaggerated claims for the success of leader decisions or actions
- Claims credit for successful ideas and outcomes produced by others
- Emphasizes positive events to distract attention from failing programs
- Limits access to negative information about leader weaknesses and failures
- Devalues and demeans critics and opponents of the leader
- Uses unconventional, dysfunctional behavior that alienates some people
- Is often absent from managing operations (too many nonrelevant activities)

Adapted from Conger (1990).

In contrast, positive charismatics have a socialized power orientation. They seek to instill devotion to ideology more than devotion to themselves. In terms of influence processes, they emphasize internalization rather than personal identification. Self-sacrifice and leading by example are used to communicate commitment to shared values and the mission of the unit, not to glorify the leader. Authority is delegated to a considerable extent, information is shared openly, participation in decisions is encouraged, and rewards are used to reinforce behavior consistent with the mission and objectives of the organization. As a result, their leadership is more likely to be beneficial to followers, although it is not inevitable if the strategies encouraged by the leader are inappropriate.

The consequences for followers are better with a positive charismatic leader than with a negative charismatic. Followers are more likely to experience psychological growth and development of their abilities, and the organization is more likely to adapt to an environment that is dynamic, hostile, and competitive. A positive charismatic leader usually creates an "achievement-oriented" culture (Harrison, 1987), a "high-performing system" (Vaill, 1978), or a "hands-on, value-driven" organization (Peters & Waterman, 1982). The organization has a clearly understood mission that embodies social values beyond mere profit or growth, members at all levels are empowered to make important decisions about how to implement strategies and do their work, communication is open and information shared, and organization structures and systems support the mission (Hayibor, Agle, Sears, Sonnenfeld, & Ward, 2011; Varella, Javidan, & Waldman, 2012; Vlachos, Panagopoulos, & Rapp, 2013). Such an organization has obvious advantages, but Harrison (1987, p. 12) contends that proponents also overlook some potential costs:

> In their single-minded pursuit of noble goals and an absorbing task, people lose their sense of balance and perspective; the end can come to justify the means. The group or organization exploits its environment, and its members—to the detriment of their health and quality of life—willingly exploit themselves in the service of the organization's purpose.

Positive charismatics can lead the organization in coping with a temporary crisis, but if prolonged for a long period of time, a single-minded achievement culture creates excessive stress and causes psychological disorders for members who are unable to tolerate this stress. If an achievement culture is created within one subunit of a larger organization, it may result in elitism, isolation, and lack of necessary cooperation with other subunits. Harrison concludes that subordinating member needs to the mission can be justified in a severe crisis, the moral equivalent of war, but under less demanding conditions a better balance between task concerns and people concerns is appropriate. Another negative side effect can occur for a charismatic leader who over-emphasizes the importance of extra-role activities, because it reduces employee job engagement (Horn, Mathis, Robinson, & Randle, 2015). Thus, while there are many potential benefits from charismatic leadership, there are also hidden costs and unintended consequences.

The Leadership Situation

Charismatic leadership is rare, and it is more likely to occur in some situations than in others. Only a limited amount of research has been conducted to learn how attributions of charisma to a leader depend on the nature of the situation and follower characteristics, but some of the findings seem important.

Crisis Situations. Charismatic leaders are more likely to emerge in crisis situations where there is fear of economic loss, physical danger, or threats to core values. For example, during the years 1915–1920 when Gandhi was back to India from a successful movement in South Africa,

India had no tall leader whom it could depend on for tis struggle of freedom against the British and Gandhi's charisma had just started showing its colors. Nevertheless, in contrast to Weber's (1947) viewpoint, Conger and Kanungo (1987) do not consider an objective crisis to be a necessary condition for charismatic leadership. Even in the absence of a genuine crisis, a leader may be able to create dissatisfaction with current conditions and provide a vision of a more promising future. To set the stage for proposing new ways, the leader may try to discredit the old, accepted ways of doing things. The impact of unconventional strategies is greater when followers perceive that conventional approaches are no longer effective. Finally, the leader may also precipitate a crisis where none existed previously to set the stage for demonstration of superior expertise in dealing with the problem in unconventional ways.

Attributional Ambiguity. The influence of charisma on leader evaluations has been shown to be greatest when the factors responsible for past performance (including leader effects on it) are inconclusive. The effects of this "attributional ambiguity" are most evident in the selection of leaders for important positions, such as when corporate board members are responsible for appointing or reappointing the CEO. If organizational performance is clearly good (or bad), evaluations of an incumbent leader tend to be positive (or negative), regardless of the leader's charisma. However, when the causes of organizational performance and leader responsibility for it are unclear, perceptions of charisma are more important for determining who is most qualified to be the next leader. To test these predictions, Jacquart and Antonakis (2015) used economic performance data and ratings of leader charisma to forecast the outcomes of presidential elections in the United States. The researchers were able to predict the past election results from 1916 though 2012 with 95% accuracy. As expected, when the performance of the national economy was clearly strong, the candidate from the incumbent party was elected, and when the economy was performing poorly, the candidate from the incumbent party was unlikely to be elected or reelected. However, when the state of the economy was ambiguous, the most charismatic candidate was elected. In a follow-up study of corporations, the researchers confirmed that CEO charisma and firm performance interact to determine leader retention. The implication is that charismatic leaders are most likely to rise to power, and remain in power, when the factors that contribute to organizational performance are ambiguous.

Follower Characteristics. Attributions of charisma also depend on follower characteristics. Howell and Shamir (2005) proposed that follower self-esteem and self-identity help to explain the type of charismatic relationship that will occur. Followers who lack a clear self-identity and are confused and anxious about their lives are more attracted to a strong leader with a personalized power orientation who can provide a clear social identity for them as disciples or loyal supporters. Examples include many members of religious cults and juvenile gangs. In contrast, followers with a clear self-concept and high self-esteem will be responsive to a leader who can explain how the mission of the group or organization is relevant to their core values. The leader may also be perceived as exceptional, but these followers will identify more with the mission and organization than with the leader.

Interaction with the Leader. Attributions of charisma are also affected by opportunity to interact directly with the leader (Meindl, 1990; Shamir, 1995). Attributions about charisma are made not only by the members of an organization, but also by outsiders who do not have an opportunity to observe the leaders closely (e.g., investors, customers, suppliers, government officials). Attributions for people who have close contact with the leader may depend more on the leader's behavior and interpersonal skills. For distant leaders, attributed charisma may depend more on evidence of exceptional achievements and the influence of individuals who promote the leader's reputation and defend controversial actions and decisions by the leader (Galvin, Balkundi, & Waldman, 2010). The frequency and nature of interactions with followers and the amount of leader position power and control also determine how distance will moderate the influence of a leader on followers. Advances in communication and social networking technology may allow physically distant followers to experience a virtual relationship that is similar in many respects to the relationship experienced by followers who are physically close to the leader.

Effects of Charismatic Leaders

To understand what is known about the effects of charismatic leaders, it is helpful to consider the diverse types of methods used to study charismatic leaders.

Types of Research on Charismatic Leaders

Different types of research methods have been used to study how charismatic leaders influence followers and the leader's organization or institution. The research methods include the analysis of biographical information about famous charismatic leaders, intensive case studies of an individual charismatic leader, survey studies with leader behavior questionnaires, and experiments in laboratory or field settings. Each method is briefly described.

Descriptive studies of charismatic leaders have used several types of information sources, including biographies that describe the leader, speeches and writings by the leader, and incidents viewed by followers and other people (e.g., Jacobsen & House, 2001; Levinson & Rosenthal, 1984; Mio, Riggio, Levin, & Reese, 2005; O'Connor, Mumford, Clifton, Gessner, & Connelly, 1995; Seyranian & Bligh, 2008; Strange & Mumford, 2002; Tichy & Devanna, 1986; Van Fleet & Yukl, 1986a; Westley & Mintzberg, 1989; Willner, 1984; Yukl & Van Fleet, 1982). In some studies, the researchers look for common attributes in leaders widely perceived to be charismatic. Other studies compare leaders widely regarded as charismatic to leaders not considered charismatic.

In the intensive case studies (e.g., Cha & Edmondson, 2006; Trice & Beyer, 1986; Weed, 1993), leaders and others are interviewed to gather information about leader behavior and its effects. The study may also involve observation of the leader, analysis of records, reports, and leader communication with others. A small number of the case studies have examined leaders who transitioned from one position to another (e.g., Roberts, 1985; Roberts & Bradley, 1988) or who experienced initial success followed by eventual failure (e.g., Finkelstein, 2003).

In the survey studies, questionnaires are used to obtain information about the behavior of leaders from subordinates and others, and information is also obtained about outcomes the leaders can influence, such as subordinate satisfaction with the leader, task commitment, organizational commitment, and performance (e.g., Conger & Kanungo, 1994; Shamir, Zakay, & Popper, 1998). However, most of the survey studies on charismatic leadership are susceptible to biases that may distort the relationships examined (Antonakis, 2018; Antonakis et al., 2016; van Knippenberg & Sitkin, 2013).

Several laboratory experiments on charismatic leadership have been conducted with university students (e.g., Awamleh & Gardner, 1999; Choi & Mai-Dalton, 1999; Halverson, Holladay, Kazama, & Quinones, 2004; Howell & Frost, 1989; Hunt, Boal, & Dodge, 1999; Jaussi & Dionne, 2003; Jung & Avolio, 1999; Kirkpatrick & Locke, 1996; Shea & Howell, 1999; van Knippenberg, D., van Knippenberg, B., 2005; Yorges, Weiss, & Strickland, 1999). In some experiments leader behavior by an actor was varied to assess the effects on participants, and in other experiments participants read written descriptions of two or more leaders and indicated their likely response to each leader. By varying the leader behaviors and situations, the effects on participants could be compared. For example, results from a laboratory study by Tskhay, Zhu, and Rule (2017) that used short videos of speakers suggest that followers form impressions of leader charisma very quickly and are highly impacted by the leader's nonverbal expressive behaviors. In field experiments with actual leaders, a training intervention to increase leader use of charismatic behaviors enabled the teams with the trained leaders to perform better than teams with leaders who did not get the training (Barling, Weber, & Kelloway, 1996; Dvir, Eden, Avolio, & Shamir, 2002).

Findings from Research on Effects of Charismatic Leaders

The research on effects of charismatic leadership has failed to yield consistent results. One reason is the use of different methods, different types of leaders, and different measures of leader effects. The essential leader traits and behaviors are not clearly identified in most theories, and the diverse conceptions of charismatic leadership make it difficult to understand and reconcile the research findings (Antonakis et al., 2016; van Knippenberg & Sitkin, 2013). Numerous studies have examined the effects of charismatic leadership, and reviews of this literature continue to be updated (e.g., Banks et al., 2017).

Another problem in interpreting results from research on effects of charismatic leaders is that both positive and negative effects are common for the same leader, and it is not always clear whether a particular outcome is beneficial or detrimental. Positive effects include influencing followers to achieve great outcomes despite major obstacles. Some of the most successful business, political, military, and social movement leaders were charismatics. The major theories of charismatic leadership emphasize the positive effects, but a number of social scientists have also considered negative effects for followers and the leader's group or organization, sometimes referred to as the "dark side" of charisma (Bass & Steidlmeier, 1999; Conger, 1989; Conger & Kanungo, 1998; Hogan, Raskin, & Fazzini, 1990; Horn et al., 2015; House & Howell, 1992; Kets de Vries & Miller, 1985; Mumford, Gessner, Connelly, O'Connor, & Clifton, 1993; O'Connor et al., 1995; Sandowsky, 1995). Negative consequences that are likely to occur in organizations led by charismatics are summarized in Table 8-2.

Two interrelated sets of consequences combine to increase the likelihood that the leader will eventually fail. Charismatic leaders tend to make more risky decisions that can result in a serious failure, and they tend to make enemies who will use such a failure as an opportunity to remove the leader from office. Leader optimism and self-confidence are essential to influence others to support the leader's vision, but excessive optimism makes it more difficult for the leader to recognize flaws in the vision or strategy. Identifying too closely with a vision undermines the capacity of people to evaluate it objectively. If other executives believe the leader

TABLE 8-2 Some Negative Consequences of Charismatic Leaders

- Being in awe of the leader reduces good suggestions by followers.
- Desire for leader acceptance inhibits criticism by followers.
- Adoration by followers creates delusions of leader infallibility.
- Excessive confidence and optimism blind the leader to real dangers.
- Denial of problems and failures reduces organizational learning.
- Risky, grandiose projects are more likely to fail.
- Taking complete credit for successes alienates some key followers.
- Impulsive, nontraditional behavior creates enemies as well as believers.
- Dependence on the leader inhibits development of competent successors.
- Failure to develop successors creates an eventual leadership crisis.

has exceptional expertise, they will be inhibited from pointing out flaws or suggesting improvements in the leader's strategies and plans (see Finkelstein, 2003). Earlier successes and adulation by many followers may cause the leader to become overconfident. In a persistent quest to attain the vision, a charismatic leader may ignore or reject early signs that it is unrealistic. How overconfidence can result in a bad decision is evident in this example about Edwin Land, the inventor of the Polaroid camera (Conger, 1989):

> Land had been correct in his earlier perception that people wanted cameras that would make instant photographs, but in 1970 he decided to develop a radical new camera (the SX-70) that would make the earlier versions obsolete. Ignoring evidence that the market demand would be very limited, Land invested a half billion dollars to develop and produce the "perfect" instant camera. This strategy proved to be unsuccessful. Sales for the first year were far below estimated levels, and several years of design changes and price cuts were necessary to gain market acceptance for the camera.

The same impulsive, unconventional behavior that some people view as charismatic will offend and antagonize other people who consider it disruptive and inappropriate. Likewise, people who remain committed to the traditional ways of doing things may be alienated by the unconventional vision espoused by most charismatic leaders. Some initial supporters may become disillusioned if the leader fails to acknowledge their significant contributions to major achievements by the group or organization. Bass (1985) noted that the response of people to a charismatic leader is likely to be polarized; the same leader arouses extreme admiration by some people and extreme hatred by others. The advantage of having some dedicated followers who identify with the leader is offset by having determined enemies, including powerful people who can undermine the leader's programs or conspire to remove the leader from office. Many charismatic political leaders have been targets of assassination attempts (Yammarino, Mumford, Serban, & Shirreffs, 2013).

Charisma is a transitory phenomenon when it is dependent on personal identification with an individual leader who is perceived to be extraordinary. When the leader departs or dies, a succession crisis is likely, and many organizations founded by a charismatic leader fail to survive this crisis (Bryman, 1992; Mintzberg, 1983). Sometimes the leader's vision can be embedded in the culture of the organization, but this approach requires a vision that continues to be relevant and appealing to members long after the leader is gone. Before departing, the leader's authority can be transferred to a designated successor through rites and ceremonies, but it is seldom possible to find a successor who will appear as extraordinary as the initial charismatic leader. In addition, a leader who fears potential rivals or is preoccupied with the mission may fail to identify a strong successor early enough to ensure a smooth transition.

The leader can also create an administrative structure that will continue to implement the vision with rational-legal authority (Weber, 1947). However, it is difficult to maintain the enthusiastic commitment of organization members when a charismatic leader is succeeded by bland bureaucrats who emphasize obedience to formal rules. Even when not actively encouraged by the leader, a formal administrative structure usually evolves in a new organization, as it grows larger and more successful. Conflicts are likely between bureaucratic administrators and the charismatic leader, and sometimes the administrators are able to wrest control of the organization away from the charismatic leader. A case study by Weed (1993) provides a vivid example:

> Candy Lightner is the charismatic founder of Mothers Against Drunk Driving (MADD). In 1980, after her daughter was killed by a drunk driver who was a repeat offender, she created MADD to lobby for stricter penalties for drunk driving in California. By 1985 she had successfully built MADD into a large national organization with 360 local chapters in

the United States and a budget of $13 million. As MADD grew its central administrative structure became more formalized. The size of the Board of Directors was increased, and its composition changed from local chapter directors who were very loyal to Lightner to professionals with a background in law, public relations, social services, and nonprofit advocacy organizations. The central staff evolved from a small circle of close friends to a larger staff of professional administrators whose primary loyalty was to the organization rather than to Lightner. By 1983 there were increasing conflicts between Lightner and other members of the central staff, who resented her autocratic style, her inconsistency about assignments, and her defensiveness about criticism or dissent. Turnover increased, and disputes erupted about her use of funds. Finally when her contract lapsed in 1985, the Board ousted Lightner from her position as president of MADD.

Another adverse consequence of charismatic leadership, and one that is somewhat counter-intuitive, is called the "awestruck effect" (Menges, Kilduff, Kern, & Bruch, 2015). In a series of three studies involving experiments and field research, Menges and colleagues found that followers of charismatic leaders were less likely to openly express their emotions than followers of supportive, noncharismatic leaders. The attempts to control their expression of emotions created problems for followers of charismatic leaders and they had more job dissatisfaction.

Learning Charismatic Leadership

The extent to which charismatic qualities can be learned has implications for leadership development (see Chapter 14), and this question was examined by Antonakis, Fenley, and Liechti (2011) in a field experiment and a laboratory experiment. In both studies the participants were taught how to use seven verbal charismatic leadership tactics and three nonverbal tactics (see Table 8-3). In the first study, middle-level managers were randomly assigned to an experimental

TABLE 8-3 Charismatic Leadership Tactics

Verbal Tactics

- *Metaphors* are figures of speech that directly refer to an object or action by mentioning another similar object or action for rhetorical effect. They are effective persuasive devices because they stir emotion, simplify the message, aid recall, and invoke symbolic meanings.
- *Stories and anecdotes* make a message understandable and memorable while inducing identification with the protagonist(s).
- *Expressions of moral conviction* communicate that the leader is a person of high moral fiber.
- *Statements that reflect the sentiments of the group* align followers with the leader by indicating that the leader shares their interests and values.
- *Setting high goals* serves as a catalyst for follower motivation.
- *Conveying confidence that goals can be achieved* increases follower self-efficacy.
- *Rhetorical questions* (to encourage engagement), *three-part lists* (to distill a message into key takeaways, provide a pattern, and instill a sense of completeness), and *contrasts* (pitting one's position against another for dramatic effect) are used to engage followers and distill the leader's message.

Nonverbal Tactics

- *Body gestures* are signals for listeners (e.g., pointing, waving a hand, or pounding a table can draw attention; a fist can reinforce power, confidence, and certitude).
- *Animated voices* can convey emotion such as surprise, happiness, passion, and excitement.
- *Facial expressions* reinforce the leader's message by conveying associated emotions.

Adapted from Antonakis, Fenley, and Liechti (2011, 2012).

condition with the charismatic leadership training or to a control group with no training. Three months later, subordinates rated the charisma of their leader. In the second study, MBA students were initially videotaped giving a speech. Then they were trained how to use the charismatic leadership tactics, and six months later they redelivered the speech. The results of both studies demonstrated that training improved ratings of leader charisma.

Implications for Organizations

A few writers have proposed the idea that charismatic leadership is a good solution for the problems of large organizations, but critics point out several reasons why it may not be feasible or desirable to have charismatic leaders occupy important positions in private and public sector organizations (Bryman, 1992; Schein, 1992; Trice & Beyer, 1993).

Charismatic leadership is risky. It is impossible to predict the result when people give too much power to an individual leader who they expect to deliver on the promise of a better future. The power is often misused while the vision remains an empty dream. History is full of charismatic leaders who caused untold death, destruction, and misery in the process of building an empire, leading a revolution, or founding a new religion.

Charismatic leadership implies radical change in the strategy and culture of an organization, which may not be necessary or appropriate for organizations that are currently prosperous and successful. It is difficult to make radical change in an organization if no obvious crisis exists and many members see no need for change. If there is more than one charismatic leader in the organization and they have incompatible visions, the organization may be torn apart by disruptive conflict. Historical accounts suggest that many charismatic leaders find it too difficult to implement their radical vision within an existing organization, and they leave to establish a new one (e.g., a new business, religious order, political party, or social movement).

Charisma is a rare and transitory phenomenon. The beneficial accomplishments of a charismatic leader may not persist after the leader departs. The early dramatic successes that make a leader appear charismatic can sow the seeds of eventual failure if overconfidence encourages risky decisions that will endanger the organization and its members.

Although research on effects of charismatic chief executives is limited, the available results suggest that charisma is not an essential attribute for their success and may even be detrimental for most of them. The descriptive research found that few leaders of successful organizations were viewed as charismatic (e.g., Bennis & Nanus, 1985; Collins, 2001a, 2001b; Kouzes & Posner, 1987; Peters & Austin, 1985; Tichy & Devanna, 1986). In a study that examined the financial performance of corporations in the years before and after a survey conducted to measure CEO charisma, financial performance was predicted by past performance but not by CEO charisma (Agle, Nagarajan, Sonnenfeld, & Srinivasan, 2006). Another study of corporations found that CEOs who appeared charismatic were able to persuade their board of directors to give them higher compensation, but these CEOs did not improve financial performance for their companies (Tosi, Misangyi, Fanelli, Waldman, & Yammarino, 2004). The longitudinal descriptive studies of charismatic leaders found that early success could be followed by dramatic failure.

Despite the adverse consequences found for charismatic leaders, they are not all doomed to fail. Success is possible when the leaders have the expertise to make good decisions, the political skill to maintain power, and the good luck to be in a favorable situation. There are many examples of charismatic leaders who established political empires, founded prosperous companies, or initiated new religious sects and retained control of them throughout their lifetime.

Transformational Leadership

Transformational leadership theory describes how effective leaders inspire and transform followers by appealing to their ideals and emotions. Early conceptions of transformational leadership were influenced by James McGregor Burns (1978), who wrote a best-selling book on political leadership. Burns contrasted transforming leadership with transactional leadership. Transforming leadership appeals to the moral values of followers in an attempt to raise their consciousness about ethical issues and to mobilize their energy and resources to reform institutions. Transactional leadership motivates followers by appealing to their self-interest and offering benefits. For a political leader, these activities include providing jobs, subsidies, lucrative government contracts, and support for desired legislation in return for campaign contributions and votes to re-elect the leader. Transactional leadership may involve values, but they are values relevant to the exchange process, such as honesty, fairness, responsibility, and reciprocity. Finally, Burns also identified a third form of leadership influence based on legitimate authority and respect for rules and tradition. Bureaucratic organizations emphasize this form of influence more than influence based on exchange or inspiration.

The process by which leaders appeal to follower values and emotions is a central feature in current theories of transformational and visionary leadership in organizations (e.g., Bass, 1985, 1996; Bennis & Nanus, 1985; Sashkin & Fulmer, 1988; Podsakoff, MacKenzie, & Bommer, 1996b; Podsakoff, MacKenzie, Moorman, & Fetter, 1990; Tichy & Devanna, 1986). In contrast to Burns, however, the newer theories of transformational leadership are more concerned with attainment of pragmatic task objectives than with the moral elevation of followers or social reform. The views of Burns on ethical leadership are discussed in Chapter 9.

Several theories of transformational or inspirational leadership were proposed, but the version of the theory formulated by Bass (1985, 1996) has influenced leadership research more than any of the others. Building on the ideas of Burns, the essence of the theory is the distinction between transformational and transactional leadership. For Bass (1985), transformational and transactional leadership are distinct but not mutually exclusive processes. With transformational leadership, the followers feel trust, admiration, loyalty, and respect toward the leader, and they are motivated to do more than they originally expected to do. The leader transforms and motivates followers by (1) making them more aware of the importance of task outcomes, (2) inducing them to transcend their own self-interest for the sake of the organization or team, and (3) activating their higher-order needs. In contrast, transactional leadership involves an exchange process in which the leader provides rewards to followers who comply with the leader's requests. This exchange process is not likely to generate commitment to task objectives. According to Bass, transformational leadership increases follower motivation and performance more than transactional leadership, but effective leaders use a combination of both types of leadership.

Leader Behaviors

Transformational and transactional leadership behaviors are described as broad categories of behavior, each with specific component behaviors. Bass (1985) initially included three types of transformational behavior. Idealized influence is behavior that increases follower identification with the leader, such as setting an example of courage and dedication and making self-sacrifices to benefit followers. Intellectual stimulation is behavior that influences followers to view problems from a new perspective and look for more creative solutions. Individualized consideration includes providing support, encouragement, and coaching to followers. A revision of the theory (Bass & Avolio, 1990a) added another transformational behavior called inspirational motivation, which includes communicating an appealing vision, and using symbols to focus subordinate effort. Yet another revision by Bass and Avolio (1997) distinguished between idealized influence behavior and attributions of charisma, but the reason for this distinction is unclear since all ratings of leadership behavior are susceptible to attribution biases.

The original formulation of the theory included two types of transactional behavior: contingent reward and passive management by exception. Contingent reward behavior includes clarification of accomplishments necessary to obtain rewards, and the use of incentives to influence subordinate task motivation. Passive management by exception includes use of contingent punishments and other corrective action in response to obvious deviations from acceptable performance standards. Another transactional behavior called active management by exception was added in more recent versions of the theory (Bass & Avolio, 1990a). This behavior is defined in terms of looking for mistakes and enforcing rules to avoid mistakes. A later version of the theory added another transactional behavior called laissez-faire leadership (Bass & Avolio, 1994). This behavior is defined as passive indifference about the task (e.g., ignoring task problems) and about subordinates (e.g., ignoring subordinate needs). It is best described as the absence of effective leadership rather than as an example of transactional leadership.

Influence Processes

The underlying influence processes for transactional and transformational leadership are not clearly explained, but they can be inferred from the description of the behaviors and effects on follower motivation. The primary influence process for transactional leadership is probably instrumental compliance (see Chapter 6). Transformational leadership probably involves internalization, because inspirational motivation includes efforts to link the task to follower values and ideals with behavior such as articulating an inspirational vision. A leader can increase intrinsic motivation by increasing the perception of followers that task objectives are consistent with their authentic interests and values (see Bono & Judge, 2004; Charbonneau, Barling, & Kelloway, 2001).

Transformational leadership also appears to involve personal identification (Horstmeier, Boer, Homan, & Voelpel, 2017). Followers may identify with the leader, imitate the leader's behavior, and embrace the values and ideals espoused by the leader. Personal identification may include follower attributions of charisma to the leader. According to Bass (1985, p. 31), "Charisma is a necessary ingredient of transformational leadership, but by itself it is not sufficient to account for the transformational process."

Other processes that may mediate the effects of transformational leadership on follower performance have been identified in research on the theory. Transformational leadership is highly correlated with trust in the leader (Dirks & Ferrin, 2002; Zhu & Akhtar, 2014). Transformational behaviors such as inspirational motivation (e.g., optimistic visioning) and individualized consideration (e.g., coaching) may increase the self-efficacy of individual subordinates (McColl-Kennedy & Anderson, 2002), the perceived meaningfulness of work (Frieder, Wang, & Oh, 2018), and the collective efficacy of teams (see Chapter 11). Intellectual stimulation may increase the creativity of individual followers (Howell & Avolio, 1993; Jung, 2001; Keller, 1992; Qu, Janssen, & Shi, 2015; Sosik, Kahai, & Avolio, 1998).

The influence process called "cascading" has been offered as a way to explain how a CEO can indirectly influence the motivation of lower-level employees in an organization

(Waldman & Yammarino, 1999). The behavior of a CEO is imitated by subordinates, and role-modeling is repeated by managers at each lower level. As yet, there is only very limited evidence for cascading of leader behaviors (Bass et al., 1987; Chun et al., 2009). There is no evidence that key CEO behaviors will be imitated by low-level managers, or that lower-level members of an organization will embrace the CEO's vision without a credible strategy and major changes in programs, reward systems, and cultural values.

Leadership Situation

According to Bass (1996, 1997), transformational leadership is considered effective in any situation or culture. The theory does not specify any conditions under which authentic transformational leadership is irrelevant or ineffective. In support of this position, the positive relationship between transformational leadership and effectiveness has been replicated for many leaders at different levels of authority, in different types of organizations, and in several different countries (Bass, 1997). The criterion of leadership effectiveness has included a variety of different types of measures. The evidence supports the conclusion that some aspects of transformational leadership are relevant for most leaders, but they are not equally effective in all situations.

As yet, there has not been much research on the way situations determine the effects of transformational leader behavior, or the effects of the specific component behaviors. A number of situational variables may increase the likelihood that transformational leadership will occur or may enhance the effect of such leadership on followers (Bass, 1985, 1996; Hill, Seo, Kang, & Taylor, 2012; Hinkin & Tracey, 1999; Howell & Avolio, 1993; Pawar & Eastman, 1997; Pettigrew, 1988; Purvanova & Bono, 2009; Waldman, Ramirez, House, & Puranam, 2001). The change-oriented components of transformational leadership are likely to be more important in a dynamic, unstable environment that increases the need for change, and such leadership is more likely when leaders are encouraged and empowered to be flexible and innovative (e.g., a decentralized organization with an entrepreneurial culture). Also, there is growing evidence that follower traits and values (e.g., conscientiousness, openness to experience, positive affectivity, learning goal orientation, core self-evaluations, self-efficacy) may determine how they respond to a leader's transformational behaviors (e.g., Den Hartog & Belschak, 2012; de Vries, Roe, & Taillieu, 2002; Ehrhart & Klein, 2001; Frieder et al., 2018; Gilmore, Hu, Wei, Tetrick, & Zaccaro, 2013; Kim, T.-Y., Liden, Kim, S.-P., & Lee, 2015; Li, Chiaburu, Kirkman, & Xie, 2013; Zhen & Peterson, 2011).

Comparison of Charismatic and Transformational Leadership

One of the most important issues for leadership scholars is the extent to which transformational leadership and charismatic leadership are similar and compatible. Some theorists treat the two types of leadership as essentially equivalent, whereas other theorists view them as distinct but overlapping processes. Even among theorists who view the two types of leadership as distinct processes, there remains disagreement about whether it is possible to be both transformational and charismatic at the same time.

Conceptual ambiguity and inconsistent definitions make it difficult to compare transformational and charismatic leadership (Antonakis et al., 2016; Sitkin & Roth, 1993). In recent years, the major charismatic theories have been revised in ways that appear to move them closer to the transformational theories. The major transformational theories have been revised to incorporate additional forms of effective leadership behavior. The term transformational has been broadly defined by some writers to include almost any type of effective leadership, regardless of the underlying influence processes. The label may refer to the transformation of individual followers or to the transformation of entire organizations.

The essence of charisma is being perceived as extraordinary by followers who are dependent on the leader for guidance and inspiration. Bass (1985) proposed that charisma is a necessary component of transformational leadership, but he also noted that a leader can be charismatic but not transformational. The essence of transformational leadership appears to be inspiring, developing, and empowering followers (although empowering is not explicit in some versions of the theory). These effects may reduce attributions of charisma to the leader rather than increase it. Thus, the essential influence processes for transformational leadership may not be entirely compatible with the essential influence process for charismatic leadership, which involves personal identification with an extraordinary leader and dependence on the leader. Some support for this distinction is provided in a study by Kark, Shamir, and Chen (2003) that found personal identification mediates the effect of the leader on follower dependence, and social identification mediates the effect of the leader on follower self-efficacy and collective efficacy.

Many of the leadership behaviors in the theories of charismatic and transformational leadership appear to be the same, but some important differences are evident as well. Transformational leaders probably do more things that will empower followers and make them less dependent on the leader, such as developing follower skills and self-confidence, delegating significant authority to individuals or teams, providing direct access to sensitive information, eliminating unnecessary controls, and building a strong culture to support empowerment. Charismatic leaders probably do more things that foster an image of extraordinary competence for the leader and increase subordinate dependence, such as impression management, information restriction, unconventional behavior, and personal risk taking.

Another likely difference between transformational and charismatic leadership involves how often each type of leadership occurs and the facilitating conditions for it. According to Bass, transformational leaders can be found in any organization at any level, and this type of leadership is universally relevant for all types of situations (Bass, 1996, 1997). In contrast, truly charismatic leaders are rare, and their emergence appears to be more dependent on unusual conditions (Bass, 1985; Beyer, 1999; Shamir & Howell, 1999). They are most likely to be visionary entrepreneurs who establish a new organization, or reformers who emerge in an established organization when formal authority has failed to deal with a severe crisis and traditional values and beliefs are questioned.

Another difference involves the way people react to the leaders. The reactions to charismatics are usually more extreme and diverse than reactions to transformational leaders (Bass, 1985). The affective reaction aroused by charismatics often polarizes people into opposing camps of loyal supporters and hostile opponents. The intense negative reaction by some people to charismatic leaders helps explain why these leaders are often targets for assassination or political tactics to remove them from office (Serban et al., 2018; Yammarino et al., 2013). Transformational leaders get a less intense reaction from followers and are unlikely to have this polarizing effect. These leaders are viewed as competent and professional but are not usually considered exciting and exceptional.

The empirical research on transformational and charismatic leadership was not designed to examine issues of comparability and compatibility for the different theories. Few studies examine underlying influence processes or go beyond the superficial, often ambiguous data provided by behavior description questionnaires (e.g., Rowold & Heinitz, 2007). The primary difference in the theories involves aspects of the relationships and influence processes that are not captured by these questionnaires. Resolution of the interesting and important question about differences in the two types of leadership requires additional research with more intensive methods. Finally, it is important to remember that broad constructs such as charismatic and transformational leadership have serious limitations, and much more can be learned about effective leadership by examining how specific traits, skills, and behaviors are relevant for the leadership situation and the desired outcomes.

Charismatic, Ideological and Pragmatic Leaders

Another theory involving charismatic leadership differentiates among three types of leaders that can emerge in situations involving crises, turbulence, and uncertainty (Hunter, Cushenbery, Thoroughgood, Johnson, & Ligon, 2011; Mumford, 2006; Mumford, Antes, Caughron, & Friedrich, 2008). In turbulent situations, leaders have more potential influence over the identification of threats and opportunities and the selection of appropriate responses. The three different types of leaders that can emerge in these situations are charismatic, ideological, and pragmatic leaders. Each type of leader can be effective, but they differ in terms of their traits, behavior, and influence processes.

The charismatic and ideological leaders are more effective in situations where there is a high level of political and ideological conflict, whereas pragmatic leaders are more effective when there is little political conflict and more emphasis on constructive problem solving.

Ideological leaders are more likely to emerge when there is a strong culture of shared values, and they can articulate a vision that embodies these values. Ideological leaders make emotional appeals to shared values and beliefs, and they involve followers in identifying strategies for resolving a crisis or attaining desirable objectives. To retain the trust of followers, ideological leaders must act in ways that are consistent with the values and vision.

The charismatic leaders appeal to emotions and articulate a vision that builds confidence that the leader can show followers how to resolve a crisis and overcome obstacles to desirable objectives. The vision appeals to some members of the organization who trust the leader and are willing to become loyal followers, but other members who do not share the leader's vision may become opponents.

The pragmatic leaders are more likely to emerge when they are perceived by followers to have the expertise and commitment necessary to guide the process of strategy formation and crisis management. Pragmatic leaders make rational appeals to followers who are able to understand and carry out proposed strategies for achieving shared objectives.

Evaluation of the Theories

The available evidence supports many of the key propositions of the major theories of charismatic and transformational leadership. Collectively, the theories appear to make an important contribution to our understanding of leadership processes. They provide an explanation for the exceptional influence some leaders have on followers, a level of influence not adequately explained by earlier theories. Specific contributions include more attention to the importance of emotional reactions by followers, the importance of symbolic behavior, and the role of the leader in making ambiguous events meaningful for followers. Earlier leadership theories did not recognize that symbolic processes and management of meaning are as important as management of things.

Despite their positive features, the theories also have some conceptual weaknesses that limit their value for understanding effective leadership (Antonakis et al., 2016; Beyer, 1999; Bryman, 1993; Mhatre & Riggio, 2014; Sitkin & Roth, 1993; Yukl, 1999b). Common weaknesses include vague constructs, insufficient description of explanatory processes, a narrow focus on dyadic processes, omission of some relevant leader behaviors, insufficient specification of situational variables, lack of attention to the relevance of the vision for organizational performance, and a bias toward heroic conceptions of leadership that attribute too much influence on outcomes to individual leaders. Some of these limitations will be explained in more detail.

Most theories of transformational and charismatic leadership lack sufficient specification of underlying influence processes. There is a need for more clarification of how the various types of influence processes interact, their relative importance, and whether they are mutually compatible. Most of the theories emphasize the influence of the leader on followers, and more attention needs to be focused on reciprocal influence processes, shared leadership, and mutual influence among the followers themselves. The theories would be strengthened by including a better explanation of how leaders enhance mutual trust and cooperation, empowerment, collective identification, collective efficacy, and collective learning. The theories should include more explanation of task-oriented functions of leaders that are essential for the effective performance of a team, and strategic functions that are essential for the financial performance of organizations. Most of the theories fail to explain the leader's external roles, such as monitoring the environment to identify threats and opportunities, building networks of contacts who can provide information and assistance, serving as a spokesperson for the team or organization, negotiating agreements with outsiders, and helping to obtain resources, political support, and new members with appropriate skills (see Chapters 3, 11, and 12).

Most of the theories focus too narrowly on dyadic processes. The charismatic and transformational theories describe how a leader can influence the motivation and loyalty of subordinates, which is relevant for understanding effective leadership. However, these theories are primarily extensions of motivation theory, and much more is needed to explain how leaders build exceptional teams or influence the financial performance and survival of an organization (Beyer, 1999; Yukl & Lepsinger, 2004). A leader may influence followers to be more motivated, creative, and cooperative, but what the followers are motivated to do and how appropriate it is for the situation are also important. Having highly motivated and loyal followers will not prevent disaster if the leader pursues unrealistic objectives or misguided strategies (Finkelstein, 2003).

The theories do not clearly specify how leadership processes are related to change, the necessary facilitating conditions for the leader to influence major change, or how initial change will affect future leadership processes. The vision may be one developed primarily by the leader or merely a minor adaptation of a vision already articulated by higher-level leaders or a previous leader. The vision may involve a call for innovative changes, or it may involve a return to traditional values that are no longer dominant determinants of strategic decisions for the organization but remain important for many members. For example, a charismatic leader may emerge as a rebel who successfully resists the implementation of major changes that are inconsistent with traditional values but may be necessary for organizational effectiveness (Levay, 2010).

The theories also lack clarity about the longer-term implications for transformational or charismatic leadership. A leader who is attributed charisma following initial success in innovative responses to threats or opportunities may lose this charisma if success is only temporary or new initiatives result in serious losses for the organization. A transformational leader may lack the cognitive skills needed to successfully deal with increasingly complex and difficult challenges as the situation changes or the person is promoted to a higher-level position.

Guidelines for Inspirational Leadership

Although much remains to be learned about charismatic and transformational leadership, the findings from the different types of research suggest some tentative guidelines for leaders who seek to inspire followers and increase their self-confidence and commitment to the mission. The guidelines (see summary in Table 8-4) are based on the theories and research findings reviewed in this chapter.

- **Articulate a clear and appealing vision.**

Transformational leaders strengthen the existing vision or build commitment to a new vision. A clear vision of what the organization could accomplish or become helps people understand the purpose, objectives, and priorities of the organization. It gives the work meaning, serves as a source of self-esteem, and fosters a sense of common purpose. Finally, the vision helps guide the actions and decisions of each member of the organization, which is especially important when individuals or groups are allowed considerable autonomy and discretion in their work decisions (Den Hartog & Belschak, 2012; Hackman, 1986; Raelin, 1989). Suggestions for developing a vision with appealing content are described in Chapter 5.

The success of a vision depends on how well it is communicated to people (Awamleh & Gardner, 1999; Holladay & Coombs, 1993, 1994; Margolis & Ziegert, 2016). The vision should be communicated at every opportunity and in a variety of ways. Meeting with people directly to explain the vision and answer questions about it is probably more effective than less interactive forms of communication (e.g., letters or e-mail messages to followers, newsletter articles, televised news conferences, videotaped speeches). If a noninteractive form of communication is used to present the vision, then it is helpful to provide opportunities for followers to ask questions afterward (e.g., use e-mail, a hotline, open meetings, or visits by the leader to department meetings).

The ideological aspects of a vision can be communicated more clearly and persuasively with colorful, emotional language that includes vivid imagery, metaphors, anecdotes, stories, symbols, and slogans. Metaphors and analogies are especially effective when they excite the imagination and engage the listener in trying to make sense out of them. Anecdotes and stories are more effective if they invoke symbols with deep cultural roots, such as legendary heroes, sacred figures, and historical ordeals and triumphs. A dramatic, expressive style of speaking augments the use of colorful language in making an emotional appeal (see guidelines for inspirational appeals in Chapter 6). Conviction and intensity of feeling are communicated by a speaker's voice (tone, inflection, pauses), facial expressions, gestures, and body movements. The appropriate use of rhyme, rhythm, and repetition of key words or phrases can make a vision more colorful and compelling. Modi prompts a higher scale of optimism and eulogizes his social policy within a spectrum of his political slogan of '*Sabka Saath, Sabka Vikas*' (collective efforts, inclusive

TABLE 8-4 Guidelines for Inspirational Leadership

- Articulate a clear and appealing vision.
- Explain how the vision can be attained.
- Act confident and optimistic.
- Express confidence in followers.
- Use dramatic, symbolic actions to emphasize key values.
- Lead by example.

growth). His light hearted remarks and catchphrases are what appeal to the mass. He maintains eye contact with the audience and modulates his voice, while laying emphasis on the important words. He stands straight and has an expansive body language. He keeps his hands in front of his chest. He does not slouch over the podium or table in front of him. His confident body language instills faith in his audience. It increases the probability of his audience buying his message as he comes across as a bold leader who knows what he is talking about.

- **Explain how the vision can be attained.**

It is not enough to articulate an appealing vision; the leader must also convince followers that the vision is feasible. It is important to make a clear link between the vision and a credible strategy for attaining it. This link is easier to establish if the strategy has a few clear themes that are relevant to shared values of organization members (Nadler, 1988). Themes provide labels to help people understand issues and problems. The number of themes should be large enough to focus attention on key issues, but not so large as to cause confusion and dissipate energy. It is seldom necessary to present an elaborate plan with detailed action steps. The leader should not pretend to know all the answers about how to achieve the vision, but instead should inform followers that they will have a vital role in discovering what specific actions are necessary.

The strategy for attaining the vision is most likely to be persuasive when it is unconventional yet straightforward. If it is simplistic or conventional, the strategy will not elicit confidence in the leader, especially when there is a crisis. Consider the example of a company that was losing market share in the face of intense competition:

> The CEO proposed to make the company's product the best in the world by improving product design and quality (the old strategy was to keep price low by cutting costs). The product would be designed to be reliable (few moving parts, durable materials, extensive product testing, quality control by every worker) as well as "user friendly" (simple operating procedures, easy-to-read displays, clear instructions). This strategy contributed to the successful turnaround of the company.

- **Act confident and optimistic.**

Followers are not going to have faith in a vision unless the leader demonstrates self-confidence and conviction. It is important to remain optimistic about the likely success of the group in attaining its vision, especially in the face of temporary roadblocks and setbacks. A leader's confidence and optimism can be highly contagious. It is best to emphasize what has been accomplished so far rather than how much more is yet to be done. It is best to emphasize the positive aspects of the vision rather than the obstacles and dangers that lie ahead. Confidence is expressed in both words and actions. Lack of self-confidence is reflected in tentative, faltering language (e.g., "I guess," "maybe," "hopefully") and some nonverbal cues (e.g., frowns, lack of eye contact, nervous gestures, weak posture).

- **Express confidence in followers.**

The motivating effect of a vision also depends on the extent to which subordinates are confident about their ability to achieve it. Research on the Pygmalion effect found that people perform better when a leader has high expectations for them and shows confidence in them (Duan, Li, Xu, &

Wu, 2017; Eden, 1984, 1990; Eden & Shani, 1982; Eden et al., 2000; Field, 1989; McNatt & Judge, 2004; Sutton & Woodman, 1989). It is especially important to foster confidence and optimism when the task is difficult or dangerous, or when team members lack confidence in themselves. If appropriate, the leader should remind followers how they overcame obstacles to achieve an earlier triumph. If they have never been successful before, the leader may be able to make an analogy between the present situation and success by a similar team or organizational unit. Review the specific strengths, assets, and resources that they can draw on to carry out the strategy. List the advantages they have relative to opponents or competitors. Explain why they are as good as or better than an earlier team that was successful in performing the same type of activity.

- **Use dramatic, symbolic actions to emphasize key values.**

A vision is reinforced by leadership behavior that is consistent with it. Concern for a value or objective is demonstrated by the way a manager spends time, by resource allocation decisions made when trade-offs are necessary between objectives, by the questions the manager asks, and by what actions the manager rewards. Dramatic, highly visible actions can be used to emphasize key values, as in the following example:

> The division manager had a vision that included relationships in which people were open, creative, cooperative, and oriented toward learning. Past meetings of the management team had been overly formal, with detailed agendas, elaborate presentations, and excessive criticism. He began a three-day meeting to communicate his vision for the division by inviting people to a beachfront ceremony where they burned a pile of agendas, handouts, and evaluation forms.

Symbolic actions to achieve an important objective or defend an important value are likely to be more influential when the manager risks substantial personal loss, makes self-sacrifices, or does things that are unconventional. The effect of symbolic actions is increased when they become the subject of stories and myths that circulate among members of the organization and are retold time and again over the years to new employees. In one example recounted by Peters and Austin (1985), the CEO personally destroyed some low-quality versions of the company's product that had been sold previously as "seconds." This widely publicized action demonstrated his commitment to the new policy that, henceforth, the company would make and sell only products of the highest quality.

- **Lead by example.**

According to an old saying, actions speak louder than words. One way a leader can influence subordinate commitment is by setting an example of exemplary behavior in day-to-day interactions with subordinates. Leading by example is sometimes called role-modeling. It is especially important for actions that are unpleasant, dangerous, unconventional, or controversial. For example, Politicians and celebrities leading by example the Swacch Bharat Abhiyan. A manager who asks subordinates to observe a particular standard should also observe the same standard. A manager who asks subordinates to make special sacrifices should set an example by doing the same. Some of the most inspirational military leaders have been ones who led their troops into battle and shared the dangers and hardships rather than staying behind in relative safety and comfort (Van Fleet & Yukl, 1986b). A negative example is provided by the executives in a large company that was experiencing financial difficulties. After asking employees to defer their expected pay increases, the executives awarded themselves large bonuses. This action created resentment among employees and undermined employee loyalty to the organization and commitment to its mission. A more effective approach would be to set an example by cutting bonuses for top executives before asking for sacrifices from other employees.

The values espoused by a leader should be demonstrated in daily behavior, and it must be done consistently, not just when convenient. Top-level leaders are always in the spotlight, and their actions are carefully examined by followers in a search for hidden meanings that may not be intended by the leader. Ambiguous remarks may be misinterpreted and innocent actions may be misrepresented. To avoid sending the wrong message, it is important to consider in advance how one's comments and actions are likely to be interpreted by others.

Summary

Attributions of charisma are the result of an interactive process between leader, followers, and the situation. Charismatic leaders use emotional, symbolic, values-based communication to arouse enthusiasm and commitment in followers. They articulate a compelling vision and increase follower confidence about achieving it. Attribution of charisma to the leader is more likely if the vision and strategy for attaining it are innovative, the leader takes personal risks to promote it, and the strategy appears to be succeeding. Other relevant behaviors have also been identified, but they vary somewhat across different theories. Some leader traits and skills such as self-confidence, strong convictions, poise, speaking ability, and a dramatic flair increase the likelihood of attributed charisma, but also important is a context that makes the leader's vision especially relevant to follower needs.

Charismatic leaders can have a strong influence on an organization, but the consequences are not always beneficial. A leader may influence followers to be more motivated and cooperative, but what the followers are motivated to do and how appropriate it is for the situation are also important. Having highly motivated and loyal followers will not prevent disaster if the leader pursues unrealistic objectives or misguided strategies (Finkelstein, 2003). Negative outcomes are likely for narcissistic charismatics with a personalized power orientation. These leaders are insensitive, manipulative, domineering, impulsive, and defensive. They consider follower devotion more important than commitment to an ideological vision. Their arrogance and excessive self-confidence encourage risky decisions that can cause the downfall of their organization. Positive charismatics seek to instill devotion to ideological goals and are more likely to have a beneficial influence on the organization. However, the high achievement culture fostered by positive charismatics may also produce some undesirable consequences if the needs of individual followers are ignored. More research is needed to discover whether it is possible to achieve the positive outcomes of charismatic leadership without the negative consequences.

Transformational leaders make followers more aware of the importance and value of the work and induce followers to transcend self-interest for the sake of the organization. The leaders develop follower skills and confidence to prepare them to assume more responsibility and have more influence. The leaders provide support and encouragement when necessary to maintain enthusiasm and effort in the face of obstacles, difficulties, and fatigue. As a result, followers trust the leader and are motivated to do more than they originally expected to do.

The empirical research on transformational leadership usually finds positive effects on follower performance, but few studies have examined the underlying influence processes that account for these effects or the reasons why some specific types of transformational and transactional behaviors are most effective for a leadership situation.

The theories of transformational and charismatic leadership emphasize that emotional processes are as important as rational processes, and symbolic actions are as important as instrumental behavior. These theories provide new insights into the reasons for the success or failure of leaders, but the underlying explanatory processes in these theories do not provide a sufficient basis for understanding how leaders can influence the long-term financial performance and survival of an organization. To understand how leaders influence organizational processes and outcomes, it is necessary to include aspects of strategic management that are not explicitly described in most charismatic and transformational theories (see Chapter 12).

Review and Discussion Questions

1. Briefly describe the key behaviors of charismatic leaders.
2. Briefly describe the influence processes involved in charismatic leadership.
3. Briefly describe verbal and nonverbal charismatic leadership tactics.
4. What problems are charismatic leaders likely to create for an organization?
5. In what type of situation is a charismatic leader most likely to be beneficial?
6. What are similarities and differences between charismatic and transformational leadership?
7. What new insights about effective leadership are provided by theories of charismatic and transformational leadership?
8. What are some guidelines for becoming more inspirational?

Key Terms

attributional ambiguity
charisma
charismatic leadership
charismatic leadership tactics
emotional contagion
impression management
internalization
personal identification
self-efficacy
social identification
symbolic action
transactional leadership
transformational leadership
vision

PERSONAL REFLECTION

Think about a leader who you have observed during your lifetime and consider to be charismatic. This leader could be someone you know personally, or a high-profile politician, business executive, religious leader, or entertainer. What types of charismatic tactics does this leader use to influence others? Do you consider this leader to be a positive or a negative charismatic leader? How effective is this leader?

CASE

Metro Bank

Marsha Brown was the new manager of a suburban office of Metro Bank. The branch office was experiencing low morale and lower productivity than expected. One of the difficulties was that the office served as an informal training center for young managers. New hires who needed experience as loan officers or assistant branch managers were assigned here for training. When they reached a certain level of competence, they were promoted out of the branch office. This practice was demoralizing to the less mobile tellers and other assistants, who felt exploited and saw no personal reward in "training their boss." After some checking with her boss and other people at corporate headquarters, Marsha concluded that it would be impossible to change this program. Her branch was one of those considered to be essential for executive development in Metro Bank.

During her first few months on the job, Marsha got to know her employees quite well. She reviewed performance records and met with each employee in the branch to talk about the person's career aspirations. She learned that many of her employees were quite capable and could do much more than they were presently doing. However, they had never seen themselves as "going anywhere" in the organization. Marsha searched for a unique vision for the branch office that would integrate the needs of her employees with the objectives of the executive development program, and in the process better serve the bank's customers. She formulated the following strategic objective: "To be the branch that best develops managerial talent while still offering quality customer service."

From this decision flowed a series of actions. First, Marsha declared that development opportunities for growth would be open to all, and she initiated a career development program for her employees. For those who wanted career advancement, she negotiated with the central training department for spaces in some of its programs. She persuaded the personnel department to inform her regularly about job openings that might interest her employees, including those not involved in the executive development program. Next, she built rewards into the appraisal system for employees who helped others learn, so that even those who did not aspire to advance would get some benefit from contributing to the new objective. To provide adequate backup in service functions, she instituted cross-training. Not only did this training provide a reserve of assistance when one function was experiencing peak workloads, it also contributed to a better understanding of the policies and procedures in other functions. Marsha also used developmental assignments with her own subordinate managers. She frequently had the assistant managers run staff meetings, represent the branch office at corporate meetings, or carry out some of her other managerial responsibilities. The changes made by Marsha resulted in major gains. By repeatedly stressing the strategic objectives in her words and actions, she gave the branch office a distinctive character. Employees felt increased pride and morale improved. Some of the old-timers acquired new aspirations and, after developing their skills, advanced into higher positions in the bank. Even those who remained at the branch office felt good about the advancement of others, because now they saw their role as crucial for individual and organizational success rather than as a thankless task. The new spirit carried over to the treatment of customers, and together with the increased competence provided by cross-training, it resulted in faster and better service to customers.

—*Written by* Gary Yukl; based on Bradford and Cohen (1984).

Questions

1. What leadership behaviors did Marsha use to change the branch office and motivate employees?
2. Describe Marsha's vision for her branch office of the bank.
3. Do you think Marsha should be classified as charismatic, transformational, or both?

CASE

Leadership Dilemmas

Srinivasan SH (popularly known as Srini) was posted as the senior divisional manager (SDM) of the Life Insurance Company's biggest division in the South Zone, the Tanjore Division. This division fell under central Tamil Nadu's agricultural belt. It was considered to be a backward division in terms of productivity of sales personnel and in terms of new business. However, the division was infamous for the strong hold of the militant trade union had over its staff. The strong union would threaten the management as well as enforce their will on the branch managers (BM) on a regular basis. With the situation being so serious, the previous two SDM's had opted out of their post within a short period of their posting.

Although an amiable person by nature, Srini was known for being straight-forward and uncompromising on his decisions for disputable issues. After his posting, Srini was warned by his colleagues about the difficulties that would lie ahead of him. Upon joining the division, he was briefed about the alarming situation created by the treacherous elements around by the incumbent SDM. The incumbent SDM was a veteran in his field, who would go out of his way to mock the trade union functionaries at all levels. Srini took stock of the situation through consultation with the marketing manager and other colleagues. It was revealed that during the first Branch Managers' Conference, the morale of the BMs was very low as they were told by the ex-SDMs to not create problem for the divisional office, and hence, they had to repeatedly concede to the illegitimate demands of the trade unions. Thus, Srini decided to meet the leaders of the various employees' informal cliques and unions and agreed to look into their problems and resolve the genuine ones that fell within his jurisdiction.

In August 2003 a new software platform was being installed in all branches of the South Zone. However, the majority trade union would not allow its implementation, because an apology was due from one of the BMs, who had insulted the divisional secretary of the union. Several rounds of discussions were held in order to reason out with the union leaders that when the larger organization interest is at stake, they should let go off their ego issues. However, there was no unanimity and success seemed impossible. This made Srini realize that the soft approach would not work and that he needed to enforce implementation. Consequently, the new software platform was implemented in the 'problem' branch as well, without the 'consent' of the majority trade union. This forceful implementation made the union feel challenged and they decided to revolt by declaring 'non-cooperation' against divisional management.

Despite given a notice in advance, majority of the staff, under the instruction from the divisional union, boycotted the staff meeting arranged during the visit of the SDMs to two branches. As a result of this disobedience and dereliction of their duties, memos were issued individually to all those who had boycotted the meeting. Angered by this, the divisional union began propaganda against the SDM. Instead of getting cowered down by this, Srini decided to utilize this opportunity in the best possible way by showing the union their proper place. He issued memos to both the president and the general secretary of the divisional union for instigating unlawful activities against the management proposing disciplinary action.

Subsequently, members from these branches to which memos were issued started growing restless, and pressurized the divisional leaders to resolve the issue at the earliest. The divisional union took up the issue with the zonal union. The zonal manager cautioned Srini that the issue might get escalated into a zonal problem, which is something he did not want. The zonal manager wanted to settle the issue as soon as possible. Srini assured him that the issue would be settled soon. The union was expecting that Srini would contact them as a result of pressure from the zonal office, but Srini was sure to not bow down to pressure and let the union have an upper hand. He conveyed a message through the personnel manager, that the SDM would be available for discussion through prior appointment, in case the union wished to talk to him. Srini decided to stay away from the headquarters for five days under the pretext of being on an official tour, for tactical reasons. Subsequently, due to the mounting pressure from its members, the trade union became very desperate as the retirement of their divisional president was also due in a month. They sought an appointment with the SDM and were granted one for the next day.

The zonal president, vice president and a few other senior dignitaries met the SDM along with the divisional secretary and urged for reconciliation. Srini agreed with their view that given the competitive external environment, it was necessary that the management and the trade union worked together for the greater good of the organization. Although, he turned down their request for withdrawal of the memos, instead he offered that if the union could guarantee that such malicious instances would not be repeated in the future, no further action would be taken. This incident served as an eye-opener for other pressure groups. Immediately, after this the agents' union was also brought to their senses. The first move was to cut their source of funds.

While the leaders were unhappy with this move, the other agents felt relieved. In response to this move, while attempts to disrupt agents' meeting were made in one of the branches, in another, a personal vilification campaign was launched against one of the tough BMs. The leaders involved were held in courts. After due processes the local secretary's agency was terminated. His attempts to get relief through courts including High Court did not succeed as records were systematically created at every stage. Development officers (DO) were served notices asking them to perform their expected duties and BMs were asked to create a record against non-performing DOs. An annual gala meeting that used to be held for all the DOs was stopped after consulting the DO's union. Instead a training and skill development program was arranged with the same budget.

By October 2003, there was noticeable difference in organization's performance. The Tanjore Division rose to the fifth position on premium growth among the 12 divisions of the Zone. Yet achieving the annual target was becoming progressively a difficult task. External competition was catching up and the Corporation had decided to concentrate on premium growth including unit linked insurance plans (ULIP) business. The Division's performance in ULIP business was poor since they had no field marketers or BMs who were competent enough to explain the ULIP products. Srini took it as a personal challenge. He organized a series of training classes and meetings in order to train a group of agents to work in this line of business. As a result, the Division saw a fair amount of improvement by December 2003, and achieved the 3rd rank in the Zone on new premium growth.

After the initial displeasure, the zonal manager seemed mightily impressed by the transformation Srini had managed to achieve in the Tanjore Division. His efforts were acknowledged and appreciated, but at the same time he was cautioned about the pace at which he reached the target would be a was a tough task to maintain, as budgeted growth rate was already the highest for the Division. Undaunted by the obstacles that lay ahead, Srini once again took up the challenge with full zeal. He organized a series of campaigns in order to boost the morale of all the functionaries. A shout-out was made to make the Division All India No. 1 in premium growth rate. All-staff meetings organized during his branch visits were addressed by him. Organizational imperatives were explained and their co-operation sought for making the Division a high performing Division. Enthusiasm amongst all functionaries could be seen and their energies were channelized for constructive purposes. When the financial year came to a close, the Division achieved the highest rank in new business premium growth in the Zone and the second highest in the country.

Another remarkable achievement during the period was the handling of a development officers' agitation against their new incentive scheme. Before it could affect the morale of the agents, the SDM decided to take the issue head on, without waiting for any direction from above. Notices, exposing the nefarious designs of the DOs in maligning their own company's product were issued.

In October, a general notice was issued to all DOs advising them to restore normalcy within three days and were warned of serious action including wage cut and withdrawal of business credit. DOs were asked to maintain daily work record. With time the fervor with which the agitation had begun, started dwindling. Open methods like *dharnas* and demonstrations were completely stopped. Initially the zonal manager felt that by not consulting the higher authorities and taking decisions arbitrarily, Srini was exceeding the brief. However, after seeing that the agitation was continuing strongly in other divisions, the zonal manager admitted in retrospect that Srini's strategy was the best. (Balakrishnan, M. R., 2007)

—*Written by* Nishant Uppal

Questions

1. Whether the strategies and actions of Srini, the SDM were correct and how the situation could have been handled differently.
2. Whether role of the zonal manager was appropriate in this case and if so why? If not what he should have actually done.

Values-Based and Ethical Leadership

Learning Objectives

After studying this chapter, you should be able to:

- Understand different conceptions of ethical leadership.
- Understand the difficulties in defining and assessing ethical leadership.
- Understand the individual and situational influences on ethical leadership.
- Understand theories of transforming, servant, spiritual, and authentic leadership.
- Understand the consequences of ethical leadership for followers and the organization.
- Understand how to promote ethical behavior and oppose unethical practices.

Introduction

Powerful leaders can have a substantial impact on the lives of followers and the fate of an organization. As Gini (2004) reminds us, the primary issue is not whether leaders will use power, but whether they will use it wisely and well. Powerful leaders can advance their own careers and economic gains at the expense of organization members and the public. Moreover, by making unethical practices appear to be legitimate, a leader can influence other members of the organization to engage in them (Beu & Buckley, 2004; Hinrichs, 2007). Interest in ethical aspects of leadership has been growing as public confidence in political and corporate leaders continues to decline. Repeated scandals about these leaders have been publicized in the news media, in books, and in movies (Kouzes & Posner, 1993; Treviño & Brown, 2014). Prominent companies with executives involved in unethical activities during the past two decades include Apple, Enron, Equifax, Global Crossing, HealthSouth, Qwest, Samsung, Scandia, Toyota, Tyco International, Volkswagen, Uber, Wells Fargo, and WorldCom (Carson, 2003; Flanagan, 2003; Treviño & Nelson, 2017). This chapter will examine different conceptions of ethical leadership, discuss ethical dilemmas commonly faced by leaders, describe leadership theories involving the effects of leader values, and identify some things leaders can do to promote ethical behavior in organizations.

Conceptions of Ethical Leadership

Despite the growing interest in ethical leadership, there is considerable disagreement about the appropriate way to define and assess it. In a scientific discipline that values objectivity, even to discuss this subject causes some people to feel uneasy. However, as Heifetz (1994) pointed out, there is no ethically neutral ground for theories of leadership, because they always involve values and implicit assumptions about proper forms of influence.

Defining Ethical Leadership

Ethical leadership has been defined in many different ways. When asked to describe ethical leaders in one study, executives identified several behaviors, values, and motives (e.g., honest, trustworthy, altruistic, fair). A key characteristic was the leader's efforts to influence the ethical behavior of others (Treviño, Brown, & Hartman, 2003; Hassan, Mahsud, Yukl, & Prussia, 2013). Examples include leader statements about the importance of ethics, communication of ethical guidelines for members of the organization, modeling ethical behavior to set a visible example for others, using ethical behavior in the assessment of performance, and criticizing or punishing unethical behavior (Brown & Treviño, 2006b; Brown & Treviño, 2014; Treviño & Brown, 2014). It is also useful to make a distinction between the ethics of an individual leader and the ethics of specific types of leadership behavior, and both types of ethics are difficult to evaluate (Bass & Steidlmeier, 1999).

Several criteria are relevant for judging individual leaders, including the person's values, stage of moral development, conscious intentions, freedom of choice, use of ethical and unethical behavior, and types of influence used. Famous leaders usually have a mix of strengths and weaknesses with regard to these criteria. One difficulty in evaluating the morality of individual leaders is the subjectivity inherent in determining which criteria to use and their relative importance. The final evaluation can be influenced as much by the qualities of the judge as by the qualities of the leader.

Judgments about the ethics of a particular decision or action usually take into account the purpose (ends), the extent to which behavior is consistent with moral standards (means), and the consequences for self and others (outcomes). The three criteria are usually considered in relation to each other, and a common issue is the extent to which the ends justify the means. For example, is deception justified when the purpose is to help another person avoid serious personal harm?

Moral standards used to evaluate behavior include the extent to which it violates basic laws of society, denies others their rights, endangers the health and lives of other people, or involves attempts to deceive and exploit others for personal benefit. Examples of behavior that is usually considered unethical in Western nations include falsifying information, stealing assets for personal use, blaming others for one's own mistakes, provoking unnecessary hostility and distrust among others, selling secrets to competitors, showing favoritism in return for a bribe, and reckless behavior that is likely to injure others. Judgments about ethical leadership vary somewhat across cultures, but researchers find that some types of leader behavior (e.g., exploiting followers) are considered improper regardless of national culture (Donaldson, 1996; Eisenbeiss & Brodbeck, 2014).

Personal Integrity and Ethical Leadership

Discussions of ethical leadership usually involve the concept of personal integrity. As noted in the chapter on leader traits and skills (see Chapter 7), integrity is an attribute that helps to explain leadership effectiveness. In cross-cultural research on the essential traits for effective leadership, integrity is near the top of the list in all cultures that have been studied (see Chapter 13). Most scholars consider integrity to be an important aspect of ethical leadership, but the meaning of integrity is still a subject of debate (Bauman, 2013; Barry & Stephens, 1998; Locke & Becker, 1998; Palanski & Yammarino, 2009; Simons, 2002; Treviño, Weaver, & Reynolds, 2006).

The most basic definition of integrity emphasizes honesty and consistency between a person's espoused values and behavior. What the leader values and how the person acts are not part of this definition, and critics contend that the values must be moral and the behavior must be consistent with a set of justifiable moral principles (e.g., Becker, 1998). A thief who believes it is morally acceptable to steal from corrupt organizations would not be classified as high in integrity. A limitation of this narrower definition is the difficulty of getting agreement about justifiable moral principles, especially when they are not the same for all cultures.

Behaviors commonly regarded as morally justifiable include observing the same rules and standards applied to others, being honest and candid when providing information or answering questions, keeping promises and commitments, and acknowledging responsibility for mistakes while also seeking to correct them. However, behaviors that appear morally justifiable can be used for unethical purposes. An example is to use kindness to gain the trust of people who will later be exploited. For this reason, it is necessary to consider a leader's intentions and values as well as behaviors when evaluating ethical leadership. To be ethical, the leader must intend no harm and respect the rights of all affected parties (Gini, 2004).

Dilemmas in Assessing Ethical Leadership

Influencing follower commitment and optimism for a task are the central aspects of most theories of effective leadership, but this influence is also the source of ethical concerns. The challenge is to determine when such influence is proper. It is easier to evaluate ethical leadership when the interests of the leader, the followers, and the organization are congruent and can be attained by actions that do not involve much risk or cost. However, in many situations the influence process may involve (1) creating enthusiasm for a risky strategy or project, (2) inducing followers to change their underlying beliefs and values, and (3) influencing decisions that will benefit some people at the expense of others. Each type of influence involves ethical dilemmas.

An important leadership responsibility is to interpret confusing events and build consensus around strategies for dealing with threats and opportunities. Sometimes success requires a strategy or project that is bold and innovative. A risky venture may result in great benefits for followers if completed successfully, but the costs can also be high, especially if the project fails or takes much longer than expected. How the leader influences follower perception of the risks and prospects for success is relevant for evaluating ethical leadership.

Most people would agree that it is unethical to deliberately manipulate followers to do something contrary to their self-interest by making false promises or deceiving them about likely outcomes. One proposed standard for ethical leadership is for the leader to fully inform followers about the likely costs and benefits of a risky venture, and ask followers to make a conscious decision about whether the effort is worthwhile. However, it is often difficult to find any objective basis for predicting the likely outcomes of an innovative strategy and project. If an obvious crisis already exists for the group or organization, expressing doubts and sharing complete information can create panic and ensure failure.

As Heifetz (1994) proposed, it is important to help people understand a problem without demoralizing them. Effective leaders do not dwell too much upon the risks or obstacles, but instead emphasize what can be accomplished with a concerted, shared effort. Hope and optimism can eventually become a self-fulfilling prophecy if combined with effective problem solving. Thus, in situations where sharing information and interpreting events involve competing values, there are complex ethical issues to be resolved. For example, should political leaders withhold information about a possible terrorist attack to avoid the risk of harm caused by mass panic?

Even more controversial is an attempt to change the underlying values of individual followers. Some writers contend that this type of leader influence is clearly unethical, even when the intended outcome is to benefit followers as well as the organization (e.g., Stephens, D'Intino, & Victor, 1995; White & Wooten, 1986). These writers question the implicit assumption that the leader knows what is best for followers, and there is concern about the misuse of power and control over information to bias follower perceptions about problems and events. A special concern is the influence of charismatic leaders on followers who are weak and insecure (Howell & Shamir, 2005).

A contrary view is that leaders have a responsibility to implement major changes in an organization when necessary to ensure its survival and effectiveness. A large-scale organizational change may not be successful without changes in member beliefs and perceptions. Effective leaders engage members and other stakeholders in a dialogue to determine what types of changes are necessary and morally right for the organization. How much influence the CEO or any other individual should try to exert on this process, and the form of the influence, are ethical questions that are yet to be resolved.

Multiple Stakeholders and Competing Values

The difficulties in evaluating the effectiveness of leaders include multiple criteria with complex trade-offs and stakeholders with partially conflicting interests. The diverse consequences of a leader's decisions and actions complicate the evaluation of ethical leadership. The same actions that benefit followers in some ways may also harm followers in other ways or at a later time. The same actions that serve the interests of some followers may be contrary to the interests of other followers. Doing what is best for one type of stakeholder (e.g., owners) may not be what is best for others (e.g., employees, customers, the community). Efforts to balance competing values and interests involve subjective judgments about rights, accountability, due process, and social responsibilities. It is more difficult to evaluate ethical leadership when stakeholders have incompatible preferences.

One traditional perspective is that managers in business organizations are agents who represent the interest of the owners in achieving economic success for the organization (Eisenhardt, 1989a). From this perspective, ethical leadership is satisfied by maximizing economic outcomes that benefit owners while not doing anything strictly prohibited by laws and moral standards. For example, the decision to move a manufacturing plant from Kansas to Mexico would be considered ethical if it would significantly improve profits, regardless of the effects on plant employees or the local economy. The pursuit of short-term profits is often used as the excuse for making strategic decisions that are harmful to many stakeholders such as employees, customers, and towns where the company has facilities.

A very different perspective is that managers should serve multiple stakeholders inside and outside the organization (Agle, Mitchell, & Sonnenfeld, 1999; Block, 1993; Donaldson & Preston, 1995; Gini, 2004; Greenleaf, 1977; Jones, Felps, & Bigley, 2007; Mitchell, Agle, & Wood, 1997; Mitchell, Weaver, Agle, Bailey, & Carlson, 2016; Paine, 1994). From this perspective, judgments about ethical leadership must take into account the extent to which a leader balances and integrates the interests of different stakeholders within the constraints imposed by legal and contractual obligations. An integrative orientation appears more ethical than supporting the faction that will provide the highest personal gain for the leader, playing stakeholders off against each other (e.g., by encouraging negative stereotyping and mutual distrust), or trying to ignore substantive conflicts of interest. The following incident described by Nielsen (1989) provides an example of the integrative approach:

> The division manager for a paper products company was confronted with a difficult problem. Top management decided to close some paper mills unless operational costs for them could be reduced. The manager was concerned that cutting costs would prevent the mills from meeting government pollution control requirements. However, unless costs were reduced, the mills would close, seriously hurting the economy of the local community. The manager decided to look for an integrative win-win solution. He asked the research and engineering people in his division to look for ways to make the mills more efficient and also reduce pollution. He asked the operations and financial people in his division to estimate how much it would cost to build better mills, and when the operations would achieve a breakeven payback. When a good solution was found, he negotiated an agreement with top management to implement the plan.

Unfortunately, when different stakeholders have incompatible objectives, an integrative solution is not always possible. Leaders of business organizations sometimes have an opportunity to support a worthy cause, even though it does not provide any short-term benefit to the financial performance of the organization. However, making this type of decision requires courage and strong convictions, because powerful stakeholders may expect a leader to protect their interests, regardless of the harm to people who are not viewed as legitimate stakeholders (Jones et al., 2007; Mitchell et al., 1997; Mitchell et al., 2016). A good example of this type of ethical dilemma is provided by Useem (1998):

> In the 1970s river blindness was one of the world's most dreaded diseases, and it had long frustrated scientists trying to stop the spread of river blindness in developing countries. Then a potential cure for the disease was discovered by researchers at Merck. The new drug (called Mectizan) would cost more than $200 million to develop, and it was needed only by people who could not afford to pay for it. When Roy Vagelos, the CEO of Merck, was unsuccessful in his effort to get governments of developing nations to agree to pay for the drug, it became obvious that Mectizan would never make any profit for Merck. Nevertheless, Vagelos decided to distribute Mectizan for free to the people whose lives depended on it. Many people in the company said the decision was a costly mistake that violated the responsibility of the CEO to stockholders. However, Vagelos believed that the decision was consistent with Merck's guiding mission to preserve and improve human life. The development of Mectizan was a medical triumph, and it helped to nearly eradicate river blindness. The humanitarian decision enhanced the company's reputation and helped to attract some of the best scientific researchers in the world to work for Merck.

Determinants and Consequences of Ethical Leadership

Two interesting research questions are the reason for differences in ethical behavior among leaders, and the consequences of ethical leadership for followers and the organization. Both questions are briefly discussed in this section of the chapter, because they are relevant for understanding the leadership theories described later in the chapter.

Individual Determinants of Ethical Leadership

Ethical leadership is related to a leader's personality traits and needs (Aquino, Freeman, Reed, Lim, & Felps, 2009; Brown & Treviño, 2006b; De Hoogh & Den Hartog, 2008; Hannah, Avolio, & May, 2011; Kish-Gephart, Harrison, & Treviño, 2010; Mumford et al., 1993; O'Connor et al., 1995; Treviño & Brown, 2014). Many of the traits related to effective leadership (see Chapter 7) are also related to ethical leadership. Unethical, abusive leadership is more likely for a person who has low conscientiousness, high neuroticism, high narcissism, and a personalized power orientation. Emotionally mature leaders with a socialized power orientation, a high level of cognitive moral development, and a strong moral identity are more likely to resist the temptation to use their power to exploit others.

Kohlberg (1984) proposed a model describing how people progress through six sequential stages of moral development as they grow from a child to an adult. With each successive stage, the person develops a broader understanding of the principles of justice, social responsibility, and human rights. At the lowest level of moral development, the primary motivation is self-interest and the satisfaction of personal needs. At a middle level of moral development, the primary motivation is to satisfy role expectations and social norms determined by groups, organizations, and society. At the highest level of moral development, the primary motivation is to fulfill internalized values and moral principles. A person at this level may deviate from norms and risk social rejection, economic loss, and physical punishment in order to achieve an important ethical objective. The Kohlberg theory of moral development is similar in many ways to Kegan's (1982) theory of psycho-social development.

Unlike physical maturation, moral development is not inevitable, and some people become fixated at a particular developmental stage (Hannah et al., 2011). A leader who is at a higher level of development is usually regarded as more ethical than one at a lower level of development. Some research indicates that cognitive moral development is related to ethical decisions in business organizations (e.g., Treviño, 1986; Treviño & Youngblood, 1990). However, a review of research on the theory found a lack of clear evidence that leadership behavior or effectiveness is related to stage of development (McCauley, Drath, Palus, O'Connor, & Baker, 2006).

Another explanation for moral behavior involves self-identity theory. A person with a strong moral self-identity is motivated to act in ways that are consistent with ethical values and beliefs (Aquino et al., 2009; Aquino & Reed, 2002; Hannah et al., 2011; Mayer, Aquino, Greenbaum, & Kuenzi, 2012; Reed, Kay, Finnel, Aquino, & Levy, 2016; Reynolds, 2006a; Skubinn & Herzog, 2016). A moral self-identity is less important as a determinant of behavior in the situation where there is a strong consensus about ethical behavior. Most people will conform to the social norms, even if they do not have a strong moral self-identity. However, if there is not a consensus about a moral issue, then judgments about ethical consequences of actions are more important as determinants of behavior.

Hannah and colleagues (2011) integrate Kohlberg's theory of moral development with work on moral self-identity to further explain how the moral capacity of organizational members determines how they think and act morally. A person's moral capacity is a function of two components: moral maturation and moral conation. Moral maturation refers to "the capacity to elaborate and effectively attend to, store, retrieve, process, and make meaning of morally relevant information" (pg. 667). Moral maturation is a function of one's moral identity, complexity, and meta-cognitive ability (i.e., the ability to reflect on one's own thought processes). Moral conation involves the "capacity to generate responsibility and motivation to take moral action in the face of adversity and persevere through challenges" (p. 667). Elements of moral conation include moral courage, moral efficacy (i.e., confidence in one's ability to take a moral stand), and moral ownership (i.e., the willingness to take responsibility for moral decisions and actions). Because moral capacity is malleable, it is possible to develop how one thinks about (moral maturation) and takes action (moral conation) to address moral issues in organizations. Hence, organizations seeking to enhance the moral capacity of their leaders should focus on developmental activities designed to strengthen moral reasoning (e.g., techniques that emphasize leader self-reflection on moral dilemmas) and moral ownership and engagement (e.g., discouraging any ambiguity about responsibility for ethical decisions; making salient the potentially injurious effects of unethical decisions).

Decisions about moral behavior are also affected by values involving the consequences of behavior and the observance of formal rules, policies, laws, and traditional practices (Aquino et al., 2009; Aquino & Reed, 2002; Reed et al., 2016; Reynolds, 2006a; Skubinn & Herzog, 2016). A person's moral identity usually emphasizes one value over the other. If consequences are more important, the person will favor actions likely to result in the greatest benefit to all affected parties. If formalism is more important, the person will be inclined to obey rules and policies. The impact of these values on behavior is most evident when there are rules or traditions about proper behavior but no strong moral consensus about it. In this situation, people with a strong moral identity and a primary concern for consequences will be the most likely to select a behavior that will result in benefits for others, even if it violates formal rules or laws. In contrast, people with a strong moral identity and primary concern for formality will be the most likely to conform with existing rules or laws, even when the behavior is likely to have adverse consequences for some people.

Situational Influences on Ethical Leadership

Ethical behavior occurs in a social context, and it can be strongly influenced by aspects of the situation (Brown & Treviño, 2006b; Mishina, Dykes, Block, & Pollock, 2010; Kish-Gephart et al., 2010; Treviño, 1986; Treviño & Brown, 2014; Treviño, Butterfield, & McCabe, 1998). A dynamic, uncertain environment and a lack of strong regulation by government may encourage more risky decisions and illegal activities intended to improve financial performance. The formal reward system can encourage and support ethical or unethical behavior by leaders and members. Unethical behavior is more likely when performance goals are unrealistically difficult, there is high pressure for increased productivity, there is intense competition for rewards and advancement, and the organization does not have strong cultural values and norms about ethical conduct and individual responsibility. The strong success-oriented culture at Enron and the compensation and performance appraisal systems that supported it encouraged employees to exaggerate results and help hide the company's growing debt (Probst & Raisch, 2005; Reynolds, 2006b). Bill George, the former CEO of Medtronic, suggested a way to deal with the temptation to use questionable actions to achieve difficult objectives (George, 2003, pp. 16–17):

> All of us who sit in the leader's chair feel the pressure to perform. Little by little, step by step, the pressures to succeed can pull us away from our core values. The irony is that the more successful we are, the more tempted we are to take shortcuts to keep it going. All leaders have to resist these pressures while continuing to perform, especially when things aren't going well. The test I used with our team at Medtronic is whether we would feel comfortable having the entire story appear on the front page of the New York Times. If we didn't, we went back to the drawing boards and re-examined our decision.

A key situational determinant of ethical behavior is the moral intensity of the issue (Jones, 1991; May & Pauli, 2002). Moral intensity refers to the saliency and strength of the issue, and for a leader it is determined by six factors: (1) the degree of consequences for others; (2) the probability that those consequences will occur; (3) whether the consequences will occur in the short-term or distant future; (4) the closeness (physical, social, cultural, and psychological) of the affected parties to the leader; (5) the extent to which the consequences are limited to only a few versus many individuals; and (6) the amount of agreement among others as to what the leader should do. Moral intensity has been shown to reduce a person's willingness to engage in questionable accounting practices (Arel, Beaudoin, & Cianci, 2012), to increase the willingness to engage in whistleblowing behaviors (Bhal & Dadhich, 2011), and to increase the amount of emotional exhaustion experienced after making the decision (Zheng et al., 2015).

Because leaders are extremely busy and juggle multiple responsibilities, they may not always be aware that issues of low or moderate intensity have ethical implications. In contrast, issues high in moral intensity (e.g., a plant closing; a hazardous product) typically command the attention of leaders. However, even for high-intensity issues, there are instances where leaders engage in questionable ethical practices simply because they fail to define the issue in ethical terms. A vivid example is provided by Denny Gioia, the recall coordinator at Ford Motor Company in 1973. Gioia made the recommendation not to recall the Ford Pinto despite the fact that the car would explode following a rear-end collision at speeds as low as 25 miles per hour, resulting in a number of fatalities. To explain his decision, Gioia (2017, pp. 101–102) suggested that he was erroneously following a well-established guide for understanding and action when faced with common and repetitive situations relevant for recall decisions:

> The beginning stages of the Pinto case looked for all the world like a normal sort of problem. Lurking beneath the cognitive veneer, however, was a nasty set of circumstances waiting to conspire into a dangerous situation. Despite the awful nature of the accidents, the Pinto problem did not fit an existing script; the accidents were relatively rare by recall standards, and the accidents were not initially traceable to a specific component failure. Even when a failure mode suggesting a design flaw was identified, the cars did not perform significantly worse in crash tests than competitor vehicles. One might easily argue that I should have been jolted out of my script by the unusual nature of the accidents (very low speed, otherwise unharmed passengers trapped in a horrific fire), but those facts did not penetrate a script cued for other features.

Follower traits and beliefs are another aspect of the situation that can influence unethical leadership. Followers are more likely to passively accept a domineering and abusive leader if they lack self-esteem and self-efficacy and do not have much confidence in their own ability to deal with threats and hardship (Howell & Shamir, 2005). Unethical leadership is more likely when people believe that formal leaders should have strong position power and obedience to formal authority is necessary. These beliefs are common in societies with strong cultural values for uncertainty avoidance and power distance (see Chapter 13). Unethical behavior is also more likely in societies where violence is prevalent, fraud and bribery are accepted, and corruption of officials is widespread (Mumford et al., 2007).

Studies of "abusive supervision" and "toxic leaders" provide insights about the conditions that make it easier for a chief executive to act in ways that are destructive for an organization and its members (Lian, Ferris, & Brown, 2012; Lipman-Blumen, 2005; Padilla, Hogan, & Kaiser, 2007). In organizations that lack mechanisms to limit the power of the chief executive, abusive leaders are more difficult to restrain or remove once they have been appointed or elected. Examples of ways to limit executive power include term limits, an independent board of directors, procedures for follower evaluation of leaders, procedures for appealing decisions made by leaders (including decisions about punishment or dismissal), and formal procedures for removing a leader who misuses power or is incompetent.

Two additional and related facets of the situation that impact ethical leadership are the ethical culture and the ethical climate of the organization. The ethical culture is defined as "a subset of organizational culture, representing a multidimensional interplay among various 'formal' and 'informal' systems of behavioral control that are capable of promoting either ethical or unethical behavior" (Treviño et al., 1998, pp. 451–452). The ethical climate refers to the perceptions employees share regarding the ethical procedures and practices of the organization (Victor & Cullen, 1988). Although these two terms sound similar, they are not the same. The ethical culture pertains to ethical beliefs, values, and assumptions of organizational members that define a set of standards for ethical behavior, whereas the ethical climate describes the shared perceptions of members regarding the organization's ethical practices and procedures. Research reveals a "trickle-down" and reciprocal effect of ethical leadership on the ethical culture of lower-level units, such that the ethical values and beliefs of top-level managers become embedded within the ethical culture of subunits, which in turn elicits higher levels of ethical leadership from subunit leaders (Schaubroeck et al., 2012). CEO ethical leadership has also been shown to shape the ethical climate of the organization, which in turn can yield higher levels of collective organizational citizenship behavior (the willingness of organizational members to help one another), depending on the climate strength (i.e., the extent to which members agree on climate perceptions; Shin, Sung, Choi, & Kim, 2015). The extent to which executive leaders practice ethical leadership plays a key role in fostering a favorable ethical climate, which encourages altruistic behavior by lower-level managers and employees when there is a strong and favorable ethical climate.

Consequences of Ethical and Unethical Leadership

Most theories of ethical leadership emphasize the importance of leader influence on followers and the ethical culture and climate of an organization, although the theories differ somewhat with regard to the criteria used to assess the effects of ethical leadership. Meta-analyses of results found in studies on the effects of ethical leadership revealed a positive relationship with ethical climate, ethical behavior, job satisfaction, job engagement, organizational commitment, organizational citizenship behaviors, organizational identification, work motivation, job performance, psychological well-being, trust in the leader, satisfaction with the leader, and perceived leader effectiveness (Bedi, Alpaslan, & Green, 2016; Hoch, Bommer, Dulebohn, & Wu, 2018; Ng & Feldman, 2015). The studies found fewer negative outcomes such as turnover intentions, employee deviance, counterproductive work behaviors, relationship conflicts, and work stress. Recent studies on ethical leadership provide evidence of additional beneficial effects, including a more favorable exchange relationship (Hassan et al., 2013; Mahsud, Yukl, & Prussia, 2010), follower perception that the work is meaningful (Demirtas, Hannah, Gok, Arslan, & Capar, 2017), work unit commitment (Hassan et al., 2013), psychological empowerment (Dust, Resick, Margolis, Mawritz, & Greenbaum, 2018), mindfulness (Eisenbeiss & van Knippenberg, 2015), and creativity (Chen & Hou, 2016). Other benefits included less follower misbehavior (Demirtas, 2015) and less emotional exhaustion (Chughtai, Byrne, & Flood, 2015; Dust et al., 2018; Zheng et al., 2015). The finding that ethical leadership by a CEO was related to better firm performance and more corporate social responsibility (Eisenbeiss, van Knippenberg, & Fahrbach, 2015; Wu, Kwan, Yim, Chiu, & He, 2015) suggests that ethical leadership at the corporate level generates both financial and societal benefits. The benefits of ethical leadership were also found in research on government agencies, and they included less absenteeism, more organizational commitment, and more willingness to report ethical problems (Hassan, Yukl, & Wright, 2014).

Abusive supervision includes using power and authority to humiliate, ridicule, bully, or otherwise mistreat subordinates (Tepper, 2000, 2007). Such behavior is usually regarded as a form of unethical leadership. A recent meta-analysis by Mackey, Frieder, Brees, and Martinko (2017) indicates that the follower consequences associated with abusive supervision are universally negative, and include poor job performance, greater emotional exhaustion, less job satisfaction, organizational commitment, and organizational citizenship behavior, and more deviant and aggressive behavior toward coworkers and the organization. For example, a study of abusive behavior by restaurant managers found that it resulted in higher employee theft and waste of food (Detert, Treviño, Burris, & Andiappan, 2007).

In research on ethical leadership, consequences are more often assessed for employees rather than for measures of organizational performance. Sometimes effects at the individual and organizational level are consistent, such as when higher employee trust and commitment also result in improved financial performance for the organization. However, in many cases leader decisions do not have consistent effects for different criteria or for different stakeholders. Some ethical decisions will benefit employees or customers but increase costs and reduce short-term financial performance for the company. Examples include providing adequate health-care benefits to employees, accepting responsibility for defective products (e.g., recalls and refunds), and keeping commitments to employees or clients despite unexpected expenses.

Conversely, some decisions and actions that improve short-term organizational performance will have adverse consequences for employees or customers. Recent examples include reducing employee rights and benefits, and outsourcing employee jobs to low-cost vendors in other countries. Another dubious practice is to reduce spending on activities that are costly but essential for longer-term performance. An example is less maintenance of equipment, despite the increased risk of costly breakdowns or accidents in the future. How unethical practices are used to inflate profits was revealed in prominent scandals over the past decade. Examples include billing the government or other customers for services that were not provided, falsifying the qualification of applicants for loans or mortgages they are not be able to repay, marketing securities with inflated quality ratings, and counting future sales revenues as current income to prop up the value of the company's stock.

Theories of Values-Based Leadership

Several prominent theories in the leadership literature have a strong emphasis on ethical leadership. The theories include transforming leadership, servant leadership, authentic leadership, and spiritual leadership. The types of values emphasized in these theories are listed in Table 9-1, and each theory is briefly described in this section of the chapter.

Transforming Leadership

As noted in Chapter 8, Burns (1978, 2004) formulated a theory of transforming leadership from descriptive research on political leaders. For Burns, a primary leadership role or function is to increase awareness about ethical issues and help people resolve conflicting values. Burns (1978, p. 20) described transforming leadership as a process in which "leaders and followers raise one another to higher levels of morality and motivation." These leaders seek to raise the consciousness of followers by appealing to ideals and moral values such as liberty, justice, equality, peace, and humanitarianism, not to baser emotions such as fear, greed, jealousy, or hatred. Followers are elevated from their "everyday selves" to their "better selves." For Burns, transforming leadership may be exhibited by anyone in the organization in any type of position. It may involve influencing peers and superiors as well as subordinates. It can occur in the day-to-day acts of ordinary people, but it is not ordinary or common.

TABLE 9-1 Explanation of Values Emphasized in Theories of Ethical leadership

Integrity: Communicates in an open and honest way, keeps promises and commitments, acts in ways that are consistent with espoused values, admits and accepts responsibility for mistakes, does not attempt to manipulate or deceive people

Altruism: Enjoys helping others, is willing to take risks or make sacrifices to protect or benefit others, puts the needs of others ahead of own needs, volunteers for service activities that require extra time and are not part of the formal job requirements

Humility: Treats others with respect, avoids status symbols and special privileges, admits limitations and mistakes, is modest about achievements, emphasizes the contributions by others when a collective effort is successful

Empathy and healing: Helps others cope with emotional distress, encourages acceptance of diversity, acts as a mediator or peacemaker, encourages forgiveness and reconciliation after a divisive conflict

Personal growth: Encourages and facilitates the development of individual confidence and ability, even when not important for the current job; provides learning opportunities despite a risk of mistakes; provides mentoring and coaching when needed; helps people learn from mistakes.

Fairness and justice: Encourages and supports fair treatment of people, speaks out against unfair and unjust practices or policies, opposes attempts to manipulate or deceive people or to undermine or violate their civil rights

Empowerment: Consults with others about decisions that will affect them, provides an appropriate amount of autonomy and discretion to subordinates, shares sensitive information with them, encourages them to express concerns or dissenting views without becoming defensive

Burns described leadership as a process in which leaders and followers influence each other as the relationships evolve over time. Transforming leadership is an influence process between individuals, but it is also a process of mobilizing power to change social systems and reform institutions. The leader seeks to shape, express, and mediate conflict among groups of people, because this conflict can be useful for mobilizing and channeling energy to achieve shared ideological objectives. Thus, transforming leadership involves not only the moral elevation of individual followers, but also collective efforts to accomplish social reforms. In the process, both the leader and followers will be changed and will begin to consider not only what is good for themselves, but also what will benefit larger collectives such as their organization, community, and nation.

Servant Leadership

Another early conception of ethical leadership builds on examples found in the New Testament (Greenleaf, 1977; Liden, Panaccio, Meuser, Hu, & Wayne, 2014; Parris & Peachey, 2013; Sendjaya & Sarros, 2002). In 1970, Robert Greenleaf proposed the concept of "servant leadership," and it became the title of a book published in 1977. Greenleaf proposed that service to followers is the primary responsibility of leaders and the essence of ethical leadership. Servant leadership in the workplace is about helping others to accomplish shared objectives by facilitating individual development, empowerment, and collective work that is consistent with the health and long-term welfare of followers. Other theorists have extended the theory to include a more explicit description of key values and the effects of servant leaders on followers and the organization (Farling, Stone, & Wilson, 1999; Graham, 1991; Liden et al., 2014; Searle & Barbuto, 2011; Smith, Montagno, & Kuzmenko, 2004). Although different questionnaires have been developed to measure servant leadership (Barbuto & Wheeler, 2006; Dennis & Bocarnea, 2005;

Ehrhart, 2004), the ones developed by Liden and associates (Liden, Wayne, Zhao & Henderson, 2008; Liden et al., 2015) have produced the strongest evidence of validity.

A servant leader must attend to the needs of followers and help them become healthier, wiser, and more willing to accept their responsibilities. Service includes nurturing, defending, and empowering followers. It is only by understanding followers that the leader can determine how best to serve their needs. Servant leaders must listen to followers, learn about their needs and aspirations, and be willing to share in their pain and frustration. The servant leader must empower followers instead of using power to dominate them. Trust is established by being completely honest and open, keeping actions consistent with values, and showing trust in followers. Greenleaf believed that followers of such leaders are inspired to become servant leaders themselves. People should prepare themselves to lead and accept the opportunity when offered. The result will be more people who serve as moral agents in society.

The servant leader must stand for what is good and right, even when it is not in the financial interest of the organization. Social injustice and inequality should be opposed whenever possible. Even the weak and marginal members of society must be treated with respect and appreciation. Greenleaf proposed that providing meaningful work for employees is as important as providing a quality product or service for the customer. He advocated that business organizations should consider social responsibility as one of the major objectives, and the board of directors should take primary responsibility for evaluating and facilitating progress on achieving this objective.

The potential benefits of servant leadership are similar to those suggested by theories of supportive and empowering leadership and theories of spiritual and authentic leadership. Leader integrity and concern for subordinates are likely to increase their trust, loyalty, and satisfaction with the leader. A favorable relationship and increased referent power for the leader make it easier to influence subordinates to carry out requests. The potential benefits derived from the development and empowerment of subordinates have been demonstrated in research on participative leadership, supportive leadership, and transformational leadership. The attempt to ensure fairness and equity can influence subordinate perceptions of distributive and procedural justice and increase their loyalty and organizational commitment. If a servant leader is able to influence other leaders to become servant leaders as well, the result may be an employee-oriented culture that attracts and retains talented, committed employees. The following example provides a good description of a servant leader (Barnabas and Clifford, 2012):

> Mahatma Gandhi experienced the sufferings of the Indians due to racial tensions in South Africa. This encouraged him to adopt the strategy of Ahimsa (non-violence) and Satyagraha (holding on to truth) and lead the Indians in their fight against racial discrimination. He started serving when he was in South Africa itself. He began by teaching Indians the English language for free, so that their living condition could improve a little. Gandhi volunteered to nurse the victims of the black plague, and the more fatal pneumonic plague, which struck Indians in South Africa, fully knowing the risks it entailed. During his stay in South Africa, the Zulu rebellion had also broken out which injured many Zulus. Since there was no one to attend the injured, Gandhi took the initiative to form the Indian ambulance corps along with twenty-three other Indians, with the permission of the Governor. This team was responsible for attending the injured and nursing them back to health. On his return to India, he led Indians to fight the British with the same weapons.

A recent meta-analysis by Hoch and colleagues (2018) demonstrated that servant leadership has positive outcomes such as improved employee job performance, more organizational citizenship behavior, work engagement, job satisfaction, organizational commitment, trust in the manager, and a more favorable leader-member exchange relationships. Despite the potential benefits from servant leadership, there may also be some negative consequences for an organization when the welfare of followers is considered more important than financial performance (Anderson, 2009; Graham, 1991). When a corporation is facing difficult economic problems and cuts in expenses are necessary to remain profitable, it is very difficult for a servant leader to balance the competing preferences of owners and employees (Schneider & George, 2011). Conflicts between financial objectives and employee welfare are less intense in nonprofit, voluntary, and public sector organizations, but even for these organizations a reduction in employee benefits may be necessary in a weak economy. More research is needed to clarify the implications of servant leadership for different stakeholders in organizations.

Spiritual Leadership

Spiritual leadership describes how leaders can enhance the intrinsic motivation of followers by creating conditions that increase their sense of spiritual meaning in the work. The popularity of books on spirituality in the workplace suggests that many people are seeking deeper meaning in their work (Carroll, 2006; Chappel, 1993; Menon, 2016; Sanders, 2017). Several types of research indicate that people value the opportunity to feel interconnected to others in a mutually supporting community of people who are collectively involved in meaningful activities (Duchon & Plowman, 2005; Pfeffer, 2003). The integration of spirituality with work is difficult if not impossible in organizations that encourage or require employees to act in ways that are inconsistent with their values (Mitroff & Denton, 1999). Consistency between personal values and work objectives is important to leaders as well as to followers.

Fry (2003) makes the point that religion usually involves spirituality, but spirituality does not need religion to be meaningful. Theories of spiritual leadership include values found in major religions (Kriger & Seng, 2005), but the theories do not explicitly include any other aspects of these religions. Confusion about the difference between spirituality and religion may be the major reason why most earlier leadership theories did not include spirituality (Fry, 2003). The theorists wanted to avoid any controversy about implied support for one favored religion.

The definition of spirituality provided by Fry (2003, 2005) includes two essential elements in a person's life. Transcendence of self is manifest in a sense of "calling" or destiny, and the belief that one's activities, including work, have meaning and value beyond being instrumental for obtaining economic benefits or self-gratification (need for power, achievement, esteem). Fellowship is manifest in the need for meaningful relationships and being connected to others in a way that provides feelings of joy and wholeness. Both elements involve altruistic love and faith. Altruistic love is associated with values or attributes such as kindness, compassion, gratitude, understanding, forgiveness, patience, humility, honesty, trust, and loyalty. Faith or hope is associated with values or attributes such as optimism, confidence, courage, endurance, persistence, resilience, and serenity.

By doing things to help people satisfy the two essential needs for transcendence and fellowship in the workplace, spiritual leaders increase the intrinsic motivation, confidence, and organizational commitment of employees. As in the case of transformational leadership, spiritual leaders can enhance the meaningfulness of the work by linking it to follower values and self-identities. In addition, spiritual leaders increase mutual appreciation, affection, and trust among members of the organization. As a result, spiritual leadership can increase cooperation, encourage collective learning, and inspire higher performance.

Much of the knowledge about spiritual leadership for leaders is provided by research on related subjects, and Reave (2005) reviewed more than 150 studies that appeared relevant for understanding spiritual leadership. A few of the studies provide evidence that the opportunity to express spiritual values in one's work is related to a person's mental health, life satisfaction, and intrinsic motivation (e.g., Chappel, 1993; Duchon & Plowman, 2005; Fry, Vitucci, & Cedillo, 2005; Milliman, Czaplewski, & Ferguson, 2003), and these findings have been reinforced by subsequent research (Chen & Li, 2013; Chen & Yang, 2012; Chen, Yang, & Li, 2012). Research in medicine and positive psychology provides evidence that altruistic love can overcome negative feelings such as fear, anxiety, anger, guilt, hatred, pride, envy, and resentment. Other studies show that a high-commitment organizational climate and highly motivated members will improve organizational performance (e.g., Harter, Schmidt, & Hayes, 2002).

Spiritual leadership theory has several limitations. How leader values and skills influence leader behavior is not clearly specified in the theory, and the processes by which leaders influence followers are not clearly explained. The relative importance of calling and fellowship and how they are interrelated is not clear. The theories include many different values, and it is not clear whether some values are more important than others, or how the values are related to leader behavior. Also unclear is how a person becomes a spiritual leader, or what types of life experiences can explain why some leaders are more spiritual than others. Even though the theorists emphasize that spirituality is distinct from religious beliefs, some religious beliefs and cultural values may encourage spiritual leadership, especially for individuals in an organization, community, or nation with strong cultural values and religious traditions. More research is needed to identify conditions that favor spiritual leadership and enhance the influence of such leaders on followers and the organization.

Authentic Leadership

The idea of authentic leadership has received a lot of research attention in recent years, and several scholars have provided versions of authentic leadership theory (e.g., Avolio, Gardner, Walumbwa, Luthans, & May, 2004; Avolio & Walumbwa, 2014; Gardner, Avolio, Luthans, May, & Walumbwa, 2005; Gardner, Cogliser, Davis, & Dickens, 2011; George, 2003; Ilies, Morgeson, & Nahrgang, 2005; Karam, Gardner, Gullifor, Tribble, & Li, 2017; Shamir & Eilam, 2005; Sidani & Rowe, 2018). The most extensively researched theory advanced by Avolio, Gardner, and colleagues (Avolio & Gardner, 2005; Gardner et al., 2005) is based on positive psychology and psychological theories of self-regulation. While several definitions of authentic leadership have been proposed (Gardner et al., 2011), the definition offered by Walumbwa and colleagues (2008, p. 94) is most accepted. They define authentic leadership as:

> A pattern of leader behavior that draws upon and promotes both positive psychological capacities and a positive ethical climate, to foster greater self-awareness, an internalized moral perspective, balanced processing of information, and relational transparency on the part of leaders working with followers, fostering positive self-development.

As this definition suggests, there are four core components included in this theory of authentic leadership: self-awareness, balanced processing of information, relational transparency, and an internalized moral component. Self-awareness refers to understanding one's own values, beliefs, emotions, self-identities, abilities, and attitudes. The self-concepts and self-identities of authentic leaders are strong, clear, stable, and consistent. In other words, these leaders know who they are and what they believe, and they have a high degree of self-acceptance, which is similar to emotional maturity (see Chapter 7).

Balanced processing of information involves the assessment of ego-related information, whether positive or negative, in a relatively unbiased fashion. Authentic leaders welcome and seek out feedback and use it to make informed decisions without becoming overly defensive. Because authentic leaders are motivated by a desire for self-improvement and self-verification, they are open to learning from feedback and mistakes. Balanced processing helps authentic leaders to make informed decisions that they consider to be the best ones for their group, organization, or society, even if doing so produces little personal benefit for the leader.

Relational transparency involves the presentation to others of the leader's true self (rather than a superficial or phony self). Organizations provide opportunities and strong incentives for leaders to manage impressions that at times may be poorly aligned with their actual traits, motives, beliefs, and values. Authentic leaders resist the temptation to misrepresent themselves for personal gain, and instead disclose work-related information in an open and transparent fashion, provided doing so does not put the safety or privacy of others at risk. Relational transparency also involves sharing one's thoughts and feelings openly, while avoiding disclosures that would be inappropriate for the workplace. Hence, followers are more likely to understand the reasons for a leader's decision and have more trust in the leader.

An internalized moral perspective refers to the extent to which a leader's decisions and conduct are guided by the leader's internal moral values and standards, even if they differ from the prevailing norms of the group, organization, or social context. Authentic leaders are motivated by their core values to do what is right and fair for followers, and these leaders value follower welfare and development. Moreover, the behavior of authentic leaders, including their espoused values, is consistent with their actual values. They do not seek leadership positions to gratify a need for esteem, status, and power, but rather to express and enact their values and beliefs. Their actions are strongly determined by their values and beliefs, not by a desire to be liked and admired or to retain their position (e.g., to be reelected).

The confidence, clarity of values, and integrity of authentic leaders enhances their influence over followers. It is easier for followers to be influenced by a leader who is perceived to be credible, focused, and confident. Followers of authentic leaders have more personal identification with the leader and more social identification with the team or organizational unit. There is also an indirect effect through influence on follower self-concepts and self-identities.

A few of the leadership behaviors used to influence followers are the same ones that are included in other leadership theories. For instance, an authentic leader may enhance follower commitment and optimism by articulating an appealing vision that reflects core values, modelling appropriate behaviors, and expressing optimism and encouragement when there are setbacks and difficulties. However, with regard to other leadership behaviors, there is less agreement among different versions of authentic leadership theory. Part of this disagreement stems from the fact that the behavior of authentic leaders will vary as a function of their backgrounds, personalities, motives, beliefs, emotions, and values. Authentic leaders may exhibit other forms of positive leadership, as long as it is consistent with their core values. Bill George (2003, p. xxii), the former CEO of Medtronic, has used the idea of "true north" for an internal compass to describe what it means to be an authentic leader:

> True North is the internal compass that guides you successfully through life. It represents who you are as a human being at your deepest level. It is your orienting point – your fixed point in a spinning world – that helps you stay on track as a leader. Your True North is based on what is most important to you, your most cherished values, your passions and motivations, the sources of satisfaction in your life. Just as a compass points toward a magnetic pole, your True North pulls you toward the purpose of your leadership. When you follow your internal compass, your leadership will be authentic, and people will naturally want to associate with you.

In most versions of the theory, an authentic relationship means that leader behavior is consistent with the leader's values, and both are consistent with follower values. However, the relative importance of the different types of consistency is unclear. If a leader's values and actions are consistent but most followers reject these values, will followers judge the leader more favorably than a leader who conforms to follower values despite not believing in them? In addition, complete transparency in revealing emotions can have unintended negative effects. For example, when it is essential to build confidence that a team can successfully deal with a serious crisis, a leader who has personal fears or doubts must be careful not to communicate these emotions in a way that will undermine follower confidence.

Follower perception of leader authenticity may be jointly influenced by the leader's ability to express emotional values skillfully enough to be credible, on the extent to which the expressed values and emotions are consistent with follower perception of the situation, and on follower ability to accurately perceive when a leader is expressing genuine emotions and values. Trust will be undermined if the leader appears genuine but the values and emotions are inappropriate for the situation, or if the values and emotions are appropriate but they do not appear to be genuine (Gardner, Fischer, & Hunt, 2009).

Like the other theories of ethical leadership, the authentic leadership theories would benefit from greater clarity in the definition of essential qualities and the explanation of influence processes (Algera & Lips-Wiersma, 2012; Cooper, Scandura, & Schriesheim, 2005; Diddams & Chang, 2012; Guthey & Jackson, 2005; Ladkin & Taylor, 2010; Nyberg, Fulmer, Gerhart, & Carpenter, 2010; Sidani & Rowe, 2018). It is unclear whether the theory is a description of attributes actually possessed by effective leaders, or only an ideal form of ethical leadership that people can hope to attain (Caza & Jackson, 2011).

Narrative reviews and meta-analyses of results from different studies (Banks, McCauley, Gardner, & Guler, 2016; Gardner et al., 2011; Hoch et al., 2018) reveal that authentic leadership is linked to several positive follower outcomes, including more work engagement, job satisfaction, satisfaction with the leader, personal identification with the leader, trust in the leader, organizational commitment, psychological empowerment, creativity, organizational citizenship behaviors, and higher job performance. In addition, authentic leadership reduces negative outcomes for followers such as job stress, counterproductive work behaviors, and turnover intentions. Positive outcomes for the leader include higher levels of psychological well-being, leader self-esteem, and leadership effectiveness. Favorable organizational outcomes have also been linked to authentic leadership, including higher levels of firm financial performance and an open organizational climate. Some preliminary evidence suggests that authentic leadership can produce beneficial outcomes for followers, leaders, and their organizations, but more research is needed to verify key propositions of the theory and resolve the paradoxes and ambiguities inherent in some aspects of the theory.

Comparison and Evaluation of Theories

The theories of servant, spiritual, and authentic leadership all share some features in common with theories of transformational and charismatic leadership (see Chapter 8), but important differences are also evident. This section will compare the various theories and identify issues that require more research and clarification.

Comparison to Transformational and Charismatic Leadership

The theories of ethical and values-based leadership have more emphasis on leader values than on leader behavior, and more emphasis on consequences for stakeholders than on enhancement of subordinate motivation and performance. For charismatic and transformational theories, these priorities are reversed. The ethical theories are primarily focused on leader values and how they affect a leader's relationship with subordinates. The types of values emphasized in the ethical leadership theories indicate that some types of leadership behavior are more relevant than others and should be consistent with the leader's values, but the theories do not specify a list of essential behaviors. The theories describe how ethical leaders can improve the lives of followers, and the leader's effects on followers have implications for improving collective performance, but maximizing performance is not a primary concern.

The initial version of transformational leadership was focused on the effects of specified leader behaviors on subordinate motivation and performance. Leader values are not explicitly specified, and there is no requirement that leader behavior (including espoused values and beliefs) must be consistent with the leader's actual values and beliefs. The transformational behaviors can be used in a manipulative way to influence follower task commitment and loyalty to the leader (Stephens et al., 1995; White & Wooten, 1986). For example, individualized consideration can be used in an inauthentic way to build subordinate loyalty to the leader and make it easier to exploit a subordinate. Inspirational motivation can be used to increase subordinate task commitment and performance even if the leader cares only about personal career advancement. Intellectual stimulation can be used to increase creative ideas that will enhance the leader's reputation (e.g., the leader may claim credit for them). Idealized influence includes leading by example and making sacrifices, but this behavior may be used to manage follower impressions and gain their trust rather than to express a leader's true concern for the mission or subordinates.

When the potential for unethical use of transformational behaviors was pointed out, the theory was modified to distinguish between authentic and inauthentic transformational leadership (Bass & Steidlmeier, 1999). Both types of leaders use transformational behaviors, but the authentic leaders have integrity and do not attempt to manipulate or exploit followers. However, even in the revised version of the theory, improvement of performance remains a stronger priority than improvement of subordinate welfare and happiness. History is full of examples of leaders who caused much suffering and misery in their dedicated pursuit of virtuous objectives (Price, 2003).

The theories of charismatic leadership described in Chapter 8 emphasized the effects of leader behavior on the motivation of followers and their relationship with the leader. As these theories evolved, there was more emphasis on leader values and socialized charismatics were differentiated from personalized charismatics (e.g., Brown & Treviño, 2006a; Howell, 1988; House & Howell, 1992). Nevertheless, follower attribution of charisma to the leader remains a central feature of the theory. In theories of servant, spiritual, and authentic leadership, the leader's values for humility, openness, and transparency in decision making and the emphasis on follower development and empowerment make it unlikely that the leader will be viewed as charismatic.

Proponents of the revised versions of transformational and charismatic leadership theories have attempted to clarify the criteria for determining when this type of leadership is ethical (e.g., Bass & Steidlmeier, 1999; Howell & Avolio, 1992), and examples of these criteria are shown in Table 9-2. The criteria appear plausible, but they may not take into account all of the complexities and dilemmas in evaluating ethical leadership. How the various criteria can be applied remains a question of discussion and debate.

Evaluation of Theories

While considerable research has been devoted in recent years to the ethical leadership theories described in this chapter, they are still at a relative early stage of development, and like most new theories there is some conceptual ambiguity (Cooper et al., 2005; Eisenbeiss, 2012; Sidani & Rowe, 2018). It is more difficult to compare and test theories that include many different types

TABLE 9-2 Suggested Criteria for Evaluating Ethical Leadership

Criterion	Ethical Leadership	Unethical Leadership
Use of leader power and influence	To serve followers and the organization	To satisfy personal needs and career objectives
Handling diverse interests of multiple stakeholders	Attempts to balance and integrate them	Favors stakeholders who can provide more benefits
Development of a vision for the organization	Develops a vision based on follower input about their needs, values, and ideas	Attempts to sell a personal vision as the only way for the organization to succeed
Integrity of leader behavior	Acts in a way that is consistent with espoused values	Does what is expedient to attain personal objectives
Risk-taking in leader decisions and actions	Is willing to take personal risks and actions to accomplish mission or achieve the vision	Avoids necessary decisions or actions that involve personal risk to the leader
Communication of relevant information	Makes a complete and timely disclosure of information about events, problems, and actions	Uses deception and distortion to bias follower perceptions about problems and progress
Response to criticism and dissent by followers	Encourages critical evaluation to find better solutions	Discourages and suppresses any criticism or dissent
Development of follower skills and self confidence	Uses coaching, mentoring, and training to develop followers	De-emphasizes development to keep followers weak and dependent on the leader

of constructs such as leader values and behaviors; follower values, perceptions, and needs; dyadic, group-level, and organizational explanatory processes; and different outcome criteria. The development of measures of values-based leadership is ongoing (Avolio, Wernsing, & Gardner, 2018; Brown, Treviño, & Harrison, 2005; Kalshoven, Den Hartog, & De Hoogh, 2011; Walumbwa et al., 2008) and more validation research is needed for them. Only a few studies have compared different theories or examined their unique implications for improving leadership in organizations. More research, including some intensive, longitudinal studies, will be needed to clarify the relationships proposed by the theories and determine their utility for explaining effective leadership.

Two recent meta-analyses provide insights into the degree of overlap between the values-based leadership theories and transformational leadership. Hoch and colleagues (2016) found that authentic and ethical leadership were both highly correlated with transformational leadership and explained little variance in key outcomes beyond that accounted for by transformational leadership. In contrast, servant leadership showed more promise as a stand-alone theory, as it was less highly correlated with transformational leadership and it explained more unique variance in work outcomes. The Banks and colleagues (2016) meta-analysis of studies on authentic leadership and transformational leadership again revealed high correlations between measures of these two types of leadership, and neither type of leadership explained much additional variance in employee attitudes and work outcomes beyond what was already explained by the other type.

The values-based leadership theories all include some of the same leader behaviors, and the theories all seek to explain how leaders can promote strong leader-follower relationships and positive organizational outcomes. Nevertheless, there are differences in the theories, as well as the follower and organizational outcomes with which they have been associated. For example, it appears that servant leadership may operate in ways that are markedly different from transformational leadership to elevate follower trust and performance. Also, preliminary evidence suggests that authentic leadership may be more important than transformational leadership as a determinant of team and organizational performance and organizational citizenship behaviors. More research and theory development is needed to both sharpen and highlight the conceptual differences between the theories, as well as their unique relationships with important outcomes.

Guidelines for Ethical Leadership

Different approaches have been used to increase ethical behavior in organizations. One approach is for individuals to encourage ethical practices and oppose unethical activities or decisions. Another approach is to use laws, professional standards, and organizational programs to increase awareness of ethical issues, encourage ethical behavior, and discourage unethical practices. The different approaches are not mutually exclusive and can be used together. Each approach will be described briefly.

Ways for Leaders to Promote Ethical Practices

Leaders can do many things to promote ethical practices in organizations (Ciulla, 2018; Hassan et al., 2013; Hassan et al., 2014; Mahsud et al., 2010; Nielsen, 1989; Treviño & Brown, 2014). The theories and research on ethical leadership suggest the following guidelines (see summary in Table 9-3):

- **Set clear standards for ethical conduct.**

Leaders can set clear standards and guidelines for dealing with ethical issues (e.g., help to establish an ethical code of conduct), provide opportunities for people to get advice about dealing with ethical issues (e.g., ethics hotline), and initiate discussions about ethical issues to make them more salient. Leaders can encourage and reinforce ethical behavior by including it in the criteria used to evaluate and reward follower performance. For example, a leader can recognize unusual examples of ethical conduct.

- **Model ethical behavior in your own actions.**

Providing advice and guidance about correct behavior on the job and avoidance of ethical problems is useful, but to reduce unethical behavior, it is essential for the leader to model proper behavior as well as espousing it (Brown & Treviño, 2014; Dineen, Lewicki, & Tomlinson,

TABLE 9-3 Guidelines for Ethical Leadership

- Set clear standards of ethical conduct.
- Model ethical behavior in your own actions.
- Help people find fair and ethical ways to resolve problems and conflicts.
- Oppose unethical practices in the organization.
- Implement and support programs to promote ethical behavior

2006). Leaders can do many things to promote honesty, fairness, mutual respect, and transparency. A leader's own actions provide an example of ethical behavior to be imitated by people who admire and identify with the leader. The examples include an honest and open examination of problems involving ethical issues, rather than attempts to ignore them or arrange a cover-up. If something said or done by the leader has unintentionally encouraged subordinates to use unacceptable practices, the error should be admitted.

- **Help people find fair and ethical ways to resolve problems and conflicts.**

One important leadership function is to influence people to acknowledge an important problem, rather than denying it, discounting the seriousness of the problem, procrastinating about corrective action, or providing fake remedies and stress-reducing diversions (Heifetz, 1994). Another important function is to help frame problems by clarifying key issues, encouraging dissenting views, distinguishing causes from symptoms, and identifying complex interdependencies. Leaders can facilitate problem solving by helping people get information, by identifying points of agreement and disagreement, and by encouraging people to find integrative solutions to conflicts. It is important to proceed at a pace that people can tolerate, because if pushed too fast, people may resort to defensive avoidance mechanisms, such as concluding that temporary relief or limited progress is a complete solution. As noted in the guidelines for leading change (see Chapter 5), it is important to ensure that people understand the difficulties that will be encountered and the self-sacrifices that will be necessary to succeed, but it is also important to build hope and optimism about finding a solution. These ideas seem especially relevant for evaluating political candidates who oversimplify problems, promise unrealistic solutions, and pander to short-term individual interests rather than collective needs.

- **Oppose unethical practices in the organization.**

Opposition to unethical practices can take many different forms, and it should be viewed as a responsibility of all people, not just formal leaders (Hinrichs, 2007; Nielsen, 1989; Treviño & Nelson, 2017). Examples include refusing to comply with unethical assignments or rules, threatening to complain to higher management, making actual complaints to higher management, threatening to publicize unethical practices to outsiders, and actually reporting unethical practices to the news media or a regulatory agency. Opposition to unethical practices is usually a difficult and risky course of action. Speaking out against injustices and opposing unethical practices may put one in danger of retaliation by powerful people in the organization. Many "whistleblowers" discover that their actions can result in dismissal or the derailment of their career in the organization.

Programs to Promote Ethical Behavior

An indirect form of leadership influence on the behavior of followers is to establish programs and systems (see Chapter 12). Many large organizations have ethical programs, and they often involve both an attempt to strengthen relevant internal values, and features to enforce compliance with ethical guidelines and policies (Treviño & Nelson, 2017; Weaver, Treviño, & Cochran, 1999). Examples of typical features of ethics programs include a formal code of ethics, an ethical committee that is responsible for developing policies and practices, methods of reporting ethical concerns to the ethics committee or top management, ethics education programs, methods to monitor ethical behavior, and disciplinary processes to deal with unethical behavior.

A study conducted in large U.S. corporations (Weaver et al., 1999) found that top executives with a strong concern for ethical behavior are more likely to implement ethical programs, and the scope of the programs is likely to be broader. A more recent study by Eisenbeiss and associates (2015) found evidence that CEO ethical leadership works through the organizational ethical culture to enhance firm performance, but only for firms with strong corporate ethics programs. The types of leadership values associated with the use of ethics programs are similar to the ones discussed earlier in this chapter. The research also indicates that responsibility for ethics should be taken seriously by all executives and not simply delegated to staff professionals. Some ways a top executive can influence the ethical climate in an organization include talking about the importance of positive values, setting an example of ethical behavior, making decisions that show integrity is as important as profits, and enforcing discipline for ethics violations.

The use of ethical programs in an organization is also influenced by environmental pressures, such as media attention for ethical failures and corporate scandals. However, it is better to avoid scandals and financial failure by being proactive and creating a strong ethical climate. An example of the type of policy that can be used to avoid problems is provided by Costco. The company ethics policy includes not accepting gifts from vendors. Costco also sends a yearly letter to the president of every vendor stating that gratuities are not accepted.

Cultural Values, Laws, and Professional Standards

Ethical leadership is also influenced by cultural values, social norms, legal requirements, and professional standards in countries where an organization is located (Eisenbeiss & Brodbeck, 2014; Svensson & Wood, 2007). It is much easier for managers to oppose unethical practices when there is strong and explicit support for such opposition and the standards for unacceptable behavior are clear rather than ambiguous (Kuntz, Kuntz, Elenkov, & Nabirukhina, 2013; Reynolds, 2006a). It is more difficult to discourage unethical behavior in countries where bribes and kickbacks, gender and religious/ethnic discrimination, child labor abuse, hazardous working conditions, unsafe products, deceptive advertising, sexual harassment, and falsifying accounting records to evade taxes are widely accepted practices in organizations. Top executives, political leaders, religious leaders, and opinion leaders in universities, the news media, and professional associations (e.g., American Management Association, Academy of Management) all can help to establish clear ethical standards and a strong concern for social responsibility in companies, nonprofit organizations, and government agencies.

Summary

Interest in ethical leadership has been increased by cynicism about the motives, competence, and integrity of business and political leaders. Conceptions of ethical leadership include nurturing followers, empowering them, and promoting social justice. Ethical leadership includes efforts to encourage ethical behavior as well as efforts to stop unethical practices. Ethical leaders seek to build mutual trust and respect among diverse followers and to find integrative solutions to conflicts among stakeholders with competing interests. Ethical leaders do not foster distrust or play favorites to gain more power or achieve personal objectives.

Determinants of ethical behavior by a leader include situational influences and aspects of leader personality such as level of cognitive moral development. Leader personality and cognitive moral development interact with aspects of the situation in the determination of ethical and unethical behavior. It is easier to understand ethical leadership when both the individual leader and the situation are considered together.

The criteria for evaluating ethical leadership include leader values and intentions, and the extent to which leader behavior is morally justifiable. Evaluation of morality for individual leaders is complicated by multiple stakeholders, diverse consequences of a leader's actions, delays in the visibility of outcomes, and disagreements about the extent to which ends justify means. The difficulties in assessing the effects of ethical and unethical leadership are increased by long delays before consequences are evident and by diverse outcomes for different stakeholders. How ethical leadership is defined and measured deserves more attention in the future.

The theories of values-based leadership emphasize the importance of integrity and ethical behavior. Ethical leaders influence followers to recognize the need for adaptive problem solving that will improve their long-term welfare rather than denying the need or settling for superficial remedies. Transforming leaders seek to raise the consciousness of followers by appealing to ideals and moral values rather than to materialistic desires or negative emotions such as fear and jealousy. Servant leadership theory explains why the primary concern of leaders should be to nurture, develop, and protect followers. Spiritual leadership theory explains how leaders can enhance the spiritual meaning in the work experienced by followers. Authentic leadership theory explains why a leader's behavior should be guided by strong positive values. In these theories, the ideal relationship of the leader with followers includes high mutual respect, trust, cooperation, loyalty, and openness. The theories all emphasize the importance of leader self-awareness (about values and beliefs) and consistency between values and behavior. The positive values or attributes in the theories are very similar, and they include honesty, altruism, kindness, compassion, empathy, fairness, gratitude, humility, courage, optimism, and resilience.

The theories of values-based leadership described in this chapter emphasize leader values more than behavior, and the long-term welfare and development of followers more than the financial performance of the organization. The theories provide important insights about effective leadership by making explicit ethical concerns that are only implicit in most other leadership theories. The theories are still evolving, and they have not been adequately tested with strong research methods. Nevertheless, some ways to encourage and support ethical practices have been identified.

Review and Discussion Questions

1. Why is it so difficult to evaluate ethics and morality for individual leaders?
2. What are some examples of ethical and unethical leadership?
3. Can unethical behavior occur for a leader who has proper values and intentions?
4. Why is it important to study ethical leadership?
5. Compare and contrast the following theories: transforming leadership, servant leadership, spiritual leadership, and authentic leadership.
6. What are some individual and situational determinants of ethical leadership?
7. What can be done to increase ethical behavior and decrease unethical practices?

Key Terms

authentic leadership
balanced processing
ethical dilemmas
ethical leadership
integrity
internalized moral perspective
multiple stakeholders
relational transparency
servant leadership
self-awareness
spiritual leadership
cognitive moral development
transforming leadership

PERSONAL REFLECTION

Which of the following ethical values are most important to you: honesty, loyalty, fairness, altruism, kindness, accountability, or transparency? If you have ever been pressured by others to compromise one or more of your important values, what aspects of the situation influenced your response? If you encounter such pressure in the future, what, if anything, would you do differently?

CASE

Tata Sons

The Tata Group is controlled by Tata Sons. Around two-thirds of the Tata Sons' income received through their holdings in various companies goes to the charitable trusts that hold a 66 percent stake in Tata Sons. The Tata trusts have contributed over ₹18,770 million in grants since 1931. These grants have been used to set up various institutions such as the prestigious Indian Institute of Science, the Tata Institute of Social Sciences, and the Tata Institute of Fundamental Research.

The leadership at the Tata Group has a repute of being ethical and value-driven, even if it has been at the cost of the group's growth at times. Responding in an interview, JRD Tata said, "I have often thought about it. If we had adopted the means some others have, we would have grown twice as big as we are today… but we would not want it any other way."

The Tata group which has been guided by its five core values—integrity, pioneering, excellence, unity, and responsibility—has always been associated with trust, reliability and commitment to the community. A code of conduct created under Ratan Tata in 1998 enshrines the company's values and core principles. It also lays down the ethical standards for the conduct of business activities by Tata colleagues and companies.

When Ratan Tata took over Tata Electronic and Locomotive Company's (TELCO) Chairmanship from Sumant Moolgaokar on April 7, 1988, tension at the Pimpri plant was simmering. Rajan Nair, who had joined TELCO as a machine miller in 1976, was the son of a trade union leader. In a span of six years, he rose to the position of general secretary TELCO Kamgar Sanghatana (TKS), one of the two TELCO workers' unions. Suspended in March 1988, he was later fired from TELCO because after a few months of his suspension, he allegedly threatened to kill a security guard. On the day he was fired, he vowed "to bring the TELCO management to its knees."

On January 31, 1989, the workers on the shop floor of the Pune plant greeted Ratan Tata with a tool-down strike. On the same day, Nair was taken into preventive custody by the local authorities but released later as the workers besieged the district court. Ratan Tata refused having played any role in Nair's arrest. Later, on March 15, 1989, Nair's men, assaulted and stabbed 22 managerial personnel across the city. Some of these even belonged to the rival union. This assault was carried out as revenge for the alleged slap that one of TKS's members had received. Ratan Tata engaged in a multi-pronged approach in order to deal with this situation. The strike came to an end on September 29, after police authorities arrested Nair and his men.

Ratan Tata, who believed that it was a victory of the principles and values for which the Tata group had always stood for, was hailed by the media as a leader par excellence. When interviewed after some years of the crisis, Tata responded by saying, "Perhaps, we took our workers for granted. We assumed that we were doing all that we could for them when probably we were not. We gave Rajan Nair—or any name—a chance to come and do what he did." The strike turned out to be a great learning lesson for Ratan Tata who decided to ensure that a trusting relationship is built between the management and the workers in the future and worked relentlessly to this effect. It was his efforts that resulted in TELCO's production increasing by 26 percent, making it the biggest company in the private sector in terms of sales. (Dua, A. K., & Rai, S., 2017)

—*Written by* Nishant Uppal

Questions

1. Which theories from this chapter can be used to explain this case?
2. Could the crisis have been prevented or avoided?
3. What other approach could Ratan Tata adopt to deal with such a crisis?
4. What was the role of Ratan Tata as leader in above crisis?

CASE

Infosys

Infosys is known for its ethical business practices and values on which leadership builds upon. The codified values are acronymed as CLIFE—Customer delight, Leadership by example, Integrity and transparency, Fairness, and pursuit of Excellence. Its co-founder and CEO, N. R. Narayana Murthy is a humble man who believes in simple living. He is of the opinion that wealth should be created in a legal, ethical, environmentally sound and sustainable way.

Narayana Murthy is a humble man who lives a simple and frugal life. He believes that wealth creation should be legal, ethical, environmentally sound and sustainable. He believes that leadership should be value-based and this belief is reflected in his leadership approach which is based on the values of transparency, transaction-based behavior, and having a clear conscience.

"Leading by example" is the most important value that is followed by the top executives at Infosys. In spite of being amongst the richest men in the country, they do not lead a lavish life. He believes that this is the most powerful way of creating trust in one's ideas. If you experience it, by choice or otherwise, no one can turn back and question your knowledge. For example, he often travelled by the company buses, so when complaints were made about bus travel, his comments on it were taken seriously, as no one could ever turn to say, "What do you know about bus travel?"

The second value, considered to be a core of the Infosys spirit, is the respect and decency with which all employees treat each other, whether in formal meetings or outside. The third value builds on this second value of mutual respect and is known as pluralism. This value stands for collective decision making which is reached upon after debating the various company issues on a regular basis. This debate however, is without exception, courteous and dignified. Murthy believes that dissent, as long as in the interest of the company and in pursuit of its excellence, is always welcome. He once said, "You can disagree with me as long as you are not disagreeable." The fourth value focuses on delivery and action. Infosys leaders promote openness, and this is reflected even in their small actions such as keeping the doors to their office always open. These values influence the company's processes—such as recruitment, selection and budgeting—thus, affecting the overall ethos of the company.

There are three more practices that support this value-based leadership at Infosys—the first is an actionable element of respect for every individual. This involves all leaders at Infosys reading and replying to each of their e-mails personally, whether it is a query, feedback, or grievance (personal or professional) from any employee. The second is the practice of making data-based decisions, or as Murthy calls it, "transaction-based" decisions. This means that the current decisions are in no way influenced by the decisions taken previously. Decisions are data driven, which helps ensures that quality of ideas is given more importance rather than where or from whom the idea comes from; this this helps foster trust in leadership. Although this is something that is practiced by a lot of Indian organizations, it is still quite unusual in the hierarchical Indian organizational culture that what is said is given more importance than who says it. Murthy explained, "If we want to create an environment of high aspirations and innovation, then people must be confident that they are in a meritocracy. There cannot be any biases, cliques, or cronyism. People must be able to say from the heart, 'If I have a good idea, it will be listened to." Lastly, the third routine lies at the heart of the culture of constant innovation at Infosys. Leaders at Infosys proactively disseminate their innovations not just within their organization, but also across the industry, in order to make them obsolete. They use their idea for the initial six months, take its advantage and then post it on their web so that it becomes accessible to everyone. According to Murthy, the reason behind this is, "Human beings have a tendency to rest on their laurels. And that is very dangerous. We strive for sustained advantage, and for that we need to constantly innovate. We proactively disseminate our innovations, and we make them obsolete." (Vries, M. F., Agrawal, A., & Treacy, E. F., 2006)

—*Written by* Nishant Uppal

Questions

1. Do you agree with Murthy's approach?
2. Would you recommend any change to the company's values and practices?

Chapter 10

Dyadic Relations and Followers

Learning Objectives

After studying this chapter, you should be able to:

- Understand why different dyadic relationships develop between a leader and subordinates.
- Understand how leaders are influenced by attributions about subordinates.
- Understand appropriate ways to manage a subordinate with performance deficiencies.
- Understand how leaders and followers attempt to manage impressions.
- Understand how attributions and implicit theories influence follower perceptions of a leader.
- Understand how followers can have a more effective relationship with their leader.

Introduction

Most of the early research on leadership behavior did not consider how much leaders vary their behavior with different subordinates. However, the discussion of delegation in Chapter 4 makes it clear that dyadic relationships are not identical for all of a leader's direct subordinates. This chapter begins with a theory that describes how a unique exchange relationship is developed with each subordinate and the implications of these relationships for effective leadership. Next, attribution theory is examined to discover how leaders interpret subordinate performance and decide how to react to it. This part of the chapter also has some guidelines on how leaders can deal with unsatisfactory performance and improve the quality of the exchange relationship.

The chapter then turns to follower-based approaches to leadership. Most leadership literature over the past half-century has focused on leaders. The attitudes and behavior of leaders have been examined in detail, but until recently, follower attitudes and behavior were only examined as an indicator of leader influence and effectiveness. Without followers there would be no leaders, and interest in studying followership has been increasing. The chapter describes follower attributions about the leader and implicit theories that influence follower perception of leader. Several impression management tactics that can be used by leaders and followers are described. The chapter also includes guidelines on how to be an effective follower while remaining true to one's values. The chapter ends with a brief discussion about integrating leader and follower roles in organizations.

Leader–Member Exchange Theory

Leader–member exchange (LMX) theory describes the role-making processes between a leader and each individual subordinate and the exchange relationship that develops over time (Dansereau, Graen, & Haga, 1975; Graen & Cashman, 1975). The basic premise of the theory is that leaders develop an exchange relationship with each subordinate as the two parties mutually define the subordinate's role. The exchange relationships are formed on the basis of personal compatibility and subordinate competence and dependability. According to the theory, most leaders develop a high-exchange relationship with a small number of trusted subordinates who function as assistants, lieutenants, or advisors. These relationships are formed gradually over a period of time, through reciprocal reinforcement of behavior as the exchange cycle is repeated over and over again. Unless the cycle is broken, the relationship is likely to evolve to the point where there is a high degree of mutual dependence, loyalty, and support.

The basis for establishing a high-quality exchange relationship is the leader's control over outcomes that are desirable to a subordinate. These outcomes include such things as assignment to interesting and desirable tasks, delegation of greater responsibility and authority, more sharing of information, involvement in making some of the leader's decisions, tangible rewards such as a pay increase, special benefits (e.g., better work schedule, bigger office), personal support and approval, and facilitation of the subordinate's career (e.g., recommending a promotion, giving developmental assignments with high visibility). In return for receiving these benefits, the subordinate in a high-quality exchange relationship provides various types of benefits to the leader (Wilson, Sin, & Conlon, 2010). The subordinate is usually expected to work harder, to be more committed to task objectives, to be loyal to the leader, and to carry out additional responsibilities such as helping with some of the leader's administrative duties. Over time, as the leader and follower deliver benefits for one another, their bond strengthens and they build trust that they can rely on one another for future benefits (Erdogan & Bauer, 2014; Law-Penrose, Wilson, & Taylor, 2015).

Drawing on his experience as CEO of General Electric, Jack Welch and his wife Suzy (2015, pp. 130–131) describe some "do's" and "don'ts" for creating "trust dividends" that forge high-quality relationships with followers:

> The first "do" is to care like crazy about your people and their work ... send the message: "I'm in this with you." Stand up for your people – in particular when they're down. Look, it's easy to cheer on subordinates when they bring you a big, breakthrough idea or log a numbers-busting year. It's after initiative flops that they need you to publicly own your earlier endorsement and take equal responsibility for its failure ... The trust-building "do" here, in other words, is to have your subordinate's back when he's on his back. The related don't is one we've seen all too often: running for the hills after a subordinate stumbles on a risky bet you'd both agreed upon ... That's just ugly: it's the kind of cowardice that reeks of self-preservation and it makes trust die in an instant. In fact, we'd go so far as to say that nothing destroys a leader's bond with his or her followers faster.

The benefits to the leader from a high-exchange relationship are evident. Subordinate commitment is important when the leader's work unit has tasks that require considerable initiative and effort on the part of some members to be carried out successfully. The assistance of committed subordinates can be invaluable to a manager who lacks the time and energy to carry out all of the administrative duties for which he or she is responsible. However, high-exchange relationships create certain obligations and constraints for the leader. To maintain these relationships, the leader must provide attention to the subordinates, remain responsive to their needs and feelings, and rely more on time-consuming influence methods such as rational persuasion, consultation, and collaboration (see Chapter 6). The leader cannot resort to coercion or heavy-handed use of authority without endangering the special relationship.

A low-quality exchange relationship is characterized by less mutual influence. These subordinates need only comply with formal role requirements (e.g., duties, rules, standard procedures, and legitimate directions from the leader), and each subordinate receives only the standard benefits for the job (such as a salary). The early version of the theory described an "in-group" of subordinates with high-quality exchange relationships and an "out-group" of subordinates with low-quality exchange relationships. Later versions of the theory did not make such a sharp dichotomy and included the possibility of a high-quality exchange relationship with all of a leader's subordinates.

A recent refinement of LMX theory seeks to further explain how high-quality exchange relationships develop over time by considering the role that affective events play during key stages of the leader–follower relationship (Cropanzano, Dasborough, & Weiss, 2017). Affective events are incidents that elicit affective reactions — either positive or negative emotions and moods — from individuals at work. Emotions are brief, intense reactions (e.g., joy, passion, elation, surprise, anger, sadness, despair, grief) to an event or person, whereas moods are longer, less intense, and are not focused on a specific event or person. Affective events are often described as the "daily hassles and uplifts" people experience that in turn influence their behavior, job attitudes, and interpersonal relationships. At the initial role-taking stage, the leader takes the initiative in relationship development by offering the member an opportunity to form a higher-quality relationship. Here, the leader's affective expressions serve as cues regarding the leader's enthusiasm for the relationship that in turn evoke emotional reactions from followers. Positive leader emotions such as happiness and joy are likely to be reciprocated by the follower and provide the foundation for further relationship development, whereas negative emotional expressions such as anger, sadness, and fear discourage relationship growth. Furthermore, leaders who are high in affective empathy, which is the ability to understand and share the emotional experiences of others, are better able to foster positive emotional connections with followers that promote relationship development. In the second role-making stage, the leader delegates promising assignments to the follower, who is expected to perform each assignment in an effective way. Throughout these interactions, leaders and followers serve as sources of affective events for one another. As the relationship unfolds, the leader's and member's feelings may begin to synchronize, as the parties come to share positive or negative feelings about one another. During the final role-routinization stage, the quality of the LMX relationship stabilizes. However, the nature of the relationship may nonetheless change based on member emotional reactions to alterations in the distribution of LMX relationships in the work group (i.e., LMX differentiation). For example, if a new member joins the work group and quickly forms a close and high-quality relationship with the leader, followers with existing LMX relationships may experience jealousy, anger, or frustration.

Research on LMX

The way in which LMX has been defined has varied substantially from study to study. Quality of an exchange relationship is usually assumed to involve such things as mutual trust, respect, affection, support, and loyalty. However, sometimes LMX is defined to include other aspects of the relationship, such as negotiating latitude, incremental influence, shared values, affect, reciprocity, obligation, and mutual trust (see Day & Miscenko, 2015; Ferris et al., 2009; Schriesheim, Castro, & Cogliser, 1999). Several different measures of LMX have been used since the theory was first proposed, making it more difficult to compare results from different studies (Liden, Wu, Cao, & Wayne, 2015).

Only a small number of studies have measured LMX from the perception of both the leader and the follower (e.g., Cogliser, Schriesheim, Scandura, & Gardner, 2009; Deluga & Perry, 1994; Liden, Wayne, & Stilwell, 1993; Markham, Yammarino, Murry, & Palanski, 2010; Phillips & Bedeian, 1994; Scandura & Schriesheim, 1994; Sin, Nahrgang, & Morgeson, 2009; Zhou & Schriesheim, 2009, 2010). It is reasonable to expect agreement about something as important as a leader–subordinate relationship, but the amount of agreement is often low, especially when there has been limited time together and limited interaction frequency. The reason for a lack of stronger agreement is not clear, but it appears to involve a difference in the basis for evaluating the relationship. Subordinate ratings of LMX are strongly influenced by how supportive and fair the leader is with the subordinate, whereas leader ratings of LMX are strongly influenced by judgments about the subordinate's competence and dependability. More research is needed to determine what LMX scores from each source actually mean and to clarify the implications of measuring exchange relationships from different perspectives.

Determinants and Consequences of LMX

Most of the research on LMX theory has examined how LMX is related to other variables. This research includes a large number of survey field studies (e.g., Erdogan, Bauer, & Walter, 2015; Gutermann, Lehmann-Willenbrock, Boer, Born, & Voelpel, 2017; Liden et al., 1993; Matta, Scott, Koopman, & Conlon, 2015; Schermuly & Meyer, 2016), a smaller number of laboratory experiments (e.g., Griffith, Connelly, & Thiel, 2011), a few field experiments (e.g., Graen, Novak, & Sommerkamp, 1982; Graen, G. B., Scandura, & Graen, M. R., 1986; Scandura & Graen, 1984), and a few studies that used observation and analysis of communication patterns within high versus low LMX relationships (e.g., Fairhurst, 1993; Kramer, 1995).

One set of studies examined factors that predict the quality of the exchange relationship for a dyad. A favorable relationship is more likely when the subordinate is perceived to be competent and has values and attitudes that are similar to those of the leader. Some personality traits for the leader and subordinate may also be related to their exchange relationship. For example, a study by Nahrgang, Morgeson, and Ilies (2009) found that high scores on extraversion and agreeableness for both leader and member predicted development of a more favorable exchange relationship in the early stages of a new team simulation exercise, presumably because these traits are associated with a more supportive and trusting style of interaction. However, after the initial period of interaction, performance was a more important determinant of LMX. Another study by Zhang, Wang, and Shi (2012) looked at how LMX was influenced by leader and follower proactive personality, which refers to the enduring tendency for people to take action to shape their environment. When both the leader and the follower possessed either high or low levels of proactive personality (i.e., high congruence), LMX quality was high along with follower work outcomes. In cases of low congruence, followers experienced lower-quality

LMX and had poorer work outcomes. The LMX relationship is especially likely to suffer when the leader values being proactive, and the follower does not, because the leader is likely to see the follower as lacking initiative.

Another set of studies examined how LMX is related to leader and subordinate behavior. When the exchange relationship is favorable, behavior by the leader is more supportive and includes more consultation and delegation, more mentoring and recognition, less close monitoring, and less domination of conversations (Erdogan & Bauer, 2014; O'Donnell, Yukl, & Taber, 2012; Yukl, O'Donnell, & Taber, 2009). The behavior of a high LMX subordinate includes more support of the leader, more honest communication with the leader, and less use of pressure tactics (e.g., threats, demands) to influence the leader. It is not clear how much a new subordinate can directly influence the role-making process, for example, by using impression management behavior, but it is likely that some subordinates are proactive about developing a favorable relationship rather than passively accepting whatever the leader decides to do.

A substantial body of research has now examined the relationship between LMX and outcomes such as subordinate attitudes and performance, and detailed reviews of research on the correlates of LMX can be found in various publications (e.g., Day & Miscenko, 2015; Epitropaki, Martin, & Thomas, 2018; Erdogan & Bauer, 2014; Erdogan & Liden, 2002; Gerstner & Day, 1997; Ilies, Nahrgang, & Morgeson, 2007; Liden, Sparrowe, & Wayne, 1997; Schriesheim et al., 1999). Meta-analytic research indicates that a favorable downward exchange relationship is associated with greater role clarity, higher job satisfaction, stronger organizational commitment, more citizenship behaviors, enhanced creativity, lower turnover intentions, less organizational deviance, superior job performance, and greater career success (Dulebohn, Bommer, Liden, Brouer, & Ferris, 2012; Gerstner & Day, 1997; Ilies et al., 2007; Martin, Guillaume, Thomas, Lee, & Epitropaki, 2016; Rockstuhl, Dulebohn, Ang, & Shore, 2012). A favorable exchange relationship is also correlated with a high level of subordinate trust, although reciprocal causality is likely (Dirks & Ferrin, 2002). Most of the research on correlates of LMX involved survey field studies, but a rare field experiment found that leaders trained to develop favorable exchange relationships with their subordinates had subsequent gains in the objective performance and satisfaction of their subordinates (Graen et al., 1982; Scandura & Graen, 1984). To incorporate the results of the initial research on outcomes, a revised version of the theory included the prescription that the leader should try to establish a special exchange relationship with all subordinates if possible, not just with a few favorites (Graen & Uhl-Bien, 1995).

A few studies also found that a leader's upward dyadic relationship affects downward dyadic relationships (Cashman, Dansereau, Graen, & Haga, 1976; Graen, Cashman, Ginsburgh, & Schiemann, 1977). A manager who has a favorable exchange relationship with the boss is more likely to establish favorable exchange relationships with subordinates. A favorable upward relationship enables a manager to obtain more benefits for subordinates and to facilitate their performance by obtaining necessary resources, cutting red tape, and gaining approval of changes desired by subordinates. Subordinates feel less motivation to incur the extra obligations of a special exchange relationship if the leader has little to offer in the way of extra benefits, opportunities, and empowerment. The research found that the effects of a manager's upward relationship were felt by subordinates regardless of their own relationship with the manager. Managers with a favorable upward relationship with their own boss were described by subordinates as having more technical skill, providing more outside information, allowing more participation in decision making, allowing more subordinate autonomy, and providing more support and consideration.

While there has been relatively little research on situational conditions affecting the development of exchange relationships (Green, Anderson, & Shivers, 1996), greater attention to the influence of contextual factors has emerged in recent years. For example, a positive work group climate and a people-oriented organizational culture have been shown to be positively related to LMX quality (Erdogan & Bauer, 2014). Furthermore, Anand, Vidyarthi, and Rolnicki (2018) found that the positive relationship between LMX and employee citizenship behaviors was stronger when the leader has more power than followers, especially when group task interdependence was high. Sui, Wang, Kirkman, and Li (2012) found that LMX differentiation contributed to higher levels of team coordination and performance for large teams, but for small teams a moderate level of LMX differentiation was optimal. Despite these advances, more research into the influence of situational variables on the quality of leader–member relationships is needed. Some aspects of the situation that are likely to be relevant include demographic attributes of work unit members, job characteristics, work unit characteristics (e.g., function, stability of membership) and type of organization. These situational variables may affect the type of dyadic relationships that occur, the underlying exchange processes, and the implications for effective leadership. For example, in a large work unit with diverse activities, it is desirable to have one or more assistant managers if the organization has not created formal positions for them, whereas an assistant manager is less important in small units with simple activities.

Cultural values in different countries (see Chapter 13) are another aspect of the situation that may be relevant for understanding the effects of LMX. In a meta-analysis by Rockstuhl and colleagues (2012), the relationships of LMX with key work outcomes were examined across 23 countries to explore the potential influence of national culture on exchange quality. Positive relationships of LMX with justice perceptions, organizational citizenship behaviors, job satisfaction, and leader trust and a negative relationship with turnover intentions were found, and these relationships were stronger in Western, individualistic cultures than in Eastern, collectivistic cultures. However, the positive relationships between LMX and organizational commitment, task performance, and transformational leadership were equally strong across cultures. These findings suggest that while higher-quality leader–member relationships tend to produce positive work outcomes, regardless of the cultural context, the benefits are most pronounced in Western and highly individualistic societies.

Evaluation of LMX Theory

LMX theory still has a number of conceptual weaknesses that limit its utility (Dienesh & Liden, 1986; Schriesheim et al., 1999; Vecchio & Gobdel, 1984). Revisions of the theory have attempted to remedy some of the deficiencies, but additional improvements are needed. The theory needs more elaboration about the way exchange relationships evolve over time. Despite the growing body of research on LMX, we still know little about how the role-making process actually occurs (Erdogan & Bauer, 2014). The theory implies that exchange relationships evolve in a continuous, smooth fashion, starting from initial impressions. The few longitudinal studies suggest that LMX relationships may form quickly and remain stable (Nahrgang et al., 2009). However, evidence from other research on dyadic relationships suggests that they typically progress through a series of ups and downs, with shifts in attitudes and behavior as the two parties attempt to reconcile their desire for autonomy with their desire for closer involvement (see Fairhurst, 1993). To resolve these inconsistencies, longitudinal research is needed, with methods that can record the pattern of interactions over time in more detail and probe more deeply into each party's changing perceptions of the relationship. Such research should focus on critical junctions in the development of the leader–member relationship to ascertain if there are tipping points that influence the upward or downward trajectory of the relationship (Erdogan & Bauer, 2014). It is desirable to examine Cropanzano and colleagues' (2017) predictions regarding the influence of affective events on the development of LMX during the role-taking, role-making, and role-routinization stages.

The theory would be improved by a clear description of the way a leader develops different dyadic relationships, how they affect each other, and how they affect group performance. Research on the antecedents and consequences of LMX differentiation was reviewed by Henderson, Liden, Glibkowski, and Chaudhry (2009). Some differentiation is likely to benefit group performance, especially if it is perceived by members as fair and appropriate to facilitate team performance (Haynie, Cullen, Lester, Winter, & Svyantek, 2014; Liden, Erdogan, Wayne, & Sparrowe, 2006). However, as differentiation increases, there may be more feelings of resentment among low-quality exchange members who believe the leader's "favorites" are getting more benefits than they deserve (McClane, 1991; Yukl, 1989). The negative effects of extreme differentiation will be greater in some types of situations than in others. For example, negative effects are more likely for an interacting team, because competition and hostility among members can undermine necessary cooperation. Leader behaviors directed at selected individuals to increase their self-efficacy and identification with the leader may have positive effects for those individuals but negative effects on group performance (Wu, Tsui, & Kinicki, 2010). The challenge for a leader is to develop differentiated relationships with some subordinates to facilitate achievement of the team's mission, while maintaining a relationship of mutual trust, respect, and loyalty with the other subordinates. It is not necessary to treat all subordinates exactly the same, but each person should perceive that he or she is an important and respected member of the team rather than a "second-class citizen." Not every subordinate may desire more responsibility, but each person should perceive an equal opportunity based on competence rather than arbitrary favoritism.

Leader Attributions About Subordinates

How a leader acts toward a subordinate varies depending on whether the subordinate is perceived as competent and loyal, or incompetent and untrustworthy. The assessment of competence and dependability is based on interpretation of the subordinate's behavior and performance. Attribution theory describes the cognitive processes used by leaders to determine the reasons for effective or ineffective performance and the appropriate reaction (Green & Mitchell, 1979; Martinko & Gardner, 1987; Mitchell, Green, & Wood, 1981; Wood & Mitchell, 1981).

Two-Stage Attribution Model

Green and Mitchell (1979) described the reaction of a manager to poor performance as a two-stage process. In the first stage, the manager tries to determine the cause of the poor performance; in the second stage, the manager tries to select an appropriate response to correct the problem. Several studies confirm the major propositions of the model (see review by Martinko, Harvey, & Douglas, 2007).

Managers attribute the major cause of poor performance either to something internal to the subordinate (e.g., lack of effort or ability) or to external problems beyond the subordinate's control (e.g., the task had inherent obstacles, resources were inadequate, information was insufficient, other people failed to provide necessary support, or it was just plain bad luck). An external attribution is more likely when (1) the subordinate has no prior history of poor performance on similar tasks; (2) the subordinate performs other tasks effectively; (3) the subordinate is doing as well as other people who are in a similar situation; (4) the effects of failures or mistakes are not serious or harmful; (5) the manager is dependent on the subordinate for his or her own success; (6) the subordinate is perceived to have other redeeming qualities (popularity, leadership skills); (7) the subordinate has offered excuses or an apology; or (8) evidence indicates external causes. Managers with prior experience doing the same kind of work as the subordinate are more likely to make external attributions, perhaps because they know more about the external factors that can affect performance (Crant & Bateman, 1993; Mitchell & Kalb, 1982). Manager traits such as internal locus of control orientation (see Chapter 7) can also influence attributions (Ashkanasy & Gallois, 1994).

The perceived reason for a problem influences the manager's response to it (e.g., Dugan, 1989; Martinko et al., 2007; Offermann, Schroyer, & Green, 1998; Trahan & Steiner, 1994). When an external attribution is made, the manager is more likely to respond by trying to change the situation, such as providing more resources, providing assistance in removing obstacles, providing better information, changing the task to reduce inherent difficulties, or in the case of bad luck, by showing sympathy or doing nothing. When an internal attribution is made and the manager determines that the problem is insufficient ability, the likely response is to provide detailed instruction, monitor the subordinate's work more closely, provide coaching when needed, set easier goals or deadlines, or assign the subordinate to an easier job. If the problem is perceived to be lack of subordinate effort and responsibility, then the likely reaction is to give directive or nondirective counseling, give a warning or reprimand, punish the subordinate, monitor subsequent behavior more closely, or find new incentives for good performance.

Other Determinants of Leader Attributions

Attributions about subordinates and the leader's reaction are affected by a leader's position power (Kipnis, Schmidt, Price, & Stitt, 1981; McFillen & New, 1979). The more position power a leader has, the more likely the leader will attribute effective performance and acceptable behavior by a subordinate to extrinsic factors (i.e., done only to gain rewards or avoid punishments) rather than to intrinsic motivation.

Research on attributions also found that the exchange relationship influences the manager's perception of a subordinate's performance (Duarte, Goodson, & Klich, 1994; Heneman, Greenberger, & Anonyuo, 1989; Lord & Maher, 1991). Leaders appear to be less critical in evaluating the performance of subordinates when there is a high-quality exchange relationship than when there is a low-quality exchange relationship. Effective performance is more likely to be attributed to internal causes for a high-quality exchange member and to external causes for a low-quality exchange member. In contrast, poor performance is likely to be attributed to external causes for a high-quality exchange member and to internal causes for a low-quality exchange member.

The leader's behavior toward the subordinate is consistent with the attribution about performance. For example, effective behavior by a high-quality exchange subordinate is more likely to be praised, and mistakes by a low-quality exchange subordinate are more likely to be criticized. Thus, the leader's perception of a subordinate tends to become a self-fulfilling prophecy. Low-quality exchange subordinates get less support, coaching, and resources, but the manager is more likely to blame them for mistakes or performance difficulties, rather than recognizing situational causes and the manager's own contributions to the problem.

The bias of many managers toward making internal attributions about poor performance by a subordinate is in sharp contrast to the self-serving bias of subordinates to blame their mistakes or failures on external factors (Martinko & Gardner, 1987). These incompatible biases make it more difficult for the manager to deal with performance problems. The manager's bias results in greater use of punitive actions, which are resented all the more by subordinates who do not feel responsible for the problem (Harvey, Martinko, & Douglas, 2006; Tjosvold, 1985). Thus, a major implication of the attribution research is the need to help managers become more careful, fair, and systematic about evaluating subordinate performance. Managers need to become more aware of the many options available for dealing with different causes of performance problems and the importance of selecting an appropriate one.

Relational Attributions

In an extension of attribution theory, Eberly, Holley, Johnson, and Mitchell (2011) introduced a third category of attributions that is especially relevant for leader–member relationships, namely attributions about the relationship itself. For example, rather than concluding that negative follower task performance is attributable to a lack of follower ability or effort (an internal attribution), or extenuating circumstances (an external attribution), a leader may identify a poor relationship with the follower as the cause. Eberly and colleagues (2011) go on to suggest that when the leader and subordinate make relational attributions for a negative outcome, they are more likely to engage in efforts to improve the relationship. A recent series of studies (Eberly, Holley, Johnson, & Mitchell, 2017) confirmed that there are cases where the leader and member both make relational attributions rather than internal or external attributions, and each person tries to improve the relationship rather than blaming the other party.

Guidelines for Correcting Performance Deficiencies

Correcting performance deficiencies is an important but difficult managerial responsibility. People tend to be defensive about criticism, because it threatens their self-esteem and may imply personal rejection. Many managers avoid confronting subordinates about inappropriate behavior or poor performance, because such confrontations often degenerate into an emotional conflict that fails to deal with the underlying problem, or does so only at the cost of lower respect and trust between the parties. Corrective feedback may be necessary to help a subordinate improve, but it should be done in a way that will preserve a favorable relationship or improve a relationship that is already strained.

Insights about the most effective way to provide corrective feedback are provided by the research on dyadic leadership processes, together with related research on counseling, feedback, and conflict. Effective managers take a supportive, problem-solving approach when dealing with inappropriate behavior or deficient performance by a subordinate. The following guidelines show how to improve communication and problem solving while reducing defensiveness and resentment (see summary in Table 10-1).

- **Gather information about the performance problem.**

Before confronting a subordinate about a performance deficiency, it is helpful to have the facts straight. It is especially important to do some fact finding when you did not directly observe the subordinate doing something improper. Gather information about the timing (when did problems occur, how many times), magnitude (what were the negative consequences, how serious were they), antecedents (what led up to the problems, what was the subordinate's involvement), and scope (did the problems occur only for the subordinate, or did others experience the same problems). If somebody else passes on information about a subordinate's unsatisfactory behavior, try to obtain a detailed account from the party who initiated the complaint. If the problem occurred previously, identify any prior actions that were taken to deal with it.

TABLE 10-1 Guidelines for Correcting Performance Deficiencies

- Gather information about the performance problem.
- Try to avoid attribution biases.
- Provide corrective feedback promptly.
- Describe the deficiency briefly in specific terms.
- Explain the adverse impact of ineffective behavior.
- Stay calm and professional.
- Mutually identify the reasons for inadequate performance.
- Ask the person to suggest remedies.
- Express confidence that the person can improve.
- Express a sincere desire to help the person.
- Reach agreement on specific action steps.
- Summarize the discussion and verify agreement.

- **Try to avoid attribution biases.**

There may be more than one reason for inadequate performance, and the leader should not assume that a performance problem is due to a lack of subordinate motivation or competence. As noted previously, a performance deficiency may be due to situational causes, internal causes, or a combination of both. Situational causes that are usually beyond the control of the subordinate include the following: shortages in supplies, materials, or personnel; unexpected or unusual events (e.g., accidents, bad weather, sabotage, lawsuits, new regulations); resource levels below budgeted levels due to last-minute cuts or shifts in priorities; and failure by people in other parts of the organization or outsiders to carry out their part of a project properly and on time. Internal causes for poor performance usually involve low motivation or deficiencies in subordinate skill. Examples of this type of problem include the following: failure to carry out a major action step on schedule, failure to monitor progress to detect a problem before it becomes serious, showing poor judgment in dealing with a problem, procrastinating in dealing with a problem until it gets worse, failure to notify superiors about a problem that requires their attention, making an avoidable error in the performance of a task, failure to follow standard procedures and rules, and acting in an unprofessional manner.

- **Provide corrective feedback promptly.**

Corrective feedback should be provided soon after the problem is noticed rather than waiting until a later time when the person may not remember the incident. Deal immediately with improper behavior that you observe, and handle other performance problems (complaints about a subordinate, substandard quality or productivity) as soon as you can conduct a preliminary investigation. Some managers save up criticisms for the annual appraisal meeting or scheduled progress review meetings, but this practice is likely to be ineffective. By delaying feedback, you lose the opportunity to deal with the problem immediately before it becomes worse. Moreover, by not responding to inappropriate or ineffective behavior, the wrong message may be sent, namely that the behavior is acceptable or not of any consequence. Finally, a person is likely to be more defensive after hearing a barrage of criticisms at the same time.

- **Describe the deficiency briefly in specific terms.**

Feedback is more effective if it involves specific behavior or specific examples of performance deficiencies. Vague, general criticism ("Your work is sloppy") may not communicate what the person is doing wrong and is easier for the person to deny. Provide specific examples of what was done, where it occurred, and when it occurred. For example, instead of saying a person is rude, point out that he interrupted you twice this week with trivial questions when you were talking to other people (describe when the incident happened and give examples). When criticizing performance, cite specific examples of unsatisfactory performance. For example, point out that two customers complained about slow service by the person's department. Avoid exaggeration such as "You are always late." Keep the description of ineffective behavior brief. The longer the person has to listen to criticism, even when constructive, the more defensive the person is likely to get.

- **Explain the adverse impact of ineffective behavior.**

Corrective feedback is more useful if it includes an explanation of the reason why a person's behavior is inappropriate or ineffective. For example, describe how the behavior causes problems for others and interferes with their work. Describe the discomfort and distress you or others experienced as a result of the person's inappropriate behavior. Describe how the person's behavior jeopardizes the success of an important project or mission and express your personal concern about it.

- **Stay calm and professional.**

It is appropriate to show concern about a performance problem or mistake, but corrective feedback should be provided without expressing anger or personal rejection. A manager who blows up, yells at the person, and makes insulting remarks (e.g., calling the person stupid and lazy) is unlikely to motivate the person to improve his or her performance. Moreover, this type of behavior impedes problem solving and undermines the relationship between manager and subordinate. Avoid accusations and insults ("Why did you do such a stupid thing?") that will make the person defensive. Criticize behavior instead of the person. Make it clear that you value the person and want to help him or her to deal with the performance problem.

- **Mutually identify the reasons for inadequate performance.**

Even after a preliminary investigation into the causes of a performance problem, you may lack important information that would change your perception of it. It is essential to listen to the subordinate's explanation for the problem, rather than jumping to conclusions about the causes. Give the person an opportunity to explain errors, inadequate performance, or inappropriate behavior. Sometimes the person may not know the reason or may make excuses rather than admitting responsibility. Be careful to differentiate between situational causes and personal causes. Personal causes of inadequate performance are harder to detect, because a subordinate is usually reluctant to admit mistakes and failures. When probing to discover these causes, ask what lessons were learned from the experience and what the subordinate would do differently if given the opportunity to go back and start over again. Keep the discussion of personal causes focused on specific behavior that was ineffective or inappropriate rather than on personal attributes such as poor judgment, irresponsibility, or lack of motivation. Mutually identify all of the important reasons in a careful, systematic manner, rather than moving immediately to a discussion of corrective actions. In doing so, be open to the possibility that the nature of your relationship with the follower contributed to the problem, and work with the follower to pinpoint aspects of the relationship that are deficient (e.g., communication, transparency, empathy, and knowledge of individual differences in values, personality, motives, and abilities).

- **Ask the person to suggest remedies.**

It is essential to get the person to take responsibility for dealing with a performance deficiency. Improvement is unlikely if the person makes excuses and denies responsibility for the problem. Commitment to improve is more likely if the person suggests ways to deal with the problem. Thus, when discussing how to correct performance deficiencies, begin by asking for suggestions rather than telling the person what to do. Use open-ended questions such as "What ideas do you have for improving performance?" and "What can we do to avoid this problem in the future?" Encourage the person to consider a variety of possible remedies, rather than focusing quickly on one narrow remedy. Try to build on the subordinate's ideas rather than merely pointing out limitations. If the subordinate fails to identify some promising remedies, try to present your own ideas as variations of the subordinate's ideas. State your ideas in a general, tentative way ("What about the possibility of . . . ?") and let the subordinate develop the details so he or she feels some ownership of the improvement plans. If you conclude that a low-quality relationship with the follower contributed to the problem, work with the follower to identify relationship-improvement behaviors that you can both target to strengthen the relationship.

- **Express confidence that the person can improve.**

A subordinate who lacks self-confidence and is discouraged about doing poorly on a task is less likely to improve. One important leadership function is to increase a person's confidence that difficult things can be achieved with a concerted effort, despite past failures. Mention the beneficial qualities that can help the person do better. Describe how others overcame similar failures or setbacks. Express confidence that the person will succeed. Research shows that subordinates perform better when the leader has high expectations for them (Eden, 1990; McNatt, 2000; Luthans, Youssef-Morgan, & Avolio, 2015).

- **Express a sincere desire to help the person.**

It is essential to communicate your intention to help the person do better. Be alert for opportunities to provide assistance to the subordinate by using your knowledge, influence, or contacts. Subordinates may be reluctant to ask for help if they believe that it is an admission of weakness. If a person's performance is being affected by personal problems (e.g., family problems, financial problems, substance abuse), be prepared to offer assistance if it is requested or is clearly needed. Examples of things that a leader can do include the following: help the person identify and express concerns and feelings, help the person understand the reasons for a personal problem, provide new perspectives on the problem, help the person identify alternatives, offer advice on how to deal with the problem, and refer the person to professionals who can provide assistance.

- **Reach agreement on specific action steps.**

It is essential to identify concrete action steps to be taken by the subordinate. If you discuss possible remedies but end the discussion without agreement on specific action steps, the person may walk away from the meeting without a clear understanding of what he or she is expected to do. Likewise, it is not enough to tell the subordinate to try to do better. Unless the person makes an explicit promise to carry out specific action steps, he or she may quickly forget about the discussion. As part of the explicit agreement, you should clearly state any action steps you will take to help the subordinate improve performance.

- **Summarize the discussion and verify agreement.**

After agreement has been reached, summarize the essence of the discussion. The purpose of a summary is to check for agreement and mutual understanding. As you end the meeting, repeat your willingness to provide assistance and indicate that you are available to discuss any additional problems or complications that may arise. You may also want to set a tentative date and time for a follow-up meeting to review progress.

Follower Attributions and Implicit Theories

Just as leaders make attributions about follower competence, followers make attributions about leader competence and intentions. Followers use information about leader actions, changes in the performance of the team or organization, and external conditions to reach conclusions about responsibility for success or failure. More attributions are made for someone who occupies a high-level position with substantial prestige and power, especially in cultures where leaders are viewed as heroic figures (Bligh, Kohles, & Pillai, 2011; Calder, 1977; Konst, Vonk, & Van der Vlist, 1999; Meindl, Ehrlich, & Dukerich, 1985; Pfeffer, 1977b).

Determinants of Follower Attributions About Leaders

Several interrelated factors determine how followers assess leader effectiveness (Awamleh & Gardner, 1999; Bligh et al., 2011; Choi & Mai-Dalton, 1999; Eberly & Fong, 2013; Ferris, Bhawuk, Fedor, & Judge, 1995; Lord & Maher, 1991; Meindl et al., 1985; Tskhay & Rule, 2018; van Knippenberg, D., van Knippenberg, B. De Cremer, & Hogg, 2004). One factor is the extent to which clear, timely indicators of performance are available for the leader's team or organization. A leader is usually judged more competent if his or her unit is successful than if it is unsuccessful. The performance trend will also influence follower assessment of the leader. A leader is more likely to be judged competent if performance is improving than if it is declining. Moreover, if performance suddenly increases (or decreases) soon after the leader's term of office begins, more credit or blame for the change will be attributed to the person than if performance remains stable or changes slowly.

Followers also consider the leader's actions. A leader who has done something that could explain a change in performance will be attributed more responsibility for it. Leaders who take direct actions that appear relevant get more credit for performance improvements than leaders who do not. Direct actions that are highly visible to followers influence attributions more than indirect actions that are not visible. The importance of direct action is increased when followers perceive an immediate crisis. A leader who acts decisively to resolve an obvious crisis is considered highly competent, whereas a leader who fails to take direct action in a crisis, or whose action has no apparent effect is likely to be judged incompetent. The uniqueness of changes made by a leader also influences attributions about the leader's competence. Leaders who make innovative changes in the strategy (what is done or how it is done) get more credit for success and more blame for failure than leaders who stick with a traditional strategy.

Followers also use information about the situation to reach conclusions about responsibility for success or failure. Improving performance is less likely to be credited to the leader when external conditions are favorable (e.g., the economy is improving and sales are up for all firms in the industry). Likewise, declining performance is less likely to be blamed on the leader when external conditions are unfavorable (e.g., a new competitor enters the market). Followers may also consider constraints on the leader's decisions and actions (e.g., new government regulations, pressure from superiors). A leader who appears to have considerable power and discretion in deciding what to do is attributed more responsibility for success or failure than a leader who is viewed as a puppet or figurehead.

Followers judge leader intentions as well as leader competence. A leader who appears to be more concerned about followers and the mission than about personal benefit or career advancement will gain more follower approval. Credibility is increased when the leader expresses strong and consistent convictions about a program or change and explains why it is necessary without exaggerating the benefits or ignoring the costs. Dedication to the organization is indicated when the leader takes personal risks to accomplish important objectives and does not benefit materially from them (Yorges et al., 1999). A leader who makes visible self-sacrifices in the service of the organization will be viewed as more sincere and committed (Choi & Mai-Dalton, 1998, 1999). In contrast, leaders who appear insincere or motivated only by personal gain get less credit for making changes that are successful, and receive more blame for making changes that are unsuccessful.

The willingness of leaders to make sacrifices for others is so crucial to securing followers' commitment that John C. Maxwell (2007, p. 222) identifies "the law of sacrifice" as one of his "irrefutable laws of leadership":

> There is a common misperception among people who aren't leaders that leadership is all about the position, perks, and power that come from rising in an organization. Many people today want to climb up the corporate ladder because they believe that freedom, power, and wealth are the prizes waiting at the top. The life of a leader can look glamorous to people on the outside. But the reality is that leadership requires sacrifice. A leader must give up to go up. In recent years, we've observed more than our share of leaders who used and abused their organizations for personal benefit — and the resulting corporate scandals that came because of their greed and selfishness. The heart of good leadership is sacrifice.

The mood of the followers can also affect attributions about leader intentions. Leaders are more likely to be seen as manipulative and self-serving if followers are in a negative mood (Dasborough & Ashkanasy, 2002). Followers also consider the extent to which the leader appears to be similar to them in terms of values, beliefs, and other qualities they consider important (e.g., religion, gender, ethnic background). Followers who identify strongly with the group or organization are likely to have more trust in a leader who appears to be "one of them" and will make more favorable attributions about the leader (Barreto & Hogg, 2017; Hogg, Hains, & Mason, 1998). The effect of perceived similarity (called "leader prototypicality") seems to be stronger for leader assessments made after a group failure than after a group success (Giessner, van Knippenberg, & Sleebos, 2009; Junker & van Dick, 2014; Peus, Braun, & Frey, 2012).

It is more difficult to assess leader competence when reliable indicators of performance are absent, followers have no opportunity to observe the leader's actions, or a long delay occurs before leader actions affect performance. Just as leaders tend to be biased toward making internal attributions about followers, followers seem to have a bias toward making internal attributions about leaders, especially when information is ambiguous. Followers usually attribute success or failure more to the leader's personal qualities (e.g., expertise, initiative, creativity, dedication) than to situational factors beyond the control of the leader. Coaches are praised when the team is winning consistently and blamed for repeated losses. The CEO of a company gets credit for increasing profits and is blamed for declining profits. The implications of follower attributions for leadership effectiveness are also discussed in Chapters 8, 11, and 12.

Implications of Follower Attributions About Leaders

How followers perceive a leader has important implications for the leader and the organization. Leaders perceived to be competent are likely to retain their position or be advanced to a higher position, whereas leaders perceived to be incompetent are likely to be replaced. Leaders who are judged to be competent gain more power and have more discretion to make changes. As explained in Chapters 6 and 12, the amount of legitimate power and discretion allowed a leader depends on the perception by followers and other stakeholders (e.g., board of directors, banks, government agencies, stockholders) that the leader has the expertise to solve important problems facing the organization. This perception depends in large part on how the leader's earlier decisions and actions are interpreted. Attributions about a leader's competence are especially important for top executives, because their long-term influence on the survival and prosperity of the organization depends on their discretion to make innovative, major changes in key areas of organization strategy (Lord & Maher, 1991).

Implicit Leadership Theories

How leaders are evaluated is affected by implicit leadership theories, which are beliefs and assumptions about the characteristics of effective leaders (Eden & Leviatan, 1975; Epitropaki, Sy, Martin, Tram-Quon, & Topakas, 2013; Junker & van Dick, 2014; Lord, Foti, & DeVader, 1984; Offermann & Coats, 2018; Shondrick, Dinh, & Lord, 2010; Tskhay & Rule, 2018). The implicit theories involve stereotypes and prototypes about the traits, skills, or behaviors that are relevant for a particular type of position (e.g., executive versus lower-level leader), context (e.g., crisis versus noncrisis situation), or individual (e.g., male versus female leader, experienced versus new leader). Implicit theories are developed and refined over time as a result of actual experience, exposure to literature about effective leaders, and other social–cultural influences (Lord, Brown, Harvey, & Hall, 2001). The implicit theories are influenced by individual beliefs, values, and personality traits, as well as by shared beliefs and values about leaders in the organizational culture and the national culture (Gerstner & Day, 1997; Junker & van Dick, 2014; Keller, 1999). Some differences in implicit theories are likely among countries with diverse cultures (see Chapter 13).

Beliefs about the ideal qualities for a particular type of leader (prototypes) influence the expectations people have for leaders and their evaluation of the leader's actions (Junker & van Dick, 2014). Implicit theories of leadership determine the perceived relevance of various types of leader behavior (Lord & Maher, 1991). Leaders who do things that are relevant for the situation but inconsistent with follower expectations may be evaluated less favorably than leaders who conform to role expectations. Follower beliefs about desirable leader qualities are influenced by gender role expectations, ethnic stereotypes, and cultural values (see Chapter 13). The same type of leader behavior may be evaluated more or less favorably depending on the identity of the leader (e.g., male versus female) and the cultural values of followers (e.g., individualism versus collectivism). Implicit theories and prototypes about ideal leaders are more important when followers agree about them and identify strongly with their group or organization (e.g., Barreto & Hogg, 2017; Hogg et al., 2006).

Implicit leadership theories, prototypes, and attributions can jointly influence ratings on leadership behavior questionnaires (Martinko et al., 2018). For example, a leader who is liked or perceived to be effective may be rated higher on behaviors in the rater's conception of an ideal leader or behaviors assumed to be relevant for performance, even though the respondent did not observe the behaviors or did not remember them correctly. If most respondents in a survey study have a similar implicit theory, their biases may influence the factor structure found for a leader behavior questionnaire. The effects of biases from prototypes and attributions can increase the correlations among behaviors considered desirable and make them appear to be part of the same meta-category. This problem complicates the interpretation of results in survey research on broadly defined conceptions of effective leaders, such as transformational leadership, authentic leadership, and servant leadership (see Chapters 8 and 9).

Impression Management by Leaders and Followers

Impression management is the process of influencing how others perceive you. Tactics such as excuses and apologies are used in a defensive way to avoid blame for weak performance or to seek forgiveness for a mistake. Other tactics are used to elicit positive affect and respect from others (e.g., Bolino, Long, & Turnley, 2016; Bolino, Kacmar, Turnley, & Gilstrap, 2008; Gardner & Martinko, 1988; Jones & Pitman, 1982; Peck & Hogue, 2018; Tedeschi & Melburg, 1984; Wayne & Ferris, 1990). Impression management tactics that seem especially relevant for the study of leadership in dyads are exemplification, ingratiation, and self-promotion.

Exemplification. This tactic involves behavior intended to demonstrate dedication and loyalty to the mission, to the organization, or to followers. Exemplification tactics used to influence bosses include arriving early and staying late to work extra hours, demonstrating effective behavior when you know the person is watching, and doing voluntary tasks that are highly visible ("organizational citizenship behaviors"). Exemplification tactics used to influence subordinates or peers include acting in a way that is consistent with espoused values ("walking the talk") and making self-sacrifices to achieve a proposed objective, change, or vision.

Ingratiation. This tactic involves behavior intended to influence the target person to like the agent and perceive the agent as someone who has desirable social qualities (e.g., friendly, considerate, caring, charming, interesting, attractive). Ingratiating behavior can take many different forms. Some examples include providing praise, agreeing with the target person's opinions, showing appreciation for the target's accomplishments, laughing at the target's jokes, showing an interest in the target's personal life, and showing deference and respect for the target person.

Self-Promotion. This tactic involves behavior intended to influence favorable impressions about your competence and value to the organization. The behavior may take the form of informing people about your achievements and talking about your skills. A more subtle form of self-promotion is to display diplomas, awards, and trophies in one's office or workspace for others to see. An indirect form of self-promotion that is similar to a coalition tactic is to get other people to talk in a positive way about your skills and loyalty.

Impression Management by Followers

Most studies on impression management have examined how followers attempt to influence bosses. Wayne and Ferris (1990) developed a self-report agent questionnaire to measure how subordinates use impression management tactics for upward influence in organizations. Their study found support for a three-factor model that included "supervisor-focused tactics" (similar to ingratiation), "job-focused tactics" (similar to exemplification), and "self-focused tactics" (similar to self-promotion).

The usual way to measure the effectiveness of upward impression management is how the boss evaluates the subordinate's competence, or the extent to which the subordinate gets favorable career outcomes such as a pay increase or promotion. The research indicates that ingratiation is often effective as an impression management tactic for upward influence (Bolino et al., 2008; Bolino et al., 2016; Higgins, Judge, & Ferris, 2003; Leary & Kowalski, 1990; Wayne & Liden, 1995). Ingratiation can increase how much a subordinate is liked by the boss and may also improve appraisals of subordinate performance. However, to be effective as an impression management tactic, ingratiation must appear to be sincere. If it seems manipulative, it will fail to have the desired effect and may have a negative effect.

The results for self-promotion tactics are less consistent, but they suggest that a negative reaction is more likely than a positive reaction (Higgins et al., 2003). A subordinate who uses this tactic too often or in an annoying way will be liked less by the boss and given a lower performance appraisal. Self-promotion is a more difficult form of impression management to pull off successfully. Unless used only infrequently and in a subtle way, self-promotion tactics are likely to be seen as bragging and conceit.

Research on the effects of upward impression management on job outcomes has some limitations that complicate interpretation of the results. An outcome such as a pay increase or job promotion may depend more on a subordinate's actual skills and performance than on the use of self-promotion tactics to focus attention on these qualifications. Moreover, the effectiveness of impression management tactics depends to a great extent on the interpersonal skills of the agent (Ammeter et al., 2002; Bolino et al., 2016; Turnley & Bolino, 2001), and these skills are also a determinant of performance. It is difficult to assess the independent effects of impression management tactics unless these other likely determinants of job outcomes are also measured, which seldom occurs in the research.

Impression Management by Leaders

Many leaders attempt to create the impression that they are important, competent, and in control of events (Pfeffer, 1977b, 1981). Successes are announced and celebrated, and failures are covered up or downplayed (Chng, Rodgers, Shih, & Song, 2015). Salancik and Meindl (1984) analyzed annual reports for a sample of corporations over a period of 18 years and found that top management consistently credited themselves for positive outcomes and blamed negative outcomes on aspects of the environment.

Impression management is especially important when constraints and unpredictable events make it difficult for leaders to exert much influence over organizational performance. Highly visible symbolic actions are one way to create the impression that a leader is dealing with problems and making progress toward attaining organizational objectives, despite delays and setbacks (Chng et al., 2015). Examples include visiting a disaster site to demonstrate active involvement and personal interest, replacing people who are blamed for a failure, creating a blue ribbon commission to study a problem and make recommendations, implementing a new policy to deal with a serious problem, and creating a new agency or position with responsibility for dealing with a serious problem. Dramatic changes in structure, policies, programs, and personnel may be relevant for solving problems and improving performance. However, it is often difficult to determine whether such changes will be beneficial, and the effects may not be known for months or years. In an effort to maintain a favorable impression, leaders who do not know how to solve a problem may be tempted to use symbolic actions that are irrelevant or even detrimental.

Impression management is also used by leaders to avoid the appearance of failure, or to shift the blame for it to other people or uncontrollable events (Chng et al., 2015). Some leaders seek to distort or cover up evidence that their strategy is not succeeding (Pfeffer, 1981; Staw, McKechnie, & Puffer, 1983). In the early stage of a developing crisis, many leaders discount the seriousness of the problem and continue with incremental approaches for dealing with it rather than proposing bold and innovative remedies. In part, the avoidance of dramatic action may be due to wishful thinking that things will get better. Even leaders who recognize an impending crisis may not have the courage to acknowledge the weakness of previous strategies and take dramatic new actions for which they will be held accountable. Many leaders with a limited term of office, such as elected officials, are tempted to put off serious problems and leave them to the next person who holds the office.

Impression management tactics can be manipulative, but some of the same behaviors can also be used in a positive way by leaders (Peck & Hogue, 2018). Praise (a form of ingratiation) can be used to build the confidence of subordinates and improve their performance. Announcing achievements that demonstrate progress in implementing a change initiated by the leader (a form of self-promotion) can increase follower optimism and commitment to make the change successful. Forms of exemplification such as showing courage, making personal sacrifices, volunteering to do extra duties, and acting consistent with espoused values are ways to lead by example and inspire follower commitment to a vision or strategy (Gardner, 2003).

Followership

The tendency to credit successful events to leaders obscures the significant contributions of followers (Baker, 2007; Epitropaki, Kark, Mainemelis, & Lord, 2017; Foti, Hansbrough, Epitropaki, & Coyle, 2017; Shamir, 2007; Uhl-Bien, Riggio, Lowe, & Carsten, 2014). Motivated, competent followers are necessary for the successful performance of work carried out by the leader's unit. Consider the following example (Kelley, 1992):

> Today most people regard the role of Thomas Jefferson in writing the Declaration of Independence as an example of effective leadership by someone who would later become one of our most famous presidents. At the time, however, Jefferson was in a follower role. He was a junior member of the committee and was assigned the task by John Adams and Benjamin Franklin. Few people outside the Continental Congress knew that Jefferson was the principal author, and he received no public recognition until eight years later when his role was explained in a newspaper article.

Followers can contribute to the effectiveness of a group by maintaining cooperative working relationships, providing constructive dissent, sharing leadership functions, and supporting leadership development. This section examines attributes of followers that influence their contribution to successful performance by the leader's team or work unit.

Follower Identities and Behavior

How followers act in a group or organization can be explained in part by their self- and social identities (Collinson, 2006; Epitropaki et al., 2017; Lord & Brown, 2004; Oc & Bashshur, 2013; Tee, Paulsen, & Ashkanasy, 2013). The follower identities are complex and not necessarily consistent. For example, the self-identity of a loyal member who follows all the norms and policies prescribed by the organization may be inconsistent with the self-identity of a courageous member who challenges bad decisions and unethical practices. Researchers have begun to study how self- and social identities help to explain how followers perceive leaders and how they comply with or resist influence attempts by leaders (e.g., Carsten, Uhl-Bien, West, Patera, & McGregor, 2010; Epitropaki et al., 2018; Uhl-Bien et al., 2014). Deference, passivity, and obedience will reflect the personality traits of followers, their relationship to the leader, the type of organization, and cultural values such as power distance (see Chapter 13).

Chaleff (1995) noted that many people define the role of follower in terms of conformity, weakness, and passivity. This negative conception is strongly influenced by early childhood experiences at home and in school, where others are responsible for our behavior but we are not responsible for their behavior. As adults, passivity in follower roles is encouraged by the fact that leaders typically are more powerful, have higher status, are older, and have more experience. The reluctance to challenge a leader is even worse for an established leader who is widely seen as brilliant and successful. Chaleff argues that it is essential to replace this negative conception of followers with a positive conception. In short, effective followers are courageous, responsible, and proactive.

The reason why courageous followers are likely to be more effective stems from the fact that all leaders have weaknesses as well as strengths. Followers can influence whether the strengths are fully utilized and the weaknesses overcome. Some of the qualities that contribute to leadership effectiveness (e.g., self-confidence, strong convictions, a passion for change) also make a leader prone to excessive ambition, risk taking, or righteousness. Followers can help the leader avoid these excesses. Rather than complaining about their leader, followers with valid concerns should help the leader to do better.

To be effective as a follower, it is necessary to find a way to integrate two different follower roles, namely to implement decisions made by a leader and to challenge decisions that are misguided or unethical. Followers must be willing to risk the leader's displeasure, but the risk can be reduced by developing a high level of mutual trust and respect. In such a relationship, a leader is likely to view criticism and dissent as an honest effort to facilitate attainment of shared objectives and values, rather than as an expression of personal rejection or disloyalty.

It takes time and effort to help a leader grow and succeed. If the leader is less competent than you or has been elevated to a position you really deserved, it is especially difficult to make this extra effort. Thus, effective followers are more likely to be people with a strong commitment to the organization and its mission. Helping a weak leader can also help a follower to develop more skills relevant for a future leadership role.

Integrating Leader and Follower Roles

Many members of an organization have the dual roles of leader and follower, and they may switch back and forth between these role identities depending on the role identities claimed by the other party (DeRue & Ashford, 2010). For example, a middle manager is the leader of an organizational unit but also a follower of a higher-level manager. How to integrate these two diverse roles is an interesting question with important implications for leadership effectiveness.

To be effective in both roles simultaneously, it is necessary to find a way to integrate them. Inevitable role conflicts and dilemmas make integration of the two roles difficult. Superiors expect the leader to represent their interests and implement their decisions, but subordinates expect the leader to represent their interests and to challenge decisions that are unwarranted or unfair. Leaders are expected to initiate and guide change, but they are also expected to encourage and support "bottom-up" changes suggested by followers. A leader is held responsible for everything that happens in the team or work unit but may be encouraged to empower followers to act on their own in resolving problems. Leaders are also expected to develop followers, which may involve gradually turning over most leadership responsibilities to one or two subordinates designated as likely successors. Issues of how to balance competing interests and resolve role conflicts deserve more attention in the leadership literature.

Self-Management

Self-management is a set of strategies used to influence and improve an individual's own behavior (Manz & Sims, 1980; Sims & Lorenzi, 1992). Self-management is based primarily on control theory. After comparing one's current condition to the desired condition, a person can use behavior in an effort to reduce any discrepancy, monitor progress to assess consequences, and make any necessary corrections in behavior. When a person determines what tasks will be done and how the work will be done, this process is sometimes called self-leadership (Manz, 1991). Self-management and self-leadership are appropriately viewed as motivation and self-regulation theories rather than as a leadership theory, but they can serve as a partial substitute for leadership. By taking more responsibility for their own lives, followers do not need to depend so much on leaders to direct and motivate them. Leaders can encourage and facilitate self-management as a way to influence follower satisfaction and development.

Self-Management Strategies

Self-management includes both behavioral and cognitive strategies (Sims & Lorenzi, 1992). The behavioral strategies include self-goal setting, self-monitoring, manipulation of cues, self-reward (or criticism), and rehearsal of planned actions. The cognitive strategies include positive self-talk and mental imagery.

Behavioral self-management strategies are useful when you are reluctant to do a necessary task or want to change your behavior. For example, set realistic goals to accomplish a task or change a behavior, including subgoals that can be achieved quickly (e.g., a goal to write the first page of a report today; a goal to get through the next hour without saying "you know" to anyone). Then, monitor your own behavior to note what you did and how others reacted (e.g., noticing each time you say something that annoys others; trying different ways of communicating ideas to see which one people respond to most favorably. Compliment yourself for doing something correctly, and reward yourself when you complete a difficult task or accomplish a goal or subgoal (e.g., go to a movie, purchase something you want). Use self-criticism or self-punishment after acting in an inappropriate way or relapsing into behavior you want to change. For example, record a conversation and for every time you say "you know" or use inappropriate language, donate a dollar to a charity. Rehearse a difficult behavior by yourself to improve skill and build confidence you can do it. Rearrange cues in the immediate physical environment; remove cues that encourage undesirable behavior and replace them with cues that encourage desirable behavior (e.g., go to a quiet place where you will not be disturbed to write a report; purchase only healthy food to avoid being tempted to eat junk food).

Cognitive self-management strategies help you to build self-confidence and optimism about doing a difficult task. One cognitive strategy is positive self-talk, which means emphasizing positive, optimistic thoughts and avoiding negative, pessimistic thoughts (Neck & Manz, 1992). An example is to interpret a difficult situation as an opportunity rather than as a problem. The confidence and determination needed to improve are more likely to be found by concentrating on what can be done to make things better than by dwelling on the difficulties or what can go wrong.

To increase positive self-talk, it is necessary to do more than just look for the silver lining in a dark cloud. It is essential to identify and suppress destructive thinking patterns, such as viewing success and failure as extreme conditions with nothing in between, exaggerating the significance of a mistake or setback, stereotyping yourself negatively, dismissing positive feedback as irrelevant ("She's just saying that to be kind"), and assuming blame for something that is not your responsibility. This type of thinking encourages overreaction to mistakes, setbacks, or periods of slow improvement in performance when you are learning a complex new activity or task. A more constructive pattern of thinking is to view performance as a continuum rather than a dichotomy, understand the process involved in learning a complex activity, look for and celebrate signs of progress, accept positive feedback, and be careful about attributing responsibility for failure. Identify destructive thoughts (e.g., "It's hopeless; even after practicing for a week I still made several mistakes") and replace them with constructive thoughts (e.g., "I improved by 20 percent this week, and with additional practice I will do even better").

Another cognitive strategy for self-management is mental imagery, which can be used instead of actually practicing a difficult task. First, you visualize yourself doing the task. Then, you imagine how it would feel to experience the satisfaction of performing it successfully. Before performing an activity, many professional athletes mentally rehearse it, carefully visualizing each movement and how it will feel (Sims & Lorenzi, 1992).

Effects of Self-Management

The consequences of self-management and self-leadership have been assessed in a variety of ways. One research method is to administer a self-report questionnaire such as the one developed by Houghton and Neck (2002), then correlate the scores with measures of each respondent's satisfaction and performance. Another method is a field experiment in which employees are trained to use more self-management, then subsequent job performance of these employees is compared to performance by a control group of employees who did not receive the training. Most studies find that individual self-management can increase satisfaction and performance (see Stewart, Courtright, & Manz, 2010; Unsworth & Mason, 2016). Effects of self-managed teams are discussed in Chapter 11.

How Leaders Encourage Self-Management

A leader can do several things to encourage and facilitate self-management by followers. Encouragement is especially important when followers are dependent on the leader for direction and are not intrinsically motivated by the work. According to some theorists (Manz & Sims, 1991; Sims & Lorenzi, 1992), a primary role of the leader is to help subordinates develop skills in self-management. Leadership activities include explaining the rationale for self-management, explaining how to use behavioral and cognitive self-management strategies, encouraging efforts to use these techniques, and providing enough autonomy to make self-management feasible. The leader should model the use of self-management strategies to set an example for subordinates. The leader should also share information subordinates need to do the work, including sensitive information about strategic plans and the financial performance of the organization. As subordinates develop skills and confidence in self-management, the leader should encourage them to take more responsibility for their own work activities.

Guidelines for Followers

The research on followers has some practical applications (Chaleff, 1995; Kelley, 1992; Whetten & Cameron, 1991). The following guidelines deal with issues such as how to improve one's relationship with a leader, how to resist improper influence from the leader, how to provide advice and coaching to the leader, and how to challenge flawed plans and policies (see Table 10-2). Underlying themes in the guidelines include maintaining credibility and trust, taking responsibility for your own life, and remaining true to your own values and convictions.

- **Find out what you are expected to do.**

It is difficult to be viewed as competent and reliable if you have role ambiguity and are unsure what you are expected to do. You may be working very hard, but doing the wrong things or doing things the wrong way. Earlier in the book, we saw that it is an important leader responsibility to clearly communicate the role expectations for subordinates. Nevertheless, many leaders fail to explain job responsibilities, scope of authority, performance standards, and the relative priority of different aspects of performance. Sometimes the message is inconsistent, such as when the leader says something is important but acts as if it is not. Sometimes the leader asks for something that is inconsistent with the needs of a client or customer. Followers should be assertive but diplomatic about resolving role ambiguity and conflict.

- **Take the initiative to deal with problems.**

Effective followers take initiative to deal with serious problems that prevent the attainment of task objectives. These problems can take many forms, such as rules that prevent attainment of task objectives, a process that does not achieve the desired results, traditions that are obsolete, conflicts between individuals with interrelated jobs, and unsatisfactory performance by someone over whom you have no authority. Taking initiative may mean pointing out the problem to the boss, suggesting ways to deal with the problem, or if necessary, handling the problem yourself. One way to gain support for changing a flawed process is to conduct a pilot demonstration to show the superiority of a different approach. Taking initiative often involves risks, but if done carefully it can make you a more valuable follower.

TABLE 10-2 Guidelines for Followers

- Find out what you are expected to do.
- Take the initiative to deal with problems.
- Keep the boss informed about your decisions.
- Verify the accuracy of information you give the boss.
- Encourage the boss to provide honest feedback to you.
- Support efforts to make necessary changes.
- Show appreciation and provide recognition when appropriate.
- Challenge flawed plans and proposals made by bosses.
- Resist inappropriate influence attempts by the boss.
- Provide upward coaching and counseling when appropriate.
- Learn to use self-management strategies.

- **Keep the boss informed about your decisions.**

Followers who take more initiative to deal with problems also have a responsibility to keep the leader informed about their actions and decisions. It is embarrassing for a leader to hear from someone else that changes have been made by you. An uninformed leader may appear incompetent to others, and lack of knowledge about ongoing changes may also adversely affect the leader's own actions and decisions. How much and how often you inform the boss about your decisions and actions is a complex issue that may be a subject of continuing discussion and revision as conditions change. Finding the right balance is much easier in a relationship of mutual trust and respect.

- **Verify the accuracy of information you give to the boss.**

An important role of followers is to relay information to their leader. Control over what information is passed on gives a follower power over the leader's perception of events and choices. It is an important responsibility for followers to provide accurate, timely information needed by the leader to make good decisions. This responsibility includes relaying bad news as well as good news. It is important to verify the accuracy of information you are trusted to obtain for the leader. Rumors, complaints, and reports of problems can have a disproportionate effect on the leader's decisions if not verified. It is also important to acknowledge when your information is limited or questionable. Rather than pretending to have expertise about a matter, say that you will look into it immediately and get back to the leader as soon as possible.

- **Encourage the boss to provide honest feedback to you.**

One way to improve mutual trust with the leader is to encourage honest feedback about your performance. If the leader is uncomfortable about expressing concerns about a subordinate's performance, it may be necessary to probe for more information. For example, ask the leader to identify the strongest and weakest aspects of your work. Ask what you can do to be more effective. After an initial response, ask if the leader has concerns about any other aspects of your performance.

- **Support efforts to make necessary changes.**

Contrary to the myth of heroic leaders, most major changes require a cooperative effort of many people in the organization. Leaders need the encouragement and support of loyal followers to overcome resistance to change in organizations. Look for opportunities to express support and encouragement to a leader who is frustrated by difficulties encountered in trying to implement necessary changes. Offer to provide assistance to a leader who is temporarily overwhelmed with new work or too preoccupied with an immediate crisis to handle other work that still must be done.

- **Show appreciation and provide recognition when appropriate.**

Leaders can feel unappreciated and taken for granted. It is appropriate to express appreciation when a leader makes a special effort to help you with a problem, represent your interests, or promote your career in the organization. It is also helpful to provide praise when the leader carries out a difficult activity successfully (e.g., negotiating a favorable contract with a client, lobbying successfully for a larger budget, finding a solution to a difficult problem, persuading superiors to authorize a proposed change). These forms of supporting are one way followers can provide feedback to the leader and reinforce desirable leadership practices. Praising the leader is a form of ingratiation that can be used in a manipulative way, but when praise is sincere it can help promote a more favorable relationship with a leader.

- **Challenge flawed plans and proposals made by bosses.**

One of the most valuable contributions a follower can make is to provide accurate feedback about the leader's plans and proposals. To minimize defensiveness, begin with a comment that shows respect and a desire to be helpful in accomplishing shared objectives. For example:

> You know that I respect what you are trying to accomplish, and I hope you won't mind if I express some honest concerns about this proposal.

Describe any obvious faults in a plan or proposal using specific terms rather than vague generalities and avoid making the critique personal. If appropriate, suggest getting reactions from other credible people before going ahead with a plan or proposal that is questionable. Following is an example:

> This change may cause some serious problems for the operations group. Shouldn't we consult with them first before going ahead with it? They are likely to have some good ideas on how to avoid problems that are not obvious to us.

Sometimes a boss may be unwilling to listen to concerns about a decision or policy that is unethical, illegal, or likely to have adverse consequences for the organization. In this situation, it may be necessary to escalate your influence attempt and use pressure tactics such as threats and warnings. Threatening to resign is one way for a follower to express deep concern over a controversial decision. However, such threats should not be used lightly, and they are appropriate only after a serious effort has been made to influence the boss in other ways, such as rational persuasion and use of coalitions. The threat should be expressed with conviction but not personal hostility. Following is a specific example:

> I cannot live with this decision, because it violates our basic principles and poses a serious risk to our people. Unless the decision can be changed, I will have no choice but to resign from my position.

- **Resist inappropriate influence attempts by the boss.**

Despite the obvious power advantage a boss holds over a subordinate, it is not necessary to comply with inappropriate influence attempts or be exploited by an abusive leader. Followers often have more counter-power than they realize, and have some things they can do to deter a leader accustomed to exploiting people who are unassertive. It is essential to challenge abuse early before it becomes habitual, and the challenge must be firm but diplomatic. Point out the use of inappropriate or manipulative influence tactics (e.g., "I don't respond well to threats" or "This offer might be misconstrued by some people as a bribe"). Insist on your rights ("It's not right to ask me to cancel my vacation plans at the last minute to do this job when other people around here have the time and skills to do it."). Remind the leader of a promise about to be violated ("Didn't you promise that assignment to me just last month?"). Point out the negative consequences of complying with an inappropriate request. For example, explain how compliance with a demand to do something immediately will interfere with your other work or jeopardize an important project.

- **Provide upward coaching and counseling when appropriate.**

Coaching is usually viewed as a leader behavior, but subordinates also have opportunities to coach the boss, especially one who is new and inexperienced. Upward coaching is easier to do when a follower has already developed a deep and trusting exchange relationship with the leader. Be alert for opportunities to provide helpful advice on technical matters (the leader may be reluctant to ask for help). Model effective behaviors the leader can learn from and imitate.

Upward counseling is awkward, but at times it is appropriate and even appreciated by a boss. One form of counseling is to help the leader understand actions that are ineffective. For example, describe how inappropriate behavior is having a different effect than the leader intended ("I'm sure you didn't mean to imply Sue is unreliable when you said . . . , but that's how she took it"). Another form of counseling is to be a good listener when the leader needs someone in whom to confide about worries and concerns. Look for opportunities to ask questions about things the leader should consider in handling a difficult problem.

- **Learn to use self-management strategies.**

As noted earlier, cognitive and behavioral strategies for self-management can be useful to increase feelings of empowerment and job satisfaction, reduce dysfunctional behavior, and improve individual performance. Self-development aids are available to guide individuals in using these strategies effectively.

Summary

Leader–member exchange (LMX) theory describes how leaders develop exchange relationships over time with different subordinates. A favorable exchange relationship is more likely when a subordinate is perceived to be competent, reliable, and similar to the leader in values and attitudes. A leader's upward influence is another important determinant of the potential for establishing a favorable exchange relationship with subordinates. The behavior of the leader and subordinate is different in favorable exchange relationships than in unfavorable exchange relationships. Exchange relationships with subordinates have implications for leadership effectiveness. Subordinate satisfaction, commitment, citizenship, creativity, and performance are usually higher when the relationship is favorable. Some differentiation of exchange relationships with subordinates may be necessary, but too much can be detrimental.

A manager's reaction to mistakes or failures by a subordinate depends in part on attributions about the reasons for poor performance. Attribution theory explains how managers interpret performance information and make judgments about the competence and motivation of a subordinate. Managers may unwittingly create a self-fulfilling prophecy if their behavior is based on a biased perception about the ability and motivation of individual subordinates. For their part, subordinates can use impression management tactics to influence the leader to view them more favorably. Followers often do things to appear competent, loyal, and reliable. When a subordinate's performance is unsatisfactory, corrective feedback is more likely to be successful if the leader is supportive rather than hostile and encourages the subordinate to take ownership of the problem.

How followers view leader competence and intentions has implications for leadership effectiveness. Followers are susceptible to the same types of attributions as leaders. A leader who takes visible actions that are followed by improvements in group or organizational performance will be viewed as more competent than one who takes no action or acts without apparent success. Leaders use impression management tactics in an effort to appear more decisive, competent, powerful, and trustworthy.

Self-management is a way for followers to become more effective as individual contributors. Self-management strategies can be used to increase confidence, spur greater effort, and manage time more effectively. One way for a leader to empower subordinates is to encourage and facilitate their self-management activities.

Followers are more likely to be effective if they view themselves as active and independent rather than passive and dependent on the leader. Followers can help make their leader more effective by providing accurate information, challenging weak decisions, resisting inappropriate influence attempts, giving support and encouragement, and providing coaching and advice.

For someone who is both a leader and a follower, it is essential to find a way to integrate the two different roles. Moreover, it is essential to find appropriate ways to share leadership functions within teams, across authority levels, and between interdependent subunits of the organization.

Review and Discussion Questions

1. Briefly explain leader–member exchange theory.
2. What are some possible benefits and costs of developing different exchange relationships?
3. Is it possible to develop different dyadic relationships and still treat everyone fairly?
4. Use attribution theory to explain how leaders interpret the reason for poor performance.
5. How can subordinates influence a leader's perceptions about them?
6. What are some guidelines for corrective feedback?
7. What factors influence follower attributions about leader competence?
8. What are some guidelines for improving effectiveness as a follower?

Key Terms

affective events
exchange relationship
exemplification
external attribution
followership
implicit theories of leadership
impression management
ingratiation
internal attribution
leader–member exchange
relational attribution
self-management
self-promotion
self-talk

PERSONAL REFLECTION

Think about your experience working for a current or previous leader and consider the quality of the leader/member relationship. To what extent did you receive valued benefits (e.g., desirable work assignments, personal support and approval, pay increases), and to what extent did they influence how hard you worked and your commitment to the leader? What was the level of trust between you and the leader?

CASE

Housefull Entertainment

Jai Nair was the production head of Housefull Entertainments, a media and entertainment company. Two months back, a new team had been formed for an upcoming project with Anjali Verma as its manager. This team was responsible for the following tasks: budgeting, scheduling, scripting, supply of talent and resources, the organization of staff, the production function itself, post-production, distribution, and marketing. While the budgeting, production and post-production segment were allotted to the two more experienced employees, the rest went to the relatively newly hired employees. Even though it had been only two months since the team had been formed, Jai expected its performance to have improved by now, since another team that was formed for another project around the same time, was performing much better than this team.

Jai received various feedback about Anjali's working style from her subordinates. He reflected on the comments made by Anjali's subordinates when they were asked about their experience of working under her. Harshvardhan who was heading the budgeting department had been working for the company for five years now. According to him, Anjali was a great manager who gave him sufficient autonomy, encouraged him to find his own solutions, and gave him space to commit mistakes and learn from them. Harshvardhan also appreciated the fact that Anjali had acknowledged and praised his efforts not just personally, but also during weekly review meetings. She had told Harshvardhan that he could expect a pay increase given his good performance and contribution to the company.

Akshara, on the other hand, who was one of the relatively new employees and was in-charge of the supply of talent and resources and organization of staff, was not very happy with her manager. Being relatively new to the nature of this job, Akshara felt she was not getting any guidance from Anjali, rather was being pushed to make her own decisions. Akshara felt that had she been a veteran at the job, she might have liked Anjali's approach, but for now the latter is insecure and unsure about her boss's (Anjali) expectations and her ability to deliver. Every time Akshara would go up to her boss with a query, she ended up getting questioned in return as to how the situation should be handled. This frustrated Akshara as she was not sure about what needs to be done, and this led Akshara avoid approaching Anjali for resolving issues. Akshara also felt that Anjali ignored mistakes as if not talking about them would make them vanish. Lastly, she felt that Anjali favoured the employees who had been working longer for the company by giving them the more interesting assignments and offering them more pay increases as well. In her feedback, Akshara also pointed out how the other new employees too had similar complaints against Anjali.

That day, at lunch, Jai decided to talk to Anjali about how things were going for her. Anjali responded that she was disappointed with the performance of the new employees and felt that only one of them was doing a good job, while the others lacked the motivation and initiative. Anjali also stated that unlike the previous manager, she made sure that she showed no favouritism. The only differentiation she showed amongst her subordinates was in the assignment of tasks, which would be based on experience. Thus, the more complex assignments were given to the more experienced employees. However, this in no way meant that the other employees did not get assignments that were not challenging or did not offer opportunity to excel. Her recent exposure to a workshop on empowerment, Anjali's aim as a manager was to provide her subordinates the autonomy they needed to learn and develop new skills for their job. She was cautious to not supervise too closely or criticise mistakes, but at the same time recognize and appreciate achievements and good efforts. Anjali felt perplexed about where she was going wrong and asked Jai for his opinion.

Questions

1. What theories from this chapter are relevant for analysing the case?
2. Evaluate Anjali's behavior as a manager, and identify effective and ineffective actions.
3. What should Jai say or do now?

CASE

American Financial Corporation

Betty Powell is the manager of human resources for American Financial Corporation, a large financial services company. When she arrived back in her office Monday after being away for a week, she discovered that a staffing report due the day before was still not finished. The report was for the vice president of the company's brokerage division, and Betty was supposed to give him the report by Wednesday.

Six weeks earlier Betty had asked Don Adams, one of her subordinates to collect the information and to write the staffing report. At that time she told him what should be included in the report and when it was due. It is not the first time Don has missed a deadline. His work is careful and meticulous, but he appears to be compulsive about checking and rechecking everything several times to avoid any mistakes.

Betty called Don and asked him to meet with her immediately. When Don came into her office, she greeted him and asked him to sit down. The following dialogue occurred.

"Don, I understand the staffing report for the brokerage division is not completed yet. The division vice president needs that report to prepare his annual budget, and he is putting a lot of pressure on me to get it to him immediately. When I gave you this assignment, you assured me that six weeks was ample time to do it."

"I'm sorry that the report wasn't ready on schedule," responded Don, "but it turned out to be much more complex than I initially expected. I had to spend extra time verifying the figures from the branch offices, because they just didn't look right. Just when I thought . . ."

"Look Don," interrupted Betty, "this is not the first time you have been late on an important project. You're supposed to be a professional, and professionals plan their work and get it done on time."

"It would not be very professional to do a report full of mistakes," replied Don. "It's important to me to do quality work that I can be proud of. It's not my fault that the branch managers don't keep accurate records."

"What types of mistakes did you find when you checked their records?" asked Betty.

"Well . . . , I didn't actually find any mistakes," replied Don, looking embarrassed, "but after I entered the information into the computer and did the preliminary analysis, I discovered that the records were missing for one of the branch offices. I lost a week waiting to get the missing information, but without it the report would not provide an accurate picture of the division's staffing needs. It's a good thing I noticed the . . . "

Betty interrupted impatiently, "Don, we have interns to do things like checking computer records and making sure they are complete. It sounds to me like you are not very efficient about managing your time. If you delegated some of these simple tasks, you wouldn't get so far behind in your work."

"The interns were busy working on the new financial reports," Don protested. "I don't get enough clerical support on any of my projects, and that's why they are sometimes late."

"Why didn't you inform me there were problems that might delay the report?" asked Betty, her voice showing she was becoming very annoyed. "I could have found you some clerical support."

Don was now becoming more defensive. "I tried to let you know last week, but you were on the West Coast for the management training workshop. I left a message for you to call me."

"Don, you have an excuse for everything, and nothing is ever your fault," Betty said sarcastically. "You seem to be incapable of planning the action steps needed to do a project like this one. You should have checked the records before you began the data analysis. As for the missing records, it wouldn't surprise me if they are buried somewhere under the piles of stuff laying around your office. You have the messiest office in the company."

Don looked sullen but did not reply. Betty continued her tirade. "Don, your career in this company is going to be very short unless you get your act together. I want that report in my hands by noon tomorrow, and no more excuses."

—*Written by* Gary Yukl

Questions

1. What did Betty do wrong prior to the meeting, and what could have been done to avoid missing the deadline?
2. What did Betty do wrong in the meeting itself, and what could have been done to make the meeting more effective?
3. What should Don have done to be more effective?

Chapter 11

Leadership in Teams and Decision Groups

Learning Objectives

After studying this chapter, you should be able to:

- Understand the processes that determine group performance.
- Understand how leaders can influence group processes and improve performance.
- Understand the types of subgroups and their effects on group processes and performance.
- Understand the leadership challenges for different types of teams.
- Understand effective procedures for leading teams.
- Understand the primary leadership functions in decision groups.
- Understand procedures for leading successful meetings.

Introduction

Most organizations have small subunits (departments, sections) that perform a functional task (e.g., production, operations, sales, accounting, research) under the supervision of an appointed manager. In many of these subunits, the members perform the same type of work, but they work alone, do not depend on each other, and need little coordination (e.g., sales representatives, professors, tax accountants, machine operators). This type of work unit is sometimes called a coacting group, because there is little role interdependence among the members.

The word team is correctly used to describe an interacting group that is small and has members with a common purpose, interdependent roles, and complementary skills. To clarify the distinction, interacting teams are found in basketball and soccer, whereas in bowling or wrestling the "teams" are actually co-acting groups. Dyadic leadership theories are useful for describing leadership in co-acting groups, but for interacting teams some additional leadership processes are needed to explain team performance.

A growing trend in organizations is to give more responsibility for important activities to teams, and in some cases they are empowered to make decisions formerly made by individual managers. Several distinct types of teams can be found in organizations, including functional work teams, cross-functional teams, self-managed teams, and top executive teams. The different

TABLE 11-1 Common Characteristics of Four Types of Teams

Defining Functional	Cross-Functional Team	Self-Managed Operating Team	Top Executive Team	Characteristic Team
Autonomy to determine mission and objectives	Low	Low to Moderate	Low to Moderate	High
Autonomy to determine work procedures	Low to Moderate	High	High	High
Authority of the internal leader	High	Low to Moderate	Low	High
Duration of existence for the team	High	Low to Moderate	High	High
Stability of the membership	High	Low to Moderate	High	High
Diversity of members in functional background	Low	High	Low	High

types of teams can be compared (see Table 11-1) with regard to duration of the team's existence, stability of team membership, functional diversity of members, authority of the internal leader, autonomy to determine the mission, and autonomy to determine work processes. The extent to which members are co-located or geographically dispersed ("virtual teams") is another basis for describing teams, but some degree of virtuality may be found in any type of team. This chapter examines what has been learned about effective leadership in functional work teams, cross-functional teams, and self-managed teams. Executive teams will be described in Chapter 12.

A related topic is leadership in the context of group meetings. As described in Chapter 4, meetings are commonly used to make decisions in organizations. Behavioral scientists have been studying leadership processes in such meetings for several decades, and practitioners have also contributed to our knowledge about the subject. The last section of the chapter examines effective leadership in meetings held to solve a problem or make a decision. The chapter begins with a description of collective processes that determine the performance of work groups and teams.

Determinants of Team Performance

In the past half century, theoretical explanations for team performance have been proposed by many scholars (DeChurch & Mesmer-Magnus, 2010; Gladstein, 1984; Hackman et al., 1976; Hewett, O'Brien, & Hornik, 1974; Kozlowski & Ilgen, 2006; McGrath, 1984; O'Brien & Kabanoff, 1981; Pearce & Ravlin, 1987; Shiflett, 1979; Wofford, 1982; Zaccaro, Rittman, & Marks, 2001). Several performance determinants have been identified for work groups and teams (see Table 11-2). Empirical studies on small groups and teams show that leaders can influence these performance determinants, and their relative importance depends on the type of team and situation (Burke et al., 2006; Hulsheger, Anderson, & Salgado, 2009; Morgeson, DeRue, & Karam, 2010). Each performance determinant and ways for leaders to influence it is briefly explained in this section of the chapter.

TABLE 11-2 Determinants of Team Performance

- Commitment to task objectives and strategies
- Member skills and role clarity
- Internal organization and coordination
- External coordination
- Resources and political support
- Mutual trust, cohesiveness, and cooperation
- Accurate, shared mental models
- Collective efficacy and potency
- Collective learning
- Member diversity

Commitment to Task Objectives and Strategies

Member commitment to task objectives and performance strategies for attaining them facilitate cooperation, innovation, and extra effort to accomplish difficult tasks (Hulsheger et al., 2009; Kotlyar, Karakowsky, & Ng, 2011; Kukenberger, Mathieu, & Ruddy, 2015; Mathieu & Rapp, 2009; Pearce & Ensley, 2004; Podsakoff, MacKenzie, & Ahearne, 1997; Ohana, 2016). Leadership behaviors that are especially relevant for increasing member commitment to shared objectives include: (1) articulating an appealing vision that links the task objectives to member values and ideals; (2) explaining why a project or new initiative is important; (3) setting task objectives that are clear and challenging; (4) planning relevant performance strategies for attaining the objectives; and (5) empowering members to participate in planning activities and developing creative solutions to problems.

In general, there is a positive correlation between member empowerment and group performance (Burke et al., 2006). However, as explained in Chapter 4, empowerment is not always successful. Many conditions can facilitate or inhibit the effects of empowerment in teams (Chen, Sharma, Edinger, Shapiro, & Farh, 2011; Cox, Pearce, & Perry, 2003; Hill & Bartol, 2016; Lorinkova, Pearsall, & Sims, 2013; Rapp, Gilson, Mathieu, & Ruddy, 2016; Seers, Keller, & Wilkerson, 2003). Examples include group size, diversity of members, geographic dispersion of members, the interpersonal skills and maturity of members, the amount of relational conflict, the nature of the task or mission, the level of team-based human resource support, the extent to which the leader is located within or outside the team, and competing loyalties of members to external constituents.

Member Skills and Role Clarity

Group performance will be higher when members have the knowledge and skills necessary to do the work, and they understand what to do, how to do it, when it must be done, and by whom (Grutterink, Van der Vegt, Molleman, & Jehn, 2013; Morgeson, Reider, & Campion, 2005). Member skills and clear role expectations are more important when the task is complex and difficult to learn, and during periods of change in team membership (Summers, Humphrey, & Ferris, 2012). A leader can do several things to improve member skills. When the team is being formed, or replacements are needed for departing members, the leader can influence the selection of new members and ensure an appropriate mix of complementary skills (Klimoski & Jones, 1995; Morgeson et al., 2010). In a newly formed team, or when the team has a new type of task to perform, the leader can clearly explain member responsibilities and relevant procedures for performing specific types of activities (Marks, Zaccaro, & Mathieu, 2000; Morgeson et al.,

2010). At appropriate times in the performance cycle, leaders can assess the skills of current members to identify any deficiencies, provide constructive feedback and coaching, and arrange for members to receive necessary instruction in other ways (e.g., from more experienced members, or in workshops and courses).

Internal Organization and Coordination

The performance of a team depends not only on the motivation and skills of members, but also on how members are organized to use their skills. The design of work roles and the assignment of people to them determine how efficiently the team carries out its work. Performance will suffer if a team has talented people but they are given tasks for which their skills are irrelevant or the team uses a performance strategy that is not consistent with member skills (Morgeson et al., 2010).

Team performance also depends on the extent to which the interdependent activities of different members are mutually consistent and synchronized. A high level of coordination is especially important when the team performs a complex task under rapidly changing conditions (Gabelica, Van den Bossche, Fiore, Segers, & Gijselaers, 2016). Coordination is determined by decisions made during the planning phase prior to the start of a new task, and a team will usually perform a new task better if members plan an explicit strategy that takes into account potential obstacles and problems that could limit performance (Courtright, McCormick, Mistry, & Wang, 2017; Fisher, 2014; Hackman & Morris, 1975; Sverdrup, Schei, & Tjølsen, 2017; Tesluk & Mathieu, 1999). Coordination is also facilitated by adjustments in member behavior during the team's performance of the task (Banks, Pollack, & Seers, 2016; Gabelica et al., 2016; Rico, Sanchez-Manzanares, Gil, & Gibson, 2008).

The increased importance of cooperation and coordination among interdependent members of interacting groups makes leadership more difficult than in co-acting work groups. A leader can do several things to ensure that necessary activities are well organized and carried out in a timely, efficient way. Relevant leadership behaviors include: (1) planning how to make efficient use of personnel and resources; (2) making contingency plans to deal with possible obstacles and emergencies; (3) involving members with relevant expertise in planning team activities; (4) leading meetings to collectively solve problems and plan activities; (5) planning how to schedule and sequence activities to avoid unnecessary delays or wasted time; (6) and actively monitoring and directing the work.

When the team performs a complex task under rapidly changing conditions, it may be necessary to have members share some of the responsibility for internal coordination. The leader can help members learn to anticipate each other's reactions to changing conditions and quickly adjust their own behavior as needed. Developing member skills about how to work together as a team is facilitated by ensuring that they understand how their roles are interrelated and by frequent rehearsal of complex activities (Morgeson et al., 2010). Training together under realistic conditions is especially important for teams that have difficult, dangerous activities to perform (e.g., combat teams, disaster relief teams, emergency medical teams, SWAT teams, firefighting teams) (Parker, Schmutz, & Manser, 2018).

External Coordination

The performance of a team also depends upon the extent to which team activities are consistent with related activities in other parts of the organization, and the importance of this external coordination increases as interdependence increases (de Vries, Walter, van der Vegt, &

Essens, 2014; Marks, DeChurch, Mathieu, Panzer, & Alonso, 2005; Marrone, 2010). It is essential for leaders to facilitate communication and coordination not only with other parts of the same organization, but also with outsiders whose decisions and actions affect the group (Ancona, 1990; Galbraith, 1973; Hogg, Van Knippenberg, & Rast III, 2012; Marks et al., 2000; Sundstrom, DeMeuse, & Futrell, 1990). Such coordination is especially important in multi-team systems, where team leaders must work with the leaders of other teams to facilitate inter-team cooperation and synchronization of task activities (Carter & DeChurch, 2014; Davison et al., 2012; Lanaj, Hollenbeck, Ilgen, Barnes, & Harmon, 2013; Murase et al., 2014).

Many specific types of leadership behaviors are relevant for improving external coordination and adaptation. Examples include: (1) maintaining a network of contacts who can provide relevant information; (2) encouraging members to develop their own networks of useful contacts; (3) consulting with other subunits about plans and decisions that affect them; (4) monitoring progress in operations involving other subunits or organizations; (5) meeting with clients or users to learn more about their needs; and (6) negotiating agreements with clients. As in the case of internal coordination, responsibility for the leadership functions can be shared by members of the team.

Resources and Political Support

Group performance also depends on getting essential resources, and political support from outside sources (Ancona & Caldwell, 1992; Druskat & Wheeler, 2003; Marrone, Tesluk, & Carson, 2007; Peters, O'Connor, & Eulberg, 1985; Tesluk & Mathieu, 1999). Relevant resources may include budgetary funds, tools and equipment, supplies and materials, and facilities. A production team cannot maintain a high level of output without a dependable supply of materials. An air force crew will be rendered ineffective if they have no jet fuel to fly their plane. Maintaining a dependable supply of resources is especially important when the work cannot be done without them and no substitutes can be found. Resource acquisition is less important for a group that needs few resources to do the work or has its own ample supply of resources.

An important leadership responsibility is to obtain essential resources, assistance, and support from outside sources (Hassan et al., 2018; Morgeson et al., 2010). Examples of relevant leadership behaviors include: (1) planning the resources required for a special project or activity; (2) lobbying with superiors or outsiders to provide additional resources; (3) influencing superiors to authorize use of unusual equipment, supplies, or materials; (4) promoting and defending the reputation of the team with superiors; (5) establishing cooperative relationships with outsiders who are a potential source of necessary resources and assistance; and (6) negotiating favorable agreements with suppliers and vendors.

Cooperation and Mutual Trust

A recent meta-analysis by De Jong, Dirks, and Gillespie (2016) documents that there is a strong relationship between intra-team trust and team performance, especially in teams characterized by high levels of task interdependence, centralized authority, and specialized member knowledge and skills. A high level of cooperation and mutual trust is more likely when members identify with the team or work unit, value their membership, and are very cohesive (Barrick, Stewart, Neubert, & Mount, 1998; Costa, Fulmer, & Anderson, 2018; Watson, Kumar, & Michaelsen, 1993; Van der Vegt & Bunderson, 2005). It is more difficult to have a high level of cohesiveness and group identification in newly formed teams, in teams with frequent changes in membership, in teams with members who represent competing subunits of the organization, in teams with members who are culturally diverse, in teams with emotionally immature members, and in teams with members who must work in close proximity for long periods of time under stressful conditions (e.g., crew of a submarine). Social identity theories of effective leadership describe the processes by which leaders help to define the identity of a group and the meaning of membership (e.g., Epitropaki et al., 2017; Fransen et al., 2015; Reicher, Haslam, & Hopkins, 2005; van Knippenberg, 2018; van Knippenberg et al., 2004). There are many ways a leader can increase mutual trust and collective identification with the team. Examples include: (1) articulating an appealing vision of what the team can jointly accomplish; (2) using symbols and rituals to make membership more unique and desirable; (3) conducting team-building activities; and (4) making recognition and rewards contingent on member contributions to team performance.

High cohesiveness can provide both benefits and risks for group decisions. A cohesive group of people with similar values and attitudes is more likely to agree on a decision, but such groups sometimes foster a phenomenon called "groupthink" (Janis, 1972; Thompson, 2014). When members of a cohesive group are unwilling to risk social rejection for questioning a majority viewpoint or presenting a dissenting opinion, the critical evaluation of ideas is inhibited and creativity is reduced. The group strives to maintain the illusion of internal harmony by avoiding open expression of disagreement, and members may agree too quickly without a complete, objective evaluation of the alternatives. Members in these groups may develop an illusion of invulnerability, which will cause them to overestimate the probability of success for a risky course of action. If the group has a shared illusion of moral superiority, it will be easier to justify a course of action that would normally be considered unethical by individual members.

Collective Efficacy and Potency

Member commitment depends in part on the shared belief of members that the team is capable of successfully carrying out its mission and achieving specific task objectives (Bandura, 2000; Guzzo, Yost, Campbell, & Shea, 1993; Pearce, Gallagher, & Ensley, 2002). This shared belief is called "collective efficacy" or "potency." Several studies provide evidence that it is related to team performance (e.g., Chen & Bliese, 2002; Gibson, 2001; Gibson, Randel, & Earley, 2000; Gully, Incalcaterra, Joshi, & Beaubien, 2002; Hu & Liden, 2011; O'Neill, McLarnon, Xiu, & Law, 2016; Pearce et al., 2002; Wu et al., 2010). Collective efficacy is likely to be higher for a team with strong member skills, a high level of mutual trust and cooperation, ample resources, and a relevant performance strategy. Prior success can increase collective efficacy, which in turn can enhance a team's subsequent performance. A downward spiral can also occur, with failure resulting in lower collective efficacy, negative affect, and additional declines in performance. High collective efficacy is desirable, but the perception of capabilities should be realistic; as noted earlier, overconfidence can encourage a team to pursue very risky strategies that will fail.

A leader can influence collective efficacy in several ways (Bass, Avolio, Jung, & Berson, 2003; Eden, 1990; Gil, Rico, Alcover, & Barrasa, 2005; Hoyt, Murphy, Halverson, & Watson, 2003; Hu & Liden, 2011; Kouzes & Posner, 1987; Lester, Meglino, & Korsgaard, 2002; Sivasubramaniam, Murry, Avolio, & Jung, 2002; Srivastava, Bartol, & Locke, 2006; Sutton & Woodman, 1989). Behaviors that influence collective efficacy include: (1) expressing optimism and confidence in the team; (2) setting realistic goals or targets that will provide an opportunity to experience early success; (3) helping the team find ways to overcome obstacles; and (4) celebrating progress and important achievements.

Accurate, Shared Mental Models

The term "mental model" is commonly used to describe conscious beliefs and implicit assumptions about the causes of performance and the best way to improve it (Cannon-Bowers et al., 1993; Gary & Wood, 2016; Klimoski & Mohammed, 1994; Senge, 1990). Research on teams found that they are likely to have higher performance if members have a shared mental model that is accurate (Dionne, Sayama, Hao, & Bush, 2010; Edwards, Day, Arthur, & Bell, 2006; Lim & Klein, 2006; Mohammed, Ferzandi, & Hamilton, 2010; Santos, Uitdewilligen, & Passos, 2015; Uitdewilligen & Waller, 2018). Problem solving is more difficult when team members have different assumptions about the cause of the problem. A shared understanding about cause-effect relationships can facilitate the development of effective strategies and plans by a team and increase member commitment to implement them. However, group performance is unlikely to improve unless the mental model is not only shared but also accurate.

Leaders can help members identify their assumptions about cause-effect relationships, determine ways to assess the accuracy of these assumptions, and jointly develop a more accurate mental model. Ways to improve understanding and agreement about causes of problems and good solutions include the following: (1) hold a meeting to discuss member assumptions and beliefs and identify any supporting evidence; (2) examine relevant publications on the subject; (3) implement more accurate measures of team processes and performance determinants; (4) conduct controlled experiments to assess cause-effect relationships; and (5) conduct after-activity reviews to improve learning from experience (see description later in this chapter). How leaders can facilitate collective learning was described in Chapter 5, and research on teams provides evidence for the importance of this leadership function (Edmondson, 2003; Marcy, 2015; Morgeson et al., 2010).

Member Diversity

The extent to which members vary with regard to personality, demographic attributes (e.g., age, gender, ethnic identity, education), and functional specialization has implications for group processes and outcomes (Joshi & Roh, 2009; Kearney, Gebert, & Voelpel, 2009; Shore et al., 2011; Srikanth, Harvey, & Peterson, 2016). Groups with diverse membership are likely to be less cohesive, because people tend to be less accepting of others who have different beliefs, values, and traditions. Diversity can also impede communication when members use different language, jargon, measures, or criteria. On the positive side, having members with different perspectives, experiences, and knowledge can result in more creative solutions to problems (Wang, Kim, & Lee, 2016). The importance of diversity for group performance varies somewhat for different types of groups and different situations (Bell, Villado, Lukasik, Belau, & Briggs, 2011; Horwitz, S., & Horwitz, I., 2007; Srikanth et al., 2016). It is easier to convert diversity into cooperative problem solving when members are highly interdependent for attainment of important shared objectives, but making it happen is a major leadership challenge. A leader with the authority to determine the membership of a work group can try to select members who are diverse in terms of their background and relevant knowledge (Mitchell et al., 2015).

Group Process Dichotomies

Some scholars have proposed a broad two-factor classification of group processes that can affect the importance of the performance determinants and the relevance of different leadership functions (Bales, 1950; Katz & Kahn, 1978; Marks, Mathieu, & Zaccaro, 2001; Morgeson et al., 2010). These process distinctions can be used to help understand effective leadership in a group or team.

One distinction is between the transition phase and performance phase of group activities. The transition phase involves determining who will be members of the group and making initial decisions about performance strategies, work assignments, and member roles in the group. If the mission, objectives, and formal leadership roles for the group are not already determined by the parent organization, then these decisions must be made as well. The transition phase is very important in a newly formed group, or when an existing group is given responsibility for a new type of project. The performance phase involves implementing and executing performance strategies, maintaining member commitment and cooperation, monitoring and assessing performance, and resolving any problems in the work. Groups typically alternate between the two phases, and the phases can overlap when unexpected problems require revision of earlier plans and decisions.

Another distinction is between internal processes versus external processes. The internal processes involve relationships among the group members and decisions about work procedures and member roles. The external processes involve interactions and relationships with the larger organization and outsiders such as clients and suppliers. Both types of processes occur during the transition and performance phases. Leadership may be provided by an elected or appointed leader, by individual members, and by an external leader in the organization with authority over group tasks, procedures, and resources.

Subgroups in Work Teams

Within many work teams, subgroups emerge due to the nature of the team's composition. An example would be a gender divide, or "fault line," between three male and three female members (Lau & Murnighan, 2005). Carton and Cummings (2012) developed a typology that distinguishes among three basic types of subgroups: (1) identity-based; (2) resource-based; and (3) knowledge-based.

Identity-based subgroups have members who share a common identity, based on demographic (e.g., gender, race/ethnicity, age, functional background) or values-based (e.g., political or religious affiliation) attributes. Subgroup processes often arise from efforts to protect the subgroup's identity, and such efforts may fragment the team's overall identity. For example, cliques of members who share lifestyle values may emerge and cause destructive rivalries to form.

Resource-based subgroups form when certain members align and achieve dominance over other members through the control of finite resources and differences in authority, power, and status. They emerge when a clear hierarchy among subgroups is apparent or when members attempt to create such a hierarchy. Interteam coalitions, factions, alliances, and blocks are examples of resource-based subgroups. Processes within resource-based subgroups often revolve around unbalanced perceptions of fairness and the centralization of power within the team. For example, because top management team members with line authority typically have more power than members who occupy staff positions, alliances among the line and staff members may form to promote their shared interests.

Knowledge-based subgroups emerge because organizations develop specialized units to address specific domains of knowledge, such as management information systems, human resource management, and accounting. Team members from different knowledge-based subgroups typically employ unique technical jargon and symbols and possess shared mental models about their work. In a subsequent field study of work teams, Carton and Cummings (2013) examined the effects of identity-based and knowledge-based subgroups on work team performance. While the presence of two identity-based subgroups created friction and adversely impacted team performance, the performance of work teams improved as the number of knowledge-based subgroups increased due to the benefits of diverse knowledge and expertise.

Functional and Cross-Functional Work Teams

Functional Work Teams

In a functional operating team, the members are likely to have jobs that are somewhat specialized but still part of the same basic function (e.g., equipment operating crew, maintenance crew, combat squad, submarine crew, SWAT team). The teams typically continue operating for a long duration of time, and the membership is relatively stable. There is usually an appointed leader who has considerable authority for internal operations and managing external relationships with other parts of the organization. Most leadership responsibilities are carried out by this formal leader, but other group members (such as an assistant leader) may perform specific leadership functions.

Effective leadership in functional work teams may require many specific types of leadership behavior. Examples of specific behaviors that can be used to influence each type of performance determinant are listed in Table 11-3. The optimal pattern of behavior is not the same for each type of functional team. The appropriate pattern of behavior will depend on the situation and the relative importance of the performance determinants at that time.

Many of the required leader behaviors in a functional work team are similar to the task-oriented and relations-oriented behaviors described in Chapter 2. If team members are not highly motivated and performance is less than it should be, then the leader may need to inspire and challenge members to increase their commitment to team objectives. If major changes are being implemented by the organization, then some change-oriented behaviors (see Chapter 5) may be needed. How much external behavior (e.g., representing, lobbying) is needed will vary depending on coordination requirements with other parts of the organization, variation in the demand for the group's products or services, and the adequacy of resources already provided by the organization. To cope with disruptions and immediate crises, some problem-solving and crisis management behaviors may be necessary (see Chapter 4).

TABLE 11-3 Leader Behaviors Influencing Performance Determinants for Teams

Leadership Behavior	Performance Determinant
Visioning, expressing confidence, celebrating progress	Task commitment, collective efficacy
Recruiting and selecting competent team members	Member skills, collective efficacy
Coaching, training, and clarifying role expectations and priorities	Member skills and role clarity, individual and collective efficacy
Planning and organizing team activities and projects	Efficiency and internal coordination, collective efficacy
Facilitating collective learning by the team	Adaptation to change, performance quality (e.g., strategies, collective efficacy)
Team building and conflict resolution	Mutual trust and cooperation, member identification with the team
Networking and external monitoring	Adaptation to change, external coordination, quality of performance strategies
Representing (promoting, lobbying, negotiating)	Resources and political support, external coordination

Cross-Functional Work Teams

Cross-functional teams are being used increasingly in organizations to improve coordination of interdependent activities among specialized subunits. The team usually includes representatives from each of the functional subunits involved in a project, and it may include representatives from outside organizations such as suppliers, clients, and joint venture partners. The team is given responsibility for planning and conducting a complex activity that requires considerable coordination, cooperation, and joint problem solving among the parties (Ford & Randolph, 1992). Examples of these activities include developing a new product and bringing it into production, implementing a new information system, identifying ways to improve product quality, planning an ad campaign for the client of an advertising agency, carrying out a consulting project, developing a new health-care program in a hospital, and developing a new MBA program in a university.

Separate cross-functional teams may be formed in an organization for different activities, projects, or clients. Some cross-functional teams may be permanent additions to the formal structure of the organization, but most of the teams are temporary and only exist until they complete their task or mission. The membership may be stable over the life of the team, or it may change as some functions become more important and others decline in importance (e.g., product development teams). The members may work for the team either on a part-time or full-time basis. In many cross-functional teams, the members are also in a functional subunit of the organization, and in some cases they are members of more than one cross-functional team.

Cross-functional teams offer many potential benefits to an organization (Ford & Randolph, 1992; Manz & Sims, 1993). The teams allow flexible, efficient deployment of personnel and resources to solve problems as they are discovered. Functional expertise is preserved because team members maintain close contact with their respective functional areas. Coordination is improved and many problems are avoided when people from different functions come together to work on a project at the same time, rather than working on it sequentially. The diversity of member backgrounds fosters communication with external sources of ideas and information, and it increases creativity in the generation of ideas and problem solutions (Keller, 2001). Working on a cross-functional team helps members learn to view a problem or challenge from different perspectives, rather than from only a narrow functional viewpoint. Members can learn new skills that will be carried back to their functional jobs and to subsequent teams.

Many organizations have reported great success with cross-functional teams. For example, a cross-functional team at Chrysler developed an innovative new subcompact (the Neon) in a record time of only 42 months and at a fraction of the cost of developing new models at other car companies (Woodruff, 1993). At Hallmark Cards, the use of teams drastically reduced the time needed to bring new holiday and greeting cards to market from more than three years to less than one year, while also improving quality and responsiveness to changing customer preferences (George & Jones, 1996). However, cross-functional teams are not always successful, and effective leadership is required to meet the challenges inherent in the use of these teams.

The same conditions that create potential advantages for a cross-functional team also create difficulties (Denison, Hart, & Kahn, 1996; Ford & Randolph, 1992). Members of cross-functional teams usually have conflicting loyalties to the team and their home department. Members may be more concerned about protecting their functional turf than about accomplishing team objectives. Decisions can become difficult and time consuming if members need to get approval from their functional superiors before agreeing to a major change. The team usually has tight deadlines to meet for completing its work, which puts additional pressure on the leader to resolve disagreements and maintain steady progress.

Meetings are time consuming, and it can be difficult to get sufficient participation from team members who also have responsibilities in a functional department or other cross-functional teams. The functional diversity of the members increases communication barriers, because each function usually has its own jargon and ways of thinking about things (Cronin & Weingart, 2007). The functional subunits represented by team members often have different objectives, different priorities, and a different time orientation. These differences can create conflicts, as shown in the following example from a large petrochemicals company (Stern, 1993):

> A team was formed to develop a better plastic resin. Members from the research department wanted to spend several months developing a new resin. Members from the production and marketing departments wanted to alter the existing product and quickly get it into production. The project was stalled for a long time because the different factions could not agree about a strategy.

Leadership in Cross-Functional Teams

Most cross-functional teams have a formal leader who is selected by higher management, because a strong leader is needed to deal with the difficult challenges facing the teams (Hollenbeck, Beersma, & Schouten, 2012). To gain commitment and resolve disagreements, the designated leader needs substantial position power and good interpersonal skills. Higher management should appoint a qualified leader and provide a clear mission, necessary resources, and political support for the implementation of ideas developed by the team.

Despite the extensive use of cross-functional project teams, research on the skills required for effective leadership in these teams is still limited. However, the research suggests that team leaders need technical expertise, cognitive skills, interpersonal and political skills, and administrative skills relevant for project management (Ehrhardt, Miller, Freeman, & Hom, 2014; Ford & Randolph, 1992; Mumford, Hunter, Eubanks, Bedell, & Murphy, 2007; Mumford, Scott, Baddis, & Strange, 2002). How each type of skill is relevant for leadership in cross-functional project teams is shown in Table 11-4.

Creativity is an important requirement for the success of most cross-functional project teams. In their review of research on leading creative teams, Mumford et al. (2002) found three themes that described essential processes: (1) idea generation, (2) idea structuring, and (3) idea promotion. These themes indicate specific roles or types of leadership behavior that are relevant for each process. With regard to idea generation, it is essential for the leader to stimulate and

TABLE 11-4 Skills Required for Leading Cross-Functional Project Teams

Technical expertise: The leader must be able to communicate about technical matters with team members from diverse functional backgrounds.

Project management skills: The leader must be able to plan and organize the project activities, select qualified members of the team, and handle budgeting and financial responsibilities.

Interpersonal skills: The leader must be able to understand the needs and values of team members, influence them, resolve conflicts, and build cohesiveness.

Cognitive skills: The leader must be able to solve complex problems that require creativity and systems thinking, and must understand how the different functions are relevant to the success of the project.

Political skills: The leader must be able to develop coalitions and gain resources, assistance, and approvals from top management and other relevant parties.

facilitate creativity by members. With regard to idea structuring, it is important for the leader to provide clear objectives for the project and explain how it is relevant for the organization, but also to allow ample autonomy with regard to how the project objectives will be attained. With regard to idea promotion, necessary resources and support for the project must be obtained from the parent organization. A more recent review by Mumford, Mulhearn, Watts, Steele and McIntosh (2017) provides further empirical evidence of the importance of these processes to team creativity and performance.

From interviews and observations of teams, Barry (1991) identified four leadership roles that appear to be essential for teams that solve problems, manage projects, or develop policies for an organization. The roles include (1) envisioning, (2) organizing, (3) social integrating, and (4) external spanning. Envisioning provides a shared objective, organizing helps the team decide how to attain it, social integrating helps to maintain internal cohesiveness, and external spanning helps to keep group decisions compatible with the needs of stakeholders outside the team. The four roles also provide a parsimonious way to describe the specific leadership behaviors used in cross-functional groups to build task commitment, develop effective performance strategies, ensure member trust and cooperation, obtain necessary resources, and maintain external coordination. A modified version of the four-role taxonomy that incorporates other findings in team leadership is shown in Table 11-5.

The relative importance of the different leadership roles varies somewhat depending on the stage of group development. For example, envisioning is especially important when the group is forming, whereas organizing is more important after the group has agreed on an objective. Even when the capacity to provide each type of leadership is present, the team will not be successful unless the leader and members understand that different patterns of leadership are needed at

TABLE 11-5 Leadership Behaviors Needed in Cross-Functional Teams

Envisioning

- Articulating strategic objectives or a vision that inspires commitment by team members
- Helping the team understand and improve their assumptions and mental models regarding the relationships among task variables
- Suggesting creative ideas and encouraging the team to consider innovative performance strategies

Organizing

- Planning and scheduling team activities to achieve coordination and meet project deadlines
- Helping the team establish standards and methods for assessing progress and performance
- Arranging and conducting meetings to solve problems and make decisions in a systematic way

Social Integrating

- Encouraging mutual trust, acceptance, and cooperation among team members
- Facilitating open communication, equal participation, and tolerance of dissenting views
- Mediating conflicts among members and helping them find integrative solutions

External Spanning

- Monitoring the external environment of the team to identify client needs, emerging problems, and political processes that will affect the team
- Promoting a favorable image of the team among outsiders
- Influencing people outside the team to provide adequate resources, approvals, assistance, and cooperation

different times. Research on cross-functional teams indicates that the leader must be flexible and adaptive as conditions change (e.g., Lewis, Welsh, Dehler, & Green, 2002).

The difficulties and obstacles facing many cross-functional teams are so great that the formal leader may be unable to carry out all of the relevant leadership roles alone. The different lines of research on leadership in cross-functional teams all indicate that success requires the efforts of multiple leaders (Barry, 1991; Cohen & Bailey, 1997; Mumford et al., 2002). Some of the internal leadership responsibilities may be shared at times with individual members of the team who have special expertise about a particular aspect of the project. However, the teams should not be self-managed. Research on the use of cross-functional project teams finds that they are less likely to be successful if they do not have a strong, designated leader, because too much time is consumed by process problems and unresolved conflicts (Cohen & Bailey, 1997).

Virtual Teams

In virtual teams, the members are geographically separated and they seldom if ever meet face-to-face (Bell & Kozlowski, 2002; Gilson, Maynard, Young, Vartianen, & Hakonen, 2015; Martins, Gilson, & Maynard, 2004). Most of the communication among members relies on computer and telecommunications technology (e.g., e-mail, texting, videoconferencing, groupware, cellular phones). There has been a rapid increase in the use of virtual teams in organizations, and some writers have predicted that they will revolutionize the workplace of the future (Ford, Piccolo, & Ford, 2017). There are several reasons for increased use of virtual teams, including the rapid pace of globalization, increased use of joint ventures, employee desire for more flexibility in work arrangements (e.g., telecommuting, independent contractors), growing emphasis on service and knowledge management activities, and need for more flexibility and innovation in product development and delivery of customized services.

Any type of team can be virtual, but the most common form is a cross-functional team. A virtual team may be either a temporary arrangement to carry out a specific task, or a more durable arrangement to carry out responsibilities such as solving technical problems, planning recurring events, coordinating activities among dispersed units of an organization, and maintaining external coordination with suppliers and clients.

Virtual teams can provide several potential benefits compared to a co-located team. With virtual teams it is possible to involve the most qualified persons who are available to work on a project or make a decision, regardless of where they are located. The membership of virtual teams is often fluid, because the technology makes it easy for people to participate in different ways only when they are needed. As compared to teams with members who work together in the same location ("co-located teams"), a virtual team is more likely to have members from different cultures, time zones, and organizations. An example of a virtual cross-functional team is a localized project group that is responsible for oil drilling in the North Sea and requires technical assistance from other teams drilling in remote locations, as well as expertise from engineers located at the organization's home office (Ford et al., 2017).

Having a diverse, fluid membership creates additional problems and unique leadership challenges that may prevent the team from realizing the potential benefits (Liao, 2017). The lack of frequent face-to-face contact makes it more difficult to monitor the performance of members, to influence members, and to develop mutual trust and collective identification. It is difficult to gain commitment from diverse members with responsibilities in their local work unit that may be more important to them. Coordination problems may be more difficult to resolve in a virtual team than in a co-located team, especially when members have highly interdependent roles and the environment is dynamic and unpredictable. The leadership challenges are increased when members represent different organizations and are located in different time zones and cultures.

In the past two decades there has been an increase in research on the differences between co-located and geographically dispersed teams (see Bell & Kozlowski, 2002; Breuer, Hüffmeier, & Hertel, 2016; Carte, Chidambaram, & Becker, 2006; Gilson et al., 2015; Kirkman, Rosen, Tesluk, & Gibson, 2004; Martins et al., 2004; Mesmer-Magnus, DeChurch, Jimenez-Rodriguez, Wildman, & Shuffler, 2011; O'Neill, Hancock, Zivkov, Larson, & Law, 2016; Pridmore & Phillips-Wren, 2011; Purvanova & Bono, 2009; Serban et al., 2015). It is likely that the same leadership roles are relevant for both types of teams, but the relative importance of these roles and how they are enacted may differ for virtual teams (Hoch & Kozlowski, 2014; Liao, 2017). More research is needed to clarify these issues.

Finally, the rapid pace of development in communication technology will have important implications for virtual teams in the near future. For example, holographic projection technology could be used to make it appear that team members are sitting around the same conference table, even though they are actually in different parts of the world. New developments in artificial intelligence may make it possible for some leadership functions to be shifted from humans to robots. As changes occur in the way virtuality is experienced by a team, earlier research findings will need to be verified and new research methods may be needed.

Self-Managed Work Teams

In self-managed work teams (sometimes called semi-autonomous work groups), much of the responsibility and authority usually vested in a manager's position is turned over to the team members (Cohen & Bailey, 1997; Hollenbeck et al., 2012; Ingvaldsen & Rolfsen, 2012; Lanaj & Hollenbeck, 2015; Millikin, Hom, & Manz, 2010; Orsburn, Moran, Musselwhite, & Zenger, 1990; Wellins, Byham, & Wilson, 1991). Most self-managed work teams are responsible for producing a distinct product or service. Any type of team can be "self-managed," but this form of team governance is typically used for teams that perform the same type of operational task repeatedly and have a relatively stable membership over time. Unlike cross-functional project teams, the members of self-managed teams typically have similar functional backgrounds (e.g., maintenance technicians, production operators). The members often take turns performing the various tasks for which the team is responsible. When members learn to perform multiple tasks, it increases team flexibility, makes the work more interesting, and provides an opportunity to learn new skills.

Self-managed teams are used most often for manufacturing work or process production, but they are finding increasing application to service work. Examples of companies that have used self-managed teams include AT&T, Colgate-Palmolive Company, Cummins Engine Company, Digital Equipment Corporation, General Electric, General Foods, Goodyear Tire and Rubber, Motorola, Procter and Gamble, TRW, Volvo, Xerox, General Motors, Dr. Reddy's and Mastek.

The parent organization usually determines the mission, scope of operations, and the budget for self-managed teams. The amount of authority for other types of decisions varies greatly from one organization to another. Each team is usually given authority and responsibility for operating decisions such as setting performance goals and quality standards, assigning work, determining work schedules, determining work procedures, making purchases of necessary supplies and materials, dealing with customers and suppliers, evaluating team member performance, and handling performance problems of individual members. The teams are usually allowed to make small expenditures for supplies and equipment without prior approval, but in most organizations any recommendations for large purchases must be approved by management. Sometimes self-managed teams are also given the primary responsibility for personnel decisions such as selecting, hiring, and firing team members, and determining pay rates (within specified limits).

Benefits and Limitations of Self-Managed Teams

Self-managed work teams offer a number of potential benefits, including stronger commitment of team members to the work, more effective management of work-related problems, improved efficiency, more job satisfaction, less turnover, and less absenteeism. Having team members cross-trained to do different jobs makes the work more interesting for members and increases the flexibility of the team in dealing with personnel shortages resulting from illness or turnover. Their extensive knowledge of work processes helps team members solve problems and suggest improvements. Finally, the changeover to self-managed teams typically reduces the number of managers and staff specialists in an organization, which lowers costs.

How many of these potential benefits are realized depends greatly on how the teams are implemented in an organization. One determinant is the amount of autonomy provided to the team, and member feelings of collective empowerment (Kirkman & Rosen, 1999; Tesluk & Matthieu, 1999). Giving authority to a self-managed team rather than to an individual leader does not necessarily result in collective feelings of empowerment. The team may use the same type of social pressure on members to conform to strict group norms and established procedures (Barker, 1993; Sinclair, 1992).

Reviews of the literature on self-managed teams (Cohen & Bailey, 1997; Goodman, Devadas, & Hughson, 1988; Kirkman & Rosen, 1999; Pearce & Ravlin, 1987) suggest that this form of employee empowerment can improve job satisfaction and team performance. However, much of the evidence is based on weak research methods or anecdotal reports published in business periodicals. Only a small number of experimental or quasi-experimental field studies have been conducted to evaluate self-managed teams (e.g., Banker, Field, Schroeder, & Sinha, 1996; Cohen & Ledford, 1994; Cordery, Mueller, & Smith, 1991; Pasmore, 1978; Pearson, 1992; Wall, Kemp, Jackson, & Clegg, 1986). These studies found some favorable outcomes for self-managed teams, but the results were not consistent from study to study and did not substantiate the large performance improvements claimed in some anecdotal reports.

Self-managed teams are difficult to implement, and they can be a dismal failure when used in inappropriate situations or without competent leadership and support (Hackman, 1986; Lawler, 1986). If interpersonal conflicts cannot be resolved in a constructive way that will ensure a high level of interpersonal trust and cooperation, then the team may restructure itself with more independent roles, thereby reducing the potential benefits and performance gains (Langfred, 2007). The research on self-managed teams suggests several conditions under which the potential advantages are likely to be realized, and they are listed in Table 11-6 (Carson, Tesluk, & Marrone, 2007; Cohen & Bailey, 1997; Goodman, Devadas, & Hughson, 1988; Hackman, 1986; Ingvaldsen & Rolfsen, 2012; Kirkman & Rosen, 1999; Lanaj & Hollenbeck, 2015; Mathieu, Gilson, & Ruddy, 2006; McIntyre & Foti, 2013; Millikin et al., 2010; Muehlfeld, van Doorn, & van Witteloostuijn, 2011; Pearce & Ravlin, 1987; Stewart et al., 2009; Sundstrom et al., 1990; Yang & Guy, 2011).

TABLE 11-6 Facilitating Conditions for Self-Managed Teams

- Clearly defined, shared objectives
- Complex and meaningful tasks
- Small size and stable membership
- Members can determine work processes
- Members have relevant skills
- Member access to relevant information
- Appropriate recognition and rewards
- Strong support by top management
- Competent external leader

Leadership in Self-Managed Teams

When describing leadership in self-managed teams, it is helpful to differentiate between internal and external leadership roles. The internal leadership role involves management responsibilities assigned to the team and shared by group members. It is typical for self-managed teams to have an internal team leader who is elected by the members, and the position may be rotated among different members on a regular basis (e.g., quarterly or annually). Whether elected or appointed, the team leader does not simply replace the former first-line manager. In self-managed teams, most important responsibilities are usually shared by group members, not concentrated in the team leader. The primary responsibility of the internal leader is to coordinate and facilitate the process of making and implementing team decisions (e.g., conduct meetings, prepare work schedules and administrative paperwork).

Internal leadership in self-managed teams can take other forms besides rotation of the team leader position among members, and the amount of shared leadership and what aspects are shared can vary significantly (Carson et al., 2007; McIntyre & Foti, 2013). One form of shared leadership occurs when members meet to discuss important matters and make a group decision. A member with relevant expertise may assume responsibility for providing coordination and direction on specific team activities. Routine administrative tasks may be assigned to individual members, or someone with a strong interest in a task may take the initiative to do it without being asked. Difficult supervisory functions such as enforcing group norms may be performed collectively, as in the following example described by Barker (1993):

> A small manufacturing company changed from traditionally managed work groups to self-managed teams. The team members collectively formulated standards of appropriate behavior. The new standards were more demanding than the earlier work rules, and compared to the supervisors of the traditionally managed work groups, the team was less tolerant of unacceptable behavior. Members first confronted an offender with a reminder of the standards or a warning to improve, then they used their coercive power to dismiss anyone who was not willing to do what was expected.

The role of an external leader involves managerial responsibilities not delegated to the team. The external leaders may be middle managers, special facilitators, or some of the previous first-line supervisors (Morgeson et al., 2010). Each external leader usually works with several teams. One leadership role that is especially important when the team is formed is to serve as a coach, facilitator, and consultant to the team. Considerable coaching and encouragement are usually necessary to get a new team off to a successful start. The type of coaching needed to facilitate shared leadership is different from providing specific advice about better procedures for doing the work. Leadership coaching includes helping members learn how to plan and organize the work, make group decisions, resolve conflicts, and cooperate effectively as a team. Most of these skills are difficult for members to learn, and it may take several months for the team to become proficient in managing its own task and interpersonal processes. During this learning period, an important function of the external leader is to build the self-confidence of team members. As the group evolves, members can gradually assume more responsibility for coaching new members and improving their own working relationships.

Another important role is to obtain necessary information, resources, and political support from the organization. Because external leaders serve as a linking pin between the team and organization, it is essential to build and maintain cooperative relationships and an effective exchange of information. The external leader must be able to influence team members to think and behave in ways that increase team effectiveness, and to influence other people in the organization to do what is necessary to facilitate team effectiveness. Unlike leaders of traditional functional teams, external leaders of self-managed teams are less likely to use their legitimate power in directive ways to influence the team; instead, they are more likely to ask questions and use influence based on their expert and referent power (Druskat & Wheeler, 2003).

A competent external leader is important for the success of self-managed teams, not only in the transition phase but also in the performance phase (Cohen, Chang, & Ledford, 1997; Gibson & Vermeulen, 2003; Morgeson, 2005; Morgeson & DeRue, 2006). As the team continues to develop, the external leader should communicate clear expectations about new responsibilities of members for regulating their own behavior. To improve external coordination in a dynamic environment, the external leader should clearly communicate objectives and changing priorities, facilitate collective learning, and continue to help the team obtain necessary resources and political support from the organization. Finally, it is often necessary for the external leader to assist the team in dealing with unusual, disruptive events, and the leader can help the team to understand the problem and coach members in how to respond effectively.

Guidelines for Leading Teams

A variety of different ways have been identified for leaders to improve member cohesiveness, cooperation, team identification, collective efficacy, and collective learning. The following guidelines based on research, theory, and practitioner insights describe team-building procedures that can be used alone or in various combinations when relevant for the situation (see also Table 11-7).

TABLE 11-7 Guidelines for Leading Teams

- Emphasize common interests and values.
- Use ceremonies, rituals, and symbols to develop collective identification.
- Encourage and facilitate social interaction.
- Inform people about group activities and achievements.
- Conduct process analysis sessions.
- Conduct alignment sessions.
- Increase incentives for mutual cooperation.
- Hold practice sessions under realistic conditions.
- Use after-activity reviews to facilitate collective learning by the team.

- **Emphasize common interests and values.**

Collective identification with a group is stronger when the members agree about objectives, values, priorities, strategies, and the need for cooperation. The leader should emphasize mutual interests, identify shared objectives, and explain why cooperation is necessary to attain them. An example of an appeal to shared values and objectives is provided by the following critical incident from the Non-cooperation movement:

> The Non-cooperation movement was a response to a lot of the British government's oppressive policies but the brutal Jallianwala Bagh Massacre in particular. Losing hope of any fair treatment from the British Government, Gandhi decided to launch the non-cooperation movement as part of India's struggle for freedom. Purchase of foreign goods was boycotted and the purchase of Swadeshi products was encouraged. The aim of this move was twofold-one, withdrawing support from the British government and two empowering Indian handicraft workers and the Indian economy that had become drained due to the influx of foreign good and export of Indian wealth to British. People were encouraged to leave their western education and jobs. All this was done however, through non-violent means. People from all walks of life joined the movement in large numbers. The value of ahimsa allowed all kinds of people to become a part of the movement, since all that was required was a simple act of boycotting anything that had its source from the British government. No special training was needed to become a part of this freedom struggle that affected and was desired by every citizen.

- **Use ceremonies, rituals, and symbols to develop collective identification.**

Ceremonies and rituals can be used to increase identification with a group and make membership appear special. Initiation rituals are used to induct new members into a group, and retirement rituals are used to celebrate the departure of old members. Ceremonies are used to celebrate special achievements or mark the anniversary of special events in the history of the group. Rituals and ceremonies are most effective when they emphasize the group's values and traditions. Symbols of group identity such as a team name, slogan, logo, insignia, or emblem may be displayed on flags, banners, clothing, or jewelry. Even a particular type or color of clothing may indicate group membership, as in the case of many urban gangs. Symbols can be effective for helping to create a separate identity for a team. Group identification is strengthened when members agree to wear or display the symbols of membership.

- **Encourage and facilitate social interaction.**

Development of a cohesive group is more likely if the members get to know each other on a personal basis and find it satisfying to interact socially. One way to facilitate pleasant social interaction is to hold periodic social activities such as dinners, lunches, and parties. Various types of outings can be used to facilitate social interaction (e.g., going to a sports event or concert together, or on a camping or rafting trip). When group members work in the same facility, social interaction can be promoted by designating a room for the group to use for meetings and coffee breaks. The room can be decorated with symbols of the group's accomplishments, statements of its values, and charts showing progress in accomplishing group objectives.

- **Inform people about group activities and achievements.**

People tend to feel alienated and unappreciated when they receive little information about the plans, activities, and achievements of their team or department. It is important to keep members informed about these things and to explain how their work contributes to the success of the mission. The social networking technology has made it much easier to keep group members informed.

- **Conduct process analysis sessions.**

Process analysis sessions involve frank and open discussion of interpersonal relationships and group processes in an effort to improve them. One approach is to ask each member to suggest ways to make the group more effective. These suggestions should focus on how members communicate, work together, make decisions, and resolve disagreements rather than on the technical aspects of the work. A similar approach is to ask each member to describe how other members could make his or her role in the group easier. The discussion should result in a list of concrete suggestions for improving working relationships. Follow-up meetings can be used to chart progress in implementing the suggestions.

It is usually better to have a trained facilitator conduct the process analysis session instead of the team leader. Discussing interpersonal relationships is more difficult than discussing work procedures, and it takes considerable skill to conduct this type of session. A team leader without training in process consultation may make team relationships worse rather than better. An outside facilitator is likely to be more objective and impartial, which is especially important if the leader is contributing to the difficulties the group has in working together.

- **Increase incentives for mutual cooperation.**

Incentives based on individual performance encourage team members to compete with each other, whereas incentives based on group performance encourage cooperation. One way to increase cohesiveness and team identification is to emphasize formal incentives such as a bonus based on improvements in team performance. Another way is to use spontaneous, informal rewards to emphasize the importance of service to the team. For example, give the members extra days off after the team completes a difficult project, especially one that involved working overtime or on weekends. Hold a special celebration party for team members and their families after the team achieves an important objective.

- **Hold practice sessions under realistic conditions.**

Team performance can be improved by holding frequent practice sessions, and they are very useful for enhancing the confidence of members that they can perform difficult tasks successfully. Unless teams regularly practice how to respond to unusual events such as crises and emergencies, performance is likely to be poor when such events eventually occur. Practice sessions are more beneficial when they are held under conditions that are as realistic as possible. When the task involves a team of people working together, it is best to have them practice complex procedures together. For example, airplane crews practice dealing with emergencies due to equipment failure. Hospital employees conduct simulations to practice dealing with large numbers of casualties from a natural disaster.

- **Use after-activity reviews to facilitate collective learning by the team.**

Collective learning from experience is more likely when a systematic analysis is made after an important activity is finished to discover the reasons for success or failure. The after-activity review (also called an "after-action review," an "after-event review," or a "postmortem") is a procedure for collectively analyzing the processes and resulting outcomes of a team activity (Ellis & Davidi, 2005; Ellis, Mendel, & Nir, 2006; Tannenbaum & Cerasoli, 2013; Tannenbaum, Smith-Jentsch, & Behson, 1998; Villado & Arthur, 2013). This process is especially useful when teams perform the same type of activity repeatedly. The objective is to identify what was

TABLE 11-8 Guidelines for Leading an After-Activity Review Session

1. Near the beginning, make a self-critique that acknowledges shortcomings.
2. Encourage feedback from others and model nondefensive acceptance of it.
3. Ask members to identify effective and ineffective aspects of team performance.
4. Encourage members to examine how group processes affected team performance.
5. Keep the discussion focused on behaviors rather than on individuals.
6. If necessary, provide your own assessment of team performance.
7. Recognize improvements in team performance.
8. Ask members for suggestions on how to improve team performance.
9. Propose improvements not already included in the team's suggestions.

Based on Tannenbaum, Smith-Jentsch, and Behson (1998).

done well and what can be improved the next time a similar activity is conducted. The members should review their initial plans and objectives for the activity, the procedures used to carry out the activity, problems or obstacles encountered in doing the activity, key decisions that were made, and the outcomes. Then the group determines how to use what was learned to improve future performance. For long projects or training simulations, it is also useful to conduct progress review sessions at convenient intermediate points. The use of after-activity reviews for evaluating activities and planning improvements is pervasive now in the U.S. Army, and it is slowly gaining acceptance in civilian organizations as well (Baird, Holland, & Deacon, 1999; Ellis & Davidi, 2005). Procedures for leading the reviews are listed in Table 11-8.

Leading Decision Groups

Groups are used frequently to solve problems and make decisions in organizations. As noted in Chapter 4, using a group to make a decision has several potential advantages over decisions made by an individual leader. Groups have more relevant knowledge and ideas that can be pooled to improve decision quality, and active participation will increase member understanding of decisions and member commitment to implement them. On the negative side, group decisions usually take longer, the members may be unable to reach agreement if they have incompatible objectives, and process problems may undermine the quality of decisions.

The process by which a group arrives at a decision is a major determinant of decision quality (Thompson, 2014). Many things can prevent a group from effectively utilizing the information and achieving its full potential. The quality of a group decision depends on the contribution of information and ideas by group members, the clarity of communication, the accuracy of problem diagnoses and predicted outcomes, the extent to which the discussion is focused on the problem, and the manner in which disagreement is resolved. Common process problems that reduce decision quality include member inhibition, groupthink, false consensus, hasty decisions, polarization, and lack of action planning for implementation.

Appropriate leadership can facilitate effective decision making by a group and help to avoid process problems (Basadur, 2004). The leadership role can be shared to some extent (Bergman, Rentsch, Small, Davenport, & Bergman, 2012), but members of decision groups often prefer to have one designated discussion leader who has primary responsibility for conducting the meeting (Berkowitz, 1953; Schlesinger, Jackson, & Butman, 1960). An effective leader ensures that the group uses a systematic decision process ("process control"), but does not dominate the discussion

TABLE 11-9 Major Types of Leadership Behavior in Decision Groups

Task Function	Specific Objective
1. Process Structuring	Guide and sequence discussion.
2. Stimulating communication	Increase information exchange.
3. Clarifying communication	Increase comprehension.
4. Summarizing	Check on understanding and assess progress.
5. Consensus testing	Check on agreement.
Group Maintenance	**Specific Objective**
1. Gatekeeping	Increase and equalize participation.
2. Harmonizing	Reduce tension and hostility.
3. Supporting	Prevent withdrawal and reduce tension.
4. Standard setting	Regulate behavior.
5. Process analyzing	Discover and resolve process problems.

("content control"). The job of conducting a meeting is a difficult one, because the group is likely to be ineffective if the leader is either too passive or too domineering. A considerable amount of skill is needed to achieve a delicate balance between these two extremes. The behaviors and procedures used to achieve this balance are discussed in the remaining sections of this chapter.

We saw in Chapter 2 that leadership behavior can be classified as task-oriented or relationship-oriented, and a similar distinction can be made for leadership behavior in group meetings. Of course, specific aspects of leadership behavior often involve both task and relationship concerns simultaneously, but the distinction helps to remind group leaders how important it is to balance task and relationship concerns in leading meetings. Several writers have proposed two-factor taxonomies of group leader behavior (Bales, 1950; Benne & Sheats, 1948; Bradford, 1976; Lord, 1977; Schein, 1969). Table 11-9 shows a simplified, composite taxonomy of task-oriented and group maintenance functions and their primary objectives.

Task-Oriented Functions

Task-oriented behavior in a group meeting facilitates the systematic communication, evaluation, and analysis of information and ideas, and it aids problem solving and decision making. Some examples of task-oriented behavior include developing an agenda for the meeting, presenting a problem to the group, asking members for specific information or ideas, asking a member to explain an ambiguous statement, helping the group understand the relevance of ideas, explaining how different ideas are related, keeping the discussion on track, reviewing and summarizing what has been said or done, checking on the amount of agreement among members, suggesting procedures for making a decision, assigning responsibility for follow-up action, and recessing or ending a meeting.

Mike Krzyewski, Head Basketball Coach at Duke University, where his teams have won five national championships, emphasizes the importance of setting standards, a key task-oriented function, to team success:

> We try to not have rules on my teams. I have what I call "standards." When I went to West Point we had a bunch of rules, all of which I didn't agree with. Usually when you're ruled, you never agree with the rules, you just abide by them. But if you have standards and if everyone contributes to the way you're going to do things, you end up owning how you do things. In my experience, the best teams have standards everyone owns (Sitkin & Hackman, 2011, p. 499).

It is not sufficient for a leader simply to carry out the behaviors; a sense of proper timing is also essential (Bradford, 1976). Any task-oriented behavior can be useless or even detrimental if it is premature or overdone. For example, summarizing too soon may discourage contribution of additional ideas on a subject, but the discussion may be excessively prolonged if the leader keeps stimulating communication instead of testing for a consensus. It is also important for the leader to have considerable skill in the use of each kind of task-oriented behavior. For example, an unskilled leader who tries to clarify a member's statement may succeed only in creating more confusion. A leader who is unskilled in summarizing may make a summary that leaves out key points and fails to organize contributions in a meaningful way.

Group Maintenance Functions

Group maintenance behavior in a group meeting increases cohesiveness, improves interpersonal relations, aids resolution of conflict, and satisfies the personal needs of members for acceptance, respect, and involvement. Some examples of group maintenance behavior include encouraging participation by quiet members, preventing dominant members from monopolizing the discussion, smoothing over conflict, suggesting compromises, asking members to resolve differences in a constructive way, using humor to reduce tension, expressing appreciation for suggestions and ideas, suggesting norms and standards of behavior, reminding the group of norms agreed upon earlier, asking members for their perception of group processes, and pointing out process problems to the group.

Just as machines need periodic maintenance to keep them running smoothly, so also do human relationships in a group. As with machines, preventive maintenance should be carried out frequently rather than waiting to do corrective maintenance after a serious breakdown. Group maintenance should be an ongoing activity designed to build teamwork and prevent the development of chronic apathy, withdrawal, interpersonal conflict, and status struggles. If allowed to develop, these problems will disrupt the task-oriented activity in a group and reduce the effectiveness of the group.

Group maintenance behavior is needed in most meetings, but it is neglected by many leaders who are unaware of its importance. Standard setting and process analyzing are the aspects of behavior least likely to occur, perhaps because they require an explicit recognition of maintenance needs. As in the case of task-oriented behaviors, the group maintenance behaviors require skill and a sense of proper timing to be performed effectively.

Who Should Perform the Leadership Functions

Behavioral scientists generally agree that task-oriented behavior and group maintenance behavior are both essential for the effectiveness of decision groups, but they disagree about who should perform these functions and about their relative priority. The traditional "leader-centered" view is that the formal leader should direct and control the activities of the group. The group leader should keep discussion focused on the task, discourage expression of feelings, and retain control over the final decision (i.e., use consultation rather than a group decision). According to Bradford (1976), this kind of group leadership may yield some favorable results but at an unacceptable price. Meetings are orderly and decisions get made, but members may become apathetic and resentful if they feel manipulated and unable to have much influence over the decisions. The result is likely to be a reduction in decision quality and member acceptance of the decisions.

With "group-centered" leadership, the role of the leader is to serve as a consultant, advisor, teacher, and facilitator, rather than as a director or manager of the group. The group maintenance functions are considered to be as important as the task-oriented functions, because feelings and interactions profoundly affect the problem-solving and decision-making processes in a group. Responsibility for both kinds of functions is shared by group members, because no one person can be sensitive to all of the process problems and needs of the group. The leader should encourage expression of feelings as well as ideas, model appropriate leadership behaviors, and encourage members to learn to perform these behaviors themselves. According to Bradford, sharing responsibility for leadership functions will improve the quality of the decisions and make members more satisfied with the group.

Bradford recognized some difficulties in implementing group-centered leadership. He noted that this kind of leadership requires considerable interpersonal skill, maturity, and trust in both the leader and group members. Some leaders are afraid to risk sharing control with group members or dealing openly with emotional behavior. These leaders may also be concerned that the new approach will make them appear weak or incompetent. Some members may be unwilling to deal openly with emotions or may prefer to avoid assuming more responsibility for leadership functions in the group. Many decision groups are only temporary and do not meet over a long enough time to develop the necessary trust, skills, and member commitment. A committee may have unwilling members who prefer to meet as seldom as possible and to assume as little responsibility as possible for committee activities. The traditional approach is often reinforced by ritual and established procedures, which represent additional obstacles to the introduction of group-centered leadership. For example, some decision groups are legally required by their charter or bylaws to follow cumbersome procedural rules (e.g., Robert's Rules of Order) that are more appropriate for large, formal groups. Despite these many obstacles, Bradford is optimistic about the prospects for successful implementation of group-centered leadership.

Guidelines for Leading Meetings

This section describes specific procedures that leaders can use to improve group effectiveness in solving problems and making decisions. The guidelines for leading meetings (see Table 11-10) are based on ideas proposed by various scholars over the years (e.g., Basadur, 2004; Janis & Mann, 1977; Jay, 1976; Maier, 1963; Mesmer-Magnus & DeChurch, 2009; Rowland & Parry, 2009; Sonnentag & Volmer, 2009; Westaby, Probst, & Lee, 2010).

TABLE 11-10 Guidelines for Leading Decision Group Meetings

- Inform people about necessary preparations for a meeting.
- Share essential information with group members.
- Describe the problem without implying the cause or solution.
- Allow ample time for idea generation and evaluation.
- Separate idea generation from idea evaluation.
- Encourage and facilitate participation.
- Encourage positive restatement and idea building.
- Use systematic procedures for solution evaluation.
- Look for an integrative solution.
- Encourage efforts to reach consensus when feasible.
- Clarify responsibilities for implementation.

- **Inform people about necessary preparations for a meeting.**

A problem-solving meeting will be more effective if people know how to prepare for it. To ensure that people plan to attend the meeting, they should be informed in advance about the time, place, and important subjects on the agenda. People who are expected to present briefings, provide technical information, or evaluate a proposal should be given clear guidance and ample time to prepare. Any reports or proposals to be studied in preparation for the meeting should be provided in advance with the agenda.

- **Share essential information with group members.**

When the problem is presented, essential facts known to the leader should be reviewed briefly, including how long the problem has been evident, the nature of the problem symptoms, and what if anything has been done about it up to that time. The amount of information that should be presented depends on the nature of the problem and the group's prior information. The information may be provided prior to the meeting, at the beginning of the meeting, or as the problem diagnosis is made. The leader should be careful to present facts with as little interpretation as possible. For example, if the problem is how to increase sales, it is better simply to review sales figures for each district than to make judgments such as "sales are terrible in the central district."

- **Describe the problem without implying the cause or solution.**

The problem should be stated objectively in a way that does not assign blame for it to some or all of the group members. Implying blame will make members defensive and reduce their willingness to help in solving a mutual problem. The problem statement should not suggest the reasons for the problem or possible solutions to it. This kind of statement would limit the consideration of different problem diagnoses by the group. Instead, the problem statement should encourage exploration of a variety of causes and a variety of possible solutions.

- **Allow ample time for idea generation and evaluation.**

The leader should plan meetings so that enough time is available to diagnose the problem, develop alternative solutions, and explore the implications and consequences of each alternative. Even when a group has members who are not inhibited, a strong majority coalition may propose a favored decision and ram it through before the critics have an opportunity to explain their concerns and gather support. The pressure of time is another reason for hasty decisions, and they often occur when a meeting is about to end and members desire to resolve matters quickly to avoid another meeting. When an important decision is being considered but time is not sufficient to evaluate solutions, the leader should try to postpone the decision until another meeting. If an immediate decision is not necessary and it is obvious that more information is needed, the leader may want to adjourn the meeting and arrange for additional information to be obtained.

- **Separate idea generation from idea evaluation.**

Research has found that idea generation is less inhibited when it is separated from idea evaluation (Maier, 1963). Procedures have been developed to reduce inhibition and facilitate idea generation in groups. With brainstorming, members are encouraged to suggest any idea about the problem that comes to mind, and no positive or negative evaluation of ideas is permitted (including scowls, groans, sighs, or gestures). The rationale is that inhibition would be reduced by deferring evaluation of ideas, domination would be reduced by making contributions brief and spontaneous, and creativity would be increased by mutual facilitation of ideas and a climate of acceptance for strange and novel ideas. Brainstorming improves idea generation in comparison with a regular interacting group, but some inhibition may still occur (Litchfield, 2008; White, Dittrich, & Lang, 1980).

The nominal group technique was developed to correct the deficiencies of brainstorming (Boddy, 2012; Delbecq, Van de Ven, & Gustafson, 1975). During a group meeting (or prior to it) the members are asked to contribute their ideas anonymously without any discussion of them. When they are finished, the leader posts the ideas for everyone to see or provides a copy of them to each member before the meeting. For a virtual group the ideas can be posted on a common web site. Group members are invited to build on ideas already listed or add new ideas stimulated by seeing the list. Then the leader reviews the list with the group to see if there are any questions about the meaning of an idea or its relevance to the objective.

In a variation of this procedure (called "brain writing"), the evaluation of ideas is postponed until a later meeting, and participants are encouraged to continue thinking about the problem and the list of suggested ideas (Michinov, 2012; Paulus & Yang, 2000). The rationale for a follow-up meeting is that members do not have adequate time to reflect upon each other's ideas when they are busy writing ideas of their own, and an "incubation" period is necessary to realize the potential for mutual stimulation of ideas.

- **Encourage and facilitate participation.**

When some members loudly advocate a particular solution and other members remain silent or fail to take a position, the silent ones are usually assumed to be in agreement. However, silence may indicate dissent rather than agreement. The leader can use appropriate gatekeeping behavior to facilitate participation and encourage serious discussion of member concerns. Each member should be encouraged to contribute ideas and express concerns, and members should be discouraged from dominating the discussion or using social-pressure tactics (e.g., threats, derogatory comments) to intimidate people who disagree with them. When computer-based groupware is available, it can be used to facilitate anonymous interaction during the posting and evaluation of ideas. After members generate ideas independently, the composite list of ideas can be displayed on each member's computer screen or smartphone. Then any member can add new ideas stimulated by seeing the list, request more information from the (anonymous) source of an idea, or suggest ways to improve an idea. Duplicate ideas can be combined if desired, and a rating procedure can be used to determine the most acceptable ideas.

- **Encourage positive restatement and idea building.**

Two procedures that are especially useful to create a more supportive climate for idea generation are positive restatement and idea building. One of the most useful techniques for nurturing new ideas is to ask group members to restate another member's idea and find something worthwhile about it before saying anything critical. In a related technique, any member who points out a deficiency or limitation of another's idea is required to suggest a way to correct the deficiency or overcome the limitation. This approach also emphasizes careful listening and constructive, helpful behavior.

- **Use systematic procedures for solution evaluation.**

Procedures have been developed to help decision groups evaluate and compare potential solutions. These procedures are especially useful when members appear to be divided into opposing factions ("polarization"), each with a different solution. With the two-column procedure, members mutually identify and post the advantages and disadvantages of each alternative (Maier, 1963). Members then discuss the advantages and disadvantages and try to agree on an overall ranking of alternatives. A similar but more detailed procedure is cost-benefit analysis. This procedure can be used when the consequences of each solution are fairly certain and it is possible to make reasonably accurate estimates of the benefits and costs in monetary terms. The analysis should be conducted in a systematic manner, and care should be taken to avoid biasing estimates of costs and benefits to support a preferred solution. After all the alternatives have been analyzed, the group selects the best one by using whatever economic criterion seems most appropriate (e.g., maximize net benefit, maximize return on investment).

- **Encourage members to look for an integrative solution.**

When a group is sharply divided in support of competing alternatives, it is sometimes feasible to develop an integrative solution that involves the best features of the rival solutions. One way to begin this procedure is to examine both alternatives closely to identify what features they have in common as well as how they differ. This comparison develops a better understanding and appreciation of the opposing alternative, especially if all group members become actively involved in the discussion. The leader should encourage participation, keep the discussion analytical rather than critical, and post the results of the comparison to provide a visual summary of the similarities and differences. It is also useful to list for each faction the essential qualities of a solution and the relative priorities of different criteria or objectives. Even when it is not possible to develop a hybrid solution, the process may help the group identify an entirely new solution that is superior to the others.

- **Encourage efforts to reach consensus when feasible.**

Voting is a common procedure for making a decision, but whenever feasible, the leader should encourage the group to try to reach a consensus rather than deciding on the basis of a simple majority. A consensus occurs when all members of the group agree that a particular alternative is acceptable, even though it is not necessarily the first choice of every member. A consensus decision usually generates more commitment than a majority decision, but more time is typically needed to make the decision, and a group consensus is not always possible. When the group has a large majority in support of one alternative, but a few dissenters still remain, the leader should carefully weigh the possible benefits of winning them over against the cost of additional discussion time. If adequate time has already been devoted to discussion of alternatives, it is seldom worthwhile to prolong the discussion merely to persuade one or two stubborn members. In this situation, the leader should take the initiative and declare that a group decision has been reached.

- **Clarify responsibilities for implementation.**

Before the meeting ends, the leader should make some provisions for implementing the decision. Necessary action steps should be specified and responsibility for each action step assigned to individuals. Many good decisions made by groups are unsuccessful simply because nobody bothers to ensure that they are implemented. If a follow-up meeting is needed, the preparations required for that meeting should be determined and responsibilities assigned. After the meeting, the leader should distribute a summary of what was discussed and decided, and what responsibilities were assigned to whom.

Summary

Organizations increasingly rely on teams to improve quality, efficiency, and adaptive change. Several types of teams are used in organizations, including functional work teams, cross-functional teams, self-managed teams, virtual teams, and executive teams (which are discussed in Chapter 12). The potential advantages of teams include more employee satisfaction and commitment, better quality of products and services, and greater efficiency and productivity. However, the benefits do not occur automatically, and successful implementation depends on the quality of leadership and some facilitating conditions.

Identity-based, resource-based, and knowledge-based subgroups often form in work teams. Subgroups can have positive or negative effects on group processes and performance, depending on their configuration (i.e., number and type) within the work team. Leaders should consider the effects of subgroups when designing and managing work teams to avoid friction between subgroups and promote cooperative relationships.

Effective leadership in teams usually requires many specific types of leadership behavior. The appropriate pattern of behavior will depend on the type of team and the relative importance of the performance determinants. Some essential leadership processes in teams include building commitment for shared objectives, identifying effective performance strategies and organizing team activities, enhancing member skills and role clarity, building mutual trust and cooperation, identifying and procuring needed resources, maintaining confidence and optimism, and facilitating external coordination.

Leadership is provided in somewhat different ways in the different types of teams. Functional work teams and cross-functional teams usually have an appointed leader with strong position power. In a self-managed team, many of the leadership roles are carried out informally and shared among the members. However, even in teams with a formal leader, it is often beneficial for other members to share responsibility for some of the leadership roles. Virtual teams have members who work in different locations and interact primarily using communications technology. Any type of team can operate with some degree of virtuality.

Team-building activities are used to increase cohesiveness, group identification, and cooperation. Some examples include emphasizing common interests and values, using ceremonies and rituals, using symbols to develop group identification, facilitating social interaction among members, informing members about group activities and achievements, and conducting process analysis sessions.

A group decision is potentially superior to a decision made by a single individual such as the leader, but many things can prevent a group from realizing its potential. Leadership is a major determinant of group effectiveness, and in the context of group meetings it includes both task-oriented and group maintenance functions. The two types of leadership functions require skill and a sense of proper timing to be effective. The leadership role is difficult, because the decision process will be adversely affected if the leader is either too passive or too domineering. To improve problem solving and avoid common process problems, a leader should present the problem in an unbiased manner, encourage the group to consider alternative conceptions of the problem, separate idea generation from idea evaluation, and use systematic procedures for solution evaluation.

Research on leadership in teams has increased in recent years, but it continues to lag behind changes in the use of teams in organizations. The extent to which effective leadership is different in virtual teams has yet to be determined, and rapid advances in technology make it difficult to predict the future relevance of results from past research.

Review and Discussion Questions

1. What factors determine the performance of a team?
2. What are the key types of subgroups and how do they impact team processes and performance?
3. What leadership processes are important for cross-functional teams?
4. Why is leadership more difficult in cross-functional teams than in functional teams?
5. What leadership roles and processes are important for self-managed teams?
6. Under what conditions are self-managed work teams most likely to be successful?
7. What can be done to improve group cohesiveness and collective identification?
8. What are the major task-oriented and group maintenance functions in decision groups?
9. What can a leader do to improve decision-making processes in a group meeting?

Key Terms

after-activity reviews
brainstorming
cohesiveness
collective efficacy
collective identification
consensus
cross-functional teams
external coordination
functional teams
group maintenance behaviors
identity-based subgroups
knowledge-based subgroups
nominal group technique
performance strategies
group potency
resource-based subgroups
self-managed teams
shared mental models
task-oriented behaviors
team building
virtual teams

PERSONAL REFLECTION

Think about your current or previous experience in a work team. Was there a single formal or informal leader of the team, or was leadership shared by team members? What task-oriented and group-maintenance behaviors were performed and who performed them?

CASE

Qwiksilver

Jeetendra Kumar was a software engineer at Qwiksilver, a mobile manufacturing company. He has been working with the company for five years now, when he was invited by Shashank Agarwal, the software whiz of the company, to join in on a new project. Jeetendra was unsure of why he was asked to be a part of the project, but he saw it as a great career opportunity and considered himself lucky to have been offered a chance to work with Shashank.

The project comprised a team of ten members in all, each specializing in a certain area needed for the completion of a new project. Shashank called for a meeting on the first day and welcomed all the team members to the project. He introduced himself after which a brief introductory round was held for the team members to know each other better. Shashank informed them how each of them had been recommended by their bosses and had been chosen because they possessed the required skills to ensure that the project turns out to be a success. Shashank told them that given the rising demand for the company's products, the volume of business was increasing and so a better decision support system was needed to manage the demand in a way that kept the manufacturing cost low, without compromising on the quality. With the increasingly competitive market, the need for a sound decision support system became all the more essential to ensure its profitability. The objective of this team thus, was to develop a new and innovative system than anything else currently available.

Shashank told them that although it was an extremely challenging an assignment, he had full faith in the abilities of his team members. He believed that if each member contributed their 100 percent, they could pull it off. Since it was going to be such a challenging and intense project, Shashank warned them that for the next nine months, nothing but this project should be the only priority in their lives. Working late nights or early mornings, over the weekends and even on other holidays could be a possibility, and so everyone should be mentally prepared. In case anyone had any reservations, they were asked to inform him by the next evening.

All except one employee, who had some family preoccupations and could not guarantee being able to stay too late at work, joined the team the next day. The work turned out to be much more intense than Jeetendra had imagined. He was mentally prepared to work late a few days but did not expect it to become a norm. The team would end up spending a lot of time together as lunch and dinner would always be ordered in and they would all eat together. In spite of the hectic working hours, the work never got to anyone, and they all felt fortunate and happy to be a part of such an important project. Shashank had such a positive work attitude that motivated and inspired the others around him as well. His enthusiasm and optimism was contagious, such that even the members who were usually dull, would get charged up.

Shashank provided the team with a clear set of objectives and specifications that were needed for the new system o that none of them go astray. However, these instructions were only meant to guide the members and keep them focused on the task and not to dictate them. They were expected to use their expertise and seek Shashank's guidance wherever needed. Even when asked for help, Shashank would give suggestions but not impose his ideas. He gave his team members the autonomy to decide exactly what they wanted to do eventually. However, he made it clear than nothing less than 100 percent effort would be accepted.

The team would meet on a regular basis to evaluate and review their progress, discuss the obstacles they were facing and try finding solutions to them. Important decisions were discussed and each member would be given the opportunity to contribute towards it. The quality of one's idea and the expertise in the area was given due consideration, and this was not based on the level of seniority in the company. Shashank's job would be to ensure that the team got whatever resources and assistance it required from the company. He would travel to interact with other companies and see whose support was needed and could be garnered for designing and implementing their new system. Prior to his trips, Shashank would appoint one of the team members to carry out internal leadership responsibilities on his behalf.

During one such occasion, Shashank appointed Jeetendra who felt very nervous to step into the leadership role. But, with Shashank's encouragement, he went ahead and managed to do the job well. Having seen Jeetendra perform the job satisfactorily, Shashank encouraged him to apply for a managerial position at the company once the current project was over.

By the end of the fifth month, there was a point where the team experienced a couple of setbacks. To prevent the team from getting disheartened and losing all enthusiasm and hope, Shashank decided to give them a pep talk. He appreciated their efforts and the progress that had been made so far. He told them the hurdles are a part of any project and that he had full faith in the ability of his team to overcome them and achieve success. He asked them to take a day off and then come back the next day to discuss ways in which the recent hurdles could be tackled. The team did exactly that, and in no time, they were able to not only overcome the obstacles, but achieve the completion of the project much before its deadline. The project was a huge success and the entire team felt extremely proud of it. They even held a party to celebrate its success.

A few days after the completion of the project, some of the team members sat together to reminisce about this project. They were all highly appreciative of Shashank as their team director and expressed their desire and hope to work with him. Based on his personal experience, Jeetendra especially credited Shashank for being a fantastic coach and facilitator. They all realized, however, that the project's success was a team effort which would not have been possible if even one of them would have not given their full effort or would have put their self-interest above the project.

—*Written by* Nishant Uppal

Questions

1. Describe the leadership behaviors Shashank used and their influence on the attitudes and behavior of the team members.
2. Compare this cross-functional project team to a self-managed operations team by identifying similarities and differences in the leadership roles.

CASE

Columbia Corporation

Columbia Corp. is a young, rapidly growing company that manufactures computer accessories and specialized components for networked computer workstations. It has some unique products and a strong reputation for quality. Sales of company products have been good, and a recent contract with a large computer company is likely to increase sales. However, along with this success the company is also experiencing some problems. Quality rejects have begun to increase, and in recent months the company failed repeatedly to meet delivery schedules.

The top executives include Matt Walsh, CEO and founder of the company, and the vice presidents of production, engineering, sales, and accounting. Walsh is a forceful manager who tightly controls important decisions in the company. The other executives are required to get his approval before making any significant changes in operations. Walsh's style has been to deal with each VP separately, rather than meeting as a group to address problems. Relationships between departments have been deteriorating for the past two years. Distrust, competition, and political maneuvering have increased, and Walsh intervenes frequently to resolve conflicts between executives. The distrust and hostility have spilled over to relationships among lower-level employees of the departments.

The Production VP believes that the rash of quality problems is the result of frequent changes in product design by the engineering department. There is little warning of these changes and insufficient time to determine how to make necessary adjustments in production methods. As for the delivery problems, the Production VP believes that the sales department makes unrealistic promises to win new customers. Production capacity has not increased fast enough to meet the growing volume of orders, and additional delays are caused by product modifications designed for customers by engineering. Another reason production is behind schedule is the decision by the Accounting VP to abruptly cancel all overtime for production employees for the remainder of this month. This action appears unwarranted, and the Production VP has asked Walsh to reverse this decision.

The Sales VP blames the late deliveries on manufacturing delays. She believes the production people spend so much time trying to correct quality problems that they can't get the product out the door. The Sales VP and the Engineering VP both believe the Production VP is set in his ways and unwilling to adapt to the special needs of important customers. The Sales VP is also upset with the Accounting VP for tightening customer credit requirements without prior notice. She only discovered the new policy when a key customer complained after credit was denied on a large order. The Sales VP believes the new policy will reduce sales, and the reduction will be blamed on her. She complained to Walsh, who apparently approved the decision without understanding the implications.

Concerned about the growing problems, Walsh asked a management consultant for advice on how get his executive team to be more effective in understanding and resolving key problems such as insufficient production capacity and declining quality.

—*Written by* Gary Yukl

Questions

1. What issues must be resolved to create an effective executive team?
2. What types of changes are needed in how Matt leads the team?

Chapter 12

Strategic Leadership in Organizations

Learning Objectives

After studying this chapter, you should be able to:

- Understand what organizational processes determine a company's performance.
- Understand how top executives can influence organizational processes and performance.
- Understand constraints on strategic leadership and conditions that make it more important.
- Understand the potential advantages of executive teams and how to use them effectively.
- Understand why it is important to monitor the external environment and how to do it.
- Understand the procedures that can be used to formulate a good competitive strategy.

Introduction

Much of the early leadership literature was concerned with supervisors or middle managers in organizations, but in more recent years there has been increased interest in "strategic leadership" by top executives (Boal & Hooijberg, 2001; Cannella & Monroe, 1997; Carter & Greer, 2013; Finkelstein, Hambrick, & Cannella, 2009; Hiller & Beauchesne, 2014). The shift in focus reflects an increased interest in understanding how executives can transform their companies to cope with globalization, increasing international competition, and rapid technological and social change.

This chapter examines what has been learned about effective leadership by top executives in organizations. The chapter begins with a description of the performance factors that determine the prosperity and survival of an organization. Next is a review of ways leaders can influence these performance determinants. Then the chapter reviews conditions that determine a need for strategic change and the amount of influence top executives are likely to have on the organization. Results are reviewed and evaluated for different types of studies that examine the influence of a chief executive officer (CEO) on organizational performance.

The chapter also explains why executive teams are relevant for understanding strategic leadership in organizations, and the effective use of executive teams is discussed. Alternative conceptions of organizational leadership are reviewed, including shared and distributed leadership, relational leadership, and complexity theory.

Two important responsibilities for top executives are monitoring the external environment to identify threats and opportunities and formulating strategy for the future survival and prosperity of the organization. These responsibilities are explained and guidelines for them are provided.

Determinants of Organizational Performance

Organizational effectiveness is the long-term prosperity and survival of the organization. To be successful, organizations must adapt to their environment, acquire necessary resources, and conduct operations in efficient ways (de Kluyver & Pearce, 2015; Katz & Kahn, 1978). Leaders can influence organizational performance in several ways, including decisions about the competitive strategy, human resources, and the management programs, systems, and organization structure. The determinants of organizational performance are closely interrelated, and leaders should understand the inherent trade-offs and potential synergies when deciding how to improve performance (Finkelstein et al., 2009; Gupta, Smith, & Shalley, 2006; He & Wong, 2004; Hiller & Beauchesne, 2014; Yukl, 2008).

Adaptation to the Environment

The effectiveness of an organization depends on responding in appropriate ways to external threats and opportunities (de Kluyver & Pearce, 2015; Porter, 1998). Adaptation is more important when the external environment is volatile and uncertain, which is likely in situations of rapid technological change, political and economic turmoil, or new threats from competitors or external enemies. A company is more likely to adapt successfully to its environment if it has a relevant competitive strategy specifying the types of products or services to offer and ways to influence potential customers or clients. Successful adaptation sometimes requires major changes in the organization's products and services, or the procedures for marketing and supplying them. A rapid response to changing conditions and new competitors is especially important for an organization with a strategy that emphasizes unique, leading-edge products or services designed to satisfy the changing needs of customers and clients.

Adaptation is enhanced by accurate interpretation of information about the environment; collective learning by members, and accurate mental models about the determinants of performance. Other determinants of adaptation include effective knowledge management (retention and diffusion of new knowledge within the organization); flexibility of work processes (capacity to change them quickly as needed); innovations in products, services, or processes; and the availability of discretionary resources (to support new initiatives and crisis management) (Coda & Mollona, 2010).

Efficiency and Process Reliability

Efficiency is the use of people and resources to carry out essential operations in a way that minimizes costs and avoids wasted effort and resources. Efficiency is especially important when the competitive strategy of the organization is to offer its products and services at a lower price than competitors, or when a financial crisis occurs and funds to support essential operations are limited (Yukl & Lepsinger, 2004). This performance determinant is less important when an organization is able to pass along cost increases to customers, or the organization is highly subsidized by the government or private investors. Efficiency can be increased by redesigning work processes, using new technology, and coordinating unit activities to avoid unnecessary a and wasted resources. However, efforts to improve efficiency by using new technology i if the cost of purchasing and operating the new technology exceeds any savings from a workforce.

Process reliability means avoiding unnecessary delays, errors, quality defects, or accidents. Examples of negative effects include theft or misuse of resources, expenses for correcting or replacing defective products or inadequate services, expenses for repairing or replacing damaged equipment, and lawsuits by customers or employees who are injured by errors, accidents, or exposure to harmful substances. Process reliability is conceptualized primarily as a component of efficiency because it usually increases costs, but sometimes it can also affect adaptation (e.g., if sales are reduced by defective products or poor service) or human resources (e.g., employees are seriously injured or killed by avoidable accidents and hazards).

Process reliability can be improved by using extra resources to ensure that quality and safety standards are maintained, products or services are delivered on time, and accidents are avoided. However, efficiency will not be improved unless the savings from improved process reliability exceed the cost of the extra resources. Sometimes it is possible to redesign products and simplify work processes in ways that will reduce errors and delays as well as the direct cost of operations (e.g., with re-engineering or Six Sigma programs).

Human Capital and Strategic Human Resource Management

The term human capital is sometimes used to describe the quality of an organization's human resources, which include the relevant skills and experience of members (Fulmer & Ployhart, 2014; Hitt & Ireland, 2002; Nyberg, Moliterno, Hale, & Lepak, 2014). Performance also depends on the motivation of members and the quality of their social relationships and networks (sometimes called social capital). Collective work is performed more effectively by people who have strong skills, strong commitment to task objectives, confidence in their ability to achieve challenging objectives, a high level of mutual trust, and strong identification with the organization and its mission (Crook, Todd, Combs, Woehr, & Ketchen, 2011; Harter, Schmidt, & Hayes, 2002; Pfeffer, 1994, 2005). Talented, dedicated employees are important for the achievement of both efficiency and innovative adaptation (Huselid, 1995; Jackson, Schuler, & Jiang, 2014; Mahsud, Yukl, & Prussia, 2011; Wright & Ulrich, 2017).

Human capital is more important when the organization is heavily dependent on people who have unique talents, require extensive training, and would be difficult to replace if they left (e.g., hospitals, consulting firms, legal firms, advertising agencies, research universities). Human capital is less important for an organization with highly automated processes and few employees, for a "virtual organization" that has outsourced most activities, or for an organization with mostly unskilled jobs and an ample supply of people willing to work for low wages.

As top executives have become more aware of the importance of human capital to organizational success, there has been an increase in efforts to align workforce skills with strategic goals. This approach is referred to as strategic human resource management (Jackson et al., 2014; Wright & Ulrich, 2017). There is a strong emphasis on alignment and coordination of the firm's human resource practices across organizational levels to ensure that human capital is deployed strategically to foster enhanced competitiveness (Jiang, Takeuchi, & Lepak, 2013). Human capital can be improved by enhancing employee skills (e.g., recruitment, selection, training), employee motivation (e.g., an inspiring vision, incentives and rewards), and the way employees are used to do the work (e.g., flexible job design, use of work teams).

Competitive Strategy

Competitive strategy includes decisions about the types of products or services to offer, the basis for appealing to potential customers (e.g., price, quality, customer service, uniqueness, patriotism), and the methods used to influence potential customers or clients (e.g., advertising, discounts, promotions). The strategy may also involve ways to obtain necessary financial resources (e.g., stocks, bonds, loans, donations), and ways to grow the organization and expand into new markets (e.g., acquisitions, mergers, joint ventures, strategic alliances, franchises). Competitive strategy is an important determinant of the financial performance and survival of business organizations (Adner & Helfat, 2003; Carmeli, Gelbard, & Gefen, 2010; de Kluyver & Pearce, 2015; Hambrick, 2007; Narayanan et al., 2011; O'Reilly, Caldwell, Chatman, Lapiz, & Self, 2010; Porter, 1980, 1998).

Leaders formulate competitive strategy with the use of change-oriented behaviors such as assessing threats and opportunities, identifying core competencies, proposing innovative strategies, and evaluating alternative strategies (de Kluyver & Pearce, 2015). Some types of programs and systems for monitoring the external environment can be used to help detect threats and opportunities and identify an appropriate strategy for the organization.

Decisions about competitive strategy have the greatest potential influence on adaptation, but they also affect the relative importance of other performance determinants and their optimal level (Hiller & Beauchesne, 2014). For example, the decision to offer lower prices as the primary basis for increasing sales and profits may require a reduction in the cost of operations (e.g., by using improved technology, by using less expensive materials, by reducing the pay and benefits of current or newly hired employees, or by outsourcing high-paying jobs to low-wage countries). The decision to provide more unique products or improve customer service may make it necessary to recruit more skilled employees or change the way current employees are trained and rewarded. Implementing a new strategy usually requires some modification of management programs, systems, and structures in the organization, and it may also involve negotiation of new agreements with other organizations (e.g., clients, distributors, suppliers, strategic partners) (Lechner & Kreutzer, 2010).

Management Programs, Systems, and Structures

Many different types of improvement programs, management systems, and structural forms can be used to influence organizational effectiveness (Yukl & Lepsinger, 2004). Most programs have as the primary objective the improvement of adaptation, efficiency, or human capital (see Table 12-1).

Several types of management programs or initiatives have been used to improve efficiency and process reliability (e.g., Benner & Tushman, 2003; DeNisi & Murphy, 2017; Ho, Chan, & Kidwell, 1999; Lahiri, 2016; Lawler, Mohrman, & Benson, 2001; Powell, 1995; van Dierendonck & Jacobs, 2012; Waterson et al., 1999). Examples include cost reduction programs (downsizing, outsourcing, just-in-time inventory), process and quality improvement programs (total quality management, Six Sigma, business process re-engineering); performance management and goal setting programs (e.g., management by objectives, zero defects); and appraisal, recognition, and reward systems that emphasize efficiency and reliability. Some programs involve the implementation of standardized procedures that provide a way to ensure that common activities are carried out in an efficient and uniform way across subunits. Another type of improvement program involves the use of new technology to automate work processes

TABLE 12-1 Management Programs, Systems, and Structures for Improving Performance

Efficiency and Process Reliability

- Performance management and goal setting programs (e.g., MBO, zero defects)
- Process and quality improvement programs (quality circles, TQM, Six Sigma)
- Cost-reduction programs (downsizing, outsourcing, just-in-time inventory)
- Structural forms (functional specialization, formalization, standardization)
- Appraisal, recognition, and reward systems focused on efficiency and process reliability

Human Capital and Strategic Human Resource Management

- Quality of work-life programs (flextime, job sharing, child care, fitness center)
- Employee benefit programs (health care, vacations, retirement, sabbaticals)
- Socialization and teambuilding (orientation programs; ceremonies and rituals; social events and celebrations)
- Employee development programs (training, mentoring, 360 feedback, education subsidies)
- Human resource planning (succession planning, assessment centers, recruiting programs)
- Empowerment programs (self-managed teams, employee ownership, industrial democracy)
- Recognition and reward programs focused on loyalty, service, or skill acquisition

Innovation and Adaptation

- Competitor and market analysis programs (market surveys, focus groups, consumer panels, comparative product testing, benchmarking of competitor products and processes)
- Innovation programs (entrepreneurship programs, quality circles, innovation goals)
- Knowledge acquisition (consultants, joint ventures, importing best practices from others)
- Organizational learning (knowledge management systems, after-activity reviews, joint ventures)
- Temporary groups for implementing change (steering committee, task forces)
- Growth and diversification programs (mergers and acquisitions, franchises, joint ventures)
- Structural forms (research departments, small product divisions, product managers, cross-functional product development teams)
- Appraisal, recognition, and reward systems focused on innovation and customer satisfaction

and reduce labor costs. Efficiency is also affected by aspects of an organization's formal structure such as formalization, standardization, and the use of functionally specialized subunits (Mintzberg, 1979).

Several types of programs have been used to improve innovation and adaptation (e.g., Damanpour, 1991; Dougherty & Hardy, 1996; Gibson & Birkinshaw, 2004; Van de Ven, Poley, Garud, & Venkataraman, 1999; Vermeulen, De Jong, & O'Shaughnessy, 2005). Examples include programs that improve understanding of customer preferences and competitor actions (e.g., market surveys, focus groups, customer panels, comparative product testing, and benchmarking of competitor products and processes). Structural forms that can increase innovation and adaptation include research and development departments, cross-functional product development teams, product managers, and semi-autonomous divisions based on products, market segments, or different types of customers (Galbraith, 1973; Mintzberg, 1979).

Many types of strategic human resource management programs and systems are used to improve human capital (Guzzo, Jette, & Katzell, 1985; Huselid, 1995; Jackson et al., 2014; Jiang et al., 2013; Kirkman & Rosen, 1997; Lawler et al., 2001; Wright & Ulrich, 2017). Employee skills can be improved with recruiting and selection programs, talent management and succession planning programs, and employee development programs (e.g., training, mentoring program, multi-source feedback, education subsidies, corporate university). Identification with the organization can be improved with quality of work-life programs (flextime, job sharing, child care, fitness center), employee benefit programs (compensation, health care, retirement, sabbaticals), socialization programs (orientation sessions, celebrations, rituals, and ceremonies), employee empowerment programs (employee stock ownership, industrial democracy), and recognition and reward programs based on loyalty, service, and skill acquisition.

Despite some dramatic successes, many improvement programs and management systems fail because they are irrelevant, poorly implemented, or incompatible with the organization's culture and competitive strategy (Abrahamson, 1996; Abrahamson & Fairchild, 1999; Beer, 1988, 2011; Benner & Tushman, 2003; Carson, P. P., Lanier, Carson, K. D., & Guidry, 2000; Narayanan & Fahey, 2013; Staw & Epstein, 2000). Management programs and systems intended to improve one performance determinant often have unintended side effects on other performance determinants, and the side effects may be positive or negative. Even if a program is able to achieve its primary objective, adverse side effects may cause it to be abandoned. However, there is considerable research evidence that strategic human resource management programs can improve organizational performance by aligning human resource practices with strategic goals (Jiang et al., 2013; Wright & Ulrich, 2017).

How Leaders Influence Organizational Performance

Leaders can do many things to influence the determinants of organizational performance, and two general approaches are described by Flexible Leadership Theory (Yukl, 2008; Yukl & Lepsinger, 2004; Yukl & Mahsud, 2010). One approach is to use leadership behaviors to directly influence individuals and groups. The task-oriented behaviors described in earlier chapters are used primarily to improve efficiency and process reliability. The relations-oriented behaviors are used primarily to improve human relations and human resources. The change-oriented behaviors are used primarily to improve innovation and adaptation to the external environment.

A second general approach is to make decisions about competitive strategy, organization structure, and management programs. Top executives usually have primary responsibility and authority for decisions about competitive strategy and the creation or modification of formal programs, systems, and structures (de Kluyver & Pearce, 2015; Finkelstein et al., 2009; Hambrick, 2007; Hambrick, Nadler, & Tushman, 1998; Hiller & Beauchesne, 2014; Hunt, 1991; Kollenscher, Eden, Ronen, & Farjoun, 2017). However, a coordinated effort by leaders at all levels in the organization is necessary to ensure that a strategy, improvement program, or new management system is effectively implemented (Raes, Heijltjes, Glunk, & Roe, 2011). Most leadership theories describe the direct influence of leader behavior on subordinate attitudes and motivation, but not the indirect influence on members derived from changing programs and systems. Over a longer period of time, top executives and other leaders in an organization can also influence cultural values with a combination of behaviors, programs, and reward systems.

Direct behaviors and decisions about strategy and programs or structures are complementary forms of leader influence (Yukl, 2008). The direct behaviors can be used to facilitate the implementation of a new strategy or program and their successful use. For example, a new training program is more likely to be successful when leaders encourage subordinates to attend the program and provide them with opportunities to use newly learned skills on the job. A new knowledge management system is more likely to be successful when employees are encouraged to input relevant information and use the system in appropriate ways. A major change in strategy is more likely to be accepted when leaders explain why it is needed and how it will benefit the organization.

Management programs and systems can enhance the effects of direct leadership behaviors (Yukl, 2008; Yukl & Lepsinger, 2004). For example, encouraging innovative thinking is much more likely to increase the development of new products and processes when an organization has a well-designed program to facilitate and reward innovation. Without such a program, employees may doubt that their creative ideas will be supported and eventually used by the organization. However, programs and structures can also limit the use of leadership behaviors or nullify the effects of this behavior. For example, it is difficult to empower subordinates when there are elaborate rules and standard procedures for doing the work. It is difficult for a leader to influence subordinates to improve customer service if there is an incentive system with rewards based entirely on the number of customers served, and faster service is achieved by reducing service quality.

Management programs and systems can also serve as substitutes for some types of direct behaviors (Yukl, 2008; Yukl & Lepsinger, 2004). For example, company-wide training programs can reduce the amount of training that managers need to provide to their immediate subordinates. Management programs and systems provide a way to ensure that common activities are carried out in an efficient and uniform way across subunits. A company-wide bonus system with clear guidelines is likely to be more equitable than having each subunit manager determine the size and frequency of bonuses and the criteria for awarding them. Training of generic skills that are relevant for all employees is likely to be more efficient and consistent if provided by expert trainers as part of a company training program rather than by many individual managers in the company.

Trade-Offs and Synergies

Complex interdependencies and trade-offs among the performance determinants create difficult challenges for leaders (Beer, 2001, 2011; Quinn, 1988; Yukl & Lepsinger, 2004). Decisions and actions that are intended to improve one performance determinant can affect the others in a positive or negative way, and unintended consequences are common. A leader who puts too much emphasis on influencing one performance determinant may have an adverse effect on another performance determinant, resulting in lower organizational performance. An example from Home Depot shows how attempts to improve efficiency can adversely affect both human relations and adaptation (Foust, 2003):

> When Bob Nardelli left GE to become the new CEO at Home Depot, he decided to cut costs by centralizing purchasing decisions, limiting the number of available items for sale, and using more part-time employees. These changes made the job of the store managers much less appealing and many quit. Customer satisfaction declined, because many of their preferred items were no longer available, and the part-time employees could not provide the type of advice valued by customers. The effect of the changes was a decline in sales and stock values for Home Depot.

When there are difficult trade-offs, it is essential to find an appropriate balance that reflects the relative priorities of the performance determinants and the potential for improving each one (Beer, 2001, 2011; Ebben & Johnson, 2005; Gibson & Birkinshaw, 2004; Quinn, 1988; Uotila, Maula, Keil, & Zahra, 2009; Yukl & Lepsinger, 2004). In some cases it is not possible to improve a performance determinant without consistent changes in the others. For example, it is difficult to improve efficiency or innovation if the necessary changes depend on employees who lack the motivation and skills necessary to achieve these objectives. Whenever possible, leaders should look for ways to enhance more than one performance determinant at the same time.

The performance of a team or organization is likely to be better when leaders are able to enhance innovative adaptation and efficiency simultaneously, which is sometimes called "organizational ambidexterity" (Boumgarden, Nickerson, & Zenger, 2012; Gibson & Birkinshaw, 2004; He & Wong, 2004; Heavey & Simsek, 2017; O'Reilly & Tushman, 2004, 2013; Patel, Messersmith, & Lepak, 2013; Tushman & O'Reilly, 1996). For example, one study (Gilson, Mathieu, Shalley, & Ruddy, 2005) found that equipment repair teams with highly skilled members (human capital) were able to achieve low costs (efficiency) as well as good customer service (adaptation) with a combination of standardized best practices and creativity in using new approaches. Success in achieving potential synergies requires a good understanding of the complex relationships among performance determinants and the consequences of decisions made to influence them. The following example illustrates how one well-known firm, 3M, successfully achieved such synergy (Paul & Fenlason, 2014).

> Throughout the twentieth century, 3M has had an unsurpassed record of breakthrough innovation and bringing new products to markets, but in 2006 the challenge facing George Buckley as the newly appointed CEO was how to achieve a balance between innovation and operational efficiency. Buckley felt it was imperative to revitalize the innovative spirit as the route to growth. He changed both the corporate strategic planning and operations planning approaches to encourage more customization of strategies in each of the businesses as well as a simultaneous reduction in the overall number of corporate initiatives. Sales of products developed in the previous 5 years, which is an indicator of future revenue and the success of R&D efforts, accounted for 32% of total revenue in 2011, up from 21% in 2005.

The task of balancing trade-offs among the performance determinants is complicated by changes in conditions affecting the relative importance of the performance determinants (Yukl, 2008; Yukl & Lepsinger, 2009). Examples include changes in economic and political conditions, new competition from other organizations, changes in customer preferences, and changes in technology that affect the processes or products of the company. A leader may achieve a good balance only to find that changing conditions have upset it again. Leaders should frequently assess the situation and determine what types of behavior, programs, management systems, and structural forms are relevant and mutually compatible. Using a particular type of behavior, program, or strategy because it proved successful in the past or for other leaders may not yield the desired results. Considerable skill is required to monitor and diagnose the situation accurately and integrate diverse leadership activities in a way that is relevant for changing conditions (Boal & Hooijberg, 2001; Hooijberg et al., 1997; Simsek, Heavy, & Fox, 2018; Yukl & Lepsinger, 2005). The following example vividly shows what can go wrong when top executives fail to understand these complexities (Finkelstein, 2003):

> In the 1980s two major problems for General Motors were contentious relations with the autoworkers union and increasing competition from low-cost, high-quality cars made by Toyota and other Japanese companies. Roger Smith, the CEO of GM, believed that the solution for improving both efficiency and quality was to replace most production workers with robots. He had a vision of GM factories operating at high speed day and night with no worker errors, no strikes, and lower labor costs. The GM executives failed to anticipate the difficulties and high cost of automating production processes, and they did not understand

that a much better solution was to use the same lean manufacturing practices that were so effective for Toyota (including supply-chain management, just-in-time inventory, and quality management practices). The cost for capital investment in new equipment and the high costs for skilled technicians to operate and maintain the equipment far exceeded any savings from downsizing the work force. The automated factories failed to provide the expected improvement in quality, and productivity actually declined during the period from 1984 to 1991. GM invested more than 45 billion dollars in automation, and this amount would have been sufficient to purchase both Toyota and Nissan.

Coordinating Leadership Across Levels and Subunits

Leadership in organizations is a process that involves many formal and informal leaders at all levels and in different subunits of the organization. The fates of different leaders are closely intertwined in complex ways, and the overall performance of the organization is likely to suffer if decisions made by different leaders are not compatible with each other (Yukl, 2008). Even though top executives have primary responsibility for strategic decisions, they are unlikely to be implemented successfully without the support and commitment of middle- and lower-level leaders in the organization (Beer, 2011; Beer et al., 1990; Huy, 2002; O'Reilly et al., 2010; Raes et al., 2011; Wai-Kwong, Priem, & Cycyota, 2001).

Even in organizations with a powerful CEO, the implementation of a new strategy or major change can be delayed by prolonged conflicts among top executives, or by resistance to change from managers at middle and lower levels. Leaders may disagree about the nature of external threats and opportunities, the reasons for past success or failure, the priorities for different objectives, the feasibility of alternative strategies, and the need for major changes. A good understanding of reasons for potential resistance is needed to identify a vision or competitive strategy that will elicit sufficient cooperation and commitment (Beer, 2011; Connor, 1995; Edmondson, Roberto, & Watkins, 2003; Kotter, 2002; Leonardi, 2015; Narayanan & Liam, 2013; Robbins & Duncan, 1988; Smith & Tushman, 2005).

It is important to understand the complex interdependencies that determine the consequences of strategic decisions for other executives and the overall organization (Hambrick, Humphrey, & Gupta, 2015). The primary responsibility for resolving disagreements and achieving integration usually falls on the CEO, but an alternative approach is to make the entire executive team responsible for integration (Kisfalvi, Sergi, & Langley, 2016). The facilitating conditions and essential processes for a "leader-centric" or "team-centric" approach are described by Smith and Tushman (2005).

It is difficult to achieve cooperation and coordination across levels and subunits in an organization unless the managers have shared ideals and values to guide their decisions (Carter & Greer, 2013). Companies with a "core ideology" that is strong and relevant are more likely to survive and be successful over a long period of time (Collins & Porras, 1997). Top management has primary responsibility for ensuring that the organization has a relevant core ideology, but leaders at all levels must help to build support for it and ensure that it is understood.

Top executives do not have a monopoly on relevant information or new ideas, and innovative changes in organizations often originate from lower levels (Marion & Uhl-Bien, 2001; Uhl-Bien & Marion, 2009; Yukl & Lepsinger, 2004). There are several ways top management can increase the involvement of middle- and lower-level managers in making strategic decisions (Barney, Foss, & Lyngsie, 2018; Denis, Lamothe, & Langley, 2001; Sundaramurthy & Lewis, 2003). Managers at different levels can be invited to participate in face-to-face or virtual meetings about strategic decisions. Task forces with representatives from different subunits and levels can be formed to develop a new initiative or determine what types of changes are necessary. Relevant programs and systems can be used to encourage and support proposals from lower-level managers for improving efficiency, adaptation, and human relations.

Situations Affecting Strategic Leadership

The opportunity of top executives to exert strong influence on the performance of an organization is greater for some situations than for others. It depends in part on the success of the organization's current strategies in achieving a high level of financial performance, on external conditions that determine if the strategies are effective, on the power of the CEO to make major changes, and on internal and external constraints that limit the decisions of the CEO (de Kluyver & Pearce, 2015; Finkelstein et al., 2009; Hiller & Beauchesne, 2014; Lord & Maher, 1991; Miller & Friesen, 1984; Simsek et al., 2018; Tushman & Romanelli, 1985; Tushman, Newman, & Romanelli, 1986). Each of these situational influences will be described briefly.

Constraints on Top Executives

How much influence top executives can have on the performance of their organization is determined in part by internal and external constraints on their decisions and actions (Bromiley & Rau, 2015; Hambrick, 2007; Hambrick & Finkelstein, 1987). One type of internal constraint involves powerful inside forces or coalitions in the organization. Power and discretion are greater when the CEO is a major owner or shareholder of the firm or when the board of directors is easily influenced to support the CEO. Discretion is also increased when surplus financial reserves are available to fund new ventures, or the firm's prosperity makes it easy to finance innovations by borrowing funds. There is less discretion when the CEO must operate in the shadow of the company founder, satisfy a dominant owner (e.g., the organization is a family-owned firm or the subsidiary of another firm), or answer to a strong board of directors with rigid ideas about the appropriate way to do things. Discretion is also limited when internal factions and coalitions have sufficient power to block changes a leader wants to make (e.g., labor unions, other executives with a strong power base), or there is a strong organization culture that is resistant to change (Windsor, 2010). Large organizations with a strong bureaucracy and standardized ways of doing things have an inertia that is difficult to overcome. People resist change that threatens their status and power, contradicts their values and beliefs, or requires learning new ways of doing things.

External constraints on the discretion of a CEO include the nature of the organization's primary products and services and the type of markets in which the organization operates (de Kluyver & Pearce, 2015). Managerial discretion is greater if the organization is in a growth industry that has rapidly increasing demand rather than flat or declining demand, if the organization's products or services can be differentiated from those of competitors (not a standardized "commodity" such as gasoline or cement), and if the organization dominates its markets and faces little or no direct competition (e.g., it is a monopoly or has a dominant share of the market). Discretion is constrained by powerful external stakeholders who can dictate conditions, as when a few major clients account for most of the company's sales, or when the company is dependent on a single source of key materials. The decisions and actions of top executives are limited by environmental regulations, labor laws, safety standards, and legal obligations. Even when the organization is a monopoly, discretion in key areas such as pricing, technology, and product changes may be severely limited by government regulation.

Environmental Uncertainty and Crises

The discretion of an executive to make major changes depends in part on how internal and external stakeholders perceive the current performance of the organization. In a crisis situation, leaders are expected to take more decisive, innovative actions (Clair & Dufresne, 2007; de Kluyver & Pearce, 2015). The potential influence of a CEO on the organization's performance is much larger when major changes in the environment threaten to undermine the effectiveness of the existing strategy or provide unusual opportunities to pursue a new strategy. A CEO who foresees the need for change and takes bold steps to deal with threats and capitalize on opportunities can have a dramatic effect on the long-term survival and effectiveness of the organization (Abdelgawad, Zahra, Svejenova, & Sapienza, 2013; Weber, 2000).

Major innovative changes in an organization are less likely to occur in periods of relative stability and prosperity. In the absence of an obvious crisis and declining performance, major changes are risky. In a relatively stable environment, changing a traditional strategy that has been effective can reduce financial performance rather than improving it (McClelland, Liang, & Barker, 2009). It is often costly to implement a new strategy, and a temporary decline in financial performance is likely as added costs are incurred and people learn new ways of doing things (Lord & Maher, 1991). Considerable time is usually required to verify the success of a major change (three to five years), and constituents may become impatient about the lack of faster progress.

When faced with gradual changes in the external environment such as new competition, new technology, or shifts in customer preferences, many executives persist too long in the belief that a previously successful strategy is still relevant (Audia, Locke, & Smith, 2000; Lant, Milliken, & Batra, 1992; Miller & Chen, 1994; Narayanan & Liam, 2013). When executives identify with the current strategy because they developed it, or their implicit assumptions about it are incorrect, then they are likely to make only incremental changes rather than major changes (Methe, Wilson, & Perry, 2000). Efforts to strengthen the current strategy by cutting costs and tightening controls often result in a temporary improvement in performance, making top management appear to be successful (Johnson, 1992). An entrenched CEO may continue to invest more resources in the current strategy rather than admit that it is failing (Staw & Ross, 1987), and such escalation of commitment by strategic decision makers has been shown to generalize across cultures (Greer & Stephens, 2001).

When organizational performance is declining and the survival of the organization is in doubt, it is common to bring in a new CEO from outside the organization with a mandate to make major changes. A new CEO usually makes some initial changes to seek immediate relief, buy time for longer-term solutions, and gain more discretion for future changes (Ma & Seidl, 2018; Schepker, Kim, Patel, Thatcher, & Campion, 2017). However, if the initial changes are costly to implement and disruptive to operations, the net effect may be a further decline in organizational performance until the benefits of the change finally begin to materialize (Gabarro, 1987; Haveman, 1992; Schepker et al., 2017). A study of NFL coaches found that major changes were more likely to be successful if the new leader had visible success in a prior position, but the study also found that leaders with a good reputation were usually more cautious about making major changes (Ndofor, Priem, Rathburn, & Dhir, 2009).

Internal and external constraints interact with each other and with the leader's personality and skills to influence the leader's behavior (Finkelstein et al., 2009; Hiller & Beauchesne, 2014). Over time pressures arise that favor a match between the type of leadership situation and the type of person filling it. The most restrictive situation is one in which internal and external constraints are so severe that the CEO is merely a figurehead who cannot implement any significant strategy changes or innovations. This type of position is unlikely to attract an ambitious, innovative leader, and the organization selection process will favor a conservative, risk-averse, compliant person.

The opposite extreme is the situation with few internal and external constraints and ample discretion. Ambitious, dynamic leaders will be attracted to this type of position. Ample discretion provides opportunities for innovative leadership but does not guarantee it. Even in a situation with few constraints, some leaders lack the cognitive skill to perceive innovative options or the motivation to pursue them.

Organizational Culture

The culture of an organization consists of shared assumptions, beliefs, and values for the members (Alvesson, 2010; Schein, 1992, 2016; Trice & Beyer, 1991, 1993). The underlying beliefs and values help members deal with problems of survival in the external environment and problems of internal integration. There may be one dominant culture for the entire organization, or the organization may have subunits with their own unique cultures. An organization's culture is a situational influence on leaders, but over time leaders can also influence culture. This section of the chapter explains the functions of culture, the relationship of culture to organizational performance, the influence of leaders on culture, and the difficulty of changing it.

Functions of Culture

A major function of culture is to help people understand the environment and determine how to respond to it, thereby reducing anxiety, uncertainty, and confusion. External issues include the core mission of the organization, concrete objectives based on this mission, strategies for attaining these objectives, ways to measure success in attaining objectives, and the reasons for unexpected events affecting the organization. Objectives and strategies cannot be achieved effectively without cooperative effort, and internal integration involves issues such as the criteria for membership in the organization, the basis for determining status and power, criteria and procedures for allocating rewards and punishments, rules or customs about how to handle aggression and intimacy, and a shared consensus about the meaning of words and symbols. The beliefs that develop about these issues serve as the basis for role expectations to guide behavior, let people know what is proper and improper, and help people maintain comfortable relationships with each other. The internal and external problems are closely interconnected, and organizations must deal with them simultaneously. As solutions are developed through experience, they become shared assumptions that are passed on to new members. Over time, the assumptions may become so familiar that members are no longer consciously aware of them. Shared beliefs and established traditions are an important cultural mechanism for ensuring stability and continuity in an organization or society, and culture can facilitate or limit efforts to make major changes in the organization (see Chapter 5).

Culture and Organizational Performance

Cultural values can enhance the performance of an organization if they are consistent with the types of processes needed to accomplish the mission and adapt to internal and external challenges (Bezrukova, Thatcher, Jehn, & Spell, 2012; Cameron & Quinn, 2011;

Gordon & DiTomaso, 1992; Harrison & Bazzy, 2017; Kotter & Heskett, 1992). For example, shared values such as flexibility, creativity, and entrepreneurial initiative can facilitate innovation and organizational learning (Baer & Frese, 2003). Shared values about reliability, meeting deadlines, error-free performance, controlling costs, and responsible use of resources, and adherence to best practices and standard procedures can enhance efficiency (Miron et al., 2004). The organization's culture may also include values that are important in the national culture (e.g., performance orientation, uncertainty tolerance), and these values can also have implications for the organization's performance (see Chapter 13). A strong corporate culture can be a weakness rather than an advantage if shared beliefs and values are not consistent with the strategies necessary for the organization to prosper and survive.

Leader Influence on Culture

The CEO of an organization usually has more influence than other individual managers, but the corporate culture reflects the influence of many different leaders over a considerable period of time (Pfeffer, 1992; Schein, 1992; Trice & Beyer, 1993; Tsui, Zhang, Wang, Xin, & Wu, 2006). The influence of an individual CEO can be substantial for the entrepreneurial founder of a successful company who has led it for many years, or for a turnaround CEO who saves a dying organization by making major changes in strategy and operating practices. The potential influence of leaders on corporate culture increases in a crisis that requires major changes, but the CEO is not the only source of this influence. When one subunit is clearly more important than the others for the continued success of the organization, key elements of its subculture may emerge and become central in the corporate culture.

Leaders can influence the culture of an organization in a variety of ways, and the effects are stronger when the different approaches are consistent with each other (Day, Griffin, & Louw, 2014; Schein, 1992, 2016). One form of leader influence on the organizational culture is the use of ideological appeals and repeated articulation of an inspiring vision for the organization or subunit. Leaders communicate their values when they make statements about values and objectives that are important and formulate long-term strategies and plans for attaining them (Hambrick & Lovelace, 2018). Written value statements, charters, and philosophies can be useful, but they have little credibility unless supported by leader actions and decisions. Leaders communicate values and expectations by highly visible symbolic actions relevant for cultural values, such as showing loyalty, self-sacrifice, and service beyond the call of duty. Even when the symbolic actions or decisions of a leader are not directly observed by most members of the organization, they can become the subject of stories and myths and be propagated widely. Leaders also communicate their priorities and concerns in their daily activity by their choice of things to ask about, measure, comment on, praise, and criticize. By not paying attention to something, a leader sends the message that it is not important. The importance of keeping decisions and actions consistent with espoused values is shown in the following example (Newstrom & Davis, 1993):

> The CEO and top executives of a small computer company in the Silicon Valley wanted to create an appropriate culture for the new company. They produced a two-page values statement describing the importance of employee involvement, open communication, high-quality products, and good customer service. The values document was posted in prominent places and distributed to company employees. However, there was a wide discrepancy between the values statement and executive behavior, and most employees knew that secrecy and expediency were the real values. Instead of open communication, meetings were used to announce decisions already made by top management, and employees were not encouraged to suggest ideas or express concerns. Getting the product out the door to customers had top priority,

regardless of possible defects. As quality problems increased, many customers became dissatisfied with the company's computers. Sales begin to decline, and two years later the company filed for bankruptcy.

Another approach for influencing culture involves the use of cultural forms such as symbols, slogans, rituals, and ceremonies (Hogan & Coote, 2014; Schein, 1992, 2016; Trice & Beyer, 1993). Rituals, ceremonies, and rites of passage can be used to emphasize core values and strengthen identification with the organization. In many organizations new members are required to make a public oath of allegiance, demonstrate knowledge of the ideology, or undergo an ordeal that demonstrates loyalty. It is common to have ceremonies to celebrate a member's advancement in rank, to inaugurate a new leader, and to acknowledge the retirement of a member. Rituals and ceremonies may also involve the communication of stories about important events and heroic actions by individuals. However, stories and myths are more a reflection of culture than a determinant of it. To be useful the story must describe a real event and convey a clear message about values.

A third way for leaders to influence culture is creation or modification of formal programs, systems, and facilities. Formal budgets, planning sessions, reports, performance review procedures, and management development programs can be used to emphasize some values and beliefs about proper behavior. Orientation programs can be used to socialize new employees and teach them about the culture of an organization. Training programs designed to increase job skills can also be used to teach participants about the ideology of the organization. Values are also communicated by the criteria emphasized in recruiting, selecting, rewarding, promoting, and dismissing people. The effect on culture is stronger if the organization provides realistic information about the criteria and requirements for success, and the personnel decisions are consistent with these criteria.

Difficulty of Culture Change

How difficult it is to change culture depends in part on the developmental stage of the organization (Schein, 1992, 2016; Trice & Beyer, 1993). The founder of a new organization has a strong influence on its culture. The founder typically has a vision of a new enterprise and proposes ways of doing things that, if successful in accomplishing objectives and reducing anxiety, will gradually become embedded in the culture. The culture in young, successful organizations is likely to be strong when it is instrumental to the success of the organization, the assumptions are internalized by current members and transmitted to new members, and the founder is still present to symbolize and reinforce the culture. The culture will evolve slowly over the years as experience reveals that some assumptions need to be modified. Eventually, as the organization matures and people other than the founder or family members occupy key leadership positions, the culture will become less uniform, and subcultures may develop in different subunits.

In general, it is more difficult for leaders to change culture in a mature organization than to create it in a new organization. One reason is that many of the underlying beliefs and assumptions shared by people in a mature organization are implicit and unconscious. Cultural assumptions are also difficult to change when they justify the past and are a matter of pride. Moreover, cultural values influence the selection of leaders and the role expectations for them. In a mature, relatively prosperous organization, culture influences leaders more than leaders influence culture. Drastic changes in cultural values are unlikely unless a major crisis threatens the welfare and survival of the organization. Even with a crisis, it takes considerable insight and skill for a leader to understand the current culture in an organization and implement changes successfully.

Research on Effects of Strategic Leadership

The effects of CEO leadership on company performance have been examined in research with different methods. Results will be reviewed for succession studies, intensive case studies, and survey studies of CEO behavior.

Studies of CEO Succession

Research on the consequences of changing the chief executive of an organization is relevant for understanding importance of strategic leadership. The research method in most succession studies is an archival field study on CEOs for a sample of business corporations, but a few succession studies have used coaches of professional sports teams. All data is from archival records, and characteristics of the successors (e.g., internal versus external) are related to changes in objective measures of organizational performance in the years before and after succession occurs (e.g., Chiu, Johnson, Hoskisson, & Pathak, 2016; Grinyer, Mayes, & McKiernan, 1990). Progress has been made in understanding the reasons for succession, how successors are selected, and the consequences of succession for the organization (Chiu et al., 2016; Georgakakis & Ruigrok, 2017; Giambatista, Rowe, & Riaz, 2005; Hutzschenreuter, Kleindienst, & Greger, 2012; Ma, Seidl, & Guérard, 2015; Marcel, Cowen, & Ballinger, 2017; Schepker et al., 2017; Sobel, Harkins, & Conley, 2007).

Narrative reviews of the succession research provide evidence that changes in the chief executive have important effects on the long-term performance of an organization (Giambatista et al., 2005; Hutzschenreuter et al., 2012). However, many limitations in the research complicate interpretation of the results, including differences in performance criteria, failure to consider effects of internal and external constraints, and failure to consider CEO skills. Many succession studies do not measure the executive's actions, the organizational processes that would explain how a chief executive influences performance, or the conditions that determine how much potential influence the leaders can have (Day & Lord, 1988; Giambatista et al., 2005; House & Singh, 1987). Nevertheless, sufficient research has accumulated over the years to allow Shepker and colleagues (2017) to conduct a meta-analysis into the relationships between CEO succession, strategic change, and firm performance. Drawing from 60 samples that reflect over 13,000 CEO successions, these researchers found that while CEO succession negatively impacted firm performance in the short-term, the effects on long-term performance depended on the amount of strategic change and whether the new CEO came from inside or outside the firm. Succession by a CEO from inside the firm was associated with long-term gains in performance and less strategic change, while hiring an outside CEO resulted in more strategic change but lower long-term performance. These findings suggest that although outside CEOs tend to produce more radical change as they attempt to shake things up in the firm, such disruption may ultimately have an adverse effect on firm performance when the outsider has an insufficient understanding of the firm and the industry.

Descriptive Studies of CEO Decisions and Actions

Several types of descriptive studies have been used to investigate the influence of CEOs on their organizations. Many different sources of information can be used, including interviews, questionnaires, company records, annual reports, and financial databases. Some researchers also use information from secondary sources such as biographies, autobiographies, and magazine articles about organizations and their leaders. Descriptive studies of chief executives usually examine the types of decisions and actions that account for the success or failure of an organization over a period of several years.

A comparative study of several organizations has been used to see if successful CEOs have a similar pattern of strategic decisions and behavior (e.g., Bennis & Nanus, 1985; Nadler et al., 1995), or if CEO actions and communications can explain why some companies have better financial performance than other companies in the same industry (e.g., Makri & Scandura, 2010; McClelland et al., 2009). An intensive case study of a single organization was used to examine how a new chief executive leads a dramatic turnaround by a company in decline (e.g., Ghosn & Ries, 2007; Wyden, 1987). A few studies examined CEOs who were initially successful but later experienced failure in order to determine the reasons for different outcomes (e.g., Finkelstein, 2003; Probst & Raisch, 2005). Descriptive studies of top executives are not limited to corporations, and some are conducted with military leaders, political leaders, or leaders of nonprofit organizations (e.g., Bennis & Nanus, 1985; Burns, 1978; Van Fleet & Yukl, 1986b).

One limitation of most descriptive studies is the difficulty in getting accurate information about the behavior of chief executives and their influence on organizational performance. Information provided by a current or former CEO may be biased by a desire to present a favorable image. Celebrity CEOs may be unwilling to reveal weaknesses and may claim more credit than is deserved for successes. Information from other sources may also be unreliable. Few members of the organization have an opportunity to directly observe most of a chief executive's actions. The people who are close to the CEO may be unwilling to discuss controversial decisions or events in which they were involved, out of loyalty, fear for their own reputation, or because of nondisclosure agreements. Even when accurate information can be obtained, it may be difficult to assess the influence of a single CEO. Many of a chief executive's strategic decisions and actions only indirectly affect the financial performance of a large company, and the effects may not be clear until several years later. Financial performance is affected by many different events and by the actions of many parties (e.g., the board of directors, other top executives, competitors, strategic partners, regulatory agencies).

Despite all the difficulties in conducting this type of research, it has provided additional evidence that CEOs can exert significant influence on the performance of their organizations. The descriptive studies also provide insights into the reasons why some chief executives are more effective than others. Successful chief executives identify important threats and opportunities for their organization, take decisive action to resolve serious problems, identify a good competitive strategy, and implement the strategy in a timely way. These CEOs also foster a strong core ideology that is consistent with the mission and strategy.

Survey Studies on CEO Leadership

Several survey studies have examined how leadership by a chief executive is related to a firm's financial performance or rated effectiveness (e.g., Agle et al., 2006; Boehm, Dwertmann, Bruch, & Shamir, 2015; Eisenbeiss et al., 2015; Jung, Wu, & Chow, 2008; Ling, Simsek, Lubatkin, & Veiga, 2008a, 2008b; Makri & Scandura, 2010; Peterson, Galvin, & Lange, 2012; Peterson, Walumbwa, Byron, & Myrowitz, 2009; Tosi et al., 2004; Waldman, Javidan, & Varella, 2004; Waldman et al., 2001; Wang, Tsui, & Xin, 2011; Zhu, Chew, & Spangler, 2005). Leadership behavior was measured with a questionnaire filled out by one or more subordinates, and behavior was correlated with measures of the company's financial performance. While most of these studies were narrowly focused on the effects of charismatic or transformational leadership by a CEO, some of the studies focused on CEO ethical or servant leadership.

The findings were not consistent across the studies, which may be due in part to large differences in the samples, the measure of leadership behavior, and the measure of organizational effectiveness. The measures of ethical, servant, charismatic, and transformational leadership were correlated with objective or perceived measures of organizational effectiveness. A few studies found that the results were dependent on situational variables such as the size and type of organization and environmental dynamism or uncertainty. None of the studies included adequate measures of performance determinants that explain how a CEO influences financial performance for a large company. Knowledge about firm performance may have biased the ratings of leader behavior. This attribution bias occurs when the CEO of a company known to have strong financial performance is rated more charismatic or transformational than CEOs for companies with weaker performance, despite no actual difference in their behavior. In one study that attempted to control for this bias by including a measure of past performance, a significant effect for CEO charismatic leadership was not found (Agle et al., 2006).

A recent study by O'Reilly, Caldwell, Chatman, and Doerr (2014) used a sample of 32 high-tech firms to explore the relationships between survey measures of CEO personality and organizational culture and objective measures of firm performance. CEOs who were very open to experience were more likely to lead firms with a culture that emphasizes adaptability. CEOs who were very conscientious were more likely to lead firms with a detail-oriented culture. CEOs who were less agreeable (more competitive and skeptical) were more likely to lead firms with a results-oriented culture. Furthermore, firms with cultures that stressed adaptability experienced more favorable levels of revenue growth, market valuations, stock analyst recommendations, reputational rankings, and employee attitudes. Firms with more detail-oriented cultures also achieved high levels of performance, as indicated by a high level of revenue growth and rankings on the *Fortune* list of most admired companies. Finally, firms with more customer-oriented cultures achieved higher market evaluations, and firms that placed an emphasis on integrity received more favorable recommendations from stock analysts. Although the study could not show causality in these relationships, the results suggest that the personalities of strategic leaders serve to shape an organization's culture and performance.

Evaluation of Research on Strategic Leadership

The research on leadership by chief executives of organizations shows that they can influence organizational processes and outcomes, but this influence varies greatly depending on the situation and the traits and skills of the leaders. The succession studies, descriptive studies, and survey studies all have limitations, and more comprehensive research is needed to accurately determine how chief executives can influence the financial performance of their firms. The research should examine a much broader range of actions and decisions by chief executives, including how they influence strategy, structure, programs, systems, and culture. The research should include measures of other relevant mediating processes and determinants of performance in addition to cultural values and member motivation, commitment, and cooperation. Other relevant mediators were described earlier in this chapter. Finally, it is essential to gather information about the influence of other top executives and leaders at middle and lower levels in the organization.

Executive Teams

All organizations have a top management group that includes the CEO and other top executives, but organizations differ greatly in the way this group operates. The traditional approach is to have a clear hierarchy of authority with a CEO (usually the chairman of the board, but sometimes the president of the organization), a chief operating officer (usually the president of the organization), and several subordinate executives (e.g., vice presidents) who head various subunits of the organization. This structure is still prominent, but an increasingly popular alternative is to share power within the top management team (Ancona & Nadler, 1989; Carmeli, Schaubroeck, & Tishler, 2011; Lin & Rababah, 2014; Ling, Wei, Klimoski, & Wu, 2015). Executives in the team collectively assume the responsibilities of the chief operating officer in managing the internal operations of the organization, and they assist the CEO in formulating strategy. Another, less common variation is the "office of the chairperson" structure in which the responsibilities of the CEO are shared, even though one executive (the chairperson) usually has more power than the others (the vice chairpersons).

Regardless of the formal structure of an organization, differences will occur in the extent to which strategic leadership is actually shared among the top executives. An organization with an executive team may have an autocratic CEO who allows other executives little influence over strategic decisions, whereas an organization with a traditional hierarchy may have a CEO who empowers other top executives to share responsibility for making strategic decisions.

Executive teams are becoming more acceptable due to their effective use in other countries (such as Japan) and a growing awareness that shared leadership can be beneficial for complex organizations in a turbulent environment. An example of an executive team with an unusual amount of shared leadership comes from Maruti Suzuki, a leading automobile manufacturer in India.

> The success of Maruti Suzuki India Ltd through all these years can be attributed to its model of paired (and shared) leadership. The model enabled the company to maintain its spot in spite of stiff competition from others. Maruti had two top executives, one from India and one from Japan. All decisions were ultimately taken jointly by the two of them. However, when the decision involved the Indian market, the opinion of the Indian executive was given precedence, while in other cases the Japanese executive's opinion was given precedence. However, in no case was the decision a solo one (The Hindu Business Line, 2012).

Potential Advantages

Executive teams offer a number of potential advantages for an organization (Ancona & Nadler, 1989; Bradford & Cohen, 1984; Eisenstat & Cohen, 1990; Hambrick, 1987; Nadler, 1998). The members often have relevant skills and knowledge that the CEO lacks and can compensate for weaknesses in the skills of the CEO. Important tasks are less likely to be neglected if several people are available to share the burden of leadership. When executives from different subunits meet regularly as a team, communication and cooperation are likely to be improved. The decisions made by a team are more likely to represent the diverse interests of organization members, and involvement in making these decisions will improve member commitment to implement them effectively.

A study by Korsgaard, Schweiger, and Sapienze (1995) found that when the CEO allowed other members of a top executive team to influence a strategic decision, the decision quality was better, the decision was perceived as more fair, team members were more committed to implement the decision, their trust in the leader increased, and they identified more with the team. A study of top management teams from 116 Israeli firms found that a high level of mutual understanding and collaboration among members (called "behavioral integration") was related to better quality of strategic decisions and more favorable ratings of organizational performance (Carmeli & Schaubroeck, 2006).

The team approach is also a way to facilitate leadership succession in large, diverse organizations. Experience in dealing with the major issues and decisions facing the organization provides opportunities for executives to develop more relevant leadership skills. Moreover, when several executives share responsibility for strategic leadership of the organization, it is easier for the current CEO and the board of directors to determine which executive in the team is most qualified to become the next CEO.

Facilitating Conditions

The potential advantages of having an executive team depend in part on the situation, and such teams are especially important when there is a complex, rapidly changing environment (Ancona & Nadler, 1989; Edmondson et al., 2003). Growing turbulence in the environment due to rapid technological changes and increased global competition has made the responsibility for developing successful strategy more difficult for many organizations. Teams are also more important when the organization has diverse but highly interdependent business units that require close coordination across units. In an organization with several diverse business units, a single leader is unlikely to have the broad expertise necessary to direct and coordinate the activities of these units.

The quality of the strategic decisions made by a team is likely to be better if the members have diverse backgrounds and perspectives, and their knowledge and skills are relevant for understanding how the organization can adapt in a dynamic, uncertain environment (Bantel & Jackson, 1989; Bjornali, Knockaert, & Erikson, 2016; Bromiley & Rau, 2015; Cannella, Park, & Lee, 2008; Murray, 1989). However, as in the research on task teams (see Chapter 11), research on top management teams (e.g., Hutzschenreuter & Horstkotte, 2013) found that task-related differences among members in educational background and experience enhance team performance, whereas performance is hindered by bio-demographic differences among members (e.g., age, nationality/ethnicity). These findings suggest that the potential benefits of diversity will not be achieved unless the team can process information and make decisions in a way that utilizes the knowledge and ideas of members. Highly divergent interests and differences in preferences and priorities regarding company objectives also make it more difficult to achieve mutual understanding (Colbert, Kristof-Brown, Bradley, & Barrick, 2008; Simsek, Veiga, Lubatkin, & Dino, 2005). It is more difficult to develop mutual trust and cooperation when team members represent subunits with different objectives or members are competing to become the successor to the current CEO.

Making strategic decisions jointly is more likely to yield high-quality decisions if the executives have an accurate, shared "mental model" about the determinants of organizational performance, their relative importance, and how they can be influenced to improve performance (Cannon-Bowers et al., 1993; Dao, Strobl, Bauer, & Tarba, 2017; Klimoski & Mohammed, 1994; Senge, 1990). More accurate models can be developed by explicit discussion of differences in how the executives view the world, by improving measures and information systems (to ensure accurate, timely information about key variables), and by conducting experiments on the effects of different types of changes and improvement programs. Relevant training in development of accurate mental models about the causes of important outcomes in complex systems is another way to improve strategic decisions by individual executives and teams (Marcy & Mumford, 2010).

Leadership of Executive Teams

Whether the potential advantages of executive teams are realized depends on the leadership provided by the CEO (Bromiley & Rau, 2015; Carmeli et al., 2011; Finkelstein et al., 2009; Eisenstat & Cohen, 1990; Lin & Rababah, 2014). Effective leadership is more likely if the CEO has relevant values, traits, and skills. For example, a comparative case study of 17 CEOs (e.g., Peterson, Smith, Martorana, & Owens, 2003) found that CEO personality was related to the top management team characteristics (optimism, cohesiveness, flexibility, and moderate risk taking), which were related in turn to a measure of financial performance.

Executive teams are more likely to be successful when the CEO selects team members with relevant skills and experience, clearly defines objectives consistent with shared values, gives the team considerable discretion but clearly specifies the limits of team authority in relation to CEO authority, helps the team establish norms that will facilitate group processes, facilitates learning of skills in working together effectively, and encourages openness and mutual trust among team members. The CEO should avoid actions that encourage competition or distrust, such as overtly making comparative evaluations among team members and meeting with individual executives to deal with issues that should be addressed by the entire team.

It is also essential for the CEO to help the team avoid process problems that can prevent them from making good decisions. If the CEO dominates decisions, the potential benefits of diverse members with relevant knowledge may not be realized. The quality of a strategic decision is likely to be better if individuals with the most expertise for that type of decision have ample influence over it. It is also important to make decisions in a timely way. The CEO should seek consensus among the executives who would be the most affected by a decision, rather than prolonging discussion in an effort to achieve consensus among all members. Here is an example of how a new CEO implemented an effective executive team (George, 2003, pp.96–97):

> To mold top executives into a well-oiled team and build agreement on major goals and objectives, we formed an executive committee that included the leaders of major company businesses and corporate staff units. Each meeting began with an executive session to discuss issues any member considered important. Then we reviewed and approved all strategies, investments, and financial plans for each business and the company as a whole. I encouraged committee members to make their positions known even on areas of the business for which they were not responsible. This open approach brought us closer together and built a strong sense of commitment to our mutual agenda. The executive committee actually voted on all major decisions of the corporation, including the release of new products before they went to market, which increased commitment to our decisions and emphasized the vital importance of product quality.

Example of a Study on Executive Teams

Eisenhardt (1989b) conducted a study of eight minicomputer firms to investigate how the speed and quality of strategic decisions were affected by the decision processes in these firms. Interviews were conducted with members of the executive team in each company to learn about the process used for important decisions, including when and how they were made. Questionnaires, company documents, and industry reports were used to obtain additional information about decision processes and company performance.

The study found that strategic decisions were both faster and better when the executive team conducted a simultaneous evaluation of several alternatives rather than using the common procedure (called "satisficing") of examining alternatives sequentially until a satisfactory one is found. An intensive decision process helped the team evaluate the strengths and weaknesses of each alternative, avoid premature commitment to a particular alternative, and identify a fallback position to use if attempts to implement the chosen alternative encountered unexpected obstacles. The executive team was more effective when it considered how a decision was related to other strategic decisions, and when it considered tactical plans (e.g., action steps, budgets, schedules) for implementing a strategic decision as part of the process for evaluating feasibility. This integrative approach appears to provide a better understanding of the alternatives and their implications, and it tends to reduce anxiety about possible adverse consequences, thereby increasing confidence in the team's evaluation and willingness to move forward with a decision.

Other Conceptions of Organizational Leadership

Some different ways of conceptualizing leadership have emerged in recent years, and they are eliciting interest among scholars who believe that the currently popular theories are too limited. Examples include shared and distributed leadership, relational leadership and social networks, and emergent processes in complexity theory. These approaches are still evolving, and as yet there is little conclusive research on them. Each approach will be described briefly.

Shared and Distributed Leadership

The theory and research on leadership have long recognized that effective leaders empower others to participate in the process of interpreting events, solving problems, and making decisions (Argyris, 1964; Likert, 1967). In most of these approaches, the focus is on the process by which focal leaders encourage and enable others to share responsibility for leadership functions. The emphasis in the traditional approaches is on using empowerment to make an individual leader more effective. An alternative view of organizations is that distributed leadership, power sharing, and political activities are inevitable in organizations, and they cannot be understood by focusing on the decisions and actions of individual leaders.

Proponents of this perspective recognize that the actions of any individual leader are less important than the collective leadership provided by many members of the organization, including both formal and informal leaders (Day, Gronn, & Salas, 2004; Friedrich, Griffith, & Mumford, 2016). Viewing leadership in terms of reciprocal, recursive influence processes among multiple leaders is different from studying unidirectional effects of a single leader on subordinates. Distributed leadership involves multiple leaders with distinct but inter-related responsibilities. Here a distinction can be made between distributed and shared leadership; while distributed leadership involves the dispersion of leadership responsibilities across individuals, these responsibilities may or may not be shared (Bolden, 2011). If the various leaders are unable to agree about what to do and how to do it (i.e., how to distribute responsibilities), performance of the team or organization is likely to suffer (e.g., Mehra, Smith, Dixon, & Robertson, 2006). Ensley, M. D., Hmieleski, K. M., & Pearce, C. L. (2006).

There are many different ways to share and distribute power and authority in organizations, and some are more successful than others (e.g., Cox, Pearce, & Perry, 2003; Ensley, Hmieleski, & Pearce, 2006; Friedrich et al., 2016; Gronn, 2002; Locke, 2003; O'Toole, Galbraith, & Lawler, 2003; Pearce & Conger, 2003). A few initial attempts to develop theories of shared leadership are promising (e.g., Ilgen, Hollenbeck, Johnson, & Jundt, 2005; Houghton, Pearce, Manz, Courtright, & Stewart, 2015; Pearce & Sims, 2000; Mayo, Meindl, & Pastor, 2003; Seers et al., 2003). In addition to the leadership literature, insights about shared and distributed leadership in organizations are provided by several other literatures (e.g., organization theory, public administration, strategic management, and social networks theory).

Several scholars have considered how shared, collective, or distributive leadership is related to team or organizational effectiveness (e.g., Brown & Gioia, 2002; Brown & Hosking, 1986; Carson et al., 2007; Denis et al., 2001; Friedrich et al., 2016; Friedrich, Vessey, Schuelke, Ruark, & Mumford, 2009; Hunt & Ropo, 1995; Lawler, 1986; Pearce & Sims, 2002; Semler, 1989). Three recent meta-analyses (D'Innocenzo, Mathieu, & Kukenberger, 2016; Nicolaides et al., 2014; Wang, Waldman, & Zhang, 2014) identified positive relationships between shared leadership and team performance. However, more research is needed on the implications of shared leadership and organizational-level outcomes such as corporate social responsibility and competitive advantage (Zhu, Liao, Yam, & Johnson, 2018). Moreover, the extent to which different types of leadership roles and decisions can be shared or distributed effectively, the conditions facilitating the emergence and success of shared leadership, and the implications for organizational design are all important questions that require more attention. Research that is intensive, descriptive, and longitudinal would make it easier to understand the complex processes involved in shared and distributed leadership.

Relational Leadership

Most theory and research on leadership view it as an influence process and focus on the actions of people designated as leaders. Relationships are acknowledged to be important in much of the leadership literature, but in "traditional" approaches the focus is on how an individual leader can develop and maintain cooperative relationships. An alternative view of leadership is to describe it as part of the evolving social order that results from interactions, exchanges, and influence processes among many people in an organization.

According to this perspective, leadership cannot be understood apart from the dynamics of the social system in which it occurs (Dachler, 1984, 1992; DeRue & Ashford, 2010; Drath, 2001; Uhl-Bien, 2006; Epitropaki et al., 2018; Uhl-Bien, Maslyn, & Ospina, 2012). Instead of the traditional focus on a single leader, scholars examine the social processes and patterned relationships that explain how collective activity can accomplish shared objectives. Organizations and other social entities (e.g., teams, coalitions, common interest groups) are defined more by the web of interpersonal relationships than by formal charters, structures, policies, and rules. The relationships are continually being modified as changes occur in the people who are involved in the collective activity, and as changing conditions elicit adaptive responses.

Leaders are defined as the people who consistently influence relationships and collective activities and are expected by others to have this influence (Hogg, 2001; Hosking, 1988; Uhl-Bien, 2006). Leadership influence is accomplished by interpreting events and explaining cause-effect relationships in a meaningful way, and by influencing others to modify their attitudes, behavior, and goals. Many different people participate in this leadership process, and their diverse and sometimes conflicting interests make it a political process involving the use of social power as well as rational and emotional appeals. Individuals develop and use social networks to gather information and build coalitions to increase their influence over decisions (e.g., Balkundi & Kilduff, 2005).

The methods most appropriate for studying relational leadership are seldom used in leadership research (Epitropaki et al., 2018; Uhl-Bien, 2006; Uhl-Bien et al., 2012). It is impossible to understand evolving relationships and reciprocal influence processes among multiple parties by analyzing data from survey studies in which most information is obtained with fixed-response questionnaires at one point in time. Instead, it is necessary to use intensive longitudinal studies and qualitative methods that allow researchers to explore different explanations of unfolding events. Examples of this type of research include Reicher et al.'s (2005) study of leadership in the BBC prison simulation and Cunliffe and Eriksen's (2011) study of the interpersonal relationships of Federal Security Directors in the United States Transportation Security Authority (TSA).

Complexity Theory of Leadership

To accurately describe effective leadership in organizations requires theories that are more complex than most of the earlier ones. Distributed leadership, relational dynamics, and emergent processes are not adequately described in the hierarchical leadership theories that focus on the influence of a chief executive or the top management team. Complexity theory involves interacting units that are dynamic (changing) and adaptive, and the complex pattern of behaviors and structures that emerge are usually unique and difficult to predict from a description of the involved units (Marion & Uhl-Bien, 2001). Complex adaptive systems are used to explain how emergent processes can facilitate adaptation by organizations to turbulent environments. The emergent processes provide an alternative explanation for organizational learning, innovation, and adaptation. However, rather than replacing hierarchical theories, it is likely that the two perspectives can be integrated to provide a more complete explanation of effective leadership in large organizations (Hunt, Osborn, & Boal, 2009; Lichtenstein & Plowman, 2009; Osborn & Hunt, 2007; Uhl-Bien & Arena, 2018; Uhl-Bien & Marion, 2009; Uhl-Bien, Marion, & McKelvey, 2007).

One version of complexity theory identifies three types of leadership processes (Uhl-Bien & Marion, 2009; Uhl-Bien et al., 2007). Administrative leadership involves actions and decisions by formal leaders who are responsible for planning and coordinating activities for the organization. Adaptive leadership is an emergent process that occurs when people with different knowledge, beliefs, and preferences interact in an attempt to solve problems and resolve conflicts. The result of this process is the production of creative ideas and new conceptions that can facilitate the resolution of conflict and an adaptive response to a threat or opportunity. Enabling leadership facilitates the process of emergent solutions by fostering interaction among people who need to be involved, increasing the interdependence among these people, supporting the value of dissent and debate, increasing access to necessary information and resources, and helping to get innovative ideas implemented in the organization. Enabling leadership also involves efforts to keep the administrative and adaptive processes consistent and mutually compatible. For example, it is essential to prevent administrative leaders from dominating or suppressing the interaction and exploration needed to produce creative solutions, but it is also important to prevent adaptive processes from creating destructive conflicts or undermining the essential mission of the organization.

Complexity theory involves emergent processes and adaptive outcomes that are often unpredictable in advance. Research is needed to learn how interactions and relationships change over time, how the historical and contextual factors affect these processes, and how the three forms of leadership interact to create adaptive outcomes for an organization (Uhl-Bien & Arena, 2018). Instead of relying on survey studies conducted at one point in time, it will be necessary to conduct intensive studies that include qualitative descriptions of the relevant processes and relationships (e.g., Lichtenstein & Plowman, 2009; Plowman et al., 2007; Schneider & Somers, 2006). Computer simulation is a useful tool for testing models based on the descriptive studies (Hazy, 2007). Examples of methods relevant for studying complexity theories of leadership are described in several publications (e.g., Hazy, 2008; Schreiber & Carley, 2008).

External Monitoring and Strategy Formulation

Two key functions for top executives in business organizations are to monitor the external environment and formulate a competitive strategy. External monitoring is needed to detect threats and opportunities for the organization, and competitive strategy guides the organization's response to threats and opportunities.

External Monitoring

Top executives need to be sensitive to a wide range of events and trends that are likely to affect their organization (de Kluyver & Pearce, 2015; Ginter & Duncan, 1990; Hiller & Beauchesne, 2014). Some representative questions likely to be important for a business organization are shown in Table 12-2. It is essential to learn about the concerns of customers and

TABLE 12-2 Questions for External Monitoring

1. What do clients and customers need and want?
2. What is the reaction of clients and customers to the organization's current products and services?
3. Who are the primary competitors?
4. What strategies are they pursuing (e.g., pricing, advertising and promotions, new products, customer service, etc.)?
5. How do competitors' products and services compare to those of the manager's organization?
6. What events affect the acquisition of materials, energy, information, and other inputs used by the organization to conduct its operations?
7. How will the organization be affected by new legislation and by government agencies that regulate its activities (e.g., labor laws, environmental regulations, safety standards, tax policies, etc.)?
8. How will new technologies affect the organization's products, services, and operations?
9. How will the organization be affected by changes in the economy (employment level, interest rates, growth rates)?
10. How will the organization be affected by changing population demographics (e.g., aging, diversity)?
11. How will the organization be affected by international events (e.g., trade agreements, import restrictions, currency changes, wars and revolutions)?

TABLE 12-3 Guidelines for External Monitoring

- Identify relevant information to gather.
- Use multiple sources of relevant information.
- Learn what clients and customers need and want.
- Learn about the products and activities of competitors.
- Relate environmental information to strategic plans.

clients, the availability of suppliers and vendors, the actions of competitors, market trends, economic conditions, government policies, and technological developments. The information may be gathered in a variety of ways (e.g., reading government reports and industry publications, attending professional and trade meetings, talking to customers and suppliers, examining the products and reports of competitors, conducting market research).

External monitoring (also called "environmental scanning") provides the information needed for strategic planning and crisis management. Grinyer and colleagues (1990) studied 28 British companies that experienced a sharp improvement in performance and a matched sample of firms with only average performance; the top management of the high-performing companies did more external monitoring (e.g., environmental scanning, consultation with key customers) and were quicker to recognize and exploit opportunities. The amount of change and turbulence in the environment will determine how much external monitoring is necessary. More external monitoring is needed when the organization is highly dependent on outsiders (e.g., clients, customers, suppliers, subcontractors, joint venture partners), when the environment is rapidly changing, and when the organization faces severe competition or serious threats from outside enemies (Ginter & Duncan, 1990; Narayanan et al., 2011; Simsek et al., 2018).

Monitoring of the external environment is usually considered more important for upper-level managers than for lower-level managers (de Kluyver & Pearce, 2015; Hiller & Beauchesne, 2014; Jacobs & Jaques, 1987; Jaques, 1989; Kraut, Pedigo, McKenna, & Dunnette, 1989; Pavett & Lau, 1983; Simsek et al., 2018). However, the difficulties involved in scanning and interpreting information about environmental changes make this responsibility one that should be shared by managers in an organization. Guidelines for external monitoring are listed in Table 12-3.

Developing Competitive Strategy

For business organizations, a major part of the strategy is how to compete effectively in the marketplace and remain profitable (Porter, 1980, 1998). Some examples of possible competitive strategies include the following: selling a product or service at the lowest price; having superior quality, customer service, or the most innovative products and services; providing a unique product or service in a segment of the market ignored by competing organizations ("niche" strategies); and being the most flexible about customizing products or services to meet each client's needs. Sometimes it is feasible to pursue a mix of strategies at the same time (e.g., have the least expensive "standard" product or service as well as the best customized versions of the product or service). Strategy may also involve the way the product or service is produced, delivered, marketed, financed, and guaranteed.

Reviews of research on strategy formulation and strategic planning by top executives show that it can improve an organization's performance, and that it is more important in a complex and dynamic environment with many threats and opportunities (Hiller & Beauchesne, 2014; Miller & Cardinal, 1994; Narayanan et al., 2011). However, a limitation of many studies on effects of strategic planning is the lack of attention to strategy content and implementation. Strategy formulation will not improve organizational performance unless the strategies are relevant and feasible, they are communicated to middle- and lower-level managers, and these managers become committed to implement the strategies.

A relevant strategy takes into account changes in the external environment, and it is realistic in terms of the organization's strengths and weaknesses. The strategy should reflect the core mission and high-priority objectives of the organization. Although strategy may include changing structure or management processes, such changes should be clearly relevant to strategic objectives. For example, it is not enough to propose downsizing, elimination of management layers, or reorganization into separate product divisions without providing a clear purpose for such changes. Unfortunately, many executives who need to improve weak short-term performance will succumb to the appeal of faddish remedies.

Guidelines for Strategic Leadership

One of the most difficult responsibilities for executives is to develop a competitive strategy for the organization, and there are no simple answers on how to do it effectively. The following guidelines (see Table 12-4) are based on relevant theory, research, and practitioner insights (Bennis & Nanus, 1985; de Kluyver & Pearce, 2015; Hiller & Beauchesne, 2014; Kotter, 1996; Nanus, 1992; Narayanan et al., 2011; Nohria, Joyce, & Roberson, 2004; Wall, S. J., & Wall, S. R., 1995; Worley, Hitchin, & Ross, 1996). The guidelines do not depict a rigid sequence of steps, but rather a set of overlapping, cyclical activities that must be interwoven in a meaningful way.

- **Determine long-term objectives and priorities.**

It is difficult to make strategic plans without knowing the objectives to be attained and their relative priority. Long-term objectives and priorities should be based on the stated mission and vision for the organization. Strategic objectives for a business organization may involve such things as maintaining a specified profit margin or return on investment, improving market share, and providing the best products or service in the industry. Strategic objectives for an organization with a humanitarian mission may include such things as finding a way to cure or prevent a disease, eliminating illiteracy in a specified population, and ending deaths from drunk driving. Strategic objectives for an educational institution may include improving the learning of essential skills, preparing students for specific careers, and increasing the number of students who graduate.

TABLE 12-4 Guidelines for Formulating Strategy

- Determine long-term objectives and priorities.
- Assess current strengths and weaknesses.
- Identify core competencies.
- Evaluate the need for a major change in strategy.
- Identify promising strategies.
- Evaluate the likely outcomes of a strategy.
- Involve other executives in selecting a strategy.

- **Learn what clients and customers need and want.**

It is essential to learn as much as possible about the specific needs and requirements of customers and what they think about the organization's products and services. It is useful to discover what they like, what they dislike, and how the products or services could be improved. Market surveys are one common source of information about clients and customers, but more personal contacts are also desirable. Some manufacturing organizations have teams of production, engineering, and sales employees from different levels of the organization visit with major clients to learn more about their needs and get ideas for product improvements (Peters & Austin, 1985). Clients and suppliers are also invited to visit the organization's facilities, meet with production and engineering personnel, and attend meetings on how to improve quality, product design, or customer service.

- **Learn about the products and activities of competitors.**

Knowledge about the products and services of competitors provides a basis for evaluating your own products and processes (a process called benchmarking), and it provides a source of good ideas on how to improve them. Detailed information about the products and services of competitors is sometimes difficult to obtain but worth the effort. Learning about competitors' products can be accomplished in a variety of ways: use them yourself, conduct comparative product testing, read evaluations conducted by product testing companies or governmental agencies, have customers directly compare the organization's products and services to those of competitors, visit the facilities of competitors, read competitors' advertising literature, and attend trade shows where competitors display and demonstrate their wares.

- **Assess current strengths and weaknesses.**

Strategic planning is facilitated by a comprehensive, objective evaluation of current performance in relation to strategic objectives and compared to the performance of competitors. Much of the information needed for this evaluation is provided by internal and external monitoring. Several types of analysis are useful. Review indicators of organizational performance for the past several years and progress toward achieving strategic objectives. Examine performance (e.g., sales, market share, costs, profits) for each product, service, and market. Identify products or services that are successful and those that are not meeting expectations. Compare the organization's products or services to those of competitors to identify strengths and weaknesses. Compare the efficiency of the organization's processes to that for similar organizations. Identify tangible resources that currently provide an advantage over competitors, such as financial assets, unique equipment and facilities, and patents on products or technology used to do the work. Identify conditions that provide an advantage, such as low operating costs, employees with relevant skills, a special relationship with suppliers, and an outstanding reputation for quality or customer service. Identify weaknesses as well as strengths, and estimate how long current strengths and weaknesses are likely to continue.

The competitive advantage to be gained from current strengths depends on how long they will last and how difficult they are for competitors to overcome or duplicate. For example, a pharmaceutical company with a patented new drug that is better and cheaper than any alternatives has a strong competitive advantage that will likely continue for several years. In contrast, a service company that devises a new and attractive promotion (e.g., special discounts) may enjoy its competitive advantage only for a few weeks or months (as long as it takes competitors to imitate it). An organization that is first into a new market has an advantage, but only if it is difficult for competitors to follow quickly. A product or service that is costly to develop but easy and cheap to duplicate offers little advantage. Capabilities should be evaluated together, not in isolation. A unique resource (e.g., an improved product or process) may offer no competitive advantage if organizational weaknesses or external constraints prevent it from being used effectively. A weakness may not be so serious if it can be corrected quickly or offset by other strengths.

- **Identify core competencies.**

A core competency is the knowledge and capability to carry out a particular type of activity (Barney, 1991). Unlike tangible resources, which are depleted when used, core competencies increase as they are used (Prahalad & Hamel, 1990). A core competency usually involves a combination of technical expertise and application skills. For example, a core competency for W. L. Gore is their expertise about a special type of material (GORE-TEX) and their capability to discover and exploit new uses for this material.

Core competencies provide a potential source of continuing competitive advantage if they are used to provide innovative, high-quality products and services that cannot easily be copied or duplicated by competitors. Core competencies can help an organization remain competitive in its current businesses and diversify into new businesses. Canon's core competencies in optics, acquired as a producer of quality cameras, enabled the company to become a successful producer of copiers, fax machines, semiconductor lithographic equipment, and specialized video systems, while continuing to be a successful producer of cameras and the first to develop a microprocessor-controlled camera. Competence in display systems, which involves knowledge of microprocessor design, ultra-thin precision casing, material science, and miniaturization enabled Casio to be successful in such diverse businesses as calculators, miniature television sets, digital watches, monitors for laptop computers, and automotive dashboards (Prahalad & Hamel, 1990).

- **Evaluate the need for a major change in strategy.**

One of the most important responsibilities of executives is to help interpret events and determine whether the organization needs a different strategy or just incremental improvements in the existing strategy. A new strategy may be needed when there is a performance crisis for the organization and established practices are not sufficient to deal with it. When a serious crisis is imminent, it is appropriate to be pragmatic and flexible rather than defensive and tradition bound in deciding how to respond. In this situation, a leader who attempts to defend the old, obsolete strategy rather than proposing necessary changes is likely to be replaced. However, proposing a different strategy when the current strategy can be easily fixed is also risky, both for the organization and the leader. A new strategy may not be needed if weak performance is caused by temporary conditions or easily resolved problems in implementing the current strategy.

- **Identify promising strategies.**

If a major change in strategy is necessary, it is better to begin by exploring a range of possible strategies. Focusing attention too quickly on one strategy will preclude finding better ones that are less obvious. Success in finding a new strategy will be greater if the quest is guided by a clear, meaningful conception of the organization's mission, long-term strategic objectives, core competencies, and current performance. Sometimes it is necessary to redefine the mission of the organization to include new activities that are relevant for the environment and the organization's core competencies, as shown in the following example (Worley et al., 1996):

Williams Company was making pipelines for transporting oil and gas, but it was losing business to larger competitors with lower costs. Recognizing that it was unlikely to find a way to compete successfully in the pipeline business, top management looked around for other opportunities to use the company's core competencies. They discovered that their piping was perfect for housing fiber-optic cable, a newly emerging market, and they could market it to cable television and telecommunications companies at a lower price than other suppliers in that industry.

- **Evaluate the likely outcomes of a strategy.**

A strategy should be evaluated in terms of the likely consequences for the attainment of key objectives. Relevant consequences include benefits and costs for the various stakeholders in the organization. The costs include the extra resources and lost productivity associated with any organizational changes necessary to support the strategy. It is difficult to forecast the consequences of a strategic change, especially when competitors can adjust their own strategies to cope with your changes. A number of procedures have been developed to assess likely customer response to a new product or service, and examples include market surveys, focus groups, and product trials in selected locations or markets.

Scenarios provide a useful way to improve the evaluation of likely consequences for a proposed new strategy (Van der Heijden, 1996). A scenario is a detailed description of what the future will be like if a proposed change or strategy is pursued. Scenarios can be developed to describe what would happen under the most and least favorable conditions, as well as under the most likely conditions. The process of developing the scenarios often provides insights about unexpected consequences of a strategy and implicit assumptions that were not realistic (Sosik, Jung, Berson, Dionne, & Jaussi, 2005).

- **Involve other executives in selecting a strategy.**

A key responsibility of executives is to make strategic decisions that will improve the organization. However, few leaders are so brilliant that they can make such decisions alone, and a competitive strategy developed with participation by the top management team is more likely to be successful than strategy developed alone by an autocratic CEO (Finkelstein, 2003; Finkelstein et al., 2009; Probst & Raisch, 2005). In the event of considerable uncertainty and disagreement about the best strategy, it is wise to select one that is flexible enough to permit later modification after more knowledge about its effectiveness can be obtained. Moderate risk taking is usually beneficial, but it is not wise to take extreme risks with irreversible decisions. Systematic procedures have been developed by scholars and consultants to facilitate the process of strategy formulation by a group of executives. One example is the scenario development procedure called "Quest" (Bennis & Nanus, 1985), which is a two-day exercise held with executives and relevant outsiders to discuss long-range opportunities and risks, and possible reactions by the organization.

Summary

The prosperity and survival of the organization depend on timely adaptation to threats and opportunities, maintaining a high level of efficiency and process reliability, practicing strategic human resource management, and having an organizational culture with shared values that are consistent with the mission and competitive strategy. The relative importance of these performance determinants for organizations, and the potential trade-offs among them, are determined by aspects of the situation such as the type of organization and the amount of change in the external environment. When changes in the external environment affect the capacity of the organization to carry out its mission, successful adaptation requires recognition of threats and opportunities, and the willingness to make changes in the processes, products, services, or the competitive strategy of the organization. Flexible, adaptive leadership is essential to deal successfully with the trade-offs, competing objectives, and changing situations. The organizational culture can facilitate or hinder efforts to make major change.

A chief executive has more potential influence on the performance of an organization when there is a crisis and the competitive strategy is no longer aligned with its environment. A major change is more likely to be successful if it is initiated before a crisis becomes serious and while the organization still has slack resources needed to make the change. However, it is more difficult to initiate a major change when there is not yet an obvious need for it. Major strategic change is most likely to be initiated by a CEO who is an external successor than by a CEO who has been in office for a long time. The different types of research described in this chapter show that despite all the constraints on top executives, they can usually have a moderately strong influence on the effectiveness of an organization. The outcome of a major change depends on what type of leadership is provided by mid-level and lower-level managers as well as by top executives, and the leadership decisions at different levels and in different subunits of the organization must be consistent and coordinated.

An executive team is more important in a complex, rapidly changing environment that places many external demands on the CEO. Teams are also more important in an organization with diverse but highly interdependent business units, because a single leader is unlikely to have the broad expertise necessary to direct and integrate the activities of these units. The member characteristics necessary for team effectiveness depend on the organizational context, the external environment, and the leadership provided by the CEO.

External monitoring provides information needed for strategic planning and crisis management. To detect threats and discover opportunities in a timely way, top management must actively monitor relevant sectors of the environment, sources of dependency for the organization, and current performance. Developing a strategy for adapting to the environment is an important responsibility for top executives, and the strategy is more likely to be effective if it builds on core competencies, is relevant to long-term objectives, and is feasible in terms of current capabilities.

Review and Discussion Questions

1. What are the major performance determinants for organizations?
2. How can leaders influence each type of performance determinant?
3. What is organizational culture and how can leaders influence it?
4. What conditions limit the discretion of a CEO?
5. What determines the effectiveness of executive teams?
6. How do shared leadership, relational leadership, and complexity theories increase our understanding of leadership in organizations?
7. Why is external monitoring important for strategic leadership?
8. What are some guidelines for strategy formulation?

Key Terms

adaptation
chief executive officer (CEO)
CEO succession
competitive strategy
complexity theory
core competencies
distributed leadership
internal and external constraints
external monitoring
flexible leadership theory
organizational culture
performance determinants
relational leadership
strategic human resource management
strategic leadership
strategic planning
top management team

PERSONAL REFLECTION

Think about an organization to which you currently belong or have previously been a member. How would you describe the organization's culture? What are its core values? How are symbols, rituals, or ceremonies used to communicate these values?

CASE

Vishal Mega Mart

Vishal Mega Mart is a fast expanding retail company in India, with several stores located across different cities. Even though its profit margins are low, it has a larger profit share in comparison to most of its competitors. This can probably be attributed to its high customer satisfaction rating. Vishal Mega Mart's strategy is to provide quality services at the lowest price possible. The Mega Mart sells products such as clothes, cookware, electrical and electronic goods, games, toys and stationery. Although there are other stores that offer products at a rate lower than Vishal Mega Mart, what gives them the edge is the superior quality of their products at reasonable prices, which result in greater customer satisfaction.

The Mega Mart indulges in very limited formal advertising and relies majorly on word of mouth of its happy customers. As a result, they end up saving a lot in terms of the marketing costs. The Mega Mart also practices a time limited supply of special discounts and bargains. What this does is increase customer excitement due to which shoppers end up purchasing products they had not intended to buy. The employees of who are responsible for procuring the stores' merchandise experiment and take big risks with luxury items because a lot of money is tied up in inventory if the items do not sell quickly. They rely on their intuition and creativity in order to identify items that may be popular and profitable. To make them more appealing to the customers, innovation in their design and packaging also plays a very important role.

Providing membership to customers for the privilege of shopping at Vishal Mega Mart provides a steady source of revenue for the company and increases customer loyalty. Vishal Mega Mart offers two types of memberships—businesses and individuals. However, the cost of their membership is slightly more than their competitors, and they have a high renewal rate. So what Vishal Mega Mart does to increase its customer base and add value to the memberships of their existing customers is to offer other services such as travel plans. On an average, a customer makes two trips to the Mega Mart per month. A lot of them even travel great distances to stock up on their supplies. Unlike its other competitors whose customers are merely looking for low priced commodities, Vishal Mega Mart's customer are usually in search of good bargains on luxury goods.

In order to minimize its costs, the company follows a no-frills approach and has a standard layout for its stores that not only helps reduce cost but also gives its customers a feeling of familiarity no matter which store they shop from. Similar products are kept across stores in different cities. Only food products vary according to the local taste. Inventory costs are reduced by having only a limited variety of product sizes, and by packaging similar products for bulk sales. For example, pack of three toothpastes, pack of five t-shirts.

Products move right from the delivery truck to the shop floor. No shopping bags are offered to the customers and the signage seems like it has been made with a cheap laser printer. Computer tracking of sales helps reduce waste and overproduction by allowing one to determine when more fresh food is required in the display cases. Along with paying its employees generously, Vishal Mega Mart also offers them excellent health benefits. The company offers its workers of all levels good opportunities for advancement. They follow the policy of promotion from within ranks (employment levels within the organization). The company is known to have one of the most loyal and productive workforces in the retail industry. This is reflected in the high level of organizational commitment and low turnover rate of its employees. As a result of low turnover, the company is able to save its cost that would have otherwise gone in recruiting and training new employees. The savings from lower turnover costs, lower employee theft and higher employee productivity, more than cover up for the generous salary that the company pays to its employees.

Hard work, respect for customers and high ethical standards form an integral part of Vishal Mega Mart's core values. Employees are encouraged to become creative and to suggest ways for improving the stores as well as the products that the company has to offer. Frequent discussions are held around the topic of improving efficiency and customer service. Employees are trained to serve customers in the best possible way, by being warm and friendly to them and helping them wherever they require assistance. For example, if a customer is looking for a product and they seek the assistance of one of the salesperson, the company employees are taught to take the customer to the product rather than merely pointing towards it or providing vague directions.

The company's founder and CEO is known for his caring attitude towards his employees. He himself is very hard working and dedicated to his job. He does not take any special privileges as a CEO and takes many steps to retain his employees as he realises the importance of having talented people work for his company. Although he expects high performance from his employees, he does not extract it through coercive or overly critical means. He meets with over a thousand Vishal Mega Mart managers and product buyers at the annual managers' conference to review the past, discuss the present, and plan the future. He also holds monthly budget meetings to talk about the importance of exercising tight cost controls, getting the details right, and adhering to the values of Vishal Mega Mart. The CEO spends almost half his time visiting either his own company's stores or that of his competitors. He tries to visit all his company stores at least once a year.

Questions

1. Explain the success of Vishal Mega Mart in terms of the three performance determinants in flexible leadership theory (adaptation, efficiency, and human capital).
2. What leadership behaviors and theories help to explain the strong influence of the CEO on the company and its continued success?

CASE

Turnaround at Nissan

In 1999, Nissan was in a state of serious decline and had lost money in all but one of the previous eight years. Only Renault's willingness to assume part of Nissan's debt saved the Japanese company from going bankrupt. As part of the deal, the French automaker appointed Carlos Ghosn to become Nissan's chief operating officer. However, there was widespread skepticism that the alliance between Renault and Nissan could succeed, or that someone who was not Japanese could provide effective leadership at Nissan.

During the three months prior to assuming the position of COO at Nissan, Ghosn met with hundreds of people, including employees, union officials, suppliers, and customers, to learn more about the company and its strengths and weaknesses. From these meetings and earlier experiences with turnaround assignments, Ghosn understood that major changes would not be successful if they were dictated by him and the experts he brought with him from Renault. Soon after assuming his new position at Nissan in June 1999, Ghosn created nine cross-functional teams and gave them responsibility for determining what needed to be done to revive the company. Such teams had never been used before at Nissan, and it was unusual in a Japanese company to involve a broad cross-section of managers in determining major changes.

The cross-functional teams examined different aspects of company operations to identify problems and recommend solutions to Ghosn and the executive committee. Several interrelated problems were identified, and they were mostly consistent with Ghosn's initial impressions. The poor financial performance at Nissan was a joint result of declining sales and excessive costs, and weak management was the primary reason for the failure to resolve these problems. Management lacked a coherent strategy, a strong profit orientation, and a clear focus on customers. There was little cooperation across functions, and there was no urgency about the need for major change.

One reason for excessive costs at Nissan was that only half of the available capacity in the company's factories was being used; production capacity was sufficient to build almost a million more cars a year than the company could sell. To reduce costs, Ghosn decided to close five factories in Japan and eliminate more than 21,000 jobs, which was 14 percent of Nissan's global workforce. To simplify production operations at the remaining factories and make them more efficient, Ghosn planned to reduce the number of car platforms by half and the number of powertrain combinations by a third. Plant closings can undermine relations with employees, and Ghosn took steps to ensure that employees knew why they were necessary and who would be affected. In general, he understood that most employees prefer to learn what would happen to them and prepare for it, rather than remaining in a state of uncertainty and anxiety. Ghosn attempted to minimize adverse effects on employees by selling subsidiaries and using natural attrition, early retirements, and opportunities for part-time work at other company facilities.

Purchasing costs represent 60 percent of the operating costs for an automaker, and Nissan was paying much more than necessary for the parts and supplies used to build its cars. After comparing expenses at Nissan and Renault, Ghosn discovered that Nissan's purchasing costs were 25 percent higher. One reason was the practice of purchasing small orders from many suppliers instead of larger orders from a smaller number of global sources. It would be necessary to reduce the number of suppliers, even though this action was unprecedented in a country where supplier relationships were considered sacrosanct. Higher purchasing costs were also a result of overly exacting specifications imposed on suppliers by Nissan engineers. The engineers who worked with the cross-functional team on purchasing initially defended their specifications, but when they finally realized that they were wrong, the team was able to achieve greater savings than expected. Excessive purchasing costs are not the type of problem that can be solved quickly, but after three years of persistent effort, it was possible to achieve Ghosn's goal of a 20 percent reduction.

Years of declining sales at Nissan were caused by a lack of customer appeal for most of the company's cars. When Ghosn made a detailed analysis of sales data, he discovered that only 4 of the 43 different Nissan models had sufficient sales to be profitable. Final decisions about the design of new models were made by the head of engineering. Designers were taking orders from engineers who focused completely on performance, and there was little effort to determine what types of cars customers really wanted. To increase the customer appeal of Nissan vehicles, Ghosn hired the innovative designer Shiro Nakamura, who became another key leader in the turnaround effort. The designers would now have more authority over design decisions, and Ghosn encouraged them to be innovative rather than merely copying competitors. For the first time in over a decade, Nissan began coming up with cars that excited customers both in Japan and abroad. Ghosn planned to introduce 12 new models over a three-year period, but the time necessary to bring a new model into production meant that few would be available until 2002.

Saving Nissan would also require major changes in human resource practices, such as guaranteed lifetime employment and pay and promotion based on seniority. Transforming these strongly embedded aspects of the company culture without engendering resentment and demoralizing employees was perhaps the most difficult challenge. The changes would primarily affect nonunionized employees at Nissan, including the managers. A merit pay plan was established, and instead of being rewarded for seniority, employees were now expected to earn their promotions and salary increases through effective performance. Areas of accountability were sharply defined so that performance could be measured in relation to specific goals. New bonuses provided employees an opportunity to earn up to a third of their annual salary for effective performance, and hundreds of upper-level managers could also earn stock options. These and other changes in human resource practices would make it possible for Ghosn to gradually replace weak middle- and upper-level managers with more competent successors.

In October 1999, Ghosn announced the plan for revitalizing Nissan. He had been careful to avoid any earlier leaks about individual changes that would be criticized without understanding why they were necessary and how they fit into the overall plan. The announcement included a pledge that Ghosn and the executive committee would resign if Nissan failed to show a profit by the end of 2000. It was an impressive demonstration of his sincerity and commitment, and it made what he was asking of others seem more acceptable. Fortunately, the primary objectives of the change were all achieved on schedule, and by 2001 earnings were at a record high for the company. That year Ghosn was appointed as the chief executive officer at Nissan, and in 2005, he would become the CEO of Renault as well.

—*Written by* Gary Yukl; based on Ghosn and Ries (2005) and Taylor (2002).

Questions

1. What was done to improve efficiency, adaptation, and human relations, and to minimize adverse side effects of the changes?
2. What effective practices were used to identify and implement necessary changes in the strategy and the organization?

Chapter 13

Cross-Cultural Leadership and Diversity

Learning Objectives

After studying this chapter, you should be able to:

- Understand why cross-cultural research on leadership is important.
- Understand the difficulties of studying cross-cultural leadership.
- Understand how cultural values are related to leader behavior.
- Understand the essentials for effective global leadership.
- Understand how gender issues have been studied and the limitations of this research.
- Understand the findings in research on gender differences in leadership.
- Understand how to manage diversity and provide equal opportunities.

Introduction

Globalization and changing demographic patterns are making it more important for leaders to understand how to influence and manage people with different values, beliefs, and expectations. Cross-cultural leadership research examines the direct or moderating influence of culture on leadership practices, processes, and effects. It is primarily a comparative approach that considers how leadership values and practices that emerge in one culture apply within other cultures. In recent years, a distinction has been made between cross-cultural leadership and global leadership as it became clear to many scholars that the world of business was moving beyond international commerce to reflect global organizations and leadership strategies (Avolio, Walumbwa, & Weber, 2009; Bird & Mendenhall, 2016; Brodbeck & Eisenbeiss, 2014). The study of global leadership is focused on the practical challenges that confront the leaders of multinational organizations (Lundby, Moriarity, & Lee, 2014). These challenges include the selection and development of leaders who possess the requisite competencies to lead people from diverse cultures in a global arena, and the identification of strategic human resource management practices that align with the organization's global strategies and goals. There has been substantial research on cross-cultural leadership, but the challenges of global leadership are mostly examined within the practitioner literature (Brodbeck & Eisenbeiss, 2014). The first part of this chapter describes key findings from research on cross-cultural leadership, and the potential application of these findings to improve the practice of global leadership.

The diversity of people in leadership positions is also increasing, and there is strong interest in studying whether the ability to provide effective leadership is related to a person's gender, age, race, ethnic background, national origin, religion, sexual preference, physical handicaps, or physical appearance (height, weight, attractiveness). There has been more leadership research on gender differences than on other types of diversity (Ospina & Foldy, 2009). The second part of the chapter examines gender differences in leadership, and the management of diversity and inclusion.

Cross-Cultural and Global Leadership

Most of the early research on leadership was conducted in the United States, Canada, and Western Europe. However, since then there has been a rapid increase in research on cross-cultural leadership and leadership in global companies (Bass, 2008; Dickson, Den Hartog, & Michelson, 2003; Dorfman, 2004; Smith, Peterson, & Thomas, 2008) (Brodbeck & Eisenbeiss, 2014; Den Hartog & Dickson, 2018). A major research question is the extent to which leadership theories developed and tested in one culture can be generalized to different cultures. A related question is the extent to which differences exist among countries with regard to cultural values that influence leader behavior, beliefs about effective leadership, and accepted management practices (Den Hartog & Dickson, 2018). This section of the chapter explains the importance of cross-cultural research on leadership, describes several different types of cross-cultural leadership research, and provides some examples of the research, including the multinational GLOBE project.

Importance of Cross-Cultural Research

Cross-cultural research on leadership is important for several reasons (Ayman & Korabik, 2010; Brodbeck & Eisenbeiss, 2014; Connerley & Pedersen, 2005; Den Hartog & Dickson, 2018; Dorfman, 2004; House, Wright, & Aditya, 1997). Increasing globalization of organizations makes it more important to learn about effective leadership in different cultures. Leaders are increasingly confronted with the need to influence people from other cultures, and successful influence requires a good understanding of these cultures. Leaders must also be able to understand how people from different cultures view them and interpret their actions. To understand these issues, it is essential to determine if a leadership theory is valid in cultures that differ from the one in which it was developed. Some aspects of a leadership theory may be relevant for all cultures, but other aspects may apply only to a particular type of culture.

Cross-cultural research also requires researchers to consider a broader than usual range of variables and processes, which can provide new insights and improve leadership theories. Research to develop or validate taxonomies of leadership behavior in different cultures can reveal new aspects of behavior that are relevant for effective leadership. Examination of cross-cultural differences may cause researchers to pay more attention to possible effects of situational variables not usually included in most leadership theories (e.g., religion, language, history, laws, political systems, ethnic subcultures). Finally, cross-cultural research poses some unique methodological challenges that may result in improved procedures for data collection and analysis.

Types of Cross-Cultural Studies

As in the case of the leadership research conducted within a single culture, much of the cross-cultural research involves leader behavior, skills, and traits. The growing body of cross-cultural research has involved different types of research objectives, designs, and methods (Brodbeck & Eisenbeiss, 2014). The most common approach has been to explain cross-cultural differences in leadership in terms of differences in cultural values. The cross-cultural research on leadership was strongly influenced by the early study of cultural values by Hofstede (1980, 1993), but since then several different sets of cultural values have been proposed (e.g., House et al., 1997; House et al., 2004; Javidan, House, Dorfman, Hanges, & Sully de Luque, 2006; Schwartz, 1992; Trompenaars, 1993). Some cross-cultural studies examine how beliefs about effective leadership behavior, skills, and traits are similar or different from one country to another. Other studies examine cross-cultural differences in the actual pattern of leadership behavior, or the effects on outcomes such as subordinate satisfaction, motivation, and performance. Only a small number of studies have examined how cultural values and leadership practices are both changing over time.

Cultural Influences on Leadership Behavior

Cultural values and traditions can influence the attitudes and behavior of managers in a number of different ways (Adler, 1997; Adler & Gunderson, 2008; Fu & Yukl, 2000; Fu, Kennedy, Tata, Yukl, & associates, 2004; Fu, Peng, Kennedy, & Yukl, 2003); House et al., 1997, 2004). The values are likely to be internalized by managers who grow up in a particular culture, and these values will influence their attitudes and behavior in ways that may not be conscious. In addition, cultural values are reflected in social norms about the way people relate to each other. Cultural norms specify acceptable forms of leadership behavior and may be formalized as social laws limiting the use of power. Most managers will conform to social norms about acceptable behavior, even if they have not internalized the norms. One reason is that deviation from social norms may result in diminished respect and increased social pressure from other members of the organization. Another reason for conformity with social norms is that the use of socially unacceptable forms of behavior is likely to undermine a leader's effectiveness.

Leadership behavior is influenced by other situational variables besides national culture (Bass, 1990, 2008; House et al., 1997, 2004). Some examples include the type of organization (e.g., profit versus nonprofit, public corporation versus private ownership), the type of industry (e.g., retailing, financial services, manufacturing, telecommunications), and characteristics of the managerial position (e.g., level and function of the manager, position power, and authority). Strong values in the organizational culture may or may not be consistent with the dominant cultural values, especially if an organization is a subsidiary of a foreign-owned company. The different determinants of leader behavior are not always congruent with each other. Some situational variables may have parallel effects across national cultures, but other situational variables may interact with national culture in complex ways.

Even when some types of leadership behaviors are not clearly supported by the prevailing cultural values and traditions in a country, it does not necessarily mean that these behaviors are ineffective. Managers who have little experience with a particular type of leadership behavior may not understand how effective it could be (House et al., 1997). When people learn that new practices are highly effective, they are likely to be widely imitated.

The values and traditions in a national culture can change over time, just as they do in an organizational culture. Cultural values are influenced by many types of changes (e.g., economic, political, social, technological). Countries in which socialism is being replaced by capitalism and an emphasis on entrepreneurship are likely to see a shift toward stronger individualism and performance-orientation values. Countries in which an autocratic political system is replaced by a democratic system are likely to become more accepting of participative leadership and empowerment in organizations. Countries in which strong gender differentiation is gradually replaced by gender equality can be expected to become more accepting of leadership practices that reflect traditional feminine attributes (e.g., nurturing, developing, building cooperative relationships). Cultural values and beliefs about the determinants of effective leadership are likely to change in consistent ways.

Cross-Cultural Research on Behavior Differences

Much of the cross-cultural research examines differences among countries with regard to typical patterns of leadership behavior. Scores on behavior questionnaires are analyzed to determine whether a type of behavior is used more in one culture or country than another. For example, Dorfman and colleagues (1997) found that American managers used more participative leadership than managers in Mexico or Korea. However, a quantitative comparison of scale means from behavior description questionnaires is complicated by methodological problems such as confounding and lack of equivalence (Brodbeck & Eisenbeiss, 2014; De Beuckelaer, Lievens, & Swinnen, 2007). For example, lower scores may be obtained in one country because the behavior items have a different meaning there, or because respondents in that culture avoid giving very high scores on a questionnaire.

A smaller number of cross-cultural studies attempts to identify qualitative differences in the way a specific type of behavior is enacted in each country. For example, one study found that positive reward behavior was important for leadership effectiveness in different cultures, but the types of behavior rewarded and the way rewards were used differed across cultures (Podsakoff, Dorfman, Howell, & Todor, 1986). Another study found differences in the way managers communicated directions and feedback to subordinates (Smith, Misumi, Tayeb, Peterson, & Bond, 1989). American managers were more likely to use a face-to-face meeting to provide directions to subordinates and to give negative feedback (criticism), whereas Japanese managers were more likely to use written memos for directions and to channel negative feedback through peers. It is important for leaders to recognize problems that are caused by cultural differences among members and need to be resolved quickly, as shown in the following example (Boot, 2011, December 17):

> An executive team was newly formed after an acquisition of a European/American company by a Japanese company. After a few weeks the first signs of tension and distrust were showing. Western team members were clinging together and forming a block against the Japanese members who acted friendly but did not share their plans or explain the changes they wanted to make. The leader met with each team member separately to discover the reasons for the tension and distrust, and these meetings revealed cultural differences in attitudes about the proper way to establish new relationships. The Japanese managers considered it appropriate to establish a friendly relationship first, and then gradually show more openness and sharing. The Western managers viewed openness and sharing as prerequisite for creating a trust-based relationship. Discussing these cultural differences with the team created a better understanding of the problem. Members realized the situation was not caused by bad intentions, and they were able to discuss ways the team could be more effective.

Cross-Cultural Research on Effects of Leader Behavior

Cross-cultural studies also examine differences in the relationship of leadership behavior to outcomes such as subordinate satisfaction and performance. For example, one study found that supportive behavior was significantly related to subordinate satisfaction and leadership effectiveness in the United States but not in Jordan or Saudi Arabia (Scandura, Von Glinow, & Lowe, 1999). Another study found that directive leadership was related to organizational commitment in Mexico and Taiwan, but not in the United States, South Korea, or Japan (Dorfman et al., 1997). Leader use of contingent rewards was related to subordinate organizational commitment in the United States, Mexico, and Japan, but not in Korea or Taiwan. Participative leadership was related to subordinate performance in the United States but not in Mexico or South Korea.

A study by Schaubroeck, Lam, and Cha (2007) examined leadership by bank branch managers in the United States and Hong Kong. They found that the transformational leadership of the branch manager (rated by subordinates) was related to branch performance (rated by higher management) in both countries. However, the effect of transformational leadership on branch performance was enhanced by power distance and collectivism values, which were higher in Hong Kong than in the United States.

A meta-analysis by Rockstuhl and colleagues (2012) examined the relationships between LMX and key work variables across 23 countries. The results revealed that while a high-quality LMX relationship was positively related to job satisfaction, organizational citizenship behavior, and leader trust and negatively related to turnover intentions, these relationships were stronger in Western as opposed to Asian cultures. However, national culture had no effect on the positive relationships between LMX and organizational commitment or task performance.

Fu and Yukl (2000) conducted a cross-cultural study on managers of a multinational company with similar manufacturing facilities in the United States and China. The study used scenarios to assess manager beliefs about the effectiveness of different tactics for influencing people in their organizations. The results indicated that confrontational tactics such as rational persuasion and exchange were viewed more favorably by American managers than by Chinese managers, although rational persuasion was still rated one of the most effective tactics in both countries. The Chinese managers had a stronger preference than American managers for indirect tactics such as giving gifts and favors prior to a request, and getting assistance from a third party. Cross-cultural differences were also found in the ways some types of tactics were commonly used. For example, when attempting to influence a peer, the American managers seldom enlisted help from others except after encountering initial resistance to a direct request. Chinese managers were more likely to ask a mutual friend to find out (in a subtle way) how a peer was likely to respond before making a direct request. This informal approach would avoid embarrassment ("losing face") for the managers and for the peer if the request was refused.

The GLOBE Project

The GLOBE project is a cross-cultural study of leadership in 60 different countries representing all major regions of the world (Chokkar, Brodbeck, & House, 2007; Dorfman, Javidan, Hanges, Dastmalchian, & House, 2012; House, Dorfman, Javidan, Hanges, & Sully de Luque, 2014; House et al., 2004; Javidan et al., 2006; Waldman et al., 2006). The acronym GLOBE means "Global Leadership and Organizational Behavior Effectiveness." The project has involved more than 150 researchers in different countries working together in a coordinated, long-term effort.

The researchers hoped to develop an empirically based theory that describes the relationships between national culture, organizational processes, and leadership. The GLOBE project also examined how leadership and cultural values are affected by other situational variables, including type of industry, economic development, type of government, dominant religions, and type of climate conditions for a country. Multiple methods of data collection were used, including survey questionnaires, interviews, media analysis, archival records, and unobtrusive measures. The strategy for sampling and analysis was designed to control for the influence of industry, management level, and organizational culture. The research included an in-depth, qualitative description of each culture as well as analyses of quantitative variables.

One important research question has been the extent to which effective leadership is similar or different across cultures, and the reasons for these differences. To compare beliefs about the importance of various traits and skills for effective leadership, managers in different countries were surveyed, and the research identified similarities and differences among countries (Dorfman, Hanges, and Brodbeck, 2004; Dorfman et al., 2012). The leader attributes that were widely viewed as effective included visionary, decisive, dynamic, dependable, positive and encouraging, excellence-oriented, honest and trustworthy, skilled administrator, and team integrator. Leader attributes that were viewed as more important in some countries than in others included ambitious, cautious, compassionate, domineering, formal, humble, independent, self-sacrificing, and willingness to take risks.

Another important research objective has been to explain how leadership beliefs and behavior are influenced by cultural values. The researchers identified nine value dimensions, including some cultural values not identified in the earlier research by Hofstede. A unique feature of the GLOBE research was to measure not only the current cultural values, but also ideal cultural values. This distinction made it possible to determine if people were dissatisfied with the current values and wanted to see a change in the future. The differences among countries for ideal values were much smaller than for actual values, and it is still not clear how to interpret the results. The next section of the chapter describes several of the value dimensions and how they are likely to be related to leadership beliefs, behavior, and development.

Cultural Values and Leadership

This section summarizes major findings in the research on the relationship of cultural values to leadership beliefs, leadership behavior, and leadership development practices. The six value dimensions to be discussed include: (1) power distance, (2) uncertainty avoidance, (3) individualism versus collectivism, (4) gender egalitarianism, (5) performance orientation, and (6) humane orientation.

Power Distance

Power distance involves the acceptance of an unequal distribution of power and status in organizations and institutions. In high power distance cultures, people expect the leaders to have greater authority and are more likely to comply with rules and directives without questioning or challenging them (Carl, Gupta, & Javidan, 2004; Dickson et al., 2003). Subordinates are less willing to challenge bosses or express disagreement with them (Adsit, London, Crom, & Jones, 1997). More formal policies and rules are used, and managers consult less often with subordinates when making decisions (Smith et al., 2002).

Participative leadership is viewed as a more favorable leadership attribute in low power distance cultures such as Western Europe, New Zealand, and the United States than in high power distance countries such as Russia, China, Taiwan, Mexico, and Venezuela (Dorfman et al., 2004). In low power distance countries, transformational (supportive and inspirational) leadership is more likely to be combined with a participative style of decision making (Den Hartog et al., 1999), whereas in high power distance countries, it is likely to be combined with a directive, autocratic style of decision making. In developing countries with a high power distance culture, people often prefer a "paternalistic" style that combines autocratic decisions with supportive behavior (Dickson et al., 2003; Dorfman et al., 1997). Sadri, Weber, and Gentry (2011) found that in low power distance cultures where interactions tend to be less formal and participative leadership is more common, leaders who displayed higher levels of empathic emotions received higher ratings of performance from their bosses than was the case in high power distance cultures.

Uncertainty Avoidance

In cultures with high avoidance of uncertainty, there is more fear of the unknown, and people desire more security, stability, and order. Social norms, tradition, detailed agreements, and certified expertise are more valued, because they offer a way to avoid uncertainty and disorder (Den Hartog et al., 1999; Dickson et al., 2003); Sully de Luque & Javidan, 2004. Examples of countries with high uncertainty avoidance include France, Spain, Germany, Switzerland, Russia, and India. Some countries with a lower concern about avoiding uncertainty include the United States, United Kingdom, Canada, Denmark, and Sweden.

When there is high uncertainty avoidance, valued qualities for managers include being reliable, orderly, and cautious, rather than flexible, innovative, and risk taking. Managers use more detailed planning, formal rules and standard procedures, and monitoring of activities, and there is less delegation (Offermann & Hellmann, 1997). There is more centralized control over decisions involving change or innovation. For example, one study found that managers in the United Kingdom expected more innovation and initiative from subordinates, whereas managers in Germany expected more reliability and punctuality (Stewart, Barsoux, Kieser, Ganter, & Walgenbach, 1994). The study also found that management development in Germany emphasized acquisition of specialized knowledge and experience in a functional area, whereas in the United Kingdom, there was more emphasis on general skills attained from a variety of job experiences. Another study of 608 firms based in Austria, Brazil, Germany, India, Singapore, and the United States found that the positive relationship between transformational leadership and absorptive capacity (i.e., the ability of a firm to explore and exploit external knowledge) was stronger in low as opposed to high uncertainty avoidance cultures (Flatten, Adams, & Brettel, 2015). These findings suggest that the efforts of transformational leaders to foster knowledge acquisition and innovation are more effective in cultures that are low versus high in uncertainty avoidance.

Individualism (versus Collectivism)

Individualism is the extent to which the needs and autonomy of individuals are more important than the collective needs of groups, organizations, or society. In an individualistic culture, individual rights are more important than social responsibilities, and people are expected to take care of themselves (Den Hartog & Dickson, 2018; Dickson et al., 2003; Gelfand, Bhawuk, Nishi, & Bechtold, 2004; Gelfand, Erez, & Aycan, 2007; Hofstede, 1980). Examples of countries with strong values for individualism include the United States, Australia, England, and the Netherlands.

The implications of collectivistic values depend in part on whether they are more important for in-groups or the larger society, but most of the cross-cultural research has emphasized in-group collectivism. The in-groups may be based on family ties, religious or ethnic background, membership in a political party, or a stable, collaborative business relationship. In a collectivistic culture, membership in cohesive in-groups is an important aspect of a person's self-identity, and loyalty to the group is an important value. People are less likely to change jobs, and members are more likely to volunteer their time to do extra work and "organizational citizenship behaviors" (Jackson, Colquitt, Wesson, & Zapata-Phelan, 2006). In turn, the groups are expected to take care of their members. Examples of countries with strong collectivistic values include China, Argentina, Mexico, and Sweden.

Because people are more motivated to satisfy their self-interests and personal goals in an individualistic culture, it is more difficult for leaders to inspire strong commitment to team or organizational objectives (Jung & Avolio, 1999; Triandis et al., 1993). The preference for rewards based on individual achievements and performance also makes it more difficult for leaders to use team-based rewards and recognition (Kirkman & Shapiro, 2000). The emphasis on individual rights and autonomy makes it more difficult to create a strong culture of shared values for social responsibility, cooperation, and ethical behavior. Because of the transitory nature of careers, selection is likely to be more important than training for ensuring that people have adequate skills.

Gender Egalitarianism

Gender egalitarianism is the extent to which men and women receive equal treatment, and both masculine and feminine attributes are considered important and desirable. In cultures with high gender egalitarianism, there is less differentiation of sex roles and most jobs are not segregated by gender. Women have more equal opportunities to be selected for important leadership positions, although access is still greater for public sector positions than in business corporations. In the absence of strongly differentiated gender-role expectations, men and women leaders are less limited in their behavior, and there is less bias in how their behavior is evaluated by subordinates and by bosses. Examples of countries with strong gender egalitarian values include Norway, Sweden, Denmark, and the Netherlands. Countries with a low level of gender egalitarianism include Japan, Italy, Mexico, and Switzerland.

Cultural values for gender egalitarianism have implications for the selection and evaluation of leaders and for the types of leadership behavior considered desirable and socially acceptable (Dickson et al., 2003; Emrich, Denmark, & Den Hartog, 2004). In cultures with strong "masculine" values for toughness and assertiveness, "feminine" attributes such as compassion, empathy, and intuition are not viewed as important for effective leadership (Den Hartog, 2004; Den Hartog & Dickson, 2018; Den Hartog et al., 1999). Participative leadership, supportive leadership, and relations-oriented aspects of transformational leadership are viewed less favorably in cultures with low gender egalitarianism. Leaders are more likely to use direct, confrontational forms of interpersonal influence rather than indirect, subtle forms of influence (e.g., Fu & Yukl, 2000; Holtgraves, 1997). Leaders whose actions display humility, compassion, or conciliation are more likely to be viewed as weak and ineffective in a "masculine" culture.

Performance Orientation

The extent to which high performance and individual achievement are valued is called performance orientation (Javidan, 2004). Related values and attributes include hard work, responsibility, competitiveness, persistence, initiative, pragmatism, and acquisition of new skills. In societies with strong performance orientation values, results are emphasized more than people. What you do is more important than who you are (e.g., gender, family, or ethnic background), and individual achievements can be an important source of status and self-esteem. Accomplishing a task effectively can take priority over individual needs or family loyalty.

In a high performance orientation culture, there is more emphasis on leader behaviors that are relevant for improving performance and efficiency. Examples include setting challenging goals or standards, developing action plans with schedules and deadlines, expressing confidence that subordinates can improve performance, developing job-relevant skills in subordinates, encouraging initiative, and providing praise and rewards for achievements. In a high performance orientation culture, the selection of members for a team with an important task is likely to be based on talent, not on friendship or family relations.

A strong concern for task performance is widely believed to be a requirement for effective leadership in any country. Economic development is aided by a strong performance orientation, but concern for improving performance may be stronger in rapidly developing countries than in a country where widespread prosperity already exists (Javidan, 2004). Cultural values may have less influence on task-oriented behavior than core organizational values and a leader's individual needs and personality traits (e.g., achievement motivation, internal locus of control). Taken together, these factors help explain the lack of consistent results in cross-cultural studies on the effects of performance orientation values.

Humane Orientation

Humane orientation means a strong concern for the welfare of other people and the willingness to sacrifice one's own self-interest to help others. Key values include altruism, benevolence, kindness, compassion, love, and generosity. These values tend to be associated with stronger needs for affiliation and belongingness than for pleasure, achievement, or power. Altruism and kindness are not limited to a person's family or ethnic/religious in-group, but instead include a humanitarian concern for everyone. Societies with a strong humane orientation encourage and reward individuals for being friendly, caring, generous, and kind to others (Kabasakal & Bodur, 2004; Schlösser et al., 2013). Such societies are likely to invest more resources in educating and training people for careers and in providing health care and social services to people. The humane values for an individual are influenced by family experiences, parenting, and religious teaching as well as by cultural norms.

Humane orientation values encourage supportive leadership behaviors such as being considerate of a subordinate's needs and feelings, showing sympathy when a subordinate is upset, providing mentoring and coaching when appropriate, offering to provide assistance when needed to deal with a personal problem, and acting friendly and accepting. A leader with strong humane orientation values is likely to be more tolerant, patient, and helpful with subordinates who make mistakes or are having difficulty learning a new task. Humane orientation values are also associated with participative leadership, servant leadership, and team-building behaviors (encouraging cooperation and mutual trust). The key values are consistent with a diplomatic, conciliatory style of conflict management that seeks to restore harmonious relations and satisfy each party's important needs. The interest in building friendly, cooperative relationships can extend to people outside of the leader's team or unit, such as developing a network of external contacts by socializing with people and doing favors for them. In some countries, humane orientation can also take other forms, such as socializing informally with subordinates and acting paternalistic with regard to the career and social welfare of subordinates and their families. India is a high power distance, low uncertainty avoidance, collectivistic, masculine, high in performance orientation, and high in humane orientation country.

Culture Clusters

The cultural value dimensions are moderately intercorrelated, and examining differences for a single value dimension without controlling for the others makes it difficult to determine their independent effects on leadership beliefs and behavior. For example, in a country that has high power distance and low uncertainty tolerance, it is not clear how much each value influences the emphasis on centralized decisions for a company. For this reason, researchers have grouped countries into clusters based on regional proximity and similarity in language, ethnic background, and religion (Dorfman et al., 2012; Gupta & Hanges, 2004; Gupta, Hanges, & Dorfman, 2002). The GLOBE researchers grouped 61 countries into 10 clusters, and a discriminant analysis confirmed that the classification of countries into clusters accurately reflected differences in the nine cultural values for each country. The nations in each cluster are shown in Table 13-1.

TABLE 13-1 GLOBE Culture Clusters

Eastern Europe	**Anglo**	**Sub-Saharan Africa**
Albania	Australia	Namibia
Georgia	Canada	Nigeria
Greece	Ireland	South Africa (black)
Hungary	New Zealand	Zambia
Kazakhstan	South Africa (white)	Zimbabwe
Poland	United Kingdom	
Russia	USA	
Slovenia		
Latin America	**Nordic Europe**	**Confucian Asia**
Argentina	Denmark	China
Bolivia	Finland	Hong Kong
Brazil	Sweden	Japan
Colombia		Singapore
Costa Rica	**Germanic Europe**	South Korea
Ecuador	Austria	Taiwan
El Salvador	Germany	
Guatemala	Netherlands	
Mexico	Switzerland	
Venezuela		
Latin Europe	**Middle East**	**Southern Asia**
France	Egypt	India
Israel	Kuwait	Indonesia
Italy	Morocco	Iran
Portugal	Qatar	Malaysia
Spain	Turkey	Philippines
Switzerland (French)		Thailand

Based on Gupta, Hanges, and Dorfman (2002).

The clusters were compared with regard to leadership beliefs, and differences were found among clusters for some of the beliefs about effective leadership. For example, participative leadership is considered more important in the Anglo, Germanic Europe, and Nordic Europe clusters than in the Eastern Europe, Southern Asia, Confucian Asia, and Middle East clusters. Showing a strong humane concern for others is considered more important for effective leadership in the Southern Asia and Sub-Saharan Africa clusters than in the Germanic Europe or Latin Europe clusters. Future research should look more closely at differences in actual leadership behavior that correspond to the differences in values and implicit theories about effective leadership.

Evaluation of Cross-Cultural Research

The research on cultural values finds important differences that are relevant for beliefs about effective leadership and actual behavior of leaders. However, conceptual and methodological weaknesses are common, and limitations in the research have been pointed out by several scholars (e.g., Brodbeck & Eisenbeiss, 2014; Jepson, 2009; Kirkman, Lowe, & Gibson, 2006; Smith, 2006). This section of the chapter summarizes the limitations and suggests some promising research questions for the future.

The conceptual frameworks used in cross-cultural research on leadership affect interpretation of results. There are differences in the cultural value dimensions proposed by different scholars, and disagreements about desirable features have not been resolved. All of the current taxonomies have limitations, and researchers continue to seek a more comprehensive and useful way to describe cultural dimensions. The reliance on broadly defined leadership behaviors in many studies makes it more difficult to get a clear picture of cross-cultural differences in behavior. To understand the joint influence of cultural and organizational values on leadership behavior, it is essential to measure specific aspects of this behavior in addition to broad categories such as participative leadership, supportive leadership, and transformational leadership. The selection of variables and interpretation of results can be biased by cultural differences among researchers in their underlying values and assumptions about human nature and organizational processes (Boyacigiller & Adler, 1991; Brodbeck & Eisenbeiss, 2014). To minimize this type of problem it is advisable to have a research team with qualified representatives from the different cultures included in the study.

Much of the early research used convenience samples from only a few countries, rather than representative samples from many different countries with controls for type of organization and type of respondent. The assumption that cultural values identified for a nation apply to all types of organizations in that country overlooks the importance of organizational culture, regional differences, and individual differences. Levels of analysis problems are caused by using an overall culture score for values to explain the behavior and performance of individuals. When cross-cultural studies have large samples, it is easy to find significant differences, and researchers have not been consistent about reporting whether the differences have much practical significance.

Another limitation in many cross-cultural studies is too much reliance on survey questionnaires. The serious biases in survey measures of leadership were explained in earlier chapters, and additional problems are common when fixed-response questionnaires are used in cross-cultural research. It can be difficult to achieve equivalence in meaning when questionnaires are translated into another language, and there are cultural differences in response biases even for scales with equivalent language (Atwater, Wang, Smither, & Fleenor, 2009; De

TABLE 13-2 Examples of Relevant Questions for Cross-Cultural Research

1. How does actual behavior of leaders differ across cultural value clusters and for different countries?
2. How are leader values and behaviors jointly influenced by personality (and developmental experiences), company culture, and national culture?
3. What types of leadership traits, skills, and developmental experiences are most useful to prepare someone for a leadership assignment in a different culture?
4. How useful is the distinction between actual and ideal cultural values for understanding implicit theories of leadership and patterns of leadership behavior?
5. What are the implications for leaders when a global organization's values are inconsistent with the social values in some countries where the organization has facilities?
6. What is necessary for effective leadership in a multi-national team with members who differ in their cultural values?
7. How fast are cultural values changing in developing countries, and how are the culture changes relevant for leadership?
8. How much agreement is there across cultures with regard to the essential requirements for ethical leadership, and what are the points of disagreement?

Beuckelaer et al., 2007; Harzing, 2006). An inherent bias in most survey research on cross-cultural leadership is the assumption that leadership is only a consequence of culture, when it is also a determinant of culture and an interpreter of culture. The use of ethnography and a detailed historical perspective are advocated as more useful approaches for research on the relationship between leadership and culture (Guthey & Jackson, 2011).

The utility of many cross-cultural studies is limited by their failure to acknowledge these problems. Even for well-designed studies, the interpretation of results is often difficult. Many studies fail to include information that could help to explain the reason for cross-cultural differences in leadership. It is useful to learn that a particular type of leadership behavior is used more often or has stronger effects in a particular culture, but it is even better to learn why. Many research questions need to be examined more closely in the future. Examples of relevant questions for future cross-cultural research on leadership are shown in Table 13-2.

Guidelines for Global Leadership

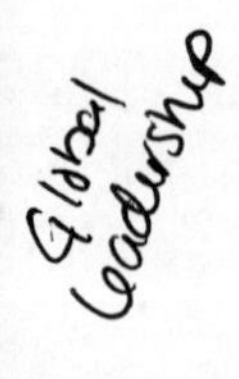

The research on cross-cultural leadership provides insights into how leadership values and practice vary across cultures, as well as how culture impacts the effectiveness of different types of leadership (Brodbeck & Eisenbeiss, 2014). The focus of global leadership involves applying these insights to meet the practical challenges facing leaders who operate in the global arena. In an increasingly interconnected and globalized world, finding and developing leaders who can effectively work across cultural and geographic boundaries is essential. While such leaders should possess the basic skills and knowledge (e.g., team-building, industry and role specific knowledge) required of most leaders, they must also possess the capacity to lead globally distributed teams and work across cultures, geographies, and time zones (Lundby et al., 2014). The following remarks from Robin Moriarity, Ph.D., regarding her role as the Managing Director of Kimberly-Clark Hong Kong, capture the challenges facing global leaders well, while suggesting an approach for addressing them:

> In today's world a global leader needs to be effective in cultures as diverse as China, India, Turkey, Brazil, Germany, Japan, South Africa, and the United States. How do you become an expert in all of those cultures? You don't. You develop personal qualities and capabilities that lead you to observe behavior, unravel nuances, build trust, and adapt your approach to be successful in a particular cultural context (Lundby et al., 2014, p. 659).

Based on emerging research and their collective experiences managing global enterprises, Kyle Lundby, Robin Moriarity, and Wayne C. Lee (2014) identify three global leadership essentials that are necessary to effectively manage in our increasingly global world. The following guidelines for global leadership reflect these essential qualities.

- **Understand your global employees.**

There are many aspects of human talent that leaders must understand to be effective. Three aspects are especially important for global leaders to understand because they differ across regions of the world: national culture, employee work preferences (e.g., desire for job security, growth opportunities, respect), and factors that engage and motivate employees. Considering the variance across national cultures and the stability of values and underlying assumptions within cultures, the subtle but strong influence of culture on the behavior of individuals and groups at work is not surprising. It is important to consider cultural differences in the preferences of employees for expected benefits and contributions at work, because this understanding can provide important insights about how to provide more effective leadership.

- **Understand the layers of complexity in your organization.**

Global organizations, like an onion, have many layers of complexity. Some, such as the industries within which the firm chooses to compete and its espoused values and norms, arise from the organization itself. Others, including different national cultures, political and economic systems, languages, and history, arise from the regions within which the organization operates. To be effective, global leaders must understand how these different aspects of the situation shape the behavior of individuals and teams at work.

- **Understand yourself.**

An understanding of the personal characteristics and practical experiences that predispose and prepare leaders to succeed in the global arena, as well as self-awareness regarding these qualities and experiences, can help global leaders to be more effective. Key among the requisite personality traits and characteristics are cultural agility (Caligiuri, 2013) and a global mindset, as they provide leaders with the perspective and flexibility required to understand and adapt their leadership within and across cultures (Lundby et al., 2014).

Although research on global leadership is limited, a study by Caligiuri and Tarique (2012) provides some preliminary insight into the kinds of personal qualities and developmental experiences that contribute to the effectiveness of global leaders. Using a sample of 420 global leaders, the study found that the personality characteristics of openness to experience, extraversion, and emotional stability coupled with work and non-work–related cross-cultural experiences, served as predictors of dynamic cross-cultural competencies such as cultural flexibility, tolerance for ambiguity, and reduced ethnocentrism. These cross-cultural competencies were positively related to supervisors' ratings of global leadership effectiveness. Overall, the findings suggest that both selection for requisite attributes and developmental cross-cultural experiences can increase the effectiveness of global leaders.

Gender and Leadership

A topic of great interest among practitioners as well as scholars is the possible difference between men and women in leadership behavior and effectiveness. A related topic of great importance is the reason for continued discrimination against women in leadership selection. This section of the chapter will briefly discuss both topics and review what has been learned about gender and leadership.

Sex-Based Discrimination

Widespread discrimination is clearly evident in the low number of women who hold important, high-level leadership positions in most types of organizations. The strong tendency to favor men over women in filling high-level leadership positions has been referred to as the "glass ceiling." Only a small number of nations have a female head of state (e.g., prime minister, president), and the number of women in top executive positions in large business organizations is also very small, although it has been increasing in recent years (Adler, 1996; Carli & Eagly, 2018; Catalyst, 2018; Chin, 2014; Powell, 2019; Ragins, Townsend, & Mattis, 1998). In the complete absence of sex-based discrimination, the number of women in chief executive positions in business and government should be close to 50 percent.

Another outcome of sex-based discrimination that has gained empirical attention over the past decade is known as the "glass cliff," which "refers to the tendency of women to be more likely to be appointed to leadership positions that are risky and precarious" (Ryan et al., 2016, p. 446). The "glass cliff" metaphor refers to "the precariousness of their roles as they teeter on the edge" (p. 447). The impetus for this research was an article in *The Times* (UK) asserting that "the triumphant march of women into the country's boardrooms ha[d] ... wreaked havoc on companies' performance" (Judge, 2003, p. 21). A series of studies was conducted to explore a more likely explanation (Bruckmüller, Ryan, Rink, & Haslam, 2014; Haslam & Ryan, 2008; Ryan & Haslam, 2007; Ryan, Haslam, Hersby, & Bongiorno, 2011; Ryan, Haslam, & Kulich, 2010). Specifically, the researchers considered if women who succeed in breaking through the glass ceiling might be especially likely to be appointed to positions with a high risk of failure. Using a combination of archival and experimental research methods, the researchers documented the existence of the glass cliff and showed that it is pervasive in both business and political organizations.

Theories of Male Advantage

Throughout the twentieth century, gender-based discrimination was supported by age-old beliefs that men are more qualified than women for leadership roles (Ayman & Korabik, 2010). These beliefs involved assumptions about the traits and skills required for effective leadership in organizations (implicit theories), assumptions about inherent differences between men and women (gender stereotypes), and assumptions about appropriate behavior for men and women (role expectations). As noted earlier, the implicit theories and gender stereotypes are also influenced by cultural values for gender egalitarianism.

A recent survey conducted by one of the country's leading HR service providers revealed that 57 percent of the overall correspondents preferred a man as their manager. What was more striking was the fact that 41 percent of the women correspondents preferred a male manager as well. The results of this survey indicate how women executives enter the workplace with one strike against them from the start (Times of India, 2017).

Theory of Feminine Advantage

A more recent controversy is fueled by claims that women are more likely than men to possess the values and skills necessary for effective leadership in modern organizations (Book, 2000; Carr-Ruffino, 1993; Grant, 1988; Hegelsen, 1990; Post, 2015; Rosener, 1990). The difference is a result of childhood experiences, parent–child interactions, and socialization practices that reflect cultural sex-role stereotypes and beliefs about gender differences and appropriate occupations for men and women (Cockburn, 1991). These experiences encourage "feminine" values such as kindness, compassion, nurturing, and sharing. Proponents of the "feminine advantage" theory contend that women are more concerned with consensus building, inclusiveness, and interpersonal relations, and they are more willing to develop and nurture subordinates and share power with them. Women are believed to have more empathy, rely more on intuition, and be more sensitive to feelings and the quality of relationships. Proponents of the feminine advantage also claim that the changing nature of leadership in organizations has increased the relevance of skills and values that are stronger in women than in men.

As with earlier claims that men are more qualified to be leaders, the claims that women are more qualified appear to be based on weak assumptions and exaggerated gender stereotypes. The evaluation of assertions about gender superiority in leadership requires a careful consideration of the findings in the empirical research. One preliminary step in this direction is provided by a study of the female leadership advantage in team settings (Post, 2015). The author posited that the advantages of female leadership may depend on the requirements for team coordination. That is, as requirements for coordination grow due to increases in team size, functional diversity, and geographic dispersion, teams with female leaders may experience higher levels of cohesion and cooperative and participative interaction norms. A survey study of 82 teams in 29 organizations found that female leadership was more positively related to cohesion for more functionally diverse and larger teams, and it was positively related to participative communication and cooperative learning for larger and geographically dispersed teams.

Explanations for the Glass Ceiling and Glass Cliff

Biased beliefs about the skills and behaviors necessary for effective leadership are one reason for sex-based discrimination. For a long time, it was assumed that effective leaders must be confident, task-oriented, competitive, objective, decisive, and assertive, all of which were traditionally viewed as masculine attributes (Powell & Butterfield, 2015; Schein, 1975; Stogdill, 1974). As shown in earlier chapters, effective leadership also requires strong interpersonal skills, and leadership behaviors traditionally viewed as feminine (e.g., supporting, developing, empowering). These skills and behaviors were always relevant for effective leadership, but now they are more important than in earlier times because of changing conditions in work organizations. As popular conceptions of effective leadership become more accurate and comprehensive, role expectations for leaders will become less gender biased.

Sex-based discrimination in leadership selection also reflects the influence of popular stereotypes and role expectations for men and women (Brescoll, 2016; Carli & Eagly, 2018; Chin, 2014; Heilman, 2001; Hoyt & Murphy, 2016). For a long time, women were assumed to be unable or unwilling to use the masculine behaviors considered essential for effective leadership. Some laboratory studies found that even when women leaders use masculine behaviors, they are evaluated less favorably than men who use them (e.g., Eagly, Makhijani, & Klonsky, 1992; Rojahn & Willemsen, 1994). However, the effects of gender stereotypes on evaluation of female managers may be overstated in laboratory studies with students.

The experience of working for men and women leaders over a period of time can reduce the effects of gender stereotypes on evaluation of the leaders (Powell, 1990). As gender stereotypes change over time in the general population, they will probably become less important as a source of biased role expectations for leaders. Unfortunately, the changes in gender role stereotypes and implicit theories have been slow, especially among male managers (Brenner, Tomkiewicz, & Schein, 1989; Epitropaki & Martin, 2004; Powell, 2019; Powell & Butterfield, 2015; Powell, Butterfield, & Parent, 2002).

Gender bias in terms of career advancement for women is quite prevalent in big corporations (Sharma and Sehrawat, 2014). Women in India still have an image of being weak, emotional and unaggressive, qualities which do are not suitable or desirable for higher level management positions. Women are unable to reach the C-level even after 40–45 years of service. Out of 1000 fortune companies, only 5 per cent of the women are serving as senior managers (Federal glass commission report, 1995). Although the number of women working in the IT sector has increased, hardly any of them are seen at top management positions (Kelkar and Shrestha, 2002; Upadhya and Vasavi, 2006).

International Business Report, a study done by Grant Thornton, reported that in the Indian workplace, the proportion of women in senior position fell from 19 percent in 2013 to 14 percent in 2014. What is more alarming was that very few Indian companies have a mentoring program for women. The situation has been worsened by the MeToo movement, post which male executives are hesitating all the more in mentoring female employees. According to a study by McKinsey & Co, female representation on executive boards of Indian companies currently stands at a meagre 5 percent.

Interest in studying barriers to advancement for women has been increasing. A study by Bell and Nkomo (2001) found that one of the major barriers (especially for black women) was limited access to social and informal networks in their organizations. A study by Babcock and Laschever (2003) found that women were less likely than men to ask for promotion and initiate the types of negotiations likely to favor it. A study by Lyness and Heilman (2006) found that women needed more of the required skills than men to advance to executive positions, and the difference was greater for the types of positions traditionally held by men. These studies and others have increased our knowledge about barriers to advancement for women, but more research is needed to determine the relative importance of different causes and how the different causes interact to limit the number of women in top leadership positions.

Current thinking also identifies several factors that combine to push female leaders toward the glass cliff (Ryan et al., 2016). First, organizations facing crises, and the accompanying uncertainty, are more likely to take risks to address the crisis, which promotes a willingness to try something new and reject the status quo. Such circumstances may open up previously blocked avenues for women to assume executive-level leadership positions. Second, women may be assumed to have certain traits and skills that make them well suited for dealing with crises situations (e.g., people skills). Third, given the inherent risks of such leadership assignments, female leaders who gain access to upper management positions may be less likely to succeed and thrive once they get there. Fourth, research on the "romance of leadership" (Meindl, 1990) suggests that observers tend to blame leaders for poor performance more than situational factors, which partially explains why organizations facing crises have high levels of turnover at the top. Fifth, in times of crisis, the leadership teams and their organizations experience high levels of pressure and scrutiny from key stakeholders and the media. Such scrutiny is especially intense in glass cliff positions, due to the combination of two rare events—a crisis and a female leader. Finally, because deposed leaders of poor performing organizations are less likely to be appointed to leadership positions in the future, the career trajectory of women who "fall off" the glass cliff may be severely hampered, which may also partly account for the persistence of the glass ceiling (Ryan et al., 2016).

Findings in Research on Gender Differences

Many studies have compared men and women leaders with regard to their leadership behavior. Reviews of this research on gender and leadership disagree about the results (e.g., Bass, 1990; Dobbins & Platz, 1986; Eagly, Darau, & Makhijani, 1995; Eagly & Johnson, 1990; Powell, 2019). Some reviewers concluded that there is no evidence of important gender differences in leadership behaviors or skills. Other reviewers concluded that there are gender-related differences for some behaviors or skills in some situations. A debate published in *The Leadership Quarterly* shows the complexity of the issues and the extent to which scholars disagree (Eagly & Carli, 2003a, 2003b; Vecchio, 2002, 2003).

Many of the early studies on gender differences in leadership behavior involved task and relationship behavior. Eagly and Johnson (1990) conducted a meta-analysis of the gender studies with actual managers and found no gender differences in the use of task-oriented behavior or supportive behavior. However, their study did find that participative leadership was used slightly more by women than by men. In a meta-analysis (Eagly, Johannesen-Schmidt, & Van Engen, 2003), women used slightly more transformational leadership behavior than men, and the primary difference was for individualized consideration, which includes supportive behavior and efforts to develop a subordinate's skills and confidence. Results for transactional leadership were mixed and difficult to interpret.

Results from studies on gender differences in leadership effectiveness are also inconsistent. Eagly et al. (1995) found no overall difference in effectiveness for men and women managers. However, when role requirements for different types of managerial positions were identified, male managers were more effective than women managers in positions that required strong task skills, and women managers were more effective in positions that required strong interpersonal skills. Because most leadership positions require both types of skills, gender is unlikely to be useful as a predictor of leadership effectiveness for these positions.

In recent years, increased research attention has focused on the relationships between gender composition on corporate boards and key organizational outcomes. Based on an extensive review of this literature, Kirsch (2018) concluded that the effect of board gender composition on firm performance was inclusive, with some studies finding positive effects, while others revealed no effects or negative effects. However, she noted that a meta-analysis by Post and Byron (2015) may help to clarify these mixed findings. The meta-analysis examined the relationships between board gender composition and firm performance as measured by both stock-based and accounting measures of performance. Stock prices are influenced by investors' perceptions, including stereotypical beliefs about the suitability of women for leadership positions. The results revealed that while the relationship between female representation on corporate boards and stock-based measures of firm performance was near zero, it was positive in countries characterized by high gender parity and negative in countries with low gender parity. One likely explanation provided for this difference was that the presence of women on boards bestows more legitimacy on firms in countries with greater gender parity. The study also found that the representation of women on the board was positively related to accounting measures of firm performance, especially in the countries with strong shareholder protections. Such protections encourage boards to use the different values, knowledge, and experience of women directors to improve board decisions and performance outcomes.

As for the ethical and social aspects of firm behavior, Kirsch (2018) concluded from her review that the available evidence indicates these outcomes are enhanced by greater representation of women directors on corporate boards. Potential explanations for these findings include gender differences, such as women's communal tendencies, ethical orientation, and predispositions for empathy and caring. However, Kirsch cautions that it is also possible that the more socially responsible firms are more likely to recruit and appoint female board members, and more research is needed to understand the nature of these relationships.

Limitations of Research on Gender Differences

Serious limitations in much of the research on gender differences complicate interpretation of the results. One major problem is the lack of a clear definition of gender (Ely & Padavic, 2007). In some cases, it refers to anatomical sex (male versus female), and in others it refers to a set of personal characteristics often associated more with one sex than with another. These conceptions of gender characteristics are not constant across studies.

In comparative studies, a major problem is contamination from extraneous variables (see Adams, 2016; Ely & Padavic, 2007; Lefkowitz, 1994). Gender is often correlated with other variables known to affect leader behavior (e.g., level, function, time in position, type of organization), and most studies of gender differences in leadership do not control for the differential effects of organizational variables on men and women leaders. People may be attracted to a profession (e.g., women to nursing, men to police work) because it involves the use of "natural" skills and behaviors, or because their opportunities are limited and their choices influenced by strong sex-role stereotypes. If a study includes more women than men in types of leadership positions that require a lot of supportive and empowering behavior, then (unless type of position is controlled) the results will seem to indicate that women leaders are generally more supportive and participative. If the study has more men in types of leadership positions that require assertive and decisive behavior, then the results will seem to indicate that men generally have more of these attributes. Unfortunately, most comparative studies reporting male–female differences do not control for this type of confounding.

Another type of biased result can occur in a comparative study that fails to take into account how organizational factors may have a differential influence on the skills of men and women who are in the same type of leadership position. For example, if strong interpersonal and political skills facilitate advancement into executive positions but the standards for selection are more difficult for women than for men, then fewer women will advance but they will have more of these skills than the men who advance. Unless this bias in taken into account, the results comparing male to female executives may be incorrectly interpreted as showing that women generally have stronger interpersonal and political skills.

Differential role expectations can also influence the measurement of leader behavior, skills, or performance for men and women in the same type of leadership position (Carli & Eagly, 2018; Chin, 2014; Eagly & Chin, 2010). For example, if most raters share common gender stereotypes, then their ratings will reflect a combination of a leader's real behavior and the biased perception of it by the raters. Thus, stereotypes about gender (or race, ethnic background, age, education) can result in inflated differences when in reality there is little or no difference.

On the other hand, for male and female leaders in similar positions, role expectations that influence leader behavior can make gender differences more difficult to discover. For example, if strong role expectations in an organization influence women to exhibit "masculine" attributes such as toughness and assertiveness, then it will be more difficult to find significant differences between men and women on these attributes. In an organization without strong role expectations, actual gender differences are more likely to emerge and be noted. Even if women in some type of leadership position have more of the relevant skills than men in that position, ratings of overall leadership effectiveness may fail to reflect this difference if the raters have different role expectations for women, or ratings are biased by the belief that women are less able to do the job effectively.

Another difficulty in evaluating results in research on gender differences in leadership is caused by the type of data analysis and reporting of results. Many studies report tests of statistical differences without reporting effect sizes. In studies with large samples, it is possible to find a difference that is statistically significant but has no practical significance. Knowing the sex of a leader is of no practical help for predicting the person's behavior or effectiveness when there are large differences within each gender group. Studies that fail to provide evidence of practical significance perpetuate exaggerated stereotypes about men and women.

The utility of meta-analyses for interpreting research on gender differences is limited when the results in the published literature are not representative. Significant but small gender differences may result from unrepresentative sampling of studies and confounding within some studies. Assessment of gender differences is seldom the primary purpose for conducting a survey field study on leadership, but most studies include gender in the demographic information about the sample. It is easy to check on any gender differences, and the popularity of the topic means that significant relationships involving gender are likely to be reported more often than non-significant relationships.

Identifying Causes and Reducing Discrimination

Most studies on gender and leadership are focused on determining if there is a difference between men and women, not on determining the cause of any differences. If the research is able to find differences with both statistical and practical significance, then it is essential to discover the reasons for them. The types of confounding and biases described earlier are one likely cause of the differences. If significant gender differences remain after these biases are removed, then a possible explanation involves biological differences created by evolutionary processes that occurred over thousands of years in primitive times (Browne, 2006; Buss, 2016; Geary, 1998; van Vugt, 2018). Another possible explanation is that differential treatment during childhood causes men and women to have different values, traits, skills, and ways of dealing with situations. Although not mutually exclusive, these explanations lead to different implications for the selection and training of leaders and the elimination of unfair discrimination. Unfortunately, most studies on gender differences in leadership provide little information about the reasons for any differences that are found. In the absence of such evidence, people are more likely to attribute gender differences to inherent biological factors than to things that could be changed.

Equally important to understanding the reasons for any real gender differences is the need to find ways to eliminate unfair discrimination. The essential skills and behaviors for effective leadership differ somewhat across situations, and some types of leadership positions may provide a slight advantage either to men or to women. However, any gender advantage is likely to be a small one, which means that gender should not be an important qualification for the position.

Female candidates are likely to be rated as less qualified than male candidates for many types of leadership positions unless accurate information about each person's skill and experience is collected and used in the selection decision (Heilman, 2001; Heilman & Haynes, 2005). To avoid bias from gender stereotypes and prejudice, a special effort should be made to ensure that the relevant skills are accurately assessed when selecting leaders. If possible, selection and promotion decisions should be made by people who understand how to avoid bias resulting from stereotypes and implicit assumptions. Affirmative action guidelines can provide helpful guidance for avoiding unfair discrimination in the selection of leaders. For leadership positions that require skills more likely to be possessed by male (or female) candidates, providing relevant training and developmental experiences to any candidates who need them will help equalize opportunities for advancement.

Summary of Leader Gender Research

More systematic and comprehensive research is needed to determine the extent of any gender differences in leadership and the reasons for them. It is essential to examine how organizational and cultural factors influence the perceptions and behaviors that shape gender identity. Given the inconsistent findings and limitations of research on gender differences in leadership, the conclusion reached by Powell (1990, p. 74) still seems correct:

> There is little reason to believe that either women or men make superior managers, or that women and men are different types of managers. Instead, there are likely to be excellent, average, and poor managerial performers within each sex. Success in today's highly competitive marketplace calls for organizations to make best use of the talent available to them. To do this, they need to identify, develop, encourage, and promote the most effective managers, regardless of sex.

Managing Diversity and Inclusion

Diversity can take many forms, including differences in race, ethnic identity, age, gender, education, physical appearance, socioeconomic level, sexual orientation, and differences associated with a person's generation (e.g., millennials). Diversity in the workforce is increasing in the United States and Europe (Chrobot-Mason, Ruderman, & Nishii, 2014; Lacey, Toossi, Dubina, & Gensler, 2017; Scott, 2018; Milliken & Martins, 1996). More women are entering traditionally male jobs, the number of older workers is increasing, and there is more diversity with regard to ethnic, religious, racial, and other types of employee differences. The increasing number of joint ventures, mergers, and strategic alliances is bringing together people from different types of organizations and national cultures. As noted in some earlier chapters, diversity and inclusion offer potential benefits and costs for a group or organization (Bell et al., 2011; Cox, 2001; Cox & Blake, 1991; Kochan et al., 2003; Ferdman, 2017; Horwitz, S. K., & Horwitz, I. B., 2007; Milliken & Martins, 1996; van Knippenberg & Schippers, 2007). A greater variety of perspectives can increase creativity, and full utilization of a diverse workforce would increase the amount of available talent for filling important jobs.

The following excerpt from *How Google Works,* written by Google Executive Chairman and ex-CEO Eric Schmidt and former Senior Vice President of Products, Jonathan Rosenberg (2014, p. 107), highlights some of the benefits to innovation and creativity that can result from a diverse workforce:

> We could go off on a politically correct tangent on how hiring a workforce that is diverse in terms of race, sexual orientation, physical challenges, and anything else that makes people different is the right thing to do (which it is). But from a strictly corporate point of view, diversity in hiring is even more emphatically the right thing to do. People from different

backgrounds see the world differently. Women, men, whites and blacks, Jews and Muslims, Catholics and Protestants, veterans and civilians, gays and straights, Latinos and Europeans, Klingons and Romulans, Asians and Africans, wheelchair-bound and able-bodied. These differences of perspective generate insights that can't be taught. When you bring them together in a work environment, they integrate to create a broader perspective that is priceless.

However, diversity can also result in more distrust and conflict, lower satisfaction, and higher turnover. An organization is less likely to have shared values and strong member commitment when it has many diverse members who identify primarily with their own subgroup. Thus, managing diversity is an important but a difficult responsibility of leaders in the twenty-first century. The desired outcome of efforts to manage and value diversity is employee inclusion, where all employees, including historically marginalized groups, feel they can openly express who they are and how they differ from others (including deep-level differences in personalities, values, and strengths) (Buengeler, Leroy, & De Stobbeleir, 2018; Ferdman, 2017; Nischii, 2013).

Fostering Appreciation and Tolerance

Leaders can do many things to foster appreciation and tolerance for diversity. Some recommended action steps for individual leaders are listed in Table 13-3. These actions can be divided into two categories that are similar to the distinction made earlier for ethical leadership behavior. Some actions seek to encourage tolerance and appreciation, whereas other actions challenge discrimination and intolerance.

Diversity training programs provide a formal approach to encourage tolerance, understanding, and appreciation (Cox, 2001; Cox & Blake, 1991). One objective of diversity training is to create a better understanding of diversity problems and the need for self-awareness about stereotyping and intolerance. Many people are not aware of their own stereotypes and implicit assumptions about diverse groups, nor do they understand that even when real differences exist, they are usually small and do not apply to many people in the group being stereotyped. Another objective of diversity training is to educate employees about real cultural or demographic differences and how to respond to them in the workplace. The specific aspects of diversity that are included vary depending on the program (e.g., ethnic background, religion, national culture, age differences, employee sex, sexual orientation, physical disabilities). It is important for people

TABLE 13-3 Guidelines for Managing Diversity and Promoting Inclusion

Encourage Tolerance and Appreciation

- Set an example in your own behavior of appreciation for diversity.
- Encourage respect for individual differences.
- Promote understanding of different values, beliefs, and traditions.
- Explain the benefits of diversity for the team or organization.
- Encourage and support others who promote tolerance of diversity.

Discourage Intolerance and Discrimination

- Discourage the use of stereotypes to describe people.
- Identify biased beliefs and role expectations for women or minorities.
- Challenge people who make prejudiced comments.
- Speak out to protest against unfair treatment based on prejudice.
- Take disciplinary action to stop harassment of women or minorities.

to understand how differences can be an advantage rather than a liability. AT&T, Accenture, Avon, Ely Lilly and Co., Hewlett-Packard, Johnson & Johnson, Marriott, Mobil Oil, Procter & Gamble, PwC, Target, and Xerox are just a few examples of companies that have used such programs. A problem with some diversity training programs is their emphasis on placing blame for discrimination rather than on increasing self-awareness and mutual understanding (Nemetz & Christensen, 1996). Leaders who implement diversity training should keep the content of the program consistent with an appealing vision of what appreciation of diversity can mean for all members of the organization.

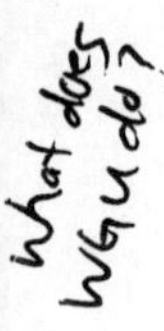

Structural mechanisms can also be helpful. Examples include (1) appraisal criteria that include diversity issues, (2) task forces or advisory committees to help identify discrimination or intolerance and develop remedies, (3) measures that allow systematic monitoring of progress, and (4) hotlines or other special mechanisms that make it easier for employees to report discrimination and intolerance. Efforts to change attitudes are more likely to be successful when diversity training is directed at people who have not already formed strong prejudices, and the organization has a culture that supports appreciation for diversity (Nemetz & Christensen, 1996).

Providing Equal Opportunity

To make full use of the talent represented by the diverse members of the organization, it is essential to eliminate constraints that prevent qualified people from selection for important positions. Many things can be done to facilitate equal opportunity and promote employee inclusion (Buengeler et al., 2018; Cox, 2001). Surveys of employee attitudes can be used to identify problems and assess progress. The organizational communications media can be used to describe what is being done to promote equal opportunity and report achievements.

The assessments used for selection and promotion decisions will be more accurate if the raters who make them are trained or otherwise helped to reduce biases caused by racial, ethnic, or gender role stereotypes. The stereotypes can include both positive and negative features, and when they lurk below conscious awareness, their influence on the interpretation and evaluation of another person's behavior is more difficult to detect (Brescoll, 2016; Carli & Eagly, 2018; Eagly & Chin, 2010; Goldberg & McKay, 2016; Hoyt & Murphy, 2016). One method for reducing this type of bias is a "structured free recall" intervention (Baltes, Bauer, & Frensch, 2007; Bauer & Baltes, 2002). The raters are asked to recall examples of both positive and negative behaviors by a candidate before rating the person's qualifications for a position.

Mentorship programs that provide adequate advice, encouragement, and assistance facilitate the advancement by women and minorities (Benschop, Holgersson, van den Brink, & Wahl, 2015). Leadership development programs should provide equal opportunities for people who want to learn relevant skills and gain valuable experience. Affirmative action programs can be helpful if they are well designed and implemented (Harrison, Kravitz, Mayer, Leslie, & Lev-Arey, 2006). The programs are likely to be less controversial and more successful if the need for them is clearly understood by the members of an organization, and ways are found to encourage affirmative action without imposing reverse discrimination.

The human resources management department usually has primary responsibility for many of the processes that affect diversity and equal opportunity, such as recruiting, selection, employee orientation, performance appraisal, training, and mentoring. However, the responsibility for providing equal opportunity should not be relegated solely to human resource staff specialists. A successful effort to improve diversity and equal opportunity requires strong support by top management and managers at all levels of the organization(Buengeler et al., 2018; Ng & Wyrick, 2011).

Other approaches for achieving equal opportunity are possible at a national level. Corporate boards of directors have only about 20 percent women members in the United States and Europe, and efforts are being made to help women penetrate this glass ceiling (Kirsch, 2018). Corporate boards determine the selection of CEOs, and more balanced boards should help to increase the number of women CEOs. Some European countries have been adopting quotas for the number of women directors (Klettner, Clarke, & Boersma, 2016; Sojo, Wood, R. E., Wood, S. A., & Wheeler, 2016). For example, Norway adopted a quota in 2002 and has already reached the mandated level of 40 percent women directors. France and Spain recently passed a similar quota. Efforts to eliminate discrimination in the selection of leaders are not limited to legal options. Organizations can iniate voluntary campaigns to increase equal opportunity, and the following example describes what an Indian company did.

> Wipro has been hiring employees with disabilities since 2010. However, they recognized that they needed to make their workspace more inclusive if they wanted to wanted to be effective. Therefore, they decided to move to a six-pronged holistic growth approach for the PwDs, rather than just having PwD representation. The six-pronged approach comprised of career, recruitment, engagement, accessibility, talent transformation, and enablement to support the 415 PwDs who represented approximately 0.38 percent of the organization's total workforce (NASSCOM, 2016).

Summary

With the rapid pace of globalization and economic development, cross-cultural leadership has become an important topic for research. Some leader attributes are considered important for effective leadership in all cultures that have been studied, but other attributes vary in importance from one culture to another. Cultural values and beliefs are likely to influence actual leader behavior, especially when they are also consistent with core values for the organization.

The amount of cross-cultural research is increasing, but the methodological difficulties in conducting this type of research are substantial. Equivalence of meaning is not assured in many studies, the sampling procedures are inadequate, controls for contaminating factors are absent, explanatory variables are not included, and interpretation of results is questionable. Faster progress may require greater use of large-scale research projects such as GLOBE.

Global leadership involves applying knowledge of cultural values and practices to address the practical challenges facing leaders who work with people from diverse cultures and across geographic boundaries. Beyond the basic knowledge, skills, and abilities required of domestic leaders, global leaders must have the capacity to lead globally dispersed teams that span cultures, geographies, and time zones. To do so requires three global leadership essentials: understanding your global talent; understanding the layers of complexity in your organization; and understanding yourself.

Sex-based discrimination in the selection and promotion of leaders continues to be a serious problem in large organizations. There are several different reasons for such discrimination, but more research is needed to understand the causes and find ways to deal with them. Many studies have examined gender-based differences in leadership behavior and effectiveness, but the findings are weak and inconsistent. Future studies need to control for effects of likely contaminating variables, report the magnitude of any significant differences that are found, and measure processes that provide insight into the reasons for the differences.

An important responsibility for leaders in this new century is the management of diversity, which can take many forms. Leaders play an essential role in helping to bring about equal opportunity and elimination of unfair discrimination in selection and promotion decisions. Leaders can do many things to encourage tolerance, promote appreciation of diversity, and foster employee inclusion in organizations. All leaders in the organization should share the responsibility for improving diversity, ensuring equal opportunity, and promoting employee inclusion. Leadership at the national level is also important in the continuing efforts to eliminate unfair discrimination and enhance inclusion for all minorities and ethnic groups.

Review and Discussion Questions

1. What are the major research questions in studies of cross-cultural leadership?
2. Why is cross-cultural research on leadership important and worthwhile?
3. What are some difficulties in conducting cross-cultural research on leadership?
4. What cultural value dimensions have been identified, and how are they related to leadership?
5. What are the essentials to effective global leadership?
6. Why is there a "glass ceiling" for women, and what can be done about the problem?
7. Why is there a "glass cliff" for women, and what factors contribute to it?
8. What can leaders do to manage diversity and promote employee inclusion in organizations?

Key Terms

collectivism
cross-cultural differences
cultural value dimensions
discrimination in personnel decisions
diversity training
gender egalitarianism
gender stereotypes
glass ceiling
glass cliff
GLOBE
Global leadership
humane orientation
inclusion
individualism
performance orientation
power distance
uncertainty avoidance

PERSONAL REFLECTION

Think of a time when you were stereotyped based on your gender, age, race, ethnicity, generation, religion, or some other attribute. Why do you think it happened and how did it affect you? What could have been done, if anything, to avoid this stereotyping and the consequences?

CASE

Aayushi and Khaitan & Co.

Aayushi got placed at the prestigious Khaitan and Co. law firm post her graduation in law from the top notch National Law University, Bangalore. Khaitan and Co. mainly handled the legal issues of corporate firms and also dealt with some pro bono cases. After working for the firm for three years, Aayushi's extraordinary performance fetched her a promotion to the position of an associate. The new position meant new set of responsibilities and Aayushi was confident about her capabilities.

Aayushi's subordinates as well as the other associates at the firm respected her. Her clients were also quite happy with her. Given her performance in the past five years at the company, it was hoped that soon Aayushi would become a partner at the company, but she knew there was a roadblock as she was the only female associate in the male dominated firm. Aayushi felt that her being a female, a lot of times her ideas went unheard, while similar ideas from a male counterpart would be often accepted and appreciated. She felt that some of the other senior associates at the firm did not see her as an equal, owing to her gender. Thus, it would often happen during meetings that her ideas or suggestions were paid attention to or were not received well either.

The firm had no mentoring programs either which would assist Aayushi in furthering her career at the firm. She did not feel accepted even in the informal network of relationships that provided opportunities for interaction with the senior associates. She was not invited to the social gatherings that were organized by the senior associates. Since she did not play pool, she was not a member of the exclusive club to which a lot of the male associates belonged.

Aayushi also felt that the projects were allotted in a biased way, with the high-profile cases always being given to the male associates. When she questioned the allotment process, she would be told that a lot of the clients preferred working with male associates. Because she was not given a lot of the high-profile cases, her performance numbers did not look as good as the numbers for some of the other male associates. As a result, two other male candidates, who had joined the firm at the same time as her, got promoted to the level of associates much before she did.

Aayushi decided to discuss her career trajectory so far and what the future holds for her, with one of the partners of the firm. The partner was surprised that Aayushi was not satisfied with her current career trajectory, and assured her that she would soon be promoted as she was considered a valuable member of the firm. However, since Aayushi saw no improvement in the way she was treated at the firm even after a year, she decided to resign, and with the help of two friends who were also law graduates from her law school, she started on her own. Soon their firm became quite successful and famous.

—*Written by* Nishant Uppal

Questions

1. What forms of gender discrimination did Aayushi experience?
2. What could Aayushi have done to overcome the obstacles she encountered?
3. What could the partner of the firm have done to create equal opportunity at his firm?

CASE

A Day in the Life of a Global Leader

When the multinational, Berlin-based auto parts manufacturer acquired the company she worked for in her native Columbia, Nathalie wasn't worried. She had risen steadily through the ranks, and felt ready for her management position. She had presumed it would be an easy transition, because she knew the industry well. However, she now managed manufacturing operations in several different countries, overseeing a "team" of plant managers. Team felt like the wrong term, as their geographic separation implied that most team communication happened through e-mail, with only occasional videoconference meetings of the whole group. Additionally, because of time zone differences, Nathalie only actually spoke to some plant managers, but with others—who worked while she slept—Nathalie had less of a personal connection. Consequently, there wasn't much of a "team feeling" so much as there were independent relationships between Nathalie and her plant managers around the world.

Today's challenges included getting information and input from her team, and building consensus on how to move forward. Nathalie had sent out draft budget projections for the unit, and asked team members to provide feedback. Three new e-mails in her inbox highlighted Nathalie's frustrations. The first, from Lingfei at a plant outside Tokyo, recommended further team discussions about the budget projections Nathalie had shared. Nathalie sensed that Lingfei didn't agree with the projections, but the e-mail never quite said that. The second e-mail, from Hasan in Indonesia, seemed vague, saying nothing about what he thought of the budgeting process, or whether the projections were remotely accurate. The third, from Christopher in England, clearly expressed frustration that the budgeting process was taking longer than scheduled, and seemed not to follow the company's standard budgeting, because of Susan's efforts to get input from the rest of the team. Christopher e-mailed that "time is money, you know." A fourth team member, Cyrille from France, had not replied by the requested deadline . . . once again.

Nathalie sighed as she looked over these e-mails. Her boss in Berlin told her yesterday that she needed to take command of her team and provide clear and consistent direction. Though she was trying, that approach was just so foreign to her. She was used to building consensus in teams with strong relationships and personal loyalty. Those sorts of relationships seemed to form naturally "back home," but hadn't happened now, and Nathalie wasn't sure where to start. She sensed issues weren't just related to specific team members, but instead to the cultures they came from. Should she try to change her style to meet their preferences, or change them to meet hers?

Source: Den Hartog & Dickson in Antonakis & Day (2018); used with permission.

Questions

1. How can Nathalie think about cultural differences that might be affecting her team without resorting to cultural stereotyping?
2. Does the lack of face-to-face communication contribute to Nathalie's problem? If so, how?
3. If we believe that cultural value differences are affecting the team's efforts, what should be Nathalie's next steps?

Chapter 14 Developing Leadership Skills

Learning Objectives

After studying this chapter, you should be able to:

- Understand the importance of leadership training and development in organizations.
- Understand the benefits and limitations of different methods for leadership development.
- Understand the individual and organizational factors that facilitate leadership training and development.
- Understand how leaders can encourage and facilitate leadership development.
- Understand some ways for leaders to develop their own skills.
- Understand why leader development should be consistent with strategic planning.

Introduction

The increasing rate of change in the external environment of organizations and the many new challenges facing leaders suggest that success as a leader in the twenty-first century will require a higher level of skill and some new competencies. To meet this need, new techniques are being invented and old techniques are being refined. Leadership development remains a multibillion-dollar business, with double-digit increases in investment among U.S. organizations in recent years, especially for small businesses (Meinert, 2014). A recent survey of more than 2,500 human resource and business leaders in 94 countries reveals that accelerating, deepening, and broadening leadership development across organizational levels is viewed as a top priority, with 86 percent of respondents reporting this need as "important" or "urgent" (Schwartz, Bersin, & Pelster, 2014).

Despite the strong interest in leadership development, organizations do not always fully assess the potential costs and returns from investments in it. To help organizations make such assessments, Avolio, Avey, and Quisenberry (2010) described how the return on leadership investment (RODI) can be estimated. They showed that, depending on the guiding assumptions, type and length of the intervention, and type of participating managers, the expected RODI ranged from slightly negative to more than 200 percent. A subsequent study by Richard, Holton, and Katsioloudes (2014) demonstrated how organizations could use a computer simulation to compute the expected RODI for leadership development programs. Their study found that leadership development programs can provide a much higher RODI than most executives realize, but organizations can incur substantial losses when such programs are implemented poorly. Together, these studies highlight the importance of effective leadership development for achieving and sustaining high organizational performance.

Leadership competencies can be developed in a number of ways, including formal training, developmental activities, and self-development activities. Most formal training occurs during a defined time period, and it is usually conducted away from the manager's immediate worksite by training professionals (e.g., a short workshop at a training center, a management course at a university). Developmental activities are usually embedded within operational job assignments or conducted in conjunction with those assignments. The developmental activities can take many forms, including coaching by the manager's boss or an outside consultant, mentoring by someone at a higher level in the organization, and special assignments that provide new challenges and opportunities to learn relevant skills (Day, 2000; Day & Thorton, 2018). Leader developmental experiences may also extend beyond the workplace to other domains (Hammond, Clapp-Smith, & Palanski, 2017). Self-development activities that are carried out by individuals on their own initiative include reading books, viewing videos, listening to audiotapes, and using interactive computer programs for skill building.

The effectiveness of training programs, developmental experiences, and self-development activities depends in part on individual attributes and organizational conditions that facilitate the learning of leadership skills and the application of this learning (Avolio & Hannah, 2008; Day & Dragoni, 2015; Day, Fleenor, Atwater, Sturm, & McKee, 2014; Day & Thorton, 2018; DeRue & Myers, 2014; Hannah & Avolio, 2010). Facilitating factors include the developmental readiness of the leader, as well as organizational attributes such as support for skill development from bosses and coworkers, reward systems that encourage skill development, and cultural values that support continuous learning. This chapter examines various approaches for leadership development and the key facilitating conditions.

Leadership Training Programs

Formal training programs are widely used to improve leadership in organizations. Most large organizations have management training programs of one kind or another, and many organizations send their managers to outside seminars and workshops (Saari, Johnson, McLaughlin, & Zimmerle, 1988). Most leadership training programs are designed to increase generic skills and behaviors relevant for managerial effectiveness and advancement. The training is usually designed more for lower- and middle-level managers than for top executives, and there is usually more emphasis on skills needed by managers in their current position than on skills needed to prepare for promotion to a higher position (Rothwell & Kazanas, 1994). However, the old pattern of selecting mostly "fast-track" managers for leadership training and providing it only once or twice during a manager's career is gradually being replaced by a series of leadership training opportunities that are available to any manager in the organization at appropriate points in the individual's career (Vicere & Fulmer, 1997).

Types of Leadership Training Programs

Leadership training can take many forms, from short workshops that last only a few hours and focus on a narrow set of skills to programs that last for a year or more and cover a wide range of skills. Many consulting companies conduct short leadership workshops that are open to managers from different organizations. Other consulting companies design leadership-training programs tailored to the needs of a particular organization. Most universities offer management development programs (e.g., executive MBA) that can be attended on a part-time basis. Many organizations compensate employees for the cost of attending outside workshops and courses. Some large organizations (e.g., Apple, Disney, General Electric, IKEA, McDonald's, Motorola, Toyota, Unilever) operate a management training center or corporate university for employees (Allen, 2014; Rio, 2018).

A number of training programs are based on the application of a particular leadership theory. Examples include training programs based on the normative decision model (Vroom & Jago, 1988), and on transformational leadership (Bass, 1996; Bass & Avolio, 1990b; Brown & May, 2012). Reviews of research on theory-based training programs find evidence that they sometimes improve managerial effectiveness (Avolio, Reichard, Hannah, Walumbwa, & Chan, 2009; Bass, 2008; Lacerenza, Reyes, Marlow, Joseph, & Salas, 2017; Latham, 1988; Tetrault, Schriesheim, & Neider, 1988). However, it is important to note that few studies determine whether improved ratings of leader behavior or effectiveness are the result of learning and applying the theory or from improvement in skills not included in the theory.

Design of Leadership Training

The effectiveness of formal training programs depends greatly on how well they are designed. The design of training should take into account learning theory, the specific learning objectives, characteristics of the trainees, and practical considerations such as constraints and costs in relation to benefits. Leader training is more likely to be successful if designed and conducted in a way that is consistent with findings in research on learning processes and training techniques (Baldwin & Padgett, 1993; Lacerenza et al., 2017; Lord & Hall, 2005; Noe & Ford, 1992; Salas & Cannon-Bowers, 2001; Tannenbaum & Yukl, 1992). The program design should take into account learning theory, the specific learning objectives, characteristics of the trainees, and practical considerations such as available time and costs in relation to benefits (see summary in Table 14-1).

Specific learning objectives at the beginning of a training program will help to clarify the purpose of the training and its relevance for trainees. In most cases it is useful to explain not only what will be learned, but also why the training is worthwhile for trainees. The training content should be clear and meaningful. It should build on a trainee's prior knowledge, and it should focus attention on important things. The training activities should be organized and

TABLE 14-1 Desirable Features for Training Programs

- Specific learning objectives
- Content based on a needs analysis
- Clear, meaningful content
- Appropriate sequencing of content
- Appropriate mix of training methods
- Opportunity for active practice
- Relevant, timely feedback
- Builds self-confidence of trainees
- Multiple delivery methods
- Multiple training sessions across regular time intervals

sequenced in a way that will facilitate learning. Training should progress from simple, basic ideas to more complex ideas, and complex material should be broken into components or modules that are easier to learn separately than simultaneously.

Many types of training methods are used in leadership programs, including lecture and discussion, role-playing, behavioral role modeling, case analysis, and simulations. The training methods should be appropriate for the knowledge, skills, attitudes, or behaviors to be learned. In selecting methods it is also important to consider the trainee's current skills, motivation, and capacity to understand complex information. Trainees should have ample opportunity to practice the skills they are learning during the training and afterward (e.g., practice using new behaviors, recall information from memory, apply principles in doing a task). Active practice should include feedback that is accurate, timely, and constructive to help trainees monitor their own progress and evaluate what they know. Trainers should communicate confidence that the training will be successful and be patient and supportive with any individuals who experience learning difficulties. Trainees should have ample opportunities to experience progress and success in mastering the material and learning the skills.

Effects of Leadership Training

Criteria for assessing the effectiveness of formal training programs include: (1) participants' attitudinal reactions (i.e., ratings of training utility and satisfaction with the training/instructors); (2) learning in the form of knowledge and skill acquisition; (3) transfer of learning whereby trainees utilize acquired skills and abilities to improve performance; and (4) results in the form of positive organizational outcomes such as lower costs, increased profits, and reduced absenteeism and turnover (Lacerenza et al., 2017). How much leadership training can affect these outcomes depends on the personality and ability of trainees, the training design and execution, and supporting conditions in the organization. The relative importance of the different determinants depends in part on the type of training and the outcome measure (see reviews by Alliger, Tannenbaum, Bennett, Traver, & Shotland, 1997; Blume, Ford, Baldwin, Huang, 2010; Taylor, Russ-Eft, & Taylor, 2009). A recent meta-analysis by Lacerenza and colleagues (2017) provided evidence of training effectiveness on the four criteria of reactions, learning, transfer, and results. Training effectiveness was enhanced by inclusion of a needs analysis, multiple delivery methods, face-to-face delivery, feedback, spaced training sessions, and on-site location of training.

Learning from Experience

Much of the skill needed for effective leadership is learned from experience rather than from formal training programs (Lindsey, Homes, & McCall, 1987; McCall, 2010a, 2010b; McCall et al., 1988). Special assignments provide an opportunity to develop and refine leadership skills during the performance of regular job duties. Coaching and mentoring can be used to help managers interpret their experiences and learn new skills. Managers can emulate the effective behaviors modeled by competent bosses (Manz & Sims, 1981; McCall et al., 1988; McCall & McHenry, 2014). Managers can also learn what not to do from observing superiors who are ineffective (Lindsey et al., 1987; McCall et al., 1988) or who engage in unethical behaviors (Brown & Treviño, 2014).

The extent to which leadership skills and values are developed during operational assignments depends on the type of experiences afforded by these assignments. The relevance of different types of experiences for the development of leadership skills was studied by researchers at the Center for Creative Leadership (CCL) (Lindsey et al., 1987; McCall et al., 1988; McCauley, 1986 and in subsequent research (e.g., DeRue & Wellman, 2009; Dragoni et al., 2014a; Dragoni, Oh, Vankatwyk, & Tesluk, 2011; Dragoni, Tesluk, Russell, & Oh, 2009; Mumford et al., 2000). The research found that learning from experience is affected by the amount of challenge in assignments, the variety of tasks and assignments, and the quality of feedback.

Amount of Challenge

A challenging situation is one that involves unusual problems to solve, difficult obstacles to overcome, and risky decisions to make. The research at CCL found that challenge was greatest in jobs that required a manager to deal with change, take responsibility for high-visibility problems, influence people without having much authority, handle external pressure, and work without much guidance or support from superiors. Some examples of challenging situations include dealing with a merger or reorganization, leading a cross-functional team or task force, implementing a major change, coping with unfavorable business conditions, turning around a weak organizational unit, making the transition to a different type of managerial position (e.g., from a functional line position to a general manager or staff position), and managing in a country with a different culture. These situations required managers to seek new information, view problems in new ways, build new relationships, try out new behaviors, learn new skills, and develop a better understanding of themselves. The CCL researchers developed an instrument called the Developmental Challenge Profile to measure the amount and types of challenge in a managerial position or assignment (McCauley, Ruderman, Ohlott, & Morrow, 1994).

Experiencing success in handling difficult challenges is essential for leadership development. In the process, managers learn new skills and gain self-confidence. However, learning from experience can involve failure as well as success. The research at CCL also found that managers who experienced adversity and failure earlier in their careers were more likely to develop and advance to a higher level than managers who experienced only a series of early successes. Types of hardship experiences found to be significant for development included failure in business decisions, mistakes in dealing with important people, career setbacks, and personal trauma (e.g., divorce, serious injury, or illness). However, experiencing failure may not result in beneficial learning and change unless a person accepts some responsibility for it, acknowledges personal limitations, and finds ways to overcome them (Kaplan, Kofodimos, & Drath, 1987; Kovach, 1989; McCall & Lombardo, 1983a, 1983b). Moreover, when the amount of stress and challenge is excessive, support and coaching may be needed to prevent people from giving up and withdrawing from the situation before development occurs.

Variety of Tasks or Assignments

Growth and learning are greater when job experiences are diverse as well as challenging. Diverse job experiences require managers to adapt to new situations and deal with new types of problems. Repeated success in handling one type of problem reinforces the tendency of a person to interpret and handle new problems in the same way, even though a different approach may be more effective. Thus, it is beneficial for managers to have early experience with a wide variety of problems that require different leadership behavior and skills. Some ways to provide a variety of job challenges include making special developmental assignments, rotating managers among positions in different functional subunits of the organization, providing assignments in both line and staff positions, and making both foreign and domestic assignments. A variety of challenges can also be designed into simulations. The effectiveness of developmental assignments and simulations designed to increase adaptability can be improved by preparing participants in advance to view problems in new ways and become more flexible in their behavior (Nelson, Zaccaro, & Herman, 2010).

Accurate, Relevant Feedback

More learning occurs during operational assignments when people get accurate feedback about their behavior and its consequences and use this feedback to analyze their experiences and learn from them. Unfortunately, useful feedback about a manager's behavior is seldom provided within operational assignments, and even when available it may not result in learning. The hectic pace and unrelenting demands make introspection and self-analysis difficult in a management job. The extent to which a person is willing to accept feedback depends on some of the same traits that are related to managerial effectiveness (Bunker & Webb, 1992; Kaplan, 1990). People who are defensive and insecure tend to avoid or ignore information about their weaknesses. People who believe that most events are predetermined by uncontrollable external forces (i.e., people who do not have a high internal locus of control orientation) are less likely to accept responsibility for failure or to use feedback to improve their skills and future performance.

The obstacles to learning from experience are greatest at higher levels of management (Kaplan et al., 1987). Executives tend to become isolated from all but a small number of people with whom they interact regularly in the organization, and these people are mostly other executives who are also isolated. Success in attaining such a high position of power and prestige tends to give executives self-confidence about their style of management, and it may progress to a feeling of superiority that causes the executive to ignore or discount criticism from others who are not so successful. Moreover, as executives become more powerful, people become more reluctant to risk offending them by providing criticism.

Developmental Activities

A number of activities can be used to facilitate learning of relevant skills from experience on the job (see Table 14-2). These developmental activities can be used to supplement informal coaching by the boss or coworkers, and most of them can be used in conjunction with formal training programs. Six of the developmental activities will be described in this section of the chapter, including multisource feedback programs, developmental assignments, mentoring, executive coaching, simulations, and personal growth programs.

TABLE 14-2 Activities for Facilitating Leadership Development

- Multi-source feedback workshops
- Developmental assessment centers
- Special assignments
- Mentoring
- Executive coaching
- Personal growth programs

Multi-Source Feedback Programs

Providing behavioral feedback from multiple sources is a widely used method for management development in large organizations (Atwater & Waldman, 1998; Day et al., 2014; Nowack & Mashihi, 2012). Other names for this method are "360-degree feedback" and "multi-rater feedback." Multi-source feedback programs can be used for a variety of purposes, but the primary one is to assess the strengths and developmental needs of individual managers. A basic assumption of feedback programs is that most managers lack accurate knowledge about their skills and behavior, and the feedback can be used to improve it. The design and use of 360-degree feedback programs is described in several books (e.g., Fleenor, Taylor, & Chappelow, 2008; Lepsinger & Lucia, 2009; Tornow & London, 1998).

In a feedback program, managers receive information about their skills or behavior from standardized questionnaires filled out by other people such as subordinates, peers, superiors, and sometimes outsiders such as clients. The questionnaires used to provide feedback may be customized for a particular organization, but most feedback workshops still utilize standardized questionnaires. Van Velsor, Leslie, and Fleenor (1997) described sixteen survey instruments commonly used in feedback workshops and reviewed the empirical evidence about the strengths and limitations of each instrument.

Feedback is likely to be more accurate when the rating questionnaire tracks behaviors that are meaningful and easy to observe. Accurate feedback also depends on gaining the cooperation of a representative set of respondents who interacted frequently with the manager over a period of time and had adequate opportunity to observe the behaviors included in the questionnaire. Respondents are more likely to provide accurate ratings if they understand the purpose of the survey, how the results will be used, and the procedures to ensure confidentiality for individuals who provide ratings. Ratings are more likely to be accurate if the feedback is used only for developmental purposes and is not part of the formal performance appraisal process (London, Wohlers, & Gallagher, 1990).

Feedback can be presented in a number of different ways, and the format of the feedback report helps to determine how clear and useful the feedback is to the recipients (Nowack & Mashihi, 2012). In most feedback interventions, each participating manager receives a report that compares self-ratings by the manager to ratings made by others, and to norms for similar managers. The ratings by others are usually provided by subordinates who report to the manager (upward feedback) and by the manager's boss. Ratings may also be provided by multiple peers and (when appropriate) by more than one boss. Providing feedback separately for each direction (e.g., subordinates, peers, superiors) can make it more informative but is only feasible when there are enough raters of each type who can observe the leader's behavior. Sometimes the feedback report includes built-in aids for interpreting the results. It is a common practice to highlight large discrepancies between what others say about a manager's behavior and self-ratings by the manager. Self-ratings that are much higher than ratings by others indicate a possible developmental need. Interpretation of feedback is facilitated by norms (e.g., percentile scores) based on a large sample of similar managers. Ratings of the manager's behavior that are well below "normal" provide another indicator of a possible developmental need.

There has been much discussion but little research on the advantages of different types and forms of feedback. Some writers have questioned the value of providing feedback based on quantitative ratings for abstract traits and vaguely defined behaviors that are difficult to observe and remember. Moses, Hollenback, and Sorcher (1993) suggested providing feedback on what the rater expects the manager would do in a well-defined, representative situation. Kaplan (1993) suggested supplementing numerical feedback with concrete examples of effective and ineffective behavior by the manager. The examples would be obtained by interviewing respondents or including open-ended questions on the survey questionnaire. An example of an open-ended question is to ask respondents what they think the manager should start doing, stop doing, or continue doing (Bracken, 1994). Quantitative feedback about a manager's current behavior can be supplemented with respondent recommendations about desirable changes in the manager's behavior.

The effectiveness of multisource feedback programs depends not only on the type and form of feedback, but also on how it is presented to managers (Kaplan, 1993; Nowack & Mashihi, 2012; Yukl & Lepsinger, 1995). Three common variations are the following: (1) managers just receive a feedback report and are left to interpret it alone; (2) managers receive a feedback report followed by a one-on-one meeting with a facilitator; and (3) managers attend a group workshop with a facilitator to help interpret their feedback reports. A field experiment by Seifert, Yukl, and McDonald (2003) found that a feedback workshop with a facilitator was more effective for changing the behavior of bank managers than merely giving them a feedback report to read. A facilitator can explain the rating categories and their relevance for leadership effectiveness, prepare participants to be receptive to behavioral feedback, encourage participants to interpret the feedback in light of their leadership situation, stress the positive aspects of feedback as well as negatives, help participants work through feelings about adverse feedback, and encourage participants to plan how to use the feedback to improve their leadership effectiveness.

Based on a review of the literature, Nowack and Mashihi (2012, p. 160) concluded: "among researchers and coaches, there is little disagreement that under the right conditions and applying evidence-based 'best practices' that 360-degree feedback can increase self-awareness and increase individual and team effectiveness." A meta-analysis by Smither, London, and Reilly (2005) of 26 studies lends support for this conclusion, as 360-degree feedback was positively related to perceived gains in performance and changes in behavior. Such improvements were most likely when recipients expressed a perceived need to change their behavior, had a positive feedback orientation, reacted positively to the feedback, believed that change was feasible, set appropriate goals for regulating their behavior, and took actions that enhance relevant skills. Recent studies have also linked the use of multisource feedback programs to improvements in human capital, financial performance, and the sustainability of a just and fair work environment (Karkoulian, Assaker, & Hallak, 2016; Kim, Atwater, Patel, & Smither, 2016). However, research also shows that when 360-degree feedback assessments and interventions are poorly designed or used for political purposes, they foster disengagement and contribute to poor individual and team performance (Nowack & Mashihi, 2012; Waldman, Atwater, & Antonioni, 1998). A meta-analysis for all types of feedback research found only a weak positive overall effect on performance (Kluger & DeNisi, 1996); in one-third of the studies, performance declined for varied reasons involving how the feedback was delivered, the recipient's personality, and the type of feedback provided.

In summary, the research shows that feedback can be effective when best practices are followed, but counterproductive when they are not (Nowack & Mashihi, 2012; Waldman et al., 1998). Feedback from other people can help a manager identify strengths and weaknesses, but the manager may not be willing or able to apply the feedback. When multisource feedback is used only for development, managers are usually not required to share the feedback with their boss or to discuss it with the raters. Some participants may dismiss negative feedback or distort its meaning (Conger, 1992; Taylor & Bright, 2011). Even when a participant acknowledges a skill deficiency and wants to improve, how to improve may not be evident.

The feedback research on managers has identified several ways to enhance the effects of feedback, including skill training, individual coaching, follow-up activities, and linking the manager's developmental action plan to subsequent appraisal and reward decisions (Bracken & Rose, 2011; Hooijberg & Lane, 2009; Luthans & Peterson, 2003; Nowack, 2009; Nowack & Mashihi, 2012; Seifert & Yukl, 2010; Seifert et al., 2003). Using more than one feedback cycle can increase the amount of improvement (Seifert & Yukl, 2010). Another way to enhance the effects of feedback is to provide individual coaching to managers for several weeks after the feedback workshop (Kochanowski, Seifert, & Yukl, 2010). Other research found that managers were more likely to improve if they held a meeting with the raters (who were subordinates) to discuss the feedback received from them (Walker & Smither, 1999). Such a meeting provides an opportunity to gain a better understanding of the reason for discrepancies in self and other ratings, and it may increase the manager's sense of accountability to make use of the feedback.

Developmental Assessment Centers

In assessment centers managerial traits and skills are measured with methods such as interviews, aptitude tests, personality tests, situational tests, a short autobiographical essay, a speaking exercise, and a writing exercise. Information from these diverse sources is integrated and used to develop an overall evaluation of each participant's management potential. The assessment center process typically takes 2 to 3 days, and some data collection may occur beforehand. Assessment centers were initially used only for selection and promotion decisions, but it was subsequently found that they are also useful for developing managers (Boehm, 1985; Munchus & McArthur, 1991).

Compared to feedback workshops, developmental assessment centers use more intensive procedures and a more comprehensive set of measures to increase self-understanding, identify strengths and weaknesses, and assess developmental needs. Information about a manager's behavior may be obtained from people who interact with the manager regularly and from observation of the manager in simulations and exercises. The facilitators also collect information about the manager's prior experience, motives, personality traits, skills, interests, and aspirations. Information about behavior and skills is integrated with information about motives, background, experience, and career aspirations to provide a more complete picture of the person's strengths, weaknesses, and potential. The rationale is that behavioral feedback alone is insufficient to change ineffective behaviors that are supported by strong motives, values, and self-concepts. Helping the person to confront weaknesses and develop a better self-understanding increases the likelihood of behavior change. Participants also receive counseling about developmental needs and career choices. To avoid the inherent dangers in this enhanced feedback, Kaplan and Palus (1994) emphasize the need for careful selection of participants to screen out people who would not benefit from it (or who may not be able to handle the stress).

Studies on participant perceptions of the benefits from developmental assessment centers and similar "feedback intensive programs" suggest that they can enhance self-awareness, help to identify training needs, and facilitate subsequent development of leadership skills (e.g., Fletcher, 1990; Guthrie & Kelly-Radford, 1998; Young & Dixon, 1996). Two studies found evidence that developmental assessment centers can improve the later performance of managers (Engelbracht & Fischer, 1995; Papa & Graham, 1991), but the results are difficult to interpret because other developmental activities were involved (e.g., skill training, special assignments, additional coaching). As with feedback workshops, developmental assessment workshops are likely to be more successful when followed by relevant training or developmental activities. In addition, the benefits of a developmental assessment center may not be limited to participants; managers who serve on the staff of these centers may also experience an increase in their managerial skills (Boehm, 1985).

Although we still do not know much about the underlying psychological processes that occur in developmental assessment centers, a recent study by Dimotakis, Mitchell, and Maurer (2017) provides some insights. The researchers found that both positive and negative developmental feedback provided through managerial assessment centers increased participants' self-efficacy regarding their ability to improve the assessed skills. Self-efficacy for improvement, in turn, was positively related to feedback-seeking behavior, which was positively linked to subsequent promotions. The results also showed that receiving social support for development and believing that one's abilities can be enhanced mitigated the potential detrimental effects of negative feedback on self-efficacy.

Developmental Assignments

Some developmental assignments can be carried out concurrently with regular job responsibilities, and Lombardo and Eichinger 1989 identified different types of special assignments that can be used to develop managerial skills in the current job. Some examples include managing a new project or start-up operation, serving as the department representative on a cross-functional team, chairing a special task force to plan a major change or deal with a serious operational problem, developing and conducting a training program for the organizational unit, and assuming responsibility for some administrative activities previously handled by the person's boss (e.g., preparing a budget, developing a strategic plan, conducting a meeting).

Other developmental assignments may require taking a temporary leave from one's regular job. Examples include working in an assessment center, serving as an understudy or staff member for an exceptional leader in another part of the organization, serving in a temporary liaison position in another organization (e.g., a client or supplier), and serving in a visiting assignment to another organization (e.g., a manager is loaned to a government agency to help implement a major change).

An example of a systematic use of developmental assignments is provided by Citibank in the 1990s (Clark & Lyness, 1991). The development of interpersonal and strategic skills was considered important to prepare managers for advancement to senior executive positions. High-potential managers were given two types of special assignments, each lasting from 3 to 4 years. One assignment involved a major strategic challenge and the other involved difficult people-management challenges.

Research on the effectiveness of developmental assignments is still limited. The longitudinal research on traits and skills (see Chapter 7) has provided evidence that diverse, challenging assignments early in one's career facilitated career advancement, and that different skills are learned from different types of challenges and hardship experiences (DeRue & Wellman, 2009; Lindsey et al., 1987; McCall et al., 1988; McCauley et al., 1994; McCauley, Eastman, & Ohlott, 1995; Valerio, 1990). Managers who have a strong learning orientation are more likely to take advantage of developmental opportunities, and they are also more likely to benefit from them (Dragoni et al., 2009). A study by Dragoni and colleagues (2014a) found that time spent in global work experiences was positively related to competency in strategic thinking, particularly for leaders who were exposed to a country culture different from that of their home country.

Most studies on effects of developmental assignments have relied on a manager's retrospective self-reports about developmental experiences and skill acquisition, but the study by

DeRue and Wellman (2009) used multiple methods. In addition to a survey measure of developmental challenges, descriptions of developmental experiences were obtained from interviews with managers. Then ratings of skill improvement by the managers were obtained from each manager's boss. The researchers found that developmental challenges increased learning up to a point, after which adding more challenge created problems that will reduce learning for some managers unless they are resolved (e.g., by providing more supportive feedback and coaching). As yet nobody has conducted an experiment comparing the effects of different types of developmental assignments in terms of measures of competencies taken before and after the assignment. We still have much to learn about what types of assignments are effective for what type of skills and what type of people.

An important research question is the amount of time required to optimize learning in developmental assignments. Brief assignments may not provide an opportunity to see the consequences of one's actions and decisions or to reflect on one's experiences and comprehend what was learned (Ohlott, 1998). On the other hand, staying in the assignment too long can result in boredom and lost opportunities for more meaningful experiences.

A related question is the optimal sequencing of developmental assignments, which is an important determinant of the amount of challenge in each assignment. Before taking on a big, difficult assignment, it is better to first learn basic knowledge and relevant skills in smaller, less challenging assignments. Otherwise, a person is likely to spend too much time learning the basic things, and may not have sufficient time to learn more complex things that are necessary for later success as a leader. Thus, attempting to move someone too quickly through different developmental assignments can be counterproductive, and the planning of developmental assignments requires careful analysis and a long-term perspective (McCall, 2004).

McCauley and colleagues (1995) suggested some ways to improve the planning and use of developmental assignments. The challenges and learning opportunities provided by each type of assignment should be matched to the manager's developmental needs, career aspirations, and learning orientation. Managers need to become more aware of the importance of developmental assignments, and they should share in the responsibility for planning them. The challenges and benefits provided by special assignments should be tracked, and this information should be related to career counseling and succession planning. After a developmental assignment is completed, it is important for a manager to reflect on the experience and identify the lessons that were learned. This process of retrospective analysis is likely to increase learning from experience, and it can be facilitated by the boss, a mentor, or a training and development professional (Ohlott, 1998).

Dechant (1994) suggested that learning from special assignments can be facilitated by preparation of a concrete learning plan. The person who has the assignment analyzes the task objectives, context, and job requirements for everyone who will be involved in the task. Skill requirements are compared with available skill resources; any gaps in necessary skills or knowledge are identified; and plans are made to acquire the skills or knowledge needed to carry out the assignment successfully. This process should increase the likelihood that a person will recognize and take advantage of learning opportunities in a special assignment. Learning needs for others are also identified and incorporated into the action plan for the assignment.

The effectiveness of developmental assignments is reduced when bias and discrimination are widespread in the organization. A variety of studies suggest that women are less likely than men to be given challenging, high-visibility assignments (e.g., Ruderman & Ohlott, 1994; Van Velsor & Hughes, 1990). Despite the existence of laws prohibiting it, discrimination based on gender, race, or age still occurs in making assignments and promotions (see Chapter 13).

Mentoring

Formal mentoring programs are used to facilitate management development in many organizations (Maxwell, 2008; Noe, 1991; Scandura & Pellegrini, 2007). Mentoring is a relationship in which a more experienced manager helps a less experienced protégé. Mentors can facilitate adjustment, learning, and stress reduction during difficult job transitions, such as promotion to one's first managerial position, a transfer or promotion to a different functional unit in the organization, an assignment in a foreign country, or assignments in an organization that has been merged, reorganized, or downsized (Kram & Hall, 1989; Zey, 1988). The mentor is usually at a higher managerial level and is not the protégé's immediate boss (McCauley & Douglas, 1998).

Research on mentors (Kram, 1985; Noe, 1988) finds that they provide a psychosocial function (acceptance, encouragement, coaching, counseling) and a career-facilitation function (sponsorship, protection, challenging assignments, exposure, and visibility). A study by Lapierre, Naidoo, and Bonaccio 2012 revealed that the provision of career support is contingent on the protégé's task performance and the extent to which the mentor's self-concept is defined in terms of relationships with significant others (i.e., the relational self-concept). Mentors with a stronger relational self-concept provided more career support, particularly for high-performing protégés. However, the mentor's relational self-concept and protégé task performance had no impact on the amount of psychosocial support provided.

Several studies show that mentoring results in more career advancement and success for the protégé (Chao, Walz, & Gardner, 1992; Dreher & Ash, 1990; Fagenson, 1989; Scandura, 1992; Turban & Dougherty, 1994; Whitely & Coetsier, 1993). A study of NCAA women's basketball coaches and assistant coaches found that the beneficial effects on protégé performance are greater when the mentor is successful and the relationship lasts for a long period of time (Tonidandel, Avery, & Phillips, 2007). Mentors may also benefit from the mentoring experience because it is likely to increase their job satisfaction and help them develop their own leadership skills. A study by Wilbur (1987) found that career advancement in a service company was predicted both by mentoring given and mentoring received. Other research revealed that senior executives were more motivated to provide mentoring when it facilitated their career development as well as that for the protégé; however, providing financial incentives for mentoring discouraged it (Walker & Yip, 2018). These findings suggest that compensation for mentoring may have unintended and detrimental effects for potential mentors who are driven by prosocial and relational motives. The Women at Wipro mentoring program proved to be effective as it increased the promotion rate (18 percent as compared to 5 percent overall) and reduced attrition amongst participants (7 percent as compared to 15 percent of the non-participant women employees). It also helped create strong bonds and wider networks for women employees to collaborate with business leaders (NASSCOM, 2016).

Despite the potential benefits from mentoring, it is not always successful. Research on conditions likely to increase the effectiveness of mentoring suggests that informal mentoring is usually more successful than a formal mentoring program (Noe, Greenberger, & Wang, 2002). The difference may be due primarily to the way a formal program is conducted, including the selection and training of the mentors. The success of a formal mentoring program is probably increased by making participation voluntary, by providing mentors some choice of a protégé, by explaining the benefits and pitfalls, and by clarifying the expected roles and processes for both mentor and protégé (Chao et al., 1992; Hunt & Michael, 1983).

Protégés can be proactive in initiating mentoring relationships rather than waiting for a mentor to select them, especially in an organization that supports this type of developmental activity. Turban and Dougherty (1994) found that protégés were more likely to initiate mentoring relationships and get more mentoring if they had high emotional stability, self-monitoring, and internal locus of control orientation. Blickle, Witzki, and Schneider (2009) found that, regardless of age, gender, or intelligence, protégés who were proactive in initiating the mentoring process secured higher levels of mentoring, income, and promotions.

Mentoring is also affected by some demographic factors such as age, gender, and race. Women and minorities have more difficulty finding successful mentoring relationships (Blake-Beard, Murrell, & Thomas, 2007; Giscombe, 2007; Ilgen & Youtz, 1986; McDonald & Westphal, 2013; Noe, 1988; Ohlott, Ruderman, & McCauley, 1994; Ragins & Cotton, 1991, 1993; Ragins & McFarlin, 1990; Thomas, 1990). Common difficulties for women include stereotypes about appropriate behavior, concern about intimacy with men, awkwardness about discussing some subjects, lack of appropriate role models, resentment by peers, and exclusion from male networks. Some of these difficulties remain even when women mentor women. Despite the difficulties, empirical studies found no evidence that gender affects the success of mentoring (e.g., Dreher & Ash, 1990; Turban & Dougherty, 1994).

In general, the research suggests that mentoring can be a useful technique for facilitating career advancement, adjustment to change, and the job satisfaction and well-being of a protégé. Mentoring also offers advantages such as stronger organizational commitment and lower turnover (Chun, Sosik, & Yun, 2012; Payne & Huffman, 2005). However, the effect of mentoring varies depending on the type of mentoring provided and the type of outcomes examined (Allen, Eby, & Lentz, 2006). As yet few studies have assessed the relationship between the characteristics of mentoring programs and different outcomes. Little is known about the skills, values, and behaviors most likely to be acquired or enhanced in a mentoring relationship, the conditions facilitating development, or the ways a mentor actually facilitates development of leadership competencies in a protégé.

Executive Coaching

In recent years individual coaching has become a popular type of developmental intervention for leaders in business organizations (Athanasopoulou & Dopson, 2018; Beattie et al., 2014; Ely, Boyce, Nelson, Zaccaro, Hernandez-Broome, & Whyman, 2010; Feldman & Lankau, 2005; Hall, Otazo, & Hollenbeck, 1999; McCarthy & Milner, 2013; Sperry, 2013). The type of leader who receives coaching is usually a high-level executive. The coach is usually a successful former executive or a behavioral scientist with extensive experience as a management consultant.

An executive coach is not a permanent mentor, and the coach is usually employed for a limited period of time ranging from a few months to a few years. Coaching may be provided on a weekly or biweekly basis, and in extreme cases, the coach may be "on call" to provide advice whenever needed. Sometimes the decision to obtain coaching is made by the executive, and other times it is made by higher management to help prepare an executive for advancement, or to prevent the person's derailment. Use of an external coach provides some advantages such as wider experience, greater objectivity, and more confidentiality. An internal coach offers other advantages, such as easy availability, more knowledge of the culture and politics, and a better understanding of the strategic challenges and core competencies.

The primary purpose of executive coaching is to facilitate learning of skills that are relevant for current or future leadership responsibilities. Coaches also provide advice about how to handle specific challenges, such as implementing a major change, dealing with a difficult boss, or working with people from a different culture. Having a coach provides the unusual opportunity to discuss issues and try out ideas with someone who can understand them and provide helpful, objective feedback and suggestions, while maintaining strict confidentiality. Executive coaching is especially useful in conjunction with techniques that provide information about developmental needs but do not directly improve skills (e.g., multisource feedback, developmental assessment center).

Executive coaching offers several advantages over formal training courses, including convenience, confidentiality, flexibility, and more personal attention. One obvious disadvantage is the high expense of one-on-one coaching, even when used for a limited time. The high cost is one reason why personal coaching is used primarily for executives. Another limitation is the shortage of competent coaches. It is important to find a coach who is able to establish a good working relationship with the executive while also remaining objective and professional. The coach should not have a personal agenda such as the desire to sell more consulting time (for an external consultant), or the desire for more power (for an internal consultant). Organizations need clear guidelines regarding the selection and use of executive coaches to avoid the potential problems with this developmental technique (Hall et al., 1999).

The executives who are being coached usually value honest, accurate feedback about strengths and weaknesses, as well as clear, relevant advice about ways to become more effective. Examples of the types of behaviors and skills that can be enhanced by a coach include listening, communicating, influencing people, building relationships, handling conflicts, team building, initiating change, conducting meetings, and developing subordinates. The coach can also provide advice about other things the executive can do to acquire relevant knowledge and skills. Guidelines for effective coaching of executives can be found in books on the subject (e.g., Boysen-Rotelli, 2018; Frisch, Lee, Metzger, Robinson, & Rosemarin, 2012). Coaching in leadership skills is not limited to individuals, and coaching the top management team collectively offers some advantages for improving shared leadership processes (Kets de Vries, 2005).

Research on the effects of executive coaching on personal development and leadership effectiveness is limited, but the evidence so far is generally favorable (Bowles, Cunningham, De La Rosa, & Picano, 2007; Dahling, Taylor, Chau, & Dwight, 2016; de Haan, Grant, Burger, & Eriksson, 2016; Grant, 2014; Kim, S., Egan, Kim, W., & Kim, J., 2013; Ladegard & Gjerde, 2014; MacKie, 2014; Perkins, 2009). The research on assessment of coaching for enhancing leadership skills is complicated by the fact that it usually involves many types of outcomes (attitudes, values, skills, behavior, performance), it is usually combined with other types of interventions and self-help activities, and it is somewhat different for each recipient and coach. Several reviews of leadership coaching studies with recommendations for future research are available (Athanasopoulou & Dopson, 2018; Beattie et al., 2014; Ely et al., 2010; McCarthy & Milner, 2013).

Simulations

Business games and simulations have been used for many years for management training. As with cases, simulations require participants to analyze complex problems and make decisions. Most business games emphasize quantitative financial information and are used to practice analytical and decision skills taught in a formal training program. The most sophisticated simulations are based on a systems model of the complex causal relationships among important variables for a particular type of company and industry. Participants work individually or in small groups to make managerial decisions about product pricing, advertising, production output, product development, and capital investment. Following is an example of one participant's experience in a computerized simulation of a start-up airline company (Kreutzer, 1993, p. 536):

> Sally stared blankly off into space. What had started out so well had turned into a nightmare. She had taken over an airline company that had three planes and gross revenues of $32 million a year, and in just four years she had grown the company to a half-billion-dollar

firm with a fleet of 100 aircraft. She had sweated over decisions in the areas of human resources, aircraft acquisition, marketing, pricing, and service scope, and in each case, her airline had triumphed. But then she had reached a turning point. Her market had collapsed. Her service quality had eroded. Losses had piled up so fast that the ability of her company to absorb them was in doubt. It would all turn around though, it had to. All she needed was one more quarter. . . . But instead of the next quarter's financial reports she received notification that her creditors were forcing her into bankruptcy. Time had run out. . . . What did I do wrong, she thought. All her decisions had seemed to make sense at the time. She reached over and pressed the save button. She would have to analyze her decisions to see what went wrong later. Right now she had another strategy she wanted to try. She hit the restart button to begin the simulation. She was back to having three planes and gross revenues of $32 million.

Large-scale simulations emphasize interpersonal skills as much as cognitive skills and decision making. A large-scale simulation typically involves a single hypothetical organization with multiple divisions (e.g., bank, plastics company). For example, the large-scale simulation (called Looking Glass) developed by the Center for Creative Leadership involves a glass manufacturing company (Kaplan, Lombardo, & Mazique, 1985; Van Velsor, Ruderman, & Phillips, 1989). Other large-scale simulations have been developed to depict specific types of organizations such as banks, insurance companies, chemical-plastics companies, and public school systems. Participants are assigned to different positions in the organization and carry out the managerial responsibilities for a period of one or two days.

Prior to the simulation, each participant is given extensive background information, such as a description of the organization's products and services, financial reports, industry and market conditions, an organization chart, and the duties and responsibilities of the position. Each participant is also given copies of recent correspondence (e.g., memos, reports) with other members of the organization and outsiders. Participants have separate work spaces but are allowed to communicate by various media (e.g., memos, e-mail) and to schedule meetings. Participants make strategic and operational decisions just as they would in a real organization. They react to each other's decisions, but unlike business games, they usually do not receive information about the financial consequences of their decisions during the simulation itself.

After the simulation is completed, participants receive feedback about group processes and their individual skills and behaviors. Feedback is usually provided by observers who track the behavior and decisions of the participants. Additional feedback can be provided by videotaping participant conversations and meetings. The facilitators help the participants understand how well they functioned as executives in collecting and processing information, analyzing and solving problems, communicating with others, influencing others, and planning strategy and operations.

What participants learn from a large-scale simulation depends in part on who participates. If participants are a "family group" of managers from the same organization, their behavior in the simulation will reflect the prevailing culture and relationships in that organization. The feedback to participants in family groups can be used to help them understand and improve their decision-making and conflict resolution processes. For example, most of the managers from one company that participated in the Looking Glass simulation made hasty decisions and looked for information to justify them, rather than carefully gathering information to determine the nature of the problem and available opportunities. During the debrief, participants became aware of their ineffective behavior and realized that it was consistent with the culture of their company.

The research on business games and simulations is still limited, but there is increasing evidence they can be very useful for leadership development (Keys & Wolfe, 1990; Leonard, 2017;

Thornton & Cleveland, 1990; Watts, Ness, Steele, & Mumford, 2018). Nevertheless, more research is needed to determine what types of learning occur and the conditions that facilitate learning. It was once assumed that interpersonal skills and problem-solving skills would be learned automatically by participants in a simulation. Now it is obvious that the potential benefits are unlikely to be achieved without extensive preparation, planned interventions with specific feedback and coaching during the simulation, and intensive debriefing with discussion of lessons learned after the simulation.

Most large-scale simulations have limitations. The short time period for the simulation makes it difficult for participants to make effective use of behaviors that necessarily involve a series of related actions over time, such as inspirational leadership, networking, team building, developing subordinates, and delegation. A possible remedy is to spread out the simulation sessions over several weeks, which also provides more opportunity for facilitators to provide feedback and coaching after each session. Improved communication technology makes it easier to use virtual meetings among team members who normally work in widely dispersed locations, which can solve some of the logistical problems of holding repeated meetings for team members over a longer period of time. There is a continuing effort to design more flexible and realistic simulations that incorporate more challenging developmental activities and provide more feedback about participant behavior and its consequences for the organization.

Personal Growth Programs

Personal growth programs are designed to improve self-awareness and overcome inner barriers to psychological growth and development of leadership competencies. These programs evolved from the humanistic psychology movement in the 1960s, and many of the founders had prior experience in programs emphasizing development of human potential, such as the Peace Corps and the National Training Laboratories in Bethel, Maine (Conger, 1993).

Personal growth workshops are based on a series of interrelated assumptions about people and leadership. One key assumption is that many people have lost touch with their inner feelings and values. Inner fears and conflicts, which are often unconscious, limit creativity and risk taking. Before one can become a successful leader, it is necessary to reconnect with one's feelings, confront the latent fears, and resolve the underlying conflicts. Another key assumption is that successful leadership requires a high level of emotional and moral development. A person with high emotional maturity and integrity is more likely to put devotion to a worthwhile cause above self-interest and become a supportive, inspiring, and empowering leader. Understanding your own values, needs, and feelings is necessary to determine whether you are able to provide this type of leadership, and indeed, whether it is really what you want to do.

Personal growth programs are usually conducted at a conference center, and the program may last from two days to a week. Participants are usually managers who do not work together, but sometimes a personal growth program is conducted for an intact management group. The programs typically include a series of psychological exercises in which participants attempt to understand their purpose for living and working and share this understanding with each other. Sometimes outdoor challenge activities are incorporated into the program to increase the experience of shared risk taking. An experienced facilitator presents conceptual models and conducts the exercises. The models usually describe how human development occurs, how organizations change over time, and the role of leadership in organizational change.

The process of developing self-understanding begins when participants are asked to explain their reasons for attending the program. In another, more intensive exercise, participants are told to imagine their company has been acquired and only the three best leaders will be retained in the newly merged organization. Each person has five minutes to prepare a two-minute appeal describing his or her positive leadership qualities and reasons to be retained (a variation of this exercise is to imagine that you are at sea in a sinking boat with a small life raft that will only allow three people to be saved). Participants discuss each appeal and vote to determine the three people who have made the most convincing case.

An important exercise near the end of most programs is for each participant to develop a personal vision for the future and present it to the rest of the group. To facilitate development of a vision, participants are encouraged to imagine they are at the end of their lives and have achieved a sense of completion and gratitude; now they must consider what they have done and how they have lived to reach that state. After each presentation, the audience provides feedback on whether they perceive the vision to be sincere and right for the person.

Personal growth programs usually involve strong emotional experiences and are more likely than most training programs to have a lasting effect on participants. The changes may include an increase in interpersonal skills relevant for leadership. However, it is also possible that some participants will change in ways that reduce leadership effectiveness (Conger, 1993). Successful leadership often involves a passionate pursuit of a vision or cause that may require sacrificing aspects of one's personal and family life. The net effect of personal growth programs that encourage people to find a better balance between their work and personal life may be to reduce commitment to the organization. Moreover, increased awareness of unconscious needs and conflicts does not necessarily result in their resolution, and the experience is sometimes more detrimental than helpful to the person.

As yet, there are few studies on the consequences of personal growth programs for leaders, followers, or the organization. Two qualitative studies (Andersson, 2010, 2012) revealed that the extent to which such programs shaped participants' personal and leadership identities varied depending upon their expectations, prior managerial experience, and the organizational context. A field experiment by Elo, Ervasti, Kuosma, and Mattila-Holappa (2014) found that the participation of line managers in a seven-and-one-half-day personal growth–oriented leadership intervention had no effect on perception of the managers' leadership by subordinates, or on the managers' own perceived well-being. Given the limited research and mixed findings provided by it, more research is needed to assess the impact of personal growth programs on leadership development.

Facilitating Leadership Development

The effectiveness of leadership development activities for an individual leader depends upon qualities of the leader and qualities of the organization. The set of individual attributes that accelerate leader development have been called developmental readiness (Avolio & Hannah, 2008; Hannah & Avolio, 2010). There is little research on how organizational attributes affect the relevance of different methods of leadership development, but the meta-analyses on methods provide clues about this question (e.g., Becker, Höft, Holzenkamp, & Spinath, 2011; Collins & Holton, 2004; Lacerenza et al., 2017; Smither et al., 2005). The effectiveness of a method will depend on the types of learning desired, the individuals who will be developed, and facilitating conditions within an organization such as support from bosses, a favorable learning climate, and a systematic process for making developmental assignments.

Developmental Readiness

Developmental readiness is a function of a person's ability and motivation to develop (Avolio & Hannah, 2008; Avolio & Hannah, 2009; Hannah & Avolio, 2010). The ability to develop is determined by a person's level of self-awareness, cognitive complexity (i.e., the ability to differentiate and integrate various types and sources of information), and meta-cognitive ability (i.e., the ability to "think about thinking"). People are more prepared for leadership development when they are able to: (1) reflect upon and understand their personal strengths and weaknesses, values, motives, emotions, and personality; (2) process both positive and negative feedback about their current and potential competencies; and (3) reflect on how their thought patterns and self-insights can be leveraged to learn from new experiences. The motivation to develop is driven by personal interests and goals, a learning goal orientation, and developmental efficacy. A commitment to engage in learning requires intrinsic motivation involving the leader's personal interests and goals. Someone with a learning goal orientation will seek new experiences and strive to learn new skills, even when failure is a possibility. Such people welcome challenges to their leadership abilities because they see them as opportunities to learn. In contrast, someone who lacks interest in acquiring the competencies necessary for effective leadership will not do the work required to develop those competencies. People with a performance goal orientation rather than a learning goal orientation see themselves as being less able to change. As a consequence, they focus more on performing current tasks than learning new skills, and they avoid situations that involve the risk of failure. Finally, developmental efficacy refers to a person's confidence in the ability to develop the knowledge, skills, abilities, and attributes needed for effective leadership. People who possess both the ability and motivation to develop are well positioned to take full advantage of the leadership development opportunities presented by their organization. A good understanding of developmental readiness can help an organization identify the members most likely to benefit from leadership development activities.

Support by the Boss

The immediate boss can facilitate development of leadership skills in subordinates (Dragoni, Park, Soltis, & Forte-Trammell, 2014b; Hillman, Schwandt, & Bartz, 1990; London & Mone, 1987; McCall & McHenry, 2014; Valerio, 1990). However, a manager who does not understand the importance of coaching and mentoring is unlikely to provide much of it to subordinates. Managers who are preoccupied with immediate crises or their own career advancement are unlikely to spend much time developing subordinates as leaders. Managers who are insecure are unlikely to develop subordinates who could become potential competitors. Development will also be impeded by managers who treat mistakes by subordinates as personal failures rather than learning experiences. Even for managers who want to develop subordinates, it is difficult to find the right balance between providing necessary guidance and encouraging them to solve problems independently. A manager who is overly protective of subordinates and fails to provide enough challenge and honest feedback to them is unlikely to be successful in developing their leadership skills.

How much encouragement and support the boss provides for training and development activities is another determinant of a person's motivation to learn and apply leadership skills (Day & Dragoni, 2015; Facteau, Dobbins, Russell, Ladd, & Kudisch, 1995; Rouiller & Goldstein, 1993; Tracey, Tannenbaum, & Kavanagh, 1995). Several things that a manager can do to enhance learning and its subsequent application are listed in Table 14-3.

TABLE 14-3 Ways to Support Leadership Training of Subordinates

Before the Training:

- Inform subordinates about opportunities to get training.
- Explain why the training is important and beneficial.
- Ask others who received the training to explain how it was useful.
- Change the work schedule to make it easier to attend training.
- Give a subordinate time off if necessary to prepare for the training.
- Support preparation activities such as distribution of questionnaires.
- Tell subordinates they will be asked to report on what was learned.

After the Training:

- Meet with the person to discuss what was learned how it can be applied.
- Jointly set specific objectives and action plans to use what was learned.
- Make assignments that require use of the newly learned skills.
- Hold periodic review sessions to monitor progress in applying learning.
- Provide praise for applying the skills.
- Provide encouragement and coaching when difficulties are encountered.
- Include application of new skills in performance appraisals.
- Set an example for trainees by using the skills yourself.

Learning Climate

The amount of management training and development that occurs in an organization depends in part on prevailing attitudes and values about development, sometimes referred to as the "learning climate" (Ford & Weissbein, 1997; Hetland, H., Skogstad, Hetland, J., & Mikkelsen, 2011). These general conditions augment the influence of the immediate boss. More leadership development is likely when individual learning is regarded as highly important for organizational effectiveness. In such an organization, more resources will be devoted to training, and more effort will be made to explicitly measure and reward learning. Managers will provide more coaching and mentoring when these activities are emphasized, measured, and rewarded. More members of the organization will be encouraged to seek opportunities for personal growth and skill acquisition. For example, a person is more likely to accept a difficult, high-risk assignment if performance in the assignment will be evaluated in terms of skill development as well as task success. A supportive organizational climate and culture also encourage managers to apply the skills they have learned in training or developmental experiences.

Many things can be done to create and maintain a supportive climate for continuous learning and development. Some examples include the following: (1) make job assignments that allow people to pursue their interests and learn new skills; (2) establish work schedules that allow enough free time to experiment with new methods; (3) provide financial support for continuing education by employees; (4) arrange special speakers and skills workshops for employees; (5) establish a sabbatical program to allow employees to renew themselves; (6) establish a career counseling program to help employees develop self-awareness and find ways to achieve their full potential; (7) establish voluntary skill assessment and feedback programs; (8) make pay increases partly dependent on skill development; (9) provide awards for innovations and improvements; and (10) use symbols and slogans that embody values such as experimentation, flexibility, adaptation, self-development, continuous learning, and innovation.

Criteria for Developmental Assignments

At present, most organizations do not make job assignments that explicitly provide adequate developmental opportunities and a logical progression of learning (Baldwin & Padgett, 1993; McCall, 2010b). The idea of using job assignments for leadership development is somewhat at odds with the traditional approach to selection and placement in an organization, which seeks a good match between manager skills and job requirements (Ruderman, Ohlott, & McCauley, 1990). It is common practice to label someone as a specialist in a particular type of activity or problem and then repeatedly assign the same types of activities or tasks to the person. It is also common for organizations to promote individuals to higher positions within the same functional specialty rather than moving them to management positions in a different functional specialty.

Assigning a challenging job to someone who does not already possess all of the necessary skills can increase development, but there is also a risk of serious mistakes and failure. Even if the person is successful, it will require a longer learning period to master the job. Thus, it is not surprising that most organizations try to select the person with the best skills for a managerial position. More leadership development is likely to occur when executives are aware of the developmental opportunities in operational assignments and value development enough to risk giving important jobs to people who have not already demonstrated success in performing them (Hall & Foulkes, 1991). Evidence from one study shows that consideration of developmental needs when making succession planning decisions is likely to result in better performance for the organization (Friedman, 1986). The global executive search firm, Egon Zehnder, helps its clients to do just that—develop executive talent with an eye toward succession, as illustrated by the following example (Fernandez-Araoz, Roscoe, & Aramaki, 2017, p. 93):

> Four years ago, Prudential PLC decided to redesign its leadership development practices to match its global ambitions. At the time, management acknowledged that the existing talent-review process was "assessment-heavy but insight light" and too focused on current capabilities. Senior leaders set out to revamp it by emphasizing rigorous succession planning across all divisions and regions. Though this change was led by the executive committee and board, development now cascades up rather than down and starts with conversations between HR leaders and line managers, who have been trained to spot future stars. Team managers openly discuss business imperatives, critical roles, and successors, all through the lens of potential, and unit leaders report back up to the group's CHRO and CEO, Tim Rolfe and Mike Wells, sharing details about why people were deemed high potentials and how over time they can grow into different roles across the organization. What have the results been? In 2016, Prudential had 19 openings in its top 100 global roles, including five at the executive committee level, and all but one were filled through internal promotions. The new approach has helped the firm find great leaders even for its most quantitative and analytical businesses, such as asset management, and allowed it to put unexpected people in highly critical roles.

Systems Perspective on Leadership Development

Leadership development is more likely to be successful when top executives have a systems perspective that takes into account related responsibilities and strategic decisions such as selection and appraisal criteria, succession planning, management systems, and competitive strategy. Training programs and developmental activities are more likely to be effective if they are compatible and used in a mutually supportive way, they prepare managers for future positions rather than focusing only on current job requirements, and they consider how to improve the collective leadership for the organization rather than focusing only on developing individuals. Developmental activities also need to be consistent with the competitive strategy, the reward system, the organizational culture, and group-level processes and values. These issues are discussed in this final section of the chapter.

Relationships Among Approaches

The distinction among formal training programs, developmental activities, and self-help activities is useful up to a point, but it implies that the categories are mutually exclusive. In fact, the different categories overlap and are interrelated in complex ways. Learning acquired from one approach can facilitate or enhance learning from the other approaches. For example, a self-help activity such as using an interactive computer program may be useful to prepare for a developmental assignment. Short courses or workshops are useful to prepare someone for a special operational assignment, or to strengthen skills identified as deficient in a developmental assessment center or feedback intervention.

Sometimes different approaches are used in conjunction with each other. Action learning projects often combine formal training with learning from experience, and participants are encouraged to use self-help activities and peer coaching to acquire additional knowledge as needed for the project. Realistic simulations can be used as a self-contained developmental experience or as part of a formal training course. Some formal leadership development courses now include behavioral feedback for participants from coworkers. Personal growth activities are also included now in some leadership courses. Special mentors can be assigned to people who have developmental assignments, or designated resource people may be available on the Internet to provide advice and coaching as needed.

There has been little research on the relative advantage of training, development, and self-help activities for different types of leadership skills. Likewise, little is known about the best way to combine training, development, and self-directed learning activities to maximize their mutual effects. A more systematic approach to the study of leadership development activities is clearly needed.

Integrating Developmental Activities

In most organizations there is little integration of leadership training and development activities with each other or with related human resources practices such as performance appraisal, career counseling, and succession planning. Decisions about what types of training and development to provide are often influenced by current fads and vendor hype rather than by a systematic analysis of essential competencies that need to be enhanced. Promotion decisions are often influenced more by a person's prior performance than by rigorous assessment of competencies needed to perform effectively in the next position. As a consequence of poor selection and development, many top executives end up derailing for weaknesses that could have been predicted in advance (Heslin & Keating, 2017; Hogan, J., Hogan, R., & Kaiser, 2011; McCall, 1998).

Planning of developmental experiences for individual managers is often haphazard and unsystematic when it is determined independently by each manager's current boss. Few organizations have a specialized position with primary responsibility for planning and coordinating the overall process of leadership development for the organization. (McCall (1992) recommended using a developmental facilitator or committee to identify essential competencies for the organization, design tracking systems to assess current skills and developmental needs of individual managers, identify assignments with high developmental potential, sponsor special training programs when needed, find ways to strengthen rewards for managers who develop subordinates, and promote greater use of developmental activities such as mentors, special assignments, and feedback workshops. Another approach is to encourage individuals to take more responsibility for actively seeking developmental experiences. Social networks can be used by an individual to learn about promising developmental assignments and to get assistance in being selected for them (Bartol & Zhang, 2007; Cullen-Lester, Maupin, & Carter, 2017).

A review of best practices in leadership development found that it is facilitated by an integrated approach that includes systematic needs analysis, alignment of development with succession planning, top management support, cultural values for personal development, a program of mutually consistent developmental activities, recognition and rewarding for improvement, and systematic assessment of effectiveness for developmental activities (Leskiw & Singh, 2007).

Leadership Development for the Organization

Most of the literature on leadership development has been focused on improving the skills and behavior of individuals. The emphasis has been on leader development rather than leadership development (Day, 2000; Day & Dragoni, 2015; Day et al., 2014; Day & Thorton, 2018). However, as the conceptualization of leadership evolves, so must ideas about leadership development (Day & Harrison, 2007; Van Velsor & McCauley, 2004). If leadership is a shared process that involves the cooperative efforts of many people, then leadership development must also consider how to prepare people to participate in this collective process. Development of individuals is still important, but there is also a need to develop effective leadership processes in teams and in organizations. Progress in understanding what must be done and how to do it will depend in part on progress in theory and research on leadership processes at the group and organizational level. It will also require more intensive, longitudinal research on ways to enhance these leadership processes.

To be optimally effective, leadership development must be consistent with an organization's competitive strategy as well as with other human resource activities (Clarke & Higgs, 2016; Day, 2000; Fulmer & Vicere, 1996; McCall, 1998; McCauley, 2001; Reichard & Johnson, 2011). Unfortunately, the developmental activities in most organizations are not based on strategic business objectives, and there is seldom any effort to determine if the activities are relevant to these objectives. The disconnect between developmental activities and strategic objectives probably reflects a lack of understanding about the interdependencies between them. We are only beginning to learn how developmental activities affect the acquisition of leadership competencies, and how the competencies are related to organizational effectiveness. In a time of rapid change, it is not easy to predict the extent to which specific competencies will continue to be relevant in the future. Thus, even when top executives realize leadership development should be guided by strategic objectives, it is difficult to design developmental systems that will meet the needs of an organization in a turbulent environment (Hall & Rowland, 2016; Holmberg, Larsson, & Bäckström, 2016; Megheirkouni, 2016). Several scholars have made suggestions on how to improve leadership development and succession planning in organizations (e.g., Fulmer & Vicere, 1996; Karaevli & Hall, 2003; London, 2002; McCall, 1998; Moxley & O'Connor-Wilson, 1998).

TABLE 14-4 Guidelines for Self-Development of Leadership Skills

- Develop a personal vision of career objectives.
- Seek appropriate mentors.
- Seek challenging developmental assignments.
- Use social networks to learn about developmental opportunities.
- Improve self-monitoring.
- Seek relevant feedback.
- Learn from mistakes.
- Learn to view events from multiple perspectives.
- Be skeptical of easy answers.

Guidelines for Self-Development

The focus of this chapter is on what organizations can do to develop the leadership skills of their members, not on what an individual can do to develop these skills. Nevertheless, as noted in the introduction to the chapter, self-help activities provide another approach to enhance leadership skills. Self-development may include diagnosing learning needs and identifying self-help techniques that are relevant and available (Orvis & Ratwani, 2010; Reichard & Johnson, 2011; Reichard, Walker, Putter, Middleton, & Johnson, 2017). Many self-help techniques are available for improving leadership, including practitioner books, instructional programs on DVDs or from on-line sources, and interactive computer programs. While some of these techniques are intended to be a substitute for formal training programs, some are used to supplement training, and others are intended to facilitate learning from experience. A study by Boyce, Zaccaro, and Wisecarver (2010) examined personality traits associated with propensity for self-development of leadership skills, but more research is needed on the effectiveness of self-learning techniques, the conditions under which they are most effective, and the extent to which they can substitute for formal instruction (Baldwin & Padgett, 1993). Table 14-4 provides some recommendations for self-development of leadership skills.

Summary

Leadership skills can be developed in several ways, including formal training programs, developmental activities, and self-development activities. Despite the massive amount of leadership training and development that occurs, there has not been enough good research to assess its effectiveness.

The importance of learning from experience on the job is now widely acknowledged, and researchers are now mapping the relationships between specific experiences and specific leadership competencies. In general, more development occurs for managers who experience challenges that require adaptation to new situations and provide opportunity to learn to deal with a variety of different types of problems and hardships. More learning also occurs when people get accurate feedback about their behavior and its consequences and use this feedback to analyze their experiences and learn from them.

Developmental techniques with the potential to increase learning from experience include multisource feedback workshops, developmental assessment centers, special assignments, mentoring, personal growth programs, and executive coaching. Although most of these developmental techniques are widely used, we are just beginning to learn what types of leadership competencies are enhanced by each technique, the optimal conditions for using a technique, and the type of people most likely to benefit from it.

The extent to which leadership competencies are acquired and used depends on the developmental readiness of the leader, type of developmental activities that occur (e.g., training, experiential learning, self-learning), and facilitating organizational conditions (e.g., boss support, learning environment). Training and development are more effective when they are mutually consistent, supported by a strong learning culture, and integrated with other human resource activities such as career counseling, staffing decisions, performance appraisal, and succession planning. Leadership development should include shared leadership processes relevant for teams and organizations, and it should be consistent with an organization's strategic objectives (Pearce, Manz, & Akanno, 2013). A systems approach to leadership development is strategically important for long-term organizational effectiveness (DeRue & Myers, 2014; Drath et al., 2008; Hall & Seibert, 1992; McCall, 1992; Kegan & Lahey, 2016; Reichard & Johnson, 2011).

Review and Discussion Questions

1. What features of a training program are likely to make it more effective?
2. What conditions facilitate learning from experience by managers?
3. How are special assignments relevant for development of leadership skills?
4. What are the likely benefits of mentoring for developing leaders?
5. What are the most effective ways to use multisource feedback workshops?
6. How is the developmental readiness of leaders affected by the ability to develop and the motivation to develop?
7. What conditions in an organization enhance leadership development?
8. What can be done to integrate the leadership training, development, and self-help activities?
9. Why is it important for the leadership development programs in an organization to be consistent with the human resource management practices and the competitive strategy?

Key Terms

developmental assignments
developmental assessment centers
developmental readiness
executive coaching
leadership development
learning climate
mentoring
multisource feedback
personal growth programs
return on development investment (RODI)
self-development
simulations

PERSONAL REFLECTION

Based on what you have learned so far about leadership and yourself from your personal reflections, how ready are you in terms of your ability and motivation to develop your leadership skills? What developmental activities (e.g., training, developmental assignments, mentoring, self-development) seem especially useful for developing your leadership skills?

CASE

Sarabhai Industries

Abhivyakti Dubey is the new HR head at Sarabhai Industries, a conglomerate with several subsidiaries. Her main job as the HR head is to monitor the personnel practices of each subsidiary and ensure that they are in line with the corporate policy and strategy. Her job also includes providing support and suggestions to each subsidiary. She has to report directly to the CEO of Sarabhai Industries.

Each subsidiary is in charge of its internal management and development. Since sufficient numbers of leaders were not found internally, the CEO wondered if a more uniform approach needed to be taken. He asked Abhivyakti to find out what steps each subsidiary had taken to develop leadership skills amongst is employees, and report back to him with recommendations for improving the leadership development process. Thus, Abhivyakti started meeting the directors of the major subsidiaries. She asked them to be prepared with a short briefing.

The first director Abhiyakti met was Arjun who was from the engineering subsidiary, and he informed Abhivyakti that his company provided its employees with only technical training, since they lacked the staff (in terms of quality) required to provide management training. Any employee interested in some managerial training or workshop for their skill-enhancement or to be equipped on-the-job as an existing manager or as a future promotion, he/she can request the company to organize it or they can attend such external workshops at the company's expense, with prior approval from their boss. Arjun told Abhivyakti that his company also provides financial assistance to its employees who are interested in pursuing a degree in management. However, the company only covers up for half of the tuition cost—the most expensive component in the complete fee strcture. However, it has also been observed that a lot of employees, after completing their management degrees would leave the company for better pay packages elsewhere.

Abhiyakti met Hamid next. He was a director from the electronics subsidiary. He informed that his company had a mentoring program in place, that provided the high-potential managers an opportunity to develop their leadership skills. Managers at each level identify a promising subordinate to mentor. This subordinate then gets personal coaching and special developmental assignments to hone his/her leadership skills. For example, in order to observe how senior managers work, and learn on-the-job about strategic issues, junior managers are placed under each executive of the company. Cross-functional projects and studying work processes in order to suggest improvements and to make junior managers more efficient are some of the other assignments that are given to the protégés. While the program seems to be a hit with the people involved in it, Hamid told Abhivyakti that the other employees who were not a part of the program felt that there was a lack of developmental opportunity for them at the company.

Finally Abhivyakti spoke to Harshita, a director from a subsidiary that dealt in consumer goods. She explained that her company provided training to the six most promising managers below the top executive level, who are selected to participate in a series of seminars that are held once a month. These managers are selected based on the executive capacity that they have demonstrated previously in their work at the company. Every month the seminar is held by one of the top executives of the company who talks about the activities at the company and his or her own area of expertise. Occasionally the company also engages an external consultant to conduct training workshops. The managers who participate in this program have given positive feedback to Harshita so far, as they feel it is quite helpful in preparing them for promotion to top management. When one employee from the program gets promoted, another takes his/her place. The only drawback of the program is the internal politics that takes place as a result of executives trying to get their protégés selected for the program.

—*Written by* Nishant Uppal

Questions

1. Identify strengths and weaknesses in leadership development at Sarabhai Industries.
2. What types of changes are most likely to improve the leadership development?
3. What additional information is needed to make a good report to the CEO?

CASE

River Bank

River Bank is a regional bank in the northeastern part of the United States. The human resource manager for River Bank asked consultants to conduct an intervention to improve the influence skills of mid-level corporate managers. The intervention included a feedback report about a manager's use of each type of influence tactic with subordinates and a training workshop to improve skills in using the influence tactics. To assess the benefits of the training workshop, the consultants compared the effects for managers who were in the workshop to the effects for a control group of managers who would not get any training until later in the year. Assignment of managers to the training group or the control group was random. A group of similar managers in another bank in the same region was used to compare the effects of the feedback and training workshop to the effects of only providing managers with a printed feedback report.

Three or more subordinates of each manager were asked to fill out a questionnaire that measures how much their manager used each of several specific influence tactics in attempts to influence the subordinates over the past few months. All individuals who provided feedback would be anonymous, and feedback results for each influence tactic would only be seen by a focal manager as the mean score for data from all the manager's subordinates. Most of the subordinates agreed to provide the requested feedback. The focal managers also filled out self-report measures on their use of the influence tactics with subordinates. The "premeasure" surveys were conducted shortly before any feedback or training was provided. The influence behavior of the managers from this premeasure was similar for the three groups of managers (training workshop, feedback only, control group). The survey on influence behavior was repeated three months after the date of the training workshop to determine if there was any change in the use of the influence tactics with subordinates.

The feedback report explained each influence tactic and compared a manager's self-perceived use of the tactic to the mean score for subordinate perception of how much the manager used the tactic. The recipient was encouraged to pay special attention to any large discrepancies between self-ratings and ratings by subordinates, or between the subordinate ratings and norms based on results for all subordinates in the company who provided data. The feedback report also explained when each tactic is most likely to be effective for influencing subordinates, peers, and bosses.

The training workshop was conducted by facilitators at the corporate headquarters for River Bank. The first part of the three-hour workshop was designed to ensure that the focal managers understood the different influence tactics and their feedback reports. The facilitators explained each section of the report and answered any questions about it. The next part of the workshop was designed to help the managers understand how the influence tactics can be used in specific situations involving influence attempts with subordinates, peers, or bosses. The managers worked in small groups to develop an influence strategy for some realistic scenarios, then the groups presented their recommendations and gave examples of what a manager would say or do in each situation.

Each focal manager reported to a single boss, and some bosses supervised more than one of the focal managers. Before the project was initiated, the immediate boss provided ratings of managerial effectiveness for each manager who reported to that boss. For this premeasure there was no significant difference in rated effectiveness for the three groups of managers (workshop, feedback only, control group). Three months after the date of the training workshop the same bosses were surveyed again and asked to rate the recent performance for each subordinate manager. There was a significant improvement in the effectiveness of the managers in the training workshop, and they also had a significant increase in their use of the most relevant influence tactics (reported by subordinates). Managers in the control group and the feedback-only condition had no change in their rated effectiveness or influence behavior. The results showed that the feedback and training workshop was successful, and that it was more effective than only providing a feedback report to managers.

—*Written by* Gary Yukl

Questions

1. What do the findings suggest about the importance of providing a feedback and training workshop, even though it is much easier and less costly to only provide managers with feedback reports?
2. What other things could be done to improve the effectiveness of the feedback and training workshop?

Chapter 15

Overview and Integration

Learning Objectives

After studying this chapter, you should be able to:

- Summarize major findings about leadership traits, skills, behavior, and influence processes.
- Understand key points of convergence in findings from the different perspectives.
- Understand similar explanatory processes in dyadic, group, and organizational theories.
- Understand what progress has been made in the research on effective leadership.
- Understand how the methods used to study leadership affect what is learned about it.

Introduction

The field of leadership has been in a state of ferment and confusion for decades. Several thousand empirical studies were conducted to understand effective leadership, but the results from most of this research are weak, inconsistent, and difficult to interpret. The confused state of the field can be attributed in large part to the sheer volume of publications, the disparity of approaches, the proliferation of confusing terms, the narrow focus of most research, the preference for simplistic explanations, and over-reliance on weak research methods. Nevertheless, the preceding chapters of this book demonstrate that despite all these problems, substantial progress has been made in learning about effective leadership.

This final chapter summarizes the major findings from earlier chapters and examines the convergence in findings across different approaches for studying leadership. Similar explanatory constructs in dyadic, group, and organizational theories are described, and some cross-level implications are identified. Progress toward identifying an integrating conceptual framework is assessed, and some essential leadership qualities are identified. Limitations in the research on leadership are briefly described and some suggestions are made for improving future research. The chapter begins with a summary of what researchers have learned about effective leadership from nearly a century of research on the subject.

Major Findings About Effective Leadership

As noted in Chapter 1, much of the research on effective leadership examines leader behavior, leader traits and skills, and leader power and influence processes, and some of the research has examined how the leadership situation influences a leader's choice of behavior and the effects of this behavior. The major findings from these different lines of leadership research are summarized briefly.

The Leadership Situation

Aspects of the leadership situation strongly influence a leader's activities and behavior. Most people in leadership positions face relentless and conflicting demands on their time. There is a constant stream of requests, problems, inquiries, and reports from the many different people who interact with a leader. The pattern of necessary interactions with people inside and outside the leader's organization is determined by aspects of the situation such as the nature of the work (e.g., repetitive or variable, uncertain or predictable) and dependencies involving the different parties. The people who interact with a leader communicate role expectations about appropriate behavior, and role conflicts are created by competing demands from different people (insiders versus outsiders, subordinates versus bosses). Role expectations and activity patterns are also affected by the nature of the position (e.g., level, function, type of unit or team), the type of organization, the culture of the organization, and the national culture. The decisions and actions of leaders are limited by many internal and external constraints, such as policies, rules, standard procedures, budgetary requirements, and labor laws.

Aspects of the situation also determine the importance of leadership and what type of leadership is needed. Despite all the situational demands and constraints on leaders, they still have choices about what aspects of the job to emphasize, how to allocate their time, and with whom to interact. Effective leaders seek to understand their situation, and they adapt their behavior accordingly. They are able to reconcile the role conflicts, and they take advantage of role ambiguity as an opportunity for discretionary action. They seek to exploit opportunities, expand their range of choices, and shape the impressions formed by others about their competence and expertise.

Leadership Behavior

More research has been conducted on leader activities and behavior than on any other aspect of leadership. The descriptive research found that effective leaders develop a mental agenda of short- and long-term objectives and strategies. The agenda is used to guide their actions, manage their time, and help them become more proactive. Effective leaders identify problems that are both important and solvable, and they take responsibility for dealing with these problems in a systematic and timely way. By relating problems to each other and to informal objectives, they find opportunities to solve more than one problem at the same time.

Effective leaders use task-oriented, relations-oriented, change-oriented, and external behaviors that are appropriate for the situation. Task-oriented behaviors are used to improve or maintain internal efficiency and coordination in a team or organization. Effective leaders plan and schedule activities in a way that will make better use of people, resources, information, and equipment. They assign tasks, determine resource requirements, and coordinate interrelated activities. They help to clarify objectives, priorities, and standards for evaluating results.

They monitor the internal operations of a group or organization to assess performance and detect problems to be resolved. They identify the likely cause of problems that can interfere with task performance and take actions necessary to resolve the problems.

Relations-oriented behaviors are used to build commitment to work objectives, mutual trust and cooperation, and identification with the team or organization. Effective leaders use a variety of different relations-oriented behaviors. They are supportive (show trust and respect) and provide recognition for accomplishments and contributions. They provide coaching and mentoring to build subordinate skills and self-efficacy. They consult with people who will be affected in important ways by a decision to discover their concerns and get their suggestions. They empower competent subordinates to resolve operational problems in their work and provide better service to customers and clients. They use team-building behaviors to increase identification with the group and build member trust and cooperation.

External behaviors are used to ensure that internal activities are coordinated with related activities in other parts of the organization, and to get necessary information, resources, assistance, and support from bosses and people outside the leader's work unit. Effective leaders build and maintain a network of cooperative relationships with outsiders who are a valuable source of information, assistance, and political support. These leaders monitor the external environment to obtain information about trends and events that can affect their work unit or organization. These leaders promote and defend the reputation of their work unit or organization, and they negotiate agreements with peers and outsiders such as clients and suppliers.

Change-oriented behaviors are used to modify objectives, strategies, and work processes and facilitate adaptation to the external environment. A major responsibility for top executives is to formulate a competitive strategy that is relevant for the external environment and consistent with the organization's core competencies and ideology. The leaders interpret external events, focus attention on threats and opportunities, and relate proposed changes to a clear, appealing vision that is relevant to follower values, ideals, and core competencies. The leaders encourage and facilitate innovative thinking and the creation, acquisition, diffusion, and application of new knowledge to improve products, services, and work processes. To gain approval and support for major change, it is usually necessary to forge a coalition of internal and external supporters. Effective leaders also empower competent change agents to facilitate effective implementation of strategic decisions throughout the organization. Symbolic actions and role modeling are used to show continued personal commitment to a new strategy or major change. Providing opportunities to experience progress and repeated "small wins" gives followers more confidence in themselves, the vision, and their leaders.

Power and Influence

Influence is the essence of leadership, and much of the activity of formal leaders involves attempts to influence the attitudes and behavior of people, including subordinates, peers, superiors, and outsiders. How much power and influence a leader needs will depend on the situation. More influence is needed to make major changes in strategy when strong resistance to change is encountered. Influence derived from position power is especially important when it is necessary to control rebels who try to disrupt the activities of the organization or criminals who want to steal its resources. Upward and lateral influence are important for the leader to provide satisfactory benefits, obtain adequate resources, facilitate the work of the team, buffer subordinates from unreasonable demands, and represent their interests effectively.

Position power is derived from aspects of the situation such as the amount of formal authority, control over distribution of rewards and punishments, control over information, and access to important people. Exclusive access to information about internal and external events provides an opportunity to interpret reality for people and influence their decisions. Influence over subordinates is enhanced by having a moderate amount of authority to make necessary changes and dispense tangible rewards and benefits. However, too much position power entails the risk that a leader will be tempted to rely on it and neglect more effective forms of influence for building commitment. Effective leaders develop referent and expert power to supplement their position power and motivate stronger subordinate commitment to tasks that require high effort, initiative, and persistence. Referent power is developed by being supportive, caring, fair, and accepting. Expert power is acquired by successfully handling internal problems and external threats.

The manner in which a leader exercises power largely determines whether it results in enthusiastic commitment, passive compliance, or stubborn resistance. Effective leaders exert both position power and personal power in a subtle, easy fashion that minimizes status differentials and avoids threatening the self-esteem of others. Effective leaders attempt to empower followers in ways that are appropriate for the situation. They use power in ethical ways and seek to integrate the competing interests of different stakeholders.

A variety of social influence techniques can be used for developing commitment tc task objectives and compliance with requests. Effective leaders use proactive influence tactics that are appropriate for the objectives, context, and relationship. These leaders also use indirect ways of influencing people, such as management systems, reward systems, improvement programs, structural forms, and facilities. Political tactics are used to influence strategic decisions, especially in situations characterized by strong disagreement about organizational objectives and priorities.

The distribution and sharing of power over decisions have important implications for leadership effectiveness in groups and organizations, especially in cultures that value democracy. Extensive participation can result in better decisions when relevant information and ideas are distributed among people who are willing to cooperate in finding a good solution, and ample time is available to use a participative process. Participants are more likely to understand and accept the decision if the decision process allows sufficient opportunity to present ideas and influence the outcome. The quality of group decisions depends to a considerable extent on whether essential leadership functions are carried out and the group is able to avoid common process problems such as hasty decisions, polarization, and groupthink. Empowerment of individuals or groups is more successful when there is agreement about objectives and priorities, a willingness to assume responsibility for making decisions, and a high degree of mutual trust.

Traits and Skills

Conceptual skills, interpersonal skills, and technical skills are needed for most leadership roles and functions. Conceptual skills are necessary to analyze problems, develop creative solutions, identify patterns and trends, differentiate between relevant and irrelevant information, understand complex relationships, and develop effective mental models. Interpersonal skills are needed to influence people, develop cooperative relationships, establish and maintain social networks, understand individuals, facilitate teamwork, and resolve conflicts constructively. Technical skills are needed to understand activities, operational processes, products and services, technology, and legal/contractual requirements. The relative importance of different skills varies greatly from situation to situation, but some specific skills are probably useful in all leadership positions.

Personality traits and core values are also relevant for understanding effective leadership. Traits determine a person's willingness to assume leadership responsibilities and tolerate the stress and relentless pressures of the job. Traits affect a leader's desire to accumulate power, influence people, develop relevant skills, and learn from feedback. Leaders with a high need for power, high self-confidence, and an internal locus of control orientation make more influence attempts, and relevant expertise and influence skills make the influence attempts more successful. Leaders with a personalized power orientation seek to accumulate more power, and they exercise it in a manipulative, impulsive, domineering manner intended to benefit themselves and gain personal loyalty from subordinates. In contrast, leaders with a socialized power orientation, altruistic values, and a high level of cognitive moral development use power to build commitment to idealized goals, and they seek to empower subordinates by sharing information and using more consultation, delegation, and development of subordinate skills and confidence.

Some traits and skills appear to be especially relevant for effective task-oriented leadership. People with high self-confidence, conscientiousness, internal control orientation, and achievement orientation are more likely to take the initiative to identify and resolve task-related problems. Cognitive and technical skills are needed for planning projects, coordinating complex relationships, directing unit activities, and analyzing operational problems. Cognitive and interpersonal skills are needed to conduct effective problem-solving meetings.

Some traits and skills appear to be especially relevant for effective relations-oriented leadership. Altruistic and humanitarian values encourage supportive leadership and concern for individual subordinates. Emotional maturity, emotional intelligence, and communication skills facilitate development of cooperative relationships and make influence attempts more effective. Personal integrity is essential for maintaining mutual trust and credibility. A socialized power orientation encourages a leader to involve subordinates in determining how to achieve task objectives. An appreciation for individual and cultural differences can help a leader facilitate cooperation and teamwork by diverse followers.

Some traits and skills appear to be especially relevant for effective change-oriented leadership. A strong achievement orientation can be a source of motivation to strive for excellence and pursue innovative improvements. Strong cognitive skills and relevant technical knowledge help a leader to recognize threats and opportunities in the external environment and formulate an appropriate strategy based on the organization's core competencies. Social and emotional intelligence help a leader determine who needs to be influenced to support change and how to do it. Political and communication skills help a leader articulate an appealing vision and persuade people that change is necessary.

The willingness and ability to learn and adapt are important requirements for effective leadership in today's uncertain and turbulent world. Effective leaders are flexible enough to adjust their behavior as conditions change, and they find ways to balance competing values and resolve role conflicts. Relevant skills and knowledge can be acquired through a combination of formal training, developmental activities, and self-learning activities. However, a person's motivation and personality also influence the desire to learn new skills, the willingness to take risks in trying new approaches, and the readiness to accept feedback about deficiencies.

Integration of Diverse Perspectives About Effective Leadership

Most leadership theories and related research have a narrow focus, and there has been limited integration of findings from the different approaches (Meuser et al., 2016). Few of the early studies on leader traits and values included measures of leadership behavior, even though it is evident that traits and values are reflected in a leader's behavior, and the behavior is necessary to explain how leaders influence follower motivation and performance. Most of the early behavior research did not include leader traits and skills, even though they influence a leader's behavior. Few behavior studies included mediating variables that would explain how leader behavior affects outcomes such as subordinate and group performance. The power-influence approach includes some research on influence tactics, but other types of leadership behavior are seldom included. Until recently, little research was conducted on the relationship of leader and follower traits to influence behavior. Finally, most situational theories examine how the situation enhances the effects of selected leader behaviors or traits, rather than taking a broader view of the way traits, power, behavior, and situation jointly interact to determine leadership effectiveness.

Despite the prevailing pattern of segmentation in research on leadership over the past half century, the number of studies that straddle more than one approach is increasing, and the different lines of research are gradually converging. Most of the findings from different lines of research are consistent and mutually supportive. When findings from different approaches are viewed as part of a larger network of interacting variables, they appear to be interrelated in a meaningful way. One useful source of integration involves the recognition that leadership in organizations is a complex process that involves many interdependent leaders at different levels of authority and multi-level explanatory processes. The next section of the chapter describes how similar explanatory processes have been used in dyadic, group, and organizational level theories of effective leadership.

Multi-Level Explanatory Processes

A comprehensive description of leadership influence requires a multilevel perspective (Eberly, Johnson, Hernandez, & Avolio, 2013; Hernandez, Eberly, Avolio, & Johnson, 2011), and similar explanatory constructs in dyadic, group, and organizational theories can be useful in developing multi-level models (Mathieu & Chen, 2010; Morgeson & Hofmann, 1999; Shepherd & Suddaby, 2017). Explanatory constructs at one level of conceptualization can serve as mediating variables for the effects of leadership at a different level, and higher-level constructs may serve as moderators for the effects of leadership on lower-level processes or outcomes. A mediating process at one level may have beneficial or adverse consequences at other levels. Most leadership theories only describe effects at one level and do not consider the possibility of inconsistent effects across levels. Table 15-1 lists several sets of constructs that are relevant for explaining effective leadership in dyads, teams, and organizations. Each set of constructs will be briefly described, and some likely multilevel effects are identified.

Motivation and Commitment

Task commitment is an important determinant of individual performance. How leaders can influence a subordinate's task commitment is the primary focus of most dyadic theories of leadership, and in many cases these theories are merely extensions of motivation theories. Influence processes such as internalization and instrumental compliance help to explain how leaders can influence subordinate task commitment. Relevant leader behaviors include inspirational appeals that link the task to the person's values and ideals, setting task goals that are specific and challenging, and explaining how high performance will result in desirable rewards and benefits.

How leaders can influence the task commitment of a team is a key feature of group-level theories of leadership. The mediating processes include leader influence on shared objectives and group norms about acceptable performance. The dyadic behaviors continue to be relevant,

TABLE 15-1 Similar Explanatory Constructs at Three Levels of Conceptualization

Dyad	Group or Team	Organization
Subordinate task commitment	Member commitment to group goals	Mission commitment by all members and subunits
Internalized values and beliefs for subordinates	Group norms and values, shared mental models	Corporate culture and core values for the organization
Subordinate trust and cooperation with leader	Trust and cooperation among members	Integration among subunits, trust of top management
Personal identification with the leader	Collective identification with the team or unit	Collective identification with the organization
Subordinate knowledge and skills	Level and diversity of team member skills	Human capital and employee talent
Role specialization for subordinate	Role specialization in the team or department	Differentiation among subunits of the organization
Subordinate self-efficacy and self-confidence	Collective efficacy or potency for the team	Shared optimism and hope among organization members
Subordinate autonomy and empowerment	Team or unit autonomy and empowerment	Decentralization and power sharing in the organization
Creativity and learning by individual subordinates	Creative problem solving, collective learning by team	Organizational learning, and innovation

but the influence processes are more complex and additional behaviors are required. Leaders must influence member commitment to shared objectives for the team, and it may be necessary to resolve disagreements among members about priorities for different objectives. For example, in temporary committees and project teams, the loyalty of members to their home units may conflict with team objectives. Sometimes it is necessary to influence members to make individual sacrifices such as a reduction in personal benefits to achieve mission objectives. Leaders of teams and work units usually have some responsibility for allocating rewards to members, and compensation policies may determine whether it is possible to provide rewards that fairly reflect member contributions to the success of the work unit.

Organizational commitment by members and commitment to mission objectives by subunits are important determinants of an organization's performance. Top executives can use the behaviors described in dyadic leadership theories, but research on close and distant leadership suggests that some of the behaviors are only effective for influencing commitment when used during personal interactions with employees. Top executives can influence members at all levels in the organization by articulating an inspiring vision and taking symbolic actions that are consistent with the vision. Decisions about compensation policies, incentive programs, and criteria for retention and promotion also provide a way for top executives to influence member motivation and commitment.

Efforts to influence member motivation are complicated by unintended consequences and competing objectives. Policies and programs that encourage competition among individuals or among subunits can have dysfunctional consequences, such as reduced cooperation and failure to share relevant information. When subunits have incompatible objectives or different priorities, conflicts can occur. For example, the marketing manager sets an objective to increase sales and encourages sales representatives to find more customers for a new product, but the production unit cannot provide sufficient amounts of the new product. Conflicts also occur when a powerful subunit has objectives that are incompatible with organizational objectives. For example, a subunit of the organization seeks to preserve activities that are now obsolete and are a waste of the organization's scarce resources. When subunits are encouraged to make strategic decisions that maximize their short-term performance, the long-term performance of the organization may suffer.

Social Identification

Personal identification by a subordinate with the leader provides potential influence (referent power) over the subordinate. However, problems will occur if loyalty to the leader is much stronger than loyalty to the mission, and the leader's objectives are not consistent with mission requirements or the objectives of the team or organization.

Collective identification by members with a team or small group has potential benefits such as greater cohesiveness and cooperation and lower turnover. Leaders can increase collective identification by helping to create a unique identity and a favorable reputation for the team. Leaders can interpret events in terms of social identities related to past experiences and shared values of followers. Symbols, rituals, and ceremonies can be used to enhance the visibility of the group and to encourage members to express their loyalty and dedication. Stories, myths, and celebration of current and past achievements can also enhance collective identification.

Despite the potential benefits, strong identification with a team or subunit also has potential risks. For example, members may be unwilling to express concerns or dissent that would improve the group's decisions. Disagreements with other subunits or with top management are more likely to escalate into serious conflicts. In extreme cases, the unit may seek to withdraw from the organization or to use political tactics to undermine opponents in the organization.

Collective identification with the organization can provide benefits in terms of increased organizational commitment, reduced turnover, and higher performance. Member loyalty is especially important for organizations that have difficulty recruiting and retaining qualified members. Top executives can build member loyalty and commitment to the organization with the same behaviors described in team leadership theories. Social identity can be enhanced by a vision that makes membership worthwhile, and by evidence of progress in achieving the shared vision. A compelling vision for the organization can also provide the basis for subunit visions that will make the work of members more meaningful and significant (even if the members provide only routine support services).

Trust and Cooperation

Dyadic theories of effective leadership usually include some aspect of mutual trust and cooperation as a key determinant of reciprocal influence. A leader can improve relations with a subordinate by the use of supportive, considerate behaviors. An important determinant of subordinate trust is the leader's integrity, which includes honesty, fairness, and consistency between actions and espoused values.

The performance of a team usually depends on mutual trust and cooperation among the members, which is more likely when members have shared values and they identify strongly with the group. To enhance and sustain cooperation, leaders can use behaviors such as emphasizing the importance of shared objectives and the need for teamwork, making rewards contingent on contributions to team performance, involving members in decisions that affect the team, facilitating the constructive resolution of disagreements, and using team-building activities.

The level of cooperation and coordination among subunits, which is sometimes called integration (Lawrence & Lorsch, 1969), is a determinant of organizational performance. It is more important when subunits of the organization are highly interdependent with regard to their operations than when the subunits are relatively independent. For example, the importance of integration is low for a company with autonomous subunits such as separate divisions for unrelated products. Integration is more difficult to achieve when the subunits differ greatly with regard to their objectives and functional specialization, or there are other sources of conflict such as cross-cultural differences for multi-national companies.

Top executives can facilitate coordination and cooperation by providing structural forms such as cross-functional teams, matrix structures, and integrator positions (e.g., product managers). Management programs can be used to encourage cooperation, such as team building activities for executives, cross-functional task forces, job rotation for executives from different subunits, and rewards based on contributions to overall firm performance. Cooperation can be increased by an inspiring vision emphasizing shared values for members of the organization, regardless of their subunit function and local objectives.

Knowledge and Skills

Job-relevant skills and knowledge are a major determinant of individual performance. If necessary, leaders can enhance these skills for an individual subordinate with dyadic behaviors such as providing instruction and coaching. A subordinate's level of skill will affect the exchange relationship between the leader and a subordinate, and it determines the feasibility of delegating more responsibility to a subordinate.

The dyadic behaviors can improve the performance of a leader's group or work unit, but other behaviors are also necessary. In addition to ensuring that all members have the knowledge and skills needed to perform their individual jobs, a leader is responsible for ensuring that members have the skills needed to operate collectively as a team. This responsibility is more difficult when members have specialized roles that require close coordination, when errors have serious consequences, and when the team must respond rapidly to crises. Relevant leader behaviors include recruiting talented members with relevant skills, developing skills that are deficient, simplifying processes to reduce errors, cross-training members on multiple tasks, encouraging peer coaching, conducting team training activities, and conducting after-activity reviews to improve team processes.

The quality of human talent ("human capital") is an important determinant of organizational performance. Talented employees are especially important for highly complex tasks requiring unique skills that are difficult to learn. Most large organizations use human resource programs and systems to improve employee skills and capabilities. Examples include recruiting and selection programs, compensation and benefits programs, training and development programs, appraisal and assessment programs, talent management programs, and succession planning programs. These management programs are seldom included in dyadic or group-level theories of leadership, except as situational variables that enhance or limit the influence of the leader or substitute for direct behaviors by leaders. For example, good company programs to select and train employees can reduce the amount of training that managers need to provide to their subordinates. Top executives in an organization have primary responsibility for decisions to implement or modify human resource programs and systems, but leaders at all levels of the organization will be involved in implementing them.

Acquiring and retaining talented employees can be expensive, and leaders must find an appropriate balance between human resource quality and costs. Leaders must decide the responsibilities for different teams, the skill requirements of team members, and assignment of jobs to members. Decisions made to maximize performance at one level may not maximize performance at other levels. Similar trade-offs occur for decisions about the allocation of scarce resources to different subunits of an organization. Resolving these trade-offs and related conflicts is another challenge for top executives.

Specialization

Most dyadic theories recognize that a primary responsibility of the leader is to assign tasks to individual subordinates who have relevant skills. How leaders plan and organize activities for the work unit is not explicitly described by the dyadic theories, so they are most useful for explaining leadership when each subordinate independently performs a similar type of task and there is little need for coordination of activities by different subordinates.

Most group-level theories recognize that a leader's task-oriented behavior includes organizing activities and designing jobs in a way that increases efficiency and makes the best use of member skills. Some degree of role specialization usually improves performance in teams and work units, but too much specialization creates problems that are difficult to overcome. As role specialization and role interdependence increase, it becomes more difficult for leaders to match member skills with job requirements and to coordinate their activities.

Specialization is an important determinant of efficiency for an organization, and it involves not only the design of individual jobs but also the design of subunits and managerial positions with responsibility for planning and coordinating subunit activities (Lawrence & Lorsch, 1969; Mintzberg, 1979). Decisions about organizing and structuring the operations of an organization are an important aspect of strategic leadership (Fredrickson, 1986). The appropriate type and amount of specialization (differentiation) depend in part on the corporate strategy and the nature of the environment. Too much specialization or an inappropriate form of it can adversely impact an organization's performance. Decisions about structural forms involve trade-offs, and it is the responsibility of top management to find an appropriate balance for competing objectives.

Decisions about structural forms and differentiation of activities will affect leadership processes and requirements in an organization. The decision to have functional subunits rather than product divisions affects the responsibilities and skill requirements for leaders at different levels in the organization. The decision to use structural forms such as cross-functional project teams creates a need for team leaders who are able to facilitate cooperation among people with different perspectives, interests, and loyalties.

Perceived Efficacy and Optimism

Confidence and optimism about the possibility of achieving difficult task objectives are motivational concepts that help explain the performance of an individual, team, or organization. When there is little hope that they will be successful, people will not be highly motivated to accomplish a difficult objective. Confidence and optimism depend on skills, task difficulty, resources, and the relative capability of competitors or opponents.

At the dyadic level, a leader can influence the self-efficacy of an individual subordinate in several ways. Examples include providing clear explanations when assigning tasks (to reduce role ambiguity), providing necessary instruction and coaching, providing necessary information and resources, providing encouragement when problems occur, expressing confidence in the ability of a subordinate to do a difficult task, and providing recognition for achievements.

In groups, collective efficacy (or potency) is the perception of members that the group can successfully carry out its task or mission. The same types of leadership behaviors just described can be used to influence collective efficacy in a team, and other relevant behaviors include making assignments that take into account member skills, planning and scheduling activities to avoid delays and meet project deadlines, and solving immediate problems (e.g., accidents, equipment failures, supply shortages, schedule changes initiated by clients or other units). Leaders can also enhance optimism with "pep talks" before difficult activities and by arranging opportunities for the team to experience success in practice sessions.

At the organizational level, collective efficacy includes optimism that a change or new strategy will be successful and confidence that top management is able to guide the organization through difficult times. Leaders can increase confidence and optimism by making inspiring speeches, acting confident and optimistic, explaining what will be done to overcome obstacles or manage crises, taking highly visible actions to deal with problems, keeping members informed about progress, and celebrating significant progress toward achievement of objectives.

Strong optimism usually increases commitment to achieve task objectives, but it may also have negative consequences. When optimism is based on wishful thinking rather than a realistic assessment of actual conditions, it can result in risky decisions or the failure to recognize serious threats that require immediate action by the team or organization in order to avoid a disaster. Negative consequences may also result when some individuals know that they have much more ability than other members of a group or organization, but they do not get more status and rewards. In this situation, self-awareness of superior ability may cause resentment or motivate a person to seek better opportunities elsewhere.

Empowerment

Empowerment involves autonomy, shared responsibility, and influence in making important decisions. Similar concepts of empowerment have been used at all three conceptual levels to explain effective leadership (Maynard et al., 2012; Seibert, Silver, & Randolph, 2004; Spreitzer, 1995; Spreitzer, 2008).

In dyadic theories, empowerment is primarily a result of a leader's use of delegation or consultation with individual subordinates. The potential benefits from this empowerment include improvements in decision quality, employee task commitment, employee initiative in problem solving, and development of employee skills. The extent to which an individual leader can empower subordinates depends in large measure on the leader's own authority, and it is difficult to empower subordinates when there are elaborate rules and standard procedures for doing the work. Other situational variables that make empowerment feasible and beneficial include a subordinate's commitment to task objectives, desire to have more influence, and knowledge that will improve decision quality.

Empowerment is more complex for teams than for dyads, and it usually means allowing the members of a team to make important task decisions collectively. Empowerment may include member influence over selection of an internal leader, the selection of new members, decisions about work procedures, the assignment of tasks to members, and evaluation of each member's performance. In extreme cases, empowerment may include determining the mission and task objectives. The charter, bylaws, or formal policies for the organization often specify how much empowerment is allowed a team or work unit and what decision processes are permitted. The situational variables that determine how much empowerment is feasible also include shared objectives and relevant expertise for members.

One primary form of empowerment for organizational leadership is decentralization of authority for important decisions to subunits and leaders at lower levels. Decentralization can help to improve the quality of decisions, reduce delays in reacting to immediate problems, and enhance development of competent leaders for promotion to higher levels. Empowerment in an organization is encouraged and facilitated by some types of structural forms and empowerment programs (e.g., subsidiaries or product divisions, self-managed teams, quality circles, innovation programs). Many political, voluntary, and professional organizations or associations have charters that empower regular members by allowing them to participate in selecting and evaluating leaders, and by giving them influence over major decisions (e.g., through direct votes or by having representatives on the board of directors).

Empowerment has both advantages and risks for organizations. Extensive decentralization to interdependent subunits means that many leaders are making interrelated decisions that must be mutually consistent to avoid detrimental effects. Empowerment of subunits that are interdependent but have different priorities increases the need for cooperation and coordination among subunit leaders (Davison et al., 2012; Gebert et al., 2003; Locke, 2003; O'Toole et al., 2003). Decentralization can be risky if subunits have objectives that are not consistent with the organization's objectives, and they are allowed to pursue risky strategies that will eventually endanger the organization. Decentralization also means forgoing some potential advantages offered by standardization of work processes and management practices. Thus, it is essential to find an appropriate mix of centralized and decentralized decisions and to ensure that relevant leadership processes occur.

Collective Learning and Innovation

An important form of leadership influence involves improvements in collective learning about effective processes and strategies. Learning is essential for improving adaptation to external change, and it is also a source of incremental improvements in efficiency and human capital. The learning occurs at individual, group, and organizational levels, and learning at each level influences learning at the other levels (Berson et al., 2006; Crossan et al., 1999).

The dyadic theories do not explicitly include collective learning as a mediating process, but some of these theories identify ways a leader can encourage and facilitate creativity by an individual subordinate. Examples include encouraging innovative thinking (intellectual stimulation), allowing enough autonomy and time to pursue creative ideas, setting innovation goals, and being receptive to subordinate suggestions about ways to improve products, services, or processes.

Theories of team leadership identify several ways leaders can influence collective learning and creative problem solving (Day et al., 2004; Mumford et al., 2002). The leadership behaviors relevant for influencing creativity by an individual are still relevant, but additional leadership behaviors are needed to explain the synergy and interactive aspects of collective learning and creative problem solving by a group. Leaders can influence the group to use systematic procedures for analyzing problems, encourage the use of helpful procedures for generating creative solutions (e.g., brainstorming), encourage discussion of a broad range of options, and prevent the team from rushing to a decision without carefully considering the potential costs and benefits (e.g., by developing best- and worst-case scenarios). Leaders can encourage group members to build on each other's ideas rather than being too critical. Relevant behaviors to facilitate collective learning include encouraging the team to experiment with competing solutions to assess their consequences and using after-activity reviews to improve group performance of repetitive tasks. Some of the leadership behaviors that facilitate creativity, collective learning, and systematic problem solving can be shared among the members of a team.

Top executives can influence collective learning and innovation in an organization (Barney et al., 2018; Damanpour, 1991; Hannah & Lester, 2009; Jung, Chow, & Wu, 2003; Popper & Lipshitz, 1998). Relevant change-oriented behaviors include encouraging the use of best practices identified elsewhere, encouraging internal development of new knowledge, providing appropriate recognition and rewards for entrepreneurial activities, encouraging diffusion of new knowledge in the organization, planning the implementation of innovations, and promoting flexibility and innovation as key values in the corporate culture. In addition to direct behaviors, top management can implement relevant programs to assess, fund, and reward learning and innovation. The success of efforts to increase learning and innovation also requires appropriate leadership by middle- and lower-level managers. Many innovative ideas emerge from lower levels, and they should be nurtured and supported by champions and sponsors who appreciate their importance, recognize their relevance, and have sufficient power to ensure they are approved and implemented effectively.

Ways to Improve Leadership Research

The choice of methods and design of studies for much of the leadership research have limited the rate of progress in learning about effective leadership. Beliefs about the most useful research methods and the type of information needed to understand leadership processes are related to biases in the conceptualization of leadership. Until recently, most leadership studies have been guided by theories of dyadic influence processes involving the effects of individual leaders on individual followers. The methods used in most leadership studies are based on questionable assumptions, and even though remedies for improving the method are available they are seldom used (Hunter, Bedell-Avers, & Mumford, 2007). This section of the chapter provides a brief description of methodological issues and limitations in many of the leadership studies conducted during the past half century.

Qualitative Versus Quantitative Methods

More leadership research uses quantitative measures of key variables such as leader behavior and the attitudes and performance of subordinates or groups. Most studies on leader behavior use questionnaires that ask subordinates to rate how often or how much a leader has been using a designated type of behavior. The subordinate responses are biased by attributions, stereotypes, and implicit theories about leadership, and several types of evidence raise doubts about the meaning and accuracy of the results (Martinko et al., 2018). Critics of this survey research contend that it has an inherent bias toward exaggerating the importance of individual leaders, and it is a weak method for studying leadership as a dynamic, shared process embedded in complex social systems.

Some scholars advocate greater use of qualitative methods (Bryman, 2004; Bryman, Bresnen, Beardworth, & Keil, 1988; Parry, Mumford, Bower, & Watts, 2014; Parry, 1998; Parry & Meindl, 2002; Schilling, 2017; Strong, 1984). One example is an intensive, longitudinal case study with data collected from a combination of two or more methods (e.g., interviews, observation, diaries, critical incidents, company records, and open-ended survey questions). The qualitative methods offer some advantages for studying leadership, but these methods also have limitations (House, 1988; Martinko & Gardner, 1985; Parry et al., 2014). Standards for the application and evaluation of qualitative methods are not as explicit as those for traditional quantitative methods, and interpretations based on qualitative methods are sometimes very subjective. Descriptions of past events may be biased by selective memory for aspects of behavior consistent with the respondent's stereotypes and implicit theories about effective leadership. Direct observation is also susceptible to selective attention and biased interpretation of events. Attribution errors may occur if an observer or interviewer has information about unit performance. When observers immerse themselves in an organization for long periods of time in an effort to understand the context and meaning of what they are seeing, they may become involved in the very processes under observation, thereby risking objectivity.

The limitations and advantages of quantitative and qualitative methods make it desirable to use a complementary combination of both methods whenever possible (Bryman, 2004; Cresswell, J. W., & Cresswell, J. D., 2018). For example, in survey questionnaire studies, researchers could interview some of the respondents to verify that the questionnaire answers are accurately measuring the intended construct and to discover the underlying reasons for some of the quantitative results. A longitudinal case study that uses interviews or observation can include quantitative questionnaires administered periodically to some of the participants.

Survey Studies Versus Experiments

Survey studies are much easier to conduct than experiments and can be completed more quickly, but they do not allow strong inferences about causality. Controlled experiments in laboratory and field settings are appropriate for many types of leadership research (Rfietzschel, Wisse, & Rus, 2017). Historically, experiments have constituted only a small proportion (less than five percent) of the thousands of studies conducted on leadership (Brown & Lord, 1999; Dipboye, 1990; Wofford, 1999), but a recent review of leadership research revealed an encouraging increase in laboratory (18 percent) and field (4 percent) experiments among studies that employed quantitative methods during the new millennium (Dinh et al., 2014). The most important advantage of an experiment is the opportunity to determine causality. In laboratory experiments, researchers can manipulate leader behavior or situational variables and assess their independent and joint effects. It is relatively easy to measure mediating processes, control for extraneous variables, and examine the effects of conditions that occur only rarely in actual organizations. However, the potential advantages of experiments may not be realized if they are poorly designed and executed. Common limitations of laboratory experiments include the use of weak manipulations, the use of tasks that do not accurately simulate realistic conditions, the use of convenience samples of students who have little work experience, and the use of brief interactions among strangers to study processes that in most organizations would involve people with established relationships.

Field experiments are more difficult to conduct than laboratory experiments but offer some unique advantages. Most field experiments involve realistic working conditions and people who have experience working together. Field experiments can be used to assess the effects of different patterns of leadership behavior, and they provide an excellent way to assess the utility of interventions used to improve leadership (e.g., training, feedback, executive coaching). Common limitations of field experiments on leadership are weak manipulations, non-random assignment of participants to experimental treatments, weak assessment of outcome variables, failure to measure mediating processes, and use of an unrepresentative sample that limits external validity. A field experiment on leadership is likely to be more useful if it is based on a relevant and well-specified model, it includes a strong and appropriate manipulation of independent variables, it includes multiple measures of relevant variables, and it is conducted over an appropriate time period. In experiments conducted to evaluate developmental interventions (e.g., feedback or coaching), it is easier to gain approval for a control group if the researcher provides an opportunity for members of the control group to participate in the intervention at a later time.

Level of Analysis

Most survey research on leadership behavior uses an individual, dyadic, or group level of analysis. Analysis at the individual level usually involves correlations between variables that are measured within individuals. For example, a subordinate's ratings of leader behavior are correlated with the subordinate's ratings of task commitment across all subordinates in the sample. Dyadic analyses usually involve data obtained from both members of a leader–subordinate dyad, such as correlating subordinate ratings of leader behavior with the leader's ratings of subordinate performance across all dyads in the sample. Group-level analyses often involve aggregating individual data to the group level. For example, the leader behavior ratings provided by several subordinates are averaged; then the composite scores for each group are correlated with other composite scores (e.g., cohesiveness, collective efficacy) or group-level measures of outcomes (e.g., group performance, turnover).

The appropriate type of analysis for quantitative data from survey studies depends on the underlying theory of leadership processes and the level of measurement for the variables. The level of data analysis should correspond to the level of measurement and the proposed relationships in the theory (Klein et al., 1994; Rousseau, 1985). Unless an appropriate level of analysis is used, the results from a study may be misinterpreted. The analysis is more complex for a multilevel theory that includes cross-level effects. Different methods for multilevel analysis are described and compared in two special issues of *The Leadership Quarterly* (see Bliese, Halverson, & Schriesheim, 2002; Yammarino & Dansereau, 2008), as well as a recent review by Dionne and colleagues (2014).

Many of the early leadership theories were vague about the level of conceptualization for each variable, and many empirical studies used data analyses that were not appropriate for the level of conceptualization (Dionne et al., 2014; Yammarino, Dionne, & Chun, 2002; Yammarino et al., 2005). When proposed relationships involve variables at different levels of conceptualization or effects that occur at more than one level (e.g., the leader's vision can affect self-efficacy of individual subordinates and collective efficacy for the team), then it may be necessary to include more than one level of analysis.

Limitations in Behavior Studies

Much of the empirical research on leadership during the past half century has involved examination of the determinants or effects of leader behavior. The lack of stronger, more consistent results in this research can be explained by examining the differences and limitations for most of the studies (Yukl, 2012; Yukl & Michel, 2015).

1. Most of the studies only examined broadly defined behaviors, the specific component behaviors were not the same in some of the studies, and the results were often reported only for the broad behaviors (e.g., task-oriented and relations-oriented). Unless the same

specific behaviors are measured and included in the analyses, it is impossible to accurately identify the individual and joint effects of the behaviors.

2. Most of the studies did not include measures of situational variables likely to influence leader behavior and the effects of the behavior, which depend to a great extent on the situation. For example, as the nature of the work becomes more variable and uncertain, detailed plans for how to do the work become less useful, whereas problem solving becomes more important. The results for effects of leader behavior will not be consistent for a set of studies with very different leadership situations.
3. Most of the studies did not examine curvilinear relationships or consider that the optimal amount of a behavior is often a moderate amount rather than the maximum amount. For example, some clarifying of work procedures is usually necessary, but too many detailed rules and regulations can have negative effects on subordinate job satisfaction and performance. In another example, the use of a moderate amount of praise for important achievements and contributions of subordinates can improve their satisfaction and task motivation, but overuse of praise for trivial achievements is likely to reduce the benefits.
4. Most of the studies did not examine the positive and negative effects of specific behaviors for multiple outcomes. Even though the specific components for a broad category of behavior may have the same primary objective, these behaviors usually affect other objectives in positive or negative ways. An example of joint positive effects is when coaching improves both task performance and interpersonal relations. An example of negative side effects is when setting a high performance goal encourages unethical and dysfunctional employee behavior such as falsification of output records or the use of improper procedures that reduce the quality of company products or services.
5. Most of the studies did not examine the joint effects of two or more specific behaviors, which can be more important than their individual effects. An example involves the joint effects of monitoring and problem solving; the potential benefits of monitoring work activities will not be achieved if the leader discovers problems but fails to take actions needed to resolve them.

Other Methodological Issues

The samples used in many leadership studies are far from ideal. The common approach is to use a convenience sample, one that is easy to get, rather than to plan the type of sample that is appropriate for the research objectives and design. For example, a sample of experienced managers from the same industry is often more useful for a survey study than a convenience sample of students with little practical experience in organizations. In comparative studies, the use of convenience samples makes it difficult to identify the effects of unmeasured variables that are confounded with the independent or dependent variables.

Many leadership studies examine events that occur during a time interval that is too brief for independent variables to have much effect on dependent variables. Longitudinal studies are needed to examine leadership processes that evolve over time, and to assess the delayed effects of leaders on a team or organization. Processes such as developing dyadic relationships, building effective teams, and leading change often require months or years of study. Unfortunately, few researchers are willing to invest that much time in a study. What usually passes for longitudinal research in leadership is a survey study with measures taken a few weeks apart, rather than an intensive examination of evolving relationships, emerging problems, protracted decisions, sequential changes, and reciprocal influence processes.

The leadership research seems to be biased toward easy methods and faddish topics. Too many studies are merely replications of earlier studies on a popular topic. One researcher publishes a study that is interesting and easy to conduct, and others imitate it with only minor variations. Too many studies lack an adequate theoretical basis to predict and explain any relationships that are found, and the results are usually inconclusive. Rather than only conducting yet another test of a weak theory, it is much better to design research that will be useful for developing better theories and practical applications. More studies should test alternative explanations, examine possible confounds, identify limiting conditions, and assess the practical significance of the results.

Table 15-2 provides an overview of the methodological biases discussed in this section of the chapter. Common features of leadership studies are contrasted with alternative and less common features. Greater use of the uncommon features would make leadership research more productive. Lowe and Gardner (2000), Gardner, Lowe, Moss, Mahoney, and Cogliser (2010), and Dinh and colleagues (2014) reached similar conclusions based on their reviews of the leadership literature.

Summary of Research Limitations

Even though many different methods of collecting information and analyzing it are available, most of the leadership research during the past half century has relied on weak methods such as survey studies with questionnaires filled out by leaders or their subordinates at one point in time. It is important to select methods that are appropriate for the type of knowledge sought, rather than merely using the most convenient methods. The research question should dictate the methodology and choice of samples, not the other way around. Each type of methodology has limitations, and it is desirable to use multiple methods whenever feasible for research on leadership (Jick, 1979; Yukl & Van Fleet, 1982). It is easier to have confidence in the results of leadership research when similar results are found for different research methods, especially if at least one method was an experiment. It is also important to consider the appropriate level of analysis for the theoretical constructs and measures. Multilevel analysis can provide new insights about leadership processes and help to determine whether parallel processes occur at different levels.

TABLE 15-2 Common and Uncommon Features in Leadership Studies

Feature	Common	Uncommon
Type of research method	Survey study	Experiment, or multiple methods
Research objective	Replication	Explore new issues
Level of processes	Individual or dyadic	Group or organizational
Time frame	Short-term	Longitudinal
Causality	Unidirectional	Reciprocal
Criterion variables	One or two	Several
Mediating variables	Few or none	Several
Data sources	Single	Multiple
Sample	Convenience	Systematic selection
Level of leader	Supervisor	Executive

General Guidelines for Effective Leadership

This book takes a broad perspective and examines many different aspects of leadership. The different ways of defining leadership, the multitude of different variables examined in the research, and the frequency of weak methods make it difficult to identify the essence of effective leadership. This section presents what seem to be the ten most important leadership functions for enhancing collective work in teams and organizations. In a large organization, the conditions that create a need for these leadership acts are played out at every level of management and in every subunit. The functions can be performed by many different members of the organization, but they are especially relevant for people who are elected, appointed, or informally recognized as leaders for a collective activity.

1. ***Help interpret the meaning of events.*** Helping people to find meaning in complex events is important, especially when the pace of change is accelerating and touching every part of our lives. Effective leaders help people interpret events, understand why they are relevant, and identify emerging threats and opportunities.
2. ***Create alignment on objectives and strategies.*** Effective performance of a collective task requires considerable agreement about what to do and how to do it. Helping to build a consensus about these choices is especially important in newly formed groups and in organizations that have lost their way. Effective leaders help to create agreement about objectives, priorities, and strategies.
3. ***Build commitment and optimism.*** The performance of a difficult, stressful task requires commitment and persistence in the face of obstacles and setbacks. Effective leaders increase enthusiasm for the work, commitment to task objectives, and confidence that the effort will be successful.
4. ***Build mutual trust and cooperation.*** Effective performance of a collective task requires cooperation and mutual trust, which are more likely to exist when people understand each other, appreciate diversity, and are able to confront and resolve differences in a constructive way. Effective leaders foster mutual respect, trust, and cooperation.
5. ***Strengthen collective identity.*** The effectiveness of a group or organization requires at least a moderate degree of collective identification. In this era of fluid teams, virtual organizations, and joint ventures, boundaries are often unclear and loyalties are divided. Effective leaders help create a unique identity for a group or an organization, and they resolve issues of membership in a way that is consistent with this identity.
6. ***Organize and coordinate activities.*** Successful performance of a complex task requires the capacity to coordinate many different but interrelated activities in a way that makes efficient use of people and resources. Effective leaders help people get organized to perform collective activities efficiently, and they help coordinate these activities as they occur.
7. ***Encourage and facilitate collective learning.*** In a highly competitive and turbulent environment, continuous learning and innovation are essential for the survival and prosperity of an organization. Members must collectively learn better ways to work together toward common objectives. Effective leaders encourage and facilitate collective learning and innovation.
8. ***Obtain necessary resources and support.*** To effectively accomplish the objectives of a group or work unit, essential resources, approvals, assistance, and political support must be obtained from the parent organization and outsiders. Likewise, the survival and prosperity of an organization depend on favorable exchanges with external parties such as clients, customers, and funding agencies. Effective leaders promote and defend the interests and reputation of their work unit and help to obtain necessary resources and support for it.

9. ***Develop and empower people.*** The performance of a group or organization is likely to be better if competent members are actively involved in solving problems and making decisions. Relevant skills must be developed to prepare people for leadership roles, new responsibilities, and major change. Effective leaders help develop the skills and confidence of people in their work unit and empower people to become change agents and leaders themselves.
10. ***Promote social justice and morality.*** Member satisfaction and commitment are increased by a climate of fairness, compassion, and social responsibility. To maintain such a climate requires active efforts to protect individual rights, encourage social responsibility, and oppose unethical practices. Effective leaders set an example of moral behavior, and they take necessary actions to promote social justice.

The State of the Field

People have been interested in leadership since the beginning of recorded history, and the study of leadership as a scientific discipline started early in the last century. The massive literature produced by this effort is beset with confusion and ambiguity, but the selective review of theory and research in this book shows that we are making substantial progress in learning about leadership. Nevertheless, much more remains to be learned. Effective leadership at all levels of society and in all of our organizations is essential for coping with the growing social, economic, and environmental problems confronting the world. Learning to cope with these problems is not a luxury but a necessity.

Progress in understanding leadership has been slower than expected from the large volume of publications and the immense amount of effort expended on leadership research. Fortunately, in recent years there has been an increase in the richness of research questions and the variety of approaches used to study them, and the field appears to be undergoing an accelerating pace of discovery. With such a vital subject, it is imperative that we continue to upgrade the quality of leadership research and theory. Faster progress will require the efforts of dedicated researchers who value discovery of useful knowledge and are willing to invest the time and effort needed to conduct good research.

Review and Discussion Questions

1. What are some points of convergence in the four major lines of research on effective leadership (traits and skills, behaviors, influence processes, situational variables)?
2. What are some of the most important findings about effective leadership in organizations?
3. What are some explanatory constructs and processes that appear similar in dyadic, group, and organizational level theories?
4. What are some biases and limitations in the way leadership is usually defined and studied?
5. What improvements could be made in the way leadership is studied?
6. What are the ten general guidelines for effective leadership in organizations?

Key Terms

field experiments
levels of analysis
multilevel explanatory processes
multi-method research
qualitative methods
quantitative methods
survey studies

REFERENCES

Abatecola, G., Mandarelli, G., & Poggesi, S. (2013). The personality factor: How top management teams make decisions. A literature review. *Journal of Management & Governance, 17*(4), 1073–1100.

Abdelgawad, S. G., Zahra, S. A., Svejenova, S., & Sapienza, H. J. (2013). Strategic leadership and entrepreneurial capability for game change. *Journal of Leadership & Organizational Studies, 20*, 394–407.

Abrahamson, E. (1996). Management fashion. *Academy of Management Review, 21*, 254–285.

Abrahamson, E., & Fairchild, G. (1999). Management fashion: lifecycles, triggers, and collective learning processes. *Administrative Science Quarterly, 44,* 708–740.

Adams, R. B. (2016). Women on boards: The superheroes of tomorrow? *The Leadership Quarterly, 27*, 371–386.

Adler, N. J. (1996). Global women political leaders: An invisible history, and increasingly important future. *The Leadership Quarterly, 7,* 133–161.

Adler, N. J. (1997). *International dimensions of organizational behavior* (3rd ed.). Cincinnati, OH: South-Western College Publishing.

Adler, N. J., & Gunderson, A. (2008). *International dimensions of organizational behavior* (5th ed.). Mason, OH: Thomson.

Adner, R., & Helfat, C. E. (2003). Corporate effects and dynamic managerial capabilities. *Strategic Management Journal, 24,* 1011–1025.

Adsit, D. J., London, M., Crom, S., & Jones, D. (1997). Cross-cultural differences in upward ratings in a multi-cultural company. *International Journal of Human Resource Management, 8,* 385–401.

Agle, B. R., Mitchell, R. K., & Sonnenfeld, J. A. (1999). Who matters to CEOs? An investigation of stakeholder attributes and salience, corporate performance, and CEO values. *Academy of Management Journal, 42*, 507–525.

Agle, B. R., Nagarajan, J. N., Sonnenfeld, J. A., & Srinivasan, D. (2006). Does CEO charisma matter? An empirical analysis of the relationships among organizational performance, environmental uncertainty, and top management team perceptions of CEO charisma. *Academy of Management Journal, 49,* 161–174.

Ahearn, K. K., Ferris, G. R., Hochwarter, W. A., Douglas, C., & Ammeter, A. P. (2004). Leader political skill and team performance. *Journal of Management, 30*, 309–327.

Ahearne, M., Matthieu, J., & Rapp, A. (2005). To empower or not to empower your sales force? An empirical examination of the influence of leadership empowerment behavior on customer satisfaction and performance. *Journal of Applied Psychology, 90,* 945–955.

Akinci, C., & Sadler-Smith, E. (2012). Intuition in management research: A historical review. *International Journal of Management Reviews, 14*(1), 104–122.

Alexander, L. D. (1985). Successfully implementing strategic decisions. *Long-Range Planning, 18,* 91–97.

Algera, P. M., & Lips-Wiersma, M. (2012). Radical authentic leadership: Co-creating the conditions under which all members of the organization can be authentic. *The Leadership Quarterly, 23*, 118–131.

Allan, P. (1981). Managers at work: A large-scale study of the managerial job in New York City government. *Academy of Management Journal, 24,* 613–619.

Allen, M. (2014). Talent management and corporate universities. *Graziadio Business Review, 17*(1), 1–6.

Allen, T. D., Eby, L. T., & Lentz, E. (2006). Mentorship behaviors and mentorship quality associated with formal mentoring programs: Closing the gap between research and practice. *Journal of Applied Psychology, 91,* 567–578.

Alliger, G. M., Tannenbaum, S. I., Bennett, W., Jr., Traver, H., & Shotland, A. (1997). A meta-analysis of the relations among training criteria. *Personnel Psychology, 50,* 341–358.

Alvesson, M. (2010). Organizational culture: Meaning, discourse, and identity. In N. M. Ashkanasy & C. P. M. Wilderom (Eds.), *The handbook of organizational culture and climate* (2nd ed., pp. 11–28). Thousand Oaks, CA: Sage.

Alvesson, M., & Sveningsson, S. (2003). The great disappearing act: Difficulties in doing "leadership." *The Leadership Quarterly, 14,* 359–381.

Amabile, T. M., Schatzel, E. A., Moneta, G. B., & Kramer, S. J. (2004). Leader behaviors and the work environment for creativity: Perceived leader support. *The Leadership Quarterly, 15,* 5–32.

Amis, J., Slack, T., & Hinings, C. R. (2004). The pace, sequence, and linearity of radical change. *Academy of Management Journal, 47,* 15–39.

Ammeter, A. P., Douglas, C., Gardner, W. L., Hochwarter, W. A., & Ferris, G. R. (2002). Toward a political theory of leadership. *The Leadership Quarterly, 13,* 751–796.

Anand, S., Vidyarthi, P., & Rolnicki, S. (2018). Leader-member exchange and organizational citizenship behaviors: Contextual effects of leader power distance and group task interdependence. *The Leadership Quarterly, 29,* 489–500.

Ancona, D. G. (1990). Outward bound: Strategies for team survival in an organization. *Academy of Management Journal, 33,* 334–365.

Ancona, D. G., & Caldwell, D. F. (1992). Bridging the boundary: External activity and performance in organizational teams. *Administrative Science Quarterly, 37,* 634–665.

Ancona, D. G., & Nadler, D. A. (1989). Top hats and executive tales: Designing the senior team. *Sloan Management Review, 31*(Fall), 19–28.

Anderson, D., & Ackerman-Anderson, L. (2010). *Beyond change management: How to achieve breakthrough results through conscious change leadership*. San Francisco, CA: Pfeiffer.

Andersen, J. A. (2009). When a servant-leader comes knocking... *Leadership & Organization Development Journal, 30,* 4–15.

Andersson, T. (2010). Struggles of managerial being and becoming: Experiences from managers' personal development training. *Journal of Management Development, 29*(2), 167–176.

Andersson, T. (2012). Normative identity processes in managers' personal development training. *Personnel Review, 41*, 572–589.

Angle, B. R., Nagarajan, J. N., Sonnenfeld, J. A., & Srinivasan, D. (2006). Does CEO charisma matter? An empirical analysis of the relationships among organizational performance, environmental uncertainty, and top management team perceptions of CEO charisma. *Academy of Management Journal, 49,* 161–174.

Ansari, M. A., & Kapoor, A. (1987). Organizational context and upward influence tactics. Organizational behavior and human decision processes, 40(1), 39–49.

Anthony, W. P. (1978). *Participative management.* Reading, MA: Addison-Wesley.

Antonakis, J. (2018). Charisma and the '"new leadership." In J. Antonakis & D. V. Day (Eds.), *The nature of leadership* (3rd ed., pp. 56–81). Los Angeles: Sage.

Antonakis, J., Ashkanasy, N. M., & Dasborough, M. T. (2009). Does leadership need emotional intelligence? *The Leadership Quarterly, 20*, 247–261.

Antonakis, J., Bastardoz, N., Jacquart, P., & Shamir, B. (2016). Charisma: An ill-defined and ill-measured gift. *Annual Review of Organizatioanl Psychology and Organizational Behavior, 3*, 293–319.

Antonakis, J., & Day, D. (2018). Leadership: Past, present, and future. In J. Antonakis & D. Day (Eds.), *The nature of leadership* (3rd ed., pp. 3–26). Thousand Oaks, CA: Sage.

Antonakis, J., Fenley, M., & Liechti, S. (2011). Can charisma be taught? Tests of two interventions. *Academy of Management Learning & Education, 10*, 374–396.

Antonakis, J., Fenley, M., & Liechti, S. (2012). Learning charisma: Transform yourself into the person others want to follow. *Harvard Business Review, 90*(6), 127–130.

Antonakis, J., Schriesheim, C. A., Donovan, J. A., Gopalakrishna-Pillai, K., Pelligrini, E. K., & Rossomme, J. L. (2004). Methods of studying leadership. In J. Antonakis, A. T. Cianciolo, & R. J. Sternberg (Eds.), *The nature of leadership* (pp. 48–70). Thousand Oaks, CA: Sage.

Anzengruber, J., Goetz, M. A., Nold, H., & Woelfle, M. (2017). Effectiveness of managerial capabilities at different hierarchical levels. *Journal of Managerial Psychology, 32*, 134–148.

Aquino, K., Freeman, D., Reed, A., II, Lim, V. K. G., & Felps, W. (2009). Testing a social-cognitive model of moral behavior: The interactive influence of situations and moral identity centrality. *Journal of Personality and Social Psychology, 97*, 123–141.

Aquino, K., & Reed, A., II. (2002). The self-importance of moral identity. *Journal of Personality and Social Psychology, 83*, 1423–1440.

Arel, B., Beaudoin, C. A., & Cianci, A. M. (2012). The impact of ethical leadership, the internal audit function, and moral intensity on a financial reporting decision. *Journal of Business Ethics, 109*, 351–366.

Argyris, C. (1964). *Integrating the individual and the organization*. New York: John Wiley.

Argyris, C. (1991). Teaching smart people how to learn. *Harvard Business Review, 69*(3), 99–109.

Argyris, C. (1998). Empowerment: The emperor's new clothes. *Harvard Business Review, 76*(3), 98–105.

Arvey, R. D., & Ivancevich, J. M. (1980). Punishment in organizations: A review, propositions, and research suggestions. *Academy of Management Review*, 5, 123–132.

Arvey, R. D., Li, W.-D., & Wang, N. (2016). Genetics and organizational behavior. *Annual Review of Organizational Psychology and Organizational Behavior, 3*, 167–190.

Arvey, R. D., Rotundo, M., Johnson, W., Zhang, Z., & McGue, M. (2006). The determinants of leadership role occupancy: Genetic and personality factors. *The Leadership Quarterly, 17*, 1–20.

Arvey, R. D., Zhang, Z., Avolio, B. J., & Krueger, R. F. (2007). Developmental and genetic determinants of leadership role occupancy among women. *Journal of Applied Psychology, 92*, 693–706.

Ashkanasy, N. M., & Gallois, C. (1994). Leader attributions and evaluations: Effects of locus of control, supervisory control, and task control. *Organizational Behavior and Human Decision Processes, 59*, 27–50.

Ashour, A. S., & England, G. (1972). Subordinate's assigned level of discretion as a function of leader's personality and situational variables. *Journal of Applied Psychology, 56*, 120–123.

Athanasopoulou, A., & Dopson, S. (2018). A systematic review of executive coaching outcomes: Is it the journey or the destination that matters the most? *The Leadership Quarterly, 29*, 70–88.

Atwater, L., & Waldman, D. (1998). 360 degree feedback and leadership development. *The Leadership Quarterly, 9*, 423–426.

Atwater, L., Wang, M., Smither J. W., & Fleenor, J. W. (2009). Are cultural characteristics associated with the relationship between self and others' ratings of leadership? *Journal of Applied Psychology, 94*, 876–886.

Audia, P. G., Locke, E. A., & Smith, K. G. (2000). The paradox of success: An archival and a laboratory study of strategic persistence following radical environmental change. *Academy of Management Journal, 43*, 837–853.

Avolio, B. J., Avey, J. B., & Quisenberry, D. (2010). Estimating return on leadership development investment. *The Leadership Quarterly, 21*, 633–644.

Avolio, B. J., Gardner, W. L., Walumbwa, F. O., Luthans, F., & Mayo, D. R. (2004). Unlocking the mask: A look at the process by which authentic leaders impact follower attitudes and behaviors. *The Leadership Quarterly, 15*, 801–823.

Avolio, B. J., & Hannah, S. T. (2008). Developmental readiness: Accelerating leader development. *Consulting Psychology Journal: Practice and Research, 60*, 331–247.

Avolio, B. J., & Hannah, S. T. (2009). Leader developmental readiness. *Industrial and Organizational Psychology: Perspectives on Science and Practice, 2*(3), 284–287.

Avolio, B. J., Reichard, R. J., Hannah, S. T., Walumbwa, F. O., & Chan, A. (2009). A meta-analytic review of leadership impact research: Experimental and quasi-experimental studies. *The Leadership Quarterly, 20,* 764–784.

Avolio, B. J., & Walumbwa, F. O. (2014). Authentic leadership theory, research, and practice: Steps taken and steps that remain. In D. Day (Ed.), *The Oxford handbook of leadership and organizations* (pp. 331–356). Oxford, UK: Oxford University Press.

Avolio, B. J., Walumbwa, F. O., & Weber, T. J. (2009). Leadership: Current theories, research, and future directions. *Annual Review of Psychology, 60*, 421–449.

Avolio, B. J., Wernsing, T. S., & Gardner, W. L. (2018). Revisiting the development and validation of the Authentic Leadership Questionaire: Analytical clarifications. *Journal of Management, 44*, 399–411.

Awamleh, R., & Gardner, W. L. (1999). Perceptions of leader charisma and effectiveness: The effects of vision content, delivery, and organizational performance. *The Leadership Quarterly, 10,* 345–373.

Axon, L., Friedman, E., & Jordan, K. (2015, July). Leading now: Critical capabilities for a complex world. *Harvard Business Publishing Corporate Learning*, 1–10. Retrieved from http://www.harvardbusiness.org/leading-now-critical-capabilities-complex-world

Ayman, R., & Korabik, K. (2010). Leadership: Why gender and culture matter. *American Psychologist, 65,* 157–170.

Ayman, R., & Lauritsen, M. (2018). Contingencies, context, situation, and leadership. In J. Antonakis & D. V. Day (Eds.), *The nature of leadership* (3rd ed., pp. 138–166). Los Angeles: Sage.

Babcock, L., & Laschever, S. (2003). *Women don't ask: Negotiation and the gender divide*. Princeton, NJ: Princeton University Press.

Baer, M., & Frese, M. (2003). Innovation is not enough: Climates for initiative and psychological safety, process innovations, and firm performance. *Journal of Organizational Behavior, 24,* 45–68.

Baird, L., Holland, P., & Deacon, S. (1999). Learning from action: Imbedding more learning into the performance fast enough to make a difference. *Organizational Dynamics, 27*(4), 19–32.

Baker, S. D. (2007). Followership: The theoretical foundations of a contemporary construct. *Journal of Leadership and Organizational Studies, 14,* 50–60.

Baker, S. (2011). Shaking up the Old Boys Club. *Bloomberg Markets,* July, 54–64.

Balakrishnan, M. R. (2007). Transformational Leadership – A Case Study. Bimaquest,VII(II). Retrieved from https://fbe.ubaya.ac.id (Accessed on January 21, 2019)

Baldwin, T. T., & Padgett, M. Y. (1993). Management development: A review and commentary. In C. L. Cooper & I. T. Robertson (Eds.), *International review of industrial and organizational psychology* (Vol. 8, pp. 35–85). New York: Wiley.

Bales, R. F. (1950). A set of categories for the analysis of small group interaction. *American Sociological Review, 15,* 257–263.

Balkundi, P., & Kilduff, M. (2005). The ties that lead: A social network approach to leadership. *The Leadership Quarterly, 17,* 419–439.

Baloff, N., & Doherty, E. M. (1989). Potential pitfalls in employee participation. *Organizational Dynamics, 18*(2), 51–62.

Baltes, B. B., Bauer, C. B., & Frensch, P. A. (2007). Does a structured free recall intervention reduce the effect of stereotypes on performance ratings and by what cognitive mechanism? *Journal of Applied Psychology, 92,* 151–164.

Bandura, A. (1986). *Social foundations of thought and action: A social cognitive theory.* Englewood Cliffs, NJ: Prentice Hall.

Bandura, A. (2000). Exercise of human agency through collective efficacy. *Current Directions in Psychological Science, 9,* 75–78.

Banker, R. D., Field, J. M., Schroeder, R. G., & Sinha, K. K. (1996). Impact of work teams on manufacturing performance: A longitudinal field study. *Academy of Management Journal, 39,* 867–890.

Banks, G. C., Engemann, K. N., Williams, C. E., Gooty, J., McCauley, K. D., & Medaugh, M. R. (2017). A meta-analytic review and future research agenda of charismatic leadership. *The Leadership Quarterly, 28*, 508–529.

Banks, G. C., McCauley, K. D., Gardner, W. L., & Guler, C. (2016). A meta-analytic review or authentic leadership and transformational leadership: A test for redundancy. *The Leadership Quarterly, 27*, 634–652.

Banks, G. C., Pollack, J. M., & Seers, A. (2016). Team coordination and organizational routines: Bottoms up—and top down. *Management Decision, 54*, 1059–1072.

Bantel, K. A., & Jackson, S. E. (1989). Top management and innovations in banking: Does the composition of the top team make a difference? *Strategic Management Journal, 10,* 107–112.

Barbuto, J. E., & Wheeler, D. W. (2006). Scale development and construct clarification of servant leadership. *Group & Organization Management, 31,* 300–326.

Barends, E., Janssen, B., ten Have, W., & ten Have, S. (2013). Effects of Change Interventions: What kind of evidence do we really have? *The Journal of Applied Behavioral Science, 50*(1), 5–27.

Barker, J. R. (1993). Tightening the iron cage: Concertive control in self-managing teams. *Administrative Science Quarterly,* 38, 408–437.

Barling, J., Weber, T., & Kelloway, E. K. (1996). Effects of transformational leadership training on attitudinal and financial outcomes: A field experiment. *Journal of Applied Psychology,* 81, 827–832.

Barnabas, A., & Clifford, P. S. (2012). Mahatma Gandhi an Indian model of servant leadership. *International Journal of Leadership Studies,* 7(2), 132–150.

Barnard, C. I. (1952). A definition of authority. In R. K. Merton, A. P. Gray, B. Hockey, & H. C. Selven (Eds.), *Reader in bureaucracy*. New York: Free Press.

Barney, J. B. (1991). Firm resources and sustained competitive advantage. *Journal of Management,* 17, 99–120.

Barney, J. B., Foss, N. J., & Lyngsie, J. (2018). The role of senior management in opportunity formation: Direct involvement or reactive selection? *Strategic Management Journal, 39,* 1325–1349.

Baron, R. A. (1989). Personality and organizational conflict: Effects of the Type A behavior pattern and self-monitoring. *Organizational Behavior and Human Decision Processes,* 44, 281–296.

Barreto, M., Ryan, M. K., & Schmitt, M. T. (2009). *The glass ceiling in the 21st century: Understanding barriers to gender equality*. Washington, DC: American Psychological Association.

Barreto, N. B., & Hogg, M. A. (2017). Evaluation of and support for group prototypical leaders: A meta-analysis of twenty years of empirical research. *Social Influence, 12*(1), 41–55.

Barrick, M. R., Stewart, G. L., Neubert, M. J., & Mount, M. K. (1998). Relating member ability and personality to work-team processes and team effectiveness. *Journal of Applied Psychology,* 83, 377–391.

Barry, D. (1991). Managing the bossless team: Lessons in distributed leadership. *Organizational Dynamics, 20*(1), 31–47.

Bartol, K. M., & Srivastava, A. (2002). Encouraging knowledge sharing: The role of organizational reward systems. *Journal of Leadership and Organizational Studies, 9*(1), 64–76.

Bartol, K. M., & Zhang, X. (2007). Networks and leadership development: Building linkages for capacity acquisition and capital accrual. *Human Resource Management Review, 17,* 388-401.

Basadur, M. (2004). Leading others to think innovatively together: Creative leadership. *The Leadership Quarterly, 15,* 103–121.

Bass, B. M. (1960). *Leadership, psychology, and organizational behavior*. New York: Harper.

Bass, B. M. (1985). *Leadership and performance beyond expectations.* New York: Free Press.

Bass, B. M. (1990). *Bass & Stogdill's handbook of leadership: Theory, research, and managerial applications* (3rd ed). New York: Free Press.

Bass, B. M. (2008). *The Bass handbook of leadership: Theory, research, and managerial applications* (4th ed). New York: Free Press.

Bass, B. M. (1996). *A new paradigm of leadership: An inquiry into transformational leadership.* Alexandria, VA: U.S. Army Research Institute for the Behavioral and Social Sciences.

Bass, B. M. (1997). Does the transactional-transformational paradigm transcend organizational and national boundaries? *American Psychologist,* 52, 130–139.

Bass, B. M., & Avolio, B. J. (1990a). Developing transformational leadership: 1992 and beyond. *Journal of European Industrial Training,* 14, 21–27.

Bass, B. M., & Avolio, B. J. (1990b). The implications of transactional and transformational leadership for individual, team, and organizational development. In W. Pasmore & R. W. Woodman (Eds.), *Research in organizational change and development,* vol. 4. Greenwich, CT: JAI Press, pp. 231–272.

Bass, B. M., & Avolio, B. J. (1994). *Improving organizational effectiveness through transformational leadership*. Thousand Oaks, CA: Sage.

Bass, B. M., & Avolio, B. J. (1997). *Full range leadership development manual for the multifactor leadership questionnaire*. Palo Alto, CA: Mindgarden.

Bass, B. M., Avolio, B. J., Jung, D. I., & Berson, Y. (2003). Predicting unit performance by assessing transformational and transactional leadership. *Journal of Applied Psychology,* 88, 207–218.

Bass, B. M., & Steidlmeier, P. (1999). Ethics, character, and authentic transformational leadership. *The Leadership Quarterly,* 10, 181–217.

Bass, B. M., Waldman, D. A., Avolio, B. J., & Bebb, M. (1987). Transformational leadership and the falling dominoes effect. *Group & Organization Studies,* 12 (1), 73–87.

Battilana, J., Gilmartin, M., Sengul, M., Pache, A.-C., & Alexander, J. A. (2010). Leadership competencies for implementing planned organizational change. *The Leadership Quarterly, 21*(3), 422–438.

Bauer, C. B., & Baltes, B. B. (2002). Reducing the effect of gender stereotypes on performance evaluations. *Sex Roles,* 47, 465–476.

Bauer, T. N., & Green, S. G., (1996). The development of leader-member exchange: A longitudinal test. *Academy of Management Journal,* 39, 1538–1567.

Bauer, T. N., & Green, S. G. (1998). Testing the combined effects of newcomer information seeking and manager behavior on socialization. *Journal of Applied Psychology,* 83, 72–83.

Baur, J. E., Haynie, J. J., Buckley, M. R., Palar, J. M., Novicevic, M. M., & Humphreys, J. H. (2018). When things go from bad to worse: The impact of relative contextual extremity on Benjamin Montgomery's positive leadership and psychological capital. *Journal of Leadership & Organizational Studies*, 25(3), 323–338.

Baum, R. J., Locke, E. A., & Kirkpatrick, S. (1998). A longitudinal study of the relation of vision and vision communication to venture growth in entrepreneurial firms. *Journal of Applied Psychology,* 83, 43–54.

Bauman, D. C. (2013). Leadership and the three faces of integrity. *The Leadership Quarterly, 24*(3), 414–426.

Beattie, R. S., Kim, S., Hagen, M. S., Egan, T. M., Ellinger, A. D., & Hamlin, R. G. (2014). Managerial coaching: A review of the empirical literature and development of a model to guide future practice. *Advances in Developing Human Resources, 16*(2), 184–201.

Becker, N., Höft, S., Holzenkamp, M., & Spinath, F. M. (2011). The predictive validity of assessment centers in German-speaking regions: A meta-analysis. *Journal of Personnel Psychology, 10*(2), 61–69.

Becker, T. E. (1998). Integrity in organizations: Beyond honesty and conscientiousness. *Academy of Management Review,* 23, 154–161.

Bedeian, A. G., & Day, D. V. (2004). Can chameleons lead? *The Leadership Quarterly, 15*, 687–718.

Bedi, A., Alpaslan, C. M., & Green, S. (2016). A meta-analytic review of ethical leadership outcomes and moderators. *Journal of Business Ethics, 139*, 517–536.

Beer, M. (1988). The critical path for change: Keys to success and failure in six companies. In R. H. Kilmann & T. J. Covin (Eds.), *Corporate transformation: Revitalizing organizations for a competitive world* (pp. 17–45). San Francisco: Jossey-Bass.

Beer, M. (2001). How to develop an organization capable of sustained high performance: Embrace the drive for results-capability development paradox. *Organizational Dynamics,* 29(4), 233–247.

Beer, M. (2011). Developing an effective organization: Intervention method, empirical evidence, and theory. *Research in Organizational Change and Development, 19*, 1–54.

Beer, M. (2014). Comments on "effects of change interventions: What kind of evidence do we really have?" *The Journal of Applied Behavioral Science, 50*, 28–33.

Beer, M., Eisenstat, R. A., & Spector, B. (1990). Why change programs don't produce change. *Harvard Business Review, 68*(6), 158–166.

Beer, M., & Nohria, N. (2000). Cracking the code of change. *Harvard Business Review, 78*(3), 133–141.

Behrendt, P., Matz, S., & Göritz, A. S. (2017). An integrative model of leadership behavior. *The Leadership Quarterly, 28*, 229–244.

Belgard, W. P., Fisher, K. K., & Rayner, S. R. (1988). Vision, opportunity, and tenacity: Three informal processes that influence formal transformation. In R. H. Kilmann & T. J. Covin (Eds.), *Corporate transformation: Revitalizing organizations for a competitive world* (pp. 131–151). San Francisco: Jossey-Bass.

Bell, B. S., & Kozlowski, S. W. (2002). A typology of virtual teams: Implications of effective leadership. *Group & Organization Management, 27,* 14–49.

Bell, E. L., & Nkomo, S. M. (2001). *Our separate ways: Black and white women and the struggle for professional identity*. Boston: Harvard Business School Press.

Bell, S. T., Villado, A. J., Lukasik, M. A., Belau, L., & Briggs, A. L. (2011). Getting specific about demographic diversity variable and team performance relationships: A meta-analysis. *Journal of Management, 37*, 709–743.

Bendahan, S., Zehnder, C., Pralong, F., & Antonakis, J. (2015). Leader corruption depends on power and testosterone. *The Leadership Quarterly, 26,* 101–122.

Benn, S., Teo, S. T. T., & Martin, A. (2015). Employee participation and engagement in working for the environment. *Personnel Review, 44*, 492–510.

Benschop, Y., Holgersson, C., van den Brink, M., & Wahl, A. (2015). Future challenges for practices of diversity management in organizations. In R. Bendl, I. Bleijenbergh, E. Henttonen, & A. J. Mills (Eds.), *The Oxford handbook of diversity in organizations* (pp. 553–574). Oxford, UK: Oxford University Press.

Benne, K. D., & Sheats, P. (1948). Functional roles of group members. *Journal of Social Issues, 4*(2), 41–49.

Benner, M. J., & Tushman, M. L. (2003). Exploitation, exploration, and process management. The productivity dilemma revisited. *Academy of Management Review, 28,* 238–256.

Bennis, W. G. (1959). Leadership theory and administrative behavior: The problem of authority. *Administrative Science Quarterly, 4,* 259–301.

Bennis, W. G., & Nanus, B. (1985). *Leaders: The strategies for taking charge*. New York: Harper & Row.

Bergman, J. Z., Rentsch, J. R., Small, E. E., Davenport, S. W., & Bergman, S. M. (2012). The shared leadership process in decision-making teams. *The Journal of Social Psychology, 152*, 17–42.

Berkowitz, L. (1953). Sharing leadership in small decision-making groups. *Journal of Abnormal and Social Psychology, 48*, 231–238.

Berson, Y., Nemanich, L. A., Waldman, D. A., Galvin, B. M., & Keller, R. T. (2006). Leadership and organizational learning: A multiple levels perspective. *The Leadership Quarterly, 17*, 577–594.

Berson, Y., Shamir, B., Avolio, B. J., & Popper, M. (2001). The relationship between vision strength, leadership style, and context. *The Leadership Quarterly, 12*, 53–73.

Beu, D. S., & Buckley, M. R. (2004). This is war: How the politically astute achieve crimes of obedience through the use of moral disengagement. *The Leadership Quarterly, 15*, 551–568.

Beyer, J. M. (1999). Taming and promoting charisma to change organizations. *The Leadership Quarterly, 10*, 307–330.

Bezrukova, K., Thatcher, S. M. B., Jehn, K. A., & Spell, C. S. (2012). The effects of alignments: Examining group faultlines, organizational cultures, and performance. *Journal of Applied Psychology, 97*, 77–92.

Bhal, K. T., & Dadhich, A. (2011). Impact of ethical leadership and leader–member exchange on whistle blowing: The moderating impact of the moral intensity of the issue. *Journal of Business Ethics, 103*, 485–496.

Bird, A., & Mendenhall, M. E. (2016). From cross-cultural management to global leadership: Evolution and adaptation. *Journal of World Business, 51*, 115–126.

Bisoux, T. (2006). The change artist. *BizEd*, November–December, 18–24.

Bjornali, E. S., Knockaert, M., & Erikson, T. (2016). The impact of top management team characteristics and board service involvement on team effectiveness in high-tech start-ups. *Long Range Planning: International Journal of Strategic Management, 49*, 447–463.

Blake, R. R., & Mouton, J. S. (1964). *The managerial grid*. Houston: Gulf Publishing.

Blake-Beard, S. D., Murrell, A., & Thomas, D. (2007). Unfinished business: The impact of race on understanding mentoring relationships. In B. R. Ragins & K. E. Kram (Eds.), *The handbook of mentoring at work* (pp. 223–247). Thousand Oaks, CA: Sage.

Blankenship, L. V., & Miles, R. E. (1968). Organizational structure and managerial decision making. *Administrative Science Quarterly, 13*, 106–120.

Blickle, G., Witzki, A., & Schneider, P. B. (2009). Self-initiated mentoring and career sucess: A predictive field study. *Journal of Vocational Behavior, 74*(1), 94–101.

Bliese, P. D., Halverson, R. R., & Schriesheim, C. A. (2002). Benchmarking multilevel methods in leadership: The articles, the model, and the data set. *The Leadership Quarterly, 13*, 3–14.

Bligh, M. C., Kohles, J. C., & Pillai, R. (2011). Romancing leadership: Past, present, and future. *The Leadership Quarterly, 22*, 1058–1077.

Blickle, G., Meurs, J. A., Wihler, A., Ewen, C., & Peiseler, A. K. (2014). Leader inquisitiveness, political skill, and follower attributions of leader charisma and effectiveness: Test of a moderated mediation model. *International Journal of Selection and Assessment, 22*, 272–285.

Block, J. (1995). A contrarian view of the five-factor approach to personality description. *Psychological Bulletin, 117*, 187–215.

Block, P. (1993). *Stewardship: Choosing service over self-interest*. San Francisco: Barrette-Koehler Publishers.

Blume, B. D., Ford, J. K., Baldwin, T. T., & Huang, J. L. (2010). Transfer of training: A meta-analytic review. *Journal of Management, 36*, 1065–1105.

Boal, K. B., & Hooijberg, R. (2001). Strategic leadership research: Moving on. *The Leadership Quarterly, 11,* 515–549.

Boddy, C. (2012). The Nominal Group Technique: An aid to brainstorming ideas in research. *Qualitative Market Research: An International Journal, 15*(1), 6–18.

Boehm, V. R. (1985). Using assessment centers for management development—Five applications. *Journal of Management Development, 4*(4), 40–51.

Boehm, S. A., Dwertmann, D. J. G., Bruch, H., & Shamir, B. (2015). The missing link? Investigating organizational identity strength and transformational leadership climate as mechanisms that connect CEO charisma with firm performance. *The Leadership Quarterly, 26,* 156–171.

Bolden, R. (2011). Distributed leadership in organizations: A review of theory and research. *International Journal of Management Reviews, 13,* 251–269.

Bolino, M., Long, D., & Turnley, W. (2016). Impression management in organizations: Critical questions, answers, and areas for future research. *Annual Review of Organizational Psychology and Organizational Behavior, 3,* 377–406.

Bolino, M. C., Kacmar, K. M., Turnley, W. H., & Gilstrap, J. B. (2008). A multi-level review of impression management motives and behaviors. *Journal of Management, 34,* 1080–1109.

Bono, J. E., & Judge, T. A. (2004). Personality and transformational and transactional leadership: A meta-analysis. *Journal of Applied Psychology, 89,* 901–910.

Book, E. W. (2000). *Why the best man for the job is a woman: The unique female qualities of leadership*. New York: Harper Business.

Bommer, W. H., Rich, G. A., & Rubin, R. S. (2005). Changing attitudes about change: Longitudinal effects of transformational leader behavior on employee cynicism about organizational change. *Journal of Organizational Behavior, 26,* 733–753.

Boot, A. (2011, December 17). Cross-cultural leadership: How misinterpretations of dishonesty can destroy team alignment. Retrieved from https://leadershipwatch-aadboot.com/2011/12/17/cross-cultural-leadership-how-misinterpretations-of-dishonesty-can-destroy-team-alignment/. Used with Permission.

Bouchard, T., Lykken, D. T., McGue, A., Segal, N. L., & Tellegen, A. (1990). Sources of human psychological differences: The Minnesota study of twins reared apart. *Science, 250,* 223–228.

Boumgarden, P., Nickerson, J., & Zenger, T. R. (2012). Sailing into the wind: Exploring the relationships among ambidexterity, vacillation, and organizational performance. *Strategic Management Journal, 33,* 587–610.

Bowen, D. E., & Lawler, E. E. (1995). Empowering service employees. *MIT Sloan Management Review, 36*(4), 73–84.

Bowers, D. G., & Seashore, S. E. (1966). Predicting organizational effectiveness with a four-factor theory of leadership. *Administrative Science Quarterly, 11,* 238–263.

Bowles, S., Cunningham, C. J. L., De La Rosa, G. M., & Picano, J. (2007). Coaching leaders in middle and executive management: Goals, performance, buy-in. *Leadership & Organization Development Journal, 28,* 388–408.

Boyacigiller, N., & Adler, N. (1991). The parochial dinosaur: Organizational science in a global context. *Academy of Management Review, 16,* 262–290.

Boyatzis, R. E. (1982). *The competent manager: A model for effective performance.* New York: Wiley.

Boyce, L. A., Zaccaro, S. J., & Wisecarver, M. Z. (2010). Propensity for self-development of leadership attributes: Understanding, predicting, and supporting performance of leader self-development. *The Leadership Quarterly, 21,* 159–178.

Boysen-Rotelli, S. (2018). *An introduction to professional and executive coaching*. Charlotte, NC: Information Age Publishing.

Bracken, D. W. (1994). Straight talk about multirater feedback. *Training and Development, 48*(9), 44–52.

Bracken, D. W., & Rose, D. S. (2011). When does 360-degree feedback create behavior change? And how would we know it when it does? *Journal of Business and Psychology, 26*, 183–192.

Braddy, P. W., Gooty, J., Fleenor, J. W., & Yammarino, F. J. (2014). Leader behaviors and career derailment potential: A multi-analytic method examination of rating source and self-other agreement. *The Leadership Quarterly, 25*, 373–390.

Bradford, D. L., & Cohen, A. R. (1984). *Managing for excellence: The guide to developing high performance organizations*. New York: John Wiley.

Bradford, L. P. (1976). *Making meetings work*. La Jolla, CA: University Associates.

Bragg, J., & Andrews, I. R. (1973). Participative decision making: An experimental study in a hospital. *Journal of Applied Behavioral Science, 9*, 727–735.

Brass, D. J. (1984). Being in the right place: A structural analysis of individual differences in an organization. *Administrative Science Quarterly, 29*, 518–539.

Brass, D. J. (1985). Technology and the structuring of jobs: Employee satisfaction, performance, and influence. *Organizational Behavior and Human Decision Processes, 35*, 216–240.

Bray, D. W., Campbell, R. J., & Grant, D. L. (1974). *Formative years in business: A long-term AT&T study of managerial lives*. New York: John Wiley.

Brenner, O. C., Tomkiewicz, J., & Schein, V. E. (1989). The relationship between sex role stereotypes and requisite management characteristics revisited. *Academy of Management Journal, 32*, 662–669.

Brescoll, V. L. (2016). Leading with their hearts? How gender stereotypes of emotion lead to biased evaluations of female leaders. *The Leadership Quarterly, 27*, 415–428.

Breuer, C., Hüffmeier, J., & Hertel, G. (2016). Does trust matter more in virtual teams? A meta-analysis of trust and team effectiveness considering virtuality and documentation as moderators. *Journal of Applied Psychology, 101*, 1151–1177.

Brief, A. P., Schuler, R. S., & Van Sell, M. (1981). *Managing job stress*. Boston: Little Brown.

Brodbeck, F. C., & Eisenbeiss, S. A. (2014). Cross-cultural and global leadership. In D. V. Day (Ed.), *The Oxford handbook of leadership and organizations* (pp. 657–682). Oxford, UK: Oxford University Press.

Bromiley, P., & Rau, D. (2015). Social, behavioral, and cognitive influences on upper echelons during strategy process: A literature review. *Journal of Management, 42*, 174–202.

Brown, D. J., & Lord, R. G. (1999). The utility of experimental research in the study of transformational and charismatic leadership. *The Leadership Quarterly, 10*, 531–539.

Brown, M. E., & Treviño, L. K. (2006a). Socialized charismatic leadership values congruence and deviance in work groups. *Journal of Applied Psychology, 91*, 954–962.

Brown, M. E., & Treviño, L. K. (2006b). Ethical leadership: A review and future directions. *The Leadership Quarterly, 17*, 595–616.

Brown, M. E., & Treviño, L. K. (2014). Do role models matter? An investigation of role modeling as an antecedent of perceived ethical leadership. *Journal of Business Ethics, 122*, 587–598.

Brown, M. E., Treviño, L. K., & Harrison, D. A. (2005). Ethical leadership: A social learning perspective for construct development and testing. *Organizational Behavior and Human Decision Processes, 97*, 117–134.

Brown, M. H., & Hosking, D. M. (1986). Distributed leadership and skilled performance as successful organization in social movements. *Human Relations, 39*, 65–79.

Brown, M. W., & Gioia, D. A. (2002). Making things click: Distributive leadership in an online division of an offline organization. *The Leadership Quarterly, 13*, 397–419.

Brown, W., & May, D. (2012). Organizational change and development: The efficacy of transformational leadership training. *Journal of Management Development, 31*, 520–536.

Browne, K. R. (2006). Evolved sex differences and occupational segregation. *Journal of Organizational Behavior, 27,* 143–162.

Bruckmüller, S., Ryan, M. K., Rink, F., & Haslam, S. A. (2014). Beyond the glass ceiling: The glass cliff and its lessons for organizational policy. *Social Issues and Policy Review, 8*(1), 202–232.

Bryman, A. (1992). *Charisma and leadership in organizations*. London: Sage.

Bryman, A. (1993). Charismatic leadership in business organizations: Some neglected issues. *The Leadership Quarterly, 4,* 289–304.

Bryman, A. (2004). Qualitative research on leadership: A critical but appreciative view. *The Leadership Quarterly, 15,* 729–769.

Bryman, A., Bresnen, M., Beardworth, A., & Keil, T. (1988). Qualitative research and the study of leadership. *Human Relations, 41,* 13–30.

Buengeler, C., Homan, A. C., & Voelpel, S. C. (2016). The challenge of being a young manager: The effects of contingent reward and participative leadership on team-level turnover depend on leader age. *Journal of Organizational Behavior, 37*, 1224–1245.

Buengeler, C., Leroy, H., & De Stobbeleir, K. (2018). How leaders shape the impact of HR's diversity practices on employee inclusion. *Human Resource Management Review, 28,* 289–303.

Bunker, K. W., & Webb, A. D. (1992). *Learning how to learn from experience: Impact of stress and coping*. Technical Report No. 154. Greensboro, NC: Center for Creative Leadership.

Burke, C. S., Stagl, K. C., Klein, C., Goodwin, G. F., Salas, E., & Halpin, S. M. (2006). What type of leadership behaviors are functional in teams: A meta-analysis. *The Leadership Quarterly, 17,* 288–307.

Burke, R. J., Wier, T., & Duncan, G. (1976). Informal helping relationships in work organizations. *Academy of Management Journal, 19,* 370–377.

Burke, W. (2002). *Organization change: Theory and practice*. Thousand Oaks: Sage.

Burns, J. M. (1978). *Leadership*. New York: Harper & Row.

Burns, J. M. (2004). *Transforming leadership: A new pursuit of happiness*. New York: Grove Press.

Buss, D. M. (2016). *Evolutionary psychology: The new science of the mind* (5th ed.). New York: Routledge.

Butler, M. J. R., O'Broin, H. L. R., Lee, N., & Senior, C. (2016). How organizational cognitive neuroscience can deepen understanding of managerial decision-making: A review of the recent literature and future directions. *International Journal of Management Reviews, 18*, 542–559.

Cain, S. (2012). *Quiet: The power of introverts in a world that can't stop talking*. New York: Crown Publishers.

Calder, B. J. (1977). An attribution theory of leadership. In B. M. Staw & G. R. Salancik (Eds.), *New direction in organizational behavior.* Chicago: St. Clair Press.

Caligiuri, P. (2013). Developing culturally agile global business leaders. *Organizational Dynamics, 42*(3), 175–182.

Caligiuri, P., & Tarique, I. (2012). Dynamic cross-cultural competencies and global leadership effectiveness. *Journal of World Business, 47,* 612–622.

Cameron, K. S., & Quinn, R. E. (2011). *Diagnosing and changing organizational culture: Based on the competing values framework* (3rd ed.). San Francisco: Jossey-Bass.

Camp, R. C. (1989). *Benchmarking: The search for industry best practices that lead to superior performance.* Milwaukee: ASQC Quality Press.

Cannella, A. A., Jr., & Monroe, M. J. (1997). Contrasting perspectives on strategic leaders: Toward a more realistic view of top managers. *Journal of Management, 23,* 213–237.

Cannella, A. A., Jr., Park, J., & Lee, H. (2008). Top management team functional background diversity and firm performance: Examining the roles of team member co-location and environmental uncertainty. *Academy of Management Journal, 51,* 768–784.

Cannon-Bowers, J. A., Salas, E., & Converse, S. A. (1993). Shared mental models in expert team decision making. In N. J. Caltellan, Jr. (Ed.), *Current issues in individual and group decision making* (pp. 221–246). Hillsdale, NJ: Lawrence Erlbaum.

Cantor, N., & Kihlstrom, J. F. (1987). *Personality and social intelligence*. Englewood Cliffs, NJ: Prentice Hall.

Carl, D., Gupta, V., & Javidan, M. (2004). Power distance. In R. J. House, P. J. Hanges, M. Javidan, P. W. Dorfman & V. Gupta (Eds.), *Culture, leadership, and organizations: The GLOBE study of 62 societies* (pp. 513–563). Thousand Oaks, CA: Sage.

Carli, L. L., & Eagly, A. H. (2018). Leadership and gender. In J. Antonakis & D. V. Day (Eds.), *The nature of leadership* (pp. 244–271). Los Angeles: Sage.

Carmeli, A., Gelbard, R., & Gefen, D. (2010). The importance of innovation leadership in cultivating strategic fit and enhancing firm performance. *The Leadership Quarterly, 21,* 339–349.

Carmeli, A., & Schaubroeck, J. (2006). Top management team behavioral integration, decision quality, and organizational decline. *The Leadership Quarterly, 17,* 441–453.

Carmeli, A., Schaubroeck, J., & Tishler, A. (2011). How CEO empowering leadership shapes top management team processes: Implications for firm performance. *The Leadership Quarterly, 22,* 399–411.

Carroll, M. (2006). *Awake at work: 35 Practical Buddhist principles for discovering clarity and balance in the midst of work's chaos*. Boston: Shambhala.

Carroll, S. J., Jr., & Gillen, D. J. (1987). Are the classical management functions useful in describing managerial work? *Academy of Management Review, 12,* 38–51.

Carr-Ruffino, N. (1993). *The promotable woman: Advancing through leadership skills*. Belmont, CA: Wadsworth.

Carson, J., Tesluk, P., & Marrone, J. (2007). Shared leadership in teams: An investigation of antecedent conditions and performance. *Academy of Management Journal, 50,* 1217–1234.

Carson, P. P., Lanier, P. A., Carson, K. D., & Guidry, B. N. (2000). Clearing a path through the management fashion jungle: some preliminary trailblazing. *Academy of Management Journal, 43,* 1143–1158.

Carson, T. L. (2003). Self-interest and business ethics: Some lessons of the recent corporate scandals. *Journal of Business Ethics, 43,* 389–394.

Carsten, M. K., Uhl-Bien, M., West, B. J., Patera, J. L., & McGregor, R. (2010). Exploring social constructions of followership: A qualitative study. *The Leadership Quarterly, 21,* 543–562.

Carte, T. A., Chidambaram, L., & Becker, A. (2006). Emergent leadership in self-managed virtual teams: A longitudinal study of concentrated and shared leadership behaviors. *Group Decision and Negotiation, 15,* 323–343.

Carter, D. R., & DeChurch, L. A. (2014). Leadership in multiteam systems: A network perspective. In D. V. Day (Ed.), *The Oxford handbook of leadership and organizations* (pp. 482–502). Oxford, UK: Oxford University Press.

Carter, S. M., & Greer, C. R. (2013). Strategic leadership: Values, styles, and organizational performance. *Journal of Leadership & Organizational Studies, 20,* 375–393.

Carton, A. M., & Cummings, J. N. (2012). A theory of subgroups in work teams. *The Academy of Management Review, 37,* 441–470.

Carton, A. M., & Cummings, J. N. (2013). The impact of subgroup type and subgroup configurational properties on work team performance. *Journal of Applied Psychology, 98,* 732–758.

Cashman, J., Dansereau, F., Jr., Graen, G., & Haga, W. J. (1976). Organizational understructure and leadership: A longitudinal investigation of the managerial role-making process. *Organizational Behavior and Human Performance, 15,* 278–296.

Castelnovo, O., Popper, M., & Koren, D. (2017). The innate code of charisma. *The Leadership Quarterly, 28*, 543–554.

Catalyst (2018). Women in the workforce: United States. http://www.catalyst.org/knowledge/women-united-states (accessed July 6, 2018).

Cavaleri, S., & Fearon, D. (1996). *Managing in organizations that learn*. Cambridge, MA: Blackwell Publishers.

Caza, A., & Jackson, B. (2011). Authentic leadership. In A. Bryman, D. Collinson, K. Grint, B. Jackson, & M. Uhl-Bien (Eds.). *The Sage handbook of leadership* (pp. 352–364). London: Sage.

Cha, S. E., & Edmondson, A. C. (2006). When values backfire: Leadership, attribution, and disenchantment in a values-driven organization. *The Leadership Quarterly, 17,* 57–78.

Chaleff, I. (1995). *The courageous follower: Standing up to and for our leaders.* San Francisco: Berrett-Koehler Publishers.

Chamberlin, M., Newton, D. W., & Lepine, J. A. (2017). A meta-analysis of voice and its promotive and prohibitive forms: Identification of key associations, distinctions, and future research directions. *Personnel Psychology, 70,* 11–71.

Chao, G. T., Walz, P. M., & Gardner, P. D. (1992). Formal and informal mentorships: A comparison on mentoring functions contrasted with nonmentored counterparts. *Personnel Psychology, 45,* 619–636.

Chappel, T. (1993). *The soul of a business: Managing for profit and the common good.* New York: Bantam Books.

Chapter 4: Benchmarking in Manufacturing Sector. (n.d.). Retrieved from https://shodhganga.inflibnet.ac.in (Accessed on January 15, 2019)

Charbonneau, D., Barling, J., & Kelloway, E. K. (2001). Transformational leadership and sports performance: The mediating role of intrinsic motivation. *Journal of Applied Social Psychology, 31,* 1521–1534.

Chaston, I., Badger, B., Mangles, T., & Sadler-Smith, E. (2001). Organizational learning style, competencies, and learning systems in small, UK manufacturing firms. *International Journal of Operations and Production Management, 21,* 1417–1432.

Chatterjee, A., & Hambrick, D. C. (2007). It's all about me: Narcissistic CEOs and their effects on company strategy and performance. *Administrative Science Quarterly, 52,* 351–386.

Chatterjee, A. A., & Hambrick, D. C. (2011). Executive personality, capability cues, and risk taking: How narcissitic CEOs react to their successes and stumbles. *Administrative Science Quarterly, 56*, 202–237.

Chen, A. S.-Y., & Hou, Y.-H. (2016). The effects of ethical leadership, voice behavior and climates for innovation on creativity: A moderated mediation examination. *The Leadership Quarterly, 27*, 1–13.

Chen, C.-Y., & Li, C.-I. (2013). Assessing the spiritual leadership effectiveness: The contribution of follower's self-concept and preliminary tests for moderation of culture and managerial position. *The Leadership Quarterly, 24*, 240–255.

Chen, C.-Y., & Yang, C.-F. (2012). The impact of spiritual leadership on organizational citizenship behavior: A multi-sample analysis. *Journal of Business Ethics, 105*, 107–114.

Chen, C. Y., Yang, C. Y., & Li, C. I. (2012). Spiritual leadership, follower mediators, and organizational outcomes: Evidence from three industries across two major Chinese societies. *Journal of Applied Social Psychology, 42*, 890–938.

Chen, G., & Bliese, P. D. (2002). The role of different levels of leadership in predicting self and collective efficacy: Evidence for discontinuity. *Journal of Applied Psychology, 87,* 549–556.

Chen, G., Sharma, P. N., Edinger, S. K., Shapiro, D. L., & Farh, J.-L. (2011). Motivating and demotivating forces in teams: Cross-level influences of empowering leadership and relationship conflict. *Journal of Applied Psychology, 96*, 541–557.

Chin, J. L. (2014). Women and leadership. In D. V. Day (Ed.), *The Oxford handbook of leadership and organizations* (pp. 733–753). Oxford, UK: Oxford University Press.

Chiu, S.-c., Johnson, R. A., Hoskisson, R. E., & Pathak, S. (2016). The impact of CEO successor origin on corporate divestiture scale and scope change. *The Leadership Quarterly, 27*, 617–633.

Chng, D. H. M., Rodgers, M. S., Shih, E., & Song, X.-B. (2015). Leaders' impression management during organizational decline: The roles of publicity, image concerns, and incentive compensation. *The Leadership Quarterly, 26*, 270–285.

Choi, Y., & Mai-Dalton, R. R. (1998). On the leadership function of self-sacrifice. *The Leadership Quarterly, 9*, 475–501.

Choi, Y., & Mai-Dalton, R. R. (1999). The model of followers' responses to self-sacrificial leadership: An empirical test. *The Leadership Quarterly, 10*, 397–421.

Chokkar, J. S., Brodbeck, F. C., & House, R. J. (2007). *Culture and leadership across the world: The GLOBE book of in-depth studies of 25 societies*. Mahwah, NJ: Erlbaum.

Chrobot-Mason, D., Ruderman, M. N., & Nishii, L. H. (2014). Leadership in a diverse workplace. In D. V. Day (Ed.), *The Oxford handbook of leadership and organizations* (pp. 683–708). Oxford, UK: Oxford University Press.

Chughtai, A., Byrne, M., & Flood, B. (2015). Linking ethical leadership to employee well-being: The role of trust in supervisor. *Journal of Business Ethics, 128*, 653–663.

Chun, J. U., Sosik, J. J., & Yun, N. Y. (2012). A longitudinal study of mentor and protégé outcomes in formal mentoring relationships. *Journal of Organizational Behavior, 33*, 1071–1094.

Chun, J. U., Yammarino, F., Dionne, S. D., Sosik, J. J., & Moon, H. K. (2009). Leadership across hierarchical levels: Multiple levels of management and multiple levels of analysis. *The Leadership Quarterly, 20*, 689–707.

Ciulla, J. B. (2018). Ethics and effectiveness: The nature of good leadership. In J. Antonakis & D. V. Day (Eds.), (pp. 438–468). Los Angeles: Sage.

Clair, J. A., & Dufresne, R. L. (2007). Changing poison into medicine: How companies can experience positive transformation from a crisis. *Organizational Dynamics, 36*(1), 63–77.

Clark, L. A., & Lyness, K. S. (1991). Succession planning as a strategic activity at Citicorp. In L. W. Foster (Ed.), *Advances in applied business strategy* (Vol. 2, pp. 205–224). Greenwich, CT: JAI Press.

Clarke, N., & Higgs, M. (2016). How strategic focus relates to the delivery of leadership training and development. *Human Resource Management, 55*, 541–565.

Coch, L., & French, J. R. P., Jr. (1948). Overcoming resistance to change. *Human Relations, 1*, 512–532.

Cockburn, C. (1991). *In the way of women*. London: Macmillan.

Coda, V., & Mollona, E. (2010). The feedback structure process and top management's role in shaping emerging strategic behavior. In P. Maxzzola & F. W. Kellermanns (Eds.), *Handbook of research on strategy process* (pp. 109–141). Cheltenhaum, UK: Edward Elgar.

Cogliser, C. C., Schriesheim, C. A., Scandura, T. A., & Gardner, W. L. (2009). Balance in leader and follower perceptions of leader-member exchange: Relationships with performance and work attitudes. *The Leadership Quarterly, 20*, 452–465.

Cohen, A., & Bradford, D. (1989). Influence without authority: The use of alliances, reciprocity, and exchange to accomplish work. *Organizational Dynamics, 17*(3), 5–17.

Cohen, M. D., & March, J. G. (1974). *Leadership and ambiguity: The American college president*. New York: McGraw-Hill.

Cohen, S. G., & Bailey, D. E. (1997). What makes teams work: Group effectiveness research from the shop floor to the executive suite. *Journal of Management, 23,* 239–290.

Cohen, S. G., Chang, L., & Ledford, G. E. (1997). A hierarchical construct of self-management leadership and its relationship to quality of work life and perceived work group effectiveness. *Personnel Psychology, 50,* 275–308.

Cohen, S. G., & Ledford, G. E., Jr. (1994). The effectiveness of self-managing teams: A quasi-experiment. *Human Relations, 47,* 13–43.

Colbert, A. E., Kristof-Brown, A. L., Bradley, B. H., & Barrick, M. R. (2008). CEO transformational leadership: The role of goal importance congruence in top management teams. *Academy of Management Journal, 51,* 81–96.

Collins, D. B., & Holton, E. F. (2004). The effectiveness of managerial leadership development programs: A meta-analysis of studies from 1982 to 2001. *Human Resource Development Quarterly, 15,* 217–248.

Collins, J. C. (2001a). *Good to great*. New York: Harper Collins.

Collins, J. C. (2001b). Level 5 leadership: The triumph of humility and fierce resolve. *Harvard Business Review, 79*(1), 66–76.

Collins, J. C., & Porras, J. I. (1997). *Built to last: Successful habits of visionary companies*. New York: HarperBusiness.

Collinson, D. (2006). Rethinking followership: A post-structuralist analysis of follower identities. *The Leadership Quarterly, 17,* 179–189.

Colquitt, J. A., Conlon, D. E., Wesson, M. J., Porter, C. O. L. H., & Ng, K. Y. (2001). Justice at the millennium: A meta-analytic review of 25 years of organizational justice research. *Journal of Applied Psychology, 86,* 425–445.

Colquitt, J. A., Scott, B. A., Rodell, J. B., Long, D. M., Zapata, C. P., Conlon, D. E., & Wesson, M. J. (2013). Justice at the millennium, a decade later: A meta-analytic test of social exchange and affect-based perspectives. *Journal of Applied Psychology, 98,* 199–236.

Combe, I. A., & Carrington, D. J. (2015). Leaders' sensemaking under crises: Emerging cognitive consensus over time within management teams. *The Leadership Quarterly, 26,* 307–322.

Conger, J. A. (1989). *The charismatic leader: Behind the mystique of exceptional leadership*. San Francisco, CA: Jossey-Bass.

Conger, J. A. (1992). *Learning to lead: The art of transforming managers into leaders*. San Francisco, CA: Jossey-Bass.

Conger, J. A. (1993). The brave new world of leadership training. *Organizational Dynamics, 21*(3), 46–58.

Conger, J. A. (1993). Personal growth training: Snake oil or pathway to leadership? *Organizational Dynamics, 22*(1), 19–30.

Conger, J. A., & Kanungo, R. (1987). Toward a behavioral theory of charismatic leadership in organizational settings. *Academy of Management Review, 12,* 637–647.

Conger, J. A., & Kanungo, R. N. (1988). The empowerment process: Integrating theory and practice. *Academy of Management Review, 13,* 471–482.

Conger, J. A., & Kanungo, R. N. (1994). Charismatic leadership in organizations: Perceived behavioral attributes and their measurement. *Journal of Organizational Behavior, 15,* 439–452.

Conger, J. A., & Kanungo, R. (1998). *Charismatic leadership in organizations.* Thousand Oaks, CA: Sage Publications.

Connelly, M. S., Gilbert, J. A., Zaccaro, S. J., Marks, M. A., & Mumford, M. D. (2000). Exploring the relationship of leadership skills and knowledge to leader performance. *The Leadership Quarterly, 11,* 65–86.

Connerley, M. L., & Pedersen, P. B. (2005). *Leadership in a diverse and multicultural environment: Developing awareness, knowledge, and skills.* Thousand Oaks, CA: Sage.

Connor, D. R. (1995). *Managing at the speed of change: How resilient managers succeed and prosper where others fail.* New York: Villard Books.

Cooper, C. D., Scandura, T. A., & Schriesheim, C. A. (2005). Looking forward but learning from our past: Potential challenges to developing authentic leadership theory and authentic leaders. *The Leadership Quarterly, 16,* 475–493.

Cooper, M. R., & Wood, M. T. (1974). Effects of member participation and commitment in group decision making on influence, satisfaction, and decision riskiness. *Journal of Applied Psychology, 59,* 127–134.

Cordery, J. L., Mueller, W. S., & Smith, L. M. (1991). Attitudinal and behavioral effects of autonomous group working: A longitudinal field study. *Academy of Management Journal, 34,* 464–476.

Costa, A. C., Fulmer, C. A., & Anderson, N. R. (2018). Trust in work teams: An integrative review, multilevel model, and future directions. *Journal of Organizational Behavior, 39,* 169–184.

Cotton, J. L. (1993). *Employee involvement: Methods for improving performance and work attitudes.* Newbury Park, CA: Sage.

Cotton, J. L., Vollrath, D. A., Froggatt, K. L., Lengnick-Hall, M. L., & Jennings, K. R. (1988). Employee participation: Diverse forms and different outcomes. *Academy of Management Review, 13,* 8–22.

Courtright, S. H., McCormick, B. W., Mistry, S., & Wang, J. (2017). Quality charters or quality members? A control theory perspective on team charters and team performance. *Journal of Applied Psychology, 102,* 1462–1470.

Cox, C. J., & Cooper, C. L. (1989). *High flyers: An anatomy of managerial success.* Oxford: Basil Blackwell.

Cox, J. F., Pearce, C. L., & Perry, M. L. (2003). Toward a model of shared leadership and distributed influence in the innovation process: How shared leadership can enhance new product development, team dynamics, and effectiveness. In C. L. Pearce & J. A. Conger (Eds.), *Shared leadership: Reframing the hows and whys of leadership* (pp. 48–76). Thousand Oaks, CA: Sage.

Cox, T., Jr. (2001). *Creating the multicultural organization: A strategy for capturing the power of diversity.* San Francisco, CA: Jossey-Bass.

Cox, T. H., & Blake, S. (1991). Managing cultural diversity: Implications for organizational competitiveness. *Academy of Management Executive, 5*(3), 45–56.

Crant, J. M., & Bateman, T. S. (1993). Assignment of credit and blame for performance outcomes. *Academy of Management Journal, 36,* 7–27.

Cresswell, J. W., & Cresswell, J. D. (2018). *Research design: Qualitative, quantitative, and mixed methods approaches* (5th ed.). Thousand Oaks, CA: Sage.

Cronin, M. A., & Weingart, L. R. (2007). Representational gaps, information processing, and conflict in functionally diverse teams. *Academy of Management Review, 32,* 761–773.

Crook, T. R., Todd, S. Y., Combs, J. G., Woehr, D. J., & Ketchen, D. J., Jr. (2011). Does human capital matter? A meta-analysis of the relationship between human capital and firm performance. *Journal of Applied Psychology, 96*, 443–456.

Cropanzano, R., Dasborough, M. T., & Weiss, H. M. (2017). Affective events and the development of leader-member exchange. *Academy of Management Review, 42*, 233–258.

Crossan, M., Lane, H., & White, R. E. (1999). An organizational learning framework: From intuition to institution.*Academy of Management, 42*, 1964–1991.

Dachler, H. P. (1984). On refocusing leadership from a social systems perspective of management. In J. G. Hunt, D. Hosking, C. A. Schriesheim, & R. Stewart (Eds.), *Leaders* *and managers: International perspectives on managerial behavior and leadership* (pp. 100–108). New York: Pergamon Press.

Dachler, P. (1992). Management and leadership as relational phenomena. In M. V. Cranach, W. Doise, & G. Mugny (Eds.), *Social representations and social bases of knowledge* (pp. 169–178). Lewiston, NY: Hogrefe and Huber.

Dahling, J. J., Taylor, S. R., Chau, S. L., & Dwight, S. A. (2016). Does coaching matter? A multilevel model linking managerial coaching skill and frequency to sales goal attainment. *Personnel Psychology, 69*, 863–894.

Dale, E. (1960). Management must be made accountable. *Harvard Business Review, 38*(2), 49–59.

Damanpour, F. (1991). Organizational innovation: a meta-analysis of effects of determinants and moderators. *Academy of Management Journal, 34,* 555–590.

Dane, E., & Pratt, M. G. (2007). Exploring intuition and its role in managerial decision making. *Academy of Management Review, 32,* 33–54.

Dansereau, F., Jr., Graen, G., & Haga, W. J. (1975). A vertical dyad linkage approach to leadership within formal organizations: A longitudinal investigation of the role making process. *Organizational Behavior and Human Performance, 13,* 46–78.

Dao, M. A., Strobl, A., Bauer, F., & Tarba, S. Y. (2017). Triggering innovation through mergers and acquisitions: The role of shared mental models. *Group & Organization Management, 42*, 195–236.

Dasborough, M., & Ashkanasy, N. M. (2002). Emotion and attribution of intentionality in leader-member relationships. *The Leadership Quarterly, 13,* 615–634.

Davis, K. (1968). Attitudes toward the legitimacy of management efforts to influence employees. *Academy of Management Journal, 11,* 153–162.

Davison, R. B., Hollenbeck, J. R., Barnes, C. M., Sleesman, D. J., & Ilgen, D. R. (2012). Coordinated action in multiteam systems. *Journal of Applied Psychology,* 97, 808–824.

Day, D. V. (2000). Leadership development: A review in context. *The Leadership Quarterly, 11,* 581–613.

Day, D. V., & Dragoni, L. (2015). Leadership development: An outcome-oriented review based on time and levels of analyses. *Annual Review of Organizational Psychology and Organizational Behavior, 2*, 133–156.

Day, D. V., Fleenor, J. W., Atwater, L. E., Sturm, R. E., & McKee, R. A. (2014). Advances in leader and leadership development: A review of 25 years of research and theory. *The Leadership Quarterly, 25*, 63–82.

Day, D. V., Griffin, M. A., & Louw, K. R. (2014). The climate and culture of leadership in organizations. In B. Schneider & K. Barbera (Eds.), *The Oxford handbook of organizational climate and culture* (pp. 101–117). Oxford: Oxford University Press.

Day, D. V., Gronn, P., & Salas, E. (2004). Leadership capacity in teams. *The Leadership Quarterly, 15,* 857–880.

Day, D. V., & Harrison, M. M. (2007). A multilevel, identity-based approach to leadership. *Human Resource Management Review, 17,* 360–373.

Day, D. V., & Lord, R. G. (1988). Executive leadership and organizational performance: Suggestions for a new theory and methodology. *Journal of Management, 14,* 453–464.

Day, D. V., & Miscenko, D. (2015). Leader-member exchange (LMX): Construct evolution, contributions, and future prospects for advancing leadership theory. In T. N. Bauer & B. Erdogan (Eds.), *The Oxford handbook of leader-member exchange* (pp. 9–28). Oxford, UK: Oxford University Press.

Day, D. V., & Schleicher, D. J. (2006). Self-monitoring at work: A motive-based perspective. *Journal of Personality, 74*, 685–713.

Day, D. V., & Thorton, A. M. A. (2018). Leadership development: The nature of leadership development. In J. Antonakis & D. V. Day (Eds.), *The nature of leadership* (pp. 354–380). Thousand Oaks, CA: Sage.

Deal, T. E. (1985). Culture change: Opportunity, silent killer, or metamorphosis? In R. H. Kilmann, M. J. Saxton, & R. Serpa, (Eds.), *Gaining control of the corporate culture* (pp. 292–330). San Francisco: Jossey-Bass.

De Beuckelaer, A., Lievens, F., & Swinnen, G. (2007). Measurement equivalence in the conduct of a global organizational survey across countries in six cultural regions. *Journal of Occupational and Organizational Psychology, 80*, 575–600.

Dechant, K. (1990). Knowing how to learn: The "neglected" management ability. *Journal of Management Development, 9*(4), 40–49.

Dechant, K. (1994). Making the most of job assignments: An exercise in planning for learning. *Journal of Management Education, 18,* 198–211.

DeChurch, L. A., Burke, C. S., Shuffler, M. L., Lyons, R., Doty, D., & Salas, E. (2011). A historiometric analysis of leadership in mission critical multiteam environments. *The Leadership Quarterly, 22,* 152–169.

DeChurch, L. A., Hiller, N. J., Murase, T., Doty, D., & Salas, E. (2010). Leadership across levels: Levels of leaders and their levels of impact. *The Leadership Quarterly, 21,* 1069–1085.

DeChurch, L. A., & Mesmer-Magnus, J. R. (2010). The cognitive underpinnings of effective teamwork: A meta-analysis. *Journal of Applied Psychology, 95,* 32–53.

de Haan, E., Grant, A. M., Burger, Y., & Eriksson, P.-O. (2016). A large-scale study of executive and workplace coaching: The relative contributions of relationship, personality match, and self-efficacy. *Consulting Psychology Journal: Practice and Research, 68*, 189–207.

De Hoogh, A. H. B., & Den Hartog, D. N. (2008). Ethical and despotic leadership relationships with leader's social responsibility, top management team effectiveness, and subordinates' optimism: A multi-method study. *The Leadership Quarterly, 19,* 297–311.

De Hoogh, A. H. B., Den Hartog, D. N., & Koopman, P. L. (2005). Linking the big five-factors of personality to charismatic and transactional leadership: Perceived dynamic work environment as a moderator. *Journal of Organizational Behavior, 26*, 839–865.

De Jong, B. A., Dirks, K. T., & Gillespie, N. (2016). Trust and team performance: A meta-analysis of main effects, moderators, and covariates. *Journal of Applied Psychology, 101*, 1134–1150.

de Jong, G., & Van Witteloostuijn, A. (2004). Successful corporate democracy: Sustainable cooperation of capital and labor in the Dutch Breman Group. *Academy of Management Executive, 18*(3), 54–66.

de Kluyver, C. A., & Pearce, J. A., II. (2015). *Strategic management: An executive perspective*. New York: Business Expert Press.

Delbecq, A. L., Van de Ven, A. H., & Gustafson, D. H. (1975). *Group techniques for program planning: A guide to nominal and delphi processes*. Glenview, IL: Scott Foresman.

Deluga, R. J. (1998). American presidential proactivity, charismatic leadership, and rated performance. *The Leadership Quarterly, 9,* 265–291.

Deluga, R. J., & Perry, T. J. (1994). The role of subordinate performance and ingratiation in leader-member exchanges. *Group & Organization Management, 19,* 67–86.

De Meuse, K. P., Dai, G., & Wu, J. (2011). Leadership skills across organizational levels: A closer examination. *The Psychologist-Manager Journal, 14*, 120–139.

Demirtas, O. (2015). Ethical leadership influence at organizations: Evidence from the field. *Journal of Business Ethics, 126*, 273–284.

Demirtas, O., Hannah, S. T., Gok, K., Arslan, A., & Capar, N. (2017). The moderated influence of ethical leadership, via meaningful work, on followers' engagement, organizational identification, and envy. *Journal of Business Ethics, 145*, 183–199.

De Neve, J.-E., Mikhaylov, S., Dawes, C. T., Christakis, N. A., & Fowler, J. H. (2013). Born to lead? A twin design and genetic association study of leadership role occupancy. *The Leadership Quarterly, 24*, 45–60.

Den Hartog, D. N. (2004). Assertiveness. In R. J. House, P. J. Hanges, M. Javidan et al. (Eds.), *Culture, leadership, and organizations: The GLOBE study of 62 societies* (pp. 395–436). Thousand Oaks, CA: Sage.

Den Hartog, D. N., & Belschak, F. D. (2012). When does transformational leadership enhance employee proactive behavior? The role of autonomy and role breadth self-efficacy. *Journal of Applied Psychology, 97*, 194–202.

Den Hartog, D. N., & Dickson, M. W. (2018). Leadership, culture, and globalization. In J. Antonakis & D. V. Day (Eds.), *The nature of leadership* (3rd ed., pp. 327–353). Los Angeles: Sage.

Den Hartog, D. N., House, R. J., Hanges, P. J., Ruiz-Quintanilla, S. A., Dorfman, P. W., Abdalla, I. A., … & Akande, B. E. (1999). Culture specific and cross-culturally generalizable implicit leadership theories: Are the attributes of charismatic/transformational leadership universally endorsed? *The Leadership Quarterly, 10,* 219–256.

Denis, J. L., Lamothe, L., & Langley, A. (2001). The dynamics of collective leadership and strategic change in pluralistic organizations. *Academy of Management Journal, 44,* 809–837.

DeNisi, A. S., & Murphy, K. R. (2017). Performance appraisal and performance management: 100 years of progress? *Journal of Applied Psychology, 102*, 421–433.

Denison, D. R., Hart, S. L., & Kahn, J. A. (1996). From chimneys to cross-functional teams: Developing and validating a diagnostic model. *Academy of Management Journal, 39,* 1005–1023.

Dennis, R. S., & Bocarnea, M. (2005). Development of the servant leadership assessment instrument. *Leadership & Organization Development Journal, 26,* 600–615.

DeRue, D. S., & Ashford, S. J. (2010). Who will lead and who will follow? A social process of leadership identity construction in organizations. *Academy of Management Review, 35,* 627–647.

DeRue, D. S., & Myers, C. G. (2014). Leadership development: A review and agenda for future research. In D. V. Day (Ed.), *The Oxford handbook of leadership and organizations* (pp. 832–855). Oxford, UK: Oxford University Press.

DeRue, D. S., & Wellman, N. (2009). Developing leaders via experience: The role of developmental challenge, learning orientation, and feedback availability. *Journal of Applied Psychology, 94*, 859–875.

Detert, J. R., Treviño, L. K., Burris, E. R., & Andiappan, M. (2007). Managerial modes of influence and counterproductivity in organizations: A longitudinal business-unit-level investigation. *Journal of Applied Psychology, 92,* 993–1005.

de Vries, R. E., Roe, R. A., & Taillieu, T. C. B. (2002). Need for leadership as a moderator of the relationships between leadership and individual outcomes. *The Leadership Quarterly, 13,* 121–137.

de Vries, T. A., Walter, F., van der Vegt, G., & Essens, P. J. M. D. (2014). Antecedents of individuals' interteam coordination: Broad functional experiences as a mixed blessing. *Academy of Management Journal, 57*, 1334–1359.

Dickson, M. W., Den Hartog, D. N., & Michelson, J. K. (2003). Research on leadership in a cross-cultural context: Making progress and raising new questions. *The Leadership Quarterly, 14,* 729–768.

Diddams, M., & Chang, G. C. (2012). Only human: Exploring the nature of weakness in authentic leadership. *The Leadership Quarterly, 23*, 593–603.

Dienesh, R. M., & Liden, R. C. (1986). Leader-member exchange model of leadership: A critique and further development. *Academy of Management Review,* 11, 618–634.

Digman, J. M. (1990). Personality structure: Emergence of the five-factor model. *Annual Review of Psychology, 4,* 417–440. Palo Alto, CA: Annual Reviews.

Dimotakis, N., Mitchell, D., & Maurer, T. (2017). Positive and negative assessment center feedback in relation to development self-efficacy, feedback seeking, and promotion. *Journal of Applied Psychology, 102*, 1514–1527.

Dineen, B. R., Lewicki, R. J., & Tomlinson, E. C. (2006). Supervisory guidance and behavioral integrity: Relationships with employee citizenship and deviant behavior. *Journal of Applied Psychology, 91,* 622–635.

Dinh, J. E., Lord, R. G., Gardner, W. L., Meuser, J. D., Liden, R. C., & Hu, J. (2014). Leadership theory and research in the new millenium: Current theoretical trends and changing perspectives. *The Leadership Quarterly, 25*, 36–62.

Dionne, S. D., Gupta, A., Sotak, K. L., Shirreffs, K. A., Serban, A., Hao, C., Kim, D. H., & Yammarino, F. J. (2014). A 25-year perspective on levels of analysis in leadership research. *The Leadership Quarterly, 25*, 6–35.

Dionne, S. D., Sayama, H., Hao, C., & Bush, B. J. (2010). The role of leadership in shared mental model convergence and team performance improvement: An agent-based computational model. *The Leadership Quarterly, 21*, 1035–1049.

Dionne, S. D., Yammarino, F. J., Atwater, L. E., & James, L. R. (2002). Neutralizing substitutes for leadership theory: Leadership effects and common source variance. *Journal of Applied Psychology, 87,* 454–464.

Dipboye, R. L. (1990). Laboratory vs. field research in industrial and organizational psychology. *International Review of Industrial and Organizational Psychology, 5,* 1–34.

Dirks, K. T., & Ferrin, D. L. (2002). Trust in leadership: Meta-analytic findings and implications for research and practice. *Journal of Applied Psychology, 87,* 611–628.

Dobbins, G. H., & Platz, S. J. (1986). Sex differences in leadership: How real are they? *Academy of Management Review, 11,* 118–127.

Donaldson, T. (1996). Values in tension: Ethics away from home. *Harvard Business Review, 74*(5), 48–49, 52–56, 58, 60, 62.

Donaldson, T., & Preston, L. E. (1995). The stakeholder theory of the corporation: Concepts, evidence, and implications. *Academy of Management Review, 20*, 65–91.

Dorfman, P. W. (2004). International and cross-cultural leadership research. In B. J. Punnett & O. Shenkar (Eds.), *Handbook for international management research* (2nd ed., pp. 265–355). Ann Arbor, MI: University of Michigan.

Dorfman, P. W., Hanges, P. J., & Brodbeck, F. C. (2004). Leadership and cultural variation: The identification of culturally endorsed leadership profiles. In R. J. House, P. J. Hanges, M. Javidan, P. W. Dorfman, & V. Gupta (Eds.), *Culture, leadership, and organizations: The GLOBE study of 62 societies* (pp. 669–719). Thousand Oaks, CA: Sage.

Dorfman, P. W., Howell, J. P., Hibino, S., Lee, J. K., Tate, U., & Bautista, A. (1997). Leadership in Western and Asian countries: Commonalities and differences in effective leadership processes across cultures. *The Leadership Quarterly, 8,* 233–274.

Dorfman, P. W., Javidan, M., Hanges, P. J., Dastmalchian, A., & House, R. (2012). GLOBE: A twenty year journey into the intriguing world of culture and leadership. *Journal of World Business, 47*, 504–518.

Dougherty, D., & Hardy, C. (1996). Sustained product innovation in large, mature organizations: overcoming innovation-to-organization problems. *Academy of Management Journal, 39,* 1120–1153.

Dragoni, L., Oh, I.-S., Tesluk, P. E., Moore, O. A., VanKatwyk, P., & Hazucha, J. (2014a). Developing leaders' strategic thinking through global work experience: The moderating role of cultural distance. *Journal of Applied Psychology, 99*, 867–882.

Dragoni, L., Oh, I. S., Vankatwyk, P., & Tesluk, P. E. (2011). Developing executive leaders: The relative contribution of cognitive ability, personality, and the accumulation of work experience in predicting strategic thinking competency. *Personnel Psychology, 64*, 829–864.

Dragoni, L., Park, H., Soltis, J., & Forte-Trammell, S. (2014b). Show and tell: How supervisors facilitate leader development among transitioning leaders. *Journal of Applied Psychology, 99*, 66–86.

Dragoni, L., Tesluk, P. E., Russell, J. E. A., & Oh, I. (2009). Understanding managerial development: Integrating developmental assignments, learning orientation, and access to developmental opportunities in predicting managerial competencies. *Academy of Management Journal, 52,* 731–743.

Drath, W. H. (2001). *The deep blue sea: Rethinking the source of leadership*. San Francisco: Jossey-Bass.

Drath, W. H., McCauley, C. D., Palus, C. J., Van Velsor, E., O'Connor, P. M. G., & McGuire, J. B. (2008). Direction, alignment, commitment: Toward a more integrative ontology of leadership. *The Leadership Quarterly, 19,* 635–653.

Drath, W. H., & Palus, C. J. (1994). *Making common sense: Leadership as meaning-making in a community of practice.* Greensboro, NC: Center for Creative Leadership.

Dreher, G. F., & Ash, R. A. (1990). A comparative study of mentoring among men and women in managerial, professional, and technical positions. *Journal of Applied Psychology, 75,* 539–546.

Drucker, P. F. (1974). *Management: Tasks, responsibilities, practices*. New York: Harper & Row.

Druskat, V. U., & Wheeler, J. V. (2003). Managing from the boundary: The effective leadership of self-managing work teams. *Academy of Management Journal, 46,* 435–457.

Dua, A. K., & Rai, S. (2017, April 28). Ratan Tata: Ethical Leadership. Retrieved from https://hbsp.harvard.edu (Accessed on January 22, 2019)

Duan, J., Li, C., Xu, Y., & Wu, C.-h. (2017). Transformational leadership and employee voice behavior: A Pygmalion mechanism. *Journal of Organizational Behavior, 38,* 650–670.

Duarte, N. T., Goodson, J. R., & Klich, N. R. (1994). Effects of dyadic quality and duration on performance appraisal. *Academy of Management Journal, 37,* 499–521.

Duchon, D., & Plowman, D. A. (2005). Nurturing the spirit at work: Impact on work unit performance. *The Leadership Quarterly, 16,* 807–833.

Dugan, K. W. (1989). Ability and effort attributions: Do they affect how managers communicate performance feedback information? *Academy of Management Journal, 32,* 87–114.

Dulebohn, J. H., Bommer, W. H., Leden, R. C., Brouer, R. L., & Ferris, G. R. (2012). A meta-analysis of antecedents and consequences of leader-member exchange: Integrating the past with an eye toward the future. *Journal of Management, 38,* 1715–1759.

Dunne, E. J., Jr., Stahl, M. J., & Melhart, L. J., Jr. (1978). Influence sources of project and functional managers in matrix organizations. *Academy of Management Journal, 21,* 135–140.

Dust, S. B., Resick, C. J., Margolis, J. A., Mawritz, M. B., & Greenbaum, R. L. (2018). Ethical leadership and employee success: Examining the roles of psychological empowerment and emotional exhaustion. *The Leadership Quarterly*. Published online before printing, doi: https://doi.org/10.1016/j.leaqua.2018.02.002

Dutt, S. (2017, June 29). Corporate India prefers man on top! | Hyderabad News – Times of India. Retrieved from https://timesofindia.indiatimes.com (Accessed on January 12, 2019)

Dvir, T., Eden, D., Avolio, B., & Shamir, B. (2002). Impact of transformational leadership on follower development and performance: A field experiment. *Academy of Management Journal, 45,* 735–744.

Eagly, A. H., & Carli, L. L. (2003a). The female leadership advantage: An evaluation of the evidence. *The Leadership Quarterly, 14,* 807–834.

Eagly, A. H., & Carli, L. L. (2003b). Finding gender advantage and disadvantage: Systematic research integration is the solution. *The Leadership Quarterly, 14,* 851–859.

Eagly, A. H., & Chin, J. L. (2010). Diversity and leadership in a changing world. *American Psychologist, 65,* 216–224.

Eagly, A. H., Darau, S. J., & Makhijani, M. G. (1995). Gender and the effectiveness of leaders: A meta-analysis. *Psychological Bulletin, 117,* 125–145.

Eagly, A. H., Johannesen-Schmidt, M. C., & Van Engen, M. (2003). Transformational, transactional, and laissez-faire leadership styles: A meta-analysis comparing men and women. *Psychological Bulletin, 129,* 569–591.

Eagly, A. H., & Johnson, B. T. (1990). Gender and leadership style: A meta-analysis. *Psychological Bulletin, 108,* 233–256.

Eagly, A. H., Makhijani, M. G., & Klonsky, B. G. (1992). Gender and the evaluation of leaders: A meta-analysis. *Psychological Bulletin, 111,* 3–22.

Earl, M. (2001). Knowledge management strategies: Toward a taxonomy. *Journal of Management Information Systems, 18,* 215–233.

Earley, P. C., & Lind, E. A. (1987). Procedural justice and participation in task selection: The role of control in mediating justice judgments. *Journal of Personality and Social Psychology, 52,* 1148–1160.

Ebben, J. J., & Johnson, C. A. (2005). Efficiency, flexibility, or both? Evidence linking strategy to performance in small firms. *Strategic Management Journal, 26,* 1249–1259.

Eberly, M. B., & Fong, C. T. (2013). Leading via the heart and mind: The roles of leader and follower emotions, attributions and interdependence. *The Leadership Quarterly, 24,* 696–711.

Eberly, M. B., Holley, E. C., Johnson, M. D., & Mitchell, T. R. (2011). Beyond internal and external: A dyadic theory of relational attributions. *Academy of Management Review, 36*, 731–753.

Eberly, M. B., Holley, E. C., Johnson, M. D., & Mitchell, T. R. (2017). It's not me, it's not you, it's *us!* An empirical examination of relational attributions. *Journal of Applied Psychology, 102*, 711–731.

Eberly, M. B., Johnson, M. D., Hernandez, M., & Avolio, B. J. (2013). An integrative process model of leadership: Examining loci, mechanisms, and event cycles. *American Psychologist, 68*, 427–443.

Eccles, T. (1993). The deceptive allure of empowerment. *Long Range Planning, 26*(6), 13–21.

Eden, D. (1984). Self-fulfilling prophecy as a management tool: Harnessing Pygmalion. *Academy of Management Review, 9,* 64–73.

Eden, D. (1990). *Pygmalion in management: Productivity as a self-fulfilling prophecy.* Lexington, MA: Lexington Books.

Eden, D., Geller, D., Gewirtz, A., Gordon-Terner, R., Inbar, I., Liberman, M., … & Shalit, M. (2000). Implanting Pygmalion leadership style through workshop training: Seven field experiments. *The Leadership Quarterly, 11*, 171–200.

Eden, D., & Leviatan, U. (1975). Implicit leadership theory as a determinant of the factor structure underlying supervisory behavior scales. *Journal of Applied Psychology, 60,* 736–741.

Eden, D., & Shani, A. B. (1982). Pygmalion goes to boot camp: Expectancy, leadership and trainee performance. *Journal of Applied Psychology, 67,* 194–199.

Edmondson, A. C. (2003). Speaking up in the operating room: How team leaders promote learning in interdisciplinary action teams. *Journal of Management Studies, 40,* 1419–1452.

Edmondson, A. C., Roberto, M. A., & Watkins, M. D. (2003). A dynamic model of top management team effectiveness: Managing unstructured task streams. *The Leadership Quarterly, 14,* 297–325.

Edwards, B. D., Day, E. A., Arthur, W., Jr., & Bell, S. B. (2006). Relationships among team ability composition, team mental models, and team performance. *Journal of Applied Psychology, 91,* 727–736.

Ehrhardt, K., Miller, J. S., Freeman, S. J., & Hom, P. W. (2014). Examining project commitment in cross-functional teams: Antecedents and relationship with team performance. *Journal of Business and Psychology, 29*, 443–461.

Ehrhart, M. G. (2004). Leadership and procedural justice climate as antecedents of unit-level organizational citizenship behavior. *Personnel Psychology, 57,* 61–94.

Ehrhart, M. G., & Klein, K. J. (2001). Predicting followers' preferences for charismatic leadership: The influence of follower values and personality. *The Leadership Quarterly, 12,* 153–179.

Eisenbeiss, S. A. (2012). Re-thinking ethical leadership: An interdisciplinary integrative approach. *The Leadership Quarterly, 23,* 791–808.

Eisenbeiss, S. A., & Brodbeck, F. (2014). Ethical and unethical leadership: A cross-cultural and cross-sectoral analysis. *Journal of Business Ethics, 122,* 343–359.

Eisenbeiss, S. A., & van Knippenberg, D. (2015). On ethical leadership impact: The role of follower mindfulness and moral emotions. *Journal of Organizational Behavior, 36,* 182–195.

Eisenbeiss, S. A., van Knippenberg, D., & Fahrbach, C. M. (2015). Doing well by doing good? Analyzing the relationship between CEO ethical leadership and firm performance. *Journal of Business Ethics, 128,* 635–651.

Eisenhardt, K. M. (1989a). Agency theory: An assessment and review. *Academy of Management Review, 14,* 57–74.

Eisenhardt, K. M. (1989b). Making fast strategic decisions in high-velocity environments. *Academy of Management Journal, 32,* 543–576.

Eisenstat, R. A., & Cohen, S. G. (1990). Summary: Top management groups. In J. R. Hackman (Ed.), *Groups that work (and those that don't)* (pp. 78–88). San Francisco: Jossey-Bass.

Ekvall, G., & Arvonen, J. (1991). Change-centered leadership: An extension of the two-dimensional model. *Scandinavian Journal of Management, 7,* 17–26.

Ellis, S., & Davidi, I. (2005). After-event reviews: Drawing lessons from successful and failed experience. *Journal of Applied Psychology, 90,* 857–871.

Ellis, S., Mendel, R., & Nir, M. (2006). Learning from successful and failed experience: The moderating role of kind of after-event review. *Journal of Applied Psychology, 91,* 669–680.

Elo, A. L., Ervasti, J., Kuosma, E., & Mattila-Holappa, P. (2014). Effect of a leadership intervention on subordinate well-being. *Journal of Management Development, 33,* 182–195.

Ely, K., Boyce, L. A., Nelson, J. K., Zaccaro, S. J., Hernandez-Broome, G., & Whyman, W. (2010). Evaluating leadership coaching: A review and integrated framework. *The Leadership Quarterly, 21,* 585–599.

Ely, R., & Padavic, I. (2007). A feminist analysis of organizational research on sex differences. *Academy of Management Review, 32,* 1121–1143.

Emrich, C. G., Denmark, F. L., & Den Hartog, D. N. (2004). Cross-cultural differences in gender egalitarianism: Implications for societies, organizations, and leaders. In R. J. House, P. J. Hanges, M. Javidan, P. W. Dorfman, & V. Gupta (Eds.), *Culture, leadership, and organizations: The GLOBE study of 62 societies* (pp. 343–394). Thousand Oaks, CA: Sage.

Engelbracht, A. S., & Fischer, A. H. (1995). The managerial performance implications of a developmental assessment center process. *Human Relations,* 48, 387–404.

Ensley, M. D., Hmieleski, K. M., & Pearce, C. L. (2006). The importance of vertical and shared leadership in the new venture top management teams: Implications for the performance of startups. *The Leadership Quarterly*, 17, 217–231.

Epitropaki, O., Kark, R., Mainemelis, C., & Lord, R. G. (2017). Leadership and followership identity processes: A multilevel review. *The Leadership Quarterly, 28,* 104–129.

Epitropaki, O., & Martin, R. (2004). Implicit leadership theories in applied settings: Factor structure, generalizability, and stability over time. *Journal of Applied Psychology,* 89, 293–310.

Epitropaki, O., Martin, R., & Thomas, G. (2018). Relational leadership. In J. Antonakis & D. V. Day (Eds.), *The nature of leadership* (3rd ed., pp. 109–137). Los Angeles: Sage.

Epitropaki, O., Sy, T., Martin, R., Tram-Quon, S., & Topakas, A. (2013). Implicit leadership and followership theories "in the wild": Taking stock of information-processing approaches to leadership and followership in organizational settings. *The Leadership Quarterly, 24*, 858–881.

Erdogan, B., & Bauer, T. N. (2014). Leader-member exchange (LMX) theory: The relational approach to leadership. In D. V. Day (Ed.), *The Oxford handbook of leadership and organizations* (pp. 407–433). Oxford, UK: Oxford University Press.

Erdogan, B., Bauer, T. N., & Walter, J. (2015). Deeds that help and words that hurt: Helping and gossip as moderators of the relationship between leader–member exchange and advice network centrality. *Personnel Psychology, 68*, 185–214.

Erdogan, B., & Liden, R. C. (2002). Social exchanges in the workplace: A review of recent developments and future research directions in leader-member exchange theory. In L. L. Neider & C. A. Schriesheim (Eds.), *Leadership* (pp. 65–114). Greenwich, CT: Information Age Publishing.

Erwin, D. G., & Garman, A. N. (2010). Resistance to organizational change: Linking research and practice. *Leadership & Organization Development Journal, 31*, 39–56.

Etzioni, A. (1961). *A comparative analysis of complex organizations*. New York: Free Press.

Evans, M. G. (1970). The effects of supervisory behavior on the path-goal relationship. *Organizational Behavior and Human Performance, 5*, 277–298.

Evans, M. G. (1974). Extensions of a path-goal theory of motivation. *Journal of Applied Psychology, 59*, 172–178.

Facteau, J. D., Dobbins, G. H., Russell, J. E. A., Ladd, R. T., & Kudisch, J. D. (1995). The influence of general perceptions of the training environment on pretraining motivation and perceived training transfer. *Journal of Management, 21*, 1–25.

Fagenson, E. A. (1989). The mentor advantage: Perceived career/job experiences of proteges versus non-proteges. *Journal of Organizational Behavior, 10*, 309–320.

Fairhurst, G. T. (1993). The leader-member exchange patterns of women leaders in industry: A discourse analysis. *Communication Monographs, 60*, 321–351.

Falbe, C. M., & Yukl, G. (1992). Consequences for managers of using single influence tactics and combinations of tactics. *Academy of Management Journal, 35*, 638–652.

Farling, M. L., Stone, A. G., & Winston, B. E. (1999). Servant leadership: Setting the stage for empirical research. *Journal of Leadership Studies, 6*, 49–72.

Fayol, H. (1949). *General and industrial management*. London: Pitman.

Fedor, D. B., Caldwell, S., & Herold, D. M. (2006). The effects of organizational change on employee commitment: A multi-level investigation. *Personnel Psychology, 59*, 1–29.

Feldman, D. C. & Lankau, M. J. (2005). Executive coaching: A review and agenda for future research. *Journal of Management, 31*, 829–848.

Ferdman, B. M. (2017). Paradoxes of inclusion: Understanding and managing the tensions of diversity and multiculturalism. *Journal of Applied Behavioral Science, 53*, 235–263.

Ferlie, E., Fitzgerald, L., Wood, M., & Hawkins, C. (2005). The nonspread of innovations: The mediating role of professionals. *Academy of Management Journal, 48*, 117–134.

Fernandez-Araoz, C., Roscoe, A., & Aramaki, K. (2017). Turning potential into success: the missing link in leadership development. *Harvard Business Review, 95*(6), 86–93.

Ferris, G. R., Bhawuk, D. P. S., Fedor, D. F., & Judge, T. A. (1995). Organizational politics and citizenship: Attributions of intentionality and construct definition. In M. J. Martinko (Ed.), *Attribution theory: An organizational perspective* (pp. 231–252). Delray Beach, FL: St. Lucie Press.

Ferris, G. R., Liden, R. C., Munyon, T. P., Summers, J. K., Basik, K. J., Buckley, M. R. (2009). Relationships at work: Toward a multidimensional conceptualization of dyadic work relationships. *Journal of Management, 35,* 1379–1403.

Ferris, G. R., Perrewe, P. L., Anthony, W. P., & Gilmore, D. C. (2000). Political skill at work. *Organizational Dynamics, 28*(4), 25–37.

Ferris, G. R., Treadway, D. C., Kolodinsky, R. W., Hochwarter, W. A., Kacmar, C. J., Douglas, C., & Frink, D. D. (2005). Development and validation of the Political Skill Inventory. *Journal of Management, 31,* 126–152.

Fiedler, F. E. (1986). The contribution of cognitive resources and leader behavior to organizational performance. *Journal of Applied Social Psychology, 16,* 532–548.

Fiedler, F. E., & Garcia, J. E. (1987). *New approaches to leadership: Cognitive resources and organizational performance.* New York: Wiley.

Field, R. H. G. (1989). The self-fulfilling prophecy leader: Achieving the Metharme effect. *Journal of Management Studies, 26,* 151–175.

Finkelstein, S. (2003). *Why smart executives fail: And what you can learn from their mistakes.* New York: Portfolio.

Finkelstein, S., Hambrick, D. C., & Cannella, A. A. (2009). *Strategic leadership: Theory and research on executives, top management teams, and boards.* New York: Oxford University Press.

Fiol, C. M., & Lyles, M. A. (1985). Organizational learning. *Academy of Management Review, 10,* 803–813.

Fisher, D. M. (2014). Distinguishing between taskwork and teamwork planning in teams: Relations with coordination and interpersonal processes. *Journal of Applied Psychology, 99,* 423–436.

Flanagan, W. G. (2003). *Dirty rotten CEOs: How business leaders are fleecing America.* New York: Citadel Press.

Flatten, T., Adams, D., & Brettel, M. (2015). Fostering absorptive capacity through leadership: A cross-cultural analysis. *Journal of World Business, 50,* 519–534.

Fleishman, E. A. (1953). The description of supervisory behavior. *Personnel Psychology, 37,* 1–6.

Fleishman, E. A. (1965). Attitude versus skill factors in work group productivity. *Personnel Psychology, 18,* 253–266.

Fleishman, E. A., Mumford, M. D., Zaccaro, S. J., Levin, K. Y., Korotkin, A. L., & Hein, M. B. (1991). Taxonomic efforts in the description of leader behavior: A synthesis and functional interpretation. *The Leadership Quarterly, 2,* 245–287.

Fleenor, J. W., Taylor, S., & Chappelow, C. (2008). *Leveraging the impact of 360-degree feedback.* San Francisco, CA: Pfeifffer.

Fletcher, C. (1990). Candidates' reactions to assessment centres and their outcomes: A longitudinal study. *Journal of Occupational Psychology, 63,* 117–127.

Floren, H. (2006). Managerial work in small firms: Summarising what we know and sketching a research agenda. *International Journal of Entrepreneurial Behavior & Research, 12,* 272–288.

Fondas, N., & Stewart, R. (1994). Enactment in managerial jobs: A role analysis. *Journal of Management Studies, 31*(1), 83–103.

Fong, K. H., & Snape, E. (2015). Empowering leadership, psychological empowerment and employee outcomes: Testing a multi-level mediating model. *British Journal of Management, 26,* 126–138.

Ford, J. D. (1981). Departmental context and formal structure as constraints on leader behavior. *Academy of Management Journal, 24,* 274–288.

Ford, J. D., Ford, L. W., & D'Amelio, A. (2008). Resistance to change: The rest of the story. *Academy of Management Review, 33,* 362–377.

Ford, J. K., & Weissbein, D. A. (1997). Transfer of training: An updated review and analysis. *Performance Improvement Quarterly, 10,* 22–41.

Ford, M. E. (1986). A living systems conceptualization of social intelligence: Outcomes, processes, and developmental change. In R. J. Sternberg (Ed.), *Advances in* *the psychology of human intelligence* (Vol. 3, pp. 119–171). Hillsdale, NJ: Erlbaum.

Ford, R. C., Piccolo, R. F., & Ford, L. R. (2017). Strategies for building effective virtual teams: Trust is key. *Business Horizons, 60*(1), 25–34.

Ford, R. C., & Randolph, W. A. (1992). Cross-functional structures: A review and integration of matrix organization and project management. *Journal of Management, 18,* 267–294.

Forrester, R. (2000). Empowerment: Rejuvenating a potent idea. *Academy of Management Executive, 14*(3), 67–80.

Foti, R. J., Hansbrough, T. K., Epitropaki, O., & Coyle, P. T. (2017). Dynamic viewpoints on implicit leadership and followership theories: Approaches, findings, and future directions. *The Leadership Quarterly, 28,* 261–267.

Foulk, T. A., Lanaj, K., Tu, M.-H., Erez, A., & Archambeau, L. (2018). Heavy Is the head that wears the crown: An actor-centric approach to daily psychological power, abusive leader behavior, and perceived incivility. *Academy of Management Journal, 61*, 661–684.

Foust, D. (2003). The GE way isn't working at Home Depot. *Business Week Online*, January 17. At WWW/businessweek.com/bwdaily/dnflash/jan2003/nf20030117-1446.htm

Fox, L. (2003). *Enron: The rise and fall*. Hoboken, NJ: Wiley.

Fransen, K., Haslam, S. A., Steffens, N. K., Vanbeselaere, N., De Cuyper, B., & Boen, F. (2015). Believing in 'us': Exploring leaders' capacity to enhance team confidence and performance by building a sense of shared social identity. *Journal of Experimental Psychology: Applied, 21*(1), 89–100.

Fredrickson, J. W. (1986). The strategic decision process and organizational structure. *The Academy of Management Review, 11*, 280–297.

French, J. R. P., Israel, J., & As, D. (1960). An experiment on participation in a Norwegian factory. *Human Relations, 13*, 3–19.

French, J., & Raven, B. H. (1959). The bases of social power. In D. Cartwright (Ed.), *Studies of social power* (pp. 150–167). Ann Arbor, MI: Institute for Social Research.

Fried, Y., & Ferris, G. R. (1987). The validity of the job characteristics model: A review and meta-analysis. *Personnel Psychology, 40,* 287–322.

Frieder, R. E., Wang, G., & Oh, I.-S. (2018). Linking job-relevant personality traits, transformational leadership, and job performance via perceived meaningfulness at work: A moderated mediation model. *Journal of Applied Psychology, 103*, 324–333.

Friedman, S. D. (1986). Succession systems in large corporations: Characteristics and correlates of performance. *Human Resource Management, 25,* 191–213.

Friedrich, T. L., Griffith, J. A., & Mumford, M. D. (2016). Collective leadership behaviors: Evaluating the leader, team network, and problem situation characteristics that influence their use. *The Leadership Quarterly, 27,* 312–333.

Friedrich, T. L., Vessey, W. B., Schuelke, M. J., Ruark, G. A., & Mumford, M. D. (2009). A framework for understanding collective leadership: The selective utilization of leader and team expertise within networks. *The Leadership Quarterly, 20,* 933–958.

Frisch, M. H., Lee, R. J., Metzger, K. L., Robinson, J., & Rosemarin, J. (2012). *Becoming an exceptional executive coach: Use your knowledge, experience, and intuition to help leaders excel.* New York: AMACOM.

Fry, L. W. (2003). Toward a theory of spiritual leadership. *The Leadership Quarterly, 14,* 693–727.

Fry, L. W. (2005). Toward a theory of spiritual well-being and corporate social responsibility through spiritual leadership. In R. Giacalone, C. Jurkiewicz, & C. Dunn (Eds.), *Positive psychology in business ethics and corporate responsibility* (pp. 47–83). Greenwich, CN: Information Age Publishing.

Fry, L. W., Vitucci, S., & Cedillo, M. (2005). Spiritual leadership and army transformation: Theory, measurement, and establishing a baseline. *The Leadership Quarterly, 16,* 835–862.

Fu, P. P., Kennedy, J., Tata, J., Yukl, G., & associates (2004). The impact of societal cultural values and individual social beliefs on the perceived effectiveness of managerial influence strategies: A meso approach. *Journal of International Business Studies*, 34, 285–305.

Fu, P. P., & Yukl, G. (2000). Perceived effectiveness of influence tactics in the United States and China. *The Leadership Quarterly, 11,* 251–266.

Fu, P. P., Peng, T. K., Kennedy, J., & Yukl, G. (2003). Examining the preferences of influence tactics in Chinese societies: A comparison of Chinese managers in Hong Kong, Taiwan, and mainland China. *Organizational Dynamics, 33*(1), 32-46.

Fulmer, I. S., & Ployhart, R. E. (2014). 'Our most important asset': A multidisciplinary/multilevel review of human capital valuation for research and practice. *Journal of Management, 40,* 161–192.

Fulmer, R. M., & Vicere, A. (1996). *Strategic leadership development: Crafting competitiveness*. Oxford: Capstone Publishers.

Fusaro, P., & Miller, R. M. (2002). *What went wrong at Enron: Everyone's guide to the largest bankruptcy in U.S. history*. Hoboken, NJ: Wiley.

Gabarro, J. J. (1985). When a new manager takes charge. *Harvard Business Review,* May–June, 110–123.

Gabarro, J. J. (1987). *The dynamics of taking charge*. Boston: Harvard Business School Press.

Gabelica, C., Van den Bossche, P., Fiore, S. M., Segers, M., & Gijselaers, W. H. (2016). Establishing team knowledge coordination from a learning perspective. *Human Performance, 29*(1), 33–53.

Galbraith, J. R. (1973). *Designing complex organizations*. Menlo Park, CA: Addison-Wesley.

Galvin, B. M., Balkundi, P., & Waldman, D. A. (2010). Spreading the word: The role of surrogates in charismatic leadership processes. *The Academy of Management Review, 35*(3), 477–494.

Ganster, D. C. (2005). Executive job demands: Suggestions from a stress and decision-making perspective. *Academy of Management Review, 30,* 492–502.

Ganster, D. C., Fusilier, M. R., & Mayes, B. T. (1986). Role of social support in the experience of stress at work. *Journal of Applied Psychology, 71*(1), 102–110.

Gardner, W. L. (2003). Perceptions of leader charisma, effectiveness and integrity: Effects of exemplification, delivery and ethical reputation. *Management Communication Quarterly, 16,* 502–527.

Gardner, W. L., & Avolio, B. J. (1998). The charismatic relationship: A dramaturgical perspective. *Academy of Management Review, 23*, 32–58.

Gardner, W. L., Avolio, B. J., Luthans, F., May, D. R., & Walumbwa, F. O. (2005). Can you see the real me? A self-based model of authentic leadership and follower development. *The Leadership Quarterly, 16,* 343–372.

Gardner, W. L., Cogliser, C. C., Davis, K. M., & Dickens, M. (2011). Authentic leadership: A review of the literature and research agenda. *The Leadership Quarterly, 22*, 1120–1145.

Gardner, W. L., Fischer, D., & Hunt, J. G. (2009). Emotional labor and leadership: A threat to authenticity? *The Leadership Quarterly, 20,* 466–482.

Gardner, W. L., Lowe, K. B., Moss, T. W., Mahoney, K. T., & Cogliser, C. C. (2010). Scholarly leadership of the study of leadership: A review of *The Leadership Quarterly's* second decade, 2000–2009. *The Leadership Quarterly, 21*, 922–958.

Gardner, W. L., & Martinko, M. J. (1988). Impression management in organizations. *Journal of Management, 14,* 321–338.

Gardner, W. L., & Schermerhorn, J. R., Jr. (1992). Strategic leadership and the management of supportive work environments. In R. L. Phillips & J. G. Hunt (Eds.), *Strategic leadership: A multiorganizational-level perspective* (pp. 99–118). Westport, CT: Quorum.

Garvin, D. A. (1993). Building a learning organization. *Harvard Business Review, 71*(4), 78–91.

Gary, M. S., & Wood, R. E. (2016). Unpacking mental models through laboratory experiments. *System Dynamics Review, 32*(2), 99–127.

Geary, D. C. (1998). *Male, female: The evolution of human sex differences*. Washington: American Psychological Association.

Gebert, D., Boerner, S., & Lanwehr, R. (2003). The risks of autonomy: Empirical evidence for the necessity of balance in promoting organizational innovativeness. *Creativity and Innovation Management, 12*(1), 41–49.

Geier, M., T. (2016). Leadership in extreme contexts: Transformational leadership, performance beyond expectations? *Journal of Leadership & Organizational Studies, 23,* 234–247.

Gelfand, M. J., Bhawuk, D. P. S., Nishi, L. H., & Bechtold, D. J. (2004). Individualism and collectivism. In R. J. House, P. J. Hanges, M. Javidan, P. W. Dorfman, & V. Gupta (Eds.), *Leadership, culture, and organizations: The GLOBE study of 62 societies* (Vol. 1, pp. 437–512). Thousand Oaks, CA: Sage.

Gelfand, M. J., Erez, M., & Aycan, Z. (2007). Cross-cultural organizational behavior. *Annual Review of Psychology, 58,* 479–514.

Gentry, W. A., Harris, L. S., Baker, B. A., & Leslie, J. B. (2008). Managerial skills: What has changed since the late 1980s. *Leadership & Organization Development Journal, 29,* 167–181.

Georgakakis, D., & Ruigrok, W. (2017). CEO succession origin and firm performance: A multilevel study. *Journal of Management Studies, 54*, 58–87.

George, B. (2003). *Authentic leadership: Rediscovering the secrets to creating lasting value*. San Francisco, CA: Jossey-Bass.

George, J. M. (1995). Leader positive mood and group performance: The case of customer service. *Journal of Applied Social Psychology, 25,* 778–794.

George, J. M., & Jones, G. R. (1996). *Understanding and managing organizational behavior*. Reading, MA: Addison-Wesley.

Gerstner, C. R., & Day, D. V. (1997). Meta-analytic review of leader-member exchange theory: Correlates and construct issues. *Journal of Applied Psychology, 82,* 827–844.

Gharajedaghi, J. (1999). *Systems thinking: Managing chaos and complexity: A platform and designing architecture*. Boston: Butterworth-Heinemann.

Giambatista, R., Rowe, W., & Riaz, S. (2005). Nothing succeeds like succession: A critical review of leader succession literature since 1994. *The Leadership Quarterly, 16,* 963–991.

Giberson, T. R., Resick, C. J., & Dickson, M. W. (2005). Embedding leader characteristics: An examination of homogeneity of personality and values in organizations. *Journal of Applied Psychology, 90,* 1002–1010.

Gibson, C. B. (2001). Me and us: Differential relationships among goal setting, training, efficacy, and effectiveness at the individual and team level. *Journal of Organizational Behavior, 22,* 789–808.

Gibson, C. B., & Birkinshaw, J. (2004). The antecedents, consequences, and mediating role of organizational ambidexterity. *Academy of Management Journal, 47,* 209–226.

Gibson, C. B., Randel, A. E., & Earley, P. C. (2000). Understanding group efficacy: An empirical test of multiple assessment methods. *Group & Organization Management, 25,* 67–97.

Gibson, C. B., & Vermeulen, F. (2003). A healthy divide: Subgroups as a stimulus for team learning behavior. *Administrative Science Quarterly, 48,* 202–239.

Giscombe, K. (2007). Advancing women through the glass-ceiling with formal mentoring. In B. R. Ragins & K. E. Kram (Eds.), *The handbook of mentoring at work: Theory, research, and practice* (pp. 549–572). Thousand Oaks, CA: Sage.

Giessner, S. R., van Knippenberg, D., & Sleebos, E. (2009). License to fail? How leader group prototypicality moderates the effects of leader performance on perceptions of leadership effectiveness. *The Leadership Quarterly, 20,* 434–451.

Gil, F., Rico, R., Alcover, C. M., & Barrasa, A. (2005). Change-oriented leadership, satisfaction, and performance in work groups:

Effects of team climate and group potency. *Journal of Managerial Psychology, 20,* 312–328.

Gilmore, P. L., Hu, X., Wei, F., Tetrick, L. E., & Zaccaro, S. J. (2013). Positive affectivity neutralizes transformational leadership's influence on creative performance and organizational citizenship behaviors. *Journal of Organizational Behavior, 34*, 1061–1075.

Gilson, L. L., Mathieu, J. E., Shalley, C. E., & Ruddy, T. M. (2005). Creativity and standardization: Complementary or conflicting drivers of team effectiveness. *Academy of Management Journal, 48,* 521–531.

Gilson, L. L., Maynard, M. T., Young, N. C. J., Vartianen, M., & Hakonen, M. (2015). Virtual teams research: 10 years, 10 themes, and 10 opportunities. *Journal of Management, 41*, 1313–1337.

Gini, A. (2004). Moral leadership and business ethics. In J. B. Ciulla (Ed.), *Ethics: The heart of leadership* (2nd ed., pp. 25–43). Westport, CT: Praeger.

Ginter, P. M., & Duncan, W. J. (1990). Macro-environmental analysis for strategic management. *Long Range Planning, 23,* 91–100.

Gioia, D. A. (2017). Reflections on the Pinto Fires Case. In L. Treviño & K. A. Nelson (Eds.), *Managing business ethics: Straight talk about how to do it right* (pp. 99–104). New York: Wiley.

Glad, B. (2002). Why tyrants go too far: Malignant narcissism and absolute power. *Political Psychology, 23,* 1–37.

Gladstein, D. L. (1984). Groups in context: A model of task group effectiveness. *Administrative Science Quarterly, 29,* 499–517.

Goldberg, C., & McKay, P. F. (2016). Diversity and LMX development. In T. N. Bauer & B. Erdogan (Eds.), *The Oxford handbook of leader-member exchange* (pp. 381–395). Oxford, UK: Oxford University Press.

Goldner, F. H. (1970). The division of labor: Processes and power. In M. N. Zald (Ed.), *Power in organizations* (pp. 97–143). Nashville, TN: Vanderbilt University Press.

Goleman, D. (1995). *Emotional intelligence: Why it can matter more than IQ*. New York: Bantam Books.

Goleman, D. (1998). What makes a leader? *Harvard Business Review, 76*(6), 93–102.

Goleman, D., Boyatzis, R., & McKee, A. (2002). *Primal leadership: Realizing the power of emotional intelligence*. Boston: Harvard Business School Press.

Goodman, P. S., Devadas, R., & Hughson, T. G. (1988). Groups and productivity: Analyzing the effectiveness of self-managing teams. In J. P. Campbell & R. J. Campbell (Eds.), *Productivity in organizations: New perspectives from industrial and organizational psychology* (pp. 295–327). San Francisco, CA: Jossey-Bass.

Goodman, P. S., & Rousseau, D. M. (2004). Organizational change that produces results: The linkage approach. *Academy of Management Executive, 18*(3), 7–19.

Goodstadt, B. E., & Hjelle, L. A. (1973). Power to the powerless: Locus of control and the use of power. *Journal of Personality and Social Psychology, 27,* 190–196.

Goodstadt, B. E., & Kipnis, D. (1970). Situational influences on the use of power. *Journal of Applied Psychology, 54,* 201–207.

Gordon, G. G., & DiTomaso, N. (1992). Predicting corporate performance from organizational culture. *Journal of Management Studies, 29,* 783–798.

Gordon, J. (2017). *The power of positive leadership*. Hoboken, NJ: Wiley.

Ghosn, C. & Ries, P. (2007). *Shift: Inside Nissan's historic revival.* Crown Publishing Group.

Gottfredson, R. K., & Aguinis, H. (2017). Leadership behaviors and follower performance: Deductive and inductive examination of theoretical rationales and underlying mechanisms. *Journal of Organizational Behavior, 38*, 558–591.

Grabo, A., Spisak, B. R., & van Vugt, M. (2017). Charisma as signal: An evolutionary perspective on charismatic leadership. *The Leadership Quarterly, 28*, 473–485.

Graen, G., & Cashman, J. F. (1975). A role making model of leadership in formal organizations: A developmental approach. In J. G. Hunt & L. L. Larson (Eds.), *Leadership frontiers* (pp. 143–165). Kent, OH: Kent State University Press.

Graen, G. B., Cashman, J., Ginsburgh, S., & Schiemann, W. (1977). Effects of linking-pin quality upon the quality of working life of lower participants: A longitudinal investigation of the managerial understructure. *Administrative Science Quarterly, 22*, 491–504.

Graen, G., Novak, M., & Sommerkamp, P. (1982). The effects of leader-member exchange and job design on productivity and satisfaction: Testing a dual attachment model. *Organizational Behavior and Human Performance, 30,* 109–131.

Graen, G. B., Scandura, T. A., & Graen, M. R. (1986). A field experimental test of the moderating effects of growth need strength on productivity. *Journal of Applied Psychology, 71*, 484-491.

Graen, G. B., & Uhl-Bien, M. (1995). Relationship-based approach to leadership: Development of leader-member exchange (LMX) theory of leadership over 25 years: Applying a multi-level multi-domain perspective. *The Leadership Quarterly, 6,* 219–247.

Graham, J. W. (1991). Servant leadership in organizations: Inspirational and moral. *The Leadership Quarterly, 2,* 105–119.

Grant, A. M. (2014). The efficacy of executive coaching in times of organisational change. *Journal of Change Management, 14*, 258–280.

Grant, J. (1988). Women as managers: What they can offer to organizations. *Organizational Dynamics, 16*(3), 56–63.

Gratton, L. (2004). *The democratic enterprise: Liberating your business with freedom, flexibility and commitment*. London: Financial Times Prentice Hall.

Green, S. G., Anderson, S. E., & Shivers, S. L. (1996). Demographic and organizational influences on leader-member exchange and related work attitudes. *Organizational Behavior and Human Decision Processes, 66,* 203–214.

Green, S. G., & Mitchell, T. R. (1979). Attributional processes of leaders in leader-member exchanges. *Organizational Behavior and Human Performance, 23,* 429–458.

Greenleaf, R. K. (1977). *Servant leadership: A journey into the nature of legitimate power and greatness.* Mahwah, NJ: Paulist Press.

Greer, C. R., & Stephens, G. K. (2001). Escalation of commitment: A comparison of differences between Mexican and U.S. decision-makers. *Journal of Management, 27*, 51–78.

Griffith, J. A., Connelly, S., & Thiel, C. E. (2011). Leader deception influences on leader–member exchange and subordinate organizational commitment. *Journal of Leadership & Organizational Studies, 18*, 508–521.

Grinyer, P. H., Mayes, D., & McKiernan, P. (1990). The sharpbenders: Achieving a sustained improvement in performance. *Long Range Planning, 23,* 116–125.

Gronn, P. (2002). Distributed leadership as a unit of analysis. *The Leadership Quarterly, 13,* 423–451.

Groysberg, B., McLean, A. N., & Nohria, N. (2006). Are leaders portable? *Harvard Business Review, 84*(5), 92–100.

Grutterink, H., Van der Vegt, G. S., Molleman, E., & Jehn, K. A. (2013). Reciprocal expertise affirmation and shared expertise perceptions in work teams: Their implications for coordinated action and team performance. *Applied Psychology: An International Review, 62*, 359–381.

Gully, S. M., Incalcaterra, K. A., Joshi, A., & Beaubien, J. M. (2002). A meta-analysis of team efficacy, potency, and performance: Interdependence and level of analysis as moderators of observed relationships. *Journal of Applied Psychology, 87,* 819–832.

Gupta, V., & Hanges, P. J. (2004). Regional and climate clustering of societal cultures. In R. J. House, P. J. Hanges, M. Javidan, P. W. Dorfman, & V. Gupta (Eds.), *Culture, leadership, and organizations: The GLOBE* *study of 62 cultures* (pp. 178–218). Thousand Oaks, CA: Sage.

Gupta, V., Hanges, P. J., & Dorfman, P. W. (2002). Cultural clusters: Methodology and findings. *Journal of World Business, 37*(1), 11–15.

Gupta, A. K., Smith, K. G., & Shalley, C. E. (2006). The interplay between exploration and exploitation. *Academy of Management Journal, 49,* 693–706.

Gutermann, D., Lehmann-Willenbrock, N., Boer, D., Born, M., & Voelpel, S. C. (2017). How leaders affect followers' work engagement and performance: Integrating leader–member exchange and crossover theory. *British Journal of Management, 28*, 299–314.

Guthey, E., & Jackson, B. (2005). CEO portraits and the authenticity paradox. *Journal of Management Studies,* 42, 1057–1082.

Guthey, E., & Jackson, B. (2011). Cross-cultural leadership revisited. In A. Bryman, D. Collison, K. Grint, B. Jackson, & M. Uhl-Bien (Eds.), *The Sage handbook of leadership* (pp. 165–178). Los Angeles, CA: Sage.

Guthrie, V. A., & Kelly-Radford, L. (1998). Feedback-intensive programs. In C. D. McCauley, R. S. Moxley, & E. Van Velsor (Eds.), *Center for Creative Leadership handbook of leadership development* (pp. 66–105). San Francisco: Jossey-Bass.

Guzzo, R. A., Jette, R. D., & Katzell, R. A. (1985). The effects of psychologically based intervention programs on worker productivity: A meta-analysis. *Personnel Psychology, 38,* 275–291.

Guzzo, R. A., Yost, P. R., Campbell, R. J., & Shea, G. P. (1993). Potency in groups: Articulating a construct. *British Journal of Social Psychology, 3,* 87–106.

Hackman, J. R. (1986). The psychology of self-management in organizations. In M. S. Pollack & R. O. Perloff (Eds.), *Psychology and work: Productivity, change, and employment* (89–136). Washington, DC: American Psychological Association.

Hackman, J. R., Brousseau, K. R., & Weiss, J. A. (1976). The interaction of task design and group performance strategies in determining group effectiveness. *Organizational Behavior and Human Performance, 16,* 350–365.

Hackman, J. R., & Morris, C. G. (1975). Group tasks, group interaction process, and group performance effectiveness: A review and proposed integration. In L. Berkowitz (Ed.), *Advances in experimental social psychology* (Vol. 8, pp. 45–99). New York: Academic Press.

Hackman, J. R., & Oldham, G. R. (1976). Motivation through the design of work: Test of a theory. *Organizational Behavior and Human Performance, 16,* 250–279.

Hall, D. T., & Foulkes, F. K. (1991). Senior executive development as a competitive advantage. *Advances in applied business strategy* (Vol. 2, pp. 183–203). Greenwich, CT: JAI Press.

Hall, D. T., Otazo, K. L., & Hollenbeck, G. P. (1999). Behind closed doors: What really happens in executive coaching. *Organizational Dynamics, 27*(3), 39–53.

Hall, D. T., & Seibert, K. W. (1992). Strategic management development: Linking organizational strategy, succession planning, and managerial learning. In D. H. Montross & C. J. Shinkman (Eds.), *Career development: Theory and practice* (255–275). Springfield, IL: Charles C. Thomas.

Hall, R. D., & Rowland, C. A. (2016). Leadership development for managers in turbulent times. *Journal of Management Development, 35,* 942–955.

Halpin, A. W., & Winer, B. J. (1957). A factorial study of the leader behavior descriptions. In R. M. Stogdill & A. E. Coons (Eds.), *Leader behavior: Its description and measurement* (pp. 39–51). Columbus, OH: Bureau of Business Research, Ohio State University.

Halverson, S. K., Holladay, C. L., Kazama, S. M., & Quinones, M. A. (2004). Self-sacrificial behavior in crisis situations: The competing roles of behavioral and situational factors. *The Leadership Quarterly, 15,* 263–275.

Ham, C., Lang, M., Seybert, N., & Sean, W. (2017). CFO narcissism and financial reporting quality. *Journal of Accounting Research, 55*, 1089–1135.

Hambrick, D. C. (1981). Environment, strategy, and power within top management teams. *Administrative Science Quarterly, 26*, 253–275.

Hambrick, D. C. (1987). The top management team: Key to strategic success. *California Management Review, 30*(1), 88–108.

Hambrick, D. C. (2007). Upper echelons theory: An update. *Academy of Management Review, 32,* 334–343.

Hambrick, D. C., & Finkelstein, S. (1987). Managerial discretion: A bridge between polar views of organizational outcomes. In L. L. Cummings & B. M. Staw (Eds.), *Research in organizational behavior* (Vol. 9, 369–406). Greenwich, CT: JAI Press.

Hambrick, D. C., Finkelstein, S., & Mooney, A. (2005). Executive job demands: New insights for explaining strategic decisions and leader behaviors. *Academy of Management Review, 30*, 472–491.

Hambrick, D. C., Humphrey, S. E., & Gupta, A. (2015). Structural interdependence within top management teams: A key moderator of upper echelons predictions. *Strategic Management Journal, 36*, 449–461.

Hambrick, D. C., & Lovelace, J. B. (2018). The role of executive symbolism in advancing new strategic themes in organizations: A social influence perspective. *Academy of Management Review, 43*, 110–131.

Hambrick, D. C., Nadler, D. A., & Tushman, M. L. (1998). *Navigating change: How CEOs, top teams, and boards steer transformation* (pp. 137–148). Cambridge, MA: Harvard Business School Press.

Hammer, T. H., & Turk, J. M. (1987). Organizational determinants of leader behavior and authority. *Journal of Applied Psychology, 72,* 647–682.

Hammond, M., Clapp-Smith, R., & Palanski, M. (2017). Beyond (just) the workplace: A theory of leader development across multiple domains. *Academy of Management Review, 42*, 481–498.

Hannah, S. T., & Avolio, B. J. (2010). Ready or not: How do we accelerate the developmental readiness of leaders? *Journal of Organizational Behavior, 31*, 1181–1187.

Hannah, S. T., Avolio, B. J., Luthans, F., & Harms, P. D. (2008). Leadership efficacy: Review and future directions. *The Leadership Quarterly, 19*, 669–692.

Hannah, S. T., Avolio, B. J., & May, D. R. (2011). Moral maturation and moral conation: A capacity approach to explaining moral thought and action. *Academy of Management Review, 36*, 663–685.

Hannah, S. T., & Lester, P. B. (2009). A multilevel approach to building and leading learning organizations. *The Leadership Quarterly, 20*, 34–48.

Hannah, S. T., & Parry, K. W. (2014). Leadership in extreme contexts. In D. V. Day (Ed.), *The Oxford handbook of leadership and organizations* (pp. 613–637). Oxford, UK: Oxford University Press.

Hannah, S. T., Uhl-Bien, M., Avolio, B., & Cavarretta, F. (2009). A framework for examining leadership in extreme contexts. *The Leadership Quarterly, 20,* 897–919.

Hansen, M. T., Mors, M. L., & Løvås, B. (2005). Knowledge sharing in organizations: Multiple networks, multiple phases. *Academy of Management Journal, 48*, 776–793.

Harrison, D. A., Kravitz, D. A., Mayer, D. M., Leslie, L. M., & Lev-Arey, D. (2006). Understanding attitudes toward affirmative action programs in employment: Summary and meta-analysis of 35 years of research. *Journal of Applied Psychology, 91,* 1013–1036.

Harrison, R. (1987). Harnessing personal energy: How companies can inspire employees. *Organizational Dynamics, 16*(2), 4–20.

Harrison, T., & Bazzy, J. D. (2017). Aligning organizational culture and strategic human resource management. *Journal of Management Development, 36*, 1260–1269.

Harter, J. K., Schmidt, F. L., & Hayes, T. L. (2002). Business-unit-level relationship between employee satisfaction, employee engagement, and business outcomes: A meta-analysis. *Journal of Applied Psychology, 87,* 268–279.

Harvey, P., Martinko, M. J., & Douglas, S. C. (2006). Causal reasoning in dysfunctional leader-member interactions. *Journal of Managerial Psychology, 21,* 747–762.

Harzing, A. (2006). Response styles in cross-national survey research: A 26-country study. *International Journal of Cross Cultural Management, 6*(2), 243–266.

Haslam, S. A., & Ryan, M. K. (2008). The road to the glass cliff: Differences in the perceived suitability of men and women for leadership positions in succeeding and failing organizations. *The Leadership Quarterly, 19*, 530–546.

Hassan, R., Mahsud, R., Yukl, G., & Prussia, G. (2013). Ethical and empowering leadership and leader effectiveness. *Journal of Managerial Psychology, 28*, 133–146.

Hassan, R., Prussia, G., Mahsud, R., &Yukl, G. (2018). How leader networking, external monitoring, and representing are relevant for effective leadership. *Leadership and Organization Development Journal, 39*(4), 454–467.

Hassan, R., Yukl, G., and Wright, B. E. (2014). Does ethical leadership matter in government agencies: Effects on organizational commitment, absenteeism, and willingness to report ethical problems. *Public Administration Review, 74,* 333–343.

Haveman, H. A. (1992). Between a rock and a hard place: Organizational change and performance under conditions of fundamental environmental transformation. *Administrative Science Quarterly, 37,* 48–75.

Hayibor, S., Agle, B. R., Sears, G. J., Sonnenfeld, J. A., & Ward, A. (2011). Value congruence and charismatic leadership in CEO–top manager relationships: An empirical investigation. *Journal of Business Ethics, 102*, 237–254.

Haynie, J. J., Cullen, K. L., Lester, H. F., Winter, J., & Svyantek, D. J. (2014). Differentiated leader–member exchange, justice climate, and performance: Main and interactive effects. *The Leadership Quarterly, 25*, 912–922.

Hazy, J. K. (2007). Computer models of leadership: Foundations for a new discipline or meaningless diversion? *The Leadership Quarterly, 18,* 391–410.

Hazy, J. K. (2008). Patterns of leadership: A case study of influence signaling in an entrepreneurial firm. In M. Uhl-Bien & R. Marion (Eds.), *Complexity leadership: Part 1* (pp. 379–415). Charlotte, NC: Information Age Publishing.

He, Z. L., & Wong, P. K. (2004). Exploration vs. exploitation: An empirical test of the ambidexterity hypothesis. *Organization Science, 15,* 481–494.

Heavey, C., & Simsek, Z. (2017). Distributed cognition in top management teams and organizational ambidexterity: The influence of transactive memory systems. *Journal of Management, 43*, 919–945.

Hegelsen, S. (1990). *The female advantage: Women's way of leadership*. New York: Doubleday/Currency.

Heifetz, R. (1994). *Leadership without easy answers*. Cambridge, MA: Belknap Press of Harvard University Press.

Heifetz, R., Grashow, A., & Linsky, M. (2009). Leadership in a (permanent) crisis. *Harvard Business Review,* 87(7/8), 62–69.

Heilman, M. E. (2001). Description and prescription: How gender stereotypes prevent women's ascent up the organizational ladder. *Journal of Social Issues, 57,* 657–674.

Heilman, M. E., & Haynes, M. C. (2005). No credit where credit is due: Attributional rationalization of women's success in male-female teams. *Journal of Applied Psychology, 90,* 905–916.

Heller, F. (2000). *Managing democratic organizations*. Dartmouth, UK: Ashgate.

Heller, F., & Yukl, G. (1969). Participation, managerial decision making, and situational variables. *Organizational Behavior and Human Performance, 4,* 227–241.

Hemphill, J. K. (1950). Relations between the size of the group and the behavior of "superior" leaders. *Journal of Social Psychology, 32*, 11–22.

Hemphill, J. K. (1959). Job descriptions for executives. *Harvard Business Review, 37*(5), 55–67.

Hemphill, J. K., & Coons, A. E. (1957). Development of the leader behavior description questionnaire. In R. M. Stogdill & A. E. Coons (Eds.), *Leader behavior: Its description and measurement* (pp. 6–38). Columbus: Bureau of Business Research, Ohio State University.

Henderson, D. J., Liden, R. C., Glibkowski, B. C., & Chaudhry, A. (2009). LMX differentiation: A multi-level review and examination of its antecedents. *The Leadership Quarterly, 20*, 517–534.

Heneman, R. L., Greenberger, D. B., & Anonyuo, C. (1989). Attributions and exchanges: The effects of interpersonal factors on the diagnosis of employee performance. *Academy of Management Journal, 32*, 466–476.

Hernandez, M., Eberly, M. B., Avolio, B. J., & Johnson, M. D. (2011). The loci and mechanisms of leadership: Exploring a more comprehensive view of leadership theory. *The Leadership Quarterly, 22*, 1165–1185.

Herold, D. M., Fedor, D. B., & Caldwell, S. D. (2007). Beyond change management: A multilevel investigation of contextual and personal influences on employees' commitment to change. *Journal of Applied Psychology, 92*, 942–951.

Hersey, P., & Blanchard, K. H. (1977). *The management of organizational behavior* (3rd ed). Englewood Cliffs, NJ: Prentice Hall.

Heslin, P. A., & Keating, L. A. (2017). In learning mode? The role of mindsets in derailing and enabling experiential leadership development. *The Leadership Quarterly, 28*, 367–384.

Hetland, H., Skogstad, A., Hetland, J., & Mikkelsen, A. (2011). Leadership and learning climate in a work setting. *European Psychologist, 16*, 163–173.

Hewett, T. T., O'Brien, G. E., & Hornik, J. (1974). The effects of work organization, leadership, and member compatibility of small groups working on a manipulative task. *Organizational Behavior and Human Performance, 11*, 283–301.

Hickson, D. J., Hinings, C. R., Lee, C. A., Schneck, R. S., & Pennings, J. M. (1971). A strategic contingencies theory of intraorganizational power. *Administrative Science Quarterly, 16*, 216–229.

Higgins, C. A., Judge, T. A., & Ferris, G. R. (2003). Influence tactics and work outcomes: A meta-analysis. *Journal of Occupational Behavior, 24*, 89–106.

Higgs, M., & Rowland, D. (2005). All changes great and small: Exploring approaches to change and its leadership. *Journal of Change Management, 5*(2), 121–151.

Hill, N. S., & Bartol, K. M. (2016). Empowering leadership and effective collaboration in geographically dispersed teams. *Personnel Psychology, 69*, 159–198.

Hill, N. S., Seo, M.-G., Kang, J. H., & Taylor, M. S. (2012). Building employee commitment to change across organizational levels: The influence of hierarchical distance and direct managers' transformational leadership. *Organization Science, 23*, 758–777.

Hiller, N. J., & Beauchesne, M.-M. (2014). Executive leadership: CEOs, top management teams, and organizational-level outcomes. In D. V. Day (Ed.), *The Oxford handbook of leadership and organizations* (pp. 556–586). Oxford, UK: Oxford University Press.

Hillman, L. W., Schwandt, D. R., & Bartz, D. E. (1990). Enhancing staff member's performance through feedback and coaching. *Journal of Management Development, 9*, 20–27.

Hills, F. S., & Mahoney, T. A. (1978). University budgets and organizational decision making. *Administrative Science Quarterly, 23*, 454–465.

Hinings, C. R., & Greenwood, R. (1988). *The dynamics of strategic change*. Oxford, England: Blackwell.

Hinings, C. R., Hickson, D. J., Pennings, J. M., & Schneck, R. E. (1974). Structural conditions of intraorganizational power. *Administrative Science Quarterly, 19,* 22–44.

Hinkin, T. R., & Schriesheim, C. A. (1989). Development and application of new scales to measure the French and Raven (1959) bases of social power. *Journal of Applied Psychology, 74,* 561–567.

Hinkin, T. R., & Tracey, J. B. (1999). The relevance of charisma for transformational leadership in stable organizations. *Journal of Organizational Change Management, 12*(2), 105–119.

Hinrichs, K. T. (2007). Follower propensity to commit crimes of obedience: The role of leadership beliefs. *Journal of Leadership and Organizational Studies, 14*(1), 69–76.

Hirst, G., Mann, L., Bain, P., Pirola-Merlo, A., & Richver, A. (2004). Learning to lead: The development and testing of a model of leadership learning. *The Leadership Quarterly, 15*, 311–327.

Hitt, M. A., & Ireland, R. D. (2002). The essence of strategic leadership: Managing human and social capital. *Journal of Leadership and Organizational Studies, 9*(1), 3–14.

Ho, S. J. K., Chan, L., & Kidwell, R. E., Jr. (1999). The implementation of business process reengineering in American and Canadian hospitals. *Health Care Management Review, 24,* 19–31.

Hoch, J. E., Bommer, W. H., Dulebohn, J. H., & Wu, D. (2018). Do ethical, authentic, and servant leadership explain variance above and byond transformational leadership? A meta-analysis. *Journal of Management, 44*, 501–529.

Hoch, J. E., & Kozlowski, S. W. J. (2014). Leading virtual teams: Hierarchical leadership, structural supports, and shared team leadership. *Journal of Applied Psychology, 99*, 390–403.

Hochwarter, W. A., Pearson, A. W., Ferris, G. R., Perrewe, P. L., & Ralston, D. A. (2000). A re-examination of Schriesheim and Hinkin's (1990) measure of upward influence. *Educational and Psychological Measurement, 60,* 755–771.

Hofmann, D. A., & Jones, L. M. (2005). Leadership, collective personality, and performance. *Journal of Applied Psychology, 90*(3), 509–522.

Hofstede, G. (1980). *Culture's consequences: International differences in work-related values.* London: Sage.

Hofstede, G. (1993). Cultural constraints in management theories. *Academy of Management Executive, 7,* 81–90.

Hogan, J., Hogan, R., & Kaiser, R. B. (2011). Management derailment. In S. Zedeck & S. Zedeck (Eds.), *APA handbook of industrial and organizational psychology, Vol 3: Maintaining, expanding, and contracting the organization.* (pp. 555–575). Washington, DC, US: American Psychological Association.

Hogan, R. J., Curphy, G. J., & Hogan, J. (1994). What we know about personality: Leadership and effectiveness. *American Psychologist, 49,* 493–504.

Hogan, R. J., Raskin, R., & Fazzini, D. (1990). The dark side of charisma. In K. E. Clark & M. B. Clark (Eds.), *Measures of leadership* (pp. 343–354). West Orange, NJ: Leadership Library of America.

Hogan, S. J., & Coote, L. V. (2014). Organizational culture, innovation, and performance: A test of Schein's model. *Journal of Business Research, 67*, 1609–1621.

Hogg, M. A. (2001). A social identity theory of leadership. *Personality and Social Psychology Review, 5,* 184–200.

Hogg, M. A., Fielding, K. S., Johnson, D., Masser, B., Russell, E., & Svensson, A. (2006). Demographic category membership and leadership in small groups: A social identity analysis. *The Leadership Quarterly, 17*, 335–350.

Hogg, M. A., Hains, S., & Mason, I. (1998). Identification and leadership in small groups: Salience, frame of reference, and leader stereotypicality effects on leader evaluations. *Journal of Personality and Social Psychology, 75,* 1248–1263.

Hogg, M. A., Van Knippenberg, D., & Rast III, D. E. (2012). Integroup leadership in organizations: Leading across group and organizational boundaries. *Academy of Management Review, 37*, 232–255.

Holladay, S. J., & Coombs, W. T. (1993). Speaking of visions and visions being spoken: An exploration of the effects of content and delivery on perceptions of leader charisma. *Management Communication Quarterly, 8,* 165–189.

Holladay, S. J., & Coombs, W. T. (1994). Communicating visions: An exploration of the role of delivery in the creation of leader charisma. *Management Communication Quarterly, 6,* 405–427.

Hollander, E. P. (1958). Conformity, status, and idiosyncrasy credit. *Psychological Review, 65,* 117–127.

Hollander, E. P. (1960). Competence and conformity in the acceptance of influence. *Journal of Abnormal and Social Psychology, 61*, 361–365.

Hollander, E. P. (1961). Some effects of perceived status on responses to innovative behavior. *Journal of Abnormal and Social Psychology, 63,* 247–250.

Hollander, E. P. (1980). Leadership and social exchange processes. In K. J. Gergen, M. S. Greenberg, & R. H. Willis (Eds.), *Social exchange: Advances in theory and research* (pp. 103–118). New York: Plenum Press.

Hollenbeck, J. R., Beersma, B., & Schouten, M. E. (2012). Beyond team types and taxonomies: A dimensional scaling conceptualization for team description. *Academy of Management Review, 37*, 82–106.

Holmberg, R., Larsson, M., & Bäckström, M. (2016). Developing leadership skills and resilience during turbulent times: A quasi-experimental evaluation study. *Journal of Management Development, 35*, 154–169.

Holtgraves, T. (1997). Styles of language use: Individuality and cultural variability in conversational indirectness. *Journal of Personality and Social Psychology, 73,* 624–637.

Hooijberg, R. (1996). A multidirectional approach toward leadership: An extension of the concept of behavioral complexity. *Human Relations, 49,* 917–946.

Hooijberg, R., Hunt, J. G., & Dodge, G. E. (1997). Leadership complexity and the development of the leaderplex model. *Journal of Management, 23,* 375–408.

Hooijberg, R., & Lane, N. (2009). Using multisource feedback coaching effectively in executive education. *Academy of Management Learning & Education, 8.* 483–493.

Horn, D., Mathis, C. J., Robinson, S. L., & Randle, N. (2015). Is charismatic leadership effective when workers are pressured to be good citizens? *The Journal of Psychology: Interdisciplinary and Applied, 149,* 751–774.

Horner-Long, P., & Schoenberg, R. (2002). Does e-business require different leadership characteristics? An empirical investigation. *European Management Journal,* 20 (96), 611–619.

Horstmeier, C. A. L., Boer, D., Homan, A. C., & Voelpel, S. C. (2017). The differential effects of transformational leadership on multiple identifications at work: A meta-analytic model. *British Journal of Management, 28,* 280–298.

Horwitz, S. K., & Horwitz, I. B. (2007). The effects of team diversity on team outcomes: A meta-analytic review of team demography. *Journal of Management, 33,* 987–1015.

Hosking, D. M. (1988). Organizing, leadership, and skillful process. *Journal of Management Studies, 25,* 147–166.

Hough, L. M. (1992). The "Big Five" personality variables—Construct confusion: Description versus prediction. *Human Performance, 5,* 139–155.

Houghton, J. D., & Neck, C. P. (2002). The revised self-leadership questionnaire: Testing a hierarchical factor structure for self-leadership. *Journal of Managerial Psychology, 17,* 672–691.

Houghton, J. D., Pearce, C. L., Manz, C. C., Courtright, S., & Stewart, G. L. (2015). Sharing is caring: Toward a model of proactive caring through shared leadership. *Human Resource Management Review, 25*, 313–327.

House, R. J. (1971). A path-goal theory of leader effectiveness. *Administrative Science Quarterly, 16,* 321–339.

House, R. J. (1977). A 1976 theory of charismatic leadership. In J. G. Hunt & L. L. Larson (Eds.), *Leadership: The cutting edge* (pp. 189–207). Carbondale: Southern Illinois University Press.

House, R. J. (1988). Leadership research: Some forgotten, ignored, or overlooked findings. In J. G. Hunt, B. R. Baliga, H. P. Dachler, & C. A. Schriesheim (Eds.), *Emerging leadership vistas* (pp. 245–260). Lexington, MA: Lexington Books.

House, R. J. (1996). Path-goal theory of leadership: Lessons, legacy, and a reformulated theory. *The Leadership Quarterly, 7,* 323–352.

House, R. J., Dorfman, P. W., Javidan, M., Hanges, P. J., & Sully de Luque, M. (2014). *Strategic leadership across cultures: The GLOBE study of CEO leadership behavior and effectivness in 24 countries.* Thousand Oaks, CA: Sage.

House, R. J., Hanges, P. J., Javidan, M., Dorfman, P. W., Gupta, V., & Associates (2004). *Leadership, culture, and organizations: The GLOBE study of 62 societies.* Thousand Oaks, CA: Sage.

House, R. J., Hanges, P. J., Ruiz-Quintanilla, S. A., Dorfman, P. W., Javidan, M., Dickson, M., & Associates (1999). Cultural influences on leadership and organizations: Project GLOBE. In W. H. Mobley, M. J. Gessner, & V. Arnold (Eds.), *Advances in global leadership* (pp. 131–233). Stamford, CT: JAI Press.

House, R. J., & Howell, J. M. (1992). Personality and charismatic leadership. *The Leadership Quarterly, 3,* 81–108.

House, R. J., & Mitchell, T. R. (1974). Path-goal theory of leadership. *Contemporary Business, 3* (Fall), 81–98.

House, R. J., & Singh, J. V. (1987). Organizational behavior: Some new directions for I/O psychology. *Annual Reviews of Psychology, 38,* 669–718.

House, R. J., Spangler, W. D., & Woycke, J. (1991). Personality and charisma in the U.S. presidency: A psychological theory of leadership effectiveness. *Administrative Science Quarterly, 36,* 364–396.

House, R. J., Wright, N. S., & Aditya, R. N. (1997). Cross-cultural research on organizational leadership: A critical analysis and a proposed theory. In P. C. Earley & M. Erez (Eds.), *New perspectives on international/organizational psychology* (pp. 535–625). San Francisco: New Lexington Press.

Howard, A., & Bray, D. W. (1988). *Managerial lives in transition: Advancing age and changing times.* New York: Guilford Press.

Howell, J. M. (1988). Two faces of charisma: Socialized and personalized leadership in organizations. In J. A. Conger & R. N. Kanungo (Eds.), *Charismatic leadership: The elusive factor in organizational effectiveness* (pp. 213–236). San Francisco: Jossey-Bass.

Howell, J. M., & Avolio, B. J. (1992). The ethics of charismatic leadership: Submission or liberation? *Academy of Management Executive, 6*(2), 43–54.

Howell, J. M., & Avolio, B. J. (1993). Transformational leadership, transactional leadership, locus of control, and support for innovation: Key predictors of consolidated business unit performance. *Journal of Applied Psychology, 78,* 891–902.

Howell, J. M., & Frost, P. (1989). A laboratory study of charismatic leadership. *Organizational Behavior and Human Decision Processes, 43,* 243–269.

Howell, J. M., & Shamir, B. (2005). The role of followers in the charismatic leadership process: Relationships and their consequences. *Academy of Management Review, 30,* 96–112.

Howell, J. P., Bowen, D. E., Dorfman, P. W., Kerr, S., & Podsakoff, P. M. (1990). Substitutes for leadership: Effective alternatives to ineffective leadership. *Organizational Dynamics, 19*(1), 21–38.

Howell, J. P., Dorfman, P. W., & Kerr, S. (1986). Moderator variables in leadership research. *Academy of Management Review, 11,* 82–102.

Hoyt, C. L., & Murphy, S. E. (2016). Managing to clear the air: Stereotype threat, women, and leadership. *The Leadership Quarterly, 27,* 387–399.

Hoyt, C. L., Murphy, S. E., Halverson, S. K., & Watson, C. B. (2003). Group leadership: Efficacy and Effectiveness. *Group Dynamics: Theory, Research, and Practice, 7*, 259–274.

Hu, J., & Liden, R. C. (2011). Antecedents of team potency and team effectiveness: An examination of goal and process clarity and servant leadership. *Journal of Applied Psychology, 96*, 851–862.

Hu, J., Wang, Z., Liden, R. C., & Sun, J. (2012). The influence of leader core self-evaluation on follower reports of transformational leadership. *The Leadership Quarterly, 23*, 860–868.

Huang, X., Iun, J., Liu, A., & Gong, Y. (2010). Does participative leadership enhance work performance by inducing empowerment or trust? The differential effects on managerial and non-managerial subordinates. *Journal of Organizational Behavior, 31*, 122–143.

Huber, G. P. (1991). Organizational learning: The contributing processes and the literatures. *Organization Science, 2,* 88–115.

Hulsheger, U. R., Anderson, N., & Salgado, J. F. (2009). Team-level predictors of innovation at work: A comprehensive meta-analysis spanning three decades of research. *Journal of Applied Psychology, 94,* 1128–1145.

Hunt, D. M., & Michael, C. (1983). Mentorship: A career training and development tool. *Academy of Management Review, 8*, 475–485.

Hunt, J. G. (1991). *Leadership: A new synthesis.* Newbury Park, CA: Sage.

Hunt, J. G., Boal, K. B., & Dodge, G. E. (1999). The effects of visionary and crisis-responsive charisma on followers: An experimental examination of two kinds of charismatic leadership. *The Leadership Quarterly, 10,* 423–448.

Hunt, J. G., & Osborn, R. N. (1982). Toward a macro-oriented model of leadership: An odyssey. In J. G. Hunt, U. Sekaran, & C. Schriesheim (Eds.), *Leadership: Beyond establishment views* (pp. 196–221). Carbondale: Southern Illinois University Press.

Hunt, J. G., Osborn, R. N., & Boal, K. B. (2009). The architecture of managerial leadership: Stimulation and channeling of organizational emergence. *The Leadership Quarterly, 20,* 503–516.

Hunt, J. G., & Ropo, A. (1995). Multi-level leadership: Grounded theory and mainstream theory applied to the case of General Motors. *The Leadership Quarterly, 6,* 379–412.

Hunter, E. M., Neubert, M. J., Perry, S. J., Witt, L. A., Penney, L. M., & Weinberger, E. (2013). Servant leaders inspire servant followers: Antecedents and outcomes for employees and the organization. *The Leadership Quarterly, 24*, 316–331.

Hunter, S. T., Bedell-Avers, K. E., & Mumford, M. D. (2007). The typical leadership study: Assumptions, implications, and potential remedies. *The Leadership Quarterly, 18,* 435–446.

Hunter, S. T., Cushenbery, L., Thoroughgood, C., Johnson, J. E., & Ligon, G. S. (2011). First and ten leadership: A historiometric investigation of the CIP leadership model. *The Leadership Quarterly, 22,* 70–91.

Huselid, M. A. (1995). The impact of human resource management practices on turnover, productivity, and corporate financial performance. *Academy of Management Journal, 38,* 635–672.

Hutzschenreuter, T., & Horstkotte, J. (2013). Performance effects of top management team demographic faultlines in the process of product diversification. *Strategic Management Journal, 34*, 704–726.

Hutzschenreuter, T., Kleindienst, I., & Greger, C. (2012). How new leaders affect strategic change following a succession event: A critical review of the literature. *The Leadership Quarterly, 23*, 729–755.

Huy, Q. (2002). Emotional balancing of organizational continuity and radical change: The contribution of middle managers. *Administrative Science Quarterly, 47,* 31–69.

Ilgen, D. R., Hollenbeck, J. R., Johnson, M., & Jundt, D. (2005). Teams in organizations. From input-process-output models to IMOI models. In S. T. Fiske, D. L. Schacter, & A. E. Kazdin

(Eds.), *Annual Review of Psychology*, Vol. 56 (pp. 517–543). Palo Alto, CA: Annual Reviews.

Ilgen, D. R., & Youtz, M. S. (1986). Factors influencing the evaluation and development of minorities. *Research in Personnel and Human Resource Management, 4,* 307–337.

Ilies, R., Morgeson, F. P., & Nahrgang, J. D. (2005). Authentic leadership and eudaemonic well-being: Understanding leader-follower outcomes. *The Leadership Quarterly, 16,* 373–394.

Ilies, R., Nahrgang, J. D., & Morgeson, F. P. (2007). Leader-member exchange and citizenship behaviors: A meta-analysis. *Journal of Applied Psychology, 92,* 269–277.

Ingvaldsen, J. A., & Rolfsen, M. (2012). Autonomous work groups and the challenge of inter-group coordination. *Human Relations, 65,* 861–881.

Isaacson, W. (2012). The real leadership lessons of Steve Jobs. *Harvard Business Review, 90*(4), 92–102.

Isenberg, D. J. (1984). How senior managers think. *Harvard Business Review, 62*(6), 81–90.

Jackson, C. L., Colquitt, J. A., Wesson, M. J., & Zapata-Phelan, C. P. (2006). Psychological collectivism: A measurement validation and linkage to group member performance. *Journal of Applied Psychology, 91,* 884–899.

Jackson, S. E., Schuler, R. S., & Jiang, K. (2014). An aspirational framework for strategic human resource management. *Academy of Management Annals, 8,* 1–56.

Jacobs, T. O. (1970). *Leadership and exchange in formal organizations*. Alexandria, VA: Human Resources Research Organization.

Jacobs, T. O., & Jaques, E. (1987). Leadership in complex systems. In J. Zeidner (Ed.), *Human productivity enhancement: Organizations, personnel, and decision making* (Vol. 2, pp. 7–65). New York: Praeger.

Jacobs, T. O., & Jaques, E. (1990). Military executive leadership. In K. E. Clark & M. B. Clark (Eds.), *Measures of leadership* (pp. 281–295). West Orange, NJ: Leadership Library of America.

Jacobs, T. O., & McGee, M. L. (2001). Competitive advantage: Conceptual imperatives for executives. In S. J. Zaccaro & R. J. Klimoski (Eds.), *The nature of organizational leadership: Understanding the performance imperatives confronting today's leaders* (pp. 42–78). San Francisco, CA: Jossey-Bass.

Jacobsen, C., & House, R. J. (2001). Dynamics of charismatic leadership: A process theory, simulation model, and tests. *The Leadership Quarterly, 12,* 75–112.

Jacquart, P., & Antonakis, J. (2015). When does charima matter for top-level leaders? Effect of attributional ambiguity. *Academy of Management Journal, 58,* 1051–1074.

Jacquart, P., Cole, M. S., Gabriel, A. S., Koopman, J., & Rosen, C. C. (2018). Studying leadership: Research design and methods. In J. Antonakis & D. V. Day (Eds.), *The nature of leadership* (pp. 411–437). Los Angeles: Sage.

James, C. R. (2002). Designing learning organizations. *Organizational Dynamics, 32*(1), 46–61.

James, L. R., & Brett, J. M. (1984). Mediators, moderators, and tests for mediation. *Journal of Applied Psychology, 69,* 307–321.

James, L. R., & White, J. F. (1983). Cross-situational specificity in manager's perceptions of subordinate performance, attributions, and leader behaviors. *Personnel Psychology, 36,* 809–856.

Janda, K. F. (1960). Towards the explication of the concept of leadership in terms of the concept of power. *Human Relations, 13,* 345–363.

Janis, I. L. (1972). *Victims of groupthink: A psychological study of foreign-policy decisions and fiascoes*. Boston: Houghton-Mifflin.

Janis, I. L., & Mann, L. (1977). *Decision making: A psychological analysis of conflict, choice, and commitment*. New York: Free Press.

Jaques, E. (1989). *Requisite organization: Thw CEO's guide to creative structure and leadership*. Arlington, VA: Cason Hall.

Jaussi, K. S., & Dionne, S. D. (2003). Leading for creativity: The role of unconventional leader behavior. *The Leadership Quarterly, 14,* 475–498.

Javidan, M. (2004). Performance orientation. In R. House, V. Gupta, P. J. Hanges, M. Javidan, & P. W. Dorfman (Eds.), *Culture, leadership, and organization: The Globe Study of 62 Societies* (pp. 239–281). Thousand Oaks, CA: Sage.

Javidan, M., House, R., Dorfman, P. W., Hanges, P. J., & Sully de Luque, M. (2006). Conceptualizing and measuring cultures and their consequence: A comparative review of GLOBE's and Hofstede's approaches. *Journal of International Business Studies, 37,* 897–914.

Jay, A. (1976). How to run a meeting. *Harvard Business Review, 54*(2), 43–57.

Jenster, P. V. (1987). Using critical success factors in planning. *Long Range Planning, 20,* 102–109.

Jepson, D. (2009). Studying leadership at cross-country level: A critical analysis. *Leadership, 5*(1), 61–80.

Jiang, K., Takeuchi, R., & Lepak, D. P. (2013). Where do we go from here? New perspectives on the black box in strategic human resource management research. *Journal of Management Studies, 50*, 1448–1480.

Jick, T. D. (1979). Mixing qualitative and quantitative methods: Triangulation in action. *Administrative Science Quarterly, 24,* 602–611.

Jick, T. D. (1993). *Managing change: Cases and concepts*. Burr Ridge, IL: Irwin.

Johnson, G. (1992). Managing strategic change—Strategy, culture, and action. *Long Range Planning, 25,* 28–36.

Johnston, M. A. (2000). Delegation and organizational structure in small businesses: Influences of manager's attachment patterns. *Group and Organization Management, 25,* 4–21.

Jones, E. E., & Pitman, T. S. (1982). Toward a general theory of strategic self-presentation. In J. Suls (Ed.), *Psychological perspectives on the self* (pp. 231–262). Hillsdale, NJ: Lawrence Erlbaum.

Jones, T. M. (1991). Ethical decision making by individuals in organizations: An issue-content model. *Academy of Management Review, 16,* 366–395.

Jones, T. M., Felps, W., & Bigley, G. A. (2007). Ethical theory and stakeholder-related decisions: The role of stakeholder culture. *Academy of Management Review, 32,* 137–155.

Joshi, A., & Roh, H. (2009). The role of context in work team diversity research: A meta-analytic review. *Academy of Management Journal, 52,* 599–627.

Judge, E. (2003). Women on board: Help or hindrance? *The Times,* November, 11, p. 21.

Judge, T. A., Bono, J. E., Ilies, R., & Gerhardt, M. W. (2002). Personality and leadership: A qualitative and quantitative review. *Journal of Applied Psychology, 87*, 765–780.

Judge, T. A., Colbert, A. E., & Ilies, R. (2004). Intelligence and leadership: A quantitative review and test of theoretical propositions. *Journal of Applied Psychology, 89*, 542–552.

Judge, T. A., Erez, A., Bono, J. E., & Thoresen, C. J. (2003). The Core Self-Evaluations Scale: Development of a measure. *Personnel Psychology, 56*, 303–331.

Judge, T. A., Piccolo, R. F., & Ilies, R. (2004). The forgotten ones? The validity of consideration and initiating structure in leadership research. *Journal of Applied Psychology, 89,* 36–51.

Judge, T. A., Piccolo, R. F., & Kosalka, T. (2009). The bright and dark sides of leader traits: A review and theoretical extension of the leader trait paradigm. *The Leadership Quarterly, 20,* 855–875.

Jung, D. I. (2001). Transformational and transactional leadership and their effects on creativity in groups. *Creativity Research Journal, 13*, 185–195.

Jung, D. I., & Avolio, B. J. (1999). Effects of leadership style and followers' cultural orientation on performance in group and individual task conditions. *Academy of Management Journal, 42,* 208–218.

Jung, D. I., Chow, C., & Wu, A. (2003). The role of transformational leadership in enhancing organizational innovation: Hypotheses and some preliminary findings. *The Leadership Quarterly, 14,* 525–544.

Jung, D. I., Wu, A., & Chow, C. (2008). Towards understanding the direct and indirect effects of CEO's transformational leadership on firm innovation. *The Leadership Quarterly, 19,* 582–594.

Junker, N. M., & van Dick, R. (2014). Implicit theories in organizational settings: A systematic review and research agenda of implicit leadership and followership theories. *The Leadership Quarterly, 25,* 1154–1173.

Kabasakal, H., & Bodur, M. (2004). Humane orientation in societies, organizations, and leader attributes. In R. House, V. Gupta, P. J. Hanges, M. Javidan, & P. W. Dorfman (Eds.), *Culture, leadership, and organization: The Globe Study of 62 Societies* (pp. 564–601). Thousand Oaks, CA: Sage.

Kaiser, R. B., Hogan, R., & Craig, S. B. (2008). Leadership and the fate of organizations. *American Psychologist, 63,* 93–110.

Kaiser, R. B., & Overfield, D. V. (2010). Assessing flexible leadership as the mastery of opposites. *Consulting Psychology Journal: Practice and Research, 62,* 105–118.

Kalshoven, K., Den Hartog, D. N., & De Hoogh, A. H. B. (2011). Ethical leadership at work questionnaire (ELW): Development and validation of a multidimensional measure. *The Leadership Quarterly, 22,* 51–69.

Kanter, R. M. (1983). *The change masters*. New York: Simon & Schuster.

Kantabutra, S. (2009). Toward a behavioral theory of vision in organizational settings. *Leadership & Organization Development Journal, 30,* 319–337.

Kaplan, E. M., & Cowen, E. L. (1981). Interpersonal helping behavior of industrial foremen. *Journal of Applied Psychology, 66,* 633–638.

Kaplan, R. E. (1984). Trade routes: The manager's network of relationships. *Organizational Dynamics, 12*(4), 37–52.

Kaplan, R. E. (1988). The warp and woof of the general manager's job. In F. D. Schoorman & B. Schneider (Eds.), *Facilitating work effectiveness* (pp. 183–211). Lexington, MA: Lexington Books.

Kaplan, R. E. (1990). Character change in executives as "re-form" in the pursuit of self-worth. *Journal of Applied Behavioral Science, 26,* 461–481.

Kaplan, R. E. (1993). 360-degree feedback PLUS: Boosting the power of co-worker ratings for executives. *Human Resource Management, 32,* 299–314.

Kaplan, R. E., & Kaiser, R. B. (2003). Developing versatile leadership. *MIT Sloan Management Review, 44*(4), 19–26.

Kaplan, R. E., Kofodimos, J. R., & Drath, W. H. (1987). Development at the top: A review and prospect. In W. Pasmore & R. W. Woodman (Eds.), *Research in organizational change and development* (Vol. 1, pp. 229–273). Greenwich, CT: JAI Press.

Kaplan, R. E., Lombardo, M. M., & Mazique, M. S. (1985). A mirror for managers: Using simulation to develop management teams. *Journal of Applied Behavioral Science, 21,* 241–253.

Kaplan, R. E., & Palus, C. J. (1994). *Enhancing 360-degree feedback for senior executives: How to maximize benefits and minimize risks*. Greensboro, NC: Center for Creative Leadership.

Karaevli, A., & Hall, D. T. (2003). Growing leaders for turbulent times: Is succession planning up for the challenge? *Organizational Dynamics, 32*(1), 62–79.

Karam, E. P., Gardner, W. L., Gullifor, D., Tribble, L. L., & Li, M. (2017). Authentic leadership and high-performance resource practices: Implications for work engagement. *Research in Personnel and Human Resources Management, 35,* 103–153.

Kark, R., Shamir, B., & Chen, G. (2003). The two faces of transformational leadership: Empowerment and dependency. *Journal of Applied Psychology, 88,* 246–255.

Karkoulian, S., Assaker, G., & Hallak, R. (2016). An empirical study of 360-degree feedback, organizational justice, and firm sustainability. *Journal of Business Research, 69,* 1862–1867.

Katz, D., & Kahn, R. L. (1978). *The social psychology of organizations* (2nd ed). New York: John Wiley.

Katz, R. L. (1955). Skills of an effective administrator. *Harvard Business Review, 33*(1), 33–42.

Katzell, R. A., Barrett, R. S., Vann, D. H., & Hogan, J. M. (1968). Organizational correlates of executive roles. *Journal of Applied Psychology, 52,* 22–28.

Kearney, E., Gebert, D., & Voelpel, S. C. (2009). When and how diversity benefits teams: The importance of team members' need for cognition. *Academy of Management Journal, 52,* 581–698.

Kegan, R. (1982). *The evolving self: Problem and process in human development.* Cambridge, MA: Harvard University Press.

Kegan, R., & Lahey, L. L. (2016). *An everyone culture: Becoming a deliberately developmental organization.* Boston, MA: Harvard Business Press.

Kelkar, G., & Shrestha, G. (2002). IT industry and women's agency: Explorations in Bangalore and Delhi, India. Gender, Technology and Development, 6(1), 63–84.

Keller, J. W., & Foster, D. M. (2012). Presidential leadership style and the political use of force. *Political Psychology, 33*, 581–598.

Keller, R. T. (1992). Transformational leadership and the performance of research and development product groups. *Journal of Management, 18,* 489–501.

Keller, R. T. (2001). Cross-functional project groups in research and new product development: Diversity, communications, job stress, and outcomes. *Academy of Management Journal, 44,* 547–555.

Keller, T. (1999). Images of the familiar: Individual differences and implicit leadership theories. *The Leadership Quarterly, 10,* 589–607.

Kelley, R. E. (1992). *The power of followership: How to create leaders people want to follow and followers who lead themselves.* New York: Doubleday/Currency.

Kelman, H. C. (1958). Compliance, identification, and internalization: Three processes of attitude change. *Journal of Conflict Resolution, 2,* 51–60.

Kennedy, J. C., Fu, P. P., & Yukl, G. (2003). Influence tactics across twelve cultures. In Advances in global leadership (pp. 127–147). Emerald Group Publishing Limited.

Kerr, S., & Jermier, J. M. (1978). Substitutes for leadership: Their meaning and measurement. *Organizational Behavior and Human Performance, 22,* 375–403.

Kessler, R. C., Price, R. H., & Wortman, C. B. (1985). Social factors in psychopathology: Stress, social support, and coping processes. *Annual Review of Psychology, 36,* 531–572.

Kets de Vries, M. F. R. (2005). Leadership group coaching in action: The Zen of creating high performance teams. *Academy of Management Executive, 19*(1), 61–76.

Kets de Vries, M. F. R., & Miller, D. (1984). *The neurotic organization: Diagnosing and changing counter-productive styles of management.* San Francisco: Jossey-Bass.

Kets de Vries, M. F. R., & Miller, D. (1985). Narcissism and leadership: An object relations perspective. *Human Relations, 38,* 583–601.

Keys, B. & Wolfe, J. (1990). The role of management games and simulation in education and research. *Journal of Management, 16,* 307–336.

Kim, H., & Yukl, G. (1995). Relationships of self-reported and subordinate-reported leadership behaviors to managerial effectiveness and advancement. *The Leadership Quarterly, 6,* 361–377.

Kim, K. Y., Atwater, L., Patel, P. C., & Smither, J. W. (2016). Multisource feedback, human capital, and the financial performance of organizations. *Journal of Applied Psychology, 101*, 1569–1584.

Kim, S., Egan, T. M., Kim, W., & Kim, J. (2013). The impact of managerial coaching behavior on employee work-related reactions. *Journal of Business and Psychology, 28*, 315–330.

Kim, T.-Y., Liden, R. C., Kim, S.-P., & Lee, D.-R. (2015). The interplay between follower core self-evaluation and transformational leadership: Effects on employee outcomes. *Journal of Business and Psychology, 30*, 345–355.

Kipnis, D. (1972). Does power corrupt? *Journal of Personality and Social Psychology, 24,* 33–41.

Kipnis, D., & Cosentino, J. (1969). Use of leadership powers in industry. *Journal of Applied Psychology, 53,* 460–466.

Kipnis, D., & Lane, W. P. (1962). Self-confidence and leadership. *Journal of Applied Psychology, 46,* 291–295.

Kipnis, D., Schmidt, S., Price, K., & Stitt, C. (1981). Why do I like thee: Is it your performance or my orders? *Journal of Applied Psychology, 66*, 324–328.

Kipnis, D., Schmidt, S. M., & Wilkinson, I. (1980). Intra-organizational influence tactics: Explorations in getting one's way. *Journal of Applied Psychology, 65,* 440–452.

Kirkman, B. L., Lowe, K. B., & Gibson, B. G. (2006). A quarter century of culture's consequences: A review of empirical research incorporating Hofstede's cultural values framework. *Journal of International Business Studies, 37,* 285–320.

Kirkman, B. L., & Rosen, B. (1997). A model of work team empowerment. *Research in Organizational Change and Development, 10,* 131–167.

Kirkman, B. L., & Rosen, B. (1999). Beyond self-management: Antecedents and consequences of team empowerment. *Academy of Management Journal, 42,* 58–74.

Kirkman, B. L., Rosen, B., Tesluk, P. E., & Gibson, C. B. (2004). The impact of team empowerment on virtual team performance: The moderating role of face-to-face interaction. *Academy of Management Journal, 47,* 175–192.

Kirkman, B. L., & Shapiro, D. L. (2000). Understanding why team members won't share: An examination of factors related to employee receptivity to team-based rewards. *Small Group Research, 31*, 175–209.

Kirkpatrick, S. A., & Locke, E. A. (1996). Direct and indirect effects of three core charismatic leadership components on performance and attitudes. *Journal of Applied Psychology, 81,* 36–51.

Kirsch, A. (2018). The gender composition of corporate boards: A review and research agenda. *The Leadership Quarterly, 29,* 346–364.

Kisfalvi, V., Sergi, V., & Langley, A. (2016). Managing and mobilizing microdynamics to achieve behavioral integration in top management teams. *Long Range Planning: International Journal of Strategic Management, 49*, 427–446.

Kish-Gephart, J. J., Harrison, D. A., & Treviño, L. K. (2010). Bad apples, bad cases, and bad barrels: Meta-analytic evidence about sources of unethical decisions at work. *Journal of Applied Psychology, 95,* 1–31.

Klein, K. J., Dansereau, F., & Hall, R. J. (1994). Levels issues in theory development, data collection, and analysis. *Academy of Management Review, 19,* 195–229.

Klein, K. J., Ziegert, J. C., Knight, A. P., & Xiao, Y. (2006). Dynamic delegation: Shared, hierarchical, and deindividualized leadership in extreme action teams. *Administrative Science Quarterly, 51*, 590–621.

Klettner, A., Clarke, T., & Boersma, M. (2016). Strategic and regulatory approaches to increasing women in leadership: Multilevel targets and mandatory quotas as levers for cultural change. *Journal of Business Ethics, 133*, 395–419.

Kletz, T. (1993). *Lessons from disaster: How organizations have no memory and accidents recur*. Houston: Gulf.

Klimoski, R., & Jones, R. G. (1995). Staffing for effective group decision making: Key issues in matching people and teams. In R. A. Guzzo & E. Salas (Eds.), *Team effectiveness and decision making in organizations* (pp. 333–380). San Francisco: Jossey-Bass.

Klimoski, R., & Mohammed, S. (1994). Team mental model: Construct or metaphor. *Journal of Management, 20,* 403–437.

Kluger, A. N., & DeNisi, A. (1996). The effects of feedback interventions on performance: A historical review, a meta-analysis, and a preliminary feedback intervention theory. *Psychological Bulletin, 119,* 254–284.

Kobe, L. M., Reitter-Palmon, R., & Rickers, J. D. (2001). Self-reported leadership experiences in relation to inventoried social and emotional intelligence. *Current Psychology, 20*(2), 154–163.

Kochan, T., Bezrukova, K., Ely, R., Jackson, S., Joshi, A., Jehn, K., et al. (2003). The effects of diversity on business performance: Report of the diversity research network. *Human Resource Management, 42*(1), 3–21.

Kochanowski, S., Seifert, C. F., & Yukl, G. (2010). Using coaching to enhance the effects of behavioral feedback to managers. *Journal of Leadership and Organizational Studies, 17*(4), 363–369.

Kohlberg, L. (1984). *The psychology of moral development: The nature and validity of moral stages (Essays on moral development,* Vol. 2). New York: Harper & Row.

Kollenscher, E., Eden, D., Ronen, B., & Farjoun, M. (2017). Architectural Leadership: The Neglected Core of Organizational Leadership. *European Management Review, 14*, 247–264.

Komaki, J. (1986). Toward effective supervision: An operant analysis and comparison of managers at work. *Journal of Applied Psychology, 71,* 270–279.

Komaki, J., Desselles, M. L., & Bowman, E. D. (1989). Definitely not a breeze: Extending an operant model of effective supervision to teams. *Journal of Applied Psychology, 74,* 522–529.

Komaki, J. L., & Minnich, M. R. (2002). Crosscurrents at sea: The ebb and flow of leaders in response to the shifting demands of racing sailboats. *Group & Organization Management, 27,* 113–141.

Konst, D., Vonk, R., & Van der Vlist, R. (1999). Inferences about causes and consequences of behavior of leaders and subordinates. *Journal of Organizational Behavior, 20,* 261–271.

Korda, M. (1975). *Power! How to get it, how to use it*. New York: Ballantine Books.

Korica, M., Nicolini, D., & Johnson, B. (2017). In search of 'managerial work': Past, present and future of an analytical category. *International Journal of Management Reviews, 19*, 151–174.

Korsgaard, M. A., Schweiger, D. M., & Sapienze, H. J. (1995). Building commitment, attachment, and trust in strategic decision-making teams: The role of procedural justice. *Academy of Management Journal, 38,* 60–84.

Kotlyar, I., Karakowsky, L., & Ng, P. (2011). Leader behaviors, conflict and member commitment to team-generated decisions. *The Leadership Quarterly, 22*, 666–679.

Kotter, J. P. (1982). *The general managers*. New York: Free Press.

Kotter, J. P. (1985). *Power and influence: Beyond formal authority*. New York: Free Press.

Kotter, J. P. (1990). *A force for change: How leadership differs from management*. New York: Free Press.

Kotter, J. P. (1996). *Leading change*. Boston: Harvard Business School Press.

Kotter, J. P. (2002). *The heart of change*. Boston: Harvard Business School Press.

Kotter, J. P., & Heskett, J. L. (1992). *Corporate culture and performance*. New York: Free Press.

Kouzes, J. M., & Posner, B. Z. (1987). *The leadership challenge: How to get extraordinary things done in organizations*. San Francisco: Jossey-Bass.

Kouzes, J. M., & Posner, B. Z. (1993). *Credibility: How leaders gain and lose it, why people demand it*. San Francisco: Jossey-Bass.

Kovach, B. E. (1989). Successful derailment: What fast-trackers can learn while they're off the track. *Organizational Dynamics, 18*(2), 33–47.

Kozlowski, S. W. J., & Ilgen, D. R. (2006). Enhancing the effectiveness of work groups and teams. *Psychological Science in the Public Interest, 7,* 77–124.

Kram, K. E. (1985). *Mentoring at work: Developmental relationships in organizational life*. Glenview, IL: Scott Foresman.

Kram, K. E., & Hall, D. T. (1989). Mentoring as an antidote to stress during corporate trauma. *Human Resource Management*, 28, 493–510.

Kramer, M. W. (1995). A longitudinal study of superior-subordinate communication during job transfers. *Human Communications Research, 22,* 39–64.

Krause, D. E. (2004). Influence-based leadership as a determinant of the inclination to innovate and of innovation-related behaviors: An empirical investigation. *The Leadership Quarterly, 15,* 79–102.

Kraut, A. I., Pedigo, P. R., McKenna, D. D., & Dunnette, M. D. (1989). The role of the manager: What's really important in different management jobs. *Academy of Management Executive*, 3 (4), 286–293.

Kreutzer, W. B. (1993). A buyer's guide to off-the-shelf microworlds. In P. M. Senge, C. Roberts, R. B. Ross, B. J. Smith, & A. Kleiner (Eds.), *The fifth discipline fieldbook: Strategies and tools for building a learning organization* (pp. 536–537). New York: Currency-Doubleday.

Kriger, M., & Seng, Y. (2005). Leadership with inner meaning: A contingency theory of leadership based on the worldviews of five religions. *The Leadership Quarterly, 16,* 771–806.

Kukenberger, M. R., Mathieu, J. E., & Ruddy, T. (2015). A cross-level test of empowerment and process influences on members' informal learning and team commitment. *Journal of Management, 41*, 987–1016.

Kuntz, J. R. C., Kuntz, J. R., Elenkov, D., & Nabirukhina, A. (2013). Characterizing ethical cases: A cross-cultural investigation of individual differences, organisational climate, and leadership on ethical decision-making. *Journal of Business Ethics, 113*, 317–331.

Kurke, L., & Aldrich, H. (1983). Mintzberg was right: A replication and extension of the nature of managerial work. *Management Science, 29,* 975–984.

Lacey, T. A., Toossi, M., Dubina, K. S., & Gensler, A. B. (2017). Projections overview and highlights, 2016–26. *Monthly Labor Review,* October.

Lacerenza, C. N., Reyes, D. L., Marlow, S. L., Joseph, D. L., & Salas, E. (2017). Leadership training design, delivery, and implementation: A meta-analysis. *Journal of Applied Psychology, 102*, 1686–1718.

Ladegard, G., & Gjerde, S. (2014). Leadership coaching, leader role-efficacy, and trust in subordinates. A mixed methods study assessing leadership coaching as a leadership development tool. *The Leadership Quarterly, 25*, 631–646.

Ladkin, D., & Taylor, S. S. (2010). Enacting the 'true self': Towards a theory of embodied authentic leadership. *The Leadership Quarterly, 21,* 64–74.

Lahiri, S. (2016). Does outsourcing really improve firm performance? Empirical evidence and research agenda. *International Journal of Management Reviews, 18*, 464–497.

Lam, C. K., Huang, X., & Chan, S. C. H. (2015). The threshold effect of participative leadership and the role of leader information sharing. *Academy of Management Journal, 58,* 836–855.

Lanaj, K., & Hollenbeck, J. R. (2015). Leadership over-emergence in self-managing teams: The role of gender and countervailing biases. *Academy of Management Journal, 58,* 1476–1494.

Lanaj, K., Hollenbeck, J. R., Ilgen, D. R., Barnes, C. M., & Harmon, S. J. (2013). The double-edged sword of decentralized planning in multiteam systems. *Academy of Management Journal, 56*, 735–757.

Landy, F. J. (2005). Some historical and scientific issues related to research on emotional intelligence. *Journal of Organizational Behavior, 26,* 411–424.

Langfred, C. W. (2007). The downside of self-management: A longitudinal study of the effects of conflict on trust, autonomy, and task interdependence in self-managing teams. *Academy of Management Journal, 50,* 885–900.

Lant, T. K., Milliken, F. J., & Batra, B. (1992). The role of managerial learning and interpretation in strategic persistence and reorientation: An empirical investigation. *Strategic Management Journal, 13,* 585–608.

Lapierre, L. M., Naidoo, L. J., & Bonaccio, S. (2012). Leaders' relational self-concept and followers' task performance: Implications for mentoring provided to followers. *The Leadership Quarterly, 23*, 766–774.

Larwood, L., Falbe, C. M., Kriger, M. P., & Miesing, P. (1995). Structure and meaning of organizational vision. *Academy of Management Journal, 38,* 740–769.

Latham, G. P. (1988). Human resource training and development. *Annual Review of Psychology, 39,* 545–582.

Latham, G. P., & Yukl, G. A. (1975). Assigned versus participative goal setting with educated and uneducated woods workers. *Journal of Applied Psychology, 60*, 299–302.

Latham, G. P., & Yukl, G. A. (1976). Effects of assigned and participative goal setting on performance and job satisfaction. *Journal of Applied Psychology, 61*, 166–171.

Lau, D. C., & Murnighan, J. K. (2005). Interactions within groups and subgroups: The effects of demographic faultlines. *Academy of Management Journal, 48*, 645–659.

Law-Penrose, J. C., Wilson, K. S., & Taylor, D. L. (2015). Leader-member exchange from the resource exchange perspective: Beyond resource predictions and outcomes of LMX. In T. N. Bauer & B. Erdogan (Eds.), *The Oxford handook of leader-member exchange* (pp. 55–66). Oxford, UK: Oxford University Press.

Lawler, E. E. (1986). *High involvement management: Participative strategies for improving organizational performance*. San Francisco, CA: Jossey-Bass.

Lawler, E. E., Mohrman, S. A., & Benson, G. S. (2001). *Organizing for high performance: The CEO report on employee involvement, TQM, reengineering, and knowledge management in Fortune 1000 companies*. San Francisco: Jossey-Bass.

Lawler, E. E., Mohrman, S. A., & Ledford, G. E., Jr. (1998). *Strategies for high performance organizations: Employee involvement, TQM, and reengineering programs in Fortune 1000 corporations*. San Francisco: Jossey-Bass.

Lawrence, L. C., & Smith, P. C. (1955). Group decision and employee participation. *Journal of Applied Psychology, 39*, 334–337.

Lawrence, P. R., & Lorsch, J. W. (1969). *Organization and environment: Managing differentiation and integration.* Homewood, IL: Richard D. Irwin.

Lazarus, R. S. (1991). *Emotion and adaptation.* New York: Oxford University Press.

Leana, C. R. (1986). Predictors and consequences of delegation. *Academy of Management Journal, 29,* 754–774.

Leana, C. R. (1987). Power relinquishment versus power sharing: Theoretical clarification and empirical comparison of delegation and participation. *Journal of Applied Psychology, 72,* 228–233.

Leana, C. R., Locke, E. A., & Schweiger, D. M. (1990). Fact and fiction in analyzing research on participative decision making: A critique of Cotton, Vollrath, Froggatt, Lengnick-Hall, and Jennings. *Academy of Management Review, 15,* 137–146.

Leary, M. R., & Kowalski, R. M. (1990). Impression management: A literature review and two-component model. *Psychological Bulletin, 107,* 34–47.

Lechner, C., & Kreutzer, M. (2010). Strategic initiatives: Past, present and future. In P. Mazzola & F. W. Kellermanns (Eds.), *Handbook of research on strategy process* (pp. 283–303). Cheltenham, UK: Edward Elgar.

Lee, A., Willis, S., & Tian, A. W. (2018). Empowering leadership: A meta-analytic examination of incremental contribution, mediation, and moderation. *Journal of Organizational Behavior, 39*, 306–325.

Lee, S., Han, S., Cheong, M., Kim, S. L., & Yun, S. (2017). How do I get my way? A meta-analytic review of research on influence tactics. *The Leadership Quarterly, 28,* 210–228.

Lefkowitz, J. (1994). Sex-related differences in job attitudes and dispositional variables: Now you see them... *Academy of Management Journal, 37,* 323–349.

Leonard, H. S. (2017). A teachable approach to leadership. *Consulting Psychology Journal: Practice and Research, 69,* 243–266.

Leonardi, P. M. (2015). Materializing strategy: The blurry line between strategy formulation and strategy implementation. *British Journal of Management, 26*(Suppl 1), S17–S21.

Lepsinger, R., & Lucia, A. D. (2009). *The art and science of 360 degree feedback* (2nd ed.). San Francisco, CA: John Wiley & Sons.

Lester, S. W., Meglino, B. M., & Korsgaard, M. A. (2002). The antecedents and consequences of group potency: A longitudinal investigation of newly formed work groups. *Academy of Management Journal, 45,* 352–368.

Levay, C. (2010). Charismatic leadership in resistance to change. *The Leadership Quarterly, 21,* 127–143.

Levinson, H., & Rosenthal, S. (1984). *CEO: Corporate leadership in action.* New York: Basic Books.

Levitt, B., & March, J. G. (1988). Organizational learning. *Annual Review of Sociology, 14,* 319–338.

Lewin, K. (1951). *Field theory in social science.* New York: Harper & Row.

Lewin, K., Lippitt, R., & White, R. K. (1939). Patterns of aggressive behavior in experimentally created social climates. *Journal of Social Psychology, 10,* 271–301.

Lewis, M. W., Welsh, M. A., Dehler, G. E., & Green, S. G. (2002). Product development tensions: Exploring contrasting styles of product management. *Academy of Management Journal, 45,* 546–564.

Li, M., Mobley, W. H., & Kelly, A. (2013). When do global leaders learn best to develop cultural intelligence? An investigation of the moderating role of experiential learning style. *Academy of Management Learning & Education, 12,* 32–50.

Li, N., Chiaburu, D. S., Kirkman, B. L., & Xie, Z. (2013). Spotlight on the followers: An examination of moderators of relationships between transformational leadership and subordinates' citizenship and taking charge. *Personnel Psychology, 66,* 225–260.

Li, W.-D., Wang, N., Arvey, R. D., Soong, R., Saw, S. M., & Song, Z. (2015). A mixed blessing? Dual mediating mechanisms in the relationship between dopamine transporter gene DAT1 and leadership role occupancy. *The Leadership Quarterly, 26,* 671–686.

Lian, H., Ferris, D. L., & Brown, D. J. (2012). Does power distance exacerbate or mitigate the effects of abusive supervision? It depends on the outcome. *Journal of Applied Psychology, 97,* 107–123.

Liao, C. (2017). Leadership in virtual teams: a multilevel perspective. *Human Resource Management Review, 27,* 648–659.

Lichtenstein, B. B., & Plowman, D. A. (2009). The leadership of emergence: A complex systems leadership theory of emergence at successive organizational levels. *The Leadership Quarterly, 20,* 617–630.

Liden, R. C., Erdogan, B., Wayne, S. J., & Sparrowe, R. T. (2006). Leader-member exchange, differentiation, and task interdependence: Implications for individual and group performance. *Journal of Organizational Behavior, 27,* 723–746.

Liden, R. C., Panaccio, A., Meuser, J. D., Hu, J., & Wayne, S. J. (2014). Servant leadership: Antecedents, processes, and outcomes. In D. V. Day (Ed.), *The Oxford handbook of leadership in organizations* (pp. 357–379). Oxford, England: Oxford University Press.

Liden, R. C., Sparrowe, R. T., & Wayne, S. J. (1997). Leader-member exchange theory: The past and potential for the future. *Research in Personnel and Human Resource Management, 15,* 47–119.

Liden, R. C., Wayne, S. J., Meuser, J. D., Hu, J., Wu, J., & Liao, C. (2015). Servant leadership: Validation of a short form of the SL-28. *The Leadership Quarterly, 26,* 254–269.

Liden, R. C., Wayne, S. J., & Stilwell, D. (1993). A longitudinal study on the early development of leader-member exchanges. *Journal of Applied Psychology, 78,* 662–674.

Liden, R. C., Wayne, S. J., Zhao, H., & Henderson, D. (2008). Servant leadership: Development of a multidimensional measure and multi-level assessment. *The Leadership Quarterly, 19,* 161–177.

Liden, R. C., Wu, J., Cao, A. X., & Wayne, S. J. (2015). Leader-member exchange measurement. In T. N. Bauer & B. Erdogan (Eds.), *The Oxford handbook of leader-member exchange* (pp. 29–54). Oxford, UK: Oxford University Press.

Likert, R. (1967). *The human organization: Its management and value.* New York: McGraw-Hill.

Lim, B. C., & Klein, K. J. (2006). Team mental models and team performance: A field study of team mental model similarity and accuracy. *Journal of Organizational Behavior, 27,* 403–418.

Lin, H.-C., & Rababah, N. (2014). CEO–TMT exchange, TMT personality composition, and decision quality: The mediating role of TMT psychological empowerment. *The Leadership Quarterly, 25,* 943–957.

Lind, E. A., & Tyler, T. R. (1988). *The social psychology of procedural justice.* New York: Plenum.

Lindsey, E., Homes, V., & McCall, M. W., Jr. (1987). *Key events in executive lives.* Technical Report No. 32. Greensboro, NC: Center for Creative Leadership.

Ling, Y., Simsek, Z., Lubatkin, M. H., & Veiga, J. F. (2008a). Transformational leadership's role in promoting corporate entrepreneurship: Examining the CEO-TMT interface. *Academy of Management Journal, 51,* 557–576.

Ling, Y., Simsek, Z., Lubatkin, M. H., & Veiga, J. F. (2008b). The impact of transformational CEOs on the performance of small- to medium-sized firms: Does organizational context matter? *Journal of Applied Psychology, 93,* 923–934.

Ling, Y., Wei, L., Klimoski, R. J., & Wu, L. (2015). Benefiting from CEO's empowerment of TMTs: Does CEO–TMT dissimilarity matter? *The Leadership Quarterly, 26,* 1066–1079.

Lipman-Blumen, J. (2005). *The allure of toxic leaders: Why we follow destructive bosses and corrupt politicians – and how we can survive them.* New York: Oxford University Press.

Litchfield, R. C. (2008). Brainstorming reconsidered: A goal-based view. *Academy of Management Review, 33,* 649–668.

Litwin, G. H., & Stringer, P. A. (1968). *Motivation and organizational climate.* Boston: Division of Research, Harvard Business School.

Locke, E. A. (2003). Leadership: Starting at the top. In C. L. Pearce & J. A. Conger (Eds.), *Shared leadership: Reframing the hows and whys of leadership* (pp. 271–284). Thousand Oaks, CA: Sage.

Locke, E. A. (2005). Why emotional intelligence is an invalid concept. *Journal of Organizational Behavior, 26,* 425–431.

Locke, E. A., & Latham, G. P. (1990). *A theory of goal setting and task performance.* Englewood Cliffs, NJ: Prentice Hall.

Locke, E. E., & Becker, T. E. (1998). Rebuttal to a subjectivist critique of an objectivist approach to integrity in organizations. *Academy of Management Review, 23,* 170–175.

Lombardo, M. M., & Eichinger, R. W. (1989). *Eighty-eight assignments for development in place: Enhancing the developmental challenge of existing jobs.* Technical Report No. 136. Greensboro, NC: Center for Creative Leadership.

Lombardo, M. M., & McCauley, C. D. (1988). *The dynamics of management derailment.* Technical Report No. 34. Greensboro, NC: Center for Creative Leadership.

London, M. (2002). *Leadership development: Paths to self-insight and professional growth.* Mahwah, NJ: Lawrence Erlbaum.

London, M., & Mone, E. M. (1987). *Career management and survival in the workplace: Helping employees make tough career decisions, stay motivated, and reduce career stress.* San Francisco, CA: Jossey-Bass.

London, M., Wohlers, A. J., & Gallagher, P. (1990). A feedback approach to management development. *Journal of Management Development, 9*(6), 17–31.

Lord, R. G. (1977). Functional leadership behavior: Measurement and relation to social power and leadership perceptions. *Administrative Science Quarterly, 22,* 114–133.

Lord, R. G., & Brown, D. J. (2004). *Leadership processes and follower self-identity*. Mahwah, NJ: Lawrence Erlbaum.

Lord, R. G., Brown, D. J., Harvey, J. L., & Hall, R. J. (2001). Contextual constraints on prototype generation and their multilevel consequences for leadership perceptions. *The Leadership Quarterly, 12,* 311–338.

Lord, R. G., DeVader, C. L., & Alliger, G. M. (1986). A meta-analysis of the relation between personality traits and leadership: An application of validity generalization procedures. *Journal of Applied Psychology, 71,* 402–410.

Lord, R. G., Foti, R. J., & DeVader, C. L. (1984). A test of leadership categorization theory: Internal structure, information processing, and leadership perceptions. *Organizational Behavior and Human Performance, 34,* 343–378.

Lord, R. G., & Hall, R. J. (2005). Identity, deep structure, and the development of leadership skill. *The Leadership Quarterly, 16,* 591–615.

Lord, R. G., & Maher, K. J. (1991). *Leadership and information processing: Linking perceptions and performance*. Boston: Unwin-Hyman.

Lorinkova, N. M., Pearsall, M. J., & Sims, H. P., Jr. (2013). Examining the differential longitudinal performance of directive versus empowering leadership in teams. *Academy of Management Journal, 56,* 573–596.

Lowe, K. B., & Gardner, W. L. (2000). Ten years of *The Leadership Quarterly*: Contributions and challenges for the future. *The Leadership Quarterly, 11,* 459–514.

Lucas, K. W., & Markessini, J. (1993). *Senior leadership in a changing world order: Requisite skills for U. S. Army one- and two-star generals*. Technical Report No. 976. Alexandria, VA: U.S. Army Research Institute for the Behavioral and Social Sciences.

Lundby, K., Moriarity, R., & Lee, W. C. (2014). A tall order and some practical advice for global leaders: Managing across cultures and geographies. In B. Schneider & K. M. Barbera (Eds.), *The Oxford handbook of organizational climate and culture* (pp. 658–675). Oxford, UK: Oxford University Press.

Luthans, F., & Lockwood, D. L. (1984). Toward an observation system for measuring leader behavior in natural settings. In J. G. Hunt, D. Hosking, C. A. Schriesheim, & R. Stewart (Eds.), *Leaders and managers: International perspectives on managerial behavior and leadership* (pp. 117–141). New York: Pergamon Press.

Luthans, F., & Peterson, S. J. (2003). 360-degree feedback with systematic coaching: Empirical analysis suggests a winning combination. *Human Resource Management, 42,* 243–256.

Luthans, F., Rosenkrantz, S. A., & Hennessey, H. W. (1985). What do successful managers really do? An observational study of managerial activities. *Journal of Applied Behavioral Science, 21,* 255–270.

Luthans, F., Youssef-Morgan, C. M., & Avolio, B. J. (2015). *Psychological capital and beyond*. Oxford, UK: Oxford University Press.

Lyness, K. S., & Heilman, M. E. (2006). When fit is fundamental: Performance evaluations and promotions of upper-level female and male managers. *Journal of Applied Psychology, 91,* 777–785.

Ma, S., & Seidl, D. (2018). New CEOs and their collaborators: Divergence and convergence between the strategic leadership constellation and the top management team. *Strategic Management Journal, 39,* 606–638.

Ma, S., Seidl, D., & Guérard, S. (2015). The new CEO and the post-succession process: An integration of past research and future directions. *International Journal of Management Reviews, 17,* 460–482.

MacKie, D. (2014). The effectiveness of strength-based executive coaching in enhancing full range leadership development: A controlled study. *Consulting Psychology Journal: Practice and Research, 66*, 118–137.

Madsen, P. M., & Desai, V. (2010). Failing to learn? The effects of failure and success on organizational learning in the global orbital launch vehicle industry. *Academy of Management Journal, 53,* 451–476.

Mahoney, T. A., Jerdee, T. H., & Carroll, S. J., Jr. (1965). The jobs of management. *Industrial Relations: A Journal of Economy and Society, 4,* 97–110.

Mahsud, R., Yukl, G., & Prussia, G. (2010). Leader empathy, ethical leadership, and relations-oriented behaviors as antecedents of leader-member exchange quality. *Journal of Managerial Psychology, 25,* 561–577.

Mahsud, R., Yukl, G., & Prussia, G. (2011). Human capital, efficiency, and innovative adaptation as strategic determinants of firm performance. *Journal of Leadership and Organizational Studies, 18,* 229–246

Maier, N. R. F. (1963). *Problem-solving discussions and conferences: Leadership methods and skills.* New York: McGraw-Hill.

Main, J. (1992). How to steal the best ideas around. *Fortune,* October 19, 102–106.

Makri, M., & Scandura, T. A. (2010). Exploring the effects of creative CEO leadership on innovation in high technology firms. *The Leadership Quarterly, 21,* 75–88.

Malviya, S. (2017, June 14). The success of Patanjali has helped the entire Ayurvedic consumer products segment. Retrieved from https://economictimes.indiatimes.com (Accessed on January 15, 2019)

Mann, F. C. (1965). Toward an understanding of the leadership role in formal organization. In R. Dubin, G. C. Homans, F. C. Mann, & D. C. Miller (Eds.), *Leadership and productivity* (pp. 68–103). San Francisco, CA: Chandler Publishing.

Manz, C. C. (1991). Leading employees to be self-managing and beyond: Toward the establishment of self-leadership in organizations. *Journal of Management Systems, 3,* 15–24.

Manz, C. C., & Sims, H. P., Jr. (1980). Self-management as a substitute for leadership: A social learning perspective. *Academy of Management Review, 5,* 361–367.

Manz, C. C., & Sims, H. P., Jr. (1981). Vicarious learning: The influence of modeling on organizational behavior. *Academy of Management Review, 6,* 105–113.

Manz, C. C., & Sims, H. P., Jr. (1993). *Business without bosses: How self-managing teams are building high performance companies.* New York: Wiley.

Manz, C. C., & Sims, H. P. (1991). SuperLeadership: Beyond the myth of heroic leadership. *Organizational Dynamics, 19*(4), 18–35.

Marcel, J. J., Cowen, A. P., & Ballinger, G. A. (2017). Are disruptive CEO successions viewed as a governance lapse? Evidence from board turnover. *Journal of Management, 43,* 1313–1334.

March, J. G. (1991). Exploration and exploitation in organizational learning. *Organization Science, 2,* 71–87.

Marcy, R. T. (2015). Breaking mental models as a form of creative destruction: The role of leader cognition in radical social innovations. *The Leadership Quarterly, 26,* 370–385.

Marcy, R. T., & Mumford, M. D. (2010). Leader cognition: Improving leader performance through causal analysis. *The Leadership Quarterly, 21,* 1–19.

Margolis, J. A., & Ziegert, J. C. (2016). Vertical flow of collectivistic leadership: An examination of the cascade of visionary leadership across levels. *The Leadership Quarterly, 27,* 334–348.

Marion, R., & Uhl-Bien, M. (2001). Leadership in complex organizations. *The Leadership Quarterly, 12,* 389–418.

Markham, S. E., Yammarino, F. J., Murry, W. D., & Palanski, M. E. (2010). Leader-member exchange, shared values, and performance:

Agreement and levels of analysis do matter. *The Leadership Quarterly, 21,* 469–480.

Marks, M. A., DeChurch, L. A., Mathieu, J. E., Panzer, F. J., & Alonso, A. (2005). Teamwork in multiteam systems. *Journal of Applied Psychology, 90,* 96--971.

Marks, M. A., Mathieu, J. E., & Zaccaro, S. J. (2001). A temporally based framework and taxonomy of team processes. *Academy of Management Review, 26,* 356–376.

Marks, M. A., Zaccaro, S. J., & Mathieu, J. E. (2000). Performance implications of leader briefings and team-interaction training for team adaptation to novel environments. *Journal of Applied Psychology, 85,* 971–986.

Marrone, J. A. (2010). Team boundary spanning: A multilevel review of past research and proposals for the future. *Journal of Management, 36,* 911–940.

Marrone, J. A., Tesluk, P. E., & Carson, J. B. (2007). A multi-level investigation of antecedents and consequences of team member boundary spanning behavior. *Academy of Management Journal, 50,* 1423–1439.

Marshall-Mies, J. C., Fleishman, E. A., Martin, J. A., Zaccaro, S. J., Baughman, W. A., & McGee, M. L. (2000). Development and evaluation of cognitive and metacognitive measures for predicting leadership potential. *The Leadership Quarterly, 11,* 135–153.

Martin, R., Guillaume, Y., Thomas, G., Lee, A., & Epitropaki, O. (2016). Leader–member exchange (LMX) and performance: A meta-analytic review. *Personnel Psychology, 69,* 67–121.

Martinko, M. J., & Gardner, W. L. (1985). Beyond structured observation: Methodological issues and new directions. *Academy of Management Review, 10,* 676–695.

Martinko, M. J., & Gardner, W. L. (1987). The leader/member attribution process. *Academy of Management Review, 12,* 235–249.

Martinko, M. J., & Gardner, W. L. (1990). Structured observation of managerial work: A replication and synthesis. *Journal of Managerial Studies, 27,* 329–357.

Martinko, M. J., Harvey, P., & Douglas, S. C. (2007). The role, function, and contribution of attribution theory to leadership: A review. *The Leadership Quarterly, 18,* 561–585.

Martinko, M. J., Mackey, J. D., Moss, S. E., Harvey, P., McAllister, C. P., & Brees, J. R. (2018). An exploration of the role of subordinate affect in leader evaluations. *Journal of Applied Psychology, 103,* 738–752.

Martins, L. L., Gilson, L. L., & Maynard, M. T. (2004). Virtual teams: What do we know and where do we go from here? *Journal of Management, 30,* 805–835.

Mathieu, J. E., & Chen, G. (2010). The etiology of the multilevel paradigm in management research. *Journal of Management, 37,* 610–641.

Mathieu, J. E., Gilson, L. L., & Ruddy, T. M. (2006). Empowerment and team effectiveness: An empirical test of an integrated model. *Journal of Applied Psychology, 91,* 97–108.

Mathieu, J. E., & Rapp, T. L. (2009). Laying the foundation for successful team performance trajectories: The roles of team charters and performance strategies. *Journal of Applied Psychology, 94,* 90–103.

Matta, F. K., Scott, B. A., Koopman, J., & Conlon, D. E. (2015). Does seeing "eye to eye" affect work engagement and organizational citizenship behavior? A role theory perspective on LMX agreement. *Academy of Management Journal, 58,* 1686–1708.

Maurer, R. (1996). *Beyond the wall of resistance: Unconventional strategies that build support for change*. Austin, TX: Bard Books.

Maxwell, J. C. (2007). *The 21 irrefutable laws of leadership: Follow them and people will follow you* (Revised and updated 10th anniversary ed.). Nashville: Thomas Nelson.

Maxwell, J. C. (2008). *Mentoring 101: What every leader needs to know*. Nashville, TN: Thomas Nelson.

May, D. R., & Pauli, K. P. (2002). The role of moral intensity in ethical decision-making: A review and investigation of moral recognition, evaluation, and intention. *Business and Society, 41,* 84–117.

Mayer, D. M., Aquino, K., Greenbaum, R. L., & Kuenzi, M. (2012). Who displays ethical leadership, and why does it matter? An examination of antecedents and consequences of ethical leadership. *Academy of Management Journal, 55*, 151–171.

Mayer, D. M., Kuenzi, M., Greenbaum, R., Bardes, M., & Salvador, R. (2009). How low does ethical leadership flow? Test of a trickle-down model. *Organizational Behavior and Human Decision Processes, 108*, 1–13.

Mayer, J. D., & Salovey, P. (1995). Emotional intelligence and the construction and regulation of feelings. *Applied and Preventive Psychology, 4*, 197–208.

Mayer, J. D., Salovey, P., Caruso, D. R., & Sitarenios, G. (2003). Measuring emotional intelligence with the MSCEIT v. 2.0. *Emotion, 3*, 97–105.

Maynard, M. T., Gilson, L. L., & Mathieu, J. E. (2012). Empowerment - Fad or fab? A multilevel review of the past two decades of research. *Journal of Management, 38*, 1231–1281.

Mayo, M., Meindl, J. R., & Pastor, J. C. (2003). Shared leadership in work teams: A social network approach. In C. Pearce & J. Conger (Eds.), *Shared leadership: Reframing the hows and whys of leadership* (pp. 193–214). Thousand Oaks, CA: Sage.

Mazutis, D., & Eckardt, A. (2017). Sleepwalking into catastrophe: Cognitive biases and corporate climate change inertia. *California Management Review, 59*(3), 74–108.

McCall, M. W., Jr. (1992). Executive development as a business strategy. *The Journal of Business Strategy, 13*(1), 25–31.

McCall, M. W., Jr. (1998). *High flyers: Developing the next generation of leaders*. Boston: Harvard Business School Press.

McCall, M. W., Jr. (2004). Leadership development through experience. *Academy of Management Executive, 18*(3), 127–130.

McCall, M. W., Jr. (2010a). Peeling the onion: Getting inside experience-based leadership development. *Industrial and Organizational Psychology, 3*, 61–68.

McCall, M. W., Jr. (2010b). Recasting leadership development. *Industrial and Organizational Psychology: Perspectives on Science and Practice, 3*, 3–19.

McCall, M. W., Jr., & Kaplan, R. E. (1985). *Whatever it takes: Decision makers at work*. Englewood Cliffs, NJ: Prentice Hall.

McCall, M. W., Jr., & Lombardo, M. M. (1983a). *Off the track: Why and how successful executives get derailed*. Technical Report No. 21. Greensboro, NC: Center for Creative Leadership.

McCall, M. W., Jr., & Lombardo, M. M. (1983b). What makes a top executive? *Psychology Today, 17*(February), 26–31.

McCall, M. W., Jr., Lombardo, M. M., & Morrison, A. (1988). *The lessons of experience*. Lexington, MA: Lexington Books.

McCall, M. W., Jr., & McHenry, J. J. (2014). Catalytic converters: How exceptional bosses develop leaders. In C. D. McCauley & M. W. McCall, Jr. (Eds.), *Using experience to develop leadership talent* (pp. 396–421). San Francisco, CA: Jossey-Bass.

McCall, M. W., Jr., Morrison, A. M., & Hannan, R. L. (1978). *Studies of managerial work: Results and methods*. Technical Report No. 9. Greensboro, NC: Center for Creative Leadership.

McCall, M. W., Jr., & Segrist, C. A. (1980). *In pursuit of the manager's job: Building on Mintzberg*. Technical Report No. 14. Greensboro, NC: Center for Creative Leadership.

McCarthy, G., & Milner, J. (2013). Managerial coaching: Challenges, opportunities and training. *Journal of Management Development, 32*, 768–779.

McCartney, W. W., & Campbell, C. R. (2006). Leadership, management, and derailment: A model of individual success and failure. *Leadership & Organization Development Journal, 27*, 190–202.

McCauley, C. D. (1986). *Developmental experiences in managerial work: A literature* *review*. Technical Report No. 26. Greensboro, NC: Center for Creative Leadership.

McCauley, C. D. (2001). Leader training and development. In S. J. Zaccaro & R. J. Klimoski, (Eds.), *The nature of organizational leadership: Understanding the performance imperatives confronting today's leaders* (pp. 347–383). San Francisco: Jossey-Bass.

McCauley, C. D., & Douglas, C. A. (1998). Developmental relationships. In C. D. McCauley, R. S. Moxley, & E. Van Velsor (Eds.), *The Center for Creative Leadership handbook of leadership development* (pp. 160–193). San Francisco: Jossey-Bass.

McCauley, C. D., Drath, W. H., Palus, C. J., O'Connor, P. M. G., & Baker, B. (2006). The use of constructive-developmental theory to advance the understanding of leadership. *The Leadership Quarterly, 17,* 634–653.

McCauley, C. D., Eastman, L. J., & Ohlott, P. J. (1995). Linking management selection and development through stretch assignments. *Human Resource Management, 34,* 93–115.

McCauley, C. D., & Lombardo, M. M. (1990). Benchmarks: An instrument for diagnosing managerial strengths and weaknesses. In K. E. Clark & M. B. Clark (Eds.), *Measures of leadership* (pp. 535–545). West Orange, NJ: Leadership Library of America.

McCauley, C. D., Ruderman, M. N., Ohlott, P. J., & Morrow, J. E. (1994). Assessing the developmental components of managerial jobs. *Journal of Applied Psychology, 79,* 544–560.

McClane, W. E. (1991). Implications of member role differentiation: Analysis of a key concept in the LMX model of leadership. *Group & Organization Studies, 16,* 102–113.

McClelland, D. C. (1975). *Power: The inner experience*. New York: Irvington.

McClelland, D. C. (1985). *Human motivation*. Glenview, IL: Scott Foresman.

McClelland, D. C., & Boyatzis, R. E. (1982). Leadership motive pattern and long-term success in management. *Journal of Applied Psychology, 67,* 737–743.

McClelland, D. C., & Burnham, D. H. (1976). Power is the great motivator. *Harvard Business Review, 54*(2), 100–110.

McClelland, P. L., Liang, X., & Barker, V. L. (2009). CEO commitment to the status quo: Replication and extension using content analysis. *Journal of Management, 36,* 1251–1277.

McColl-Kennedy, J. R., & Anderson, R. D. (2002). Impact of leadership style and emotions on subordinate performance. *The Leadership Quarterly, 13,* 545–559.

McCrae, R. R., & Costa, P. T. (1999). A five-factor theory of personality. In L. Pervin & O. P. John (Eds.), *Handbook of personality: Theory and research* (2nd ed., pp. 139–153). New York: Guilford.

McCrae, R. R., & Costa, P. T., Jr. (2008). Empirical and theoretical status of the Five-Factor Model of personality traits. In G. J. Boyle, G. Matthews, & D. H. Saklofske (Eds.), *The SAGE handbook of personality theory and assessment* (Vol. 1, Personality theories and models, pp. 273–294). Los Angeles: Sage.

McDonald, M. L., & Westphal, J. D. (2013). Access denied: Low mentoring of women and minority first-time directors and its negative effects on appointments to additional boards. *Academy of Management Journal, 56,* 1169–1198.

McFillen, J. M., & New, J. R. (1979). Situational determinants of supervisor attributions and behavior. *Academy of Management Journal, 22,* 793–809.

McGill, M. E., Slocum, J. W., Jr., & Lei, D. (1993). Management practices in learning organizations. *Organizational Dynamics, 22*(1), 5–17.

McGrath, J. E. (1984). *Groups: Interaction and performance*. Englewood Cliffs, NJ: Prentice Hall.

McGregor, D. (1960). *The human side of enterprise.* New York: McGraw-Hill.

McIntyre, H. H., & Foti, R. J. (2013). The impact of shared leadership on teamwork mental models and performance in self-directed teams. *Group Processes & Intergroup Relations, 16*(1), 46–57.

McLean, B., & Elkind, P. (2003). *Smartest guys in the room: The amazing rise and scandalous fall of Enron*. Portfolio/Penguin Group USA.

McLennan, K. (1967). The manager and his job skills. *Academy of Management Journal, 3,* 235–245.

McNatt, D. B. (2000). Ancient Pygmalion joins contemporary management: A meta-analysis of the result. *Journal of Applied Psychology, 85,* 314–322.

McNatt, D. B., & Judge, T. A. (2004). Boundary conditions of the Galatea effect: A field experiment and constructive replication. *Academy of Management Journal, 47,* 550–565.

Megheirkouni, M. (2016). Factors influencing leadership development in an uncertain environment. *Journal of Management Development, 35*, 1232–1254.

Mehra, A., Smith, B., Dixon, A., & Robertson, B. (2006). Distributed leadership in teams: The network of leadership perceptions and team performance. *The Leadership Quarterly, 17,* 232–245.

Meinert, D. (2014). Leadership development spending is up. *HR Magazine*. Retrieved from https://www.shrm.org/hr-today/news/hr-magazine/pages/0814-execbrief.aspx

Meindl, J. R. (1990). On leadership: An alternative to the conventional wisdom. In B. M. Staw & L. L. Cummings (Eds.), *Research in organizational behavior* (Vol. 12, pp. 159–204). Greenwich, CT: JAI Press.

Meindl, J. R., Ehrlich, S. B., & Dukerich, J. M. (1985). The romance of leadership. *Administrative Science Quarterly, 30,* 78–102.

Menges, J. I., Kilduff, M., Kern, S., & Bruch, H. (2015). The awestruck effect: Followers suppress emotion expression in response to charismatic but not individually considerate leadership. *The Leadership Quarterly, 26,* 626–640.

Menon, D. (2016). *Spirituality at work: The inspiring message of the Bhagavad Gita.* Mumbai, India: Yogi Impressions.

Meredith, J. R., & Mantel, S. J., Jr. (1985). *Project management: A managerial approach.* New York: John Wiley.

Mesmer-Magnus, J. R., & DeChurch, L. A. (2009). Information sharing and team performance: A meta-analysis. *Journal of Applied Psychology, 94*, 535–546.

Mesmer-Magnus, J. R., DeChurch, L. A., Jimenez-Rodriguez, M., Wildman, J., & Shuffler, M. (2011). A meta-analytic investigation of virtuality and information sharing in teams. *Organizational Behavior and Human Decision Processes, 115*, 214–225.

Methe, D. T., Wilson, D., & Perry, J. L. (2000). A review of research on incremental approaches to strategy. In J. Rabin, G. J. Miller, & W. B. Hildreth (Eds.), *Handbook of strategic management* (2nd ed., pp. 31–65). New York: Marcel Dekker.

Meuser, J. D., Gardner, W. L., Dinh, J. E., Hu, J., Liden, R. C., & Lord, R. G. (2016). A network analysis of leadership theory: The infancy of integration. *Journal of Management, 42*, 1374–1403.

Meyer, A. (1982). How ideologies supplant formal structures and shape responses to environments. *Journal of Management Studies, 19,* 45–61.

Mhatre, K. H., & Riggio, R. E. (2014). Charismatic and transformational leadership: Past, present, and future. In D. V. Day (Ed.), *The Oxford handbook of leadership and organizations* (pp. 221–240). Oxford, U.K.: Oxford University Press.

Miao, Q., Newman, A., & Huang, X. (2014). The impact of participative leadership on job performance and organizational citizenship behavior: Distinguishing between the mediating effects of affective and cognitive trust. *The International Journal of Human Resource Management, 25*, 2796–2810.

Michael, J., & Yukl, G. (1993). Managerial level and subunit function as determinants of networking behavior in organizations. *Group & Organizational Management, 18,* 328–351.

Michinov, N. (2012). Is electronic brainstorming or brainwriting the best way to improve creative performance in groups? An overlooked comparison of two idea-generation techniques. *Journal of Applied Social Psychology, 42* (Suppl 1), E222–E243.

The military balance. (2010). London: International Institute for Strategic Studies.

Miller, C. C., & Cardinal, L. B. (1994). Strategic planning and firm performance: A synthesis of more than two decades of research. *Academy of Management Journal*, 37, 1649–1665.

Miller, D. (1990). *The Icarus paradox*. New York: Harper-Collins.

Miller, D., & Chen, M.-J. (1994). Sources and consequences of competitive inertia. *Administrative Science Quarterly, 39,* 1–23.

Miller, D., & Friesen, P. H. (1984). *Organizations: A quantum view*. Englewood Cliffs, NJ: Prentice Hall.

Miller, D., Kets de Vries, M. F. R., & Toulouse, J. (1982). Top executive locus of control and its relationship to strategy, environment, and structure. *Academy of Management Journal, 25,* 237–253.

Miller, K. I., & Monge, P. R. (1986). Participation, satisfaction, and productivity: A meta-analytic review. *Academy of Management Journal, 29,* 727–753.

Miller, D., & Toulouse, J. (1986). Chief executive personality and corporate strategy and structure in small firms. *Management Science, 32,* 1389–1409.

Miller, S. M., Lack, E. R., & Asroff, S. (1985). Preference for control and the coronary-prone behavior pattern: 'I'd rather do it myself.' *Journal of Personality and Social Psychology, 49*, 492–499.

Milliken, F. J., & Martins, L. L. (1996). Searching for common threads: Understanding the multiple effects of diversity in organizational groups. *Academy of Management Review, 21,* 402–433.

Millikin, J. P., Hom, P. W., & Manz, C. C. (2010). Self-management competencies in self-managing teams: Their impact on multi-team system productivity. *The Leadership Quarterly, 21*, 687–702.

Milliman, J., Czaplewski, A., & Ferguson, J. (2003). Workplace spirituality and employee work attitudes: An exploratory empirical assessment. *Journal of Organizational Change Management, 16,* 426–447.

Miner, J. B. (1975). The uncertain future of the leadership concept: An overview. In J. G. Hunt & L. L. Larson (Eds.), *Leadership frontiers* (pp. 197–208). Kent, OH: Kent State University Press.

Miner, J. B. (1978). Twenty years of research on role motivation theory of managerial effectiveness. *Personnel Psychology, 31,* 739–760.

Miner, J. B. (1985). Sentence completion measures in personnel research: The development and validation of the Miner Sentence Completion Scales. In H. J. Bernardin & D. A. Bownas (Eds.), *Personality assessment in organizations* (pp. 145–176). New York: Praeger.

Mintzberg, H. (1973). *The nature of managerial work.* New York: Harper & Row.

Mintzberg, H. (1979). *The structuring of organizations: A synthesis of research.* Englewood Cliffs, NJ: Prentice Hall.

Mintzberg, H. (1983). *Power in and around organizations*. Englewood Cliffs, NJ: Prentice Hall.

Mintzberg, H., Raisinghani, D., & Theoret, A. (1976). The structure of "unstructured" decision processes, *Administrative Science Quarterly, 21*, 246–275.

Mio, J. S., Riggio, R. E., Levin, S., & Reese, R. (2005). Presidential leadership and charisma: The effects of metaphor. *The Leadership Quarterly, 16,* 287–294.

Miron, E., Erez, M., & Naveh, E. (2004). Do personal characteristics and cultural values that promote innovation, quality, and efficiency compete or complement each other? *Journal of Organizational Behavior, 25,* 175–199.

Mishina, Y., Dykes, B. J., Block, E. S., & Pollock, T. (2010). Why "good" firms do bad things: The effects of high aspirations, high expectations, and prominence on the incidence of corporate illegality. *Academy of Management Journal, 53,* 701–722.

Misumi, J., & Peterson, M. (1985). The performance-maintenance (PM) theory of leadership: Review of a Japanese research program. *Administrative Science Quarterly, 30,* 198–223.

Mitchell, R., Boyle, B., Parker, V., Giles, M., Chiang, V., & Joyce, P. (2015). Managing inclusiveness and diversity in teams: How leader inclusiveness affects performance through status and team identity. *Human Resource Management, 54*, 217–239.

Mitchell, R. K., Agle, B. R., & Wood, D. J. (1997). Toward a theory of stakeholder identification and salience: Defining the principle of who and what really counts. *Academy of Management Review, 22*, 853–886.

Mitchell, R. K., Weaver, G. R., Agle, B. R., Bailey, A. D., & Carlson, J. (2016). Stakeholder agency and social welfare: Pluralism and decision making in the multi-objective corporation. *Academy of Management Review, 41*, 252–275.

Mitchell, T. R. (1973). Motivation and participation: An integration. *Academy of Management Journal, 16,* 670–679.

Mitchell, T. R., Green, S. C., & Wood, R. E. (1981). An attributional model of leadership and the poor performing subordinate: Development and validation. In L. L. Cummings & B. M. Staw (Eds.), *Research in organizational behavior* (Vol. 3, pp. 197–234). Greenwich, CT: JAI Press.

Mitchell, T. R., & Kalb, L. S. (1981). Effects of outcome knowledge and outcome valence on supervisor's evaluation. *Journal of Applied Psychology, 66,* 604–612.

Mitchell, T. R., & Kalb, L. S. (1982). Effects of job experience on supervisor attributions for a subordinate's poor performance. *Journal of Applied Psychology, 67*, 181–188.

Mitroff, I. I. (2004). *Crisis leadership: Planning for the unthinkable.* Hoboken, NJ: Wiley.

Mitroff, I. I., & Denton, E. A. (1999). *A spiritual audit of corporate America: Multiple designs for fostering spirituality in the workplace*. San Francisco, CA: Jossey-Bass.

Mohammed, S., Ferzandi, L., & Hamilton, K. (2010). Metaphor no more: A 15-year review of the team mental model construct. *Journal of Management, 36,* 876–910.

Morais, F., Kakabadse, A., & Kakabadse, N. (2018). The chairperson and CEO roles interaction and responses to strategic tensions. *Corporate Governance: The International Journal of Business in Society, 18*(1), 143–164.

Morgeson, F. P. (2005). The external leadership of self-managed teams: Intervening in the context of novel and disruptive events. *Journal of Applied Psychology, 90,* 497–508.

Morgeson, F. P., & DeRue, D. S. (2006). Event criticality, urgency, and duration: Understanding how events disrupt teams and influence team leader intervention. *The Leadership Quarterly, 17,* 271–287.

Morgeson, F. P., DeRue, D. S., & Karam, E. P. (2010). Leadership in teams: A functional approach to understanding leadership structures and processes. *Journal of Management, 36,* 5–39.

Morgeson, F. P., & Hofmann, D. A. (1999). The structure and function of collective constructs: Implications for multilevel research and theory development. *Academy of Management Review, 24,* 249–265.

Morgeson, F. P., Reider, M., & Campion, M. (2005). Selecting individuals in team settings: The importance of social skills, personality characteristics, and teamwork knowledge. *Personnel Psychology, 58,* 583–611.

Morse, J. J., & Wagner, F. R. (1978). Measuring the process of managerial effectiveness. *Academy of Management Journal, 21*, 23–35.

Morse, N. C., & Reimer, E. (1956). The experimental change of a major organizational variable. *Journal of Abnormal and Social Psychology, 52,* 120–129.

Moses, J., Hollenbeck, G., & Sorcher, M. (1993). Other people's expectations. *Human Resource Management, 32,* 283–297.

Moxley, R. S., & O'Connor-Wilson, P. (1998). A systems approach to leadership development. In C. D. McCauley, R. S. Moxley, & E. Van Velsor (Eds.), *Center for Creative Leadership handbook of leadership development*. San Francisco: Jossey-Bass, pp. 217–241.

Muehlfeld, K., van Doorn, J., & van Witteloostuijn, A. (2011). The effects of personality composition and decision-making processes on change preferences of self-managing teams. *Managerial & Decision Economics, 32*, 333–353.

Muffet-Willett, S. L., & Kruse, S. D. (2008). Crisis leadership: Past research and future directions. *Journal of Business Continuity & Emergency Planning, 3,* 248–258.

Mulder, M., deJong, R. D., Koppelaar, L., & Verhage, J. (1986). Power, situation, and leaders' effectiveness: An organizational study. *Journal of Applied Psychology,* 71, 566–570.

Mulder, M., Ritsema van Eck, J. R., & de Jong, R. D. (1970). An organization in crisis and noncrisis conditions. *Human Relations, 24,* 19–41.

Mulder, M., & Stemerding, A. (1963). Threat, attraction to group, and need for strong leadership: A laboratory experiment in a natural setting. *Human Relations, 16,* 317–334.

Mumford, M. D. (1986). Leadership in the organizational context: Some empirical and theoretical considerations. *Journal of Applied Psychology, 16,* 508–531.

Mumford, M. D. (2006). *Pathways to outstanding leadership: A comparative analysis of charismatic, ideological, and pragmatic leaders.* Mahway, NJ: Erlbaum.

Mumford, M. D., Antes, A. L., Caughron, J. J., & Friedrich, T. L. (2008). Charismatic, ideological, and pragmatic leadership: Multi-level influences on emergence and performance. *The Leadership Quarterly, 19,* 144–160.

Mumford, M. D., & Connelly, M. S. (1991). Leaders as creators: Leader performance and problem solving in ill-defined domains. *The Leadership Quarterly, 2,* 289–315.

Mumford, M. D., Espejo, J., Hunter, S. T., Dedell-Aveers, K., Eubanks, E. L., & Connelly, S. (2007). The sources of leader violence: A comparison of ideological and non-ideological leaders. *The Leadership Quarterly, 18,* 217–235.

Mumford, M. D., Friedrich, T. L., Caughron, J. J., & Byrne, C. L. (2007). Leader cognition in real-world settings: How do leaders think about crises? *The Leadership Quarterly, 18,* 515–543.

Mumford, M. D., Gessner, T. L., Connelly, M. S., O'Connor, J. A., & Clifton, T. C. (1993). Leadership and destructive acts: Individual and situational influences. *The Leadership Quarterly, 4,* 115–147.

Mumford, M. D., Hunter, S. T., Eubanks, D. L., Bedell, K. E., & Murphy, S. T. (2007). Developing leaders for creative efforts: A domain-based approach to leadership development. *Human Resource Management Review, 17,* 402–417.

Mumford, M. D., Marks, M. A., Connelly, M. S., Zaccaro, S. J., & Reiter-Palmon, R. (2000). Development of leadership skills: Experience and timing. *The Leadership Quarterly, 11,* 87–114.

Mumford, M. D., Mulhearn, T. J., Watts, L. L., Steele, L. M., & McIntosh, T. (2017). Leader impacts on creative teams: Direction, engagement and sales. In R. Reiter-Palmon (Ed.), *Team creativity and innovation* (pp. 131–166). Oxford, UK: Oxford University Press.

Mumford, M. D., Scott, G. M., Baddis, B., & Strange, J. M. (2002). Leading creative people: Orchestrating expertise and relationships. *The Leadership Quarterly, 13,* 705–750.

Mumford, M. D., & Strange, J. M. (2002). Vision and mental models: The case of charismatic and ideological leadership. In B. J. Avolio & F. J. Yammarino (Eds.), *Transformational and Charismatic Leadership: The road ahead* (Vol. 2, pp. 109–142): Elsevier Science Ltd.

Mumford, M. D., Todd, E. M., Higgs, C., & McIntosh, T. (2017). Cognitive skills and leadership performance: The nine critical skills. *The Leadership Quarterly, 28,* 24–39.

Mumford, M. D., Watts, L. L., & Partlow, P. J. (2015). Leader cognition: Approaches and findings. *The Leadership Quarterly, 26,* 301–306.

Mumford, T. V., Campion, M. A., & Morgeson, F. P. (2007). The leadership skills strataplex: Leadership skill requirements across organizational levels. *The Leadership Quarterly, 18,* 154–166.

Munchus, G., III, & McArthur, B. (1991). Revisiting the historical use of the assessment centre in management selection and development. *Journal of Management Development, 10*(1), 5–13.

Murase, T., Carter, D. R., DeChurch, L. A., & Marks, M. A. (2014). Mind the gap: The role of leadership in multiteam system collective cognition. *The Leadership Quarterly, 25,* 972–986.

Murray, A. I. (1989). Top management group heterogeneity and firm performance. *Strategic Management Journal, 10,* 125–141.

Munyon, T. P., Summers, J. K., Thompson, K. M., & Ferris, G. R. (2015). Political skill and work outcomes: A theoretical extension, meta-analytic investigation, and agenda for the future. *Personnel Psychology, 68,* 143–184.

Nadkarni, S., & Herrmann, P. (2010). CEO personality, strategic flexibility, and firm performance: The case of the Indian business process outsourcing industry. *Academy of Management Journal, 53,* 1050–1073.

Nadler, D. A. (1988). Organizational frame bending: Types of change in the complex organization. In R. H. Kilmann & T. J. Covin (Eds.), *Corporate transformation: Revitalizing organizations for a competitive world* (pp. 66–83). San Francisco: Jossey-Bass.

Nadler, D. A. (1998). Leading executive teams. In D. Nadler, J. Spencer, & Associates (Eds.), *Executive teams* (pp. 3–20). San Francisco: Jossey-Bass.

Nadler, D. A., Shaw, R. B., Walton, A. E., & Associates (1995). *Discontinuous change: Leading organizational transformation.* San Francisco, Jossey-Bass.

Nahavandi, A., Mizzi, P. J., & Malekzadeh, A. R. (1992). Executives' type A personality as a determinant of environmental perception and firm strategy. *Journal of Social Psychology, 132,* 59–67.

Nahrgang, J. D., Morgeson, F. P., & Ilies, R. (2009). The development of leader–member exchanges: Exploring how personality and performance influence leader and member relationships over time. *Organizational Behavior and Human Decision Processes, 108,* 256–266.

Nair, S. K., & Yuvaraj, S. (2000). Locus of control and managerial effectiveness: A study of private sector managers. Indian Journal of Industrial Relations, 41–52.

Nanus, B. (1992). *Visionary leadership: Creating a compelling sense of direction for your organization*. San Francisco: Jossey-Bass.

Narayanan, V. K., & Fahey, L. (2013). Seven management follies that threaten strategic success. *Strategy & Leadership, 41*(4), 24–29.

Narayanan, V. K., Zane, L. J., & Kemerer, B. (2011). The cognitive perspective in strategy: An integrative review. *Journal of Management, 37,* 305–351.

NASSCOM. (2016, March 15). Making diversity work: Key trends and practices in the Indian IT-BPM industry. Retrieved from https://www.pwc.in (Accessed on January 12, 2019)

Ndofor, H. A., Priem, R. L., Rathburn, J. A., & Dhir, A. K. (2009). What does the new boss think? How new leaders' cognitive communities and recent "top-job" success affect organizational change and performance. *The Leadership Quarterly, 20,* 799–813.

Neck, C. P., & Manz, C. C. (1992). Thought self-leadership: The influence of self-talk and mental imagery on performance. *Journal of Organizational Behavior, 13,* 681–699.

Nelson, J. K., Zaccaro, S. J., & Herman, J. L. (2010). Strategic information provision and experiential variety as tools for developing adaptive leadership skills. *Consulting Psychology Journal: Practice and Research, 62,* 131–142.

Nemetz, P. L., & Christensen, S. L. (1996). The challenge of cultural diversity: Harnessing a diversity of views to understand multiculturalism. *Academy of Management Review, 21,* 434–462.

Newman, W. H., & Warren, K. (1977). *The process of management*. Englewood Cliffs, NJ: Prentice Hall.

Newstrom, J., & Davis, K. (1993). *Organizational behavior: Human behavior at work*. New York: McGraw-Hill.

Nevis, E. C., Dibella, A. J., & Gould, J. M. (1995). Understanding organizations as learning systems. *Sloan Management Review,* Winter, 73–85.

Ng, E. S. W., & Wyrick, C. R. (2011). Motivational bases for managing diversity: A model of leadership commitment. *Human Resource Management Review, 21*, 368–376.

Ng, T. W. H., & Feldman, D. C. (2015). Ethical leadership: Meta-analytic evidence of criterion-related and incremental validity. *Journal of Applied Psychology, 100*, 948–965.

Nicolaides, V. C., LaPort, K. A., Chen, T. R., Tomassetti, A. J., Weis, E. J., Zaccaro, S. J., & Cortina, J. M. (2014). The shared leadership of teams: A meta-analysis of proximal, distal, and moderating relationships. *The Leadership Quarterly, 25*, 923–942.

Nielsen, R. P. (1989). Changing unethical organizational behavior. *Academy of Management Executive, 3*(2), 123–130.

Nischii, L. H. (2013). The benefits of climate for inclusion for gender-diverse groups. *Academy of Mangement Journal, 56*, 1754–1774.

Noe, R. A. (1988). An investigation of the determinants of successful assigned mentoring relationships. *Personnel Psychology, 41,* 457–479.

Noe, R. A. (1991). Mentoring relationships for employee development. In J. W. Jones, B. D. Steffy, & D. W. Bray (Eds.), *Applying psychology in business: The manager's handbook and hum,an resource professionals* (pp. 475–482). Lexington, MA: Lexington Press.

Noe, R. A., & Ford, J. K. (1992). Emerging issues and new directions for training research. In K. Rowland & G. Ferris (Eds.), *Research in personnel and human resource management* (Vol. 11, pp. 345–384). Greenwich, CT: JAI Press.

Noe, R. A., Greenberger, D. B., & Wang, S. (2002). Mentoring: What we know and where we might go. In G. R. Ferris & J. J. Martocchio (Eds.), *Research in personnel and human resources management* (Vol. 21, pp. 129–173). Oxford, England: Elsevier.

Nohria, N., Joyce, W., & Roberson, B. (2003). What really works. *Harvard Business Review, 81*(7), 42–2.

Nowack, K. M. (2009). Leveraging multirater feedback to facilitate successful behavioral change. *Consulting Psychology Journal: Practice and Research, 61,* 280–297.

Nowack, K. M., & Mashihi, S. (2012). Evidence-based answers to 15 questions about leveraging 360-degree feedback. *Consulting Psychology Journal: Practice and Research, 64*, 157–182.

Nyberg, A. J., Fulmer, I. S., Gerhart, B., & Carpenter, M. A. (2010). Agency theory revisited: CEO return and shareholder interest alignment. *Academy of Management Journal, 53*, 1029–1049.

Nyberg, A. J., Moliterno, T. P., Hale, D., Jr., & Lepak, D. P. (2014). Resource-based perspectives on unit-level human capital: A review and integration. *Journal of Management, 40*, 316–346.

O'Brien, G. E., & Kabanoff, B. (1981). The effects of leadership style and group structure upon small group productivity: A test of a discrepancy theory of leader effectiveness. *Australian Journal of Psychology, 33*(2), 157–158.

O'Connor, J., Mumford, M. D., Clifton, T. C., Gessner, T. L., & Connelly, M. S. (1995). Charismatic leaders and destructiveness: A historiometric study. *The Leadership Quarterly, 6,* 529–555.

O'Donnell, M., Yukl, G., & Taber, T. (2012). Leader behavior and LMX: A constructive replication. *Journal of Managerial Psychology, 27*(2), 143–154.

O'Neill, T. A., Hancock, S. E., Zivkov, K., Larson, N. L., & Law, S. J. (2016). Team decision making in virtual and face-to-face environments. *Group Decision and Negotiation, 25*, 995–1020.

O'Neill, T. A., McLarnon, M. J. W., Xiu, L., & Law, S. J. (2016). Core self-evaluations, perceptions of group potency, and job performance: The moderating role of individualism and collectivism cultural profiles. *Journal of Occupational and Organizational Psychology, 89*, 447–473.

O'Reilly, C. A., III, Caldwell, D. F., Chatman, J. A., & Doerr, B. (2014). The promise and problems of organizational culture: CEO personality, culture, and firm performance. *Group & Organization Management, 39*, 595–625.

O'Reilly, C. A., Caldwell, D. F., Chatman, J. A., Lapiz, M., & Self, W. (2010). How leadership matters: The effects of leaders' alignment on strategy implementation. *The Leadership Quarterly, 21*, 104–113.

O'Reilly III, C. A., Doerr, B., & Chatman, J. A. (2018). "See you in court": How CEO narcissism increases firms' vulnerability to lawsuits. *The Leadership Quarterly, 29*, 365–378.

O'Reilly, C. A., III, & Tushman, M. L. (2004). The ambidextrous organization. *Harvard Business Review, 82*(4), 74–81.

O'Reilly, C. A., III, & Tushman, M. L. (2013). Organizational ambidexterity: Past, present, and future. *Academy of Management Perspectives, 27*, 324–338.

O'Toole, J. (1995). *Leading change: Overcoming the ideology of comfort and the tyranny of custom*. San Francisco: Jossey-Bass.

O'Toole, J., Galbraith, J., & Lawler, E. E., III (2003). The promise and pitfalls of shared leadership: When two (or more) heads are better than one. In C. L. Pearce & J. A. Conger (Eds.), *Shared leadership: Reframing the hows and whys of leadership* (pp. 250–267). Thousand Oaks, CA: Sage.

Oc, B. (2018). Contextual leadership: A systematic review of how contextual factors shape leadership and its outcomes. *The Leadership Quarterly, 29*, 218–235.

Oc, B., & Bashshur, M. R. (2013). Followership, leadership and social influence. *The Leadership Quarterly, 24*, 919–934.

Offermann, L. R., & Coats, M. R. (2018). Implicit theories of leadership: Stability and change over two decades. *The Leadership Quarterly, 29*, 513–522.

Offermann, L. R., & Hellmann, P. S. (1997). Culture's consequences for leadership behavior: National values in action. *Journal of Cross Cultural Psychology, 28*, 342–351.

Offermann, L. R., Schroyer, C. J., & Green S. K. (1998). Leader attributions for subordinate performance: Consequences for subsequent leader interactive behaviors and ratings. *Journal of Applied Social Psychology, 28*, 1125–1139.

Oh, I.-S., & Berry, C. M. (2009). The five-factor model of personality and managerial performance: Validity gains through the use of 360 degree performance ratings. *Journal of Applied Psychology, 94*, 1498–1513.

Ohana, M. (2016). Voice, affective commitment and citizenship behavior in teams: The moderating role of neuroticism and intrinsic motivation. *British Journal of Management, 27*, 97–115.

Ohlott, P. J. (1998). Job assignments. In C. D. McCauley, R. S. Moxley, & E. Van Velsor (Eds.), *Center for Creative Leadership handbook of leadership development* (pp. 127–159). San Francisco: Jossey-Bass.

Ohlott, P. J., Ruderman, M. N., & McCauley, C. D. (1994). Gender differences in manager's developmental job experiences. *Academy of Management Journal, 37*, 46–67.

Orsburn, J. D., Moran, L., Musselwhite, E., & Zenger, J. H. (1990). *Self-directed work teams: The new American challenge*. Homewood, IL: Business One Irwin.

Orvis, K. A., & Ratwani, K. L. (2010). Leader self-development: A contemporary context for leader development evaluation. *The Leadership Quarterly, 21*, 657–674.

Osborn, R. N., & Hunt, J. G. (2007). Leadership and the choice of order: Complexity and hierarchical perspectives near the edge of chaos. *The Leadership Quarterly, 18,* 319–340.

Osborn, R. N., Hunt, J. G., & Jauch, L. R. (2002). Toward a contextual theory of leadership. *The Leadership Quarterly, 13*, 797–837.

Osborn, R. N., Uhl-Bien, M., & Milosevic, I. (2014). The context and leadership. In D. V. Day (Ed.), *The Oxford handbook of leadership and organizations* (pp. 589–612). Oxford, UK: Oxford University Press.

Ospina, S., & Foldy, E. (2009). A critical review of race and ethnicity in the leadership literature: Surfacing context, power, and collective dimensions of leadership. *The Leadership Quarterly, 20,* 876–896.

Packard, T., & Shih, A. (2014). Organizational change tactics: The evidence base in the literature. *Journal of Evidence-Based Social Work, 11*, 498–510.

Padilla, A., Hogan, R., & Kaiser, R. B. (2007). The toxic triangle: Destructive leaders, susceptible followers, and conducive environments. *The Leadership Quarterly, 18,* 176–194.

Paglis, L. L., & Green, S. G. (2002). Leadership self-efficacy and managers' motivation for leading change. *Journal of Organizational Studies, 23,* 215–235.

Palanski, M. E., & Yammarino, F. J. (2009). Integrity and leadership: A multi-level conceptual framework. *The Leadership Quarterly, 20*, 405–420.

Papa, M. J., & Graham, E. E. (1991). The impact of diagnosing skill deficiencies and assessment-based communication training on managerial performance. *Communication Education, 40,* 368–384.

Park, J., & Hassan, S. (2018). Does the influence of empowering leadership trickle down? Evidence from law enforcement organizations. *Journal of Public Administration Research and Theory*, 28(2), 215–225.

Parris, D. L., & Peachey, J. W. (2013). A systematic literature review of servant leadership theory in organizational contexts. *Journal of Business Ethics, 113*, 377–393.

Parry, K. W. (1998). Grounded theory and social process: A new direction for leadership research. *The Leadership Quarterly, 9*, 85–105.

Parry, K. W., & Meindl, J. R. (2002). *Grounding leadership thoery and research: Issues, perspectives, and methods*. Greenwich, CT: Information Age Publishing.

Parry, K. W., Mumford, M. D., Bower, I., & Watts, L. L. (2014). Qualitative and historiometric methods in leadership research: A review of the first 25 years of *The Leadership Quarterly. The Leadership Quarterly, 25*, 132–151.

Pasmore, W. A. (1978). The comparative impacts of sociotechnical systems, job redesign, and survey feedback interventions. In W. A. Pasmore & J. J. Sherwood (Eds.), *Sociotechnical systems: A sourcebook* (pp. 291–301). La Jolla, CA: University Associates.

Patchen, M. (1974). The locus and basis of influence on organizational decisions. *Organizational Behavior and Human Performance, 11,* 195–221.

Patel, P. C., Messersmith, J. G., & Lepak, D. P. (2013). Walking the tightrope: An assessment of the relationship between high-performance work systems and organizational ambidexterity. *Academy of Management Journal, 56,* 1420–1442.

Pauchant, T., & Mitroff, I. (1992). *Transforming the crisis-prone organization: Preventing individual, organizational, and environmental tragedies*. San Francisco: Jossey-Bass.

Paul, K. B., & Fenlason, K. J. (2014). Transforming a legacy culture at 3M: Teaching an elephant how to dance. In B. Schneider & K. M. Barbera (Eds.), *The Oxford handbook of organizational clmate and culture* (pp. 569–583). Oxford, UK: Oxford University Press.

Paulus, P. B., & Yang, H.-C. (2000). Idea generation in groups: A basis for creativity in organizations. *Organizational Behavior and Human Decision Processes, 82,* 76–87.

Pavett, C., & Lau, A. (1983). Managerial work: The influence of hierarchical level and functional specialty. *Academy of Management Journal, 26,* 170–177.

Pawar, B. S., & Eastman, K. K. (1997). The nature and implications of contextual influences on transformational leadership: A conceptual examination. *Academy of Management Review, 22,* 80–109.

Payne, S. C., & Huffman, A. H. (2005). A longitudinal examination of the influence of mentoring on organizational commitment and turnover. *Academy of Management Journal, 48,* 158–168.

Pearce, C. L., & Conger, J. A. (2003). *Shared leadership: Reframing the hows and whys of leadership*. Thousand Oaks, CA: Sage.

Pearce, C. L., & Ensley, M. D. (2004). A reciprocal and longitudinal investigation of the innovation process: The central role of shared vision in product and process innovation teams (PPITs). *Journal of Organizational Behavior, 25,* 259–278.

Pearce, C. L., Gallagher, C. A., & Ensley, M. D. (2002). Confidence at the group level of analysis: A longitudinal investigation of the relationship between potency and team effectiveness. *Journal of Occupational and Organizational Psychology, 75,* 115–119.

Pearce, C. L., Manz, C. C., & Akanno, S. (2013). Searching for the holy grail of management development and sustainability: Is shared leadership development the answer? *Journal of Management Development, 32,* 247–257.

Pearce, C. L., & Sims, H. P., Jr. (2000). Shared leadership: Toward a multi-level theory of leadership. *Advances in interdisciplinary studies of work teams* (Vol. 7, pp. 115–139). Greenwich, CT: JAI Press.

Pearce, C. L., & Sims, H. P., Jr. (2002). Vertical versus shared leadership as predictors of the effectiveness of change management teams: An examination of aversive, directive, transactional, transformational, and empowering leader behaviors. *Group Dynamics: Theory, Research, and Practice, 6,* 172–197.

Pearce, J. A., II, & Ravlin, E. C. (1987). The design and activation of self-regulating work groups. *Human Relations, 40,* 751–782.

Pearson, C. L. (1992). Autonomous workgroups: An evaluation at an industrial site. *Human Relations, 45,* 905–936.

Peck, J. A., & Hogue, M. (2018). Acting with the best of intentions… or not: A typology and model of impression management in leadership. *The Leadership Quarterly, 29*, 123–134.

Perkins, G., Lean, J., & Newbery, R. (2017). The role of organizational vision in guiding idea generation within some contexts. *Creativity and Innovation Management, 26*(1), 75–90.

Perkins, R. D. (2009). How executive coaching can change leader behavior and improve meeting effectiveness: An exploratory study. *Consulting Psychology Journal: Practice and Research, 61,* 298–318.

Peters, L. H., O'Connor, E. J., & Eulberg, J. R. (1985). Situational constraints: Sources, consequences, and future considerations. *Research in Personnel and Human Resource Management, 3,* 79–114.

Peters, T. J. (1987). *Thriving on chaos: Handbook for a management revolution*. New York: Harper Collins.

Peters, T. J., & Austin, N. (1985). *A passion for excellence: The leadership difference*. New York: Random House.

Peters, T. J., & Waterman, R. H., Jr. (1982). *In search of excellence: Lessons from America's best-run companies*. New York: Harper & Row.

Peterson, R. S., Smith, D. B., Martorana, P. V., & Owens, P. D. (2003). The impact of chief executive officer personality on top management team dynamics: One mechanism by which leadership affects organizational performance. *Journal of Applied Psychology, 88,* 795–808.

Peterson, S. J., Galvin, B. M., & Lange, D. (2012). CEO servant leadership: Exploring executive characteristics and firm performance. *Personnel Psychology, 65*, 565–596.

Peterson, S. J., Walumbwa, F. O., Byron, K., & Myrowitz, J. (2009). CEO positive psychological traits, transformational leadership, and firm performance in high-technology start-up and established firms. *Journal of Management, 35,* 348–368.

Peterson, T. O., & Van Fleet, D. D. (2008). A tale of two situations: An empirical study of behavior by not-for-profit managerial leaders. *Public Performance & Management Review, 31,* 503–516.

Petrenko, O. V., Aime, F., Ridge, J., & Hill, A. (2016). Corporate social responsibility or CEO narcissism? CSR motivations and organizational performance. *Strategic Management Journal, 37*, 262–279.

Pettigrew, A. M. (1972). Information control as a power resource. *Sociology, 6,* 187–204.

Pettigrew, A. M. (1988). Context and action in the transformation of firms. *Journal of Management Studies, 24,* 649–670.

Pettigrew, A. M., Ferlie, E., & McKee, L. (1992). *Shaping strategic change in large organizations: The case of the National Health Service*. London: Sage.

Pettigrew, A. M., & Whipp, R. (1991). *Managing change for competitive success*. Oxford, England: Blackwell.

Peus, C., Braun, S., & Frey, D. (2012). Despite leaders' good intentions? The role of follower attributions in adverse leadership–A multilevel model. *Zeitschrift für Psychologie, 220*(4), 241–250.

Pfeffer, J. (1977a). Power and resource allocation in organizations. In B. Staw & G. Salancik (Eds.), *New directions in organizational behavior* (pp. 235–265). Chicago: St. Clair Press.

Pfeffer, J. (1977b). The ambiguity of leadership. *Academy of Management Review, 2,* 104–112.

Pfeffer, J. (1981). *Power in organizations.* Marshfield, MA: Pittman.

Pfeffer, J. (1992). *Managing with power: Politics and influence in organizations*. Boston, Harvard Business School Press.

Pfeffer, J. (1994). *Competitive advantage through people*. Boston: Harvard Business School Press.

Pfeffer, J. (2003). Business and the spirit: Management values that sustain values. In R. A. Giacalone & C. L. Jurkiewics (Eds.), *The handbook of workplace spirituality and organizational performance* (pp. 29–45). New York: M. E. Sharpe.

Pfeffer, J. (2005). Producing sustainable competitive advantage through the effective management of people. *Academy of Management Executive, 19,* 95–106.

Pfeffer, J., Cialdini, R. B., Hanna, B., & Knopoff, D. (1998). Faith in supervision and the self-enhancement bias: Two psychological reasons why managers don't empower workers. *Basic and Applied Social Psychology, 20,* 313–321.

Pfeffer, J., & Moore, W. L. (1980). Average tenure of academic department heads: The effects of paradigm, size and department demography. *Administrative Science Quarterly, 25,* 387–406.

Pfeffer, J., & Salancik, G. R. (1974). Organizational decision making as a political process: The case of a university budget. *Administrative Science Quarterly, 19,* 135–154.

Phillips, A. S., & Bedeian, A. G. (1994). Leader-follower exchange quality: The role of personal and interpersonal attributes. *Academy of Management Journal, 37,* 990–1001.

Pink, D. H. (2009). *Drive: The surprising truth about what motivates us*. New York: Riverhead Books.

Plowman, D. A., Solansky, S., Beck, T. E., Baker, L., Kulkarni, M., & Travis, D. V. (2007), The role of leadership in emergent self-organization. *The Leadership Quarterly, 18*, 341–356.

Podsakoff, P. M., Dorfman, P. W., Howell, J. P., & Todor, W. D. (1986). Leader reward and punishment behaviors: A preliminary test of a culture-free style of leadership effectiveness. In R. N. Farmer (Ed.), *Advances in international* *comparative management* (Vol. 2, pp. 95–138), Greenwich, CT: JAI Press.

Podsakoff, P. M., MacKenzie, S. B., & Ahearne, M. (1997). Moderating effects of goal acceptance on the relationship between group cohesiveness and productivity. *Journal of Applied Psychology, 82,* 974–983.

Podsakoff, P. M., MacKenzie, S. B., Ahearne, M., & Bommer, W. H. (1995). Searching for a needle in a haystack: Trying to identify the illusive moderators of leadership behaviors. *Journal of Management, 21,* 422–470.

Podsakoff, P. M., MacKenzie, S. B., & Bommer, W. H. (1996a). Meta-analysis of the relationships between Kerr and Jermier's substitutes for leadership and employee job attitudes, role perceptions, and performance. *Journal of Applied Psychology, 81,* 380–399.

Podsakoff, P. M., MacKenzie, S. B., & Bommer, W. H. (1996b). Transformational leadership behaviors and substitutes for leadership as determinants of employee satisfaction, commitment, trust, and organizational citizenship behaviors. *Journal of Management, 22*, 259–298.

Podsakoff, P. M., MacKenzie, S. B., Moorman, R. H., & Fetter, R. (1990). Transformational leader behaviors and their effects on follower's trust in leader, satisfaction, and organizational citizenship behaviors. *The Leadership Quarterly, 1,* 107–142.

Podsakoff, P. M., Niehoff, B. P., MacKenzie, S., & Williams, M. L. (1993). Do substitutes for leadership really substitute for leadership? An examination of Kerr and Jermier's situational leadership model. *Organizational Behavior and Human Decision Processes, 54,* 1–44.

Podsakoff, P. M., & Schriesheim, C. A. (1985). Field studies of French and Raven's bases of power: Critique, reanalysis, and suggestions for future research. *Psychological Bulletin, 97,* 387–411.

Popper, M., & Lipshitz, R. (1998). Organizational learning mechanisms: A structural and cultural approach to organizational learning. *Journal of Applied Behavioral Science, 34,* 161–179.

Porter, L. W., & Lawler, E. E. (1968). *Managerial attitudes and performance*. Homewood, IL: Irwin-Dorsey.

Porter, L. W., & McLaughlin, G. B. (2006). Leadership and the organizational context: Like the weather? *The Leadership Quarterly, 17,* 559–576.

Porter, M. E. (1980). *Competitive strategy: Techniques for analyzing industries and competitors*. New York: Free Press.

Porter, M. E. (1998). *Competitive strategy: Techniques for analyzing industries and competitors*. New York: The Free Press.

Post, C. (2015). When is female leadership an advantage? Coordination requirements, team cohesion, and team interaction norms. *Journal of Organizational Behavior, 36*, 1153–1175.

Post, C., & Byron, K. (2015). Women on boards and firm performance: A meta-analysis. *Academy of Management Journal, 58,* 1546–1571.

Powell, G. N. (1990). One more time: Do female and male managers differ? *Academy of Management Executive, 4,* 68–75.

Powell, G. N. (2019). *Women and men in management* (5th ed). Los Angeles, CA: Sage.

Powell, G. N., & Butterfield, D. A. (2015). Correspondence between self- and good-manager descriptions: Examining stability and change over four decades. *Journal of Management, 41*, 1745–1773.

Powell, G. N., Butterfield, A. D., & Parent, J. D. (2002). Gender and managerial stereotypes: Have the times changed? *Journal of Management, 28,* 177–193.

Powell, T. (1995). Total quality management as competitive advantage: a review and empirical study. *Strategic Management Journal, 16,* 15–37.

Prahalad, C. K., & Hamel, G. (1990). The core competence of the corporation. *Harvard Business Review, 68*(3), 79–91.

Preston, P., & Zimmerer, T. W. (1978). *Management for supervisors*. Englewood Cliffs, NJ: Prentice Hall.

Price, T. L. (2003). The ethics of authentic transformational leadership. *The Leadership Quarterly, 14,* 67–81.

Pridmore, J., & Phillips-Wren, G. (2011). Assessing decision making quality in face-to-face teams versus virtual teams in a virtual world. *Journal of Decision Systems, 20,* 283–308.

Probst, G., & Raisch, S. (2005). Organizational crisis: The logic of failure. *Academy of Management Executive, 19*(1), 90–105.

Pryor, A. K., & Shays, M. (1993). Growing the business with intrepreneurs. *Business Quarterly, 57*(3), 42–49.

Purvanova, R. K. & Bono, J. E. (2009). Transformational leadership in context: Face-to-face and virtual teams. *The Leadership Quarterly, 20,* 343–357.

Qu, R., Janssen, O., & Shi, K. (2015). Transformational leadership and follower creativity: The mediating role of follower relational identification and the moderating role of leader creativity expectations. *The Leadership Quarterly, 26,* 286–299.

Quinn, J. B. (1980). Formulating strategy one step at a time. *Journal of Business Strategy, 1,* 42–63.

Quinn, R. E. (1988). *Beyond rational management: Mastering the paradoxes and competing demands of high performance*. San Francisco: Jossey-Bass.

Quinn, R. E., Faerman, S. R., Thompson, M. P., McGrath, M., & St. Clair, L. S. (2006). *Becoming a master manager: A competing values approach* (4th ed.). New York: Wiley.

Quinn, R. E., Spreitzer, G. M., & Hart, S. L. (1992). Integrating the extremes: Crucial skills for managerial effectiveness. In S. Srivastva and R. E. Fry (Eds.), *Executive and organizational continuity* (pp. 222–252). San Francisco: Jossey-Bass.

Raelin, J. A. (1989). An anatomy of autonomy: Managing professionals. *Academy of Management Executive, 3,* 216–228.

Raes, A. M. L., Heijltjes, M. G., Glunk, U., & Roe, R. A. (2011). The interface of the top management team and middle managers: A process model. *Academy of Management Review, 36,* 102–126.

Rafferty, A. E., & Griffin, M. A. (2006). Perceptions of organizational change: A stress and coping perspective. *Journal of Applied Psychology, 91,* 1154–1162.

Ragins, B. R., & Cotton, J. L. (1991). Easier said than done: Gender differences in perceived barriers to gaining a mentor. *Academy of Management Journal, 34,* 939–951.

Ragins, B. R., & Cotton, J. L. (1993). Gender and willingness to mentor in organizations. *Journal of Management, 19,* 97–111.

Ragins, B. R., & McFarlin, D. B. (1990). Perceptions of mentoring roles in cross-gender mentoring relationships. *Journal of Vocational Behavior, 37,* 321–339.

Ragins, B. R., Townsend, B., & Mattis, M. (1998). Gender gap in the executive suite: CEOs and female executives report on breaking the glass ceiling. *Academy of Management Executive, 12*(1), 28–42.

Rahim, M. A. (1988). The development of a leader power inventory. *Multivariate Behavioral Research, 23,* 491–503.

Rahim, M. A. (1989). Relationships of leader power to compliance and satisfaction with supervision: Evidence from a national sample of managers. *Journal of Management, 15,* 545–556.

Rahim, M. A., & Afza, M. (1993). Leader power, commitment, satisfaction, compliance, and propensity to leave a job among U.S. accountants. *Journal of Social Psychology, 133,* 611–625.

Randolph, W. A. (1995). Navigating the journey to empowerment. *Organizational Dynamics, 23*(4), 19–32.

Rapp, T. L., Gilson, L. L., Mathieu, J. E., & Ruddy, T. (2016). Leading empowered teams: An examination of the role of external team leaders and team coaches. *The Leadership Quarterly, 27,* 109–123.

Raskin, R., & Hall, C. S. (1981). The narcissistic personality inventory: Alternate form reliability and further evidence of construct validity. *Journal of Personality Assessment, 45,* 159–162.

Raskin, R., Novacek, J., & Hogan, R. (1991). Narcissistic self-esteem management. *Journal of Personality and Social Psychology, 60,* 911–918.

Rauch, C. F., & Behling, O. (1984). Functionalism: Basis for an alternate approach to the study of leadership. In J. G. Hunt, D. M. Hosking, C. A. Schriesheim, & R. Stewart (Eds.), *Leaders and managers: International perspectives on managerial behavior and leadership* (pp. 45–62). Elmsford, NY: Pergamon Press.

Raven, B. H. (1965). Social influence and power. In I. D. Steiner & M. Fishbein (Eds.), *Current studies in social psychology* (pp. 371–381). New York: Holt, Rinehart & Winston.

Reave, L. (2005). Spiritual values and practices related to leadership effectiveness. *The Leadership Quarterly, 16,* 655–687.

Reed, A., II, Kay, A., Finnel, S., Aquino, K., & Levy, E. (2016). I don't want the money, I just want your time: How moral identity overcomes the aversion to giving time to prosocial causes. *Journal of Personality and Social Psychology, 110,* 435–457.

Reh, S., Van Quaquebeke, N., & Giessner, S. R. (2017). The aura of charisma: A review on the embodiment perspective as signaling. *The Leadership Quarterly, 28,* 486–507.

Reichard, R. J., & Johnson, S. K. (2011). Leader self-development as organizational strategy. *The Leadership Quarterly, 22,* 33–42.

Reichard, R. J., Walker, D. O., Putter, S. E., Middleton, E., & Johnson, S. K. (2017). Believing is becoming: The role of leader developmental efficacy in leader self-development. *Journal of Leadership & Organizational Studies, 24,* 137–156.

Reicher, S., Haslam, S. A., & Hopkins, N. (2005). Social identity and the dynamics of leadership: Leaders and followers as collaborative agents in the transformation of social reality. *The Leadership Quarterly, 16,* 547–568.

Reitz, H. J. (1977). *Behavior in organizations.* Homewood, IL: Irwin.

Resick, C. J., Whitman, D. S., Wengarden, S. M., & Hiller, N. J. (2009). The bright-side and the dark-side of CEO personality: Examining core self-evaluations, narcissism, transformational leadership, and strategic influence. *Journal of Applied Psychology, 94,* 1365–1381.

Reynolds, S. J. (2006a). Moral awareness and ethical predispositions: Investigating the role of individual differences in the recognition of moral issues. *Journal of Applied Psychology, 91,* 233–243.

Reynolds, S. J. (2006b). A neurocognitive model of the ethical decision-making process: Implications for study and practice. *Journal of Applied Psychology, 91,* 737–748.

Rfietzschel, E. F., Wisse, B., & Rus, D. (2017). Puppet masters in the lab: Experimental methods in leadership research. In B. Schyns, R. J. Hall, & P. Neves (Eds.), *Handbook of methods in leadership research* (pp. 48–72). Cheltenham, UK: Edward Elgar Publishing.

Richard, B. W., Holton, E. F., III, & Katsioloudes, V. (2014). The use of discrete computer simulation modeling to estimate return on leadership development investment. *The Leadership Quarterly, 25,* 1054–1068.

Richards, D., & Engle, S. (1986). After the vision: Suggestions to corporate visionaries and vision champions. In J. D. Adams (Ed.), *Transforming leadership* (pp. 199–214). Alexandria, VA: Miles River Press.

Rico, R., Sanchez-Manzanares, M., Gil, F., & Gibson, C. (2008). Team implicit coordination processes: A team knowledge-based approach. *Academy of Management Review, 33,* 163–184.

Rio, A. V. E. (2018). The future of the corporate university. *Chief Learning Officer, 17*(4), 36–56.

Robbins, S. R., & Duncan, R. B. (1988). The role of the CEO and top management in the creation and implementation of strategic vision. In

D. C. Hambrick (Ed.), *The executive effect: Concepts and methods for studying top managers* (Vol. 2, pp. 205–233). Greenwich, CT: JAI Press.

Roberson, Q. M., Moye, N. A., & Locke, E. A. (1999). Identifying a missing link between participation and satisfaction: The mediating role of procedural justice perceptions. *Journal of Applied Psychology, 84,* 585–593.

Roberts, N. C. (1985). Transforming leadership: A process of collective action. *Human Relations, 38,* 1023–1046.

Roberts, N. C., & Bradley, R. T. (1988). Limits of charisma. In J. A. Conger & R. N. Kanungo (Eds.), *Charismatic leadership: The elusive factor in organizational effectiveness* (pp. 253–275). San Francisco: Jossey-Bass.

Rockstuhl, T., Dulebohn, J. H., Ang, S., & Shore, L. M. (2012). Leader–member exchange (LMX) and culture: A meta-analysis of correlates of LMX across 23 countries. *Journal of Applied Psychology, 97,* 1097–1130.

Rojahn, K. M., & Willemsen, T. (1994). The evaluation of effectiveness and likability of gender-role congruent and gender-role incongruent leaders. *Sex Roles, 30,* 109–119.

Rosener, J. (1990). Ways women lead. *Harvard Business Review, 68*(6), 119–125.

Rosenthal, T. L., & Pittinsky, T. L. (2006). Narcissistic leadership. *The Leadership Quarterly, 17,* 617–633.

Rothwell, W. J., & Kazanas, H. C. (1994). Management development: The state of the art as perceived by HRD professionals. *Performance Improvement Quarterly, 7*(1), 40–59.

Rotter, J. B. (1966). Generalized expectancies for internal versus external control of reinforcement. *Psychological Monographs: General and Applied, 80*(1), 1–28.

Rouiller, J. S., & Goldstein, I. L. (1993). The relationship between organizational transfer climate and positive transfer of training. *Human Resource Development Quarterly, 4,* 377–390.

Rousseau, D. M. (1985). Issues of level in organizational research: Multi-level and cross-level perspectives. In L. L. Cummings & B. M. Staw (Eds.), *Research in Organizational Behavior* (Vol 7, 1–37). Greenwich, CT: JAI Press.

Rowland, P., & Parry, K. (2009). Consensual commitment: A grounded theory of the meso-level influence of organizational design on leadership and decision-making. *The Leadership Quarterly, 20*, 535-553.

Rowold, J., & Heinitz, K. (2007). Transformational and charismatic leadership: Assessing the convergent, divergent, and criterion validity of the MLQ and CKS. *The Leadership Quarterly, 18,* 121–133.

Rubin, R. S., Dierdorff, E. C., Bommer, W. H., & Baldwin, T. T. (2009). Do leaders reap what they sow? Leader and employee outcomes of leader organizational cynicism about change. *The Leadership Quarterly, 20*, 680–688.

Ruderman, M. N., & Ohlott, P. J. (1994). *The realities of management promotion*. Technical Report No. 157. Greensboro, NC: Center for Creative Leadership.

Ruderman, M. N., Ohlott, P. J., & McCauley, C. D. (1990). Assessing opportunities for leadership development. In K. E. Clark & M. B. Clark (Eds.), *Measures of leadership* (pp. 547–562). West Orange, NJ: Leadership Library of America.

Rus, D., Van Knippenberg, D., & Wisse, B. (2012). Power and self-serving behavior: The moderating role of accountability. *The Leadership Quarterly, 23,* 13–26.

Ruvio, A., Rosenblatt, Z., & Hertz-Lazarowitz, R. (2010). Entrepreneurial vision in nonprofit vs. for-profit organizations. *The Leadership Quarterly, 21,* 144–158.

Ryan, M. K., & Haslam, S. A. (2007). The glass cliff: Exploring the dynamics surrounding the appointment of women to precarious leadership positions. *Academy of Management Review, 32,* 549–572.

Ryan, M. K., Haslam, S. A., Hersby, M. D., & Bongiorno, R. (2011). Think crisis—think female: The glass cliff and contextual variation in the think manager–think male stereotype. *Journal of Applied Psychology, 96*, 470–484.

Ryan, M. K., Haslam, S. A., & Kulich, C. (2010). Politics and the glass cliff: Evidence that women are preferentially selected to contest hard-to-win seats. *Psychology of Women Quarterly, 34*, 56–64.

Ryan, M. K., Haslam, S. A., Morgenroth, T., Rink, F., Stoker, J., & Peters, K. (2016). Getting on top of the glass cliff: Reviewing a decade of evidence, explanations, and impact. *The Leadership Quarterly, 27*, 446–455.

Saari, L. M., Johnson, T. R., McLaughlin, S. D., & Zimmerle, D. M. (1988). A survey of management training and education practices in U.S. companies. *Personnel Psychology, 41*, 731–743.

Sabherwal, R., & Becerra-Fernandez, I. (2003). An empirical study of the effects of knowledge management processes at the individual, group, and organizational levels. *Decision Sciences, 34,* 225–260.

Sacks, D. (2009). John Mackey's Whole Foods vision to reshape capitalism. *The Fast Company,* December 1.

Sadri, G., Weber, T. J., & Gentry, W. A. (2011). Empathic emotion and leadership performance: An empirical analysis across 38 countries. *The Leadership Quarterly, 22*, 818–830.

Sagie, A., & Koslowsky, M. (2000). *Participation and empowerment in organizations*. Thousand Oaks, CA: Sage.

Salancik, G. R., Calder, B. J., Rowland, K. M., Leblebici, H., & Conway, M. (1975). Leadership as an outcome of social structure and process: A multidimensional analysis. In J. C. Hunt & L. L. Larson (Eds.), *Leadership frontiers* (pp. 81–101). Kent, OH: Kent State University Press.

Salancik, G. R., & Meindl, J. R. (1984). Corporate attributions as strategic illusions of management control. *Administrative Science Quarterly, 29,* 238–254.

Salancik, G. R., & Pfeffer, J. (1977). Who gets power and how they hold on to it: A strategic contingency model of power. *Organizational Dynamics, 5*(3), 3–21.

Salas, E., & Cannon-Bowers, J. A. (2001). The science of training: A decade of progress. *Annual Review of Psychology, 52*, 471–499.

Salas, E., Rosen, M. A., & DiazGranados, D. (2010). Expertise-based intuition and decision making in organizations. *Journal of Management, 36,* 941–973.

Salovey, P., & Mayer, J. (1990). Emotional intelligence. *Imagination, Cognition, and Personality, 9,* 185–211.

Sanders, J. O. (2017). *Spiritual leadership: Principles for excellence for every believer* Chicago, IL: Moody Publishers.

Sandowsky, D. (1995). The charismatic leader as narcissist: Understanding the abuse of power. *Organizational Dynamics, 24*(4), 57–71.

Santos, C. M., Uitdewilligen, S., & Passos, A. M. (2015). Why is your team more creative than mine? The influence of shared mental models on intra-group conflict, team creativity and effectiveness. *Creativity and Innovation Management, 24*, 645–658.

Sariol, A. M., & Abebe, M. A. (2017). The influence of CEO power on explorative and exploitative organizational innovation. *Journal of Business Research, 73*, 38–45.

Sashkin, M., & Fulmer, R. M. (1988). Toward an organizational leadership theory. In J. G. Hunt, B. R. Baliga, H. P. Dachler, & C. A. Schriesheim (Eds.), *Emerging leadership vistas* (pp. 51–65). Lexington, MA: Heath.

Sayles, L. R. (1979). *Leadership: What effective managers really do… and how they do it*. New York: McGraw-Hill.

Scandura, T. A. (1992). Mentorship and career mobility: An empirical investigation. *Journal of Organizational Behavior, 13,* 169–174.

Scandura, T. A., & Graen, G. B. (1984). Moderating effects of initial leader-member exchange status on the effects of leadership intervention. *Journal of Applied Psychology, 69,* 428–436.

Scandura, T. A., & Pellegrini, E. K. (2007). Workplace mentoring: Theoretical approaches and methodological issues. In T. D. Allen & L. T. Eby (Eds.), *The Blackwell handbook of mentoring: A multiple perspectives approach* (pp. 71–91). Malden: Blackwell Publishing.

Scandura, T. A., & Schriesheim, C. A. (1994). Leader-member exchange and supervisor career mentoring as complementary constructs in leadership research. *Academy of Management Journal, 37,* 1588–1602.

Scandura, T. A., Von Glinow, M. A., & Lowe, K. B. (1999). When East meets West: Leadership "best practices" in the United States and Middle East. In W. H. Mobley, M. J. Gessner, & V. Arnold (Eds.), *Advances in global leadership* (pp. 235–248). Stamford, CT: JAI Press.

Schaubroeck, J. M., Hannah, S. T., Avolio, B. J., Kozlowski, S. W. J., Lord, R. G., Treviño, L. K., Dimotakis, N., & Peng, A. C. (2012). Embedding ethical leadership within and across organizatinal levels. *Academy of Management Journal, 55,* 1053–1078.

Schaubroeck, J., Lam, S. S. K., & Cha, S. E. (2007). Embracing transformational leadership: Team values and the impact of leader behavior on team performance. *Journal of Applied Psychology, 92,* 1020–1030.

Scheibehenne, B., & von Helversen, B. (2015). Selecting decision strategies: The differential role of affect. *Cognition and Emotion, 29*(1), 158–167.

Schein, E. H. (1969). *Process consultation: Its role in management development*. Reading, MA: Addison-Wesley.

Schein, E. H. (1992). *Organizational culture and leadership* (2nd ed.). San Francisco: Jossey-Bass.

Schein, E. H. (2016). *Organizational culture and leadership* (5th ed.). San Francisco: Jossey-Bass.

Schein, E. H. (1993). How can organizations learn faster? The challenge of entering the green room. *Sloan Management Review, 34,* 85–90.

Schein, V. E. (1975). Relationships between sex role stereotypes and requisite management characteristics among female managers. *Journal of Applied Psychology, 60,* 340–344.

Schein, V. E. (2001). A global look at psychological barriers to women's progress in management. *Journal of Social Issues, 57,* 675–688.

Schermuly, C. C., & Meyer, B. (2016). Good relationships at work: The effects of Leader–Member Exchange and Team–Member Exchange on psychological empowerment, emotional exhaustion, and depression. *Journal of Organizational Behavior, 37*, 673–691.

Schepker, D. J., Kim, Y., Patel, P. C., Thatcher, S. M. B., & Campion, M. C. (2017). CEO succession, strategic change, and post-succession performance: A meta-analysis. *The Leadership Quarterly, 28*, 701–720.

Schilling, J. (2017). Qualitative content analysis in leadership research: Principles, process and application. In B. Schyns, R. J. Hall, & P. Neves (Eds.), *Handbook of methods in leadership research* (pp. 349–371). Cheltenham, UK: Edward Elgar.

Schlesinger, L., Jackson, J. M., & Butman, J. (1960). Leader-member interaction in management committees. *Journal of Abnormal and Social Psychology, 61,* 360–364.

Schlösser, O., Frese, M., Heintze, A.-M., Al-Najjar, M., Arciszewski, T., Besevegis, E., … & Zhang, K. (2013). Humane orientation as a new cultural dimension of the GLOBE project: A validation study of the GLOBE Scale and out-group humane orientation in 25 countries. *Journal of Cross-Cultural Psychology, 44*, 535–551.

Schneider, M. & Somers, M. (2006). Organizations as complex adaptive systems: Implications of complexity theory for leadership research. *The Leadership Quarterly, 17,* 361–365.

Schoen, S. H., & Durand, D. E. (1979). *Supervision: The management of organizational resources*. Englewood Cliffs, NJ: Prentice Hall.

Schreiber, C. & Carley, K. M. (2008). Network leadership: Leading for learning and adaptability. In M. Uhl-Bien & R. Marion (Eds.), *Complexity leadership: Part 1*. Charlotte, NC: Information Age Publishing, pp. 291–331.

Schriesheim, C., & Kerr, S. (1974). Psychometric properties of the Ohio State leadership scales. *Psychological Bulletin, 81*, 756–765.

Schriesheim, C. A., Castro, S., & Cogliser, C. C. (1999). Leader-member exchange (LMX) research: A comprehensive review of theory, measurement, and data-analytic procedures. *The Leadership Quarterly, 10,* 63–113.

Schriesheim, C. A., & Hinkin, T. R. (1990). Influence tactics used by subordinates: A theoretical and empirical analysis and refinement of the Kipnis, Schmidt, and Wilkinson subscales. *Journal of Applied Psychology, 75,* 246–257.

Schriesheim, C. A., Neider, L. L., & Scandura, T. A. (1998). Delegation and leader-member exchange: Main effects, moderators, and measurement issues. *Academy of Management Journal, 41,* 298–318.

Schwartz, J., Bersin, J., & Pelster, B. (2014). *Global human capital trends: Engaging the 21st-century workforce*. Westlake, TX: Deloitte University Press.

Schwartz, S. H. (1992). Universals in the content and structure of values: Theoretical advances and tests in 20 countries. In M. P. Zanna (Ed.), *Advances in Experimental Social Psychology* (Vol. 25, pp. 1–65). New York: Academic Press.

Schweiger, D. M., Anderson, C. R., & Locke, E. A. (1985). Complex decision making: A longitudinal study of process and performance. *Organizational Behavior and Human Decision Processes, 36,* 245–272.

Schyns, B., Hall, R. J., & Neves, P. (Eds.). (2017). *Handbook of methods in leadership research.* Cheltenham, U.K.: Edward Elgar Publishing.

Scott, C. L. (2018). Historical perspectives for studying diversity in the workplace. In M. Y. Byrd & C. L. Scott (Eds.), *Diversity in the workforce: Current issues and emerging trends* (pp. 28–48). New York: Taylor & Francis.

Searle, T. P., & Barbuto, J. E. (2011). Servant leadership, hope, and organizational virtuousness: A framework for exploring positive micro and macro behaviors and performance impact. *Journal of Leadership & Organizational Studies, 18,* 107–117.

Seers, A., Keller, T., & Wilkerson, J. M. (2003). Can team members share leadership? Foundations in research and theory. In C. L. Pearce and J. A. Conger (Eds.), *Shared leadership: Reframing the hows and whys of leadership* (pp. 77–102). Thousand Oaks, CA: Sage.

Seibert, S. E., Silver, S. R., & Randolph, W. A. (2004). Taking empowerment to the next level: A multiple-level model of empowerment, performance, and satisfaction. *Academy of Management Journal, 47,* 332–349.

Seibert, S. E., Wang, G., & Courtright, S. H. (2011). Antecedents and consequences of psychological and team empowerment in organizations: A meta-analytic review. *Journal of Applied Psychology, 96*, 981–1003.

Seifert, C., & Yukl, G. (2010). Effects of repeated feedback on the influence behavior and effectiveness of managers: A field experiment. *The Leadership Quarterly, 21,* 856–866.

Seifert, C., Yukl, G., & McDonald, R. (2003). Effects of multisource feedback and a feedback facilitator on the influence behavior of managers toward subordinates. *Journal of Applied Psychology, 88,* 561–569.

Self, D. R., & Schraeder, M. (2009). Enhancing the success of organizational change: Matching readiness strategies with sources of resistance. *Leadership & Organization Development Journal, 30,* 167–182.

Semler, R. (1989). Managing without managers. *Harvard Business Review, 67*(5), 76–84.

Sendjaya, S., & Sarros, J. C. (2002). Servant leadership: Its origin, development, and application in organizations. *Journal of Leadership & Organizational Studies, 9*(2), 57–64.

Senge, P. M. (1990). *The fifth discipline: The art and practice of the learning organization*. New York: Doubleday/Currency.

Serban, A., Yammarino, F. J., Dionne, S. D., Kahai, S. S., Hao, C., McHugh, K. A., … Peterson, D. R. (2015). Leadership emergence in face-to-face and virtual teams: A multi-level model with agent-based simulations, quasi-experimental and experimental tests. *The Leadership Quarterly, 26*, 402–418.

Serban, A., Yammarino, F. J., Sotak, K. L., Banoeng-Yakubo, J., Mushore, A. B. R., Hao, C., McHugh, K. A., & Mumford, M. D. (2018). Assassination of political leaders: The role of social conflict. *The Leadership Quarterly, 29,* 457–475.

Seyranian, V., & Bligh, M. C. (2008). Presidential charismatic leadership: Exploring the rhetoric of social change. *The Leadership Quarterly, 19,* 54–76.

Shamir, B. (1991). Meaning, self, and motivation in organizations. *Organization Studies, 12,* 405–424.

Shamir, B. (1995). Social distance and charisma: Theoretical notes and an exploratory study. *The Leadership Quarterly, 6,* 19–47.

Shamir, B. (2007). From passive recipients to active co-producers: Followers' roles in the leadership process. In B. Shamir, R. Pillai, M. C. Bligh, & M. Uhl-Bien (Eds.), *Follower-centered perspectives on leadership* (pp. ix–xxxix). Greenwich, CT: Information Age Publishing.

Shamir, B., & Eilam, G. (2005). "What's your story?" A life stories approach to authentic leadership development. *The Leadership Quarterly, 16,* 395–417.

Shamir, B., House, R. J., & Arthur, M. B. (1993). The motivational effects of charismatic leadership: A self-concept based theory. *Organization Science, 4,* 577–594.

Shamir, B., & Howell, J. M. (1999). Organizational and contextual influences on the emergence and effectiveness of charismatic leadership. *The Leadership Quarterly, 10,* 257–283.

Shamir, B., Zakay, E., Breinin, E., & Popper, M. (1998). Correlates of charismatic leader behavior in military units: Subordinates' attitudes, unit characteristics, and superiors' appraisals of leader performance. *Academy of Management Journal, 41,* 387–409.

Sharma, P. N., & Kirkman, B. L. (2015). Leveraging leaders: A literature review and future lines of inquiry for empowering leadership research. *Group & Organization Management, 40*, 193–237.

Sharma, S., & Sehrawat, P. (2014). Glass Ceiling for Women: Does it exist in the Modern India? Journal of Organisation and Human Behavior, 3(2).

Shea, C. M., & Howell, J. M. (1999). Charismatic leadership and task feedback: A laboratory study of their effects on self-efficacy and task performance. *The Leadership Quarterly, 10,* 375–396.

Shepherd, D. A., & Suddaby, R. (2017). Theory building: A review and integration. *Journal of Management, 43*, 59–86.

Sherman, H. (1966). *It all depends: A pragmatic approach to delegation*. Birmingham: University of Alabama Press.

Shetty, Y. K., & Peery, N. S. (1976). Are top executives transferable across companies? *Business Horizons, 19*(3), 23–28.

Shiflett, S. C. (1979). Toward a general model of small group productivity. *Psychological Bulletin, 86,* 67–79.

Shin, Y., Sung, S. Y., Choi, J. N., & Kim, M. S. (2015). Top management ethical leadership and firm performance: Mediating role of ethical and procedural justice climate. *Journal of Business Ethics, 129*, 43–57.

Shipper, F., & Wilson, C. L. (1992). The impact of managerial behaviors on group performance, stress, and commitment. In K. Clark, M. B. Clark, & D. P. Campbell (Eds.), *Impact of leadership* (pp. 119–129). Greensboro, NC: Center for Creative Leadership.

Shondrick, S. J., Dinh, J. E., & Lord, R. G. (2010). Developments in implicit leadership theory and cognitive science: Applications to improving measurement and understanding alternatives to hierarchical leadership. *The Leadership Quarterly, 21,* 959–978.

Shore, L. M., Randel, A. E., Chung, Beth G., Dean, M. A., Ehrhart, K. H., & Singh, G. (2011). Inclusion and diversity in work groups: A review and model for future research. *Journal of Management, 37*, 1262–1289.

Sidani, Y. M., & Rowe, W. G. (2018). A reconceptualization of authentic leadership: Leader legitimation via follower-centered assessment of the moral dimension. *The Leadership Quarterly*. Online before print, doi: https://doi.org/10.1016/j.leaqua.2018.04.005

Simon, H. (1987). Making managerial decisions: The role of intuition and emotion. *Academy of Management Executive, 1,* 57–64.

Simons, D. (2002). Behavioral integrity: The perceived alignment between managers' words and deeds as a research focus. *Organization Science, 13,* 18–35.

Sims, H. P., Jr., & Lorenzi, P. (1992). *The new leadership paradigm: Social learning and cognition in organizations*. Newbury Park, CA: Sage.

Simsek, Z., Heavy, C., & Fox, B. C. (2018). Interfaces of strategic leaders: A conceptual framework, review, and research agenda. *Journal of Management, 44*, 280–324.

Simsek, Z., Veiga, J. F., Lubatkin, M. H., & Dino, R. N. (2005). Modeling the multi-level determinants of top management team behavioral integration. *Academy of Management Jounal, 46,* 69–84.

Sin, H.-P., Nahrgang, J. D., & Morgeson, F. P. (2009). Understanding why they don't see eye to eye: An examination of leader-member exchange (LMX) agreement. *Journal of Applied Psychology, 94,* 1048–1057.

Sinclair, A. (1992). The tyranny of a team ideology. *Organization Studies, 13,* 611–626.

Singh, P., & Leskiw, S. L. (2007). Leadership development: learning from best practices. *Leadership & Organization Development Journal, 28*, 444–464.

Sitkin, S. B., & Hackman, J. R. (2011). Developing team leadership: An interview with coach Mike Krzyzewski. *Academy of Management Learning & Education, 10,* 494–501.

Sitkin, S. B., & Roth, N. L. (1993). Explaining the limited effectiveness of legalistic "remedies" for trust/distrust. *Organization Science, 4*, 367–392.

Sivasubramaniam, N., Murry, W. D., Avolio, B. J., & Jung, D. I. (2002). A longitudinal model of the effects of team leadership and group potency on group performance. *Group & Organization Management, 27,* 66–96.

Skordoulis, R., & Dawson, P. (2007). Reflective decisions: the use of Socratic dialogue in managing organizational change. *Management Decision, 45*, 991–1007.

Skubinn, R., & Herzog, L. (2016). Internalized moral identity in ethical leadership. *Journal of Business Ethics, 133*, 249–260.

Smith, B. N., Montagno, R. V., & Kuzmenko, T. N. (2004). Transformational and servant leadership: Content and contextual comparisons. *Journal of Leadership & Organizational Studies, 10*(4), 80–91.

Smith, D. K., & Alexander, R. C. (1988). *Fumbling the future: How Xerox invented, then ignored, the first personal computer*. New York: William Morrow.

Smith, K. W., & Tushman, L. M. (2005). Managing strategic contradictions: A top management model for managing innovation streams. *Organization Science, 16,* 522–536.

Smith, P. B. (2006). When elephants fight the grass gets trampled: The GLOBE and Hofstede projects. *Journal of International Business Studies, 37,* 915–921.

Smith, P. B., Misumi, J., Tayeb, M., Peterson, M., & Bond, M. (1989). On the generality of leadership styles across cultures. *Journal of Occupational Psychology, 62,* 97–109.

Smith, P. B., Peterson, M. F., Schwartz, S. H., Ahmad, A. H., & Associates (2002). Cultural values, sources of guidance, and their relevance to managerial behavior: A 47-nation study. *Journal of Cross-Cultural Psychology, 33*(2), 188–208.

Smith, P. B., Peterson, M., & Thomas, D. C. (2008). *The handbook of cross-cultural* *management research*. Thousand Oaks, CA: Sage Publications, Inc.

Smither, J. W., London, M., & Reilly, R. R. (2005). Does performance improve following multisource feedback? A theoretical model, meta-analysis, and review of empirical findings. *Personnel Psychology, 58,* 33–66.

Snyder, M. (1974). Self-monitoring of expressive behavior. *Journal of Personality and Social Psychology, 30,* 526–537.

Snyder, N., & Glueck, W. F. (1980). How managers plan: The analysis of managers' activities. *Long Range Planning, 13,* 70–76.

Sobol, M. A., Harkins, P., & Conley, T. (Eds.) (2007). *Linkage Inc.'s* best practices *for succession planning: Case studies, research, models, tools*. San Francisco, CA: Pfeiffer.

Sojo, V. E., Wood, R. E., Wood, S. A., & Wheeler, M. A. (2016). Reporting requirements, targets, and quotas for women in leadership. *The Leadership Quarterly, 27,* 519–536.

Sonnentag, S., & Volmer, J. (2009). Individual-level predictors of task-related teamwork processes: The role of expertise and self-efficacy in team meetings. *Group & Organization Management, 34*, 37–66.

Sosik, J. J., Jung, D. I., Berson, Y., Dionne, S. D., & Jaussi, K. S. (2005). Making all the right connections: The strategic leadership of executives in high-tech organizations. *Organizational Dynamics, 34*(1), 47–61.

Spector, P. E. (1986). Perceived control by employees: A meta-analysis of studies concerning autonomy and participation at work. *Human Relations, 39,* 1005–1016.

Sperry, L. (2013). Executive coaching and leadership assessment: Past, present, and future. *Consulting Psychology Journal: Practice and Research, 65*, 284–288.

Spreitzer, G. M. (1995). Psychological empowerment in the workplace: Dimensions, measurement, and validation. *Academy of Management Journal, 38,* 1442–1465.

Spreitzer, G. M. (2008). Taking stock: A review of more than twenty years of research on empowerment. In C. Cooper and J. Barling (Eds.), *Handbook of organizational behavior* (pp. 54–72). Thousand Oaks, CA: Sage.

Spreitzer, G. M., McCall, M. W., Jr., & Mahoney, J. D. (1997). Early identification of international executive potential. *Journal of Applied Psychology, 82,* 6–29.

Srikanth, K., Harvey, S., & Peterson, R. (2016). A dynamic perspective on diverse teams: Moving from the dual-process model to a dynamic coordination-based model of diverse team performance. *Academy of Management Annals, 10*, 453–493.

Srivastava, A., Bartol, K. M., & Locke, E. A. (2006). Empowering leadership in management teams: Effects on knowledge sharing, efficacy, and performance. *Academy of Management Journal, 49,* 1239–1251.

Stahl, M. J. (1983). Achievement, power and managerial motivation: Selecting managerial talent with the job choice exercise. *Personnel Psychology, 36,* 775–789.

Stamp, G. (1988). *Longitudinal research into methods of assessing managerial potential*. Alexandria, VA: U.S. Army Research Institute.

Staw, B. M., & Epstein, L. D. (2000). What bandwagons bring: effects of popular management techniques on corporate performance, reputation, and CEO pay. *Administrative Science Quarterly, 45,* 523–556.

Staw, B. M., McKechnie, P. I., & Puffer, S. M. (1983). The justification of organizational performance. *Administrative Science Quarterly, 28,* 582–600.

Staw, B. M., & Ross, J. (1987). Behavior in escalation situations: Antecedents, prototypes, and solutions. In B. M. Staw & L. L. Cummings (Eds.), *Research in organizational behavior* (Vol. 9, pp. 39–78). Greenwich, CT: JAI Press.

Steinmann, B., Dörr, S. L., Schultheiss, O. C., & Maier, G. W. (2015). Implicit motives and leadership performance revisited: What constitutes the leadership motive pattern? *Motivation and Emotion, 39*(2), 167–174.

Stephens, C. W., D'Intino, R. S., & Victor, B. (1995). The moral quandary of transformational leadership: Change for whom? *Research in Organizational Change and Development, 8,* 123–143.

Stern, A. (1993). Managing by team is not always as easy as it looks. *New York Times,* July 18, B-14.

Stewart, G. L., Courtright, S. H., & Manz, C. C. (2009). Self-leadership: A multilevel review. *Journal of Management, 37,* 185–222.

Stewart, R. (1967). *Managers and their jobs.* London: MacMillan.

Stewart, R. (1976). *Contrasts in management.* Maidenhead, Berkshire, England: McGraw-Hill UK.

Stewart, R. (1982). *Choices for the manager: A guide to understanding managerial work.* Englewood Cliffs, NJ: Prentice Hall.

Stewart, R. (1991). Chairmen and chief executive: An exploration of their relationship. *Journal of Management Studies, 28,* 511–527.

Stewart, R. (2002). Managerial behavior. In M. Warner (Ed.), *International encyclopedia of business and management* (2nd ed., pp. 4083–4099): Thomson Learning.

Stewart, R., Barsoux, J. L., Kieser, A., Ganter, H. D., & Walgenbach, P. (1994). *Managing in Britain and Germany.* London: St. Martin's Press/ MacMillan.

Stogdill, R. M. (1974). *Handbook of leadership: A survey of the literature.* New York: Free Press.

Stogdill, R. M., Goode, O. S., & Day, D. R. (1962). New leader behavior description subscales. *Journal of Psychology, 54,* 259–269.

Stone, T. H., & Cooper, W. H. (2009). Emerging credits. *The Leadership Quarterly, 20,* 785–798.

Strange, J. M., & Mumford, M. D. (2002). The origins of vision: Charismatic versus ideological leadership. *The Leadership Quarterly, 13,* 343–377.

Strange, J. M., & Mumford, M. D. (2005). The origins of vision: Effects of reflection, models, and analysis. *The Leadership Quarterly, 16,* 121–148.

Strauss, G. (1962). Tactics of lateral relationship: The purchasing agent. *Administrative Science Quarterly, 7,* 161–186.

Strauss, G. (1963). Some notes on power equalization. In H. J. Leavitt (Ed.), *The social science of organizations: Four perspectives* (pp. 40–84). Englewood Cliffs, NJ: Prentice Hall.

Strong, P. M. (1984). On qualitative methods and leadership research. In J. G. Hunt, D. M. Hosking, C. A. Schriesheim, & R. Stewart (Eds.), *Leaders and managers: An international perspective on managerial behavior and leadership* (pp. 204–208). New York: Pergamon Press.

Strube, M. J., Turner, C. W., Cerro, D., Stevens, J., & Hinchey, F. (1984). Interpersonal aggression and the Type A coronary-prone behavior pattern: A theoretical distinction and practical implications. *Journal of Personality and Social Psychology, 47,* 839–847.

Sturm, R. E., Taylor, S. N., Atwater, L. E., & Braddy, P. W. (2014). Leader self-awareness: An examination and implications of women's under-prediction. *Journal of Organizational Behavior, 35,* 657–677.

Sully de Luque, M. S, & Javidan, M. (2004). Uncertainty avoidance. In R. J. House, P. J. Hanges, M. Javidan, P. W. Dorfman, & V. Gupta (Eds.), *Culture, leadership, and organizations: The GLOBE study of 62 societies* (pp. 602–653). Thousand Oaks, CA: Sage.

Summers, J. K., Humphrey, S. E., & Ferris, G. R. (2012). Team member change, flux in coordination, and performance: Effects of strategic core roles, information transfer, and cognitive ability. *Academy of Management Journal, 55,* 314–338.

Sundaramurthy, C., & Lewis, M. (2003). Control and collaboration: Paradoxes of governance. *Academy of Management Review, 28,* 397–415.

Sundstrom, E., DeMeuse, K. P., & Futrell, D. (1990). Work teams: Applications and effectiveness. *American Psychologist, 45,* 120–133.

Sutton, C., & Woodman, R. (1989). Pygmalion goes to work: The effects of supervisor expectations in a retail setting. *Journal of Applied Psychology, 74,* 943–950.

Svensson, G., & Wood, G. (2007). Sustainable leadership ethics: A continuous and iterative process. *Leadership & Organization Development Journal, 28,* 251–268.

Sverdrup, T. E., Schei, V., & Tjølsen, Ø. A. (2017). Expecting the unexpected: Using team charters to handle disruptions and facilitate team performance. *Group Dynamics: Theory, Research, and Practice, 21*, 53–59.

Sy, T., Horton, C., & Riggio, R. (2018). Charismatic leadership: Eliciting and channeling follower emotions. *The Leadership Quarterly, 29,* 58–69.

Szabla, D. B. (2007). A multidimensional view of resistance to organizational change: Exploring cognitive, emotional, and intentional responses to planned change across perceived change leadership strategies. *Human Resource Development Quarterly, 18*, 525–558.

Tannenbaum, R., & Schmidt, W. H. (1958). How to choose a leadership pattern. *Harvard Business Review, 36*(2), 95–101.

Tannenbaum, S. I., & Cerasoli, C. P. (2013). Do team and individual debriefs enhance performance? A meta-analysis. *Human Factors, 55*(1), 231–245.

Tannenbaum, S. I., Smith-Jentsch, K., & Behson, S. J. (1998). Training team leaders to facilitate team learning and performance. In J. A. Cannon-Bowers & E. Salas (Eds.), *Making decisions under stress: Implications for individual and team training* (pp. 247–270). Washington, DC: American Psychological Association.

Tannenbaum, S. I., & Yukl, G. (1992). Training and development in work organizations. *Annual Review of Psychology, 43,* 399–441.

Taylor, A. (2002). Nissan's turnaround artist. *Fortune International (Europe), 145*(4), 46.

Taylor, J., & Bowers, D. (1972). *The survey of organizations: A machine-scored standardized questionnaire instrument*. Ann Arbor: Institute for Social Research, University of Michigan.

Taylor, P. J., Russ-Eft, D. F., & Taylor, H. (2009). Transfer of management training from alternative perspectives. *Journal of Applied Psychology, 94*, 104–121.

Taylor, S. N., & Bright, D. S. (2011). Open-mindedness and defensiveness in multisource feedback processes: A conceptual framework. *Journal of Applied Behavioral Science, 47*, 432–460.

Tedeschi, J. T., & Melburg, V. (1984). Impression management and influence in the organization. In S. B. Bacharach & E. J. Lawler (Eds.), *Research in the sociology of organizations* (Vol. 3, pp. 31–58). Greenwich, CT: JAI Press.

Tee, E. Y. J., Paulsen, N., & Ashkanasy, N. M. (2013). Revisiting followership through a social identity perspective: The role of collective follower emotion and action. *The Leadership Quarterly, 24*, 902–918.

Tepper, B. J. (2000). Consequences of abusive supervision. *Academy of Management Journal, 43,* 178–190.

Tepper, B. J. (2007). Abusive supervision in work organizations: Review, synthesis, and research agenda. *Journal of Management, 33*, 261–289.

Tesluk, P. E., & Mathieu, J. E. (1999). Overcoming roadblocks to effectiveness: Incorporating management of performance barriers into models of work group effectiveness. *Journal of Applied Psychology, 84,* 200–217.

Tetrault, L. A., Schriesheim, C. A., & Neider, L. L. (1988). Leadership training interventions: A review. *Organizational Development Journal, 6*(3), 77–83.

Thambain, H. J., & Gemmill, G. R. (1974). Influence styles of project managers: Some project performance correlates. *Academy of Management Journal, 17,* 216–224.

Tharenou, P., Latimer, S., & Conroy, D. (1994). How do you make it to the top? An examination of influences on women's and men's managerial advancement. *Academy of Management Journal, 37,* 899–931.

The Hindu Business Line. (November 21, 2012). *Shared Leadership is the secret of Maruti 's success*. Retrieved from https://www.thehindubusinessline.com (Accessed on August 30, 2019)

Thomas, B. (1976). *Walt Disney: An American tradition*. New York: Simon & Schuster.

Thomas, D. A. (1990). The impact of race on manager's experiences of developmental relationships (mentoring and sponsorship): An intra-organizational study. *Journal of Organizational Behavior, 11,* 479–492.

Thomas, K. W., & Velthouse, B. A. (1990). Cognitive elements of empowerment: An "interpretive model" of intrinsic task motivation. *Academy of Management Review, 15,* 666–681.

Thomason, G. F. (1967). Managerial work roles and relationships (Part 2). *Journal of Management Studies, 4,* 17–30.

Thompson, L. L. (2014). Team decision making: Pitfalls and solutions. *Making the team: A guide for managers* (5th ed., pp. 162–194). Boston: Pearson.

Thornton, G. C., III, & Cleveland, J. N. (1990). Developing managerial talent through simulation. *American Psychologist, 45,* 190–199.

Tichy, N. M., & Devanna, M. A. (1986). *The transformational leader*. New York: John Wiley.

Tjosvold, D. (1985). The effects of attribution and social context on superiors' influence and interaction with low performing subordinates. *Personnel Psychology, 38,* 361–176.

Tonidandel, S., Avery, D. R., & Phillips, M. G. (2007). Maximizing returns on mentoring: Factors affecting subsequent protégé performance. *Journal of Organizational Behavior, 28,* 89–110.

Tornow, W. W., & London, M. (Eds.) (1998). *Maximizing the value of 360-degree feedback: A process for successful individual and organizational development*. San Francisco: Jossey-Bass.

Tornow, W. W., & Pinto, P. R. (1976). The development of a managerial job taxonomy: A system for describing, classifying, and evaluating executive positions. *Journal of Applied Psychology, 61,* 410–418.

Tosi, H. L., Misangyi, V. F., Fanelli, A., Waldman, D. A., & Yammarino, F. J. (2004). CEO charisma, compensation, and firm performance. *The Leadership Quarterly, 15,* 405–420.

Tost, L. P., Gino F. & Larrick, R. P. (2013). When power makes others speechless: The negative impact of leader power on team performance. *Academy of Management Journal*, 56, 1465–1486.

Tracey, J. B., Tannenbaum, S. I., & Kavanagh, M. J. (1995). Applying trained skills on the job: The importance of the work environment. *Journal of Applied Psychology, 80,* 239–252.

Trahan, W. A., & Steiner, D. D. (1994). Factors affecting supervisors' use of disciplinary actions following peer performance. *Journal of Organizational Behavior, 15,* 129–139.

Treviño, L. K. (1986). Ethical decision making in organizations: A person-situation interactionist model. *Academy of Management Review, 11,* 601–617.

Treviño, L., & Brown, M. E. (2014). Ethical leadership. In D. V. Day (Ed.), *The Oxford handbook of leadership and organizations* (pp. 524–538). Oxford, UK: Oxford University Press.

Treviño, L. K., Brown, M., & Hartman, L. P. (2003). A qualitative investigation of perceived ethical leadership: Perceptions from inside and outside the executive suite. *Human Relations, 56,* 5–37.

Treviño, L. K., Butterfield, K. D., & McCabe, D. L. (1998). The ethical context in organizations: Influences on employee attitudes and behaviors. *Business Ethics Quarterly, 8,* 447–476.

Treviño, L., Butterfield, K. D., & McCabe, D. M. (1998). The ethical context in organizations: Influences on employee attitudes and behaviors. *Business Ethics Quarterly, 8*, 447–476.

Treviño, L., & Nelson, K. A. (2017). *Managing business ethics: Straight talk about how to do it right* (7th ed.). New York: Wiley.

Treviño, L. T., Weaver, G., & Reynolds, S. J. (2006). Behavioral ethics in organizations: A review. *Journal of Management, 32,* 951–990.

Treviño, L. K., & Youngblood, S. A. (1990). Bad apples in bad barrels: A causal approach. *Journal of Applied Psychology, 75,* 378–385.

Triandis, H. C., McCusker, C., Betancourt, H., Iwao, S., Leung, K., Salazar, J. M., … Zaleski, Z. (1993). An etic-emic analysis of individualism and collectivism. *Journal of Cross-Cultural Psychology, 24*, 366–383.

Trice, H. M., & Beyer, J. M. (1986). Charisma and its routinization in two social movement organizations. In B. M. Staw & L. L. Cummings (Eds.), *Research in organization behavior* (Vol. 8, pp. 113–164). Greenwich, CT: JAI Press.

Trice, H. M., & Beyer, J. M. (1991). Cultural leadership in organizations. *Organization Science, 2,* 149–169.

Trice, H. M., & Beyer, J. M. (1993). *The cultures of work organizations*. Englewood Cliffs, NJ: Prentice Hall.

Trompenaars, F. (1993). *Riding the waves of culture: Understanding cultural diversity in business*. London: Brealey.

Tskhay, K. O., Zhu, R., & Rule, N. O. (2017). Perceptions of charisma from thin slices of behavior predict leadership prototypicality judgments. *The Leadership Quarterly, 28,* 555–562.

Tskhay, K. O., & Rule, N. O. (2018). Social cognition, social perception, and leadership. In J. Antonakis & D. V. Day (Eds.), *The nature of leadership* (3rd ed., pp. 221–243). Los Angeles: Sage.

Tsui, A. S., Zhang, Z., Wang, H., Xin, K. R., & Wu, J. B. (2006). Unpacking the relationship between CEO leadership behavior and organizational culture. *The Leadership Quarterly, 17,* 113–137.

Turban, D. B., & Dougherty, T. W. (1994). Role of protégé personality in receipt of mentoring and career success. *Academy of Management Journal, 37,* 688–702.

Turnley, W. H., & Bolino, M. C. (2001). Achieving desired images while avoiding undesirable images: Exploring the role of self-monitoring in impression management. *Journal of Applied Psychology, 86,* 351–360.

Tushman, M. L., Newman, W. H., & Romanelli, E. (1986). Convergence and upheaval: Managing the unsteady pace of organizational evolution. *California Management Review, 29*(1), 29–44.

Tushman, M. L., & O'Reilly, C. A. III. (1996). Ambidextrous organizations: Managing evolutionary and revolutionary change. *California Management Review, 38*(4), 8–29.

Tushman, M. L., & Romanelli, E. (1985). Organizational evolution: A metamorphosis model of convergence and reorientation. *Research in Organizational Behavior, 7,* 171–222.

Uhl-Bien, M. (2006). Relational leadership theory: Exploring the social processes of leadership and organizing. *The Leadership Quarterly, 17,* 654–676.

Uhl-Bien, M., & Arena, M. (2018). Leadership for organizational adaptability: A theoretical synthesis and integrative framework. *The Leadership Quarterly, 29*, 89–104.

Uhl-Bien, M., & Marion, R. (2009). Complexity leadership in bureaucratic forms of organizing: A meso model. *The Leadership Quarterly, 20,* 631–650.

Uhl-Bien, M., Marion, R., & McKelvey, B. (2007). Complexity leadership theory: Shifting leadership from the industrial age to the knowledge era. *The Leadership Quarterly, 18,* 298–318.

Uhl-Bien, M., Maslyn, J., & Ospina, S. (2012). The nature of relational leadership: A multitheoretical lens on leadership relationships and processes. In D. V. Day & J. Antonakis (Eds.), *The nature of leadership* (2nd ed., pp. 289–330). Los Angeles: Sage.

Uhl-Bien, M., Riggio, R. E., Lowe, K. B., & Carsten, M. K. (2014). Followership theory: A review and research agenda. *The Leadership Quarterly, 25*, 83–104.

Uitdewilligen, S., & Waller, M. J. (2018). Information sharing and decision-making in multidisciplinary crisis management teams. *Journal of Organizational Behavior, 39,* 731–748.

Ulrich, D., Jick, T., & Von Glinow, M. A. (1993). High impact learning: Building and diffusing learning capability. *Organizational Dynamics, 22*(1), 52–66.

Unsworth, K. L., & Mason, C. M. (2016). Self-concordance strategies as a necessary condition for self-management. *Journal of Occupational and Organizational Psychology, 89*, 711–733.

Uotila, J., Maula, M., Keil, T., & Zahra, S. A. (2009). Exploration, exploitation, and financial performance: Analysis of S&P 500 corporations. *Strategic Management Journal, 30,* 221–231.

Upadhya, C., & Vasavi, A. R. (2006). Work, culture, and sociality in the Indian IT industry: a sociological study. Final report submitted to NIAS-IDPAD, Bangalore.

Urwick, L. F. (1952). *Notes on the theory of organization*. New York: American Management Association.

Useem, M. (1998). *The leadership moment: Nine stories of triumph and disaster for us all*. New York: Times Books, pp. 10–42.

Vaill, P. B. (1978). Toward a behavior description of high-performing systems. In M. W. McCall, Jr., & M. M. Lombardo (Eds.), *Leadership: Where else can we go?* (pp. 103–125). Durham, NC: Duke University Press.

Valerio, A. M. (1990). A study of the developmental experiences of managers. In K. E. Clark & M. B. Clark (Eds.), *Measures of leadership* (pp. 521–534). West Orange, NJ: Leadership Library of America.

Van de Ven, A., Poley, D., Garud, R., & Venkataraman, S. (1999). *The innovation journey*. New York: Oxford Press.

Van der Heijden, K. (1996). *Scenarios: The art of strategic conversation*. New York: John Wiley.

Van der Vegt, G. S., & Bunderson, J. S. (2005). Learning and performance in multidisciplinary teams: The importance of collective team identification. *Academy of Management Journal, 48,* 532–547.

Vanderslice, V. J. (1988). Separating leadership from leaders: An assessment of the effect of leader and follower roles in organizations. *Human Relations, 41,* 677–696.

van Dierendonck, D., & Jacobs, G. (2012). Survivors and victims, a meta-analytical review of fairness and organizational commitment after downsizing. *British Journal of Management, 23*, 96–109.

Van Fleet, D. D., & Yukl, G. (1986a). A century of leadership research. In D. A. Wren (Ed.), *One hundred years of management* (pp. 12–23). Chicago: Academy of Management.

Van Fleet, D. D., & Yukl, G. (1986b). *Military leadership: An organizational perspective*. Greenwich, CT: JAI Press.

van Knippenberg, B., & van Knippenberg, D. (2005). Leader self-sacrifice and leadership effectiveness: The moderating role of leader prototypicality. *Journal of Applied Psychology, 90,* 25–37.

van Knippenberg, D. (2018). Leadership and identity. In J. Antonakis & D. V. Day (Eds.), *The nature of leadership* (3rd ed., pp. 300–326). Los Angeles: Sage.

van Knippenberg, D., & Schippers, M. C. (2007). Work group diversity. *Annual Review of Psychology, 58,* 515–541.

van Knippenberg, D., & Sitkin, S. B. (2013). A critical assessment of charismatic-transformational leadership research: Back to the drawing board? *Academy of Management Annals, 7,* 1–60.

van Knippenberg, D., van Knippenberg, B., De Cremer, D., & Hogg, M. A. (2004). Leadership, self, and identity: A review and research agenda. *The Leadership Quarterly, 15,* 825–856.

Van Velsor, E., & Hughes, M. W. (1990). *Gender differences in the development of management: How women managers learn from experience*. Technical Report No. 145. Greensboro, NC: Center for Creative Leadership.

Van Velsor, E., & Leslie, J. B. (1995). Why executives derail: Perspective across time and cultures. *Academy of Management Executive, 9*(4), 62–72.

Van Velsor, E., Leslie, J. B., & Fleenor, J. W. (1997). *Choosing 360: A guide to evaluating* *multi-rater feedback instruments for management development*. Greensboro, N.C.: Center for Creative Leadership.

Van Velsor, E., & McCauley, C. D. (2004). Our view of leadership development. In C. D. McCauley & E. Van Velsor (Eds.), *The center for creative leadership handbook of leadership development* (2nd ed., pp. 1–22). San Francisco: Jossey-Bass.

Van Velsor, E., Ruderman, E., & Phillips, A. D. (1989). The lessons of the looking glass: Management simulations and the real world of action. *Leadership & Organizational Development Journal, 10,* 27–31.

van Vugt, M. (2018). Evolutionary, biological, and neuroscience perspectives. In J. Antonakis & D. V. Day (Eds.), *The nature of leadership* (pp. 189–217). Los Angeles: Sge.

Varella, P., Javidan, M., & Waldman, D. A. (2012). A model of instrumental networks: The roles of socialized charismatic leadership and group behavior. *Organization Science, 23,* 582–595.

Vecchio, R. P. (2002). Leadership and the gender advantage. *The Leadership Quarterly, 13,* 643–671.

Vecchio, R. P. (2003). In search of the gender advantage. *The Leadership Quarterly, 14,* 835–850.

Vecchio, R. P., & Gobdel, B. C. (1984). The vertical dyad linkage model of leadership: Problems and prospects. *Organizational Behavior and Human Performance, 34,* 5–20.

Vecchio, R. P., Justin, J. E., & Pearce, C. L. (2010). Empowering leadership: An examination of mediating mechanisms within a hierarchical structure. *The Leadership Quarterly, 21,* 530–542.

Vera, D., & Crossan, M. (2004). Strategic leadership and organizational learning. *Academy of Management Review, 29,* 222–240.

Vermeulen, P. A. M., De Jong J. P. J., & O'Shaughnessy, K. C. (2005). Identifying key determinants for new product introductions and firm performance in small service firms. *The Service Industries Journal, 25,* 625–640.

Vicere, A. A., & Fulmer, R. M. (1997). *Leadership by design*. Boston: Harvard Business School Press.

Victor, B., & Cullen, J. B. (1988). The organizational bases of ethical work climates. *Administrative Science Quarterly, 33,* 101–125.

Villado, A. J., & Arthur, W., Jr. (2013). The comparative effect of subjective and objective after-action reviews on team performance on a complex task. *Journal of Applied Psychology, 98,* 514–528.

Vlachos, P. A., Panagopoulos, N. G., & Rapp, A. A. (2013). Feeling good by doing good: Employee CSR-induced attributions, job satisfaction, and the role of charismatic leadership. *Journal of Business Ethics, 118,* 577–588.

Vries, M. F., Agrawal, A., & Treacy, E. F. (2006, January 09). The Moral Compass: Values-based Leadership at Infosys. Retrieved from https://hbsp.harvard.edu(Accessed on January 22, 2019)

Vroom, V. H., & Jago, A. G. (1978). On the validity of the Vroom-Yetton model. *Journal of Applied Psychology, 63,* 151–162.

Vroom, V. H., & Jago, A. G. (1988). *The new leadership: Managing participation in organizations*. Englewood Cliffs, NJ: Prentice Hall.

Vroom, V. H., & Yetton, P. W. (1973). *Leadership and decision making*. Pittsburgh: University of Pittsburgh Press.

Wagner, J. A., & Gooding, R. Z. (1987). Shared influence and organizational behavior: A meta-analysis of situational variables expected to moderate participation-outcome relationships. *Academy of Management Journal, 30,* 524–541.

Wagner, J. A., III, Leana, C. R., Locke, E. A., & Schweiger, D. M. (1997). Cognitive and motivational frameworks in U.S. research on participation: A meta-analysis of primary effects. *Journal of Organizational Behavior, 18,* 49–65.

Wai-Kwong, F., Priem, R., & Cycyota, C. (2001). The performance effects of human resource managers' and other middle managers' involvement in strategy making under different business-level strategies: the case in Hong Kong. *Human Resources Management, 12,* 1325–1346.

Wainer, H. A., & Rubin, I. M. (1969). Motivation of research and development entrepreneurs: Determinants of company success. *Journal of Applied Psychology, 53*, 178–184.

Waldman, D. A., Atwater, L. E., & Antonioni, D. (1998). Has 360-degree feedback gone amok? *Academy of Management Executive, 12,* 86–94.

Waldman, D. A., Javidan, M., & Varella, P. (2004). Charismatic leadership at the strategic level: A new application of upper echelons theory. *The Leadership Quarterly, 15,* 355–380.

Waldman, D. A., Ramirez, G. R., House, R. J., & Puranam, P. (2001). Does leadership matter? CEO leadership attributes and profitability under conditions of perceived environmental uncertainty. *Academy of Management Journal, 44,* 134–143.

Waldman, D. A., Sully de Luque, M., Washburn, N., & House, R., … & Associates (2006). Cultural and leadership predictors of corporate social responsibility values of top management: A GLOBE study of 15 countries. *Journal of International Business Studies, 37,* 823–837.

Waldman, D. A., & Yammarino, F. J. (1999). CEO charismatic leadership: Levels-of-management and levels-of-analysis effects. *Academy of Management Review, 24,* 266–285.

Walker, A. G., & Smither, J. W. (1999). A five-year study of upward feedback: What managers do with their results matters. *Personnel Psychology, 52,* 393–423.

Walker, D. O., & Yip, J. (2018). Paying it forward? The mixed effects of organizational inducements on executive mentoring. *Human Resource Management*. Published online before print, March 15, 2018. doi: 10.1002/hrm.21901

Wall, S. J., & Wall, S. R. (1995). *The new strategists: Creating leaders at all levels*. New York: Free Press.

Wall, T. D., Kemp, N. J., Jackson, P. R., & Clegg, C. W. (1986). Outcomes of autonomous workgroups: A long-term field experiment. *Academy of Management Journal, 29,* 280–304.

Walter, F., Cole, M. S., & Humphrey, R. H. (2011). Emotional intelligence: Sine qua non of leadership or folderol. *Academy of Management Perspectives, 25*(1), 45–59.

Walumbwa, F. O., Avolio, B. J., Gardner, W. L., Wernsing, T. S., & Peterson, S. J. (2008). Authentic leadership: Development and validation of a theory-based measure. *Journal of Management, 34*, 89–126.

Wang, D., Waldman, D. A., & Zhang, Z. (2014). A meta-analysis of shared leadership and team effectiveness. *Journal of Applied Psychology, 99*, 181–198.

Wang, H., Tsui, A. H., & Xin, K. R. (2011). CEO leadership behaviors, organizational performance, and employee attitudes. *The Leadership Quarterly, 22,* 92–105.

Wang, X.-H. F., Kim, T.-Y., & Lee, D.-R. (2016). Cognitive diversity and team creativity: Effects of team intrinsic motivation and transformational leadership. *Journal of Business Research, 69*, 3231–3239.

Warren, D. I. (1968). Power, visibility, and conformity in formal organizations. *American Sociological Review, 6,* 951–970.

Wasmuth, W. J., & Greenhalgh, L. (1979). *Effective supervision: Developing your skills through critical incidents.* Englewood Cliffs, NJ: Prentice Hall.

Waterson, P. E., Clegg, C. W., Bolden, R., Pepper, K., Warr, P. B., & Wall, T. D. (1999). The use and effectiveness of modern manufacturing practices: A survey of UK industry. *International Journal of Production Resources*, 37, 2271–2292.

Watson, W. E., Kumar, K., & Michaelsen, L. K. (1993). Cultural diversity's impact on interaction process and performance: Comparing homogeneous and diverse task groups. *Academy of Management Journal, 36*, 590–602.

Watts, L. L., Ness, A. M., Steele, L. M., & Mumford, M. D. (2018). Learning from stories of leadership: How reading about personalized and socialized politicians impacts performance on an ethical decision-making simulation. *The Leadership Quarterly, 29*, 276–294.

Wayne, S. J., & Ferris, G. R. (1990). Influence tactics, affect, and exchange quality in supervisor-subordinate interactions: A laboratory experiment and field study. *Journal of Applied Psychology, 75*, 487–499.

Wayne, S. J., & Liden, R. C. (1995). Effects of impression management on performance ratings: A longitudinal study. *Academy of Management Journal, 38,* 232–260.

Weaver, G. R., Treviño, L. K., & Cochran, P. L. (1999). Corporate ethics programs as control systems: Influences of executive commitment and environmental factors. *Academy of Management Journal, 42,* 41–57.

Webber, R. A. (1980). *Time is money: The key to managerial success*. New York: Free Press.

Webber, R. A. (1981). *To be a manager.* Homewood, IL: Irwin.

Weber, J. A. (2000). Uncertainty and strategic management. In J. Rabin, G. J. Miller, & W. B. Hildreth (Eds.), *Handbook of strategic management* (2nd ed., pp. 203–226). New York: Marcel Dekker.

Weber, M. (1947). *The theory of social and economic organizations*. Translated by T. Parsons. New York: Free Press.

Weed, F. J. (1993). The MADD queen: Charisma and the founder of mothers against drunk driving. *The Leadership Quarterly, 4,* 329–346.

Weick, K. E., & Sutcliffe, K. M. (2001). *Managing the unexpected: Assuring high performance in an age of complexity*. San Francisco, CA: Jossey-Bass.

Welch, J., & Welch, S. (2015). *The real-life MBA: Your no-BS guide to winning the game, building a team, and growing your career*. New York: Harper Collins.

Wellins, R. S., Byham, W. C., & Wilson, J. M. (1991). *Empowered teams: Creating self-directed work groups that improve quality, productivity, and participation*. San Francisco: Jossey-Bass.

Westaby, J. D., Probst, T. M., & Lee, B. C. (2010). Leadership decision-making: A behavioral reasoning theory analysis. *The Leadership Quarterly, 21*, 481–495.

Westley, F., & Mintzberg, H. (1989). Visionary leadership and strategic management. *Strategic Management Journal, 10,* 17–32.

Whetten, D. A., & Cameron, K. S. (1991). *Developing management skills*. New York: Harper-Collins.

White, L. P., & Wooten, K. C. (1986). *Professional ethics and practice in organizational development: A systematic analysis of issues, alternatives, and approaches.* New York: Praeger.

White, S. E., Dittrich, J. E., & Lang, J. R. (1980). The effects of group decision-making process and problem-situation complexity on implementation strategies. *Administrative Science Quarterly, 25,* 428–440.

Whitely, W. T., & Coetsier, P. (1993). The relationship of career mentoring to early career outcomes. *Organization Studies, 14,* 419–441.

Wikoff, M., Anderson, D. C., & Crowell, C. R. (1983). Behavior management in a factory setting: Increasing work efficiency. *Journal of Organizational Behavior Management, 4,* 97–128.

Wilbur, J. (1987). Does mentoring breed success? *Training and Development Journal,* November, 38–41.

Williams, M. J. (2014). Serving the self from the seat of power: Goals and threats predict leaders'' 'self-interested behavior. *Journal of Management*, 40, 1365–1395.

Willink, J., & Babin, L. (2017). *Extreme ownership: How U. S. Navy SEALs lead and win*. New York: St. Martin's Press.

Willner, A. R. (1984). *The spellbinders: Charismatic political leadership*. New Haven: Yale University Press.

Wilson, K. S., Sin, H., & Conlon, D. E. (2010). What about the leader in leader-member exchange? The impact of resource exchanges and substitutability on the leader. *Academy of Management Review, 35,* 358–372.

Windsor, D. (2010). The politics of strategy process. In P. Mazzola & F. W. Kellermanns (Eds.), *Handbook of research on strategy process* (pp. 43–66). Cheltenham, UK: Edward Elgar.

Wofford, J. C. (1982). An integrative theory of leadership. *Journal of Management, 8,* 27–47.

Wofford, J. C. (1999). Laboratory research on charismatic leadership: Fruitful or futile? *The Leadership Quarterly*, 10, 523–529.

Wofford, J. C., & Liska, L. Z. (1993). Path-goal theories of leadership: A meta analysis. *Journal of Management, 19,* 857–876.

Wong, C.-S., & Law, K. S. (2002). The effects of leader and follower emotional intelligence on performance and attitude: An exploratory study. *The Leadership Quarterly, 13,* 243–274.

Wood, R. E., & Mitchell, T. R. (1981). Manager behavior in a social context: The impact of impression management on attributions and disciplinary actions. *Organizational Behavior and Human Performance, 28,* 356–378.

Woodruff, D. (1993). Chrysler's Neon: Is this the small car Detroit couldn't build? *Business Week,* May 3, 464–476.

Woodward, H., & Bucholz, S. (1987). *Aftershock: Helping people through corporate change*. New York: John Wiley.

Worley, C. G., Hitchin, D. E., & Ross, W. L. (1996). *Integrated strategic change: How OD builds competitive advantage*. Reading, MA: Addison-Wesley.

Wright, P. M., & Ulrich, M. D. (2017). A road well traveled: The past, present, and future journey of strategic human resource management. *Annual Review of Organizational Psychology and Organizational Behavior, 4,* 45–65.

Wu, J. B., Tsui, A. S., & Kinicki, A. J. (2010). Consequences of differentiated leadership in groups. *Academy of Management Journal, 53,* 90–106.

Wu, L.-Z., Kwan, H. K., Yim, F. H.-k., Chiu, R. K., & He, X. (2015). CEO ethical leadership and corporate social responsibility: A moderated mediation model. *Journal of Business Ethics, 130,* 819–831.

Wu, Y.-C. (2010). An exploration of substitutes for leadership: Problems and prospects. *Social Behavior and Personality, 38,* 583–595.

Wyden, P. (1987). *The unknown Iacocca*. New York: William Morrow.

Xu, X.-D., Zhong, J. A., & Wang, X.-Y. (2013). The impact of substitutes for leadership on job satisfaction and performance. *Social Behavior and Personality, 41,* 675–685.

Yammarino, F. J. (1994). Indirect leadership: Transformational leadership at a distance. In B. M. Bass & B. J. Avolio (Eds.), *Improving organizational effectiveness through transformational leadership* (pp. 26–47). Thousand Oaks, CA: Sage.

Yammarino, F. J., & Dansereau, F. (2008). Multi-level nature of and multi-level approaches to leadership. *The Leadership Quarterly, 19,* 135–141.

Yammarino, F. J., Dionne, S., & Chun, J. U. (2002). Transformational and charismatic leadership: A levels-of-analysis review of theory, measurement, data analysis, and inferences. In L. L. Neider & C. A. Schriesheim (Eds.), *Leadership* (pp. 23–63). Greenwich, CT: New Information Age Publishing.

Yammarino, F. J., Dionne, S. D., Chun, J. U., & Dansereau, F. (2005). Leadership and levels of analysis: A state-of-the-science review. *The Leadership Quarterly, 16,* 879–919.

Yammarino, F. J., & Gooty, J. (2017). Multi-level issues and dyads in leadership research. In B. Schyns, R. J. Hall & P. Neves (Eds.), *Handbook of methods in leadership research* (pp. 229–255). Cheltenham, UK: Edward Elgar Publishing.

Yammarino, F. J., Mumford, M. D., Serban, A., & Shirreffs, K. (2013). Assassination and leadership: Traditional approaches and historiometric methods. *The Leadership Quarterly, 24*, 822–841.

Yang, D. J. (1992). Nordstrom's gang of four. *Business Week,* June 15, 122–123.

Yang, S.-B., & Guy, M. E. (2011). The effectiveness of self-managed work teams in government organizations. *Journal of Business and Psychology, 26*, 531–541.

Yeung, A. K., Ulrich, D. O., Nason, S. W., & Von Glinow, M. A. (1999). *Organizational learning capability: Generating and generalizing ideas with impact*. New York: Oxford University Press.

Young, D., & Dixon, N. (1996). *Helping leaders take effective action: A program evaluation*. Greensboro, NC: Center for Creative Leadership.

Yorges, S. L., Weiss, H. M., & Strickland, O. J. (1999). The effect of leader outcomes on influence, attributions, and perceptions of charisma. *Journal of Applied Psychology, 84,* 428–436.

Yukl, G. (1981). *Leadership in organizations*. Englewood Cliffs, NJ: Prentice Hall.

Yukl, G. (1989). *Leadership in organizations* (2nd ed.). Englewood Cliffs, NJ: Prentice Hall.

Yukl, G. (1990). *Skills for managers and leaders: Text, cases, and exercises*. Englewood Cliffs, NJ: Prentice Hall.

Yukl, G. (1993). *Leadership in organizations* (8th ed.). Boston: Pearson.

Yukl, G. (1997). *Effective leadership behavior: A new taxonomy and model*. Paper presented at the Eastern Academy of Management International Conference, Dublin, Ireland.

Yukl, G. (1999a). An evaluative essay on current conceptions of effective leadership. *European Journal of Work and Organizational Psychology, 8,* 33–48.

Yukl, G. (1999b). An evaluation of conceptual weaknesses in transformational and charismatic leadership theories. *The Leadership Quarterly, 10,* 285–305.

Yukl, G. (2008). How leaders influence organizational effectiveness. *The Leadership Quarterly, 19,* 708–722.

Yukl, G. (2009). Leading organizational learning: Reflections on theory and research. *The Leadership Quarterly, 20,* 49–53.

Yukl, G. (2012). Effective leadership behavior: What we know and what questions need more attention. *Academy of Management Perspectives, 26*, 66–85.

Yukl, G., & Becker, W. (2007). Effective empowerment in organizations. *Organization Management Journal, 3*(3), 210–231.

Yukl, G., Chavez, C., & Seifert, C. F. (2005). Assessing the construct validity and utility of two new influence tactics. *Journal of Organizational Behavior, 26,* 705–725.

Yukl, G., & Falbe, C. M. (1990). Influence tactics and objectives in upward, downward, and lateral influence attempts. *Journal of Applied Psychology, 75,* 132–140.

Yukl, G., & Falbe, C. M. (1991). The importance of different power sources in downward and lateral relations. *Journal of Applied Psychology, 76,* 416–423.

Yukl, G., Falbe, C. M., & Youn, J. Y. (1993). Patterns of influence behavior for managers. *Group and Organization Management, 18,* 5–28.

Yukl, G., & Fu, P. (1999). Determinants of delegation and consultation by managers. *Journal of Organizational Behavior, 20,* 219–232.

Yukl, G., Fu, P. P., & McDonald, R. (2003). Cross-cultural differences in perceived effectiveness of influence tactics for initiating or resisting change. *Applied Psychology: An International Review, 52,* 68–82.

Yukl, G., Gordon, A., & Taber, T. (2002). A hierarchical taxonomy of leadership behavior: Integrating a half century of behavior research. *Journal of Leadership and Organization Studies, 9,* 15–32.

Yukl, G., Guinan, P. J., & Sottolano, D. (1995). Influence tactics used for different objectives with subordinates, peers, and superiors. *Group and Organization Management, 20,* 272–296.

Yukl, G., Kim, H., & Chavez, C. (1999). Task importance, feasibility, and agent influence behavior as determinants of target commitment. *Journal of Applied Psychology, 84,* 137–143.

Yukl, G., Kim, H., & Falbe, C. M. (1996). Antecedents of influence outcomes. *Journal of Applied Psychology, 81,* 309–317.

Yukl, G., & Lepsinger, R. (1995). 360-degree feedback: What to put into it to get the most out of it. *Training,* December, 45–50.

Yukl, G., & Lepsinger, R. (2004). *Flexible leadership: Creating value by balancing multiple challenges and choices.* San Francisco, CA: Jossey-Bass.

Yukl, G., & Lepsinger, R. (2005). Why integrating the leading and managing roles is essential for organizational effectiveness. *Organizational Dynamics, 34*(4), 361–375.

Yukl, G., Lepsinger, R., & Lucia, A. (1992). Preliminary report on development and validation of the influence behavior questionnaire. In K. Clark, M. B. Clark, & D. P. Campbell (Eds.), *Impact of leadership* (pp. 417–427). Greensboro, NC: Center for Creative Leadership.

Yukl, G., & Mahsud, R. (2010). Why flexible and adaptive leadership is essential. *Consulting Psychology Journal, 62*(2), 81–93.

Yukl, G., & Michel, J. (2015). A critical assessment of research on effective leadership behavior. In Neider, L., & Schriesheim, C., (eds.), *Research in management, Vol. 10: Advances in authentic and ethical leadership.* Charlotte, NC: Information Age Publishing, pp. 209–229.

Yukl, G., O'Donnell, M., & Taber, T. (2009). Leader behaviors and leader member exchange. *Journal of Managerial Psychology*, 24(4), 289–299.

Yukl, G., Seifert, C., & Chavez, C. (2008). Validation of the extended Influence Behavior Questionnaire. *The Leadership Quarterly, 19,* 609–621.

Yukl, G., & Tracey, B. (1992). Consequences of influence tactics used with subordinates, peers, and the boss. *Journal of Applied Psychology, 77,* 525–535.

Yukl, G., & Van Fleet, D. (1982). Cross-situational, multi-method research on military leader effectiveness. *Organizational Behavior and Human Performance, 30,* 87–108.

Yukl, G., Wall, S., & Lepsinger, R. (1990). Preliminary report on validation of the managerial practices survey. In K. E. Clark & M. B. Clark (Eds.), *Measures of leadership* (pp. 223–238). West Orange, NJ: Leadership Library of America.

Yun, S., Samer, F., & Sims, H. P., Jr. (2005). Contingent leadership and effectiveness of trauma resuscitation teams. *Journal of Applied Psychology, 90,* 1288–1296.

Zaccaro, S. J. (2007). Trait-based perspectives of leadership. *American Psychologist, 62,* 6–16.

Zaccaro, S. J. (2012). Individual differences and leadership: Contributions to a third tipping point. *The Leadership Quarterly, 23*, 718–728.

Zaccaro, S. J., & Banks, D. (2004). Leader visioning and adaptability: Bridging the gap between research and practice on developing the ability to manage change. *Human Resource Management, 43*, 367–380.

Zaccaro, S. J., Dubrow, S., & Kolze, M. (2018). Leader traits and attributes. In J. Antonakis & D. V. Day (Eds.), *The Nature of leadership* (pp. 29–55). Thousand Oaks, CA: Sage Publications Inc.

Zaccaro, S. J., Foti, R. J., & Kenny, D. A. (1991). Self-monitoring and trait-based variance in leadership: An investigation of leader flexibility across multiple group situations. *Journal of Applied Psychology, 76,* 308–315.

Zaccaro, S. J., Gilbert, J. A., Thor, K. K., & Mumford, M. D. (1991). Leadership and social intelligence: Linking social perspectiveness and behavioral flexibility to leader effectiveness. *The Leadership Quarterly, 2,* 317–342.

Zaccaro, S. J., Mumford, M. D., Marks, M. A., Connelly, M. S., Threlfall, K. V., Gilbert, J. A., et al. (1997). *Cognitive and temperament* *determinants of army leadership*. Technical Report MRI 97–2. Bethesda, MD: Management Research Institute.

Zaccaro, S. J., Rittman, A. L., & Marks, M. A. (2001). Team leadership. *The Leadership Quarterly, 12,* 451–484.

Zaleznik, A. (1977). Managers and leaders: Are they different? *Harvard Business Review, 55*(5), 67–78.

Zey, M. G. (1988). A mentor for all reasons. *Personnel Journal,* January, 46–51.

Zhang, X., & Bartol, K. M. (2010). Linking empowering leadership and employee creativity: The influence of psychological empowerment, intrinsic motivation, and creative process engagement. *Academy of Management Journal, 53,* 107–128.

Zhang, Z., Ilies, R., & Arvey, R.D. (2009). Beyond genetic explanations for leadership: The moderating role of the social environment. *Organizational Behavior and Human Decision Processes, 110,* 118–128.

Zhang, Z., Wang, M., & Shi, J. (2012). Leader-follower congruence in proactive personality and work outcomes: The mediating role of leader-member exchange. *Academy of Management Journal, 55*, 111–130.

Zhen, Z., & Peterson, S. J. (2011). Advice networks in teams: The role of transformational leadership and members' core self-evaluations. *Journal of Applied Psychology, 96*, 1004–1017.

Zheng, D., Witt, L. A., Waite, E., David, E. M., van Driel, M., McDonald, D. P., ... & Crepeau, L. J. (2015). Effects of ethical leadership on emotional exhaustion in high moral intensity situations. *The Leadership Quarterly, 26*, 732–748.

Zhou, X., & Schriesheim, C. A. (2009). Supervisor–subordinate convergence in descriptions of leader-member exchange (LMX) quality: Review and testable propositions. *The Leadership Quarterly, 20,* 920–932.

Zhou, X., & Schriesheim, C. A. (2010). Quantitative and qualitative examination of propositions concerning supervisor–subordinate convergence in descriptions of leader-member exchange (LMX) quality. *The Leadership Quarterly, 21,* 826–843.

Zhu, Y., & Akhtar, S. (2014). How transformational leadership influences follower helping behavior: The role of trust and prosocial motivation. *Journal of Organizational Behavior, 35*, 373–392.

Zhu, W., Chew, I. K. H., & Spangler, W. D. (2005). CEO transformational leadership and organizational outcomes: The mediating role of human-capital-enhancing human resource management. *The Leadership Quarterly, 16,* 39–52.

Zhu, J., Liao, Z., Yam, K. C., & Johnson, R. E. (2018). Shared leadership: A state-of-the-art review and future research agenda. *Journal of Organizational Behavior, 39,* 834–852.

AUTHOR INDEX

A

B

C

D

E

G

H

I

J

K

L

M

N

O

P

Q

R

S

T

U

V

Van Velsor, E., 174, 191, 195, 381, 385, 389, 396

W

Y

Z

SUBJECT INDEX

D

E

F

G

H

I

J

K

L

P

R

S